DRAGON SLAYER

Sons of Rome Book III

By

Lauren Gilley

The Sons of Rome Series

"The Stalker"

White Wolf

Red Rooster

Dragon Slayer

Golden Eagle
(coming soon)

DRAGON SLAYER

ISBN-13: 9781795208420

Copyright © 2019 by Lauren Gilley

Cover design copyright © 2019 by Lauren Gilley

HP Press®
Atlanta, GA

Dear Reader,

The book you are about to read is a work of fiction, as you well know. But you might *not* know how closely it follows the true events of the life of the real Vlad Dracula.

I must confess a bit of a long-term, persistent fascination with the man history refers to as "the Impaler." His name comes up, invariably, whenever someone mentions vampires; this is part of the reason, lifelong lover of vamps, and wolves, and dark, Gothic monsters that I am. But begin to dig, even a little, and one is struck by his sheer force of will. In a collective past rife with negotiators, deal-makers, and opportunists, Vlad stands out as implacable; singular in his hatred and focus. Yet, unlike the conquerors of the world, he sought not to take over the world, but merely to hold his ground. Villain? Monster? Some say yes, though many of his smallfolk loved him. Relentless, and intolerant, yes, but, as already stated – fascinating.

Vlad was always intended to be a part of my Sons of Rome series, and I always meant for him to be Val's brother. But it wasn't until I began researching in earnest, in the last few years, that I stumbled upon the unbelievable true story of Vlad, his baby brother, and their involvement with the Ottoman Empire. A true story that doesn't make its way often to the silver screen, nor even the documentary screen, nor Western history books. Suddenly, it all started to make sense, and Vlad went from mythical beast, to furious, badly wronged prince, who, while his actions can't be excused, his hatred could at least be explained. Dare I say understood. I then realized that I didn't just want to fold him into my larger narrative – which I have done – but also to shed some light on his little talked-of true story. As closely as I could, I have within this novel stuck to the facts of Vlad's life, and his wars.

But this is, of course, a story of the paranormal, and I have tweaked some details to suit my own mythology. In the Sons of Rome series, Vlad, and his little brother Val (Radu), are purebred vampires. Their father, Vlad Dracul, is, in my story, an alias for the presumed-dead Remus, co-founder of Rome, twin to Romulus. And so in this novel, Vlad and Val are, quite literally, sons of Rome.

Many other true figures from Vlad's time appear within these pages, the most notable of which is the Ottoman sultan Mehmet, known as the Conqueror. He was Vlad's great nemesis, but it has been my attempt to style the sultan as Vlad's antagonist, and not the villain of this book. Indeed, my overall approach with this series is not one of casting heroes against villains, but to write in-depth character epics, in which the audience can decide or even debate the morality of the main characters, and those they struggle against.

Alright, I've bent your ear enough at this point. It's my one request that you go forward into this novel with an open mind, reserving judgement on our two brothers until the end. And it is my great hope that you enjoy the journey. I don't say this often, but I am incredibly proud of this book; writing it has been a singular experience.

Good luck, dear reader. I'll see you on the other side.

~Lauren
(Feb. 2019)

Characters of Relevance We've Met So Far:

Prince Valerian: known to history as Radu Dracula, former prince of Wallachia, heir to Vlad Dracula. Vampire.

Prince Vlad Dracula: known as "Tepes," or "The Impaler." Prince of Wallachia. Vampire.

Fulk le Strange: Baron Strange of Blackmere. Werewolf.

Annabel le Strange: Baroness Strange of Blackmere. Werewolf.

Dr. Edwin Talbot: head of the Ingraham Institute. Human.

Mia Talbot: friend of Valerian. Edwin Talbot's daughter.

Major Jake Treadwell: disabled former military officer in the employ of the Ingraham Institute.

Sergeant Adela Ramirez: disabled former military officer in the employ of the Ingraham Institute.

Captain Nikita Baskin: former Chekist captain in the Soviet Union. Vampire sired by Rasputin.

Sasha Kashnikov: companion to Nikita. Former Soviet weapon. Werewolf.

DRAGON SLAYER

"Pray, think that when a man or prince is powerful and strong at home, then he will be able to do as he wills. But when he is without power, another one more powerful than he will overwhelm him and do as he wishes."

~ Vlad Tepes Dracula, in a letter to the mayor of Brasov, 1457

"I am young and rich and favored by fortune, so I intend to surpass Caesar, Alexander, and Hannibal by far."

~ His Imperial Majesty Sultan Mehmet, "the Conqueror"

Prologue

Tîrgoviște, Wallachia
1439

He woke to the pain of his brother's elbow in his ribs.

"Val," Vlad murmured, half-asleep. "Stop kicking me."

"Oh." Val blinked up at the ceiling, the faint shadows from the fireplace that flickered over it. "Sorry."

Vlad sighed and rolled toward him. The furs flapped, letting in a shaft of cold air that made Val gasp. But then his brother wriggled closer until there was no room for anything save soft shirts, body heat, and warm, sleep-sour breath between them.

The lantern Mother had left on the desk had all but burned down, only the last sputtering fraction of the wick. The fire crackled low in the grate, a diffuse glow that washed up over the bed where the two brothers slept together beneath a heap of furs and blankets to keep warm in the winter-chilled palace. There was just enough light for Val to make out his brother's face, the glimmer of his cracked-open eyes through a screen of tousled dark hair.

"Where did you go this time?" Vlad asked, sounding more awake now.

The dream still clung to him. The dream that wasn't a dream at all, but a *visit*. "I don't know," he said. "There was gold everywhere. And columns. Tapestries. I think it was a palace. There was a man. A prince, maybe."

Vlad grunted in obvious disappointment. He liked specifics.

The very first time Val went dream-walking, it was to see his brother. His nurse had tucked him in for a nap, the sun high above, the light of his bedroom pure and without shadows. Val's mouth still tasted of berries and cream, and his muscles burned pleasantly from playing, and his eyes had closed the moment his head touched the pillow.

But then, suddenly, he'd found himself awake. And out of bed. Standing in the center of the room where Vlad sat perched on a stool at a low, book-loaded table, reading from a tome almost as big as he was. Vlad had jumped, startled, his serious reading-face dissolving into an expression of intense shock. And then he'd frowned and huffed angrily. "You're supposed to be napping."

"I…I am. Or…I was."

Vlad slid off the stool with a sigh, and came around the table, reaching for Val's hand. "I'll take you back," he said.

But his hand passed straight through Val's. As if it wasn't even there.

Val stared down at his own small hand, agape, as he watched his fingers blur and swirl, like smoke, before resettling and becoming solid again.

Solid-looking.

Vlad let out a string of curses he'd learned from the wolves, no doubt, and tried again. The same thing happened.

Vlad was in the process of stepping right *through* him when Fenrir poked his head into the room and startled both of them with one of his booming laughs.

"Dream-walking is it, my lords?" Fenrir was very old, and very wise, even if father said he was a "great stupid lout of a wolf," and he'd explained to them that Val was still very much upstairs in their shared bed, that this was his mind projecting itself.

"Not all vampires have the gift," he'd said, "but some do. *You* do, your grace." And he'd bowed low, beard swaying, so that Val had a view of the top of his head.

Val had laughed, and tried to clap his hands together, but of course he wasn't really there, so that hadn't been possible.

In the months since that first discovery, the dream-walking had happened with greater consistency. Mother had promised he'd someday be able to choose his destination, to drop into his strange not-dreams at will, and go visiting with others of their kind across vast distances. But so far, it happened when it wanted to happen.

He thought Vlad might have been jealous of his skill, but Vlad never said so. He only asked about his travels, pumping him for details, trying to experience it vicariously.

Vlad's nose wrinkled. "Are you sure it wasn't Father again?"

"No, it wasn't him. This prince wasn't speaking Romanian."

"Father speaks lots of languages."

"But it *wasn't* Father."

"Uncle, then?"

"*No*, it–"

Footsteps in the hall. Their mother's scent reached them before the door swung open. They both froze; Vlad's dark eyes went comically wide. Candlelight stretched across the floor and Mother entered with a soft, musical chuckle.

"Boys," she chided, coming to sit on the side of the bed. The candle's glow fell over them, gentle as the hand she smoothed across each of their foreheads in turn. "I seem to remember putting two handsome princes to bed two hours ago." When Mother scolded, it was always with a smile, and it always made Val want to promise that he'd never step so much as a single toe out of line ever again.

"Val went dream-walking," Vlad said, shifting onto his back so they were both looking up at Mother's quietly radiant face.

Her hair fell in thick gold waves to her waist, the ends trailing across the blankets. "Oh? Where did you go, darling?" She pushed Val's hair out of his eyes, smile impossibly warm.

"He doesn't know," Vlad said.

"I don't know," Val echoed. "I was by the sea. I could smell the salt. And there was a man – very tall, and handsome, and he had curly dark hair. I think he was important."

"Hmm, he sounds important," Mother agreed, smoothing his hair again. "What else do you remember?"

He felt his face scrunch up as he fought to recall. Every time he dream-walked, it became easier to recall the details. The first few times had left him foggy, his thoughts distorted. But the more he walked, the more pieces he was able to bring back with him. Now, tonight, he remembered a velvet night sky studded with stars, the distant shush and slap of gentle waves. He remembered buildings packed cheek-by-jowl, smooth pale stone that gleamed in the moonlight, architectural angles that reminded him of…

He gasped. "Greek. They were speaking Greek." The man he thought might be a prince, bent over a wooden table with another man, a silver plate dotted with burning, melting candles. They'd spoken in Greek.

"Ah." Mother's smile became proud. The same smile she bestowed on Vlad when he slid down from his horse's bare back, a brace of hares clutched in one small hand. "My son the triumphant hunter," she would always say. She looked at Val like that now. "Did you go to Byzantium, love?"

"I…" He wracked his brain, searching, searching. He'd made a noise, a quiet clearing of his throat, and the two men had turned around in their chairs to look at him, looking startled. Humans were always startled by what he could do.

But before that, before they'd noticed him, one man had called the handsome, curly-haired stranger by his name.

"Constantine," he said. "That was his name."

Mother *beamed*. "My clever boy. You went all the way to the seat of the emperor."

Val felt himself smiling in return.

"Wow," Vlad breathed beside him, breath warm where it tickled Val's neck.

Byzantium. Constantinople. The eastern seat of the Roman Empire. A fitting destination, he supposed, for a son of Rome.

~*~

An Empire Away

Nightfall in the palace gardens of Edirne smelled of a strange blend of orange blossom and healing wolfsbane. The climate here was that of Eastern Europe, of Wallachia, and Transylvania, and Hungary. But the Turks had brought plants from farther east with them, and architecture and customs as well. Overhead, the sky wheeled dark and star-studded. A breeze stirred the flames of the torches; they scudded and smoked, and lit the way with bright flickers. Mehmet admired the patterns on his bare toes as he walked down the pebbled path, wending his way beneath the shadows of climbing roses.

He still missed his mother, living with her and the other women in the harem. But it was time for him to start acting like a man, as Father had said. And men didn't hang off their mother's skirts.

Did men eavesdrop, though? He hoped they did, because that's what he was doing now, moving toward the low murmur of voices just ahead beneath a wisteria bower. One belonged to his father, but the other was a stranger.

Silent from long months of practice, Mehmet skirted one of the bower's stone support columns and ducked down into the shadows of a decorative hedge. When he peered through the leaves, he saw two figures standing in the flickering torchlight: his father's familiar stocky build, and a tall, lean stranger, a hood hiding most of his face. Mehmet caught the wet gleam of dark eyes, and the end of a prominent nose.

They spoke in Turkish. "I'm afraid," Father was saying, "that I fail to understand your reasoning for this, my lord. Generous gifts are not given without the expectation of reciprocity."

The stranger chuckled. "You really think me so mercenary, Your Majesty?"

Father didn't join in his laughter. "I know who you are, and what you've done."

"Ah. You disapprove, then."

"I did not say that."

The stranger rolled his weight back onto his heels, obviously surprised.

"Sometimes," Father continued, "it's a man's own flesh and blood that stands in the way of his empire, and steps must be taken."

A gleam of teeth beneath the hood as the stranger smiled. "Then we understand one another."

Father cocked his head. "I understand much of you. Still. Choosing my son, when you have nephews – that I do not understand."

It was quiet a moment, save the rustle of leaves and the pounding of Mehmet's heart behind his ribs.

"My nephews are fine boys," the stranger said at last. "But they are content. They lack...*imagination.*"

Mehmet didn't know why, but he shivered.

The hooded face turned toward him. "Speaking of which, it seems your son has joined us."

17

Oh no! He'd tried so carefully to be quiet.

Father turned toward his hiding spot, expression shifting from surprise to outrage. "Mehmet–" he started.

The stranger lifted a staying hand. "No, it's alright. Don't scold the boy. Mehmet, come out now, you're not in any trouble."

He hesitated, thinking of the mullahs and their riding crops, their assertions that they would make a mannerly boy of him for the sultan.

The stranger pushed his hood back and revealed a high forehead, and strong jaw, bold cheekbones. Fierce and beautiful, like one of the Greek statues he admired so much. "Come here, Mehmet," he said, smiling, "let me look at you."

Mehmet left his hiding place, brushing leaves from his kaftan, trying to look as upright and respectable as possible – a waste after hiding, but he wanted, suddenly, to impress this man.

The man looked down at him, and his smile widened. In the dancing torchlight, his eyes seemed to glow. "Hello, Mehmet. My name is Romulus, and I think you and I shall be great friends."

1

ONLY MY MIND

Denver, Colorado
Present Day

The first time it happened, Mia was coming off a twelve-hour day at the barn. She'd climbed into her first saddle at six, schooled four horses, handled a tricky lameness exam with a client's horse and a man-diva of a vet who sniffed at her contemptuously every time she asked a question, and then she started teaching lessons. At some point, Donna shoved half a peanut butter sandwich into her grubby hand and said, "Eat that before you fall over." When she got home, bone-weary and ready for bed by seven p.m., she'd noticed a big greasy spot of peanut butter on the collar of her polo. Figured.

She took an obscenely hot shower, threw her schooling clothes in the direction of the hamper, and reheated a Tupperware of leftover pasta. Hair still wet, she collapsed into her comfiest chair, dinner and a glass of wine on the side table, favorite ugly socks on her feet, her current vampire novel du jour in one hand. It was a boring evening; the kind a busy trainer/working student gunning for the pro circuit lived for.

And then, suddenly, it wasn't.

She glanced up from her book, intent on spearing a difficult hunk of chicken with her fork, and froze.

A man stood in the center of her living room.

Her fork fell out of her hand, landing on the edge of the plate with a clatter.

The first thing she noticed was his hair. It was impossible *not* to notice: long, full, pale gold waves that fell nearly to his waist.

Then the eyes: blue.

The face: narrow and regal.

The clothes: red velvet, and a black fur cloak, and knee-high polished boots.

He was stunning.

He was impossible.

Slowly, Mia set her book aside on the table.

The man wasn't looking at her, was instead inspecting the room around him, making a slow turn in the center of the rug, tilting his head side to side as he took in her TV, Ikea furniture, and overloaded bookshelf. He stopped, finally, blue eyes widening, and stepped in closer to inspect the titles on the spines.

Later, much later, she would remember the way it was the books that had captured his interest first, and she'd carry that little kernel of gold with her for the rest of her life.

But for now, she had an intruder in her apartment, and the closest weapon to hand was the lamp on the table beside her. Slowly, slowly, she leaned over and wrapped her fingers around the base. It was a chunky faux-bronze thing that she thought was supposed to look antique, and it was heavy. She gave it an experimental tug and it eked toward her a half-inch, shade wobbling alarmingly. She bit her lip, wincing. It would take both hands, but she thought it would make a good projectile. She'd get only one shot, though, so it had to count.

"Hmm," the man hummed, back still to her, "you can throw that if you like, but it won't do any good."

She snatched it up in both hands, heart leaping wildly, and chucked it at him.

He didn't move, but the lamp didn't strike him. It seemed to pass *through* him, his back and shoulders swirling like smoke a moment, then resettling. The lamp crashed against the bookshelf; a handful of well-loved hardbacks toppled to the floor, pages crumpling. The frame of the shelf had cracked.

Silence, save the rough scrape of Mia's breath in and out of her lungs. *Holy shit*, she thought. *What the...*

The man turned, unhurried. A sharp little smile lifted one corner of his mouth. "I did warn you."

A dozen potential questions gathered on the back of her tongue, but what left her mouth was, "What are you?"

His smile widened; the lamplight caught on sharp, white canines. "Oh, well. This is *interesting*." He tipped his chin down, and his eyes flashed, and he leaned toward her in a way that sent goosebumps rippling down her arms. There was such an inherent threat in his posture. Like the villains in her favorite novels.

"Stop." She threw up a hand, as if that could keep him back. "Just…" She couldn't breathe. "Stop."

He relaxed a fraction, head pulling back on his slender, pale neck. "I can't actually touch you, you know. Not even if I wanted to." To demonstrate, he reached behind him and passed a spectral hand through a shelf on her bookcase.

I'm dreaming, she thought with sudden relief. She'd been even more tired than she thought, and she'd passed out in the chair; probably dropped her book; probably spilled her wine.

Or what if it's worse than a dream? an insidious voice whispered in the back of her mind.

No. She couldn't think that. Not right now.

She was dreaming.

And yet…

"What are you?" she repeated.

He smiled, but it was softer this time, almost delighted. "You could have asked all sorts of things, you know. Who. Why. What are my intentions. But you went straight to *what*." His smile became almost a grimace, but he folded his arms and cocked his hips in obvious challenge. "What am I? I'm many things. A prince. A prisoner. A brother. A legacy. But that's not what you meant, is it?"

"You look…" Her eyes moved over his glorious hair, his fine features, his elegant clothes. Beautiful. "…like an elf."

But that wasn't right, and when he smiled again, she saw his canines, that sharp flash, and knew. "Close, darling," he said. "But not quite."

Mia took a deep breath that did nothing to calm her pounding heart. She glanced over at the book she'd laid on the table; its cover depicted a long-haired vampire in medieval armor, arms around a human woman.

She exhaled in a rush. "Of course there's a vampire in my living room," she muttered, gaze flicking back to the intruder. "Of course."

His grin was blinding. He sketched a deep, formal bow, hair sliding over his shoulders in gorgeous disarray. "Prince Valerian of Wallachia, ma'am. It's a pleasure."

She blinked at him. "What kind of accent is that?" Because if she was dreaming, why not play along? It was the most entertaining thing that had happened to her in months.

He sighed. "I've just told you. Wallachian." When she continued to stare, he said, "That's in Romania, darling."

"Ah."

"I speak many languages, though. English, obviously. And I'm fluent in Slavic – written form, mostly; all the books were in Slavic when I was a boy – and Latin; Russian; French; Turkish; Greek. A little Italian."

Breathe, Mia reminded herself. "Okay. Um. So you're a vampire."

"Quite."

"Can you…turn into smoke? Is that what this is?" She gestured to him.

"Smoke?" His nose wrinkled and his lip curled. "No. This isn't smoke. It's an astral projection."

"Okay."

"I'm not really here, you see. Only my mind." He tapped the side of his head. Then glanced around the room again. "Where *is* here, actually?"

"Denver, Colorado."

"Fascinating," he hummed, but looked more concerned than fascinated. He turned back to her, clasping his hands behind his back; the movement pulled his cloak wide, revealing broad shoulders and a tiny waist encased in brocaded red velvet. "You haven't introduced yourself."

"Because this isn't real."

He tilted his head. "Of course it is."

They stared at one another – studied one another. One of those long moments, stretched out slow like taffy. Almost sweet in the way she relished it. A moment for a careful decision: continue the charade? Or go call her doctor?

In the way of all drowning people, Mia grabbed for the charade.

"So…you're a Romanian prince, huh?"

He smiled again, a kind of smile he hadn't shown her yet, full of gladness. "What's your name?"

"Mia. Mia Talbot." She held out her hand, like an idiot.

His brows jumped, and for one fast second, he looked like he'd been slapped. But then his expression melted back to the way it had been, and he stepped forward. "Mia." He extended his hand toward hers, slow and careful, and she marveled at the way his narrow fingers passed right through hers. "Pleased to meet you. You can call me Val."

2

VAMPIRE

"If you're not really here, then where are you?"

Val sat on the end of her kitchen island — at least he appeared to, swinging his booted feet and frowning down at them in contemplation. He'd left off the cloak and velvet coat this time, was dressed in a simple shirt with a vest over it, the cuffs trailing laces. His hair caught the evening sunlight that slanted through the windows, rivers of gold spilling over his shoulders. "In a cell," he said, and his voice had lost all the bright spark it had held only moments before, when he'd asked what she was making for dinner.

It had been a week since he first appeared in her apartment, and he'd returned every day since. Shortly after she arrived home from the barn, once she'd showered and changed, he materialized in the living room, beautiful and smiling.

On the first day, she knew this was a bad sign. At the very best, she'd gone batshit crazy and invented herself a handsome imaginary friend to combat the quietly crushing loneliness she refused to acknowledge. At the worst...

She couldn't think about the worst.

By the third day, when Val appeared between the turning of two pages, cross-legged and splendid on the rug, she'd felt a traitorous swooping in her stomach. She was looking forward to his impossible visits. To his questions about her books, and her favorite TV shows, and her job. Learning she was a horse trainer had lit his face up like Christmas morning. "Are you *really*?" She'd ended up pulling down one of her horse albums, full of photos chronicling her equestrian journey from the days of jodhpur straps all the way to last year's regional win.

He'd tried to touch the album page, divot marring his smooth brow when his fingers passed through. "But you sit the horse so well," he'd murmured. "You're a natural."

She'd blushed at the quiet praise.

So far, they hadn't talked about anything serious. Why waste a good imaginary friend on mundane drama? But he looked tired today, shadows like soft indigo paint smudges lingering beneath his eyes. So the question slipped out.

Mia stood at the island chopping veggies, and she set her knife down. "A cell?"

"Yes." His boot heels drummed soundlessly against the cabinet face.

"Val," she said carefully, moving around to the end of the island so she could see his face. "Are you in jail?"

He didn't answer a moment, gaze still trained on the floor, chest lifting as he took deep breaths through his mouth. When he spoke, his voice was almost a growl, bitter and hurt. "Does that matter? Are you one of *those* people?" He lifted his head, eyes flashing; his fangs were more prominent than normal. "Do you take incarceration for guilt without knowing the circumstances?"

She'd spent her whole life communicating with creatures who couldn't speak; learning the little body language tells.

Val bared his teeth in a challenge...that was also a way to brace for rejection. His words taunted, but his eyes begged. And doubted.

"No," she said, simply, and returned to her vegetables. "If you're innocent, you shouldn't be locked up. But thanks for making assumptions about me."

It was silent a beat save the clean slice of the knife through bell pepper.

Then Val turned to look at her over his shoulder, mouth gone soft, eyes wide. "Oh."

"Do you want to talk about it?"

"Not...especially."

"Okay. So don't." She scraped the peppers over with her knife and started in on the squash.

Silence stretched for so long that she thought he might have fritzed out. Every evening, after she'd loaded the dishwasher and her eyelids started to flag, he would always say, "You're tired. I've kept you long enough." He would bow, smile one final time, and then disappear. She'd nearly jumped out of her skin the first time, but by now it was normal.

This whole thing was becoming alarmingly normal.

She really needed to call her doctor and set up an appointment.

Finally, she said, "Did I tell you how Brando's tempi changes are coming along?" and was ashamed to admit to herself how badly she hoped he was still here.

He said, "No, you haven't." Clear relief in his voice.

Mia smiled.

~*~

"I was born in 1435," he said when she asked him how old he was.

Mia paused with her coffee cup halfway to her lips. Her imagination was very specific, she'd give it that. "So..." she mused, doing the math in her head. "Five-hundred-eighty-three." A staggering thought, even if it was a fictional one. He looked twenty-five at most. "So vampires really are immortal, I guess."

"Quite." He'd been sitting cross-legged, and kicked his legs out, leaning back on his hands.

Mia sat opposite, back braced against the sofa. She couldn't help but notice that the velvet was back tonight, in all its intricate glory. "Is that what you were wearing when you..." *Were captured*, she left unsaid.

"Oh no." He waved one long-fingered hand. A massive ruby ring on his middle finger seemed to catch the light. "I bargained this from a French aristocrat in 1802." He gave her one of his sharp grins. "I just had to have it."

"What kind of bargaining power does a prisoner have?"

His smile stretched, until it was all teeth. "He wanted immortality. I told him I'd turn him in exchange for his beautiful outfit."

"And did you?"

"Of course not. I drained him dry and tried to escape."

She glared at him. "You're horrible."

"And yet you're the one sitting here talking to me. What does that make you?"

26

"Well, after that little murder confession, I'm thinking it makes me an accessory after the fact."

He rolled his eyes and groaned. "Oh, you humans and your moral indignation."

"Murder warrants some indignation."

He huffed a sigh. "He was one of my jailors, and a horridly perverted one, too."

She lifted a single brow.

"And we're back to incarceration."

"You won't tell me what you were locked up for."

"Hmm. No, I won't." He glanced away, pretending to inspect the blank TV screen, but Mia could see the downward quirk at the corner of his mouth.

Who'd ever heard of a self-indulgent hallucination who pouted? He acted the age that he looked, not the age he actually was.

"1435," she said, because he was too beautiful to frown. "I'm not much of a historian. Did you live in a castle?"

He brightened a fraction, turning back to her. "Yes, the palace at Tîrgovişte. I don't really remember anything from Sighişoara, before. Mother always said it was very provincial. But Tîrgovişte was lovely. Father had just been confirmed as Prince of Wallachia, and the city was always teeming. My brothers – Mircea and Vlad, both older – were training to be knights. Mircea was the eldest, and he was being groomed as Father's heir, you know. Vlad wanted to be a military man." He chuckled. "He was martial from birth, I think."

Vlad. The named pinged something in her memory banks.

She wasn't a historian, no, too busy with juggling her riding dreams alongside first high school, then her tumor, then her recovery, then college. She'd majored in communications, intent on using the degree to manage the riding school she wanted to some day run. And though she loved to read, she didn't force herself toward educational tomes; she read novels, to unwind, to slip into the skins of women with daring, dangerous, wondrous lives.

But she'd always loved vampire novels.

Romania. Prince. Vampire. *Vlad.*

"…I had this pony," Val was saying, but trailed off, brows pinching together, when he saw her face. "What?"

Mia's next breath rattled a little in her throat; a shiver moved beneath her skin as she pushed to her feet and walked across the room to the bookshelf. She ran a fingertip along the spines, searching, chanting *no way, no way, no way* in her head.

"What?" Val repeated. "Is something wrong?" He sounded worried.

"Your brother…Vlad…" Most of her collection consisted of secondhand paperbacks, but she had a whole shelf dedicated to the titles she loved so much she'd bought them in hardback collectors' editions. She found the one she wanted and pulled it out, turning the cover toward Val with shaking hands. "Your brother Vlad, as in this guy?"

It was her gorgeous, leather-bound version of Bram Stoker's *Dracula*.

Val's eyes narrowed as he read the title. Then he smiled. A closed-mouthed, tight, sideways smile laced with an emotion too faint for her to place. "Ah, yes." His tone seemed carefully modulated. "I always forget they named a book after him."

Mia let her hands fall to her sides because her arms felt weak, heavy book thumping against her thigh. "You're shitting me."

"It's all fiction. Stoker's character is nothing like my brother. Nothing that happens in the book is true."

Nothing about this *conversation* was true.

"Dracula is real," she said, deadpan in an effort to keep a meltdown at bay, "and he's your brother."

"Yes."

She sat down hard on the floor and covered her face with her hands. "I have to call my doctor," she whispered to herself, stomach clenching.

"Why?" Val's voice said, right in front of her, and she startled so hard she whacked her head on the bookshelf.

He winced in sympathy and eased back a fraction; he knelt on the rug in front of her, hands on his thighs, limned in golden evening light.

Mia let her hands fall into her lap. "This isn't real," she said. "*You're* not real." The words scraped her throat, and she hated them, but there was no sense letting this play out any longer.

His mouth fell open; he wore a slapped expression. "I – I – I *am* real." He pressed his lips together, jaw clenching tight; she saw the tendons leap beneath his fine skin. "Don't say that, I'm *real!*"

"How? How could you possibly be? Vampires don't exist outside of books."

His lips skinned back off his teeth; he opened his mouth…and *snarled*. An aggressive punch of sound, like the tigers she'd seen once at the zoo. No human could have made that sound.

Mia startled again, whacked her head *again*.

The sound cut off immediately, and Val lifted both hands like he meant to touch her. They realized at the same moment that that wasn't possible; he froze, and she caught her instinctive flinch.

His hands went back to his thighs and he let out a long, slow exhale, shoulders drooping. His gaze dropped to the rug. "Sometimes I wonder," he murmured, "if I really am dead. Or if I've been buried, and I'm only dreaming. Maybe this is purgatory; centuries of never being able to touch, or taste, or smell…until I've paid off my debts."

"Val–" she started.

And he disappeared.

3

AS LONG AS YOU'LL HAVE ME

"Mia? *Mia.*"

"What? Oh." She gave herself a mental shake. She was standing in the center of the outdoor arena, sun beating down hot on her face and neck, vision gone blurry behind the lenses of her sunglasses. She was in the middle of teaching a lesson, and she'd spaced out. Again.

Her student, Monica, had pulled her horse up to a halt right in front of Mia, and was currently staring at her with obvious concern, brows drawn together beneath the brim of her helmet. "Mia, are you okay?"

"Yeah. I'm–" The ground tilted dangerously beneath her, and she braced a hand against the horse's – poor, sweet Gephardt – shoulder to keep her balance. "Fine," she said. But she wasn't. Black spots crowded the edges of her vision, and a prickling cold erupted beneath her skin.

Gephardt nudged her shoulder.

"It's really hot out here," Monica said. "Maybe you should go sit in the shade a second. Get some water."

Mia closed her eyes. Monica was right, but Mia hated the fact that she had to be coddled and sent to sip cold drinks like a novice who didn't know her own body's limits.

Her head swam, and she managed a nod. "Yeah. Maybe. Okay. I'm sorry–"

"It's fine," Monica assured. "Geppie needs a walk break anyway."

When Mia managed to tip her head back and crack her eyes open, Monica gave her a reassuring smile.

Ugh.

"Alright," she said, and stepped back from Gephardt's solid shoulder; managed to walk over to the edge of the arena and the pop-up canopy tent they kept there for just such a purpose. Javier had filled the cooler there with fresh ice and the usual array of drinks: water, Gatorade, Coke, orange juice. Mia sat down in one of the camp chairs and made herself down half a blue Gatorade, stomach churning afterward.

In the arena, Monica let out Gephardt's reins and the bay stretched his neck gladly, long walking strides eating up the distance across the sand.

Mia was in serious danger of passing out.

Last night, she'd spent half an hour staring at the place on the rug where Val had knelt in front of her, willing him to return. He hadn't, and so she'd spent those thirty minutes replaying his growl – that's what it had been: a growl. There was no other word for it. And then, after, his utterly crestfallen expression. The heavy sadness that had pressed lines into his smooth face.

This was getting so out of hand; she could no longer pretend that he was imaginary: this was a flat-out, off the charts hallucination.

But.

But…

She'd tugged the hardback copy of *Dracula* into her lap, opened it to the first page, and started reading. She'd read it a number of times, gaining some new insight on each read, coming away from the classic with a tweaked interpretation.

She'd read in fits and starts last night, skipping passages and whole pages. Finally, halfway through, she'd pulled out her phone and Googled Dracula. The usual nonsense results popped up: the count in his high collar, black-and-white movie stills, dozens of variations, plus fanart and fanfiction.

She'd refined her search to *real Dracula*. That had yielded a very different result.

Romanian prince born in 1431. Prince of Wallachia. Dubbed "The Impaler" thanks to his penchant for impaling victims on wooden stakes.

There were paintings.

Vlad had indeed had two brothers, one older and one younger. Mircea…

And Radu.

She'd stood up, left her phone on the floor, and gone straight to bed. She'd stared up at the ceiling in the dark and given herself a stern talking-to. It was time to drop this stupid shit. She needed a vacation, or to go on a date. Or, what was most likely to happen, to stop reading so damn many books about made-up stuff and focus instead on qualifying for regionals. The spring show season was melting into summer, and she had a long way to go.

Val was someone she'd conjured for her own amusement, because she clearly wasn't keeping busy enough.

(A tiny voice whispered: *Val might be a new tumor playing kickball with your brain.*)

She'd rolled over, slammed her eyes shut…and not slept a wink.

Now here she was, dehydrated, exhausted, and miserable, about to faint in the middle of a lesson she was *teaching*; she wasn't even *riding*.

She really did feel terrible.

She downed the rest of the Gatorade and, leaning against the fence for support, managed to finish Monica's lesson. Her student kept shooting her concerned glances, and Mia broke one of her own rules: rather than walk through her usual post-lesson debrief while Monica cooled down, she patted Gephardt's neck and said a simple, "Good job."

The walk back to the barn felt like a hike, though the ground was level. She stopped once she was in the shade, hand braced on a stall front, breathing through her mouth while she fought the phantom weight on her chest.

"Mia." The sharp clip of bootheels rebounded off the stall fronts like gunshots.

Mia lifted her head, already wincing, as her boss, Donna, bore down on her, long, ballerina legs carrying her across the bricks so fast it made Mia's head spin.

"Javi said you were feeling poorly," Donna said, blunt as usual. "What's wrong? Do I need to send you home?"

"No," Mia said, aiming for firm, falling somewhere a little south of that. "Just a little overheated. I'm fine." She let go of the blanket bar she was holding and stood up straight to prove her point. She wobbled a little.

Donna's eyes narrowed; her ponytail was so tight that the movement shifted her entire hairline forward a fraction. "You're keeping up with your regular doctor's appointments?"

"Yes," Mia said, too fast, too sharp.

Donna's eyes narrowed further. "Come down to my office. We need to have a talk."

Shit.

Mia followed her, wishing her own hips and legs were so miraculously lean, dreading the conversation about to unfold.

Four years ago, Mia had emailed her résumé, five recommendation letters, and a video compilation that included the most awkward, painful interview of her life, to the one and only Donna Masters, already knowing she didn't have a prayer of landing the working student job of her dreams. She'd fallen out of her chair when Donna herself called to offer her the job and ask how fast she could get her horse and all her worldly possessions to Denver.

The past four years had been a whirlwind of riding, teaching, schooling, and learning more than she'd ever imagined. A two-time Olympian, daughter of two trainers, and a passionate horsewoman, Donna expected nothing less than perfection from the people in her employ. She was a fair boss – but an exacting one. The last thing Mia wanted was to show the kind of weakness that she had so far today.

Donna led them into her office, a small square room with a view of the front pasture, its walls covered in framed photos, commemorative plaques, and ribbons. It was better organized than Mia's office, more of a showpiece, with elegant leather couches and an elaborate antique French desk; a place where Donna could entertain high-dollar clients. There was a mini fridge in one corner, above it a massive framed poster of Donna at her last Olympics, astride the now-retired Key Largo.

"Sit down." Donna waved at one of the couches as she dropped down behind her desk and shifted a stack of printouts over. "Have some water if you haven't already."

Gatorade still sloshing in her empty stomach, Mia eased down onto the couch. "I'm fine."

"Where is that – ah, remind me to call Adrianna after this. We need to talk about the next steps in Lancelot's training schedule."

"Yes, ma'am."

Maybe this wouldn't be so bad. Maybe Donna wanted to talk horses, and–

Donna straightened the last bit of paperwork and lifted her head, gaze laser-focused on Mia's face, sculpted brows somehow judgmental. "You don't look well."

Damn.

"I didn't get much sleep last night." Not a lie. "And I wasn't keeping up with my water intake."

Donna stared at her. "Mia, one of the things we agreed on when you started here was that you would look after your health. I might be a hard bitch, but I'm not heartless – if you're having problems–"

"I'm not," Mia said, too firmly.

Donna sighed delicately through her nostrils. "You can talk to me, you know. If something's wrong."

But Mia couldn't. What would she say: *I've been seeing this beautiful man who claims to be a vampire every night, and I'm afraid he's a brain tumor-induced hallucination. I'm too scared to go to the doctor and get a scan, because another tumor means more treatment, more surgery. Another tumor means I can't keep working for you.*

She took a deep breath and said, "Donna, I appreciate the concern, but I swear I'm okay. If something changes, I'll tell you. But I need to drink some water and get to my next lesson."

Donna held her gaze a long, unblinking moment, corner of her mouth twitching downward. Then she nodded. "Alright. Remind Asa to lengthen his stirrups this time."

"Ma'am." Mia got to her feet and made a hasty escape before Donna could change her mind.

~*~

She kept the fluids going the rest of the day, stayed in the shade as much as possible, and forced down a lunch of takeout chicken and veggies that Javier ordered from their favorite café.

By the time she climbed into her truck and headed home, she felt tired, but pleasantly so. Strong, fit, and not like a fainting flower at all.

It really was just the heat, she decided. She turned up the radio and resolved to think about something else.

Which inevitably sent her thoughts spinning back toward Val.

The root of her problem, she decided between red lights, was basic loneliness. She got along with Donna, with Javi and the grooms. She enjoyed her students. But everyone around her was either much older, much younger, or happily married. Donna wasn't the sort of trainer who kept lots of young students around. "I don't want a bunch of gossip and drama," she had said, dismissively, when Mia asked about the possibility of other working students. Mia didn't want gossip and drama either – and she'd seen plenty of both in her lifetime of equestrian sports – but at the end of every day, she became acutely aware that she didn't know anyone in Denver with which to hang out recreationally.

She read a lot.

Watched a lot of Netflix.

Most nights she was so tired that the thought of going out made her want to cry anyway, so what was the problem?

The problem was she didn't have any friends at this stage in her life. She was twenty-eight, and bi-weekly phone calls with her mom were the highlight of her social calendar.

It made a crazy kind of sense that she'd invented her own charming, gorgeous man to talk to every night. Why try online dating when you could ogle a sleek blond with fangs?

Crazy or not, she *wanted* to see him.

She parked, went up to her little one-bedroom, locked herself in, flipped on the lights. Slid a single-serve frozen lasagna into the oven, showered, toweled her hair. And all the while she was composing an apology to Val in her head. If he showed back up, well…she was going to enjoy his company and stop questioning it. It could be her little secret. No one had to know she was losing her marbles.

She tugged on leggings, a t-shirt, and socks, and stepped out of her bedroom to find the object of all her obsessive thoughts lying across her sofa, his head tipped back over the arm so his hair spilled down to the floor. His brows quirked, and his mouth curved the tiniest fraction, a hopeful little smile.

Mia's heart clenched, and oh no, she was in *trouble*.

"Hi," she said.

"I'm sorry about last night."

"Me too."

"Did I frighten you?" he asked, softly.

"A little bit."

"I didn't mean to."

She nodded.

"You look tired. What's wrong?"

She took a deep, shuddering breath. The truth hurt, badly, but it proved to be the easiest thing to say. "When I was in high school, I had a brain tumor. The chemo, and radiation, and surgery almost killed me. The doctors didn't know if I'd ever be able to ride again. But I beat it, and I can. And now..." Her voice cracked. "You're here, and I'm afraid you're just another hallucination. That you're another tumor."

His expression did something complicated, pain pressing grooves around his mouth. He rolled over onto his stomach, hair falling to frame his face. He reached one elegant hand toward her. "I'm sorry you were sick. There are lots of people who would say that I'm a cancer – but I'm not *your* tumor. I'm real. I promise you that."

She stared at his hand a long moment – a hand she couldn't touch. She couldn't get close enough to feel his body heat, to bury her face in the softness of his hair and breathe in the smell of it. Couldn't trace a finger down the pale column of his throat and feel the beating pulse there. Couldn't ask him to find her own pulse in turn, to sink his fangs in it and drag her down to some dark plane where she was strong and whole.

But she could allow herself this indulgence.

Shaking, she stepped forward, reaching out to him. Her hand passed right through his, and she held it there, inside the swirling smoke that had been his fingers. "Will you keep coming back?" she asked.

He smiled, soft. "As long as you'll have me."

4

EVERDALE

"It's cavalry movements. But…no battle. Just presentation. Beauty and strength for the sake of enjoyment alone. It's *wonderful*," Val gushed, eyes glued to the TV screen. He sighed dreamily, like a pining lover. "I wish this had existed in my day."

"Uh huh." Mia extended her legs out across her yoga mat, leaned forward and wrapped her hands around her feet. The deep stretch tugged at a sore spot in her lower back, and she winced.

"That, there," Val said. She snuck a glance at the screen and saw footage from last week, her putting Brando through a rough attempt at a canter pirouette.

"Pirouette," she supplied. "Or, an attempt at one."

"Lovely," he breathed, transfixed. And then, wistful, "I had a mare once who did them beautifully. A little Arabian, bright red with white markings." He sighed. "God, I miss riding."

Mia pulled up out of her stretch and stared at him a moment: the sparkle in his eyes, the naked longing on his face. "Hey."

It was so much worse when he turned his head to look at her, the way her chest grabbed and squeezed. A long tendril of golden hair slipped from behind his ear and unfurled down his shoulder.

She cleared her throat. "I can't do anything about the riding. But." This was such a bad idea. "Do you wanna come to the barn with me?"

Such a bad idea.

But the way his face lit up made it worth the risk.

~*~

Mia went to change into breeches and a crisp white Everdale Farms polo, and when she got back to the living room, tote bag slung over one shoulder, Dansko clogs dangling from her fingers, she came to a grinding halt.

Val had changed, too.

Over his breeches, we wore an embroidered blue tunic, cinched around his narrow waist with a worn, brown leather belt. His boots were different, too, brown, scuffed, and bearing old horse sweat stains along the insides of the shafts. His hair lay over one shoulder in a single, tidy braid.

He tipped his head to the side, and she realized she'd been staring like an idiot.

"What?" he asked.

She swallowed. "Where'd you get the change of clothes?" She thought her voice sounded mostly normal.

"Oh. It's just..." He shut his eyes, and his whole being seemed to shimmer. In the wake of the ripples, he wore his red velvet again. Another shimmer, and he was in heavy chain mail with leather shoulder guards, metal gauntlets and greaves, his hair braided in a tight crown around his head. A last shimmer, and it was the blue tunic, brown boots, and single braid once more.

Mia gasped. "Wow."

Val's eyes opened, and he grinned. "Astral projection, remember? I can look however I want."

"...Good to know." Her palms were a little clammy with something like excitement, but she didn't dare set down her clogs and wipe them on her breeches. That would be too smitten-schoolgirl of her. "Ready to go?"

"Yes!" His fangs flashed when his smile turned delighted.

"Wait. Can you ride in the truck?"

His smile dimmed, grew thoughtful. "I believe so. We shall see, I suppose."

And here came the big question: "Will anyone else be able to see you?"

Fangs again. "Not if I don't want them to."

Right. Because he was a...

Nope. She wasn't thinking about that. She was living in the gorgeous, enjoyable moment. "Okay. Let's go."

~*~

It wasn't until they were down in the parking lot, standing beside her truck, that she realized maybe someone born in 1435 and kept as a prisoner most of his life wouldn't know anything about modern transportation.

"This is yours?" he asked, nodding to the dusty blue Ford with the Everdale sticker on the window and the trailer hitch set under the bumper. A single crease had formed between his brows, his mouth set in a neutral line.

"Yes. Do you know what a car is?"

"Yes," he snapped, before she'd even finished speaking. Then the neutral line became a frown, and the tips of his ears turned a delicate pink. "I just...it's rather large, isn't it?" A note of doubt crept into his voice, and paired with the pink ears, she had to bite back a smile.

"It's a standard size for a truck," she explained. "You can't tow a horse trailer with a sports car."

"Of course," he saw, but the groove between his brows deepened in puzzlement. He clearly had no idea what she was talking about at all.

"Look at it this way," she said. "If you're not really here, you can't really fly through the windshield if I slam on the brakes, right?"

His head whipped around, braid flying. "*What?* That happens?"

"Only when people don't wear their seatbelts. And don't worry, I'm a very good driver. It won't happen at all." She prayed she hadn't just jinxed herself. "You'll be perfectly safe."

His brows shot up. "As you pointed out, I'm not here. What about you? What if you throw yourself through the – the – wind...thing?"

Oh damn, he was too cute.

She suppressed her smile into something soothing, or so she hoped. "I'll wear my seatbelt. And I won't slam on the brakes. It'll be fine. Come on, I do this every day." She tried to nudge his arm, forgetting she couldn't until his elbow was swirling like smoke.

He frowned and turned back to the truck. "Traveling by horse is much safer."

"That is not even a little bit true."

"It is!"

"Val, if you'd rather not go—"

"I'm going. How dare you take back your invitation?" Before she could tell him that she'd done no such thing, and that he was being ridiculous, he melted through the passenger door like something out of *Casper* and situated himself in the seat. He shot her a narrow-eyed, challenging look through the window.

Mia chuckled and went around to get behind the wheel.

He held himself stiffly, head pressed back against the rest, hands folded together in his lap, back ramrod straight. She didn't know how it was possible to be so uncomfortable when you weren't even really here, but he seemed to manage that.

When they were out on the road, headed toward the farm, Mia said, "Have you ever ridden in a car before?"

He made an unhappy sound in his throat. "I've been transported in vehicles, yes."

When he didn't elaborate, she cast a glance across the cab and saw that he was staring out the window, expression withdrawn.

"What sort of vehicle?" she asked.

"I was blindfolded, I didn't get to see."

"Oh."

"I wasn't given a seat. I was thrown in like luggage."

Because he was a prisoner.

Mia swallowed and said, "I'm sorry."

"Yes, well, being sorry doesn't change anything." He took a quick, deep breath, and his tone sounded forced afterward. "Tell me about the farm."

"Everdale? Gosh, it's gorgeous." And it was. Before Donna offered her the job, Mia had been convinced she would only ever lay eyes on such a place through *Dressage Today* photo spreads. The barn was done up like a Colorado mountain house, with heavy timbers under the eaves and fat stone columns. Like most top-dollar equestrian centers, it boasted big box stalls, hot-and-cold washracks with heaters and fans, an indoor arena, offices, a lounge, a bathroom, and the tack room to end all tack rooms. But unlike so many farms, it had pastures, too: eighty acres of them, all the fences stained black. Mia had never ridden so many horses a day, from freshly-started four-year-olds to schoolmaster lesson horses in need of a tune-up between students. It was exhausting and amazing, and she gushed on about it until she was breathless and she was slowing the truck to turn in at the gates.

"Sorry." She felt a blush staining her cheeks. "I got kind of carried away." When she snuck a glance at Val, he was smiling almost wistfully, gaze fond.

"You're passionate about what you do. I like that."

She blushed harder and steered them up the lazy curves of the driveway, fence flashing past, toward the barn.

Val leaned forward in his seat. "Oh, it's lovely."

"Isn't it?" She parked beside Javier's Jeep, killed the engine, and then turned in her seat to really look at her spectral passenger.

Val's gaze was directed out the window, to the front pasture where three mares and their two-month-old foals grazed. Well, the mamas grazed, tails swishing lazily at flies. The foals were engaged in a rollicking game of something like tag, darting and dodging between their mothers, nipping at one another, gamboling on their too-long legs. Val watched the scene with a smile, face bathed in morning light, his skin smooth and fine. From behind, she could see the start of his braid, at the nape of his neck, the heavy golden strands plaited together to reveal a vulnerable patch of skin just behind his ear; it looked like it would be silky-soft to the touch. If she could touch him. If he was here.

She bit back a sigh. "I would love to give you a tour. Introduce you to all the horses. But it'll look like I'm talking to myself…"

He turned to face her, smile small and rueful. "Yes, I know. Don't worry about me. I won't be a bother."

"I didn't think you would be. I wanted to apologize in advance, though, for not being able to talk to you like I want."

One of his hands opened in his lap, lifted a fraction – he'd wanted to reach for her, she thought – and then eased back down. He smiled again, and it didn't quite reach his eyes. "Seeing will be enough."

She swallowed with sudden difficulty. *Where are you? How can I help you?*

41

She gathered her keys and said, "Follow me, then."

~*~

Val had assured her that he could keep himself cloaked from everyone but her, and that appeared to be true. At one point, she'd glanced up and seen Javi lead a horse right through Val. She'd gaped…but Javi hadn't seemed to notice.

Val shot her a wink.

The usual daily chaos swept her up in its tide, and she didn't get the chance to worry about how Val was faring. She taught two lessons, schooled two of the five-year-olds, and ate the sandwich Donna brought her. She snuck glances of Val: him peering into stalls; him standing in the shade of the pop-up tent beside a client who didn't notice him; him staring out across the fields, untouched by the breeze, his gaze open and heartbroken.

She lost track of him for a while. But he reappeared in the early evening, when Mia finally climbed aboard Brando for her own lesson. He stood at the rail, projecting the image of having his arms folded over the top board, gaze trained on her as Donna sat down on the mounting block. Mia sent him a quick, small smile.

He returned it, but there were shadows under his eyes. A tiredness she hadn't seen before. And his face didn't seem as solid, his skin translucent. With a start, she realized that she could see the barn *through* him. He was fading.

"Mia," Donna said. "Did you hear me?"

"What? Yes, sorry." She gave herself a firm mental shake. She needed to focus; her horse and her instructor and her sport deserved better attention than she'd paid it today.

Putting Val out of her mind – a difficult task, more troubling than she was ready to admit – she gathered her reins and squeezed Brando into a swinging warm-up trot, encouraging him to stretch through the neck and back with gentle pressure on the bit.

Unlike her coach and mentor, Mia hadn't been born to the equestrian life. Her father, already a prominent scientist when she was born, had bounced the family from university to

42

university…that was before the divorce…trying to earn grant money to start up his own facility. Mia and her mom had been left to their own devices for the most part, and Mom, Kate, had tried to make up for Mia's absent father through a variety of mother-daughter activities. They'd tried ballet together, and jazz, and tap. Painting, and ceramics, and even soccer. But they went for riding lessons when Mia was six, and that was it. End of story. Mia didn't want to do anything but ride after that.

Edwin and Kate divorced when Mia was ten. Edwin got his grant, and Kate got Mia.

And Mia got a mother who scraped, and saved, and sacrificed so that her daughter could chase her Olympic dreams. Mia had been a barn rat, mucking stalls, polishing tack, wrapping legs. She'd exercised horses, broken colts, driven tractors. She'd fetched coffee, and lunch, and whips, and used her own t-shirt to wipe the snot from the nose of her trainer's horse right before they went into the show ring. Her chiropractor said she had the neck of someone who'd been in a terrible car crash, after years of riding, and lifting, and working her fingers to the bone.

And now here she was. *DT* had actually interviewed her a few months ago. Interviewed *her*. "I'm so proud of you, baby," Kate said over the phone every time they talked. Because Mia had beaten a brain tumor, and all the odds, and that Olympic dream wasn't really out of reach anymore.

So she wasn't born in the saddle, but after an early childhood of moving from city to city, the saddle had been the first place that felt like home. From the calluses in her palms, to the busted capillaries in her knees, she was a horsewoman to her bones. On the back of the horse, nothing else mattered.

Today, like every day, she shifted her weight back, shortened her reins, and when Brando responded – lifting his back, surging to meet her halfway – she forgot all her earthly worries. There was no possible new tumor, no Val, no distractions. She asked, and Brando answered; they danced.

"Good," Donna said. "Less inside rein, more outside leg, *yes*."

Mia could sense the pirouette, an electricity that lived beneath her skin, and Brando's. A power ready to be unleashed if she could just tap into it the right way. She half-halted, slowed, slowed, slowed, adjusted the flexion.

Hold, release, hold, release. Abs, outside rein, seat, leg…

Almost. It wobbled. The shape was right, even the steps, but it was too big. Not tight and clean enough.

"That was too big," Donna called.

"Yeah," Mia panted.

"Again."

She gave it three more tries, then Donna sent her off to do an extended trot down the center line – Brando had beautiful extensions, with incredible reach and flipped toes, and he knew it, too. He swiveled his ears and snorted in obvious pride when they reached the rail and turned.

Mia laughed, patted his neck, and slowed him to a walk. That was one of Donna's fixed rules: always end on a good note. Always do something last that the horse does well. She was convinced they all had egos and, well, she wasn't wrong.

Mia let the reins slide through her fingers and walked down the long side of the arena to her trainer.

Donna had a water bottle in one hand for Mia, and a sugar cube in the other hand for Brando. "It's coming along," she said. "Next time we'll try to spiral into it from a ten-meter circle. All the mechanics are there, it's just not confirmed."

"Yeah, sounds good."

Donna patted her knee, a rare show of physical affection. "You'll get there." Then she tipped her head back and peered up at Mia through her sunglasses. "How are you doing today?" she asked, tone softer and more concerned than Mia had ever heard. It was disconcerting.

"I…why?" Mia blurted. She gripped the water bottle too tightly and felt it bend between her fingers.

Donna studied her a long, inscrutable moment, eyes hidden behind dark lenses. "Just checking," she finally said, and drew back.

Mia thought she'd acted normally today…but maybe not.

~*~

She caught up with Val later, after she'd cooled down and then bathed Brando. She walked the big bay out to hand-graze him in an open patch of grass behind the barn, and Val ambled over from his place at one of the picnic tables.

He looked almost sickly up close: skin sallow, eyes smudged with shadows, the whole image of him unsteady, flickering at the edges.

Her pulse skipped. "Val, what's wrong?"

He turned to look at Brando, wet flanks gleaming in the evening light. He lifted a hand and laid it against Brando's side – tried to. He let it hover there, half-in and half-out, tangled vapors.

Brando lifted his head and snorted, twisted his head around and looked right at Val, eyes white-rimmed.

"Shh," Val whispered.

Brando waited another moment, then flicked his tail and resumed grazing.

"I'm tired, I guess," Val said, voice soft. "I've never dream-walked for an entire day like this. Well," he amended. "Not in a long time." He lifted his head and looked at her with flagging eyelids. "I had to leave, in the middle of the day. They brought my meal and woke me." Pained smile. "I came back."

"Yeah." She wanted to touch him, press her hand to his forehead and see if he felt as feverish as he looked. "Do you need to…um, wake up? I guess? Or go back?"

"I do. Soon." He blinked slow, swayed on his feet. Made an effort to look her in the eye and force a trembling grin. "Thank you for showing me this place. It's wonderful."

"You're welcome." It felt like the absolute least she could do. Insufficient.

"You ride beautifully."

"Oh. Well. Thank you."

"I'll see you tomorrow, Mia." He bowed, and was gone.

She let out a deep breath. "Bye, Val."

5

TIPPING, AND THEN FALLING

Sometimes he appeared in the mornings, sometimes in the evenings, sometimes along the rail while she was riding. Sometimes it was velvet, other times rough tunics she thought must have come from his own time, and occasionally in modern clothes. But Val visited in some way every single day. Like riding, like teaching, like eating, and sleeping, and unrolling her yoga mat, he became a part of her routine. Familiar as her well-worn boots; beautiful as the summer sunset; more engaging than any of the novels on her shelves.

"Are you lonely?" he asked one day, apropos of nothing.

Mia looked up from her tablet and blinked at him in surprise. He'd shown up in jeans and a t-shirt today; she'd recognized the outfit as one worn by a model in a Macy's catalogue she'd left sitting out on her kitchen counter: artfully destroyed denim with slits in the knees, and a clinging plain gray v-neck that showed off stark collarbones and pale skin. He lay on the floor beside her, and his shirt had ridden off to reveal a stretch of lightly-toned stomach and sharp hipbones.

Mia forced her gaze up to his face and he flashed a quick grin to show he knew where her eyes had gone first.

"What?" she asked.

His expression grew thoughtful. "I asked if you were lonely."

"I heard you." Self-consciousness moved like an itch beneath her skin. "I just don't know why you asked."

He tilted his head, hair rustling against the carpet. "You live alone. I haven't seen you spend time with any friends. Or a lover."

Heat filled her face. "Well that's rude as hell."

"It's only an observation, darling." His eyes were soft, the same faded blue as his jeans. "You're beautiful. You could have your pick of lovers if you wanted one."

"Ugh. Okay." She rubbed at the blooming tension between her brows so she didn't have to see him *looking* at her like that and *saying things* like that. "We're not having a conversation about lovers. And don't use that word. It's…" Too intense for today's casual handling of love, sex, and relationships. "Corny," she said, instead.

Val breathed a laugh and she heard him sit up. "Too late." When she dropped her hand, he was sitting beside her, almost in front of her, their faces level and much too close. It made her wish he was really here, that she could feel the heat of his skin and breath. "Now I'm interested."

She glared at him. The best she could, anyway. He was irrepressible cute when he smiled like that. "No."

"Yes."

"Why?"

"Why not?" he countered. "We're friends. I want to know more about you." His smile dimmed a fraction. "We are friends, aren't we?"

"I see you every day. If that doesn't count as friends, I don't know what does."

"An excellent point." He brightened again. "Now tell me all about your salacious love life. I'm dying to know." He propped his chin on his fist and batted his lashes at her.

She groaned. "It's not salacious." When he only blinked at her expectantly: "I've had two boyfriends. If you could call them that." She shrugged, uncomfortable. "Not much to tell. I was busy with horse stuff, they were busy with their stuff. Neither one was serious. We parted ways amicably."

He seemed displeased.

"What?"

"That's unacceptable."

She huffed a laugh. "Excuse me?"

"It ended amicably? How? They just let you go? Like absolute fools?"

"What were they supposed to do? Hit me over the head and keep me captive? That's illegal, Middle Ages Man," she tried to joke.

But Val was serious. He leaned in closer – close enough to the see the darker striations in his eyes; close enough to see a thin, pale scar at his hairline she hadn't noticed before, a silvery line

47

that caught the sunlight. "Mia, why didn't they fight to keep you?" he asked earnestly. "Why not?"

"Because they didn't love me."

He held her gaze a moment, his own stern. "*Idiots*," he finally said, like a curse, and flopped back down to the rug.

~*~

"Killed by sunlight–"

"Wrong."

"…aversion to crosses–"

"My brother is a Roman Catholic."

"What about the garlic thing?"

Val snorted. "Absolutely not."

"And we've already established you can't turn into smoke." Mia tried to keep her grin in check. Val sat cross-legged on her kitchen island, eyes slanted almost shut, nose lifted to a comically superior angle. He looked every inch the prince in his traditional Romanian formalwear. "But what about turning into a bat?"

His eyes and mouth sprang open, an expression of such blended offense, dismay, and horror that Mia couldn't help the laugh that punched out of her.

"Oh my God, your *face*!"

"You're horrid," he said, sniffing disdainfully. "Here I am trying to disabuse you of all the ridiculous notions you've picked up from novels, and you mock me." He splayed a hand over his heart, pressed the back of the other to his forehead. "Poor me, locked away in a cell for centuries, and you treat me so cruelly, when I've only offered you friendship and wisdom."

Mia's laugh died down to a low, tense chuckle. It was easy to forget, in moments like the one just before, that he was being held against his will. That his visits to her were the only positive human contact he ever had.

Still in his dramatic, disparaging pose, Val cracked one eye open to peer at her. "What?"

"Val," she said, growing serious, setting down her wineglass. "Where are you? I mean, where are you really?"

He let his hands fall slowly to his lap. "It doesn't matter."

"Are you in Romania?"

"No. Mia–"

"Maybe I could come visit you in person."

His reaction, the abject horror that flashed across his face, startled her. "No. No, no, absolutely not."

"Val–"

"No!"

She waited a beat, then said, patiently, "In modern-day prisons, prisoners can receive visitors."

His face flushed. "I'm not *in* a modern-day prison."

A shiver moved down her spine. "Val, where are you?" She said it with a touch of desperation now.

His jaw set, and he stared at the wall a long moment. Finally, he said, "Virginia," and then vanished.

~*~

It was a coincidence, she told herself.

Val was in Virginia.

Her father was in Virginia.

Val was a Romanian vampire prince being held as a prisoner.

Her father was a scientist so obsessed with his work he'd allowed his family to fall apart.

Virginia was a whole state; there was no way they'd ever crossed paths. That their lives in Virginia were in any way connected.

But it was the sort of coincidence that nagged at her; that followed her into her dreams, until those dreams became nightmares.

~*~

She was sipping at an Instant Breakfast shake the next morning when Val's voice sounded behind her: "I didn't mean to run off yesterday."

49

Mia was so startled she choked. She managed to swallow, and snagged a paper towel off the roll on the counter to wipe at her chin.

"Sorry," Val said, "I didn't mean to scare you."

But when she turned around, she saw that his shoulders quaked with silent laughter, a smile hidden behind his hand.

He wore blue today, she noticed absurdly.

"Jerk," she accused.

His eyes danced. For a moment, and then his hand fell away, and his smile dimmed, and he grew more serious. "I am sorry, though. About yesterday. I shouldn't have shouted at you."

"You didn't shout," she said. Almost, but not quite. And she'd seen the emotion flickering across his face, hard to name. "But I was just trying to help."

His mouth quirked to the side. He took a deep breath and let it out slow. She got the impression he'd practiced this. "I appreciate that you were trying to show me a kindness. That you would even consider…" He looked down at his hands and shook his head. "I don't understand…But I am no regular prisoner, Mia." He lifted his head again, gaze so direct she felt herself wanting to take a step back from it. "I am considered volatile, and dangerous; traitorous, and untrustworthy."

"Are you those things?" She couldn't really believe, afterward, that she'd asked such a thing.

He stared at her steadily. "What do you think?"

Careful. She wanted to be so careful here. "I think," she said, slowly, "that real traitors never claim to be traitors."

A thin, humorless smile touched his mouth. It was a beautiful mouth; lips thin but shapely, mobile, petal pink.

"And I think danger is relative."

He released a single breath of quiet laughter. "Well, aren't you the optimist?"

"No. I'm someone who's spent weeks getting to know you. And I think wherever you are must really suck if you want to come dog my boring heels every day."

He bristled. "You think – you think that's what I'm doing? *Dogging your heels?*" He frowned. "You think I'm pathetic–"

"Val, no. Please calm down. Okay."

He folded his arms and turned away from her, glaring at a cabinet face.

"I love spending time with you. I wish—" She caught herself before she could admit that she wished they had more time. That he could stay through the night; that she could open her eyes each morning and find him sleep-rumpled and gorgeous on the pillow next to her. He went very still, listening. "Every day it gets a little harder to think about you locked up in a cell somewhere. I hate it, Val. I wish I could change things for you."

The corner of his mouth ticked up, a bitter smile. "No need wasting wishes on me."

"I want to help you," she said, and it sounded like a plea.

"You can't. I'm locked in silver cuffs, and chains, and buried in the dungeon of a manor house out in the woods."

Mia couldn't help it; she gasped.

Val turned back to her, eyes bright with checked emotion. "Yes, darling. I am a horror. A monster who has to be locked in a cage." He tilted his head, smile cutting. "And no one better get too close to the bars, lest my bloodlust get the best of me."

All at once, she realized what he was doing.

She put her hands on her hips. "You're trying to scare me off," she accused.

His smile stayed fixed, but he blinked. "Am I?"

"You're doing a shitty job of it too, by the way."

He took a few huffing breaths, obviously offended.

Mia rolled her eyes. "Oh my God, don't be stupid, Val."

"I'll have you know that I—"

"You asked yourself if I was lonely. You noticed I have zero social life. It's just me, and the horses, and my books. You," she faltered a second, chest tightening, afraid that admitting this would make her too vulnerable; would make the cramping of her stomach when she thought of him locked up in an actual *dungeon* somehow worse. She swallowed and pressed on. The time for cowardice had come and gone weeks ago. "You make every single day brighter. Every evening, when I unlock the door, I worry that it'll be the night that you're not here. And then you show up, and I…" She felt a furious blush stain her face. "And it feels like this amazing, secret, wonderful thing that I don't have to share with anyone. That's all mine." *You feel like you're all mine*, she didn't say.

Throughout her speech, his expression had slowly blanked over...and then begun to warm, touched with wonder. He licked his lips. "I..."

"I'm sorry that you're in a cell. In a dungeon. In cuffs." Her voice cracked, the pain in her stomach spiking. What he'd said horrified her. "And I wish you'd let me help. That I could do something. But you won't, so..." She shrugged. "Do you really want to scare me off? Or do you want to keep doing this?"

Whatever it was. As impossible as it seemed.

He swallowed. "I don't...I don't want to scare you away."

"Good. 'Cause like I said, you were doing a real shitty job of it," she tried to tease.

But his smile bloomed sweet and pleased. "Alright."

~*~

Her next USDF Regional qualifying show was two weeks away, and Donna had reduced her lesson workload so she could concentrate on getting Brando and herself ready for the competition.

Brando was having a stiff day – it happened, same as with human athletes – and so they'd worked on stretching, elasticity, and some simple gymnastics over cavaletti poles. Now, Brando stood clipped in crossties while Mia cold-hosed his front legs, freshly-showered body drying in the breeze of a box fan.

"I think he's starting to recognize me," Val said. He stood at Brando's head, smiling softly as the gelding stretched his neck and reached toward him with his nose, nostrils flared. Val held up his hand for a sniff, and though that wasn't possible, Brando tested the air anyway, bobbing his head in approving fashion. Val smiled, bright as the afternoon sun.

"He likes you," Mia said, feeling soft and warm and hopeless.

"Hmm," Val hummed, eyes sliding over. "Hopefully that's mistress-approved." He called her Brando's mistress, which she found helplessly charming. She had been thinking for a while now that whoever taught him English had been British, the very proper way he referred to things and composed his sentences.

"Mistress-approved," she confirmed.

Val lowered his hand. He and the horse regarded one another, quiet and affectionate on both sides. It was quiet save the droning of the fan and the splashing of the water on the rubber floor mat.

"This show's local, you know," she said after a moment, after she'd worked up the courage – which was stupid, because they were together all the time, and they couldn't even touch, so how was asking him to come to a show anything out of their strange ordinary? "If you wanted to come watch–"

She shouldn't have been nervous, because before the words were even out of her mouth, Val was beaming at her. "Yes! I won't be any trouble at all."

"I know." She smiled back.

~*~

Somewhere between reading aloud to him, and describing the taste of ice cream; between falling asleep on her sofa to the sound of his story about the time he and his brother got stuck on a parapet during a rousing game of medieval hide-and-seek, and the almost-crippling fear that one day he'd disappear, Mia realized that she had fallen in love with him. It was stupid, and painful, but unavoidable. She promised herself she wouldn't let it wreck her.

But that was a pretty lie.

~*~

"Will your family be there?" he asked the night before the show, when she was lint-rolling her black wool coat.

She paused, lint-roller suspended against the coat's shoulder, and let her eyes flick up and over the ironing board she'd unfolded, and to Val, where he sat cross-legged in her squishy old reading chair, chin cupped in his linked hands. His gaze was curious, imploring. She glanced away from it, smoothing the roller down the left sleeve again, lips pressed together against her initial, knee-jerk question: *You haven't ever met my father, have you?*

One of the problems with realizing that she was in love with him was that there was still *so much* she didn't know about him (like if he was even real, an obnoxious inner voice pointed out). She didn't really know anything about his family, and he didn't know anything about hers.

"No. Mom couldn't get off work, and Dad hasn't been in the picture for a long time. So." She shrugged, tried to look casual about it. Inwardly, her pulse kicked up a notch. Whether he was a regular boy you met at a coffee shop, or a noncorporeal vampire prince who could float through walls, it turned out telling the guy you loved about your family was a bit nerve-wracking.

He was silent a beat – a beat too long. "The two of you don't get along?"

When she looked at him again, his pleasant half-smile seemed off: affixed to his face, unnatural.

She snorted and returned her attention to her jacket. "I haven't spoken to him in five years. Yeah. We don't get along. Sure."

"May I ask why?" His smile wasn't the only thing off; his voice was too.

Slowly, Mia set the roller on the ironing board. A shiver stole down her backbone; a premonition. One she chose to ignore for the moment. "The long answer," she said, "is that he's a biologist with about a dozen degrees, and all he's ever cared about is work. He was never home; he never remembered birthdays, or any holidays, really. He spent one whole Christmas in his lab. When he got home," she breathed a humorless laugh, remembering, "Mom started yelling at him and he just…shrugged. He never yelled back. He wouldn't fight with her." Her face heated; she'd said too much. "Short answer: he's an emotionless asshole who never loved us. So. No. We don't get along. I don't think he even remembers I exist."

"And you believe that?"

"What?"

"That he doesn't know you exist? In my experience, even terrible fathers have regrets."

She lifted her brows. "Speaking from personal experience?"

He grimaced. "Yes."

In a careful voice, she said, "You never talk about your family."

He blinked. "That's not true."

"You tell me about being a little boy in Tîrgovişte," she pressed, gently. "About you and Vlad as boys. But nothing after that."

He glanced away, throat rippling as he swallowed. "It isn't a pleasant story."

"But I would listen if you wanted to tell it."

A pause. "I don't."

"Okay, fair enough. But the offer stands if you change your mind."

~*~

She slept poorly. Her usual show nerves were overlaid with a sick ball of dread that turned over and over in her stomach like a stone. Val was under no obligation to tell her about his past…but the longer they went without discussing it, the more convinced she became that it was truly terrible.

Later, she told herself sternly. *Worry about that later.* She had two blue ribbons to win.

Her alarm went off at four, and she was too busy rushing between bedroom and bathroom, getting ready, to worry about whether Val would appear before she left for the barn. She'd told him the address of the park – "What, do you have some sort of psychic GPS?" – and the barn number. He could find her; right now, she needed to focus.

"Get deeper in the corner," she murmured to her reflection as she braided her hair with the help of a lot of styling cream. Flyaways were an equestrian's worst enemy. "Half-halt, half-halt-squeeze…" Donna's instructions to her turned into a mantra. Her stomach felt tangled with too many butterflies.

She grabbed a PowerBar she was too nervous to eat, and the cooler she'd packed last night, and hit the road in the pitch blackness before dawn. When she got to Everdale, all the barn lights were on, blazing against the dark, the truck and trailer rig lit up with happy orange running lights. Donna had hooked up the four-horse; Mia had packed all her tack in the dressing room the night before.

It was thirty minutes of controlled chaos: Mia and her three fellow bleary-eyed-but-wired students woke and fed their horses; brushed them; wrapped their legs for travel; secured their leather head guards between their ears, attached to their sheepskin-padded halters. They all checked the tack room one last time to make sure they hadn't forgotten anything. Chuckled nervously with one another; show day camaraderie. Then Donna appeared, in fawn full-seats, white farm polo, and sunglasses…even though it was still dark out. She clapped her hands, once. "Let's load up, ladies."

Horses were led, snorting a little in anticipation of the trailer and early hour, to the ramp and loaded up. Then it was off for the park.

Dawn bloomed with the slow, purple unfurling of spring iris over the show barns, warm and honeyed.

Mia fastened Brando's girth on the loosest holes, the first of several adjustments, and let out a long, slow breath that quavered at the end. Damn, she was *nervous*.

A soft, fond, familiar voice spoke from behind her. "I don't know why you're worried. You're the best horseman here."

Mia turned, already smiling, butterflies in her stomach surging up toward her throat, and found Val with his arms crossed, leaning back against the stall wall, one booted foot propped behind him. His hair was pulled back at the crown, loose down his back, highlighting his cut-glass cheekbones and narrow, knife-edged jaw.

"You don't know that," she said, tone softer than the mocking one she'd aimed for. He was *here*. And suddenly she wasn't nervous anymore; she was excited to show him what she could do. "You haven't seen anyone else here ride. Also, *Donna Masters* is three stalls over."

He shrugged. "Your hands are quieter."

Mia…blinked at him. She'd shown him some old Olympic video of Donna, had gushed about how she couldn't believe she got to work for one of her childhood idols. And Val had just said she had quieter hands. She didn't know what to do with that.

"Pfft," she scoffed, turning back to tighten the girth another notch. "Flatterer."

"You think so?" He moved to stand beside her, spectral hand hovering over Brando's side. "I'm unfailingly honest, actually. It's always been one of my worst traits."

Mia sent him a sideways glance, expecting to find a smirk, a teasing little wink. Instead, Val stared at Brando's shiny bay coat, brows pinched, mouth tucked at a thoughtful angle.

"Thank you," she said. "That's…one of the nicest things anyone's ever told me."

"Then that." His head turned, blue gaze falling on her unforgivingly. "Is a terrible shame."

She felt heat gathering in her cheeks. She wanted to kiss him right now. Reach up to trace those cheekbones with careful fingertips, slide her hands into the silken curtain of his hair, pull him down and *kiss* him.

Truly unhelpful thoughts at the moment.

"Mia," Donna said from the open stall door, and Mia whipped around.

Her trainer frowned at her. "Who are you talking to?"

"Uh…" *This amazing guy who you can't see right now.* "No one, just Brando." The lie tasted greasy on her tongue.

Donna's frown twitched; she didn't believe. "Are you about ready? It's time to head down to the warm-up arena."

"Yeah, coming." Mia tightened the girth for the last time and Brando tossed his head.

She turned back to Val, quickly, and he flashed her a toothy grin and a wink. "What is it modern Americans say? Break a leg?"

~*~

Brando always got a little wiggy in the warm-up ring. He was a serious horse, ordinarily, with a tremendous work ethic, and a touch of true sweetness that he expressed through gentle nudges of his nose and polite requests for ear scratches. But the things that made him a stellar athlete also made him nervous, and the hustle and bustle of almost a dozen horses moving through portions of their tests got his back tense and his neck bowing. He blew sharp little snorts with every step, eyes flicking wildly back and forth.

"You're alright." She kept up a low, steady stream of reassurances. They trotted along the rail, her reins slack, and eventually his ears stayed tipped toward her, listening, and his topline slowly relaxed into the stretch until his gait was loose and swinging.

The walkie-talkie clipped to her boot crackled and Donna's voice came through: *"Good. Bring him in toward the center and let's do some collected canter work."*

Mia flashed a thumb-up toward the rail in acknowledgement and gathered her reins. At the rail, Val stood undetected at Donna's side, elbows propped on the top board, chin in one hand, smile almost dreamy.

Her stomach did a little flip.

Ugh, focus.

A space opened up in the very center of the arena, and she maneuvered Brando into it, pressing him into an easy canter. She let him stretch a moment, then closed her legs and deepened her seat; adjusted the rein pressure. His neck lifted and he collected beautifully; he felt like a coiled spring beneath her, energetic and ready for the next movement.

"Outside rein," Donna said through the walkie. *"There, yes. When he feels ready, let's see a few lead changes."*

Without much space to work, Mia steered him into a careful turn and started down the next long side. Dizziness touched her, just a second. Nerves, must be. She should have eaten more earlier. The PowerBar was becoming a lead ball in her stomach.

Focus.

She tightened her right hand, half-halted, shifted her weight, and, when the moment was right, slid her legs, one forward a fraction, one back, changed the flexion, and...Brando executed a perfect flying change.

"Perfect," Donna confirmed.

Mia grinned, gave him a quick pat on the neck, and set up another.

Tried to, at least. Her vision blurred between one blink and the next, and she felt her balance tipping. Shit, she was dizzy.

She shook her head – which didn't help – half-halted and tried again.

This one was shakier; it took Brando two strides to make the change, lagging, like he was waiting for her.

"Hmm. Not so clean. Let's try…"

Mia didn't hear what Donna said next because a buzzing like cicadas filled her head. She tipped to the side, the arena seeming to tilt around her, and Brando broke into a sloppy trot, and then walk, startled by her loss of balance.

Her stomach rolled, and sweat prickled across her skin beneath her tight, white show clothes. Thank God she wasn't in her black coat yet; she would have swooned.

"Mia," Donna said through the walkie.

Her gorge was rising. She tugged Brando to a graceless halt and leaned forward, mouth open and panting. Waiting for the vomit that didn't seem to want to come. The ground blurred and spun beneath her, and she closed her eyes.

No, no, no, no, no she chanted inwardly. Because now she knew it wasn't the PowerBar, or nerves, or the heat of the morning. No, this was something she'd been dreading for weeks, ever since Val first showed up.

Speaking of…

"Mia!" she heard him shout, and wondered if anyone else could hear him now.

Then Donna's voice: "Mia! Mia, oh, shit!"

Other voices around her: the others riders asking if she was okay.

"There's an ambulance over by the show ring!" someone shouted.

Mia closed her eyes; the world spun; her stomach cramped. The cicada buzz became a wailing siren.

"Mia," Val again, up close, pleading. "What's wrong, darling?"

Donna: "Who the fuck are you?"

Falling off was going to hurt, Mia thought. And then she was tipping, and then falling, and she blacked out before she hit the ground.

6

SYMPTOM

She woke to the gentle beeping of hospital machines: a sound she knew well. For a moment, she squeezed her eyes shut, willing the noise away. Praying it was just a nightmare. But her back was sore from her fall; a bruise throbbed on her hip. And her throat was scratchy, and she had to pee, and yes, she was definitely here.

With a deep sigh, she opened her eyes.

All hospital rooms looked more or less the same. This was a private one, small, but blessedly only boasting one bed, a TV, and a door that led into a bathroom. There was a window, the sky beyond dark and star-studded; lamps had been left on low settings, the overhead lights off.

Her mother sat in the chair beside the bed.

"Mom?" Her voice came out a startled croak.

Kate threw her magazine aside on the table and leaned forward, almost falling off her chair, to touch Mia's face, tears filling her eyes that she hastily blinked away. "Hey, sweetie, there you are. How're you feeling?"

Sluggish, Mia thought, eyelids heavy and mind lagging. "How," she started, and her throat was too dry to continue; she coughed, arm too heavy to lift in time, just coughing into the air like a mannerless heathen.

"Here." Kate plucked a water cup from the bedside table and brought the straw to Mia's lips. The water tasted metallic – maybe that was just her tongue – but she sipped it down greedily until her mom pulled it back. "Not too much, or it'll make you sick."

Mia blinked against the sudden sting in her eyes. Kate had said the same thing when she was a teenager, the last time her life had become nothing but a whirlwind of hospitals. "What happened?" she asked, voice an embarrassing chirp. "You're supposed to be in New York."

"Well, I *was*," Kate said gently, easing back into her chair, hand finding Mia's among the bedclothes. "But Donna called, and I hopped onto the first available flight."

Flight? Oh…

"Donna said you blacked out and fell off of Brando in the warm-up arena," she continued. "He was standing still, and Donna managed to catch your head." Her sandy brows pinched together and she let out an unsteady breath; her voice remained calm, though. She had lots of practice being the parent of a sick child. "Someone ran to get the paramedics who were there for the show. By the time they got there, you – you had started seizing."

"I had a *seizure*?" Mia gasped. That explained the full-body soreness and weakness.

"A bad one, so I hear." She attempted a weak smile, and squeezed Mia's hand.

Mia swallowed, dry throat sticking. "Mom, how long was your flight?" That wasn't her real question, and Kate knew it.

"You've been asleep for nine hours, baby."

"Shit." She let go of the tension she'd been holding, the attempt to hold her head up off the pillow, and sank down into the mattress. Nine hours. Plenty of time. The show was over; Donna would have taken Brando back to the farm and put him away; would have had to deal with her other three students, the ones who didn't fall off and seize in the middle of the warm-up ring.

"What'd the doctor say?"

Kate winced, fractionally; if Mia had blinked, she would have missed it.

"Mom." Mia hated the way her voice shook. "It's been nine hours. I had to have had a CT scan."

"You did," Kate said with a deep, unsteady exhale. She reached to smooth Mia's hair back, touch tender. "But…" She sighed again, face falling. "Baby. They…they found something."

Mia held her mother's watery gaze a moment, searching for a lie that wasn't there; Kate would never lie about this sort of thing. It was just a fruitless wish.

Mia rolled her head away, gaze flying up to the ceiling, the silver sprinkler heads there.

"Oh, honey," Kate said brokenly. "I'm so sorry."

Mia waited for the pain to hit. The tears, the crushing pressure in her chest. The outrage and the fear. But instead, it seemed like a black hole opened up in her chest, sucking up all of her emotion so that she felt…nothing. Nothing at all.

Kate slowly released her hand. "I'm gonna go tell them you're awake. Be right back."

Mia saw her mother dabbing tears as she slipped from the room. There was a call button they could have used; getting the doctor was a chance for Kate to get her emotions under control in the hallway; she'd never liked falling apart in front of her daughter.

Mia wouldn't have minded right now, though. She had no tears of her own to contribute. She had nothing.

It was quiet a few seconds, just the beep of the monitors, and then, softly, hesitantly, "Mia?"

She turned her head – her neck hurt terribly – and saw Val standing against the wall, by the window. He wore his red velvet, the outfit he'd bargained a man for – a man he'd then killed. And really, what was her brain thinking conjuring someone like him as a fantasy? She couldn't have just imagined a handsome firefighter? Maybe a bookish professorial type? Even one of her favorite fictional characters. No, her dumb, diseased brain wanted her to have pretend conversations with Dracula's brother, who was chained up in a basement somewhere, for crimes so terrible he'd never explained them.

She'd let this go on way, way too long.

She sighed and turned away from him; her neck hurt too much to keep staring.

"Mia?" he said again, voice almost childlike. He came closer, but she couldn't hear him; his footfalls made no sound, and his clothes didn't rustle, because he wasn't really here.

He never had been.

Slowly, he leaned over the bed, so his face was suspended above hers, his hair a gleaming curtain falling around sharp features. His eyes almost seemed to glow in the dim light.

If it was possible, she would have reached up and gathered his hair in her hands, even if she was weak and shaky. Would have pulled him in close by it, to feel the heat of his forehead against her own, the warmth of his breath on her face.

But he wasn't real.

"Are you alright?" he asked, face pinched. He looked near tears. "You fell, and no one could wake you, and I couldn't ask anyone—"

"I have another tumor," she said, and she shut her eyes, not able to look at him anymore. She couldn't keep clinging to this hallucination – because that's exactly what he was, what she'd always secretly suspected him to be. A symptom of her illness.

"Mia," he breathed.

She refused to open her eyes. This had to end. She was ending it. She'd been betrayed by her own brain – by her tumor – and she couldn't allow that.

"You're not real," she said. "You were always just the tumor."

He made a quiet, hurt sound. "Is that really what you believe?" Just a whisper. Soft and broken.

"Yes."

When she finally opened her eyes again, he was gone.

~*~

Donna came to visit her the next day during lunch, in the break between lessons. The moment she walked through the door, Mia was hit with conflicting waves of relief and guilt. Relief because her mom had gone to the cafeteria and, unlike Kate, Donna would be pragmatic and unemotional, sympathetic without being tearful. And guilt, because who was teaching Mia's lessons? Schooling the horses under her care? Who would give Brando his daily handful of Sweet Lumps? He was addicted to those stupid, hard, pink treats.

"No, no, no," Donna said as she dropped her purse – it was really a small Ariat tote bag, and no doubt full of hair ties, test booklets, protein bars, and horse cookies – and came to fall gracefully into the visitor chair. "I can feel you gearing up for an apology, and just don't, okay? *I'm* the one who's sorry."

She was dressed in charcoal breeches and an UnderArmour athletic tank, boots and spurs, her hair back in its usual severe ponytail. With her sunglasses perched on her head, Mia could see that her eyes were dry and clear, but that real apology tweaked her features.

Mia frowned at her. "Why would you be sorry?"

Donna lifted her brows to say *really?* "Mia, my job is to look after the horses in my care, *and* the humans. Horses and students. You've been acting strange and unwell for weeks. And I saw it. And I ignored it, and let you tell me you were fine. I could see you wobbling out there, and I didn't–" Her ever-present confidence faltered, for the first time in Mia's memory. "I caught your head," she said, cupping her hands around empty air in demonstration. "It didn't hit the ground. But. I should have gotten there sooner. I never should have even let you get in the saddle yesterday."

"Donna–"

"I'm sorry, Mia. You've been sick. I'm your trainer, and I should have done something about what I noticed."

Mia swallowed with difficulty, throat tight. "I can't lose this job," she said, pleading. "It's my dream. I can't–" Something jagged threatened to shake loose in her chest, tear her open. She swallowed, and swallowed, and willed it away until she was just a void again. A black hole of nothingness inside.

"You're not losing your job," Donna said. "I promise. We can work out something going forward that will allow you time off for treatment, or surgery, if that's what happens. Do you know yet?"

"No." And then she finally felt something, and it was cold dread. "I don't care about treatment, I can just–"

"Mia," Donna cut her off, firm. "This isn't up for negotiation. You're sick, and you need treatment."

She thought about last time, about her hair falling out in big clumps on her pillow every night; about throwing up in the middle of class; about the relentless headaches, dizziness, mood swings. The terror of the surgery; the slow, painful recovery.

She hiked herself a little higher up on the pillows. "What if I refuse treatment?"

Donna gave her a sharp look...then checked it. "Wait and see what the doctor says, hm?" She got to her feet. "I'll let you get some rest. Don't worry about Brando. Javi's spoiling him rotten and I'll ride him this week."

"'Kay. Thank you."

"Let me know how things are going." She offered a tight, awkward smile as she headed for the door.

She stopped, though, lingering with her hand on the knob, and cast a look back over her shoulder, frowning. "Oh, one thing I've been wondering. Do you know who that was in the ring with us? He was calling your name. Screaming it, actually. Thought he was gonna faint."

A wave moved through her, a surge of something between dread and panic that threatened to rip apart her carefully taped seams, send all those jagged pieces slicing through her. She went through a series of swallows again, breathing past the sharp pain until it dissipated. "Who?"

"That guy." Donna snorted. "The pretty one with the long hair and the Halloween costume. He work at a Ren Faire or something?"

"I..." Val. Donna had seen Val. "I don't know what you're talking about."

Donna's frown deepened; she looked like she started to say something else, drawing in a breath. But then she gave a little headshake and said, "Huh. Oh well. Rest up. Eat your Jell-O." She gave an awkward smile and slipped out.

~*~

Donna had seen Val.

~*~

Dr. Patel stood at the foot of her bed, hands clasped together, expression one of practiced sympathy and gravity. He had a warm bearing, and a gentle voice, and was one of the preeminent neurosurgeons in this part of the country. So when he said, "Mia, I'm very sorry..." Mia knew that he spoke the truth.

Her tumor was inoperable.

Too risky; too much chance of cutting into some life-sustaining part of her brain.

There was a chance radiation could shrink it…

Mia stared down at her hands.

"Oh, sweetheart," Kate murmured, voice tear-choked.

Mia's voice came out detached, oddly calm. "How long do I have."

"It's hard to say," Dr. Patel said.

Because they didn't know.

~*~

Donna *had seen Val.*

~*~

Mia let her duffel bag slide down off her shoulder and hit her bedroom floor with a thump. She sat down hard on the edge of the bed and just…

Stared at the wall. Took a breath.

She had another tumor.

She was dying.

Donna had seen Val. Those were the three most pressing issues weighing on her mind at the moment.

Mom had flown back home that morning; she'd had another realtor cover her clients for the week she was in Denver, but she was losing commissions, which she needed, and Mia was feeling better; had urged her mother over and over again to leave until Kate finally caved with a grief-stricken look. Mia had tried to smile at her. "I have time." And she did…just probably not a whole lot of it.

Donna wasn't happy, but Mia had been firm. If she didn't have but a few more months to be her real self, she wanted to spend that time doing what she loved best. Spending time with the people she loved best.

That wasn't a long list. Kate was going to close up the house in New York, get her affairs in order, and come back to Denver. Mia would see Donna every day. And that just left...

"Val?" she said, just a whisper. She felt stupid, but she had to try. Donna *had seen him*.

She took a deep breath and continued. "I don't know if you can hear me, or if you even want to. If you don't, I get that. I...hell, I denied that you exist, and..." She bit her lip, not willing to admit that it had taken someone else laying eyes on him for her to believe what he'd been telling her all along. "But. I miss you. So much. And I wondered if, maybe, if you don't hate me, you might—"

He materialized two feet in front of her, swirling into existence, unbearably beautiful. Unbearably sad.

Her chest squeezed. "Val. You came."

The barest hint of a smile lifted at one corner of his mouth; the expression didn't touch his eyes, flat and low-lidded with unhappiness. "You called, didn't you?"

She had the sense of balancing on an edge; if she said the wrong thing, he'd disappear again, maybe for good this time. She couldn't bear to risk that. So she took a breath and kept her voice soft, careful, affectionate. "I didn't think you could hear me, though."

The tiny smile twisted, became mocking. "I have plenty of time to sit alone and contemplate my captivity. What else do I have to do but pine and listen? Waiting like a maiden in a tower."

Except he wasn't in a tower, was he? But a basement. She imagined it: windowless, slimy stone walls. And he'd said chains, too, hadn't he? Oh, God.

She swallowed the lump in her throat. "I'm glad you're here. I wanted a chance to apologize for the things I said to you at the hospital. I never should have—" He didn't meet her eyes, instead studied a place on the rug. "You *are* real. I know that. I shouldn't have said otherwise. I was angry, and scared" — no, really, she'd been nothing, fighting the void — "and I lashed out at you. You didn't deserve that, and I was wrong. I'm sorry."

He held still a moment, not even blinking. And when he lifted his head, he moved as if it was heavy on his neck. Something about his edges weren't right…as if they bled. She squinted and saw the tiny feelers of smoke lifting from his shoulders. The projection wasn't strong, it didn't want to hold. She must have made a face, or some kind of noise. She caught her hand lifting away from the bed, wanting to reach for him.

He nodded. "Do you want to see what I really look like?" Before she could answer, he *flickered*, like the image on an old TV, and then he was no longer the polished prince he'd always presented. He was no longer even standing.

He sat cross-legged on the floor, hands in his lap. Like the first time he'd appeared, it was his hair that caught her eye first. Not the sleek cascade, or the tidy braid, but a greasy, snarled rat's nest that poured over his shoulders in knots. Frizzy and unkempt, and dull. Gaunt-faced, glassy-eyed, he wore heavy smudges of dirt, and raw, reddish patches that might have been burns or bruises. His clothes were rags, rotting off of his body. His long, beautiful fingers were grubby. And his wrists, she noted, were connected by a length of chain, and two heavy, flashing silver cuffs. Those cuffs were the only clean things on his person.

She knew she made a sound this time, low and choked, a sudden sob caught in her throat. "*Val.*"

"This is me," he said, turning his palms up. The chains hooked to his cuffs rattled. "Behold: Radu the Handsome. Prince. Hostage. Whore. Brother-killer." His smile was a horrible, emotionless facsimile.

She trembled silently a moment, and then she realized the shaking wasn't fear; it was rage. She wanted to throttle whoever held him captive. "Who did this to you?" she asked, and the ferocity in her tone lifted his head, widened his eyes a fraction, so he almost looked alive again.

He blinked at her a few times. "It doesn't matter–"

"Yes it does!"

Another blink. He shrugged and looked down at his grimy palms. "The first time – the initial capture – that was Vlad's people. His Familiar, and his humans, and they knew – they knew how to subdue me. They kept me for a while, and then passed me along to some monks…" He shook his head. "It's been many people. It doesn't matter."

She wanted to scream. Wanted to throw up. She curled her hands into fists and squeezed until her nails bit into her palms.

"Is it true?" he asked. "Are you–"

She shut her eyes, briefly, because how did her traitorous brain even begin to compare to *five-hundred-years* of captivity? But he'd asked, and he sounded like the answer matter. She nodded and met his gaze. "Yeah. Inoperable brain tumor. They can try chemo and radiation, but…They don't think that will do anything but buy me some time, and I…" She took a deep breath and pushed past the wall of emotion that threatened to crowd out the nothingness inside her. "Whatever time I have left, I want to enjoy it. Not lie around in a hospital being sick."

He stared at her with open sorrow. "Oh, Mia. I'm sorry."

"I'm sorry, too."

There was nothing else to say after that. They sat there in companionable, if grievous silence. Until exhaustion pulled her down sideways onto the bed.

Val was still sitting there, watching her, when her eyes finally closed.

~*~

She was awakened an indeterminate amount of time later by the ringing of her phone. She floundered a moment, slapping across the bed for it, noting in the process that Val was gone, and that the time flashing on her nightstand clock read 3:14 a.m. She squinted at the phone screen, trying to place the unfamiliar number, and finally just thumbed to answer; Dr. Patel had said he wanted to pass her case along to another specialist in Pennsylvania, and maybe…

Her sleep fog evaporated and she realized no doctor would call her in the wee hours just as she was saying, "Hello?" heart thudding fast now. This wasn't a professional call. Maybe a wrong number…

"Hello? Mia?" her father's voice asked, and suddenly she was wide awake.

She scrambled up onto her knees and gripped the headboard tight with her free hand. Her lungs contracted, and she fought to keep her breath slow and regular as it left her mouth. She didn't want him to know that he caused her any kind of anxiety. "Dad," she greeted, with what she hoped was a neutral tone.

Silence a beat, one she wasn't willing to fill with idle chatter. She felt a stab of betrayal; obviously, Kate had called him.

"Your mother called me," he said, finally, in confirmation. "Honey, I'm—"

"No pet names. We don't have that kind of relationship."

"Oh." He sounded startled. Off-kilter. "Oh, okay. Well." A breath that sounded pained, almost a whimper.

It angered her. *He* was the one who'd abandoned *them*. He didn't get to act hurt.

"Mia, I'm so terribly sorry. This is just…it's devastating."

Mia closed her eyes, because the worst part, the absolute *worst*, was that he sounded sincere. Actually devastated. And he'd always had this soft, pleasant voice to go with his soft, pleasant face. Not a tall man, nor an imposing one; always smiling, wire-framed glasses always spotless and reflecting the light, screening his eyes – and whatever emotion might have lurked in them – from view. He bore all the superficial markers of a good father, but he hadn't been one. Not ever. Somehow, she'd always found his unfailing politeness more offensive than outright cruelty.

"Yeah, well, I figured this would happen someday," she said. "Not a surprise, really. It's fine."

"No. No, it's not fine at all." Heavy emotion; he sniffled audibly, and her hand tightened on the phone. "But it *could* be."

Her anger caught, suspended for a moment in surprise. "What?"

"Mia, I know that you and your mother never saw the importance of my work—"

"You never saw the importance of *us*." A low blow, but a satisfying one.

"That's not true," he said, smoothly. "I always loved you both, dearly, but your mother couldn't be patient. She couldn't see that I was on the edge of a breakthrough."

She didn't snap back this time; what was the use? Every time her mother asked him for even a scrap of time, he politely told her that she couldn't possibly understand the magnitude of his research. How earth-shattering it would be. But he never told them anything about it; spent all his time at the lab; cut down their intelligence and understanding in a thousand little smiling slights.

"The last few years," he continued, excitement coloring his voice now, "we've made some marvelous progress. There's a new drug – a wonder drug! Mia, my colleague in New York attached a donor foot to a wounded war vet, administered this drug to her, and her body accepted the new limb. Flawlessly. We've returned a man's sight. We've – we've–"

"Not interested."

"No! No, Mia, listen to me, please! Let me explain. This is truly, truly a miracle drug. It's not chemo, honey. It won't make you sick. There aren't any side effects at all! It's not available to the public yet, but I'm the initiator of the trial; if you come here to Virginia, to the lab, I can administer it. Honey, this serum *eats tumors*."

She allowed herself a moment of hope. To imagine that what he was talking about was true. A miracle, tumor-eating drug with no side effects.

She shook her head. "You sound insane."

"I know I do, I know. And if I told you the kind of research it took to create this drug, you'd think I sounded even more insane. But, Mia, I'm telling you the truth. I can cure you. You'll be strong, and whole, and you can live your life."

"I could never get onto the trial."

"You're not *listening*. You don't have to be a part of the trial. You can just walk in."

"That's not how this sort of thing works."

"I don't have to play by other people's rules."

Her breathing had accelerated, she noticed, and fought to even it out again. This was…it…

"I don't believe you." She meant it as a forceful statement, but it left her lips as a murmur. She'd believed crazier things; she believed Val existed. So why not believe this?

It was more that she didn't *trust* this. Him. Didn't trust Edwin Talbot to do anything for her out of the kindness of his heart.

"Please believe," he pleaded. "Please."

"What's the catch?"

"Pardon?"

"The catch, Dad. You act kind, but you aren't. If you have some miracle drug that you want to give to me? There's an ulterior motive. What is it?"

He took a deep breath that rattled across his end of the connection. "Mia. I can't believe you think…"

"Thanks for the offer, but I'm going back to sleep."

"No, wait! Please just tell me you'll consider it. You don't have much time. Let me do this for you. I…I know I couldn't be the father you wanted. But I can help you now. Please let me do at least that much."

She hung up.

The silence afterward seemed crushing. She could hear the fridge droning out in the kitchen, just audible beneath the crashing of her own heart against her ribs.

She knelt there for a long time, trying to decide if she should believe him. A part of her wanted to, desperately. A part of her that knew her time was short; and a part of her who had never forgiven the father that abandoned them.

But a larger, more insistent part knew that, father or not, Edwin wasn't to be trusted. He didn't do things for other people. Not even his own daughter.

Angry, confused, sweating a little, she slid back down and clicked off the lamp.

It was a long time before sleep found her.

7

WISH YOU WERE HERE

Donna let her hang out at the barn as much as she wanted, still taught her lessons, and let her ride Brando – in the indoor, where it was shady and the ceiling fans were going –, but she'd been officially banned from working. Mia hated being cut off like that, ostracized. The other students gave her sympathetic looks; all of her own students had called to express their condolences. Monica had baked her cookies. It was like everyone was paying their respects before she was even dead, and it got under her skin.

But there were bittersweet moments of goodness. She'd never gotten to spend so much one-on-one time with Brando. Riding him, bathing him, grooming him for long hours, working Show Sheen through his tail until it was gleaming and tangle-free.

She hand-grazed him now, on a low hill overlooking the rest of the farm, the Rockies a dark stamp along the horizon. Mia sat in the grass, lead-line held loosely in one hand, other wrist propped on her raised knee. The wind played with Brando's mane, sweeping his forelock off his face, so she could see the bright white star that lay beneath.

Val lay on his back beside her, hair spilling across the grass, gaze trained on the tattered clouds that trailed by lazily overhead. He wore his modern jeans and tee ensemble today; Mia kept glancing over for glimpses of sharp hipbones.

They'd been quiet for several moments, just enjoying the sunshine and one another's company. But then Val's head rolled toward her and he said, "There's *nothing* they can do?"

She didn't have to ask for clarification. She took a quick breath, nerves shivering low in her belly. She hadn't told him about her father's offer yet. Since that first phone call, Edwin had left three voicemails and sent her five texts. Outright begging now. *Please, Mia. Let me help you.*

She shuddered.

Val noticed, sitting up suddenly, gaze going intense. "What?"

"My…" She had to wet her lips. "Remember how I said that I don't get along with my father?"

She could never smell him, never sense him like she could a real person who was truly there. But she had the sudden sense that he stiffened. His voice came out flat. "Yes." His eyes were trained to the side of her face, though. Very blue in the sunlight. "I remember."

"Remember how I also said he was a scientist?"

"Yes."

"Well, he…he called me. The other night. When I got back home from the hospital. He said that he – well, I never knew what he was working on. He would never tell us, only that it was important." Shit, she was babbling. "Anyway, he said that he'd been developing an experimental drug serum. Miracle drug, he called it. He said that if I went to Virginia, he could give it to me, and that it would shrink the tumor. That it would *cure* me." She finally turned to meet Val's gaze, and was startled by it; the raw, unnamable emotion in it. "I don't even know how that's possible," she said, just a murmur, pinned by his wild expression.

He swallowed several times, throat bobbing, and glanced away; his eyes darted back and forth, gaze shifting across the grass. He looked paler – more like his true color, the day he'd shown her how he *really* looked.

"Val?"

"That…that…" He panted, mouth open, flash of pink tongue sliding over his fangs. "Yes, okay. Yes." He looked at her again, eyes feverish. "You should take him up on it. Let him give you the medicine. Yes…"

Mia frowned. "Val–"

"No! No, wait!" He shut his eyes, shook his head, winced. "Side-effects," he hissed mostly to himself.

"He said there weren't any."

His eyes popped open. He reached to grab her shoulders, but the touch never came, hands flickering above her, trying and failing to land. "You can't know that," he said, frantic now. "There are side effects. Everything has consequences, Mia, *everything*. Especially miracles. Those never come without strings."

She'd never wanted to touch him so badly. "I know. Believe me, I know."

They stared at one another, her questioning, him reaching.

"I don't want to do it," she said. "I don't trust him."

His mouth pulled to the side, half-grin and half-grimace. "I understand."

And somehow, she thought that he did.

~*~

"Hi, sweetie," Kate greeted when Mia opened the door. She had three suitcases on the ground at her feet, enough clothes and personal effects for an extended stay. An extended stay that *wasn't enough time.*

Mia stepped back and opened the door, knowing a pang of guilt, and a deep, deep frustration. "Here, let me get your bags. It's the least I can do since I couldn't pick you up." She wasn't allowed to drive anymore, doctor's orders. She'd been taking Ubers everywhere, and Javi had given her rides to and from the barn.

Kate waved her off as she stepped inside, juggling the handles of the three rolling cases expertly. "No, no, I've got them."

Mia closed the door, locked it, and reached for one of the suitcases – which her mother promptly pulled out of her reach. She didn't want Mia exerting herself, not even wheeling a bag across the floor. It stung more than it should have, her pride getting the best of her.

"I can still do normal things, Mom." Except for drive. Or ride unsupervised. Or leave the house without texting someone before and after. Fuck. She was an invalid.

"I know sweetie, I know," Kate hummed. "Where am I sleeping, on the foldout?"

~*~

Mia hadn't spent this much time with her mother in years. Kate had always been the best kind of sick-patient parent: always trying to find normal, distracting things to do, not hovering or making her feel like she was made of glass. They played countless games of doubles solitaire at the kitchen table sipping wine; watched all their old favorite rom-coms; went for long walks on the nature trail that started just at the edge of the apartment complex's property, enjoying the first cool touch of fall on sunkissed summer skin. Mia hadn't realized just how much she missed her mom until now.

But Kate being around all the time meant that Val couldn't be, and that…bothered her more than it probably should have. She debated telling her mother about her spectral visitor, but ultimately decided "Mom, I'm in love with a vampire who can only visit me mentally" wasn't the best way to prove that her tumor was under control.

Val had other ideas, though.

"I'm very charming, though," he said, pacing back and forth across the living room rug one afternoon while Kate was at the grocery store. He wore the velvet today, sable cloak – she'd asked, and he'd said it was real sable, inspired by his adventures in Russian dream-walking – flung out behind him with one long arm so that it rippled around his calves in dramatic fashion. He turned to her, posed with his shoulders and hips cocked, head tipped to the side, grinned toothily and winked at her.

"Hmm, yes, very charming," she deadpanned.

He huffed. "*Very*. Women love me. Men, too. Who wouldn't?" He tossed his hair, and she couldn't hide her laugh anymore.

He smiled in response, a smile that started cutting and wicked and all playboy…and melted into something soft and true.

It warmed her. "You know I would love to introduce you to Mom. But, um, I think she might…"

"Run screaming?" he suggested.

"Probably, yeah."

He sighed and threw himself at the counter, sprawling all the way across it like he'd swooned. "Always so terrifying," he said with mock anguish. He cracked an eye and looked up at her through a screen of hair. His tone changed, became serious. "*You're* not terrified of me, are you?"

"No. Why would I be?"

"Hmm, no. Of course you wouldn't be." Another tone shift. Now he sounded airy, dismissive. Like a prince. A shield, she thought. Or a disguise. "I'm not here after all, am I? So I can't very well…" He opened his mouth, and as she watched, his fangs seemed to elongate, descending so that they were unmistakable.

She thought she understood, then. "I'm not afraid of you because – and don't take this the wrong way – you're not scary. I trust you, whether or not I can actually touch you."

His mouth closed slowly, and he pushed up so he was propped on his elbows, expression morphing into one of wonder. "Do you mean that?" he asked, a little breathless.

"Yes."

He smiled, small and pleased, and his cheeks turned a delicate pink. "Oh. Well. That's…" He cleared his throat. "Say, did I ever tell you about the Scottish laird who thought I was a woman?" He gave her the cheeky, salacious grin again, and that was fine, because she'd seen the real one.

~*~

Val liked to talk. He seemed to like the sound of his own voice – and why not, it was a lovely voice – and he enjoyed telling stories. In their stolen moments, when Kate was out, or even, sometimes, when Kate was asleep and Mia couldn't seem to keep her eyes closed, they sat up against her headboard and whispered back and forth. Val told piecemeal stories from his childhood and his captivity. He bragged, and he ragged on his brother, and he never said anything too deep, too personal, too painful.

But Mia was beginning to form a picture in her mind gathered from the scraps, filling in the blank places with all the things he *didn't* say. And she was starting to think that something far more terrible than simple imprisonment had happened to him.

It started to bother her, like a sore tooth, or a hangnail; a small, but tender kind of pain that nagged and nagged.

During one of their late-night chats, she turned to him, fixed him with a serious look, and Val cut off mid-sentence. "Hey," she said, wishing she could lay her hand over his in reassurance. He looked startled. "You know that if there was ever anything…anything really bothering you" – shit, she was so lame, saying this all wrong, but pressed on – "that you could tell me about it, right? You can tell me anything."

He stared at her a moment, gaze tracking over her face, searching. Then glanced away. Swallowed. "Yes, I know."

"And I really do mean anything. If…if there's anything you think talking about would help with."

"Yes," he said again, faraway now. Drawing into himself.

But she didn't think he would tell her.

~*~

It was a tiny apartment, but the bathtub was deep. Sometimes, Mia even took advantage of that fact.

Her mother, steadfast in her daily support, always kind, even when Mia grew frustrated to the point of tears with her own traitorous body, had an old sorority sister who lived in Denver. Only ten minutes from Mia's place, in fact. So tonight, feeling tired, and sore, but mostly stable, Mia had shooed her mother out the door, insisting she go spend time catching up with an old friend. "You shouldn't have to play nursemaid all the time."

"Oh, honey." Kate had touched her cheek, eyes glazing over, briefly. "I don't think of it like that at all."

But she'd gone, and Mia was grateful to have a few hours alone.

Well…mostly alone.

She'd called for Val, feeling a little stupid for it, while she stood in her kitchen. Had called a few times, and then waited. When he didn't show, she decided not to sit around moping after him. She poured herself a glass of wine, and went to run a bath full of lavender-scented salts.

It proved to be an excellent idea, once she was totally submerged, sinking down until her chin touched the surface of the warm water. The heat immediately went to work on her stress-knotted muscles, and the towel she'd folded to put behind her head gave her just enough support to allow her neck to relax.

She'd just closed her eyes when she heard, "This is a terrible idea, really."

She sat upright with a gasp, water slopping over the edge of the tub, and reached instinctively to cover her breasts. Val sat on the edge of the counter, ankles hooked together, kicking lightly back and forth. There was no sound of his boot heels rapping the cabinet face, though, of course. He wore his red velvet; she suspected he knew it was her favorite of his usual outfits. And he held one hand clapped over his eyes.

She breathed out, and let some of her sudden tension ebb. "Are you...?"

"I haven't seen anything, I assure you. I'm merely concerned for your wellbeing."

"Right."

"For instance." He tilted his head, and she had the sense he could see right through his hand. Considering said hand, like the entire rest of him, was nothing but a mental projection, there was a good chance that was true. "What if you should have another of those awful seizures, here alone, and slip down into the water and drown? Bathtubs can be dangerous, you know."

"Yeah, I know." She snorted, and settled back against her towel again, letting her hand slide back into the water. Truth told, she wouldn't mind terribly if he *did* look; with her brain tumor back, there was no sense wasting time lying to herself: if he were here now in the flesh, she'd grab him by the hand and pull him down into the water with her. It warmed her even more than the water to have him here with her now; she wanted him with her all the time, really. "But I'm okay right now, and this is heavenly."

She realized her mistake the moment the words left her mouth.

"Oh, shit, Val, I didn't mean—"

He grinned, sad but sincere, beneath his hand. "It's alright, darling. Monster I may be, but I want you to enjoy heavenly things, whether I'm able to or not." His voice softened a fraction, full of impossible gentleness – heavy with something like grief. She saw his throat move as he swallowed. "You deserve it."

She felt a lump form in her own throat to know that he cared. He was a centuries-old vampire who visited her through impossible psychic powers, but he was real, and he cared about her, and she could cry because of it. She sniffed, and blinked a few times.

Val cracked his fingers, and peeked through with one blue eye. "Please don't cry."

She sniffed again, harder and shook her head. "I'm not, I'm not. It's fine. I'm sorry."

"Don't apologize. You have *nothing* to apologize for." Then he pressed his fingers shut again.

God, he was precious.

"Val, you don't have to keep covering your eyes."

He lifted his chin, voice going prim. "I believe you're naked, are you not?"

"Do you know anyone who takes a bath with clothes on?"

One fine brow arched into view above his hand.

"I don't mind if you don't. Honestly."

Slowly, he lowered his hand to his lap. And smirked. "Darling, I assure you: I'm hardly the blushing virgin."

"You're blushing a little bit, though," she pointed out with a giggle, and didn't feel quite so self-conscious about being totally bare beneath the water.

His cheeks were indeed a little pink, but he smoothed his smile into something unconcerned, haughty, and got slowly to his feet.

She'd barely touched her wine, but her tongue felt loose. The warm water, she thought, or maybe having him here in the intimacy of her bathroom, while she lay naked and vulnerable.

She didn't *feel* vulnerable, though. She said, "I like the way you stand." She would have died if she'd said that six months ago, but it was true. He had this catlike grace, and he cocked his hips like he knew he was sexy. "And that's not just the tumor talking."

His smile became a smirk – an attractive one – and he took two panther-like steps toward her, hips rolling. "I didn't think it was." Another step, and the movement pulled his coat tight against his waist, highlighting its narrowness; and his breeches pulled tight in other areas, highlighting things that were definitely not narrow. "Perhaps I stand that way on purpose. To arouse you."

She snorted – but it was a weak sound, and she knew it. She felt a heat gathering low in her belly, a tightening. And a fluttering in her chest. Shit, it had been a long time. Too long.

"Perhaps," she echoed, faintly. "That's sweet of you."

He grinned, fangs sharp points, and his pupils dilated as he came closer, and closer still. "Not really." His gaze made a slow journey from her face, down to the water, over her body beneath it. She'd pulled her knees up a fraction, and they shadowed the place between her legs, just enough that he wouldn't be able to see it. But his gaze shifted down her legs, to her toes, and back up, over her pale belly, and breasts, and down her sunburned arms.

"I like the way you sit a horse," he said, eyes finally returning to her face, "and I'd ask if you do that to arouse me, but I know you don't. You're only wonderful at it, and *that* arouses me."

Her mouth fell open, and she breathed out a shivery little exhale. Her blood was thrumming, and the heat in her belly had become an empty ache. She wanted – a dozen specific fantasies flickered through her mind, each rawer and dirtier than the last.

She wet her lips, and his gaze followed the movement of her tongue. "Val," she said, voice low and rough. "Come here."

He sank down – gracefully, always graceful – to his knees beside the tub and rested his forearms on its edge, his face only a few inches from hers. Eyes dark pools, fangs elongated and teasing at his lower lip as he breathed roughly through an open mouth.

She was panting, too. "Val, please."

"I can't touch you, darling," he said, pained. "I wish – God, you have no idea how much I–" He closed his eyes a moment, swallowed, expression almost a grimace. When he opened his eyes again, they were nothing but pupil, the blue only a thin ring. "I can't touch you," he said again, "but you can touch yourself."

And...*oh.*

She could do that.

She wanted to do that.

Her hands shifted under the water.

"Go slow, love," he murmured, like his throat was tight.

A tightness she felt in her own throat; her whole body felt tight. She had to wet her lips again. "Where should I start?"

He reached with one spectral hand, and hovered it just beneath her ear. "If I were here, I would touch you everywhere. I'd start right here, at your lovely throat."

The words sent a thrilled shiver through her. Of course a vampire would go for the throat first. Would he sink his fangs? Drink her blood? No, no, she didn't think so. She knew he wouldn't. But the thought of those sharp points scraping lightly over her pulse left her reeling, and she pressed wet fingertips to the side of her neck.

Val let out an explosive breath, a little hiss at the end, utterly transfixed.

Her skin came alive under her own touch in a way it never had, made electrifying by the weight of his gaze. She trailed her fingertips down, and felt her pulse flutter. Swallowed with an audibly click when she reached the ultra-sensitive hollow at the base of her throat. She pretended it was his touch; pretended she could feel the heat of his breath as he leaned in even closer, as her hand slipped beneath the surface of the water.

"You're so utterly feminine," he murmured around a low, pulsing growl when she cupped her breasts in both hands. They felt heavy, swollen, her nipples drawn tight, despite the heat of the water. She plucked at her nipples and lifted into the sensation with a little gasp.

"*Yes*," he said.

And as he moved lower: "I love your hips. I love that little bit of softness, there, on your belly, and just inside your thighs. God, you're such a woman and I *love* it."

"Val." Her heart hammered behind her ribs; the rush of blood in her ears loud as a faucet left running.

"Lower."

She went lower, a punched-out sound leaving her throat. She was wet already, slick in a way that had nothing to do with the water, and she teased apart her lips while her thumb pressed into her clit.

Val reached into the water, then. The second his hand made contact, it curled into mist, but he kept going, all the way up to his shoulder. So that, had he been there, his hand would have joined her between her legs. She pushed a finger inside her sex and pretended it was his.

His voice came rough, frantic. "I bet you're so warm in there. I bet you're hot. And tight. And wet. I want to taste you."

She let her head fall back, eyes going to the ceiling, the soft glow of lamp-shattered light across the plaster. Added a second finger.

"Yes, more. I would stretch you, work you open. And then – and then my cock. I'd split you open." He gasped, desperate, broken breaths. "*Mia*. Does it feel good? Do I feel good to you?"

"You feel amazing," she said on a moan, and stroked deep, deep as she could, wishing it was deeper. Wishing it was him.

Her arm flexed with the effort, and she heard the soft slap of the water as it lapped at the edges of the tub. Heard her own choppy breathing, and his. Imagined the weight of his body over hers, hot breath, and wet tongue, and the bite of his fingertips into her waist, the sharp press of narrow hipbones on the insides of her thighs. Slick slide of skin, a frictionless slide between her legs. Split open, like he'd said. The *image* that conjured, God.

He growled, the quiet rumble of a big cat. "Mia," he said again. "Come for me."

She did, back arching, chest heaving up out of the water, sex tightening like a vise around her fingers. She closed her eyes, and stars burst behind the lids.

An orgasm like a full-body spasm, one that brought only pleasure, and wiped every bit of pain and worry from her system. She made a noise, something embarrassing and high-pitched. But she didn't care; she gave herself over to it completely.

It was a slow comedown, muscles unlocking one at a time. She slumped back, boneless, so weak she was afraid she couldn't get out of the tub, now, and blinked her eyes open.

Val's face hovered over hers, expression reverent.

"Thank you," he whispered. "You're perfect."

"Thank *you*," she countered. And then emotion rose in her, a post-coital tide of endorphins crashing. "I wish you were here."

He smiled like it hurt to do so. "I know, my love. So do I."

~*~

Some days there were headaches. Vicious, throbbing, relentless headaches that made her flinch away from the sun and brought tears to her eyes. Those days were the worst – those were the days that she couldn't do the things she wanted to do…the days when she started to wonder if, maybe, just maybe, Val wasn't real after all. That she'd dreamed him up, and then dreamed Donna telling her that she'd seen him.

She was having one of those awful headache days when she took a tumble off Brando, and Donna banished her to the office. Alone, surrounded by all the ribbons and awards that marked a life she wouldn't get to live any longer, she put her head in her hands and gave in to the tears.

Val appeared, then.

"My imaginary friend," she called him, hating herself for letting the words slip, hating the sad way he tilted his head.

He disappeared suddenly, after that, vanished without a sound.

She didn't see him again for three weeks.

8

SHOW ME

Mia brushed Brando with long strokes of the body brush, flicking her wrist at the end, little puffs of dust rising up toward the sunlight spilling through the stall window. He huffed contentedly and leaned into the pressure. His coat gleamed, penny-bright, his new autumn hair coming in darker than his washed-out summer coat.

Grooming a horse was the most soothing activity of which she knew. But she couldn't stem the tide of worry for Val. Alone with only Brando's warm presence and her own thoughts for company, she couldn't stop replaying their last interaction, wondering if she'd finally managed to push him away for good, too overcome by pain and misery to say the kind things he so obviously needed to hear.

But even worse was the thought that he wasn't coming to visit because he couldn't. Early on in their relationship, the first time she brought him to the barn and he spent all day there, he'd fritzed out for a while, and been tired in the evening, telling her it had taken too much energy to maintain an astral projection for that long.

Maybe he was tired.

Or maybe, a dire voice whispered in the back of her mind, something had happened to him.

She lifted the brush and started another stroke–

"*Mia.*" A ragged gasp behind her. A pained, choked voice.

She dropped the brush and whirled, bumping back into Brando as she lost her balance.

Val stood at the open stall door, in his tattered prison clothes, his hair wild and greasy. His eyes *glowed*, dilated and feverish.

"Oh my God–" Mia started.

"Mia," Val said again, his voice raw, like he'd been screaming. "Listen to me. I don't know how long I'll have, but I have to–" He paused to catch his breath, panting. "I have to tell you this. I can't..."

"It's okay. Take your time."

"No, I can't! There is no time!"

"Val." Her heart raced; she felt its sharp tattoo under every inch of skin. "What's going on?"

He gulped a few more breaths, and then drew upright, a valiant effort to compose himself. "Your father's drug. You haven't agreed to take it yet, have you?"

"No. But why–"

"*Don't.* You can't. There's a good chance it will kill you."

"*What?*"

He closed his eyes a moment, sighing. "Christ, I should have told you all this from the start." When he looked at her again, he said, "Forgive me, darling. You'll hate me after this, for keeping things from you, but I had to know first. I had to be sure."

"Sure of what?" He was scaring her now.

"That you aren't like him. That you're genuine."

She felt like she'd been slapped. Offended, shocked, worried, a whole tangle of things. "Val, what the hell–"

"I know your father. He's the one keeping me prisoner these days."

Mia...

Couldn't process it.

It hit her like a wave. Over her head, all around her, filling her lungs. It didn't feel like she took a breath for a full minute, and when she finally did, it was a gasp.

That coincidence, the one that had worried her weeks ago...it wasn't a coincidence after all.

"Your father," Val went on, tone resigned, heavy, "is the biologist in charge at the Ingraham Institute of Medical Technology. His drug isn't a drug at all; it's a serum he's made out of vampire blood. My blood, and my brother's. He bought me from my last captors, and then he finally found Vlad in Romania and dug him up. The drug works – on some people. But it isn't a true turning, and without being turned, some of the recipients...well...it doesn't go well. They die. Painfully."

Mia opened her mouth and no sound came out.

He gave her a wry smile, gaze miserable. "I knew who you were the day we met. When you told me your last name. And now Talbot knows I've been visiting you. He'll punish me, and he's sending people here now to collect you. To take you to Virginia for treatment."

"Val," she said, helplessly, shaking now. "I don't – how can you–"

"Shh." He took a step closer. "It's alright. It's fine if you hate me, everyone does. Just one more thing. There's something I want to try." He lifted both hands. "I don't know if it will work. I might not be strong enough. But I don't think we'll see each other again, and I want to show you. I want someone to know – I want *you* to know. I owe you that at least, I think. No one knows the real story. No one's ever seen it. Not all of it."

He gritted his teeth, bracing himself. "I'm sorry," he said. "It's – some of it is – well, I'm sorry. But I don't think I've got the energy to skip over the bad parts. I don't know how much you'll see, or if I can…"

His past, she realized. He wanted to show her what had happened to him. The reason he was locked up, and starved; the reason her father was keeping him, manipulating him.

"It's alright," she whispered. "Show me."

He shut his eyes…and surged toward her.

Mia gasped. She saw a bright white flash, felt a powerful burst of coldness steal across her body.

And then…

Then…

9

A BOUQUET OF FLOWERS

Tîrgovişte, Capital of Wallachia
1439

"Vlad! Vlad, wait for me!" Val panted as his small legs worked and his arms pumped and he struggled to catch up to his older brother. Vlad was only four years his senior, but they were a dramatic four years for boys who were four and eight, and Vlad had always been sturdy and large for his age. Val, by contrast, was a pale, slow-growing, delicate thing. "No bigger than a bouquet of flowers," Fenrir's wife and mate, Helga, liked to say, smiling and ruffling his golden hair. Vlad hadn't meant to run off and leave him, Val didn't think, but his legs were so much longer, so much stronger. And now Val was alone as he rounded the corner and saw that Vlad was long gone.

He took a ragged breath and redoubled his efforts, soles of his boots slapping across the stone floor.

The scents of the palace household flowed through his sinuses, down into his lungs. He smelled his parents, and Father's wife, who was Mircea's mother; smelled his brothers, and the family wolves, their mates. Smelled the maids, and nurses, and Father's human advisors; smelled fresh bread baking three floors down in the kitchen. And very near, just around the next corner, a scent and a sound – the steady thump of a heartbeat – he sensed–

"Got you!" Fenrir crowed, scooping Val up in both arms, tossing him into the air, so his head almost brushed the ceiling, and then catching him securely against his chest, held tight in his strong embrace.

Val shrieked in delight. Father could dismiss Fenrir as dumb and huge all he liked, but Val loved him. He was Val's favorite wolf.

89

"Where are you off to in such a hurry, little prince?" Fenrir asked, still holding him. He began to walk in the direction Val had been heading, his much-longer strides eating up the distance.

"Vlad said I could go with him into the city. There's going to be acrobats!" His stomach swooped excitedly at the thought.

"Oh, well, you won't want to miss that," Fenrir said, and lengthened his stride.

It was a warm, bright summer day, and though the windows were set at sparse intervals, all the shutters were flung wide to let in the heat, and the corridor swelled with light, the stones the color of toasted bread, warm even through the soles of Val's boots – when he'd been walking, anyway. Now, carried securely in Fenrir's arms, he had a rare, high view of the tapestries on the walls; a glimpse out the windows, as they passed, of the bailey, and the moat, and the red tiled rooftops of Tîrgoviște spreading out down the hill, a wide stretch of packed humanity, the hustle and bustle of commerce and busy commoners, all the way to the jagged peaks that stood ink-blank against the horizon.

The capital city of his father's principality may have been the only home he could remember, but he still found it irrepressibly lovely.

"Are you done with your lessons for the day?" Fenrir asked as they reached the stairwell and started down.

"Um, well…" Val fidgeted. He didn't want to lie. So he said, "Mostly." His tutor *had* ended their lesson. After the fifth time he asked if Val was feeling well – "Radu, are you well?" and that name, his father's picked name for him, had set him into a fresh batch of wriggling in his chair – the tutor had sighed and said, "Clearly, you're distracted today. Go on. I saw your brother walk past the doorway three times already."

Val hadn't wasted any time after that.

But though he had waited at first, loitering outside the study where Val had been attending to his Greek and Latin lessons, Vlad hadn't been able to wait anymore, far outdistancing him.

Sometimes it wasn't much fun being the youngest.

At the bottom of the spiral staircase, Val and Fenrir encountered Father's preferred wolf, Cicero, named for the

Roman orator, in company with his packmate, Caesar, and Val's oldest brother, Mircea.

Father's wolves had been with him, according to Mother, for centuries. Loyal Familiars who served as confidants, generals, political advisors, and, even, friends. They'd been Dacian, originally, bearing Dacian names. Father had renamed them for Roman notables, and he'd taught them all the languages he knew, given them access to the finest tutors and books, so that they could be of greater use to him. They were unfailingly loyal. They took the protection of the heir, though Mircea was half-human, very seriously.

Too seriously, in Val's opinion. They rarely smiled, and Mircea rarely did so either in their company.

"Mircea!" he called. "Vlad's taking me to see the acrobats. Come with us!"

Mircea smiled the warm, but regretful smile that had become the only one he exercised. Val thought he had vague memories of his oldest brother when they still lived in Sighișoara, before the palace, before father was officially sanctioned as prince. A toddler's fuzzy memories, snatches of sounds, and colors, but he remembered Mircea laughing, and leaping, and being a child. He was the heir now, officially, and all he ever did was train and study.

"I'm afraid I can't, Radu."

Val frowned at the name.

"But I'm sure you'll have more fun without me." He rolled his eyes, first to the left and then to the right, indicating his wolf escort.

Fenrir broke out in a hearty chuckle.

Cicero and Caesar shared a glance over top of the heir's head.

But Val frowned. "We'll miss you." And he already did, a tug of regret in his gut. Vlad's friends were never unkind to him...but they weren't outright welcoming either. Not like Mircea, who always went out of his way to ensure Val felt included, asking for his opinion, even though he probably hadn't earned the right to give it.

"Send my regards," Mircea said, reaching up to pat Val fondly on the cheek. "Have fun. Be careful with my favorite brother, Fen!" he called as he and his wolf escort retreated toward the stairs.

"No worries on that, your grace," Fenrir assured, and off they went again.

They caught up with Vlad in Mother's garden, on the hedge-lined path that led past the stables toward the gate. Vlad had come to a stop, kicking at stray pebbles, impatient as he waited. He glanced up with a nod that seemed to say *finally* when they appeared, Val riding on Fenrir's shoulders by that point. Two human men-at-arms waited a few paces away, arms folded, relaxed and awaiting their little prince's orders. This was their into-the-city escort, Val knew.

"What kept you?" Vlad asked.

You were too fast, Val thought. But that was something a baby would say. So he said, "We ran into Mircea. He said he can't come."

Vlad snorted. "When does he ever? Come on."

The men-at-arms made to fall in.

"I'll take them," Fenrir said, setting Val down on his feet beside his brother.

One of the guards shrugged, but Val thought he looked relieved.

The afternoon stretched out before them as they walked through the gates, across the bridge, and headed down the motte's slope toward the city proper, a glorious, too-warm, high-summer day filled with the thrum and call of humanity, the sun a bright discus overhead. Val held a bit of his brother's sleeve pinched between his thumb and forefinger, and felt a not-unpleasant prickling of sweat beneath his clothes, cool drops gathering at the back of his neck under his hair, sliding down between his shoulder blades. He loved the heat; though his fair skin would flush, and if left too long in the sun without a hat, or a cup of water, or a stolen bit of shade he was wont to faint, he liked the way summer made everything feel so alive. Winter was a dead season; not without its charms – Mother's soothing voice as she read to them, the crackle of logs, the scent of wine, and pipe smoke, and the raucous shouts of wolf laughter and conversation. But winter was all indoors, shut up against the snow, and his hands cracked and bled in the dry air. Summer, though, summer was ripe, and unrushed, and all the green things thrived.

Val breathed deep through his nose, and he could smell *everything*, scents tripping over one another in their haste to be identified. As the city swallowed them, Val could smell the hundreds and hundreds of scent markers of human commoners; the vegetables and freshly-butchered meats on offering in the market stalls; tobacco smoke; fresh flowers; sweat and offal; and best of all, the competing savory and sweet flavors of the vendor food being hawked with enthusiastic shouts.

Fenrir drew some looks, in part for his size, in part for his mass of curly red hair, but mostly because he wore the finely-tailored red tunic, breeches, and knee-boots of the princely household. It was probably Fenrir that Vlad's friends spotted first, a moment before a skinny arm shot through the crowd.

"Vlad!" Marcus shouted, shouldering his way between bodies, dragging Nicolae along behind him. "There you are. Finally! We'll have to hurry, they've already started – oh," he said, voice falling flat at the end when he spotted Val.

Val pinched Vlad's sleeve tighter, gathered it in his whole hand, squeezed until his knuckles went white.

Marcus – ten and tall for his age, broad-shouldered and already starting to resemble the man he would become – turned to look over his shoulder at Nicolae, who made a helpless sort of gesture in response. Marcus turned back, looking at Vlad – just at Vlad. "You brought your brother?"

Two days ago, Vlad had dumped a handful of fireplace ashes down the back of Val's shirt – and caught a single blow from Father's riding crop across the backs of his thighs for the effort. But that was nothing new; he would stick wet fingers in Val's ears, and muss his hair on purpose, and had blamed mud tracked on the rug on Val. "Brother things," Mother would say with a shake of her head.

But here now, in front of his friends, Vlad drew himself up like a bristling cat, stuck out his chin, puffed up his chest, and said, "So what if I did?"

Marcus and Nicolae exchanged another look, one Val had no hope of interpreting.

"Alright," Nicolae said. "Follow us."

Fenrir was able to bull his way through the crowd, the four boys following along in his wake. The tight press of bodies around them, the overwhelming headiness of so much scent at once, tightened a sensation almost like panic in Val's belly. He held the back of Fenrir's tunic with one hand, Vlad's sleeve with the other. Vlad shot him a dark look, like he thought he was acting like a baby, but didn't shake him off.

"I hear there's women in this troupe," Marcus said with a laugh. "From the Far East. And they're *naked*."

Nicolae chuckled.

Vlad said, "You're lying."

"It's just what I heard!"

"What you hoped, you mean," Nicolae said, and *then* Vlad laughed.

"You'll see," Marcus grumbled. "They'll be naked, and then you'll have to cover little Baby Radu's eyes."

That *name*.

Val faltered a step…but then Vlad took his hand from his sleeve, slid it into his own, their fingers laced. Vlad's palms were callused and tough from riding and training. Only eight, but he could gallop bareback, down a hare with a bow from horseback, and wield a short sword meant for a much older boy.

Val caught himself, letting his brother's strong grip tow him along, and the name didn't bother him so badly.

The crowd parted around Fenrir, at first because of the sheer spectacle of him, and then because they noted, sometimes with quiet gasps and exclamations, the two boys who trailed behind him. One dark and one light, hands clenched tight. One sallow and harsh like their father, one golden and slight as their mother.

Finally, they reached the edge of the throng, and the square where the acrobats had already begun their performance.

Vlad breathed a quiet, self-satisfied laugh. "I don't see anyone naked, Marc."

"Shut up."

They settled into a familiar argument, Marcus's insecurities playing off Vlad's sureness, but Val wasn't paying attention. He could only stare, open-mouthed, at the spectacle before him.

If not for his vampiric sense of smell, he wouldn't have known whether the five lithe, androgynous humans leaping over one another were male or female. But he flagged two women, and three men, all of their faces painted, dramatic lines of kohl giving them cat's eyes. They wore beaded and belled crimson costumes, gauzy and diaphanous, long sleeves swirling like flags as they lifted one another, and sprung into wild jumps and twists.

They moved like birds, like fairies. Like creatures who weren't nailed down to the earth.

Free, he thought, unbidden. They looked free.

His hand tightened, a spasm flex of excitement.

And Vlad squeezed back.

~*~

His name.

It probably shouldn't have mattered, but it did. To him, at least.

Mother had told them the story often, one of their frequent requests at bedtime, when the winter wind howled through the cracks in the shutters and they weren't quite ready for her to blow out the candle and slip off to her own bed. The story of the tourney at which she'd first laid eyes on their father. When, tall and regal, head held high, shoulders squared, he'd ridden into the arena on a prancing chestnut destrier and captured her heart with a single wink. Vlad II, back from his apprenticeship…maybe not quite like anyone expected, though no one could have said what he was supposed to look like. Mother told them how, up in the stands, flanked by Fenrir and Helga, she'd leaned out over the rail to toss a favor into the sawdust: a heavy golden belt buckle that Father still wore every day.

Mother had been a purebred vampire, and so had Father, and they'd scented it on one another, irrevocably drawn together right away. He'd reined his horse up right in front of her, smiled up at her from beneath his visor.

"What is the fair lady's name?"

"I see no fair lady." She'd smiled wide enough to flash her fangs. *"But my name is Eira."*

Mother talked fondly and at length about that tourney, Father's indomitable strength, skill, and horsemanship. He'd unseated every opponent at the joust. Conquered totally in the melee.

Mother told them what none of the cheering spectators had known that day, what Father had told her later, in the candlelit dark of a bedchamber amid warm, tousled sheets: that he wasn't Vlad II, son of Mircea at all. That he was Remus, twin brother of Romulus, co-founder and one-time-heir of Rome. That he'd hidden from his brother for centuries, that he'd found a purpose and a calling here, in the shadow of the Carpathians, and that he wanted the chance to be the kind of benevolent and thoughtful ruler he'd been too callow to appreciate before.

Mother never talked about what happened after. About her Remus – her *Vlad Dracul*– having to marry the eldest daughter of Alexandru the Good, Prince of Moldavia. That Princess Cneajna had borne him a son, half-human. A political obligation, Father called it. Though he did love his half-human son, Mircea, named for his own pretend father. And most of all he loved Eira, his Viking shieldmaiden, who had eventually taken him back into her bed.

Eira birthed two purebred sons. The first she named Vladimir.

"It isn't a Wallachian name," Vlad chastised her gently.

"It's not?"

"No, my love, it's Russian."

And so her Vladimir was renamed Vlad III by his father.

And everyone save their household wolves thought he was the son of Cneajna, who locked herself most often in her room with a book and a cup of wine, indifferent to the unfaithfulness of her husband.

So when Val was born, Eira brought his small face up to hers, and kissed his forehead, and said, *"You will be my Valerian. My precious boy."*

And when father proclaimed him Radu, Mother wouldn't play along.

To the people of Wallachia, and Moldavia, and Transylvania, and to all the visiting dignitaries who arrived at the palace, Dracul's youngest son was Radu.

But Val was *Val* in his head. And in his mother's smiling mouth. And in the gentle, reassuring squeeze of his brother's hand.

And his name mattered. It always would. Because the world didn't care about the truth, but the people who loved him did. And those were the only people whose good opinions he valued.

~*~

Val couldn't suppress a yawn as Mother tugged his nightshirt down over his head.

She chuckled. "My sleepy little prince tonight, hm? Too much fun today?" She smoothed his shoulder-length hair down with several long, gentle passes of her hand.

"Mama, it was amazing," he declared, going limp and flopping backward on the bed. "They were so beautiful. And the way they *moved*." He lifted a hand and swept it through the air in demonstration. "Can I be an acrobat?"

"Well." She lifted his legs and tucked them beneath the covers, pulled the blankets up to his chin. "You're already a prince, and I think that's pretty special, don't you?"

He made a face.

She smiled and perched on the side of the bed. "Think of it this way: a prince can hire acrobats to come entertain him whenever he wants."

"Hmm." Small consolation.

"Where is your brother?"

As if summoned, Vlad walked in, already dressed for bed. He went to the washstand in the corner of the room and scrubbed his face with the still-steaming water from the bowl. He came to bed pink-cheeked and heavy-eyed.

"Another sleepy son," Eira said fondly, gathering him close for a moment, kissing his dark, silky hair.

97

"No I'm not," he protested, and then yawned hugely.

"Of course not. Up you get. Go on."

By the time they were settled, both of them beneath the covers and snuggled up shoulder-to-shoulder, Helga had arrived in the threshold, bearing a wooden tray.

"Ready, mistress?" she called.

"Yes, Helga, thank you," Mother said, and took the two small gilt cups the female wolf offered her.

Helga tucked the empty tray beneath her arm and gave both boys a warm, motherly smile. "Enjoy, my lords. That's fresh from my Fenny."

"Thank you," they choroused, dutifully, and Helga left, wide hips rolling like a ship at sea.

They sat up against the pillows and Mother handed them each a cup. The hot, salty scent of blood curled up from it, the metal warm in Val's palms. A thirst he hadn't felt before quickened; his mouth filled with saliva.

"Drink up," Mother encouraged, and he buried his nose in the cup, opened his mouth and gulped it down like a savage. In all things he was delicate, nothing but a little bouquet, but the blood...the blood...

It hit his tongue like velvet, his belly like wine. It tasted of every wonderful thing, and also of home, and safety, and pack, their beloved wolf's blood offered freely to nourish their bodies. It felt *right*.

Blood was a gift, mother always said. Not something to which they had a right. Being a vampire wasn't a right. Her name meant merciful, and she was.

When the cup was empty, Val pulled off of it with a deep gasp. His chest pumped as he fought to catch his breath; he licked the last salty traces of blood off his lips and wished for more.

Beside him, he felt Vlad vibrating with the same craving, his shoulder quaking where it pressed against Val's. "Mother—" His voice came out low, and hoarse, full of wanting.

"No, no," she murmured, taking the cups from their lax fingers. "That was the perfect amount for two growing boys. Now it's time to sleep."

Vlad grumbled, but when Val slipped down to lie flat, he followed suit.

Mother smoothed the blankets over their chests. "Now, are my little princes getting too old for bedtime stories?"

"No," they chorused immediately, and she smiled.

"Alright, then, have I told you–" She cut off, head tilting, and Val heard the sound of rapid footfalls in the corridor.

Helga burst in a moment later, still carrying the tray, wild-eyed and breathless. Val could smell fear on her.

"My lady, it's the prince, he–"

Father.

Eira stood, instantly tense. The usual softness of her posture melted into a straight-backed, alert stance, feet braced wide apart on the floor. "What is it? What's happened?"

But Val could already feel a low thrum of panic in the palace, like the buzzing of insects, hopping from wolf to wolf, to Helga, to Mother, to his own suddenly-queasy stomach.

Helga braced her free hand against her side, as if she had a stitch. She huffed and puffed, but managed, "It's his brother. His brother's here."

Vlad sat bolt upright in the bed. "Uncle Romulus?"

A low, angry growl pulsed through the room, and at first, Val didn't realize the sound came from his mother. Then he saw her eyes flash, and her fangs slide down to peek from beneath her lip. "Where?" she asked, in a voice she never used with the two of them.

Val shrank sideways into Vlad, who put an arm around his shoulders.

Helga straightened, hand falling to her side. "In his grace's study, my lady, but he doesn't want–"

"I don't care what he wants," Eira said. "Not if *he's* here. Go and fetch Fenrir, bring him to the study. Cicero is there already, I assume?"

"Yes, my lady, but–"

"Now, Helga. Please."

The wolf muttered something distressed under her breath, but hastened to do as told.

When Mother turned back to the bed, her expression softened a fraction. "Go to sleep, the two of you. I'm going to help your father."

Vlad pushed the blankets down, gathering himself to climb out of bed. "But, Mother–"

"You will *stay here*. Is that understood? Look out for your brother. Neither of you are to leave this room." Her gaze was ferocious.

Vlad seemed to shrink down in his nightshirt a little. "Yes, Mama."

She glanced between the two of them, expression stony, implacable. This was no gentle encouragement, nor a request. It was an order: *stay put.*

"Don't leave the room," she said again, and finally left them, shutting the door firmly in her wake.

They sat for a moment, pressed together, not breathing. The candle flame guttered, nearly went out, and recovered in the sudden flurry of wind current left by the slamming door. Its light licked up the walls, across the ceiling and the bed, unsteady flickers that seemed to echo Val's erratic heartbeat.

Finally, Val said, "How did he find us?"

Vlad snorted – but it was a shaky snort, and his arm tightened around Val's shoulders. Val could feel his fear, sense it, even if Vlad would never admit to being afraid. "Father's a *prince.* He isn't exactly hiding."

No, he wasn't, but it had been so long. And he went by Vlad Dracul now. Only the smallest handful of individuals knew that Father was also Remus, and even those only knew because Father had told them, not because they'd known him then, back when the first king of Rome tried to have him executed.

Val wanted to feign braveness, like his brother, but at the moment, cold terror washed through him, obliterating the chance. "Do you – do you think he'll hurt Father?"

"Probably not. Why would he? That was centuries ago." But there was doubt in his voice. Uncle Romulus had been a shadow lying over their lives, a faceless threat, the imagined monster under the bed. "And besides: Fenny and Cicero, and Caesar would never let anything happen to Papa."

Very true.

"Damn it," Vlad muttered. "I want to see what happens, though."

An idea struck Val then. A brilliant one. "I could go."

"What? No." Vlad turned to him, frowning, his arm slipping off Val's shoulders. "You saw her. She'll box your ears if she catches you out of bed." She'd never lifted a hand to them in anger, which was perhaps why her expression minutes before had rattled them so.

"But I won't *be* out of bed." He tapped a knuckle against his temple. "Only my mind will."

Vlad looked interested. For a moment, and then he frowned again. "You can't ever dream-walk when you want. And you can't choose where you go. It'll never work."

"It might. I've been practicing."

"You have? When?"

Val felt his face color. "At night. Just sometimes. When you're asleep."

Vlad's frown twitched sideways, caught between pleased with the development, and sore for being left out, Val thought. "Can you do it?"

"I think so." A few nights before, he'd gone to visit Constantine on purpose. He hadn't been able to hold it long, but he'd set a destination and carried it out.

He wriggled down beneath the covers now, closing his eyes, willing his nerves to let go of his tightly clenched muscles. "If Mother comes, wake me up," he said, and concentrated on his breathing. Vlad said something, but it was distant, and mumbled, and Val was already slipping away.

Dream-walking, he'd learned in his own self-directed experiments over the last few months, wasn't a case of actually dreaming. Sometimes it happened when he was asleep, but falling asleep wasn't the key. He had to *go under* instead, willingly climb onto the plane where his thoughts, and image could traverse beyond the physical. So in that sense, it was really like *crossing over* instead. He still wasn't sure how the mechanics of it worked. All he knew was that a stillness came over him, frightening at first, and then he had the sense of falling; a flash of light, and then he was rising, wind in his hair, and then he was...

Standing in the corner of his father's study, and there was the low, rolling sound of a half-dozen wolves growling.

Val pressed back into the shadows and tried to make himself even smaller than he was.

Vlad Dracul's study was a large, airy room, prone to draftiness in the winter, its ceilings high enough that the two fireplaces were necessary to keep it warm. Tonight, summer cool as fresh melon, and almost as sweet, the shutters were thrown wide, letting the breeze in to play with the candle flames, the velvet sky beyond embroidered with stars. A fire burned on one of the hearths, adding to the glow of the candles, and in the diffuse, warm light, Val could see that every wolf of the household was present, standing shoulder-to-shoulder, a wall between Father and the newcomer that Val couldn't see yet. There was Cicero, and Caesar, their packmates Mihai, and Vasile. Fenrir, and his son, Vali. The wolf captain of the guard, Ioan. If the threat wasn't clear in their growling – and it was – then it was in their posture: heads ducked, throats guarded, shoulders bunched and ready to pounce. Or to shift. They were all in human shape, now, but Val knew they would shift in a moment, ready to rend and tear with fangs and claws.

Father looked ready for bed, in a nightshirt and elaborate dressing gown; he'd tugged on boots, and pushed his hair back with his hands, though water droplets glimmered faintly at the dark ends. He'd just had a bath. His profile, clean and regal as ever, betrayed an expression Val had never seen on him before, the corners of his mouth turned down, the creases at the corners of his eyes more pronounced.

Father took a deep breath, chest lifting beneath the heavy brocade of the dressing gown. "It's alright, boys," he said, voice soothing. "Let him through."

Cicero turned to regard him, brows knit together in clear question.

Father nodded, and then the wolves parted, like the Red Sea.

A man stepped forward, and Val remembered that Father was a twin.

Romulus, first king of Rome, looked alarmingly like his brother. But harsher, in Val's estimation. Sharper, his angles more dramatic. He wore a long black cloak with the hood pushed back, and beneath it his clothes were dark and unremarkable.

Val shivered.

"Brother," Romulus said, a smile twisting his mouth to a cruel angle. "It's been a while."

"Centuries, even," Dracul said.

Romulus chuckled. A dry sound, like leaves rustling. Like a man with a mouth full of grave dirt. "Come now, don't look at me like that. You said yourself it's been centuries – let's let bygones be bygones. All our bad blood is in the past now." He held out both arms. "I've come to congratulate my little brother on all his accomplishments, and his new title. The Dragon. I like that." He grinned, fangs flashing.

He made to step forward, but Caesar barred his path, growling low in his throat.

"Caesar," Father said, softly. "It's alright."

Another chuckle. "Caesar, eh? You haven't gotten too far from your roots, have you?"

Father laid a hand on Caesar's shoulder and urged him to the side, careful, kind. His brows knit, his face a portrait of concern, he said, "It's good to see you, Romulus."

The twins studied one another a long, fraught moment.

Then Romulus inhaled, nostrils flaring, and turned toward the far corner of the room, the chair where Val noticed his mother was seated, Helga standing behind her. "Ah," he said. "I see your beloved is here. Or. Well." He tipped his head. "I *smell*."

Val bit back hard on the sound that rose in his throat, and watched his mother get slowly, gracefully to her feet, her head held aloft at a challenging angle.

"My lady," Helga whispered, frightened, hands clenching into useless fists.

"My mate," Father said. "Eira."

"Mate," Romulus said, and then turned to Father, grinning. "But not wife? Does the princess know she bore you only one son, or have you compelled her to think that the other two are hers as well?"

Growling filled the room.

Father looked as if he'd been struck.

Val felt as if he had been.

Only the family knew the real nature of the prince and princess's relationship. Only the wolves, undyingly loyal, knew that Eira was mother to Vlad and Val.

"What, you thought I wouldn't be able to tell? You've been away from our kind for too long, brother. There are four vampires under this roof, and one half-breed."

"Perceptive as always," Father said.

"It would seem so. I've also noticed that your youngest son is a dream-walker."

Dracul frowned. "How could you possibly know that?"

"Because he's standing right over there." He nodded toward Val's hiding place, and all eyes swept his direction.

Oh no.

"Valerian," Mother gasped.

Father charged toward him in three long strides, expression thunderous. "Radu, what are you—"

A flash, a sense of falling, and Val opened his eyes to his bedchamber, Vlad propped on one arm and leaning over him, watching his face.

"Well?" he said immediately.

Val tried to swallow, but his throat was too dry. His heart beat wildly against his ribs, and his palms prickled with fear sweat. "I got caught."

Vlad sighed. "Stupid."

"Uncle Romulus is…" He'd been smiling, and laughing, but.. "He's wrong."

Vlad's dark brows knitted together. "What do you mean 'wrong'? What did he say?"

"No, he just…" Val frowned to himself, frustrated with his inability to communicate. His uncle hadn't done anything, or even really said anything, but he'd sensed a threat. Too obscure for his four-year-old mind to grasp properly, or to classify.

The quick rap of footfalls echoed out in the hallway, and Vlad's eyes went comically wide. "Mother," he whispered, and flopped down beside Val, closing his eyes and feigning sleep.

Val closed his eyes, too, and hoped he wasn't in too much trouble.

10

ECHOES OF AN EMPIRE

Romulus purchased a two-story white stone house in Tîrgovişte and, for all intents and purposes, seemed eager to reacquaint himself with his brother. He began visiting the palace regularly, though he never stayed long, and Mother was always hovering nearby, displeasure writ clear on her face.

"He brings us presents," Val said one afternoon, sitting cross-legged in a puddle of sunshine in the center of Constantine Palaiologos's solar while the emperor pored over a document at the table. "He brought me a little wooden horse." He didn't have it now, because he couldn't carry things with him when he dream-walked, not even the images of them. At least not yet. He was still basking in the joy that came with being able to pick a destination and send himself there, across rivers, and lakes, and sharp mountain peaks.

"That's thoughtful of him," Constantine murmured, distracted. He read with one fingertip skimming down the page in front of him, chewing at his lip in thought.

Val climbed up from the floor and walked over to stand beside his chair, look over his shoulder and squint at the Greek letters.

It had taken a matter of months, but slowly the emperor had stopped startling like he'd seen a ghost every time Val appeared in his chambers. Maybe other boys would have found it amusing, to see the Roman Emperor shout and fling his papers and stumble over his own feet; he'd pulled down a tapestry once. But it saddened Val. Once, to his great shame, he'd burst into tears. That was the visit in which the emperor had gathered his composure and approached him, face going soft.

"Oh dear. Well. Don't cry." He'd patted the air above Val's shoulders, awkward. "Hell. I don't know anything about children. Can you stop crying?" He'd tried to touch Val's shoulder, and his hand had passed right through. "Christ, you're a *ghost*."

106

Val had wiped his face — his not-real face and his not-real tears — and choked down the rest of his childish sobs, peering up at Constantine's shocked countenance. "I'm not a ghost," he'd said. "And I'm not a demon." He'd felt a burst of frustration, then. "I'm a real boy. I'm a prince. Son of Vlad Dracul of Wallachia, and I'm not here, I'm dream-walking."

Val still wasn't sure if Constantine actually believed him, but the man had stopped startling out of his chair when Val appeared, and he was always kind and conciliatory. Val enjoyed visiting him; he'd begun treating him as a sort of confessional. Father was always talking about outside third-party opinions, and Val supposed that's what Constantine was for him.

"I'm glad I'm not an emperor," Val said now, as Constantine read. "You're always busy."

"Yes, well, I'm not really emperor. Only until my brother gets back from Rome, remember?"

Val wrinkled his nose. "*Will* you be emperor one day?" He didn't want to have to think of him as *pro tempore*. As of this moment, Constantine was ruling Constantinople, a symmetry that Val found pleasing. To his mind, the title wasn't as meaningful as the actions; if Constantine's brother John was so great, why wasn't he here now?

"I suppose I might be," Constantine said with a shrug. "John doesn't have any children. And." Here he looked up from his reading, finally, grinning, and shot Val a wink. "I *am* the favorite brother."

Val smiled back in response. "That's what Mircea always says: that I'm his favorite brother."

"Always a good thing." His expression grew serious again, gaze narrowing. "There's three of you, right? Three brothers?"

Val smiled, pleased that he'd remembered. Once they'd finally gotten past the I'm-not-a-ghost-or-a-demon stage, Constantine had admitted that he knew little of Wallachian politics or the royal family.

"Yes," he said. "Mircea's the oldest, and the heir. He's always busy doing heir things. And then there's Vlad, and I'm the youngest." He felt his smile tug a little sideways. "I won't ever be an emperor, or even a real prince. If anything happens to

Mircea..." A lump formed in his throat, suddenly, and he swallowed, blinking against the prickle of tears. He heard the wolves whispering sometimes, muttered, angry stories about the Ottoman raids into Transylvania, the gold demanded, the janissaries taken, the pretty young women and beautiful boys stolen in the night. It was a dangerous time for princes; he worried for his oldest brother. "Then Vlad would be heir," he said, hollow and afraid now.

"Well," Constantine said gently, drawing his gaze back. "It's not much fun being in charge of things. So really, you're lucky. You get to enjoy all the fun parts of being a prince without any of the hassle. Right?"

A ghost of his former smile tugged at Val's mouth. "Right."

He stepped away from Constantine's chair and moved to sit on the edge of the table, legs swinging. It was a trick he'd been working to perfect: he couldn't lift anything, or touch anyone, but if he concentrated, and stretched his magic, he could sit on solid surfaces...or at least project his image on top of them, so that he looked like he was really present in the room, and no longer had to stand in the center of the floor.

When he was settled, and sure that he wasn't about to flicker out of existence and wake up on the rug in front of the hearth back home, he glanced up, expecting to see Constantine poring over his reading again. Instead, the emperor *pro tem* was studying Val, a thoughtful look on his face.

"Your Majesty?" Val asked.

That earned him a tiny smile. "Valerian, your father has a treaty with the Ottomans, doesn't he?"

"Yes, sir. Monetary tribute, additions to the Janissary Corps, and raiding rights," he rattled off from memory.

"Is there..." Constantine started, and then sighed and cut himself off with a shake of his head. "Forgive me. You're only a child."

Val frowned. Folded his arms. "I'm not a baby."

"I said 'child,' not 'baby.' And I shouldn't be bothering you with this anyway." He went back to his ledger with an air of finality.

Val lingered a while longer, until he began to feel stretched-thin and shaky. It took an immense amount of energy to maintain a projection like this. His body, lying prone in the palace back home, began to recall his conscience, reminding him that he needed to eat. Soon Vasile would come collect him for archery practice, where Vlad would no doubt show him up.

"I need to leave now," he said, the first time he'd spoken in long minutes.

"Princely duties?" Constantine asked, teasing, lifting his head.

"Archery."

"Ah. Have fun, then, little prince."

"Your Imperial Majesty," Val said with a little bow, and then let go of the projection.

He always came back to his body as if physically across the distance; a sense of rushing wind, and mountains and rivers flashing beneath his feet. A dizzy spin. And then he cracked his eyes and was looking at the cold grate, feeling the softness of carpet beneath his cheek, the stickiness of drool at the corner of his mouth.

He pushed himself upright on trembling arms and heard the brisk footfalls that heralded Vasile's arrival. A cursory knock sounded at the door before it creaked open.

"Your grace," Vasile started, and Val could sense the bristling of his figurative hackles when he spotted Val on the floor, unsteady and no-doubt pale. "Are you unwell?"

Val forced himself upright, blinking back the black spots that crowded his vision, and turned to face the concerned wolf. "Fine," he said, "only walking."

~*~

To no one's surprise, Vlad made a mockery of everyone else's archery attempts.

The targets were set up on the palace lawns, thick wooden planks secured to a frame, backfilled with tightly-packed hay. Someone, probably Ioan, had painted crude human torsos and heads over the bullseyes, pretend Ottomans at which to aim. The three princes were staggered; Vlad's target was the farthest, and Val's was the shortest distance, with Mircea in the middle.

"That's just embarrassing," Mircea said with a deep, tired sigh, lowering his bow and staring glumly at his target. It bristled with arrows, none of which were close to the center.

Val didn't look at his own target – all of his arrows were in the grass, none of them having reached their destination – and instead glanced toward Vlad. Watched his serious expression; watched the wind toy with loose wisps of his shoulder-length dark hair; watched him draw his arm back in one fluid movement, hold, breathe, and release. A faint whistle, and then a thunk and a twang as the arrow found its mark. Dead center.

"A natural, your grace," Vasile said with quiet pride.

Val snapped his head around to see that Father had joined them. Dracul, Cicero beside him, his constant shadow, stood in the shade cast by the stable behind them, arms folded, smile tugging at the corners of his mouth. His gaze rested on Vlad as his middle son lowered his bow and turned to face his audience.

"Well done," Father said.

Vlad nodded, once, and tucked loose hair behind his ear with a quick movement. "Thank you, Father." His expression was careful, but his eyes shone. Pleased, proud.

Val wanted to be just like him in four years. Wanted it the way he wanted fresh fruit, or Mother's hugs, or to see the first cherry blossoms in the spring. A want so sweet it ached.

Nicolae had said once that Val was jealous, but he wasn't, oh no, he wasn't.

Father's gaze shifted, then, to Val, and his smile softened. "How've you been faring, Radu?"

Val ducked his head, cheeks heating. "Not well. Sir," he mumbled.

"He's doing fine," Mircea piped up. "He's just got to grow into his bow a little more, and then he'll be Wallachia's own Robin Hood, wait and see."

Val lifted his face and found his brother smiling at him with warm encouragement. He smiled back, grateful.

"I'll bet you're right," Father said.

Hands landed on Val's shoulders, starling him; a warm body pressed up against his back. Vlad: he recognized the scent of his skin and sweat and hair, the same scents pressed into the pillows of their shared bed.

"Here," he said, breath warm across Val's ear. "We'll do it together."

Val clumsily nocked another arrow; his brother's arms came around him, hands closing over his smaller ones, adjusting his grip. Val went through the motions, but it was really Vlad, his strength, his surety, that drew the bow and aimed the shot.

"Ready?" Vlad whispered in his ear.

Val nodded.

They let go together, and the arrow flew straight to the target, landing on the bullseye like a lover's smacking kiss.

It wasn't Val's achievement, not truly, but it *felt* like it, the burst of excitement in his chest. He cheered, and Vlad clapped him on both shoulders.

"Well done," he murmured.

Val spun and flung his arms around his brother's middle, hugged him tight.

"Father!" he shouted. "Did you see? Did you—"

He and Vlad both stilled in the same moment. A new scent reached them: Uncle Romulus.

Val pulled back, slowly, though Vlad left a hand on his shoulder, fingers curling tight in the fabric of his shirt. Holding him there. *Stay here beside me.* It gave Val the courage to peer around Vlad and search for their uncle.

Romulus stood several paces from Father, projecting a relaxed demeanor, one booted foot cocked, hands resting lightly on his hips. He didn't acknowledge the aggressive stare Vasile drilled into the side of his head. His gaze was fixed on Mircea, who'd gone totally still, bow clenched in white-knuckled hands. Val could smell the first acrid notes of fear lifting off his oldest brother's skin.

"You should adjust your stance," Romulus suggested.

Mircea took a rattling breath. "S-sir?"

"His stance is fine," Vasile snapped, growling softly.

Romulus snorted. "If he was full-blooded, or a wolf like you, yes, it would be. But he's half-mortal. He needs to adjust his stance to make up for the strength he lacks. Here." He stepped forward, and though Mircea's brows jumped, he didn't flinch away. "Face the target, yes, like that. Nock your arrow."

Mircea did as told, feet braced wider, elbow tilted at a higher angle at Romulus's urging.

"Now. Take a breath. Hold it. And then release."

Bullseye.

Mircea stared goggle-eyed at the target.

Romulus chuckled. "Perhaps you should invest in a mortal archery instructor, eh brother?"

Vlad's hand tightened again, a little spasm on Val's shoulder.

~*~

"You were frightened," Val said the next day, sitting across from Mircea at a book-loaded table.

Sunlight fell through the open window at Mircea's back, turning his shaggy hair into a copper halo around his face. He turned the page and sighed. "What do you mean?" But he fidgeted in his chair a little, and his denial was just a token; Val already knew the truth.

"Uncle Romulus." Val lowered his head so his chin was propped on the back of one hand, low enough that the sun couldn't slant into his eyes, and he could watch Mircea's gaze grow distant, no longer reading, only staring at the page in front of him. "You were afraid of him."

Mircea chewed his lip a moment, eyes still glued to the book, then finally gave up with another sigh. Propped an elbow on the table and leaned sideways, gaze troubled when he lifted it to Val. "But you were too, weren't you? This is *Romulus*. He tried to *kill* Father...probably even thought he succeeded." He shook his head, and Val thought he was struggling with the notion of vampires again.

His father was one, his brothers were; he was on, if not friendly, at least cordial terms with Eira. He knew all the wolves,

112

had watched them shift. He *knew* immortals...but Val thought sometimes it overwhelmed him.

His gaze sharpened, suddenly, coming back to Val's and pinning him in place. "What does he smell like?"

"What?"

Mircea wrinkled his nose. "You can all, I don't know, tell what a person's intentions are, can't you? You can smell their...emotions, or something?"

"I..." It wasn't something easily put into words. He couldn't smell intent, or emotions. It was more that a person's intent had a way of affecting their heartrate, the tang of their sweat. It was a sense. He'd been born with it, and explaining it to mortals was difficult. He had to try, though, for his brother. "He...there's something *wrong*," he said, reiterating what he'd said to Vlad before, frustrated with his own lack of understanding.

"Wrong?" Mircea's brows jumped.

"I don't know." Val shook his head, but of course that didn't clear it. "I can't tell. There's just...something."

Mircea studied him a moment, giving him a chance to come to some great revelation, then finally offered a lopsided smile. "It's alright. Sometimes bad feelings are unfounded."

"Sometimes," Val echoed, but he couldn't return the smile.

~*~

He dream-walked to his father's study by accident one night. His projection manifested in a dark corner, as if his subconscious was trying to be sneaky. He heard his father's and uncle's voices, engaged in tense discussion.

"...sultan is fairly peaceable, as far as sultans go," Romulus was saying.

"There's nothing *peaceable* about it from where I'm sitting," Father said, tone sharp-edged. "Wallachia and Transylvania are their pathway into Western Europe, and it's a path they're eager to take."

"Fuck Western Europe. What has it ever done for you? I'm telling you: Murat is an old man, and grows weary of war. But his heir...he's only Vlad's age, but he's already got his eye set on the

Red Apple. Mark my words, when he's sultan, he'll march on Constantinople, and he'll succeed. Afterward, once Rome falls—"

"Rome will *never* fall."

Romulus chuckled. "Brother, it's as good as already fallen. But that doesn't concern you, and your territories. If you would heed the advice of an older brother who was once your king, I would tell you this: cooperate with the Ottomans. Let them have whatever they want."

"And if what they want is my life?"

It was quiet a beat; a gentle wind rattled the shutters.

Val's pulse pounded in his ears. He heard his father's pulse as an echo, a rapid drumbeat.

"It won't come to that," Romulus said at last, soothing. "The Turks want the world. It's better to be a man living in that world, than a corpse living under it. Remember that."

Val closed his eyes and willed himself back to his bedchamber, to the small body burrowed against Vlad's side. While he was dream-walking, he'd tucked himself in tight to his brother's ribs, fingers curled to claws that gripped his shirt tight. He came awake and realized that he was panting, rapid breaths that turned the air beneath the covers humid and too-close.

Vlad stirred. "What?" he asked, sleepily.

"Nothing," Val said, "sorry." Because he was only four, and he didn't understand wars and territories yet, and he thought that, maybe, if he pretended he hadn't heard what Romulus had said, he wouldn't have to find out if it was true.

~*~

It nagged at him, though, that conversation, like a canker sore that he couldn't stop poking at. A week later, he found himself in Constantine's solar again, hiding behind a low table full of decanters and wine goblets, as the *pro tem* discussed something with his chief advisor. Over the past few months, Val had come to learn, through eavesdropping, that George Sphrantzes was Constantine's closest friend, his most trusted and loyal of helpmates. Val wanted to meet him, but then they'd have to go through the whole not-a-ghost argument again.

At every visit, Val made sure that Constantine was alone before he revealed himself. But today, worry throbbing in the back of his mind like a headache, he decided he couldn't wait.

"Your Majesty," he said, stepping out into the open, and the conversation cut off abruptly.

Both men turned to look at him, Constantine with mild surprise – maybe even a dash of worry – and Sphrantzes with something more like startled annoyance.

"A little young to be a messenger, isn't he?" Sphrantzes asked, already turning back to the map spread out on the table.

But Constantine frowned, gaze searching Val's face. "Is something the matter, Valerian? You look frightened."

Because he was. He swallowed with difficulty and walked closer to the table, booted feet silent on the stones. "My uncle." The words scraped at his throat, like he'd swallowed bones, and he forced them out through suddenly-chattering teeth. The fear closed over him like a shroud. "I heard him talking. The Ottomans – Your Majesty, the Ottomans are coming for Constantinople. Not – not Murat," he stumbled over the name, uncertain, "but his heir. The next sultan. My uncle, he knows things, he's – he's–"

Sphrantzes turned around with an impatient snort. "Constantine, who is this? We don't have time–"

"George." He silenced his friend with a wave. "This is Vlad Dracul's son."

"He *what*–"

"Shh." Constantine came to crouch in front of Val, his expression soft and rapt all at once. "What is it, little prince? What did you learn?"

Val took a deep, heaving breath, trying to calm down. "The Ottomans are going to try to attack the city," he said all in a rush. "Uncle thinks they'll win!"

Constantine offered a sad sort of smile. "It won't be the first time they've attacked. This is a very old fight, Val."

Sphrantzes came up behind the emperor, scowling down at Val. "What do you mean this is Vlad Dracul's son? Is Dracul here? In Byzantium?"

Constantine ignored him, so Val did too. "But, Uncle Romulus said–" He caught himself, teeth snapping shut, but too late. No one outside the family was supposed to know who exactly his uncle was, and he'd just blurted it out in a fit of panic.

Constantine sucked in a breath. "Your uncle *who?*"

Before Val could answer, Sphrantzes leaned down and reached for Val's shoulder.

Val winced, and a second later Sphrantzes stumbled back after his hand passed right through Val's body. He panicked as calmly as a man who thought he'd just touched a ghost could panic, Val thought.

"What – how – but–" He clutched Constantine's sleeve and tried to drag him away. "A demon! This is a portent of disaster! The Turks–"

Constantine stood and clapped a hand over his friend's mouth, silencing him. His own mouth smoothed, a smile barely suppressed. "George, how long have we been friends?"

Sphrantzes made a gesture with his eyebrows that left Constantine nodding.

"Yes, exactly. And in that time have I lied to you? Deceived you?"

He deflated with a muffled sigh and shook his head.

Constantine removed his hand and gestured to Val. "This young man has been visiting me for several months now," he said, his smile fond enough to ease some of Val's panic. "George, meet Prince Valerian, son of Vlad Dracul, Prince of Wallachia. Valerian, this is my closest friend, George Sphrantzes."

Val sketched a shaky, but correct bow.

"And Val," Constantine said, gaze narrowing, "I think there's some things you've neglected to tell me, isn't there?"

Val took a deep breath, and, ignoring the look of utter disbelief on Sphrantzes face, decided that he had to tell the truth. He trusted Constantine, for better or for worse. He'd come to him for a reason, he was convinced.

He said, "Well, actually…"

11

A BRACE OF HARES

1441

"It's because of what you are," Mother explained one sunny afternoon. She was in the kitchen garden, gathering sprigs of herbs and laying them gently in the basket she carried hooked over one arm. In her simple blue dress, hair bound in a loose braid, she looked more like a palace maid than the mother of two princes. Which, Val conceded with a pang of sadness, was exactly what everyone beyond the household wolves thought she was. He hated the charade, hated it for her most of all, but whenever he expressed concern, she brushed it off.

"Do you see that rosemary?" she asked, pointing to the raised bed situated behind the tomato stakes. "Fetch me a pinch of that, darling."

Though six now, Val was still helplessly tiny, and he slipped right between the stakes, sure-footed as a deer. Vlad's friends called him a fairy. Mother called him beautiful, and perfect, and golden, so it was no small wonder he'd sought her out in her garden, rather than accompany Vlad into town.

Also, he'd had questions.

His day's language lesson had concluded with his tutor leaning back in his chair and blinking at Val in obvious surprise. "Your progress is...remarkable. For someone your age," he'd said.

Was it? Val had been brought up speaking Romanian in the palace, the informal, unwritten dialect of Wallachia. But he could also speak and read Slavic, French, Hungarian, Greek, and Italian. He could read Old Church Slavonic and was fluent in spoken Slavic. He could speak Russian, and was working on his Cyrillic letters now. Vlad had the same gift for languages, and they tested one another, holding conversations that flitted from one language to the next, probing and teasing and searching for weak spots, for badly conjugated verbs and mispronunciations. Mircea had been taught the same languages, but he struggled at times, especially with Greek and Italian.

"*Is* it remarkable?" he asked his mother.

He returned to her side and laid the rosemary sprig gently in the basket, on top of bundles of sage, and lavender, and lemongrass.

Mother raked her long nails through his hair, tidying the pieces that had slipped from the loose knot gathered at his nape. "You're a vampire, darling," she said, fond and patient, smiling down at him brighter than the midday sun. "One day you'll be much stronger, and faster, and agile than any human. It only stands to reason that you learn quickly, too."

He cocked his head to the side. "I never thought of that."

She rested her palm on the top of his head. "That's because you're humble, darling, and that's a very good thing." Her hand shifted to his shoulder and squeezed. "We're different from humans, but we aren't better. Always remember that."

He nodded. "Yes, Mama."

She looked at him a long moment; he had the sense she was really trying to drive the point home. Then her hand fell away and she turned back to her thriving plant life. "*Come*," she said in Russian, "*let's hear what you've been learning.*"

~*~

Where he excelled at languages, swordsmanship was another matter entirely.

The next afternoon, he sat on a wooden bench in the practice yard, sweat gathering beneath his dirt-smudged tunic, watching Vlad spar with Fenrir's son, Vali.

The boys were mismatched in size, Vali a good head taller than Vlad, but when the blunted practice blades clashed together, Vlad more than held his own when it came to strength.

Sunlight flashed along the steel. A parry, a block. A step forward, a step back. The bright ring of metal meeting metal again and again. Dust kicked up around their boots, clung to the shiny sweat on their arms and faces.

Vlad's braid kept coming loose, one wisp at a time, and he reached up impatiently to swipe his arm across his forehead. Hair clung to his temples; a muscle in his jaw clenched as he lunged again, powering past Vali's intended block and catching the wolf boy in the arm with the blunted edge of his sword.

"Agh!" Vali's arm went limp – Val knew from experience the awful pins-and-needles sensation that came with being struck there – and he staggered back, clutching at his wrist with his free hand. His face was red, and he breathed in ragged bursts. "Yield, yield!" he exclaimed when Vlad made to advance again.

Vlad nodded, quietly pleased, and let his sword arm fall to his side. He smoothed the loose hair back from his face with his other hand and a stable boy hurried forward with a water bucket and a ladle.

"Excellent," Fenrir said, hands propped on his hips, beaming. Then he turned to Val. "Alright, young sir."

"Ugh," Val groaned.

"Come now, let's see a little enthusiasm."

Val dragged himself upright, his sword weighing heavy on his arm and shoulders. Or maybe that was just the dread.

Vlad passed him on his way to the bench, and knocked their shoulders together. "Don't be a baby," he said lightly.

Val kicked dust at his retreating back.

"Valerian," Fenrir sang. "Front and center, let's go."

Grudgingly, Val took his place, and saw that he'd be facing off with Vali, too. Vali, who was sweaty, tired, and still wincing from Vlad's blow, but for whom Val wasn't enough of a challenge to warrant sitting out this bout.

A discouraging notion.

Vali offered him a tired smile. "It's alright. I'll go easy on you."

Val frowned. "You don't need to."

Vali hefted his sword. "Alright." But his smile was still kind and placating.

Val shored up his stance, trying desperately to mimic the sure way that Vlad stood. Rolled his shoulders, gripped the pommel of his sword in both sweat-damp hands.

"Make your move, Val, on the offensive," Fenrir said.

119

Val moved. Too slow, too clumsy. Hesitating. And Vali put him on his back in the dirt with seemingly no effort.

Val stared up at the sky, tried to catch his breath, and sighed. He was a third son, and what was a third son good for if not as a soldier?

He'd have to find another way to earn his bloodline, he supposed.

~*~

Riding, though. Now there was a talent. In that he and Vlad were evenly matched.

A half-length ahead of him, Vlad wound his finger's tight in his horse's mane and leaned low over the gelding's neck, urging him faster.

Val laughed, a sound snatched immediately away by the wind, and pressed his face into his mare's neck, knees gripped tight to her bare sides. He fed her another bit of rein, clucked, and urged her on with a gentle press of his heels.

Vlad's horse, Storm, was fast.

But Val's Dancer was faster.

She took the extra rein with relish and lengthened her stride, neck stretched out flat. Val held on for dear life, laughing wildly as she managed to overtake Storm in just a few strides.

Vlad glanced over as they past, teeth bared, lips forming angry curses Val couldn't hear.

Val laughed and Dancer surged ahead, the bit in her teeth.

They rode in a field, the sky a vast blue stretch above them, birds flinging themselves up from the tall grass and taking flight as the thunder of hooves approached. The horses, well used to these races, didn't spook; they carried their boys across the long, flat stretch, already slowing as they neared the tree line.

Val sat back, closed his thighs, and checked the reins with reluctance. Dancer slowed to a canter, then a trot, then, true to her name, danced in place, tossing her head a few times. He patted her damp neck. "Good girl. What a good girl."

She danced a little more, preening.

Vlad reined up beside them, boy and horse both blowing through dilated nostrils. "You cheated."

Val laughed. "How?"

"That horse would do anything for you," Vlad said, sulking. "And you know it."

"That's not cheating. That's good horsemanship."

"Brat."

They turned the horses around and settled them at a walk, reins loose. Storm and Dancer stretched their necks out long and low, blowing, catching their breath. Val felt the familiar heave of the mare's ribs beneath his legs.

"Can you, though?" Vlad asked, out of nowhere.

When Val glanced over, he saw that his brother was playing with bits of Storm's mane, scowling at his own hands.

"Can I what?"

Vlad flicked him an impatient look. "Talk to her? To Dancer. You can – you can dream-walk. Can you talk to animals too?"

"Oh." The question caught him off guard. "I don't think so." He frowned. "No. We can't *talk*. But I can tell she loves me, and I think she knows I love her. I get on well with animals."

"I noticed." It could have been a scoff, but wasn't. Vlad glanced away, out across the waving grass, thoughtful line pressed between his brows. "You're only six, and you can already do so much. Who knows how much power you really have?" He sounded melancholy. "I don't think I have *any* power." The last just a whisper.

Val's sudden shock was so strong that Dancer came to a halt, head lifting. She craned around and nudged the toe of his boot with her nose. "What?" It was almost – almost *distressing* to hear Vlad say something like that. "What are you talking about?"

Vlad shrugged and wouldn't look at him.

"Vlad, you're a vampire, and a prince, and you're going to be the best warrior in all of Eastern Europe. You're the best archer, and the best swordsman, and you could probably beat Fenrir up with your bare hands right now. What do you mean you don't have any *power*?"

"I–" Vlad started, and then went still. Storm came to a sudden halt. "Shh."

Slowly, slowly, slowly, he unslung the bow from his back and drew an arrow from the small quiver buckled around his shoulders.

They returned to the stable a half-hour later with a brace of hares slung over Storm's withers. They hadn't had a chance to resume their conversation about power, but Vlad seemed looser after the two kills; the line had smoothed between his brows.

At least until Vali came running up to them, red-faced, panting. He stopped and pitched forward, braced his hands on his knees.

"What?" Vlad snapped, and sounded every inch the lofty prince.

Power, Val thought with an inward snort. The way Vali's eyes widened in a brief flicker of panic was all the proof anyone needed that Vlad was destined to be the most powerful creature in the whole palace.

Vali straightened. "Your mother – sent for you – guests tonight – banquet."

"And she wants us to wash the horse smell off ourselves," Vlad said, already sliding down off Storm's back. "Yes, tell her we're coming."

Vali hurried off.

Val lingered a moment, idly stroking the fine strands of mane at Dancer's withers. Watching his brother drag the hares off his horse and stroke Storm's nose with a rare, fond smile. He smiled less often, now. He had grown lanky, thin, pale. Dark shadows lingered beneath his eyes.

"Come on, little brother," Vlad said.

Val shook himself and slid down to join him. "Who do you think the guests are?"

"I suppose we'll find out soon enough."

~*~

Freshly-scrubbed, pink-faced, and buttoned into fancy dinner velvets and glossy boots, Val joined his brothers, father, and Princess Cneajna at the high table that evening. His eyes sought his mother, first, an old familiar spark of guilt and longing flaring in his chest.

Two long wooden tables sat perpendicular to the high table, creating a horseshoe shape in the midst of the wide hall. Candles blazed in the iron chandeliers, and in the candelabrum along the walls, and on the tables, suffusing the room with warm, flickering light. Eira, dressed in rich gold, sat at the near end of the table to the left, surrounded by the family wolves and their mates and offspring, smiling in response to something Fenrir had said. She caught Val watching her and sent him a reassuring smile.

He smiled back, weakly, wishing she was up here with the rest of his family. Their family.

The high table was packed to capacity, though, even if it had been appropriate for Eira to join them. Father's guest tonight was the governor of Transylvania, John Hunyadi.

A tall, sturdy man with a bull neck and a headful of thick auburn hair, he sat between Mircea and Dracul, gesturing animatedly as he spoke.

Val kept leaning forward to peek around Vlad and sneak glimpses of him. Politically-motivated dinners were a near-constant thing in the palace, but Hunyadi was an anti-Ottoman hero of near-mythic proportions at this point.

Val kept playing Uncle Romulus's words over and over in his mind: *Give them whatever they want.* And now Father was at table with a man who believed just the opposite.

Nervous sweat began to gather between his shoulder blades.

Which of course Vlad could sense. He elbowed him. "What?"

Val shook his head.

Vlad kicked him under the table. "*What?*"

"*Nothing.*"

Vlad sulked a moment, and then his brows jumped and he leaned in closer. Val could *smell* the supposed great idea lifting off him before he said, "I've got a great idea."

Val groaned.

"No, listen." A tiny smile tugged at Vlad's mouth now, and the dark circles beneath his eyes faded in the sudden glow of his eyes themselves. Once he set a goal, he followed it through, no matter how ill-advised. "They won't talk about anything serious until later, in Papa's study. You have to dream-walk and spy on them."

Val's stomach shriveled. "But–"

"You do it all the time!" Vlad hissed. "You go all the way to Constantinople! And you're too afraid to go into Father's study?" He lifted a single brow in challenge. "Coward."

Val huffed in irritation. "Last time–"

"Listen." Vlad leaned even closer; his breath smelled of the wine he'd snuck from Mircea's cup. "Everyone always says you're a baby." His eyes blazed. "Don't prove them right."

Val forced himself to take a measured breath. To think.

After the incident with eavesdropping on the night of Romulus's first visit, Val had been expressly prohibited from dream-walking his way into private conversations. If he wasn't asked into Father's study, then he wasn't allowed.

But as the only dream-walker in the family, no one knew which means to take to prevent him from doing it again. There were no wards, no silver tokens – that would have hurt everyone. So Val technically *could*...

If he wasn't a baby.

Vlad's gaze was stern – and desperate with curiosity. He wanted, viciously, to be a part of the discussion, to be a prince who could contribute to the family, to the principality. Power, he'd said. He was a child, still, and not the heir, and he felt powerless.

Val sighed. "Alright, I'll do it."

Vlad's grin was manic. And grateful. Val would do anything for that grin, even stupid things. Maybe *especially* stupid things.

~*~

Vlad was obvious and an idiot. After the third fake yawn, Mother shot him a narrow-eyed glance.

"Long day, my Vladimir?" she asked, reaching to smooth his hair.

"We went riding," he said, and smothered another massive, pretend yawn in his elbow.

Val rolled his eyes from his fireside chair.

"I shot two hares," Vlad continued, slumping sideways across the sofa, head propped on one listless hand. "Val beat me in a race, the little shit."

"Don't call your brother that," Eira said, immediately, and Val hid his laugh in his shirt collar.

Vlad huffed a quiet "sorry, Mama" under his breath. Then made a great show of dragging himself to his feet. "I should probably turn in."

"Yes, dear, if you're really that tired."

Vlad trudged toward the doorway, dragging his toes. His faux exhausted face was the dumbest and funniest thing Val had ever seen. He paused with one limp hand on the doorframe, and turned to look back over his shoulder. "Val should turn in, also. He's tired. Right?" His façade slipped a moment, dark brows slanting down at threatening angles.

Val bit the inside of his cheek, but managed not to crack a smile. "Yes," he said, levelly, "I'm very tired." He got up slowly, to prove the point, but without Vlad's theatrics. Here was another area in which he succeeded over his brother: acting.

Eira sighed once, short and sharp, and when Val darted a glance to her found that she looked terribly unimpressed. "Whatever you boys are doing, I don't care so long as you don't break anything, hurt yourselves, or anger your father."

Well, Val could say they weren't going to do two of those things.

"Yes, Mama," they said as a unit, and then ducked out into the hall.

"I mean it!" she called after them.

When they were far enough away for vampire ears, Val said, "You were really stupid."

Vlad shoved him sideways into the wall. And took off at a sprint, laughing back over his shoulder.

Val growled and followed.

They hadn't shared a bedchamber in some months, a change Val hated. He'd known the split was coming, and that it made sense. They were both growing up, and more importantly, Vlad was becoming a man. A slightly-scrawny, pale man, but a man nonetheless. He was beginning his official apprenticeship as a knight, and was well on his way to becoming a warrior of legend. It was time to leave childish things behind, including sharing a bed with his clingy little brother.

And Val knew that, as a prince in his own right, it was time to start thinking more like his brothers.

But he was six. And he'd never slept alone until a few months before, and he missed the warmth and weight that came with having his brother beside him. It still hit him with a fresh wave of surprise and loneliness every time he walked into his bedchamber, with only his clothes hung up in the wardrobe, and only one comb on the dressing table. Only his boots lined up at the end of the bed. The linens always cold when he slipped between the covers.

Tonight, he stuttered on the threshold, the now-normal melancholy hitching, jumping, and then leaving him. Vlad was right on his heels, pushing the door shut and climbing up onto the bed with him. He was grinning by the time they settled.

"What?" Vlad asked. He was impatient, bristling with anticipation.

"Nothing." Val lay down with his head on the pillow and folded his arms over his middle. Took a deep breath. "Alright." He shut his eyes. "Wake me if someone comes."

"I will."

It took longer than it usually did to go under. The excitement of the evening, his heartbeat racing from running, the thrill of doing something forbidden…and the fear. Vlad had no hesitation when it came to disobedience, but it always made Val's stomach squirm.

Down, down, down, he thought. He envisioned the fall, and the subsequent rise, and then he was doing it, and found himself in the cool dark plane that existed between his physical body and his destination. And then it was down again, his blood calling him back to earth, and he opened his eyes as he coalesced in a dark corner of his father's study.

Cicero and Caesar stood sentry on either side of the door, backs flat to the wall, gazes carefully blank. They missed nothing, Val knew.

In fact, Cicero cocked his head, and his eyes swept slowly up to meet Val's gaze.

Val winced, and he almost bolted, almost went flying back to his body. But he made a pleading face and shook his head. *Please don't say anything.* The wolf gave him a long, penetrating look, then turned his head away.

Val let out a deep breath and looked toward Father's desk.

Dracul sat behind it, Mircea at his side, and Hunyadi had been given a lavish chair across from them. A pitcher of rich red wine sat in the center of the desk, and all three of them held cups, though Mircea's pressed-together lips and white cheeks revealed that he wasn't drinking his. He was nervous; if Val had been there in person, he would have been able to smell the apprehension on him.

Val wasn't even there, and *he* was apprehensive.

Remus of Rome was a literal living legend. But right now, tonight, Father was Vlad Dracul, and even if he was a good and fair prince, he wasn't the celebrity in the room. No, that honor went to John Hunyadi. Who currently studied Father with a shrewd gaze.

Everything Val had ever heard about the man hit him all at once. He was purported to be charming, and Val had seen him dancing tonight – with Mother, even, smiling at her as he spun her across the clean-swept stones once the trestle tables had been cleared away. He was said to be a wealthy man – the Holy Roman Emperor borrowed from *him*, as opposed to the other way around. And Father said he was ambitious; that he wanted not merely to defend Christendom, but that he wanted all of Eastern Europe for himself and for his sons.

"Ambition is a thing that gets men killed," Father had said once, his frown deep and contemplative. *"Or, maybe worse: gets a man ruined."*

Val tried to steady his breathing and settled in to watch.

127

"A lovely dinner," Hunyadi said, voice deceptively conversational.

Father lifted his cup and took a slow swallow of wine. "I'll be sure to pass your compliments along to our cook."

"You do that."

"It's an honor to have you here with us, my lord," Mircea said, voice paler and meeker than Val was used to. Half-human or not, Mircea was the most rational and easygoing of the three of them, the one with the best manners. But tonight he had shrunk down into himself, and the idea chafed at Val.

"Aren't you the perfect little prince," Hunyadi said with a soft laugh. His voice was kind, and not mocking, his smile genuine.

Mircea's gaze fell to his lap.

"Your eldest?"

"Yes." Father's voice held the barest note of impatience. "My heir: Mircea. You saw his brothers at dinner."

"Named for your father, I take it."

A tiny pause, only half a breath. "Yes. Of course."

"You mentioned your other sons…"

Father tensed, a fast flicker of muscle leaping in his jaw.

"The little one," Hunyadi said, drawing it out slow, "is golden." His brows lifted, a quiet asking for confirmation. For explanation. "And neither you nor your wife are, Dracul."

Mircea lifted his head, eyes wide and startled.

Father eased slowly back in his chair, hands clenched tight on its arms. "Why have you come, Hunyadi? What do you want from me?"

"Come, let's not be so crass about it—"

"Make reference to my golden son again, and I will show you crass."

A long, tense silence.

The candle flames danced, shadows leaping up the walls.

Val's belly clenched and cramped, and he wished he was corporeal so he could grab onto the chair beside him. He'd never seen Father like this.

Hunyadi held his gaze a moment, expression placid, then nodded. "I need to move my troops through Wallachia. Across the Danube and into Ottoman territory. I'm on a mission from my king – we're renewing the crusade that Albert abandoned, and I'm here to ask for your assistance, Vlad Dracul."

Father blew out a breath. "I was afraid of as much. I'm sorry, but I can't help you."

The charming façade slipped for the first time that night. Hunyadi's smile fell away, and he leaned forward in his seat. "What do you mean? Why not?"

"I signed a treaty with Sultan Murat, and I won't go back on it."

Hunyadi sneered. "You would honor an agreement you made with those barbarians?"

"A treaty is a treaty."

"You would side with *them* over *me*? Over the rest of Europe?"

Father sighed with barely-checked frustration. "Wallachia is the border between their lands and Europe. I am their neighbor. If I allow you through, that will be seen as a violation of the treaty, and he will put my entire principality to the sword. My people will suffer. My family. Don't ask me to make that kind of decision. You can crusade all you want, but you won't have any participation from me. I'm sorry, John, but this is what I have to do."

Hunyadi's hands curled into fists; his jaw clenched. His voice was calm, though. It sent a little chill skittering down Val's back. "I think you'll end up regretting that decision."

Val shut his eyes and returned to his body. He swam up from the haze and opened his eyes to find that his head was resting in Vlad's lap, Vlad peering down at him expectantly, hair hanging down around his face.

"Well?" he asked.

Val let out a sigh, exhausted and yet almost dizzy with nerves. "He wants Father to let him cross the Danube. He's trying to get another crusade started."

Vlad frowned. "What did Father say?"

"He said no."

12

GALLIPOLI

"I'm leaving you my bell, Mama," Val told Eira before they departed, and put the bit of dinted bronze into her cupped palm.

She'd smiled at him. "Won't you need it with you, on your trip?"

"No. You keep it. And if you need me, you can ring it, and I'll come find you." He'd said so in a fit of uncommon bravery, little chest puffed out, wanting to be the man that his older brothers already were.

Eira had hugged him close, and kissed his forehead, and wished him safe travels in an uncharacteristically tight voice. She was worried, he knew, and it had pained him to leave her behind.

But this was such an *adventure*.

Their party rode down a narrow, dusty roadway carved along a narrow ledge, only wide enough to ride two abreast. To the left, an uneven hillside of heaped boulders, laced with scrub grasses and stunted olive trees. To the right, a downward slope thick with brambles; effective barriers on both sides.

Val clutched tight to his reins, and willed Dancer not to trip.

"Stop being so frightened," Vlad admonished.

Val dared take his eyes off the trail long enough to shoot his brother a dark look. "I'm not."

"Uh-huh. That's why your knuckles are white."

He attempted to relax his hands a fraction.

"We'll be there soon," Vlad relented. "And then you can finally see what a sultan looks like."

"Oh, yes," Val said, perking up as he remembered. He'd never been in the saddle for such long stretches, and he was sore, and tired, and nervous about the drop-off beside them. He'd forgotten his initial excitement at the outset of the journey: he'd finally get to see the sultan.

A messenger from Edirne had arrived in Tîrgovişte several weeks before, bearing a summons from Sultan Murat, leader of the Ottoman Empire. He'd learned of John Hunyadi's visit, and, in elegantly subtle terms, had suggested he questioned Dracul's loyalty. He wanted a meeting. A confirmation of their treaty, a show of goodwill, and a chance to speak face-to-face. He would have his heir, the young Mehmet, with him, he said, and asked if Dracul might bring his sons as well, so the boys could meet. *They'll be allies someday, when you and I are dead and in the ground*, the missive read.

They rode now to Gallipoli, and an audience with the sultan who controlled their father's alliances and military actions.

Val was excited. And he was torn.

They rode a moment in silence, hooves clopping loudly on the hard-packed road. Val snuck another glance at his brother, and found Vlad scowling beneath the hood of his cloak.

"Why are you angry?" Val asked. He could feel his brother's aggression, radiating off of him like the heat from a fire, and it dimmed his own anticipation.

Vlad snorted. "Because I don't want to meet the sultan."

"Because of Father?"

Vlad answered with a question of his own: "Why should I want to meet the man who subjugates us?"

Val had no answer for that, and lapsed back into silence.

The trail sloped down, and narrowed farther, so they had to ride single-file, and lean back in their saddles, counterbalancing the horses' forward momentum. The land to the right leveled off, its brambles shoulder-high, and tightly-woven enough that daylight couldn't penetrate the boughs and thorns. A cloud scudded across the sun, shading them, and the wind changed direction, suddenly.

That was when Val caught the scent of humans. Many of them, and not in their party. A group come to greet them, Val thought. The sultan's men.

At the head of the line, Cicero halted, and threw up a hand to signal them.

Val reined his mare in hastily, nearly colliding with the rump of Vlad's horse.

"What–" he started.

But Vlad twisted his head around, nostrils flared, eyes wild. "Ambush," he whispered.

And then the rocks on the hillside beside them moved, and stood up, and revealed themselves as men clad in brown and gray, faces wrapped, skin around their eyes painted black.

The cry went down the line: "Ambush!"

"Val, run!" Vlad shouted.

Val spun Dancer – tried to. He yanked the reins around, and she collided with the mount of the guard behind them. The mare shied hard, tripped, and Val gripped the saddle tight with his legs to stay aboard.

Scrape of steel on leather as swords were drawn; shouts of men, frantic; blooming scent of anxious sweat.

Attackers leapt down off the hillside into their midst, dozens of them, like the land itself coming alive and rolling over them like a landslide.

Val froze, pulse drumming in his ears, hands going wet and weak on the reins. Dancer tried to bolt, tried to squeeze past the horse behind and make a run for it. But the way was blocked.

Dancer reared.

And a hand latched onto Val's foot, which had come out of the stirrup in the madness, and strong arms dragged him down out of the saddle.

The world tilted. He screamed, or thought he did; he could hear nothing but the awful hammering of his heart.

He hit the ground with a teeth-rattling thud, all the breath leaving his lungs. Flat on his back, shocked into stillness for one horrible, critical moment, he saw a face appear above his own, blotting out the light. Another, and then another.

He finally sucked in a breath. "Vlad! Papa!"

He wanted his mother, a powerful, instinctual urge to press his face into her throat and be hugged.

He tried to flip onto his belly, tried to get away. Men shouted, horses screamed, dust swirled around him.

Then a foot caught him in the ribs.

Pain exploded in his head, and then he was gone.

13

NOT COPS

Present Day

Mia returned to herself with a deep, desperate gasp. It felt like she fell, and then landed, suddenly, her knees threatening to give out. She blinked black spots from her vision and fought to get her racing pulse under control.

"Wha…" she panted. "What was…"

Her surroundings resolved themselves slowly, seeming to tilt around her. She was in Brando's stall, still, one hand braced on the boards of the wall, the other clutched at the base of her throat where a low ache made itself known.

With sweat-damp, clumsy fingers, she dug her phone out of her jeans pocket and checked the time. She'd come in to groom Brando around three, and it was only fifteen after. A quarter hour had passed, but it had felt like years.

The dream. The vision…whatever it was. It had seemed so *real.* She'd been inside Val's head, had seen life through his eyes.

His four-year-old eyes.

His life in fifteenth century Romania.

"Holy shit," she whispered, wobbling dangerously as dizziness washed over her. "Holy shit, holy shit, holy shit."

Then her panic derailed.

Because *where the fuck was Val now?*

"Val?" Her voice cracked. "Val?" She took a step, and stumbled forward, tripped over the track that housed the stall door, and almost face-planted in the middle of the barn aisle. Louder, not caring if anyone heard or thought she was insane: "Val?! Where are you?"

"Mia."

She whipped around and found Donna bearing down on her. She was flanked by two strangers, a man and a woman. Both in dark, nondescript clothes.

Mia shivered, and she didn't know if it was the aftereffects of her vision, or something else.

133

"Mia," Donna repeated, face set at unhappy angles. "Are you alright?"

No. No, she wasn't even a little bit alright. "I…" Her breath still huffed in and out, chest tight. "I don't…" Her gaze skipped to the strangers. Their stern expressions, their squared shoulders. The guns on their hips.

"Why are the cops here?" she asked, still too scrambled for any tact.

Donna sighed, like she was weary, but her gaze was electric with an emotion Mia had never seen on her before. It took her a moment to realize it was anxiety, and her own fractious heartbeat accelerated another notch. "They aren't cops," Donna said, admirably even-toned. "This is Major Treadwell and Agent Ramirez. They work with your father."

Oh God.

She remembered Val's spectral hands making a grab for her shoulders, the naked terror on his face. If Dad was holding Val against his will, chained up in some basement, then these expressionless droids with guns were the sort of people guarding him.

She drew herself as upright as possible; Donna steadied her with a hand at her elbow. "I don't have anything to say to either of you," she said. "Tell my father I don't want anything to do with him."

The man, Treadwell, frowned politely. She detected something beneath, though, something pained. "With all due respect, ma'am, you don't exactly have a choice in the matter. We have reason to believe you've been consorting with a dangerous prisoner. We're going to have to take you in."

Donna spun around, hand already lifted, finger aimed at his chest. "What? Uh-uh. Oh hell no. I said you could talk to her, not take her in. If you're not cops, you can't do that anyway. Fuck you, buddy." It was the most emotion she'd ever displayed.

Major Treadwell frowned at her a moment, then shifted his gaze around her to Mia. "Miss Talbot," he said, tone aiming for reasonable. "Your father's apprised us of your medical situation. He only wants to help you, and it's imperative that you cease all contact with this prisoner immediately."

"Did you just–" Donna spluttered. "Don't you dare act like I'm not here, asshole! This is my barn, and you can't–"

"Don't get hysterical, ma'am," the woman, Agent Ramirez, said, hand settling on her gun.

Red-faced, Donna opened her mouth to respond–

And Mia put a hand on her shoulder and squeezed. "It's alright, Donna." She was afraid for her boss, suddenly. These people had God knew what kind of jurisdiction, but anyone willing to lock up a centuries' old vampire prince? It was safe to say that they weren't too worried about the law of the land. Or, worse, they were far, far out of reach of regular law enforcement. Whatever was happening, this was her family, her fault, and her problem. "I'll talk to them, at least." Her heart slammed against her ribs, but she forced herself to be calm. "Is it alright if we use your office?"

Donna twisted to look at her, outwardly furious. And afraid. "Mia," she tried.

Mia shook her head and forced a tiny smile. "I can handle it."

Donna held her gaze a long moment, but finally nodded. "I think I left Brando's door open."

"I'll check," Donna said, and grabbed Mia's hand, giving it a brief, crushing squeeze before she headed down the barn aisle.

Inwardly quaking, Mia folded her arms, fixed the two strangers with her best unimpressed look, and said, "Follow me."

The back of her neck prickled with awareness as she led them there. Without turning her head, she scanned the stalls and washracks they passed for any sign of Val, but he was gone. If astral projection sapped his energy, she had no idea how draining showing her his past had been. She had the sense that she'd only seen a part of what he wanted her to, that they were only getting started, and that, for some reason, his consciousness had been snatched away from her. With every step, her panic mounted. Where was he? Was he alright? Was he being punished?

But she had to keep her wits; had to stay calm if she wanted to help Val.

She still had her phone in her hand, and she opened up her video camera as discreetly as possible before she shoved it back in

135

her pocket. Whatever they were about to say to her, she wanted it recorded.

By the time she reached the office and ushered Treadwell and Ramirez inside, she'd begun to formulate a plan, resolve settling like lead in her belly.

She heeled the door shut, and then leaned back against it, arms folded.

Ramirez went to peer out the window, gapping the blinds with her fingers, and then settled in a loose stance, one hand propped on her hip.

Treadwell, by contrast, perched on the edge of the leather sofa. Trying to look nonthreatening, Mia decided, like she was a horse liable to spook.

He started to speak, and Mia ran right over him.

"You think I'm fraternizing with a dangerous prisoner? Tell me about this person, then. Who is it?"

The question hit him like a slap. His mouth opened and his expression went comically blank.

Ramirez picked up the slack. "Don't get cute. You know exactly who we're talking about."

Mia stared at her a moment. The other woman was medium height, lean, her fitted dark clothes showing off compact muscles and a fighter's grace. With her dark hair pulled back in a severe ponytail, and her brows tucked low over her eyes, she looked a bit like one of the female henchmen in an action movie. But sharp. And very much real. And staring Mia down.

Mia took a breath. "You're trying to get me to admit to something, right? I think it's only fair you tell me what."

He frowned at her, considering. "Alright."

"What?" Ramirez hissed.

Treadwell ignored her. "You know exactly what – *who* – I'm talking about, right? Otherwise you wouldn't be this defiant. If I walked up to any random civilian and accused them of fraternizing with the enemy, they'd be outraged and frightened. You just look angry. So you're either" – he started listing things off on his fingers – "guilty, trying to throw us off the scent, or he's filled your head with so much bullshit that you actually feel protective of him. Which I understand is his MO."

Mia took a deep breath, and tried to think. There was a way to handle this if she insisted on denial.

And there was a way to handle this if she wanted to help Val.

An outsider might have blamed it on her terminal diagnosis, but that wasn't why she chose Val. No, it went deeper and simpler than that: because she loved him, and she wasn't sure anyone else did at the moment.

She exhaled, steady now. "I wasn't sure I believed it – I guess I didn't want to. Because how, in this day and age, does something like that go on, unnoticed, *allowed* by whatever higher authority is supposed to prevent that sort of thing."

Ramirez's scowl shifted a fraction, became uncertain.

Treadwell's brows jumped.

"What sort of people keep a man locked up for over five-hundred years?"

Treadwell clenched his jaw, muscle jumping in his cheek, and winced, like the movement pained him. "The kind of people who know exactly what a monster he is."

Her chest *ached*. But she kept her voice calm. "You're admitting it, then: that you're keeping him prisoner."

"The Institute is," Ramirez said. "We just follow orders."

"The prisoner you've been talking to–" Treadwell started.

"He has a name. And a title."

"Not anymore he doesn't. Valerian is a violent, dangerous, manipulative liar. Whatever he's been showing you, that's not the real him."

She thought of the golden-haired boy who loved his brothers. Who picked rosemary sprigs for his mother. Who needed his brother's help to hold a bow steady, but who could race a horse bareback across uneven terrain at age six. She thought of his pain, and confusion, and fear at Gallipoli. Of the way he'd cried out for his father, and wished for his mother, the day the sultan took him.

She was so unspeakably angry she didn't trust her voice. Pushed the words out through her teeth. "My father wants me to come to Virginia so bad? Fine. When do we leave?"

14

KNIFE FOR KNIFE

The Ingraham Institute
Virginia

There was a stark difference, Vlad had come to realize in the past few months, between knowing that you were immortal, and *understanding* that you were.

He'd been born a vampire, and he'd been brought up to know exactly what that meant. Had sipped blood first from his mother's wrist, and then from a golden cup – rich wolf blood that filled him with strength and stamina – and then from humans. Some willing, some not. No matter.

He wielded a sword with the strength of ten mortals. Could survive grievous wounds. *Had* survived them, the worst of which was the last, the one dealt him by his brother.

He'd known that vampires could come back from almost anything. If the heart was intact, still beating, however faintly, a vampire could go to sleep in a close, dark place and take all the time they needed to heal. When they were whole, a wolf could wake them. Sometimes hours passed, sometimes days. Sometimes years. Sometimes centuries. Father had done that. And clearly, so had Romulus.

So he knew what immortality meant.

But not with this kind of firsthand certainty until he was sitting upright on a slab of metal, blinking against bright lights, assaulted by a tangle of unfamiliar smells and a rapid back-and-forth in a language he didn't fully understand.

English, some part of his still-sluggish brain had supplied. The language of Britain.

Learning the language, as it turned out, had been the least difficult adjustment in this new century.

He'd been surrounded by a terrible abundance. There had been plenty of blood, human and wolf, offered to him in tall cups, and plenty of rich, belly-filling food. Plenty of water, and wine, and fruit juices, and something the humans called Gatorade.

Plenty of clothes, though they were thin, and tight, contouring to the shape of his body in a way that would have scandalized the people of his own time.

Plenty of incomprehensible devices that mortals used to communicate, and tabulate data, and treat one another medically. A nervous, sputtering young man in a long white coat and spectacles had attempted to show Vlad how to use a little glowing rectangle that he called an iPhone, squeaking in surprise when Vlad plucked it from his hand. He could use it, but he didn't like it.

He didn't like anything about this time.

Except having the chance to spar.

"You're slow," he said, stepping back and lowering his sword a fraction when it became apparent that the Baron Strange would collapse if Vlad carried through with his next strike. "Out of practice, or out of shape?"

"Both," le Strange panted, letting his sword arm drop and reaching with the other to wipe the sweat from his forehead. He'd tied his long hair back – scratch that, his wife had doubtless braided it for him – but the fight had loosened it, and long strands clung to his sweaty neck. He plucked at them with a grimace. His white sleeveless shirt was translucent, clinging to him. He looked ready to fall over, his arms shaking.

Pathetic, Vlad thought.

Fulk le Strange was a wolf with a reputation, one that Vlad had heard murmurings of as a boy. When Fenrir would sit them down by the fire and tell tall tales of other immortals. Heartless, unflinching, vicious – le Strange was a legend among wolf kind. As old as he was, as strong as he was, he should have been backing Vlad across the packed sawdust of the training ring, giving as good as he got.

When the wolf leant forward and braced his free hand on one knee, gulping air, Vlad turned away, sneering, disgust sour on the back of his tongue. He went to the wall and the table there, where cloths, whetstones, his scabbard, and an assortment of other blades waited.

139

"I expected better from you," Vlad said over his shoulder, reaching for his whetstone. "Either the stories I heard of you as a boy were never true, or you've gone soft."

His fingers had just closed over the stone when something else caught his eye, the gleam of unremarkable steel. He dropped the stone, laid his sword out on a towel, and instead picked up the knife he'd knocked out of the Russian vampire's hands weeks ago.

It was one of a matched pair, both of them laid out beside one another. Black handles; sharp, straight, functional blades perfect for stabbing. Combat knives, Fulk had explained to him before. They dated back to the nineteen-forties, apparently. Soviet made – whatever that meant.

"Well," le Strange said behind him, getting some of his breath back. He sounded wry. "When one loses a bloodthirsty master, one tends to become less bloodthirsty by default."

"It's your wife that's the problem," Vlad said, mostly to himself. He didn't really care, fixated on the knife in his hands as he turned around and leaned back to brace his hip against the table. "She's your softness." He lifted his gaze in time to see that le Strange had bared his teeth, tendons standing out in his neck as he strained with sudden, barely-checked aggression. He smoothed his face over when Vlad's eyes touched him, though. "The Russian," Vlad said, showing him the knife. "What do you know about him?"

Fulk shook his head. He went to lay his own sword down, and picked up a bottle of water. When he'd drained half of it in one gulp, he said, breathless, "I know what you know. I read the files, same as you. Former Captain of the Soviet secret police put in charge of a top-secret military weapon. Turned by Rasputin's blood." He shrugged and turned the cap of the water bottle over in his hand a few times. "I know he was willing to die on your sword to save his wolf."

At this he looked up, a guarded glance through his lashes, weighing.

Vlad snorted, dismissive. "That wasn't *his* wolf. He wasn't bound."

Le Strange smiled, small and unhappy. "Even worse, then. The wolf is his softness."

140

Vlad extended a single finger and rested the knife on it. Perfectly balanced. "He comes from an age of gunpowder, and not of blades?"

Le Strange sighed. "Yes."

"I could tell he was inexperienced. Still. He fought well, considering."

"Yes, and I'm sure he'd hold such a compliment dear. Coming from you, especially."

Vlad flicked his fingers toward the wolf. Let him snark and snap if he wanted to. "I'm thinking of his potential as a soldier. I can fight this war alone, but the odds would be better if I didn't have to."

A soft sound as the wolf set the bottle down. He lifted his head, gaze direct now. "If you need generals, maybe you should start by freeing your brother and asking him." His look was openly challenging.

Vlad shrugged and pushed off from the table, curling his hand around the hilt of the knife. "Maybe I will."

Le Strange made a soft, shocked sound as Vlad turned his back on him.

"Wipe my sword down and put it away, wolf."

"I'm not your Familiar," he shot back.

"No," Vlad agreed as he slipped through the door. "Not yet."

~*~

"Your grace!" a familiar, obnoxious voice called out as Vlad crossed the main floor of the basement, headed for the staircase. Le Strange had informed him that there was no such thing as royalty here in America, but that hadn't stopped Dr. Talbot from calling him by his honorific.

He paused and turned a flat look on the man. "What?"

Dr. Talbot quailed a little, but that was normal. "Your grace," he repeated, visibly drawing himself up to his full, unimpressive height. "I've had word from the mage. He's coming to—"

"What mage?"

141

"The – the one I've told you about. The father of the girl we had here, for a time." He frowned, no doubt remembering the failure to retain the little redheaded witch. "The Necromancer, they call him."

"They?"

"Other immortals. Some of them."

"Hmm," Vlad hummed, but felt a small inward twinge of unease. He'd heard of the Necromancer, same as he had the Baron Strange. At one time, they'd been the left and right hands of the same vampire.

Their hatred for one another was legendary.

"Why would he come here?" Vlad asked.

"He's been traveling. But when I told him about losing the girl…" He twisted his hands together a moment, distraught. He took a breath and regathered his composure. "Anyway, it's just as well. Your punishment" – his gaze flicked up, carefully constructed behind the lenses of his spectacles – "seems to have damaged the tracking spell the Necromancer placed on your brother. Even if he were to dream-walk again, we'd no longer be able to tell where he goes, and who he visits. While he's here, he can cast it again. Perhaps next time," he said, delicately, "it would be prudent to not use *quite* so much electricity."

"Yes," Vlad agreed. "When will he arrive? This Necromancer?"

"In a few days' time."

Vlad nodded. "Fine." He turned and resumed course for the stairs. A few days would give him enough time to figure out what to do with a man purportedly able to raise the dead.

~*~

Pain can only be tolerated for a finite spell. Eventually, the body and the mind part ways; the brain's way of sparing the physical form the sensation. Mortal or immortal, the only difference was a matter of duration. Just because vampires could survive terrible injury, mortals tended to think they didn't feel pain the same way.

But they did.

Being a vampire, Vlad knew this. And he'd attached the cuffs, and collar, and electrical leads anyway.

It could have been hours, or days. For a stretch, Val's world was pain, and only pain. The incandescent, blinding pain of electrocution.

At some point, it stopped, because all things stopped eventually.

When he woke next, he was a charred, trembling wreck in the corner of his cell, too weak to even push the hair from his eyes or check the nature of the wound where Vlad's sword had bit through muscle and bone.

Instead, he tilted his head back against the stone wall, shut his eyes, and put every ounce of pathetic strength into dream-walking. He went to see Mia, so that he could explain. It might be the last chance he had to see her, and he had to make her see that he was real, that he could be honest, no matter what anyone thought. And, selfishly, he wanted someone to know the real story.

And he wanted to see her face again.

But he wasn't strong enough. He showed her his abduction, that horrible moment in Gallipoli when his life went sideways, and then the blackness swallowed him. Exhaustion, pure and simple.

The next time he woke it was to the sound of a disapproving voice saying, "Sir, I'm sorry, but you don't have clearance to—" The speaker cut off with an *oomph*. Val, even behind crusty, closed eyelids, swimming in drowsiness, recognized the sound of someone's back hitting the wall.

And then: "Let me through." Vlad. Low and commanding.

Vlad. *No, no, no, no.* Val curled in on himself; a whimper got caught in the back of his throat, too tired to even voice it properly. He was so tired, and he hurt so much, and *no, no, no, no.*

Flight instincts kicked in as he heard the key turn in the lock. Of course the guards were letting Vlad through; he didn't have the power to compel; there were no mind tricks. It was simply his presence. His implacable stare, the reputation that still, alarmingly, dogged his heels in the twenty-first century.

Get up, get up, he thought, desperate, but his body wouldn't cooperate. He managed to crack his eyes open a slit, just in time to get a blurry glimpse of Vlad's boots as he came to stand over him. He opened his mouth to croak out some pitiful insult, but his throat was too dry, his tongue stuck to the roof of his mouth.

Vlad's clothes rustled softly as he crouched down. And then…

Then.

A touch on his head. The gentle weight and warmth of a palm; he could feel it even through his tangled hair. And he squeezed his eyes shut, ashamed, because even after all that had happened, he could scent his brother, recognize his touch, and his muscles unclenched. Family. Safety. But it had never been safe, and Vlad didn't want them to be family.

Vlad's hand withdrew, and here it came: more pain. Val braced himself as much as he could, muscles feebly tightening in anticipation.

But there was no pain. Only Vlad's hands, turning him over onto his back, and then his strong arms sliding under Val's knees and behind his shoulders, and he was being lifted. His soreness spiked when he was moved, and he hissed, awash with pain – but it wasn't intentional, was it? It was…it was…

Tears pushed at his eyelids, and he kept them shut tight as Vlad walked out of the cell, carrying him, Val's head tucked into his chest. He smelled like modern human laundry, and sweat, and steel…and like his brother. Like Wallachia. Like home.

"Sir," the guard tried again.

Vlad growled, deep and threatening. Val felt it rumble through his cheek.

There were no more protests from the guard.

Val drifted, teeth gritted against the pain of being moved, but lulled by the rhythm of his brother's familiar gait. Vlad seemed to walk forever. Through the labs that, only a few weeks ago, Val had broken through. They rode in the elevator. Went up more stairs.

He fell asleep at some point, or maybe passed out. When he managed to pry his eyes open again he heard the rush of water, the sound contained within a small space, and his eyes were filled with…with…

"Sunlight," he breathed, voice the barest croak of sound.

"Hmm," Vlad murmured. He set him down, gently, gently, on a hard surface, sitting upright, his back braced against something smooth and cool.

He blinked and let his head roll to the side, scanning the room. It was a bathroom, all white tile and black marble. He was sitting on the counter, leaning against the mirror. To his right was a massive claw-foot tub filling with steamy water. And above it, a leaded-glass window. Sunlight spilled in, a pure white shaft of it, gleaming across the clean, expensive fixtures.

He'd seen the sun in all its iterations while he dream-walked. But seeing it in person, now, falling through the diamond-shaped panes of a window, glimmering on the surface of the water, was like a religious experience.

He lifted one shaking hand and held it up before him, fingers spread so the sunlight slipped between them, limned them in silver.

"Why?" he asked, and looked to his brother. His voice shook, his body shook.

Vlad's cruel features were as implacable as always. But his eyes hinted at warmth and softness. "When was the last time they bathed you?"

He wet his lips. "I...I don't know."

"Can you stand?"

"No."

Vlad nodded and went to turn the taps off. The rushing of water left behind a bristling silence, filled only with the occasional plunk of a stray droplet, and Val's unsteady, open-mouthed breathing.

Vlad returned. "Here," he said, and reached for the tattered hem of Val's shirt. He undressed him efficiently, but carefully, his sword-callused hands gentle. And when Val was naked, lifted him into his arms again and lowered him slowly into the full bath.

The water was startlingly hot, and Val clutched at his brother's arms, hissing when it touched his skin. He was sore all over, bruised and tender, and at first it hurt badly.

"Wait," he breathed when Vlad started to lift him back out. "Just..." And it began to ease. Began to soothe him. Vlad settled him all the way in, so his head rested on the edge of the tub, his body submerged beneath the surface.

The water clouded with dirt and grease almost immediately. His long, knotted hair floated, golden kelp waving gently as he fidgeted and the water lapped around his knees.

Val shut his eyes, tilted his head back, and tried to breathe slowly through his mouth. The heat, and the wet, and the tender way his brother had carried him up here…it was too much. He…

His chest hitched, and his throat ached, and he didn't understand any of this.

"Why are you doing this?" he whispered. "Vlad, if you're just going to hurt me…" Then he couldn't stand this small kindness first. Going back to pain and filth after this – it would kill him.

He was aware of Vlad settling down on his knees beside the tub. Of him leaning in, pressing his face into the side of Val's head, breathing deep through his nose. "It's gone," he said.

"What? What's gone?"

Vlad's hand settled over his, where it gripped the edge of the tub. "Val, do you remember meeting the mage they call the Necromancer?"

He struggled to think, eyes opening again, searching Vlad's face for cues. His brother looked so *soft*. As soft as he ever could, the mean bastard. Without the mustache he'd adopted as an adult, he looked more like the narrow-faced, pale-skinned brother Val had shared a bedchamber with for the first five years of his life. It grounded him.

"It was before they found you," he said, remembering. "They had me – had me at the New York facility then. He came to see me. Red hair. Cocky smile. He smelled *old*."

"He *is* old," Vlad agreed. "And very powerful. I smelled his magic on you the first time I came to visit you in the dungeon."

"You smelled his…" Val felt his mouth drop open, and his eyes sprang wide. "*What?*"

Vlad nodded, mouth a thin, grim line. "He cast some sort of spell over you. I don't know how. But he was spying on your dreams. How else do you think these idiot mortals found your friends? The mage was walking behind you, your constant shadow."

Spied on. And he hadn't known.

He *hadn't known.*

Nauseated suddenly, he pitched forward. Tried to. His hand slipped on the wet porcelain and the water rushed up to meet his face.

Vlad caught him with one steadying hand on his shoulder. "You didn't know."

"I didn't…I didn't…how…" He hyperventilated.

"It's gone now," Vlad said. "I burned it out of you."

Val lifted his head, hair dripping water, and met his brother's gaze. "You burned it…" And then he understood, breath catching. "You *burned it out of me.*"

"I did. And he won't get the chance to cast it again."

Emotion crashed over Val like a wave. He drew his knees up and pressed his face to them. Closed his eyes tight, but the tears came anyway, hot and relentless, dripping down his face and into the bathwater. He opened his mouth to take a breath, and a sob spilled out, painful and choked.

Vlad didn't speak, but his arm was strong and grounding around Val's shoulders. He held him, and Val cried and cried, until he cried himself to sleep.

~*~

He came to warm and dry, curled up on his side amid downy sheets, head resting on a pillow that smelled of lavender and his brother's skin. He knew Vlad was there beside him, and opened his eyes to find him sitting propped up against the headboard, legs stretched out in front of him, reading a book with a thoughtful frown. His expression reminded Val of their boyhood, of long tutoring sessions bent over tomes written in Greek and Latin and Slavic, trying to make sense of the tangled knots of history, religion, and art.

"Did you dry my hair?" Val asked, feeling it soft and silky and fresh-smelling against his neck.

Vlad closed the book on one finger and looked over with the mildest interest. It was probably a look that sent the humans running, but it was a rather sweet expression, Val knew from experience. "It was wet. The humans have this device–" He made a face, and a gesture with his hand that mimicked a gun.

Val felt a smile tug at his mouth. "A hair dryer?"

Vlad frowned, shrugged, and glanced away. "It's useful."

"So I've heard." He chuckled, just a weak little gust that tweaked at sore muscles in his chest. He felt a pull at the edges of his healing wound, and winced. "It's funny," he said, breathless now as the pain tugged at him, "all these humans think I'm the liar, and you're the straightforward one. They've got it all wrong."

"I'm not a liar," Vlad countered, turning back to him. "I'm only patient."

"That's one word for it. And you never met a grudge you couldn't hold forever. Atlas carried the world on his shoulders, but you carry all the world's grudges, brother."

"I'm patient," Vlad repeated. "I waited five-hundred years to pay you back for this." He reached to pull the collar of his shirt aside and reveal the faint white scar across his shoulder, a near mirror-image of the wound he'd given Val.

"That's not patient, that's vengeful!" Val countered with a disbelieving laugh.

"Revenge requires patience," Vlad said seriously, and Val lost it.

He pressed his face into the pillow, wincing as each laugh shook his battered body, but unable to stop. There were tears in his eyes when he finally managed to come to a gasping, snorting halt, still chuckling. "God above. You are an unchanging asshole."

"I count it among my strengths."

"Of course you do. What is it you used to say?"

"An eye for an eye," Vlad stared, and Val chorused along on the rest: "A scar for a scar, a knife for a knife."

The last of his laughter melted away, leaving him achy and hollow. "I put you in the ground to keep them from killing you outright."

"I know you did."

Val's next breath left his lungs on a shiver. "They'll never let me go, will they?" He hated how small and pathetic his voice sounded, but there was nothing to be done for it. At the moment, he felt small and pathetic, too.

Vlad's dark brows slanted low, shifting from their usual sternness to outright hostility. "Do you trust me?"

"I have always *wanted* to trust you, brother."

"Trust me now. And be patient."

"No one is as patient as you."

"No. But try." Vlad leaned over to put the book on the nightstand, and then slid down until he lay on his back, head on the neighboring pillow. When he reached for Val's hand, Val gave it up to him with hesitation.

Vlad's mouth twitched; it could have been a rueful smile. "Here," he said, and pulled Val's hand up so that the palm was pressed to his forehead. "Take me walking with you. Into the past. I think…" A note of uncertainty stained his voice, foreign and unsettling. "I think we misunderstand each other."

Dread and excitement flickered under Val's skin; chased like lightning through his veins. "I don't think I'm strong enough for that now. I–"

Vlad's other hand was suddenly shoved under his nose, tipped back, the wrist exposed. Blue veins twined together like vines under his pale skin, throbbing with a strong pulse.

Val clenched his jaw and felt his fangs descend; saliva pooled on his tongue.

"Drink," Vlad said, like a command. "And then show me."

"You still think you're the boss of everyone, don't you?" Val huffed.

"That's because I am."

"Insufferable." Val reached to curve his slimmer, more elegant hand behind his brother's and brought the tempting wrist to his lips. He looked up, one last time, searching Vlad's face for a lie or a trap. But Vlad stared steadily back, the same quietly encouraging face he'd used when they were boys in the training yard back home.

Home. Oh, he wanted to go *home*.

149

He bit, slow but sure, and when his fangs pierced flesh, velvet blood welled up to fill his mouth.

The guards he'd drained a few weeks before had hit his starved system like a narcotic. But this was on another plane entirely. This was home, and brother, and family, and strength, such impossible strength.

He only took a little, until his skin was buzzing and his lips were throbbing and he thought he could have scaled the façade of the manner house with nothing but finger- and toenails for support. Then he eased back, licked the wound until it started to seal.

Vlad's forehead felt warm and grounding beneath his other hand. "How far back do you want to go?" he asked.

"How far did you get with your mortal?"

Val sighed. "You know about her?"

"Everyone here does. The spell, remember?"

"Damn it."

"Talbot sent minions to fetch her."

"He–" Val made a flailing move to leap out of bed.

Vlad grabbed him around the waist and pinned him down, pressing Val's hand tight to his forehead. "*Later.* Right now you need to show me."

Val forced himself to take a breath. Vlad was right. If they were going to work together…

A hysterical laugh bubbled to life in his chest.

"What?" Vlad demanded.

"Nothing, nothing. Alright." He resettled. They were closer now, close enough to see what Val had always known: that though they looked sometimes brown, or sometimes gray, Vlad's eyes were in fact the color of hammered gold. Like a wolf. He would have made a spectacular wolf; vampirism was a genetic waste.

"Alright," Val said again. "To Adrianople, then."

Vlad bared his teeth in a silent snarl, but Val closed his eyes. Thought about going down, down…and then up, and then *back*.

Back to the place where the real hell had started.

15

HONORED GUESTS

Adrianople, called Edirne by the Ottomans
Capital of the Ottoman Empire
1441

Their captors knew they were vampires. That was the panic-inducing thought that continued to cycle through Vlad's brain.

He'd come to the first night in a tent, chained to a stake, and in the light of a brazier had seen that his cuffs were of a heavy, solid silver, and that Val still lay unconscious beside him. Who bound a ten-year-old boy with silver? Someone who knew he was a vampire.

The men who had entered the tent wore the garb of Ottoman foot soldiers. Some looked Turkish, others seemed to be Mongols. One was blond, his nose aquiline, his eyes blue: a Western convert. They had brought him food, but they had not spoken to him. Vlad had roused his brother, though Val whimpered and tried to curl in on himself; he'd been struck in the ribs first, Vlad remembered, and the silver was slowing his healing.

The Ottomans talked in low voices, in Turkish, and Vlad had understood only the occasional word. All that time he'd spent studying Greek, but they weren't headed for Byzantium now, were they?

The trip took days, and when they were on the horses, rough sacks were put over their heads so they couldn't see the paths they took, could only sway in the saddle as their party climbed steep slopes and splashed across mountain streams.

The brothers were forced to share a horse. Vlad sat in front, Val behind him, Val's arms around his waist and cuffed together in front of Vlad's stomach. Vlad was cuffed too, and unable to hold the reins. Their cuffs were chained together. Ropes had been run loosely beneath the horse's belly, connecting their feet, ensuring that Vlad couldn't tip them off the side and onto the trail and make a break for it. Nor, should the rope break, could he run with his brother hugging him like this.

It was a thorough, well thought out containment. All he could so was sit, breath stiflingly hot inside the hood, and try to map their route in his head, trying to remember turns, counting strides, for all the good it would do. He had to try *something*. Make some sort of plan. When they stopped to rest, he tried to wriggle his hands loose from the cuffs. At mealtimes, he eyed their captors, searching their belts for knives, wondering if he could just get close enough…

But they were careful, and they gave him no openings.

Neither he nor Val had the power to compel, not that Val was any use, alternating between crying and sleeping.

"You have to stop," Vlad hissed at him one night. "Eat your food. *Shut up.*"

Val looked up at him with huge, betrayed blue eyes.

"We're escaping," Vlad whispered. "But you have to stop being such a baby and help me."

Val's lip quivered, and his eyes filled with fresh tears, but he nodded and wiped his face on his filthy sleeve. When he pushed his hair back, he revealed ugly purple bruises at his hairline, one on his forehead, one just behind his ear.

Vlad saw red.

Vampire or not, his brother was just a tiny thing, with slender wrists and a skinny neck, and skin that bruised like overripe fruit. He could be subdued with a word. With a *look*. And someone had struck him, again and again.

Vlad would figure out which one of these men had done that, and make him pay.

But first he had to have a plan. And he couldn't form a plan if Val kept *crying*. His brother's distress triggered something ugly and primal, a side of him that was all fangs and claws, violence and knee-jerk reactions. A plan required rational thought.

Val made a valiant effort to stop crying, but try as he might, Vlad couldn't figure out a way to escape.

One night, the blond one brought their dinner, and Vlad spoke to him in Slavic: "Where are you taking us?"

The man's gaze flicked up; he'd understood. In the same language, he answered, "You'll find out soon enough."

Vlad bit back a curse and forced his expression to smooth. He couldn't snarl, or show his fangs, not now. That wouldn't help the plan. "What happened to our father?"

The man shrugged and retreated to the other side of the tent, where his comrades were watching the boys with a mixture of curiosity and amusement.

Vlad did growl then, just a little, before he clamped it down tight. He wished Mircea were here; he was the diplomatic one.

Days passed, until his body was ungodly sore from being strapped to a saddle, and he spent so much time under a hood that the sun became too bright. They rode, and they ate their meager rations – when Val tried to starve himself, Vlad reminded him that they couldn't escape if they were too weak to stand – and finally, they arrived somewhere loud and bustling that stank of humanity.

The horses' hooves clattered over cobblestones, and they climbed one last hill. Shouts hailed their arrival: staccato, rote greetings from guards, the same as when he reentered the palace grounds after a day spent in Tîrgovişte.

Vlad realized where they must be, and his heart sank.

The ropes on his ankles loosened, and he was dragged off the horse. Val let out a yelp as he was dragged along too, and then fell to their knees on a bed of sharp gravel stones, Val's arms tightening around Vlad's waist.

Vlad's hood was ripped off, and dappled sunlight assaulted his eyes.

They were in a tree-lined courtyard. Vlad saw benches, and reflecting pools edged with spills of bright flowers. A group of stable boys moved forward to take the horses. A set of doors shaped like a keyhole waited at the top of a shallow flight of stairs, and in front of them stood a man in elaborate robes, hair covered by a snow-white turban. He spoke to the captors in Turkish, quick and dismissive. The blond one came to drag them up to their feet, but he left the cuffs attached – a wise move on his part, an infuriating one from Vlad's perspective.

153

Then the man turned his gaze to Vlad and said, in Slavic, "Welcome to Edirne, your graces."

They'd been brought to the Ottoman capital, then.

In the heart of enemy territory.

~*~

In 1437, Vlad Dracul sighed a treaty with the Ottoman Sultan, Murat, that made Wallachia a vassal state of the empire. In exchange for their promise of peace, the Wallachians were assured trade and diplomatic relations, and some semblance of autonomy. In addition to cooperation, Dracul would provide a yearly monetary tribute, as well as a selection of able-bodied boys destined for the sultan's Janissary Corps.

Vlad knew this, had been briefed on it as both a student and a prince. And he also knew that his father – turning John Hunyadi away despite his own personal sympathies – had upheld the treaty, and never broken it.

And yet here they were.

The sultan received them in an audience chamber with soaring, painted ceilings, and brightly-colored tiles on the floors, tapestries on the walls. Multiple fountains filled the vast space with the musical splash of water. Massive, glazed urns boasted flowers and ferns. The plants nearly disguised the armored janissaries that lined the walls, spears propped against their shoulders.

Mama would love this, Vlad thought, faintly. Though she wouldn't love the circumstances. Then he pushed all such soft thoughts aside. He was a hostage – and he didn't plan on being one for long.

He and Val had been separated, their hands re-cuffed in front of them. The walked side-by-side. Val stared at his dusty boots, still sniffling occasionally; he trembled like a new foal and reeked of fear.

For his part, Vlad held his head high, his shoulders thrown as far back as the cuffs would allow, and faced the puppet master behind their abduction as they were marched forward to a low dais where a gathering of men awaited them.

154

They were advisors and scribes; a messenger boy, bare-chested under an embroidered vest. All wore jewel tones, rich fabrics, and elaborate turbans, each unique, displaying the wearer's individual aesthetic.

Sultan Murat II was seated. That was the only thing that distinguished him from his viziers. A compact, tidy man, he was even handsome, though unremarkably so; he wore the usual neatly trimmed beard and white muslin turban. His dress was that of royalty: an indigo kaftan with gold embroidery and buttons, gold silk şalvar, a kusak of bright teal around his waist.

One of the soldiers stopped Vlad with a hand on his shoulder, the other on Val's. Then he pushed them down to their knees on the tiles, so they knelt before the sultan and his retinue.

Vlad growled – he couldn't help it, and these men already knew what he was. Why hide it? Why not show them that he was well aware he was a monster, and ready to make use of that fact?

A flat palm struck him *hard*, right in the ear. For a moment, his vision whited out and the pain of the strike was a burst of light, and then a sharp sting, and then a faded red roar that echoed through his entire head.

Vlad gritted his teeth and breathed through it. He wouldn't give any of them the satisfaction of crying out.

Val did, though, a soft little exclamation. "Vlad!"

Shut up, Vlad thought, wildly, even as his own head rang. *Shut up, shut up, or they'll hit you, too!*

His vision cleared, spots receding off to the edges, and he saw that the man who'd first welcomed them stood before him now, frowning. A vizier, or a mullah. Something.

"Do not speak to the sultan," the man said in Slavic, voice vibrating with contained fury. "And don't you dare growl, you immortal, amoral dog. You are no creature of God. Do not sully our sultan with your profanity. You should be grateful to even be in his presence. You should kiss the floor and–"

"Ali," a voice called out, low and commanding.

The man's teeth clicked together with an audible snap. He stepped back, and revealed that it was the sultan who'd spoken, his unreadable gaze pinned on Vlad.

155

"I am perfectly capable of speaking for myself," Murat said in flawless Romanian. Then, to Vlad: "I welcome you to Edirne, Vlad Dracula." He looked at Val. "Radu Dracula. The sons of the prince of Wallachia." Back to Vlad: "Trust that you are here in a gesture of goodwill. Your father has been, up to now, quite agreeable in our negotiations. Your presence here ensures that such agreeable conduct will continue. You will be fed, and cared for, and educated, as befits any prince. In exchange for such luxuries, I expect your cooperation and good behavior." He tilted his head to the side. "Do we understand one another?"

Hostages, Vlad thought. They were political hostages, here to ensure that Father never betrayed his Ottoman masters.

Vlad took a deep breath and said, "Understanding doesn't automatically lead to cooperation."

He was struck again, across the back of his head this time. He tasted blood.

Val let out a frightened, strangled sound.

Shut up!

"That's enough," the sultan said. "He can't agree to anything if his mind's addled."

Vlad braced a hand on the floor. The tile beneath was blue and white, patterned like flowers. Or stars. Blood dripped from his lip in regular splats, the bright crimson a contrast.

"Prince Vlad," the sultan said from above him. "You can resist this if you want to, but it will be easier for you if you don't. Easier for both of you."

Head still ringing, it took a moment for the sultan's words to sink in, but when they did...

A chill skittered down Vlad's back. That was how they would manipulate him, then: by threatening his little brother.

He lifted his head, and found the sultan staring at him.

"Do we understand one another?" Murat asked again, voice smooth and cool.

Vlad swallowed a mouthful of his own blood. "Yes, Your Majesty."

~*~

They were taken to a bathing chamber, one with a sunken center full of steaming water, tiled in cool blue. Very Roman, Vlad thought, before his clothes were stripped off and he was shoved unceremoniously in. Val tumbled in after him, yelping. Vlad steadied him with a hand on his small shoulder and pulled them out deep into the water, until their heads were the only things breaking the surface.

Through the haze of steam, Val looked at him with tear-filled eyes. "Vlad," he whispered. "I want to go home."

"I know, but we can't." *Not yet*, he added silently. Because they were only boys, and it would take time to formulate an escape plan. But as slaves joined them, with sweet-smelling oils and floral soaps in their hands, Vlad made a vow that someday, hopefully soon, he would get his brother out of this beautiful prison, and take him home.

After, when they were scrubbed pink and clean, dressed in soft silk kaftans and şalvar, they were escorted to a chamber with barred windows that looked down on an elaborate garden below. Two beds were made up, in the Turkish style, a series of doubled-over and stacked carpets cushioned with silk and satin, across from a washstand with basin and ewer, a wardrobe full of clothes. Ottoman clothes.

Their guard, a stiff-backed, armored contrast to the lavishness of the palace, said, "You will be sent for in the morning," in Slavic, and then retreated. He closed the door behind him, and a key grated in the lock. When his footsteps had receded down the hall, Vlad said, "Fuck," with great feeling.

Val, who'd been valiantly fighting his tears for hours, dissolved into silent, body-wracking sobs, his hands covering his face.

"Oh, Valerian," Vlad sighed, and crossed the room to pull his brother into his arms. Val buried his face immediately into Vlad's chest, his little arms going around his waist. His breath rushed hot and quick through the buttonholes of Vlad's kaftan, fanning across his chest.

Vlad held him close and smoothed a hand through his soft golden hair, still damp from the bath, smelling of roses and lavender. "Listen to me," he urged. "I know this is terrible, and

157

frightening. But I'm going to get us free. I promise you that. You just have to trust me and not draw any attention to yourself."

Val mumbled something.

"What?"

"What happened to Father?"

Vlad took a deep breath, and tried not to let it shake on the exhale. "I don't know," he said, which was mostly the truth. He feared Father had been tortured for information – a prospect made more likely by the fact that someone had told Murat that they were vampires. Did they know Father was? Had they pinned him down, as his blood gushed across the stones, and cut out his heart? "I'm sure he's fine," he told Val.

"Will he come for us?" he whimpered into Vlad's collarbone. "He will, won't he?"

"Maybe."

Vlad looked up, over his brother's head, and out the grilled window, into the garden below, melting into rich sunset golds and indigos as the shadows grew long. The high, smooth white walls gleamed faintly, sheer and shiny, as if polished. Not a toe-hold in sight.

He took a deep breath and forced his panic down deep in his gut. No doubt it would eventually fester, might boil and rise to choke him, a black sickness of worry and dread. But for now, it settled, a cold lump that he could still breathe around.

"I'm sure Father will negotiate our release. This is how this sort of thing works. We'll be kept here a bit, and when Father pays, the sultan will send us back."

But will he? a tiny voice asked in the back of his mind.

~*~

Dawn saw Vlad at the window, his elbows braced on the wide stone sill, skinny arms draped through the elaborate silver bars. Watching the sun rise in vibrant pinks and oranges above the tumbling deciduous forests around the Ottoman capital. Beyond the onion domes and spires of mosques, beyond the unclimbable palace walls, the land reminded him of home. The sharp tang of pine needles and the breathless quality of mountain air.

But inside, everything he could touch was foreign.

It was Sultan Murat, he recalled, who'd changed the city's name – formally, among the Turks – to Edirne. Before, the Latin name by which he knew it, it had been called Adrianople, named for the Roman emperor Hadrian, that visionary engineer who'd designed the wall by the same name.

The heir was here, Vlad thought, being educated. And the hostages of the Ottoman court. Of which they were now two.

A sound from the pallet behind him drew his attention and he put his back to the sunrise to see the faint light play across his sleeping brother's face.

If it had been up to Vlad, he would have sat on the floor, back to the wall all night, and kept watch. But Val had been exhausted, and tearful, and hadn't been able to bear sleeping alone. So they'd settled down on a single pallet together; Vlad had woken a few minutes ago with Val's head shoved up under his chin, his little hands clutching tight to his kaftan. Exhaustion was the only thing that had kept the boy from waking when Vlad extricated himself and slipped away.

Vlad studied him now, heartsick. Tears had dried on Val's cheeks, their tracks tight and shiny in the early light. The top few buttons of his kaftan had come loose during the night, and the garment gapped now, revealing a delicate wedge of throat, pulse beating in its hollow. His fingers clutched tight at a pillow, knuckles white.

The problem was, Vlad had heard stories. The kinds of stories the wolves had whispered to one another, followed sometimes by shudders or uncomfortable laughter. The kinds of stories children weren't supposed to overhear. He'd heard what sometimes happened to beautiful little boys who were abducted and taken as hostages.

Vlad, with his almost gaunt face, and his gangly limbs, and his dark eyes with even darker smudges beneath, was not the sort of boy that anyone had ever called beautiful.

But Val was.

Women were always wanting to pinch his cheek, and men awkwardly mistook him for a girl more oft than not. And then there had been the looks that made Vlad's blood boil – the careful, slanted, breath-held looks of people, boys their age and grown men alike, who set eyes on Val and *wanted* him. Sometimes it was a nameless longing, but others it dripped with intent.

Because Valerian was beautiful. And so Vlad's stomach ached now, because terrible, terrible things happened to beautiful boys in war.

As if sensing that he was being watched, Val shifted and opened his eyes a crack. He made a low, inquiring sound that was all vampire, and not at all human.

Vlad answered, a soft rumble in his throat like a lion cub, then crossed to the pallet and sank down to his knees. "We can't make noises like that. They'll know we're not mortal."

Val blinked a few times, clearing his vision, and then sat up, frowning and rubbing his eyes. "I thought they already knew? The cuffs were silver." His sleeve slipped down to reveal the still-pink mark of one of them.

Vlad suppressed a growl. "Well. The sultan knows, at least. And maybe some of the others. But we don't know *how many* know. It's safer to pretend we're mortal." Because if some unsuspecting fool tried to kill them, they probably wouldn't succeed that way.

"Al-alright," Val murmured, and swallowed, Adam's apple bobbing hard. "I'm...Vlad, I'm really scared." His breath hitched, and his lip trembled, and his eyes filled with fresh tears.

He couldn't keep doing this, Vlad thought. Emotion was weakness. Tears inspired cruelty.

And Vlad wanted to bite throats and claw open stomachs when his baby brother was upset like this. He couldn't *think*.

So his voice came out harsh when he said, "You have to stop that."

Val's mouth fell open, expression slack with surprise. The tears swelled, and they were tears of hurt now, caused by his own brother.

Vlad hated that. Hated himself for causing it. And the anger fell out of his mouth as an order. And an insult. "Don't be a baby, Val. What good do you think crying's going to do? Do you *want* to draw attention to yourself?"

"N-n-no—"

"No more crying, Val, I mean that. It's time to grow up. Can you do that?"

His watery blue eyes fell to the floor, the plump cushions and rugs under their knees. He said, very softly, "Yes, brother."

Vlad heard the sound of footsteps out in the hall, distant but coming closer. He moved around Val, put himself between his brother and the door. By the time a key turned in the lock, and the portal swung inward, he was on his feet, hands balled into fists at his sides, a growl barely checked behind his teeth.

But it was only a slave, bearing a breakfast tray. He looked up, startled by the aggression in Vlad's stance, and hastened to set the tray between two colorful rugs that Vlad realized were mats for sitting and eating.

A janissary lingered at the door, hand on the knob, sword at his hip and flat gaze trained on Vlad. "Eat," he suggested. "Before they come to drag you in front of the mullahs."

The slave scurried out, and then the door was pulled shut and relocked.

~*~

When they were alone, Vlad could admit that his stomach was gnawing on itself he was so hungry. The tray, when he approached it, smelled of strange humans, but not of anything harmful. And better: it smelled of meat...and of blood.

Still, he approached it slowly, balanced on his toes, and pulled the lids off the dishes in a quick flurry, jerking back to avoid any kind of a trap.

All that looked up at him was breakfast.

Two platters heaped with soft warm flatbread, and roasted lamb, and cups of water, and tea, and heated sheep's blood. He wanted to refuse it; to cast the whole tray against the wall and watch the cups break, and the blood spray bright across the floor. But he needed his strength, and so did Val.

"Come eat, brother," he ordered, and settled down cross-legged on one of the rugs.

Val hurried to sit beside him, pressed tight to his side, shaking, breathing shallow.

161

Vlad pressed a cup of blood into his hand. "Drink." And he did.

By the time their bellies were full, another slave had brought a ewer of hot water, and the same janissary as before told them to wash their hands and faces in the little bowls provided for the purpose. Vlad helped Val wash the last sticky residue of blood from his mouth, and finger-combed his hair with damp fingers, but refused to wash his own greasy face.

Fuck what the sultan wanted.

Because during breakfast, he'd begun to form a partial plan. If he played the role of the rebellious boy, the one who talked back and didn't follow orders, then golden Val would look sweet and obedient by contrast. Vlad would earn the punishments all for himself, because he could endure them…

And because he would *enjoy* being disobedient.

When the janissary came back – with a friend this time – to cuff them and lead them away, he took a look at Vlad's messy hair and no-doubt shiny face and shook his head a fraction. "You'll probably regret that."

Vlad shrugged.

Their escorts marched them down a long hallway with pale stone walls and more painted tile floors. Open windows let in shafts of morning sunlight, white-gold, heatless. They went down a gentle half-turn of a staircase and then down another hall, a parallel of the one above, in reverse. Vlad twisted his hands, testing the cuffs. They didn't break the skin, but they would if he twisted any harder, and he could feel the cold, dulling drone of the silver, a soundless buzzing that turned his arms numb all the way down to the bone.

They were led through an open archway out into a patch of garden, down a short, gravel path to an open pavilion, flooded with sunlight, its tile floors laid with more woven mats like the ones they'd used at breakfast. Three rows of rugs, lined up neatly with a view of a courtyard. At the edges: trunks, heaps of scrolls, and stacks of heavy books.

Some things were universal everywhere, and Vlad knew right away that this was a schoolroom.

Two men with gray beards and long cream robes over their kaftans waited for them, and the janissary guards sent the boys forward with firm nudges.

The man on the left raked Vlad up and down with an emotionless gaze and said something in Turkish.

Vlad ground his molars together and shook his head.

"This is your language, yes?" the man said in perfect Romanian.

Vlad thought his teeth might crack if he clenched his jaw any tighter.

Val said, "Yes, sir," just a whisper.

"What other languages do you speak?"

"Greek, and Latin, and Slavic, and Russian, and a little bit of Italian, if we have to."

The man's look was neither impressed nor unimpressed. "You will learn Turkish as well. That is the language of our sultan, and of your new home."

"No." Vlad said.

The man stared at him. "No?"

"No, I won't learn Turkish. This will *never* be my home."

Vlad was aware of several things: Val staring at him, big-eyed, and shocked, and imploring; the other man moving, pacing slowly around them; the janissaries' boots scraping on the floor as they made to start toward him.

The man in front of him, stoic as a lake in winter, lifted a single hand to halt their progress. Unconcerned. "You will learn many things," he said, "and you can resist all you like, but that will only make it more difficult. More difficult, but not impossible. We are here to educate you, but we will punish you if we must."

Vlad balled his hands into useless fists and bared his teeth. Between them, he hissed, "When my father–"

The blow caught him across the backs of his knees. Sharp, and hot, and stinging. A riding crop, he thought dully, as his knees buckled and he fell to them on the hard tiles, the rest of his threat leaving his mouth as a bitten-back cry.

He sucked in a gasp, and said, "You–"

The next strike landed like a brand on the back of his neck, just under his hairline.

163

Vlad was proud that he didn't make a sound this time. He bit his tongue until he tasted blood, and pitched forward to brace his fists awkwardly on the tile.

Above him, the old man said, "I am Mullah Sinan, and this is Mullah Hamiduddin. Tomorrow morning, you will clean your face and hands when the slave brings you water, and you will come to this room with a willing and respectful attitude. Do you understand?"

The leather tip of the riding crop touched his cheek.

"Yes," he gritted out.

When he finally snuck a look at Val, his brother's eyes were glittered with unshed tears.

16

A PROPER EDUCATION

The first day they were tutored, and took their meals in private, just the two of them, and their guards, and the stone-faced mullahs. It was a good thing they didn't have to eat with utensils, Vlad thought savagely, because he couldn't have worked a knife with his hands cuffed together.

But tomorrow, Sinan told them like a warning, they would begin their education in earnest, alongside the court's other "political guests." A "proper education," he said.

Vlad barely managed to suppress his snort.

When they were finally alone, dressed in linen nightshirts, cuddled up together on one pallet because Val still couldn't bear to sleep alone, Vlad allowed himself a moment of weakness. The door was locked, and a cool evening breeze sifted through the bars on the window, and it had never been more obvious that they were a long, long way from home.

Vlad shut his eyes, pressed his face down into his brother's hair, and breathed deep. Under the floral notes of unfamiliar soap, he sought the smell of Val's skin, and with it the sense memory of home fires, and Mother's singing, and Mircea's patient smiles.

"Vlad?" Val whispered.

Vlad tightened his arms around him in answer, and knew that it was a bad idea. He had to put some distance between them, to show Val that it was best he learn to stand on his own two small feet, and be strong, learn to be a man instead of a boy. But right now, all Vlad could be was weak.

Val's voice trembled when he said, "Why did you do that today?"

Vlad didn't need to ask for clarification. He swallowed, and felt something stick in his throat. "They're not my masters, and I will not go quietly."

"But, Vlad…" His hands tightened in Vlad's shirt, shaking, bony knuckles digging into Vlad's ribs. "They *hurt* you."

"No, they didn't." His neck and his knees stung, but that was already healing; he felt the faint itch of fading bruises already. "Not in any way that matters."

~*~

The next morning, they were marched to the same schoolroom, but this time they weren't alone with the mullahs.

The rugs were occupied with boys today. Some looked Val's age, and others were clearly in their early teens, gangly, with prominent apples in their throats and awkward patches of stubble on their chins. These were the Ottoman hostages, the children of important Eastern European leaders.

One boy, Vlad noted as they were ushered in, was older than the others. Twenty, maybe, already a man, tall and strongly built, with European features and wheat-colored hair. He stood against a column of the pavilion, arms folded, casual and negligent. His gaze betrayed nothing as it followed them into the room.

And then–

Vlad came to an abrupt halt and felt Val do the same beside him. Over the perfume of blooming flowers that wafted in through the open archways, over the fear, anxiety, and boredom of the other boys, a very distinct, very unexpected scent reached Vlad's nose. If he'd been searching for it, he would have detected it halfway across the garden. As it was, it hit him now, like a physical blow, and raised all the fine hairs on the back of his neck and arms.

There was a vampire in this room.

Male. Young. And a whiff of…of something…familiar.

Val made a soft whimpering sound beside him, an inhuman, questioning sound.

"Hush," Vlad whispered.

"Move," the janissary behind them said, and pushed them down onto rugs.

At a rug at the front of the assemblage, two rows ahead, an auburn-haired Turkish boy twisted lazily around and sent Vlad a look from beneath his shiny black lashes. Vlad's age, but handsome, fine featured. His kaftan was an extravagant affair.

He smiled, sideways and sly, showing just enough teeth to flash one sharp fang.

"Brother," Val murmured beside him, fearful. "Who is that?"

He was the reason the people here knew to cuff them with solid silver and bring them blood with breakfast. The reason boys who growled like tigers weren't anything to scream about. And Vlad had a feeling–

Sinan slapped a riding crop into his palm in front of the Ottoman boy. "Mehmet," he snapped.

Vlad swallowed. "I think," he whispered back, "that's the heir."

The boy faced forward, and the janissary cuffed Vlad lightly across the back of the head, and it was time for the day's lessons to begin.

Or, he thought it was.

Mullah Sinan's gaze lifted to the entryway and Vlad heard shuffling footsteps, and the heavier tread of an adult. Without turning his head, he watched from the corner of his eye as two boys were led forward by a slave. They were both small, and shared the same hair color and bone structure: brothers.

Both wore bandages wound round their heads, covering their eyes. They held hands, clinging tight, knuckles bloodless.

Warm breath brushed across Vlad's ear. The janissary, leaning down to speak Slavic in his ear. "Stepan and Gregor Brankovic. Serbian princes. They were caught writing letters to their father," he said, without inflection, "and the sultan had their eyes burned out with a hot iron. You'd do well to learn from their lesson."

The slave helped the boys to rugs, guided their heads gently so they faced the mullahs. No books or writing tablets awaited them. How could they read without eyes?

Vlad closed his own hands into fists. *Let him try to burn my eyes out*, he thought, viciousness curdling the breakfast in his stomach. *Let him try.*

~*~

Vlad was a reluctant student, but he was an intelligent one.

A routine developed. In the mornings, all the hostages – and the heir – were educated on the Quran, history, geography, and politics.

In the afternoons, Vlad and Val had Turkish lessons.

Vlad picked it up the way he picked up all languages, the way Father had described as being like a bucket in a well: "efficiently, thoroughly, brimming over."

But his understanding didn't make him cooperative. He couldn't comprehend the gall of these people; that they thought he would go meekly along with their plans to domesticate and educate him. That he would pray over their holy book, and eat their food, wear their clothes, learn their customs, and willingly agree to this imprisonment. It offended him on a visceral level. Wouldn't it be more honorable to be thrown in a cell and deprived of food and water? To be chained to a dirty wall and left to wallow in his own filth?

To go along with them felt disloyal not only to his family, but to his homeland. To be a happy hostage was unthinkable.

So.

"Now repeat it back to me," Mullah Effendi said. He was a former Serbian prisoner of war who'd fully assimilated. A prisoner no longer, but an educator of boy prisoners.

Vlad looked down at the book that lay open on the low writing table in front of him. He could read the majority of it, and what words he didn't understand could be figured out easily enough with context clues.

He lifted his head, and stared at the man.

"Repeat it back to me," Effendi said.

In Romanian, Vlad said, "No."

Slowly, deliberately, Effendi picked up the riding crop that rested beside his own open book. "Repeat it back to me," he said for the third time.

"Vlad," Val whispered from his own rug, where he studied with his own tutor; too far to touch, his voice reaching like a hand. "Brother, just say it. *Please.*"

A darted glance proved that Val had his lip caught between his teeth, gaze wide and imploring. *Begging*, really.

"Radu," Mullah Iyas reprimanded quietly, and Val turned his attention back to his tutor. He really was the sweetest, most cooperative child.

Vlad might have obeyed then, just to wipe the worry and fear from his brother's face. He was thoroughly convinced his little brother could stop a war with that pitiful look.

But to do so would show that Val was his weakness – which it was. And weaknesses could be exploited; could be made to suffer for the sake of manipulation.

That couldn't happen. Not ever.

So Vlad turned his shoulder to his brother, blanked his face, and said, "No," yet again.

~*~

The crop left angry red welts that, despite his healing abilities, faded slowly, painful when his clothes shifted over them.

But he could bear it. If not gladly, then at least willingly.

That night, Vlad curled up on his side on his pallet, facing the window, his back to his brother. He listened to Val's near-silent footfalls as he crept up close and then knelt down on the cushions behind him.

"Vlad," he said, just a sad breath of sound. "Are you hurt badly?"

Vlad took a breath in through his mouth, shallow, so the bruised skin over his ribs didn't stretch too much.

As if a handful of bruises were the real pain.

"Go to sleep, Radu," he said.

Behind him: a gasp, low and shocked. "*Vlad.*"

Mother had given him the name Valerian. He loved that name – loved that it was a *sign* of her love. Vlad had never minded that Val was the favorite, and he'd always used his real name, the one he preferred.

"Vlad," he said again, voice choked with tears. "Why would you–"

"Go to sleep."

169

Long moments passed, Val struggling not to cry. And then he finally shifted away and went to lie on his own, as-of-yet-untouched pallet.

Vlad listened to him quietly cry himself to sleep. He never slept at all, himself; he watched the stars wink out, one by one, until pink dawn touched the sky and it was time to rise and play hostage again.

17

BOYS AT COURT

A great kindness. That was how Sinan described it when he informed them that they would not be forcibly converted.

A slave showed Vlad to a folly in the midst of the palace gardens, a lovely white stone structure with open doors at either end, vaulted timber ceilings, all crawling with ivy and climbing mountain roses. Someone had fashioned wooden pews, and a large, plain wood cross hung above one door, beneath it a makeshift altar with the melted stumps of candles. The chapel, the place was called, somewhere for non-converts to pray.

The slave gave a little aborted bow and retreated, leaving Vlad alone with the jasmine-scented air and the echoing sense that, despite all odds, something holy did indeed dwell here.

He wasn't in the mood for holy, though.

He threw himself down onto a pew and scowled up at the cross. "A great kindness," he mimicked. "Fuck you."

He gave it a moment, expecting to be struck dead.

Instead, a voice spoke up behind him. "Your Turkish is almost flawless. Remarkable."

Romanian, Vlad registered.

The man had spoken to him in Romanian!

Heart racing, suddenly, Vlad twisted around and saw that the man who knew his language was the oldest of the hostage boys at court. The one with long wheat-colored hair and a decent beard growing in. His posture mirrored that in which Vlad had first seen him: arms folded, leaning negligently back against the wall.

He tamped down his flurry of excitement. "Who are you?"

The young man studied him a moment, expression guarded in a way that Vlad actually found reassuring. In this instance, away from prying eyes, a little caution went a long way toward earning Vlad's trust.

Finally, he pushed off the wall and extended his right hand for a shake. "My name's George Castrioti. Of Albania. You're Vlad Dracul's son, right?"

Vlad stared at the proffered hand. And then the boy's face. He felt a tug somewhere under his ribs, the pull to talk, to trust, to *confide*. He'd been pushing Val away more steadily each day – they slept separately now, and Val looked to him for comfort less and less – and the thought of stealing even half a conversation with someone who wasn't a captor made him ache.

But he frowned and said, "They don't call you George."

The boy's hand dropped, but he smiled and shrugged. Kicked off the wall and came to rest with both palms leaned casually against the back of the pew. Nothing about his body language nor his scent spoke of a threat, but still, Vlad didn't relax.

"They don't, you're right," he agreed. "They call me Iskander now. Iskander Bey. That's how the Turks refer to Alexander the Great."

Vlad felt his brows jump. "Oh, and you're great?"

He shrugged again, an offhand gesture, dismissive. "I don't know. The sultan seems to think I'm a fierce warrior, though. As far as monikers go, it's not such a bad one." He offered a smile. "But you're welcome to call me George."

Vlad turned away. No one had smiled at him since his arrival here, and he didn't know what to do with it now.

George pulled back – Vlad expected him to leave – but then he came around the end of the pew and sat down beside Vlad, a reasonable arm span between them.

Curiosity got the best of Vlad – the kind that burned, the kind that made him angry, that left his teeth grinding and his voice tight. Most emotions led to anger for him; he didn't understand why, and he hadn't figured out how to control it yet. "How old are you?" he asked, ducking his head when he heard the bite to the words.

But George answered easily, unperturbed. "Twenty-one. The oldest here, by far."

Surprise wiped the frown from Vlad's face. He lifted his head. "But why have they kept you so long?"

"Several reasons, I suspect. He needed to keep a tight rein on my father. And I was" – he grinned and it was more a baring of teeth, a low chuckle building in his throat – "not the most cooperative hostage at first. I took some convincing to behave. You know what that's like."

Vlad hummed an agreeing sound.

"Also, I managed to convince them that I'd converted, and I think they want to make sure that I really have."

Vlad blinked. "You did *what*? But – why–?"

George studied him a moment, gaze narrowing. He offered a less friendly smile, one that was calculating. "I'm playing the long game here, Vlad. You might want to consider doing the same." He stood, and his expression smoothed. "I'll let you pray in peace, then. See you at supper."

"See you..." Vlad murmured. He twisted around in his pew and watched him walk away, noting the breadth of his shoulders, the way even the loose sleeves of his kaftan couldn't hide the muscle development in his arms. A warrior worthy of the title Iskander?

Maybe.

Vlad wasn't at all sure what had just happened.

~*~

Val was ashamed. No, he was worse than that, but he didn't think there was a proper label for the knot of shame that sat heavy in his belly, weighing every breath and darkening every thought. The majority of his energy went to keeping himself from crying; checking tears with rapid blinks and biting his tongue until it bled.

Vlad hated him. And he didn't know *why*. And he *needed* him.

He never called him by his real name anymore. Their captors had known him as Radu from the start, but not Vlad, never Vlad. And now Vlad wouldn't touch him, or look at him, or assure him that everything would be alright. That they would get fee, and run home.

They weren't friends anymore. Weren't *brothers*.

Val had always been told that vampires weren't like wolves – they weren't pack animals, and tended toward solitary existences. More like cats. But he felt like a wolf now, deprived of his pack, without the chance for closeness, and skin contact and the familiar scents of home. Maybe he wasn't a wolf, but he wasn't a human, either, and he wanted, needed, to be in close contact with someone he loved. To be held, and soothed, and allowed to smell the faint copper traces of his own kind.

Now, curled up on his side, he looked at his brother's shape, a dark lump limned in silver moonlight. They were separated by only a meter, but it felt like a chasm.

"Vlad?" he whispered, and even that felt like an obscene amount of sound.

Vlad didn't respond. He wasn't asleep – Val was too aware of his heartbeat and knew that it was only resting, not dreaming – but he refused to acknowledge Val in any way.

Only a meter away, and unreachable.

"Vlad?" One more time, though it was pitiful. He was so *alone*...

A thought struck, then. How had it not struck already?

In the chaos of being captured, and hauled across the mountains on horseback, amidst the emotional tumult of all that had occurred, he hadn't ever thought to try dream-walking. He hadn't been calm enough to settle down and reach for the astral plane, and when he slept, it was with total exhaustion.

Now, though, with a full belly, his anxiety settled by the routine of this new terrifying reality, he thought he might be able to manage.

The more he thought of it, the more he realized that he needed to. That he had to reach out to Father, and ask when they could return, and see Mother, hear her sweet voice singing.

He wasn't wearing cuffs. In the dark, he could just make out the faint lines where the silver had chafed his wrists.

He took a deep breath and resettled on his pillow. Thought about releasing the tension from his body, one muscle at a time. Shut his eyes and cleared his mind. Wiped it clean and then searched for the stars...

It was dizzying; he was out of practice. But when he opened his eyes it was to the familiar view of his mother's bedchamber.

She'd always preferred soft, feminine colors – flower colors. Her four-poster bed was draped with lavender Turkish silk, soft minks, a sable lap rug from Russia. The tapestries on the walls wove gentle golds, and sky blues, and petal pinks: garden scenes, horses, birds on fruit tree branches.

Eira sat in a straight-backed chair by the fire, though it was a warm evening, staring unseeing into the flames, hair molten in its glow.

Val's heart squeezed. "Mama," he breathed, tremulous and tear-choked.

She leapt up from her chair with a little cry of alarm, whirling to face him. Wide eyes, and open mouth, and another cry, this one anguished and choked and elated all at once. "Valerian," she whispered, and nearly tripped over her long skirt in her haste to get to him.

She went to her knees in front of him, reaching. And he reached for her, and then–

Smoke. His arms turned to smoke when they touched, swirling. Because he wasn't really here.

Eira lowered her hands slowly to her lap, and Val's eyes filled with tears. He'd known he was dream-walking, that it wasn't possible to make real contact, but he ached for it. For her arms, and her warmth, and her scent, and her pulse beating beneath his ear.

"Mama," he said again, and his projection solidified again as the tears spilled over and poured down his face.

"Darling. Oh, my precious boy." She clenched her hands into fists on her thighs, and her eyes glimmered as tears filled them. But she smiled at him. Beamed. It was etched with worry and anguish, but it was the most beautiful thing he'd seen in weeks. "Val, sweetheart, I'm here. I'm right here. I'm so proud of you for finding me."

He sniffled, and hiccupped, and tried unsuccessfully to catch his breath.

"Is your brother with you? Are you together? Are you safe?" Her voice trembled on the last word. She looked afraid to know the answer.

He took a few hitched breaths, cleared his throat. He didn't want her to worry like this; had to get the words out. He hadn't thought it would hurt this much to see her. "We – we, y-yes, we're together." Except Vlad hated him. "And we're s-s-safe." No one had struck him with a crop yet. "We're at the sultan's court."

"Oh." A soft gasp. She shook her head, and pushed the brittle smile wider. "You look – you look well. They must be feeding you."

"They know – Mama, they know we're vampires."

She bit her lip, hard, until it drew blood. "Oh, darling…"

Talking helped; his tears slowed, and his throat grew clearer. "The heir is, too. His father isn't – the sultan. So he's not purebred, he must be turned, but they give us blood, and they made us wear silver cuffs when we traveled, and–" He was out of breath. "Mama, I want to come home. Is Father coming for us? Is he negotiating with the sultan?"

Her face crumpled. Her eyes shut, and tears slipped down her face. "Your father…sweetheart." She opened her eyes again, the look in them painful to see. "He's not here. The Ottomans are holding him. Mircea is the prince *pro tem* until he's released."

"…what?"

"The sultan's envoy brought us the missive. Remus is being held until they're sure he can be trusted to keep to the treaty. I had hoped that he was with you boys, but…"

Val took shallow breaths through his mouth. If Father wasn't here…if he was being held, too…

He swallowed a sudden swell of nausea. "He's not here. Mama, he's *not here*."

"I know, baby."

"How…then how…how will he get us home?"

She moved to touch him again, and caught herself just before her fingertips breached the illusion of his face. She was still crying, but silently, and her expression firmed. "Val. Love. I need you to listen to me, and listen carefully, alright?"

Emotions slid over one another like layers of oil; he was adrift. But he would do anything for his mother, anything, so he nodded.

"Your father will do everything he can to secure your release," she said, and her tears finally dried, voice taking on the steel tone of the Viking shieldmaiden she'd been long ago. "But he can't do anything that's immediate. He has to come home first.

It will take time to convince his captors that he is loyal to them, and to formulate a new treaty that will allow you and Vlad to return to us. You – *we* must all be patient. And careful."

She gestured with one hand, and he knew that, if she was able, she would have smoothed his hair back from his face, tucked it lovingly behind his ears. "I need you and your brother to be on your best behavior, to learn as much as you can, but to keep your heads down and stay safe. Don't draw any undue attention. Mircea and I are drafting letters to the sultan – if he'll read them." She huffed. "Mircea is a good prince, but he's young, and he's scared. So I need your help, alright darling? I need you to be my eyes and ears in Adrianople. That's where you are, right?"

"Yes'm."

She nodded, resolved. Fixed him with a serious look. "I *will* get you back, Val. You, and Vlad, and your father. I will. I promise you that."

He had absolute faith. "I know you will, Mother."

Then the resolve crumbled into grief, and fear, and shining, shining love. "I love you, precious boy. I love you so, so much, more than anything."

He felt fresh tears sting his eyes. "I love you, Mama."

"Give my love to your brother for me, please."

"I will." Though…maybe Vlad didn't want it.

She stood up and straightened her skirts. "Can you stay a little longer? You should come talk to Mircea and tell him what you know."

"Okay."

Mircea tried to embrace him, and his face fell when he remembered that he couldn't.

Val "sat" by his desk for nearly an hour, telling him what little he'd learned at the Ottoman court so far, and sometime after that he faded, waking on his pallet in Edirne as the sun was breaking over the horizon, the first pale light of dawn stealing across the tile floors.

Vlad still lay on his side, facing away, and Val sighed. *Hurry, Mama,* he thought. *I don't know how long we have.*

~*~

177

"Radu," Gregor said with his usual soft-voiced hesitance. A gentle prompt.

"Oh. Right, sorry." Val forced his gaze away from the scene unfolding in the training yard – Vlad and Iskander Bey sparring with blunted practice swords, the clang of the metal ringing off the stone walls – and turned his attention back to the book he held in his lap. It was a collection of Turkish stories for children, and at another time he might have been enjoying it – might have reveled in his ability to read a new language so fluently – but dread was pooled low in his belly. This was their training time, and he knew that, sooner or later, he would be forced to give up his role as reader and pick up a practice sword of his own.

He began to read again, and beside him on the bench, the eyeless boy relaxed a fraction and leaned in so their shoulders touched. Propped together. His brother didn't want him anymore, but there were others who appreciated him. A small comfort in a sea of anticipated hurts.

He read until a shadow fell across him. Then his tongue got stuck to the roof of his mouth and he looked up to see Iskander standing over him, sandy hair glued to his neck with sweat, smile wide and straight.

"Your turn, Radu," he said. "Up you go and pick out a sword."

Val set the book aside slowly, stealing a glance at his brother.

Vlad stood in the center of the yard, wiping his forehead with his sleeve, sword held in his other hand. His hair had been braided before, but was sliding loose after his exercise, clinging to his temples, and jaw, and throat.

Separated for the past few weeks – even just figuratively – Val now realized that he was able to see his brother with fresh eyes, and that Vlad was changed. Taller, more muscular. His neck thicker, his jaw squarer. Not a man, but no longer a child. His shirt clung to his arms, his shoulders and biceps taut with new muscle.

A slave brought him a water cup and he drank half of it, and poured the rest over his head, fangs visible when he opened his mouth and panted.

"Radu," Iskander said, snatching his attention. He frowned now, concerned. "Are you well?"

"Yes. Yes, sorry. Here." He set the book gently in Gregor's hands. "I'll be back in a little while. Okay?"

"O-okay," the boy said, hands clenching tight around the book.

Val stood and made his way to the wooden rack where the blunted practice swords waited, already dreading his lesson…and eyes trained on his brother.

If Vlad felt his gaze, he didn't show it, retreating to another bench and sitting on it heavily, accepting a second cup of water, gaze trained on the packed dirt and sawdust of the ground.

He didn't look at Val once.

Disheartened, Val picked a sword – the lightest one of the bunch, one that hopefully wouldn't pull on his arms and shoulders much. Unlike Vlad, he wasn't getting broader or more muscular, was instead growing lean and more graceful, if that was even possible. Not the ideal dimensions of a warrior who hoped to work his way free of enemy territory.

When he turned, Iskander waited for him, smile slight, but encouraging, tone warm. "Are you ready?"

Val hitched up his drooping shirtsleeves and nodded. He brought his sword up to the correct angle and approached the center of the yard warily, already braced for an attack.

The sword master, a grizzled janissary, watched from a post leaning against the wall, unconcerned. Iskander had taken over the lessons before the brothers' arrival, one of the other boys had said, and the sword master rarely intervened in the lessons anymore.

This was an improvement, in Val's eyes, because Iskander was kind, and a patient teacher. But he was still much older, larger, and stronger, and Val still didn't have the hang of swordplay.

As if he could sense this – and he was oddly perceptive for a mortal – Iskander tilted his head to the side and gave Val a considering look. "Let's try something new today."

"Oh…okay…"

Iskander's smile widened, and softened. "It's alright, I promise. I want you to close your eyes, and try to relax for me.

179

Can you do that? Take deep breaths. In and out, nice and slow, yes, like that."

When he registered the praise, Val realized he had in fact closed his eyes, and that his breaths were deep and regular, and that some of the awful tension bracketing his spine had begun to ease. Iskander 's voice was low and smooth, his Turkish spoken with a slight Slavic accent. *I'm like you*, that accent said. *Here against my will, but see how well I've adjusted?*

Val took a breath in, and let it out. In and out.

"Now," Iskander said, "I want you to envision yourself. Envision me, and the yard, and your sword. Imagine the dance. Because that's what it is, sword-fighting – it's a dance. Imagine that I strike, and that you parry. Think about your foot placement; the weight of the blade in your hand. Think about the shock up your arms when the blades meet. Imagine yourself doing it *well*. This isn't a battle, Radu. It's only a dance. And you're a good dancer, yes?"

"Yes," Val murmured, because he was, and because he could *see* it suddenly: dodging, and spinning, and parrying, and slicing, his small feet quick across the ground, sawdust swirling around his ankles, clinging to his sweaty shins.

And then...

Whirling stars, and orange flames, and oh, he was traveling, dream-walking, heading for home, for Mother, and Mircea, and he was–

"Radu," Iskander said, and Val opened his eyes, and anger boiled up inside him, and he *struck*.

The return to this plane, and the bright afternoon sun after the dark, was dizzying, but his footwork was sure as he advanced on Iskander – the interloper who'd pulled him from his trip home – with a sure swing that would have startled him at another time. He couldn't wield a sword like that; at least, he hadn't been able to before. But now...

Iskander stepped back – *danced* back – and laughed, smile delighted as he brought his own sword up to parry Val's attack. "*Good*. Come on, yes!"

The bright sound of metal meeting metal, the sharp cry of steel crashing together. The shock of impact up his arms, just as

Iskander had said... Val pressed his attack a few minutes before he realized that through his haze of sweat and adrenaline and flying dust...he was smiling. This was exhilarating. Was this the way it felt for Vlad? This rush of delight and aggression?

Iskander retreated in a circle around the yard, letting Val hack at him with passionate, if amateurish determination. Then he braced his feet and held his ground, began to push back a little bit.

At home, Val would have retreated then, but now, with his blood up, he gritted his teeth and tightened his sweaty palms on the hilt of his sword, and met the older boy strike for strike.

"Good," Iskander said again, and he sounded winded. "Left leg back – there, yes, good."

It was only a training exercise, and the first in which Val hadn't had his sword knocked out of his hand within the first minute, but when Iskander finally lowered his blade and stepped back, grinning at him, he felt triumphant.

Val smiled, and laughed, and tasted sawdust on his lips when he wet them. He forgot himself a moment, so high on this brief success. "Vlad, did you see? Did you see me?" he asked, turning to his brother.

Vlad's face was like a bucket of cold water dumped over his head. Closed-off, his mouth twisted, a displeased notch between his brows.

Oh, that was right. Vlad hated him now.

Val felt his smile falling, his stomach lurching, the joy fading.

And then someone began to clap behind him. A slow clap, too loud in the momentary quiet of the training yard.

On Val's next deep breath, he caught a whiff of blood – of vampire – and tension stole over him once more as he turned to face the heir.

Mehmet Çelebi, heir of the Ottoman Empire, was rumored to have been born of a Greek mother. His braided hair gleamed red-brown in the sunlight, his eyes the pale, bright green of glass. Val hadn't been able to see much of his father in him, with his aquiline nose, and his narrow, winged brows, his elegant, long-fingered hands.

181

He never tried to hide his fangs; they were always a little too prevalent, like now, as he continued to clap and walked into the center of the circle to join them. Smiling. He smiled like he knew a secret that others would kill to learn.

"Well done, little one," he said in Slavic. "You're finally learning how to handle a sword." His smile stretched, fangs winking in the sunlight, and Val wanted to take a step back.

"Radu is improving every lesson," Iskander said, tone gone cold and flat. "Everyone is."

"Yes, yes," Mehmet said with a dismissive little wave. His green gaze stayed pinned on Val. "But *this* one. He wasn't made for fighting. Much too pretty." He tilted his head, and the movement held none of the soft concession it had when Iskander had done it earlier. This was all calculation, gaze sweeping down to Val's boots and then slowly back up to his face. "Look at that hair. Like spun gold."

"If you'd like to spar," Iskander said, "just give me a moment to catch my breath, and I'll–"

"No. I want to spar with this one."

Val hadn't ever seen Iskander look startled, but he did now. "You can't–" He caught himself. "Your grace…"

Mehmet turned his head slowly, gaze low-lidded, almost lazy. But flashing like fire. "Are you arguing with me, Iskander Bey?" he asked mildly.

Iskander's hand tightened on his sword hilt, and Val smelled a spike of aggression in his sweat. But he shook his head and said, "No, your grace."

Wait, Val wanted to tell him. *Stay here with me!*

But Iskander was a hostage after all, and he withdrew, going to hang up his sword and accept water from a slave.

Val wanted to look at his brother, but Vlad hated him now…

"Don't worry, little one," Mehmet said as he went to select a practice sword of his own. "I wouldn't dare put a mark on your pretty face."

Val choked on his next breath.

"Come now." Mehmet stepped toward him, twirling his sword. "Would you refuse the request of the heir?"

A question to which there was no answer.

"No," Val breathed, anxiety already skating across his nerves, tightening his stomach.

"Alright, then." Mehmet slid into a ready stance. "Let's begin."

Val wanted to turn tail and run. But. This was the heir. And he was a long way from home.

He adjusted his feet, and lifted his sword.

"*En garde*," Mehmet said with a smile, and attacked.

Val lifted his sword. Too late, too slow, he knew–

Sharp *clang* of metal against metal.

Scent of home, family, brother. Because Vlad had leapt up and thrown his shoulder in front of Val, had stopped Mehmet's sword with his own.

The collision echoed, bouncing off the utter stillness of the training yard. And then Val heard his brother growl, low like a panther. "Don't touch him," he rumbled. "Don't you fucking *touch* my brother."

Mehmet stared at him a moment, expressionless for once. And then a smile slowly bloomed. He chuckled. "Oh. So you do care, huh? We can work with that."

Vlad opened his mouth and *snarled*.

"Brother–" Val started, and was elbowed backward. He landed hard on his backside in the sawdust, and had to scramble out of the way as the two princes broke apart, swords held at the ready.

"That doesn't sound very civilized," Mehmet taunted.

Vlad roared, and ripped his sword back; lunged forward with a vicious strike.

This was no training exercise, Val knew. His brother wanted blood. Two rival male vampires, no matter how young, would only relent when one was too badly wounded to lift his arms.

"Vlad," he tried again, but it was no use.

Vlad moved with every ounce of his viciousness, his movements a blur, snarling the whole time.

The heir began with a smile…that soon became a grimace. Vlad was stronger, faster, and a far superior swordsman.

183

Val scrambled over to the wall, right beside Iskander. "We have to stop them," he whispered. "Iskander!"

But the older boy didn't look desperate the way that Val felt, not even troubled. No, he looked thoughtful, damp hair held off his forehead with one hand, the other resting on his hip.

"Iskander!" Val tried again, louder this time.

And Iskander…smiled. Just a slow curling at the corners of his mouth. "Huh," he said under his breath.

In the center of the yard, Vlad pushed Mehmet back with a sequence of quick, brutal strikes. The blunted steel hissed and cracked as it was met again and again. Sweat gleamed on their brows; both had their teeth bared, gritted, fangs in full view.

The heir tripped, and went down on one knee.

Vlad lifted his sword high, prepared to strike.

Val didn't want to watch, but couldn't look away.

The old janissary moved, finally, and took a few lurching strides toward them. "Hey, that's enough!"

The movement caught Vlad's attention. He turned his head – just a fraction, but it was enough.

"Vlad!" Val shouted. Iskander caught him by the back of the collar as he tried to rush toward his brother.

Mehmet brought his sword up, a vicious swing. Val heard his brother's ribs break, the awful faint *snap* of bone breaking under clothes and flesh.

Vlad staggered back a step.

"Mehmet," the janissary warned.

The heir surged to his feet, smiling again, face sweat- and dirt-streaked. "Don't ever take your eyes off me, hostage," he panted. "That's a grave mistake." And his next swing was aimed at Vlad's head.

~*~

Val was aware of darkness, and a sense that the floor was falling out from under him. When he opened his eyes, he was in a shaded, sweet-smelling place, and he saw a familiar curly-headed figure bent over a table, quill in-hand as he composed a letter.

184

He'd fainted, he realized, and in that faint, he'd wound up dream-walking.

He scrambled upright with a gasp.

Constantine turned toward him, the quill falling from his hand and rolling across the desk. "Valerian. What are you–" He stood, and moved forward, hands outstretched as if to offer help. He pulled up, though, when he remembered.

Val knew he looked a fright: sweaty, dust-smeared, hair falling down around his face. He tugged at his shirt and tried to sniff back his impending tears. "Your Imperial Majesty."

Constantine made a sound that was half laugh, and half sigh. "I'm still not the emperor, Val. I'm not even emperor *pro tem* anymore; John's back from Rome."

"He…" Val was too distraught and tired to make much sense of that.

Constantine spread his arms wide, inviting a look around the room…which proved not to be the palace solar in which Val had visited him before. This room was lavish, yes, but it was much smaller, cozy even, and the incoming golden sunlight fell across piles of books, and a dusty mantlepiece, and a half-dozen mismatched chairs.

"John is back from Rome," Constantine repeated, gentler this time, as if speaking to a frightened child – which he *was*. "We're at Mistra, son. I'm the despot here now."

It shouldn't have been possible – given that he wasn't physically here – for Val's legs to give out. But give out they did, and he sat down hard on the stone floor, elbows landing on his thighs. "I…"

"Are you alright? You don't look well. What's happened?"

Val wasn't really listening; he was marveling. "I found you," he said, and looked down at his hands, at the floor, at the rich Turkish rugs laid out across it.

Constantine crouched down in front of him so they were on eye level, concerned. "Yes, you did."

"No, don't you see – I thought I had to walk to a place, but it's people! I dream-walked to you, even though you weren't in the palace anymore! I–" His excitement caught, like a sleeve snagging on a door handle, and the blooming joy dissolved like the dust that layered his boots. "Your Majesty," he said, fresh tears burning his eyes. "It's so terrible!"

"What is?"

Val took a hitched breath and then told him everything. The meeting that was a trap in Gallipoli, their capture, their trek to Edirne. In too-fast, unsteady pulses between breaths, Val spilled the whole story, right down to today's sparring lesson gone horribly wrong.

"He struck Vlad, and I – I think I fainted, I..." He clenched his hands into fists, and bit his lip so hard he tasted blood. "I fainted just like the baby I am. Because I'm *useless*. And now my brother might be dead, and I'm lying in the sawdust like an *idiot*."

"Val. Valerian," Constantine said, and shifted forward, catching Val's attention. "Can you look at me?" His handsome features were twisted with sympathy, a grave sadness etched into the lines around his eyes. "I'm very sorry," he said, and Val knew that he meant it. "I'm sorry you've been taken hostage, and your father and brother as well. And I'm sorry that I can't be of any help to you."

"Oh, well, I understand. I don't need you to – to – to do anything, I just–" He bit his lip again, mouth full of blood-taste, on the verge of sobbing. "I only – I – I was scared, and..."

"It's alright." Constantine hugged him. Did his best to, anyway. He put his arms in a circle around Val's shaking shoulders, close enough to block the room from sight, but not so close that Val's projection dissipated into smoke. "I'm sorry," he repeated, so gently, and that made Val cry even harder. "It's alright. You can cry. I'm sorry."

Val wanted, instinctually, desperately, to put his arms around a friendly neck, press his face into a kind chest, and feel an embrace. To feel the warmth and caring of a person who didn't mean him any harm. But all he could do now was band his arms around his middle and let the sobs shake him to pieces.

Softly, Constantine said, "You can always come to visit me when you need to see a friendly face."

Val closed his eyes because it was too much, too much–

And his body called him back.

He tumbled through the stars and woke on the ground, his head pillowed on someone's strong leg, his mouth full of his own blood.

He scrambled to get up. "Vlad!"

Hands caught him by the shoulders. "Easy, easy now," Iskander said. "Just rest a minute until you get your bearings back."

"But Vlad." As the black spots cleared from his vision, the training yard began to take shape in front of him. Iskander had moved him up against the wall, in a patch of shade, and if the cool water trickling down into his collar was anything to go by, had been mopping his face and throat with a wet cloth.

Vlad was gone, as were all the other boys…save the heir.

Mehmet knelt on the ground, his sword laid across his lap. Hair clung to his face, skin sun-dark and shiny with sweat. He breathed raggedly through his mouth – his smiling mouth. Blood flecked his cheeks, and the bridge of his nose, and his throat – grisly freckles.

When Val met his gaze, he laughed, breathless. "What, do you think I killed him? I only hit him in the head." He lowered his own head, and looked up at Val from beneath slanted brows. "Your brother needs to learn his place, little one. Today was a lesson. Nobody gets in the way of what I want."

"Your grace," the sword master said, stepping up and offering a hand down to the future sultan.

Mehmet held Val's gaze a long, uncomfortable moment, then put his practice sword in the master's hand and climbed to his feet without assistance. "Don't worry, Radu," he called over his shoulder as he headed for the arched doorway that led into the weapons room, "I don't have any interest in *fighting* you."

Val swallowed thickly, the taste of his own blood threatening to gag him. Cold sweat prickled at his hairline and it had nothing to do with his fainting spell.

"What does he mean?" he asked, turning a look up and around to Iskander.

He got a grim frown and a shake of a head in response. "Stay away from him, Radu. Don't do anything to catch his attention."

"But...I haven't."

The hands tightened on his shoulders. "I know. I'm sorry."

"Where's Vlad? Is he...?"

"Breathing, when they carried him off. I suspect he's in the infirmary. Just like I suspect..." He lifted a brow, knowing. "That neither of you boys is altogether human, are you?"

~*~

In years past, Vlad had spent a probably-embarrassing amount of time wondering what it would be like if he could dream-walk like his brother. Val had explained it to him, talked about vast spaces, and pinpricks of light like stars, and the sense of flying. Like a dream, he'd said. But that wasn't any help, because Vlad dreamed of concrete things: the scent of rain, the feel of a horse beneath him, the taste of Helga's sweetcakes fresh from the oven. The way his muscles burned pleasantly when he drew a bowstring, or swung a sword. The taste of fresh blood over his tongue – once he'd dreamed of a hunt he'd taken with Fenrir, when the big wolf had shifted into his shaggy four-legged shape and helped him fell a deer. Fenrir had lay on the still-alive beast, and Vlad had crept up, quiet, careful, and bared his fangs, set his teeth in the stag's neck. That day he'd drunk *living* blood, pumping across his tongue in pulses, the beat of the animal's heart, and he'd dreamed of it often, afterward.

But he couldn't control his dreams. Couldn't go visit with the people he wanted to see, convey messages he needed to send. He couldn't control himself in his dreams, couldn't stop the awful coursing anger; most nights he screamed through dreams that were really nightmares, and woke to find his throat tight, phantom leftover threads of his subconscious fury.

This sleep, now, was dreamless. He woke to dizziness, and pain, and heavy eyelids that he cracked open slowly. It was dusk, the light angled and thick, a dull blue shaft that slanted over the bed where he lay. His head throbbed, and his chest ached, and there was a sharp pain that undercut both of those hurts: the familiar sensation of bone knitting faster than was humanly possible.

Three broken ribs, he thought. A skull fracture, for sure, the way the pain blossomed bright and white and sent stars wheeling across his vision. Huh. Were these anything like the stars Val meant when he talked about the astral plane?

An amused thought, just before nausea overwhelmed him and he jackknifed upright, shouting as the movement jerked his ribs. A physician materialized beside the bed, bowl held ready to catch the watery bile that Vlad vomited up.

The room spun and he shut his eyes. *Mama*, he thought, once, piteously. He wanted his mama.

"You should rest, young lord," the physician said in Slavic.

He put a hand to Vlad's shoulder and helped him to lie back down. Carefully, Vlad eased his eyes open again. The ceiling swayed above him, and the bed seemed to tilt.

He knew three things:

The heir wanted to fuck Valerian.

An heir of whom Vlad had just made an enemy for life.

And if it was the last godforsaken thing he did in his miserable life, Vlad was going to kill him.

18

LIVING BLOOD

It was three days before Vlad was able to be up and about on his own, bandages wound round his head and chest.

Three days without lessons.

Three days without any contact with Val.

When he shuffled into the schoolroom, he saw Val's narrow shoulders stiffen; saw his nostrils flare and knew that, though he gritted his teeth and stared resolutely ahead, he'd sensed Vlad's entrance.

He was angry, then. Good.

Vlad recalled the sound of his own name ringing across the training yard three days ago, a terrified cry from his brother. *Vlad!* Like the world was ending. Maybe it had been selfish to allow Val to see him injured like that – it was – but he told himself it was to spare what would have happened if he hadn't intervened. The heir looked on Val with open lust, and Val, innocent as a lamb, didn't recognize that particular craving, not even when it picked up a sword and offered to spar with him.

He'd been going to keep his distance, Vlad decided. But then came Mehmet, with his boldly showcased fangs, and his open want, and Vlad couldn't *be* anything but an enraged big brother. So enraged that he'd fought blindly, and allowed an opening.

It had been three days since he'd taken blows that would have killed a mortal boy, and now Val was the one turning away and ignoring, feigning hate.

He supposed that was the plan all along. But not…

In the front row, Mehmet turned a fraction to glance back over his shoulder, expression closed-off, one green eye gleaming. He had glass eyes: they reflected, but they projected nothing of their own light.

…now this wasn't just about surviving as hostages.

Vlad slipped into the back row, settling gingerly on crossed legs, teeth gritted against the jostling of his ribs.

Beside him, George spoke quietly, eyes trained ahead, lips barely moving. "Didn't expect you up and about so soon."

Vlad opened the book in front of him with one hand – the side that wouldn't pull at his healing fractures. "I heal quickly."

"I can see that."

Vlad didn't want to cooperate, but he found, as the morning ticked slowly into afternoon, and Mullah Sinan's voice droned onward, that he didn't have the strength to be rebellious today. One lick from the crop would send him back to the infirmary – or make him pass out, something that seemed more and more a possibility the longer he sat swaying on his mat.

In the last three days, Vlad had come to realize something. Either the heir had never been seriously injured after his turning, or the Ottomans didn't care that he was weak; maybe they even wanted him that way. Because they'd given him his daily cup of sheep's blood, but when his bones knit themselves back together this quickly, it required a massive amount of energy. Ordinarily, a vampire in his shape would need to either drop into a deep sleep, or feed round the clock. And feed on something stronger than sheep's blood.

When he was four, he broke his arm falling off his horse. A bad break; he'd come to and found the bone had split the skin, a jagged, red-streaked stump of white protruding just beneath his elbow. Cicero had reset the bone, and then fed him straight from his own vein. Regular doses of wolf blood had left him fully-healed within a week's time.

But right now, the room spun lazy circles around him.

"You're pale," George said, once.

"I'm fine," Vlad said, and swallowed down his rising gorge.

He pushed through the day, forcing food down his throat, mumbling answers to questions during his lessons. The mullahs lifted their brows in surprise when he offered none of his usual vitriol, but every answer given was correct, so they didn't lift the crop to him. The sword master excused him from sparring, and the archery master took one look at his pale face and sent him away.

When he was free, finally, he dragged himself to the chapel and fell into a pew. It was the only place he could think to go where he might be alone. And he had to be alone, because he couldn't fall to bits in front of anyone – not his brother, and certainly not his enemy.

He finally let go of the tension that was all that held him together and slumped forward, arms braced on the back of the pew in front of him. Sweat slid down his face, and down his spine, and he breathed in ragged gulps. Black spots crowded his vision. What would happen if he passed out here? Would anyone come find him? How badly would he be beaten?

"...Vlad?"

Awash in his own weakness and pity, he hadn't sensed anyone approach, and now there was a voice in his ear, and breath against the side of his face.

Vlad tried to leap to his feet, to turn, brace himself for a fight. But he ended up sprawled across the flagstone floor, one arm held up as a useless shield, a pained shout catching between his teeth as his ribs pulled.

But it was only George, hands held out in a gesture intended to calm. "I said your name several times," he said apologetically. "You didn't seem to hear."

Vlad warred with himself a moment. He wanted to get to his feet and walk away. To say something cruel. To give in to his constant, simmering anger...

But he was exhausted, and shaking, and...

He slowly lowered his arm and just...slumped sideways. Rested his face against the back of the pew in front of him.

George's brows pinched together in a look of sad concern. "You're like Mehmet, aren't you?"

Vlad growled. It was a pathetic little sound, but inhuman all the same. "I am *nothing* like Mehmet."

George tipped his head. "I meant that you're not – not mortal, are you? You're something else."

Vlad tried to rally his scattered thoughts and studied the other hostage a moment. This could be a trap – a way for the Ottomans to get him to give up his secrets; send in the friendly face to tease secrets out of him. But his vampirism wasn't a secret, was it?

He sighed. "I'm a vampire."

192

To his credit, George only blinked a few times, and then finally gave a slow nod. "Alright."

"Alright? That's all you have to say to that?"

George seemed to consider his next words. He sat back in his pew, hands folded together in his lap. His gaze was shrewd. "There was a time," he said, finally, "when the heir hoped to make a friend of me. He didn't come to Edirne until he was eleven – he spent his boyhood in Amaysa. When he arrived, the moment we met, there was something about him that...troubled me. It's true that princes are spoiled, and tend to grow up both too fast and too slow all at once. They have women too early, and a sense of maturity too late. But Mehmet was like no eleven-year-old I'd ever met. Composed, cold, always guarded. But also lustful, and malicious."

He shuddered. "I didn't dare push him away outright. And because of that, I got to see a side of him that – well, let's say his behavior isn't boyish.

"He never told me what he was exactly, but he feeds from the women in the seraglio. Puts fangs in their throat and drinks their blood and ruts against them." He tipped his head the other way, gaze narrow. "But I don't get that sense from you or your brother."

Vlad's skin crawled. He took a few shallow breaths through his mouth. He shouldn't say more. But he'd already come this far...

"My brother and I are born vampires. Purebred. Natural. The sultan is human, which means Mehmet was turned as a child. That never ends well. Turned adults are one thing. But."

George stared at him a long moment, and then nodded. "Can you tell who turned him?"

"No. Not without tasting his blood, and that only works if I recognize the blood."

"Barbaric," George said, but not with any heat or disgust. "You really do need blood to survive."

Vlad didn't answer.

"And I'm willing to bet that human blood is more potent than animal."

"Hmm," Vlad murmured. He might be spilling his guts, but he had *some* sense of self-preservation left. Werewolf blood was the strongest, the best, part of the ancient symbiotic relationship that had begun on the banks of the Tiber.

"They aren't letting you feed from the women, I know. What do they give you instead? Chickens? Goats?"

"Sheep," Vlad bit out.

"Is that enough?"

"When you're healthy it is."

"So that's why you're so sickly right now."

Vlad glared at him. "It takes a lot of energy to heal broken bones."

George glanced away, up toward the cross on the wall. "When you feed," he said, the words drawn out. "Do you kill the – thing – you're feeding from?"

"Some do. I never have." Vlad growled again. "What the hell does that even matter? Why do you care?"

George didn't answer right away. He stared into the middle distance a long moment. Then, finally, nodded and turned back, jaw set at a resolute angle. "If it'll help, you can feed from me."

"Wha...*what*?" Shock gave Vlad enough strength to stagger to his feet, though he had to clutch the pew for balance. "Are you insane? Why the hell would you offer to do that?"

George sat forward, and dropped his voice. "Remember how I told you I'm playing the long game? I'm also realistic: when I'm released, I'll go home to Albania, and no matter the willingness and might of the army I plan to raise, I am only one man, and we will be but one vassal state. I'll need allies, Vlad. And I think maybe you hate these men more than I do." He smiled, a wicked line like a knife slice across his face. "I want to help you, yes, but believe me, it's in my own best interest to keep you alive and well."

He stuck out a hand, the same one Vlad had declined to clasp before. "This is what happens behind enemy lines. Hostages with a common purpose make alliances. There's no reason we can't help each other."

Vlad stared at his hand – the hangnails, the sword calluses – and slumped a little more into the pew. He felt the blood draining out of his face, receding from the healing crack in his skull that needed it so badly. Felt the floor tilt; felt his knees threaten to give. His voice shook. "You don't – you don't k-kn-know what you're offering."

"No, I do." George reached up and began unbuttoning his kaftan, and *oh*, that was *bad*. "I'm offering you a drink."

Vlad slammed his eyes shut, and swayed where he stood, gripping the pew so tight he heard his knuckles crack. "You don't – your *throat*? Are you insane?" Even though his eyes were shut, he could hear the shifting of fabric, the faint low thump of a healthy pulse. Could smell skin, and sweat, and blood, blood, blood, *freely offered* blood. "I've never fed from a human before. What if I can't stop? What if I kill you?"

"I'm trusting you not to."

"But *why*?" He opened his eyes and found George watching him calmly, his kaftan unbuttoned all down the throat.

"I already told you: I need an ally." He pulled the collar down, exposed the tempting column of his throat. The vein pulsed there. "And I'm trusting you because no matter how thirsty you are for blood, you're *hungrier* for release. For returning to your homeland. If you kill me, they'll thrash you to within an inch of your life – at the very least. They might even kill you. They certainly won't educate you, and arm you, and make you an officer, and eventually send you back home as their intended puppet."

"They–" Vlad gasped. "But they–" His mind reeled; he was too tired to make sense of what the Albanian boy had just said. "But they won't…"

"They will. That's what they plan to do with me, and it's what they plan to do with you. Sway you to their cause, and send you back to Wallachia to rule according to their wishes."

He couldn't – he couldn't *think*. And there was a throat *right there,* being offered, and he…

"Vlad," George said, gently this time. He patted the bench beside him. "You can barely stand. Just–" and here came the first sign of hesitance, doubt flickering through his eyes "–don't take too much, okay? I have to be able to walk out of here."

195

Vlad fought it – really he did. But there were some fights that could not be won by will alone, and this was one of them. One time, Vlad told himself, and sank slowly, shakily down onto the pew. His fangs descended, and saliva gathered at the back of his mouth, and gooseflesh broke out down his arms and back. Anticipation. Bloodlust.

His vision had already gone hazy, George just a blurred shape in front of him, but he managed to say, "My ribs."

"What?"

"If I try to take too much – if I won't stop – then hit my ribs. Here." He ghosted a hand over his side to demonstrate. "And push me away."

Sound of George swallowing. "Alright."

And then Vlad couldn't wait anymore.

He shifted forward, hands finding the boy's shoulders, and hauled himself up into his lap, gracelessly. He pressed his face down, seeking with nose and lips, and found the pulse point on his throat.

He breathed there a moment, open-mouthed, and felt the skin beneath his lips flicker, like a horse twitching beneath a fly.

"Vlad–"

He bit. It had been a long time since he put his teeth in something – some*one* – but he remembered the punch of fangs through flesh, the way blood boiled up into his mouth. Wolf blood was the best, the strongest, and its richness had always filled him with comfort. This, though, this human blood, tasted exotic and thrilling, like flower nectar.

Vlad closed his eyes, dimly aware of the obscene growl that rumbled in his throat, and drank.

It was a tide on which he floated. He didn't know for how long. All his hurts faded into the blurred edges of his consciousness, along with rational thought and restraint, leaving only the blood, and his suddenly-empty stomach, and the building pressure down low in his hips, the tingling in his spine.

But something broke through the haze, finally; a hand touched his neck, and awareness came tumbling back, almost painful. Vlad opened his mouth, retracted his fangs, and let the hand ease him away from his source of nourishment.

He blinked, and George slid into focus. Even in his haste, Vlad had been careful, and the wound was neatly done: tidy punctures. It would bruise, but that was inevitable. As he watched, a few pulses of blood seeped out and trickled down George's throat toward his as-of-yet-untouched kaftan.

Vlad braced a hand on his thigh, pitched forward and caught the rivulets with his tongue. Chased them back up to the bite and then began to lick the mark with methodical steadiness. He already felt better, his head clearer, his limbs stronger. The thirst was slaked enough that he could tamp it down and focus now on healing, rather than harming.

Still, George jerked beneath him at the first swipe of Vlad's tongue. His voice was steady, though, when he said, "What are you doing?"

"I have to seal it," Vlad explained between licks. "Or the blood will ruin your clothes."

"Oh." George shifted a little, but then settled, and waited. "Alright."

When Vlad pulled back, the bleeding had stopped, and the messy raw wound looked only like two punctures and the purple-blue indentations of the rest of his teeth. Not a drop of blood had been spilled, save the last bit that he licked off his lips before flopping backward and lying along the pew, breathing heavily through his mouth. He was dizzy, but not sick-dizzy, like he had been before; this was the headrush of slowly fading euphoria.

Rustle of fabric: George buttoning up his kaftan, no doubt. Creak of the pew as he stood, footsteps, and then George appeared standing above him, bite now hidden by his collar, expression guarded.

Vlad draped an arm over his eyes and concentrated on the pulses of energy moving like lightning through his veins. "Thank you for the drink," he said, still breathless. "It worked wonders."

A beat passed before George said, "You're welcome." Then, hesitant: "Is it...are you always like...like this?" He coughed politely.

"Like what? Wildly aroused?" Vlad snorted. "No. Only when it's living blood. Other times it's just a nice pleasant warmth."

197

"Oh. Well." Even without looking, Vlad could imagine the discomfort on his face.

Vlad barked a rude laugh. "I wouldn't have fucked you, if that's what you're worried about. I don't like other boys that way."

"Yes. Well. Um. Alright…"

Vlad lifted his arm a fraction and peeked up at him. For once, George didn't look like the much-older pseudo-uncle of the group, instead red-faced, and uncertain, and awkward.

Vlad chuckled and covered his eyes again. For the first time since their capture, he wasn't blisteringly angry about something. No, he was flying instead, sky-high and pleasantly tired, and sated. The arousal was a dull itch, something that might be fun to explore, but which wasn't pressing the more his heartbeat slowed.

"Go back to your studies, Iskander Bey," Vlad said, tone imperious. "Before I change my mind."

He laughed out loud when he heard George's hurried footsteps across the flagstones.

~*~

Four days later, Vlad walked up to Mehmet in the practice yard and fixed him with a dark look. They were both fresh from their studies, neither sweaty nor winded yet. The heir was in the process of wrapping his wrists, to brace them for the sparring to come.

Vlad said, "I want a rematch."

All conversation stopped around them; there was only the trill of birds from beyond the walls.

Mehmet finishing tying off his bandages at his leisure, and then cast a glance to his left, toward George, and then right, toward the sword master – who was currently occupying the only patch of shade in the yard, head ducked down in disinterest.

Then he looked at Vlad. Crooked smirk, fangs flashing. "Are you speaking to me, Wallachian?"

Vlad very pointedly didn't growl. "I don't see anyone else here I might have a grudge against, do you?"

"Heh." The heir breathed a laugh. But his eyes were hard, jewel-bright. "You're confident, I'll give you that."

198

"I'm a better swordsman than you, too."

"Then why'd I beat you half to death last time?"

"I got distracted. It won't happen again." The back of his neck itched; he could feel Val's gaze on him from across the yard, but he would not turn. Would not react to the slow-blooming fear-scent coming from that direction.

"Boys," George tried.

Mehmet stood from the bench in one quick motion, and sliced a hand through the air, silencing the older boy. "Stay out of this, hostage."

George sighed. Vlad thought he might have thrown up his hands, but didn't turn his head to look. "Fine. So be it."

Vlad, chosen practice sword already in his hand, backed away toward the center of the yard. Kept his eyes trained on Mehmet as the heir went to the wall where the weapons were kept and selected one after several long moments of deliberation.

"Your weapon won't make a difference," Vlad taunted. "I'll beat you regardless."

Mehmet chuckled, and finally drew a length of bright, ringing steal from a scabbard left propped against the wall.

Vlad's pulse kicked. That was no practice sword, was instead a sharpened blade.

Mehmet turned toward him, sunlight gliding down the length of his sword. He adopted an innocent expression. "A problem?"

Vlad settled into a ready stance, his blunted sword held in a sure grip. "No."

"Mehmet," George started to protest, and then apparently thought better of it, falling silent.

"Well?" Vlad said.

Mehmet grinned. Lifted his sword. In a delighted voice too low for anyone else to hear: "You know, I think your brother missed you while you were healing. He looked so lonely. All by his pretty lonesome..."

Vlad tightened his grip on his sword and refused to take the bait. Mehmet wanted him to take the first swing, but he wouldn't do it. He'd learned his lesson last time, and he was patient. Had always been patient.

He edged to the right, circling, slow, forcing Mehmet to turn with him. "Tell me." His voice was even. "Does your holy book allow you to find boys 'pretty'?"

Mehmet's smile became a baring of teeth, instead. "You wish to talk of religion?" Words laced with insult.

"No," Vlad said. "My grandfather was a god. I don't give a *fuck* about your religion."

"The god of what? Submission? Servitude?"

"God of *War*," Vlad growled, and made his first move.

A vicious swing, one that Mehmet blocked just in time. He grunted when their blades clashed. A high metallic screech as Vlad powered past the block and his sword slid against the other one.

Mehmet leapt back, and they faced off again. The heir was panting now, sweat gleaming at his temples from just one meeting.

Vlad took a measured breath and moved against him again.

In the time since their last encounter, Vlad had realized something. Mehmet was an ambitious, clever, learned boy. An ideal heir in that respect. And he was a vampire, so he was strong, and quick; a formidable opponent to be sure.

But Vlad was a son of Rome. Brought up like a Spartan child; taught to fight, and shoot, and ride, and run, and kill. And he wasn't an heir. He was a second son. And second sons were bred for one purpose: war.

When he thought about it like that, his previous defeat was an embarrassment.

He wouldn't make the same mistake twice.

Vlad launched an aggressive offensive, strike after strike, cutting in from a new angle each time, pushing forward with sure steps. Mehmet could only parry and block, stumbling back. He bared his teeth, and the tendons stood out in his neck as he worked to deflect the kind of blows that would cut even with a dulled blade; that would shatter bones. Vlad wasn't training anymore, and he knew it.

Vlad had pushed the heir an entire circle of the training yard when he felt his strength begin to flag. Even vampires couldn't go forever. He needed a break, now, before his arms started to shake and he left himself an opening.

He dropped low, under Mehmet's intended block and swept his blade at his ankles. It connected.

Mehmet shouted and went down, turning the fall into a controlled tuck and roll. He popped up a few meters away, unsteady on his feet, breathing hard through his mouth, fangs fully extended.

"Yield?" Vlad asked.

Mehmet growled; loud, and deep, and panther-like. There would be no mistaking what he was after this. If any witness hadn't already known, they would know now.

What the hell. Vlad growled back.

A soft gasp, off to the side. "Brother." Val.

Vlad ignored it. This time, he let Mehmet come to him.

A run, a leap, a high, arcing swing.

Vlad dodged it neatly and brought his own sword up, a flash of silver in the sunlight. He heard the crunch of bone as Mehmet's shoulder shattered.

The heir yelled and went to his knees. His arm hung at an unnatural angle. He braced the knuckles of his other hand down in the sawdust, sword hilt still gripped in his fist.

Vlad paced around him. "You were turned," he said, "and I was born. That's a very big difference, *your grace.*"

When Mehmet lifted his head…he was smiling. Teeth stained red with blood where he'd bit his tongue. "Wouldn't you like to know who turned me?" he asked, his laughter pained, tight. "It's a fascinating story."

"Not interested." Vlad lifted his sword.

Shouts now, from the onlookers, finally. Because this was him raising arms against an opponent who'd fallen. Dimly, a voice in the back of his head warned him what would happen if he struck the prince while he was down. He'd be flogged. Probably killed.

Did he care?

No.

But…

The long game, George had said. *Patience.* Because one day they would send him home as their trained dog, and—

It was a moment of hesitation, and that was all Mehmet needed.

He pushed up onto one knee, and brought his sword with him.

Vlad parried, shoved him away, kicked him in the ribs –

"Stop," someone was saying behind him, over and over, an angry adult voice.

Mehmet tried to run him through, sun winking off the sharp edge of his sword.

Vlad avoided the stab, but he tripped, and went down hard on one elbow.

Mehmet made a triumphant sound, and Vlad kicked him again, in the hand this time. Fingers broke with a little snap. Mehmet snarled, an animal sound of mixed fury and pain, and then, suddenly, neither of them was armed, and they were grappling in the dirt like beasts. Fangs, and claws and struggling lungs, and hate, hate, hate.

Vlad felt blunt nails rake his skin, and hard heels kick at his belly, and he didn't care, because he just wanted to kill this boy. The rank smell of another vampire, a rival, filled his sinuses and he *hated* him.

"Damn you, stop it!" A hand latched onto the back of Vlad's collar; he was aware that it was George, and that he was about to be pulled away from his opponent.

Vlad found Mehmet's throat and bit him.

This was a mistake. Because when the blood filled his mouth – oily, putrid, wrong – he realized, immediately, who had turned this boy.

Vlad went limp and let George drag him backward, opening his lips, letting the blood run out, down his chin, his throat. Spitting it, wanting it off his tongue.

Mehmet – bloody, and filthy, and winded, face pale with shock – laughed at him, eyes glazed. "Do you see now?" he taunted, wheezing. "Do you understand, Vlad? Your uncle sends his regards."

It was Romulus.

Romulus had turned the sultan's heir.

~*~

They stripped off his kaftan and shirt and had him press his hands flat to a wall. A janissary did the caning, because his arms were stronger. Vlad bit his tongue, and the insides of his cheeks, but he did not scream.

He pissed blood for the next twenty-four hours, but he didn't weep over it.

They took him to a cramped room with a sloppy pallet. He wasn't to be allowed to sleep alongside his brother anymore, who, they told him, was being moved to one of the pavilions that housed the other hostages. But he didn't fret.

As his bruises faded, and the marks healed, Vlad could only think of the foul taste of a rival's blood in his mouth, flavored with the blood his uncle had pressed to his tongue with a single pricked fingertip, so that he might know it in the future.

So that he'd know it in this inevitable moment, Vlad now knew.

Romulus had turned Mehmet, but he didn't understand *why*.

No…that wasn't strictly true. He knew why Romulus *would*…why *anyone* would…he just hadn't thought…

He rolled over, teeth clenched against the painful welts on his back, and stared out through the barred window. A cloudy, starless night had fallen across the mountains, the sky indigo and rain-scented. He thought of his father's regal profile, his gentle smiles, the flicker of his lashes as he read a Latin volume and chewed thoughtfully at the inside of his lip. The legend of Remus was no legend at all, but his real life, his real past; an oversight and trust that had warred within him in his new life as Vlad II. Did he raise his sons with love? Or bring them up to question everything?

Vlad thought the result shook out somewhere in the middle. Vlad was suspicious, Val trusting and sweet, and Mircea fell somewhere between, the well-balanced heir.

But all of them had distrusted Romulus. The king who'd tried to kill their father.

And all of them had sipped his blood, and called him "uncle," and wanted to believe that – without a throne – he was a changed man.

But he'd turned the Ottoman heir.

Who was their enemy…at the very least their liege lord. And…

And Vlad could find no justification for that outside of treachery.

Sleep came slowly that night, and was filled with helpless nightmares.

The next morning, he chose a rug directly behind his brother; gritted his teeth and refused to handle himself gingerly despite the pain that flared from healing bruises.

"Radu," he started, and when that earned him only a stiffening of narrowed shoulders, whispered, "Valerian."

Val was seated, as usual, between the Serbian princes Stepan and Gregor. For the first few weeks of the brothers' captivity, the Serbian princes had been attended by a slave during their lessons. Val had, through innate kindness, adopted the role for them. So when Val turned, the other boys turned as well, though they couldn't see Vlad.

"Not you, idiots," he hissed at them, and they hastily faced forward again. They knew his voice; they'd listened to him snarl and growl and beat the heir with a practice sword. Vlad wondered if they'd heard the shattering of bone, the way that he had.

Val's pretty face was carefully composed; guarded. It pained Vlad to see, but he knew it was for the best. He might always be golden and beautiful, but he could at least harden himself.

Vlad crooked a finger. *Closer.*

Val hesitated a long moment, gaze screened by his lashes – so long that Vlad began to fear the mullahs would enter and take the crop to the back of his neck. But finally, Val leaned in and said, "What?"

"The next time you go walking, I need you to take a message home. I got a taste of his blood – I know who turned Mehmet."

"Who?"

"Uncle Romulus."

Val's cool mask slipped. His brows leapt, and his mouth fell open. Not just fear, but terror bloomed on his skin, a sudden sweat that was acrid to Vlad's nose. "What? Are you – are you–"

"I'm sure. He had us taste his blood remember?" That was something that had dogged his nightmares. "I think he'd already done it then, and he wanted us to know." He felt the grim lines of his expression. "He knew we would get captured. Or maybe even helped to orchestrate it."

"But..." Val's breath came in quick little pants. "Why would he...?"

"Because he's tainted, and he always has been." And he was, but Vlad knew that wasn't the whole truth. There was something else there, something he was missing. Romulus might very well be the sort of man who enjoyed the suffering of others – and clearly he was. Perhaps he was jealous that he was now unknown and exiled, while father was a prince, with a family, a loyal contingent of wolves.

But something prickled at the back of Vlad's mind. The understanding that he was, after all, still just a boy, and that Romulus was working a scheme that he didn't yet fully comprehend.

"He turned our enemy," Val whispered, eyes glazed, face slack. "Our enemy. And set us against him." He gripped the fabric of his own kaftan, knuckles white.

"I need you to go walking tonight," Vlad repeated. "I need you to warn Mother, warn Mircea. Father, if you can find him. Tell the wolves. Tell them what we're dealing with. If Romulus is at the palace..."

And he hadn't thought of *that* until just now. He swallowed an unsteady breath. "Can you do that?"

Val pushed his hands through his hair, grimacing. But he said, "Yes. As soon as I can, I will."

It would have to be enough, because that was all Vlad could do.

~*~

George found him in the chapel that afternoon. "Mehmet's healing well, they say," he said as he dropped down onto the pew beside Vlad. "Then again, they wouldn't say if he wasn't. So. Anyone's guess, really."

Vlad nodded to himself.

George sighed. "What happened to being patient, Vlad?"

"I am patient. But I needed to settle the score."

Another sigh, weary and long-suffering.

"You disagree?"

"No, I…no," George admitted. When Vlad said nothing else, George prompted, "So that was it? A beating for a beating? That was your plan?"

Strange as it seemed, the older boy seemed not only curious, but lost, too. Searching for answers.

"I did want to beat him, yes," Vlad said. "I also needed to know how strong he was." He left off the part about the blood. He'd come as close to trusting Iskander Bey as he ever had anyone, but there were some things he would never voice to someone outside his immortal family.

"Yes? And what were your findings on that matter?"

Vlad smirked. "He might be immortal, but he's not as strong as me." And there was something *wrong* in his blood. Romulus's famous taint. He had not a single bred child, and now Vlad thought he understood why.

"And now what will you do?" Less curiosity, more test.

Vlad turned to face him, brows raised.

"Press your strength advantage? Kill him?"

"Speak plainly."

George chuckled. "You are stubborn." Then it faded. "When Mehmet first came to court, before I knew what he was, I thought I could have killed him. During practice, during a sparring session, just like yesterday. Now, I know that he could have healed—"

"The heart."

"What?"

"Vampires can overcome even the most grievous of wounds – save those mortal to the heart. Cut it out, ruin it beyond repair: it's the heart that counts."

George's face went blank with surprise. "Huh."

"Just thought I'd pass that along."

"Alright. Yes. Well. As I was saying, I could have. Or at least tried. But I didn't. Because it isn't just about the immediate victory. If I'd killed Mehmet, they would have impaled me and mounted me on the wall as an example to the others. And then another heir would have been chosen. Legitimacy isn't an issue with the Ottomans; Murat doubtless has other get, or could have gotten more. The empire would have ruled on, Mehmet or no. That kind of assassination wouldn't have helped my people – nor any of the people forced to live as vassals.

"But," he continued, eyes shining, "if Mehmet is beaten in the field, if the empire is forced out, that *will* make a difference. I meant what I said before about the long game. It isn't about me, here and now, or you, or any of us hostages. It's about fighting for the freedom of our people."

"That…makes sense."

Tone wry, George said, "Then why do I have the feeling I'll have to remind you of the fact often?"

Vlad shrugged. "I'm just stubborn."

~*~

Val dream-walked to Father's study that night. It was late, but a dozen candles flickered, the room dancing with light. Mircea sat at the desk; the heavy wooden piece with its ornate chair had always suited father, but looked comically large swallowing up Val's brother. Like a boy playing pretend – only it was real, and all the more tragic for it.

Val cleared his throat as he stepped up to the desk, so as not to startle him.

Mircea jumped a little anyway, but recovered quickly, smiling tiredly when he laid eyes on Val. "Little brother," he greeted.

"Hello, Mircea." Val noted the lines on his brother's face, the crinkles at the corners of his eyes that hadn't been there before. "I've…" He faltered; it seemed cruel to lay more at his feet, when the desk was piled high with ledgers and correspondence.

"What, Radu? What is it?"

By the door, a shadow moved; Cicero, shifting his weight. Val was glad to see the wolves were watching after the new prince, even if he was only half-vampire.

Val didn't know what his face was doing, but when he looked at Cicero, made contact with his glinting golden eyes, the wolf stepped away from his post and came forward.

"What?" he asked, tone gentler than Val was used to from him. A grave sadness lay etched in his face; his bound master had been taken, and he struggled with the itch and pull of instinct.

Val took a deep breath and looked back and forth between them. "I have to tell you something. I told you the heir was a vampire? Well, Vlad got a taste of his blood–"

Cicero made a low noise that Val could have sworn was proud.

Mircea groaned and put a hand to his forehead. "Oh, *Vlad*…"

"We know who turned him now," Val continued. "It was Romulus."

Both of them froze. The only movement in the room was the dance of candle flames.

Then Cicero growled.

"Are you certain?" Mircea asked, but his white-rimmed eyes and his shaking hand proved that he already believed.

"Vlad's always certain."

Mircea sat back, hands braced on the desk. "This changes things," he muttered. "This…this is…"

Cicero crossed to the window in three long strides and peered out into the night, growling low, figurative hackles raised.

"Has Uncle been back here?" Val asked. "Since we were taken?"

Mircea shook his head and seemed to gather his wits. "No, not since then. He sent a note via courier, asking if I needed anything, saying I should call on him if–" He shuddered. "Damn it, Father should never have let him in the palace! He should have turned him away the second he dared to show his face. Once a brother-killer, always a brother-killer. He hasn't changed at all!"

Cicero latched the shutters and came back to the desk, shaking his head. "Your father has a forgiving spirit." He didn't say what he truly meant, but Val could read his tone well enough: *your father is a sentimental fool.*

"But I just don't understand – *why*," Mircea said. His eyes had glazed over. When he ran his hands through his sable hair, he tugged at it, hard; it had to hurt, but he didn't seem to notice.

Cicero glanced at Val, and then at Mircea, gaze knowing, sympathetic. He also looked like he thought they were stupid boys. He sighed. "Romulus has never been able to have an heir." He waited, expecting them to pick up the story. When they didn't: "Your father didn't tell you? Of course not." A sigh. "He's sterile. He can't breed an heir. But he wanted one – or he used to, back in the Roman days. He was obsessed, Remus says."

Val stared at him. "You think Mehmet is – is his *heir*?"

Mircea's mouth fell open. "If – if he wanted an heir–" he spluttered. "Why not name one of the three of us?"

"You misunderstand me, your grace," Cicero said, bowing his head in deference. "Romulus doesn't have any property or riches – he has no legacy. But I think…" He hesitated. Wolves – especially bound wolves – took subservience seriously.

"Go on," Mircea said, gently, "I want to hear your thoughts, Cicero."

The wolf lifted his head, expression steely. "It isn't my place to say so, your grace, because I don't know it for a fact. But I think that Romulus wants to gain some property. A seat of power. He could fight someone for it…or he could appoint an already powerful boy as his heir and then take it from him, when the time is right."

Slowly, Mircea reached for the cup at his elbow – the rosy glow of wine – and brought it to his lips. Drained it dry in one long gulp, head thrown back. "God," he breathed after, hand clenched tight around the cup. "My God, I think you're right. This is – this is disturbing. It's *untenable*."

"Does he hate us?" Val asked Cicero. His heart throbbed in his chest, uneven, lurching beats. "Does he really?"

Cicero sent him an apologetic look. "I don't know. He might. Then again, it might just be his nature. He's the son of a god, and I'm just a wolf. I won't pretend to understand."

A dark thought occurred. "Father's gone," Val said. He breathed so quick and unsteady that his voice fluttered. "Father's gone, and maybe that's – maybe Uncle means to march on Wallachia, maybe he already has his army, maybe this is just–"

The top of his head swirled up into mist.

Cicero pulled his hand back, expression oddly unguarded; caught out with dismay. "Apologies, your grace." He'd been trying to lay a steadying hand on his head. To comfort him.

Fenrir, as Mother's wolf, had always been affectionate and familiar with him and Vlad. But Cicero, as Father's, trusted confidante and battle consultant, had always seemed cool and removed; Val had sensed that he didn't care about the plight of boys.

But he'd been wrong. This sudden show of caring brought tears to his eyes. He blinked them away and did his best to control his voice. "Cicero, do you think Romulus's plan was to have Father removed so that he could take Tîrgovişte for his own?"

"I suspect not," he said, grimly. "If he was going to move against us, he would have done so in the early days, before Mircea was officially installed, while there was chaos. And also." Here he looked pained. "I think Wallachia is too small for his great ambition. If you'd waited this many centuries to make your move, would you settle for one vassal state? Or would you want the whole empire?"

It made horrifying sense.

"You're right," Mircea said. He looked at his cup, as if willing it to refill itself. "You are absolutely right."

Something tugged at Val's guts. His edges thinned.

He made a noise in his throat, and the others looked at him.

"My body," he said. "I have to go back. Someone's–"

And then he was gone, spinning away through the stars, opening his eyes to his dark room in the palace at Edirne.

A figure stood over him, limned in faint silver by the moonlight beyond the window bars. Val couldn't make out the face, but he didn't need to; he could smell that it was Mehmet.

Dread boiled up in his stomach, cold and fast. He swallowed the urge to retch. He clutched at the bedclothes, caught between fleeing and pulling them over his head. Where would he

run if he even tried to? He didn't think it was possible to run away
from a prince in his own palace.

"Shh," Mehmet murmured, and sank down on the edge of
his pallet. The moonlight caught the white of bandages on his
healing shoulder. Carved a line down his face: deep-set eye, high
cheekbone, strong jaw losing the last of its puppy fat to manhood.
His mother was Greek, all the rumors said; he looked it now. "It's
alright, little one. Don't be frightened."

Frightened wasn't the word for it. Every sense he possessed
told him to get as far away from him as possible – as far away
from his pulsing energy as possible. Even when he smiled, teeth
gleaming, Val read a threat into it. No, he was *terrified*.

"What were you dreaming of just now?" Mehmet asked.
"Your lips were moving. And your brows were unhappy." He
leaned forward – Val held his breath and pressed back into the
pillow – and touched the space between them, the little worried
groove there. "Was it a nightmare?"

"Y-yes."

Mehmet pulled back with a murmured sound of sympathy.
He rested his hand on the edge of the feather mattress, right
beside Val's knee. "I have nightmares, too. The slaves tell me I
shout in my sleep sometimes."

Val's heartbeat tapped out a rhythm in his fingertips, his
throat; he felt it pound in his temples.

"Radu." His voice was hesitant in a way Val had never heard
before. Heavy and introspective. "You...you know what I am.
Don't you? Because you're the same thing."

Val held still.

"I can smell that you are. I can almost – I can almost *taste*
it." He inhaled deeply. "That's been the strangest part of all this,
the way everything is so intense. Your brother said that the two
of you were born, and not turned. Is that so?"

He didn't want to answer, but he didn't think he had a
choice. "Yes."

"So that means both of your parents are vampires? My." He
smiled again. "That's incredible. Your father is Remus isn't he?
Brother to the first king of Rome?"

"I...I don't think I'm supposed to talk about that."

211

When Mehmet laughed, it was a boy's laugh. "You're darling. What a sweet boy." He moved his hand, so it covered Val's knee; his tiny knee, the cap of which could have fit twice over in the heir's cupped palm. It burned warm through the covers. "Your loyalty to your family is an admirable trait, Radu. But perhaps misplaced here. It was your uncle who turned me. Surely Vlad told you this?" He cocked his head, lifted a single brow.

Val nodded.

"Doesn't that make us family, after a fashion?"

"I...don't know."

"Well, I think it does. My father is my father, but isn't Romulus a sort of second father? The one who sired me into a new sort of life?"

"I suppose."

Mehmet smiled again. "Romulus spoke so fondly of his nephews. He wanted us to be friends. To be brothers. Family." He was beaming, moonlight glinting off his teeth. "It's what I want as well."

Vlad will never be your friend, Val wanted to say.

Romulus means to topple us with you – and then the world.

But he saw sincerity in that smile, heard it in the gentle laugh. Maybe Mehmet didn't know. Maybe he was just another chess piece on the board.

The heir squeezed his knee and then stood; he held himself at awkward angles, still sore from his beating. "You should go back to sleep. I'm sorry I disturbed you."

That's alright, Val started to say, but he couldn't form the words. He watched Mehmet walk to the door, and tried, unsuccessfully, to interpret the look thrown his way before the heir slipped out.

Much later, he would know that gaze had been predatory, and always question if he could have stopped the things that happened next.

19

OATH

1443

The bay mare was small-boned but quick, fleet-footed as a mountain goat. She flew across the grass, despite his weight. When he looked at his reflection in the mirror – lithe, ropey with muscle, sharp-faced and snakelike – Vlad didn't think he looked heavy. But muscle counted more than fat; he tweaked the left rein with a flick of his fingers and the mare ducked that way. He could feel her tiring, but she was determined; maybe as determined as him. She was a hunter's mount, and the hunt was not yet finished.

Overhead, his falcon wheeled, still searching.

And then she dove.

Vlad rode to the edge of the tree line, slowing his mare to a canter, then a trot, and finally halting her right at the edge. He listened for the sounds a human could never have heard: the rustle of wings, the shifting of leaves. He lifted his gauntleted arm and the falcon came winging out between branches, hare clutched in her talons. She dropped onto his arm and let him take the rabbit from her, and feed her a bit of meat from the pouch at his belt.

"There's a pretty girl," he murmured, and swore the bird preened.

Someone whistled for him, and he turned to see a rider cantering toward him across the field. In the distance, the palace walls rose in an unbroken white line, monolithic and impenetrable.

The rider was George, nearly as winded as his blowing horse.

"What?" The falcon shifted nervously on his arm, and he tightened his fist around her jesses.

George reined up alongside him, expression guarded in that careful way that meant he had news. "The sultan–" He hesitated, frowning. "The sultan has sent for you. I intercepted the slave on his way to get you. You have a formal audience."

Vlad felt his features tighten. He tamped down on a growl, lest it spook his animals. "Why? What news from the north?"

George shook his head. "I don't know. But there is…something else. You should talk to him. And you should hurry."

~*~

He handed his horse off to a groom and washed hastily in the fountain of the stable yard. Pushed his damp hair off his face and followed the nervously waiting slave with water dripping down into his collar and off his cuffs.

Sultan Murat awaited him in a far corner of the shady part of the garden. A vine-choked pergola shielded a bench beside a chuckling fountain, and that was where the sultan sat, clothed all in white to combat the heat, gazing serenely into the tumbling water. Two guards and a vizier stood at attention a short distance away.

The vizier leaned forward as Vlad approached, and hissed, "Watch yourself, boy. This is an honor beyond imagining. If you so much as raise a finger toward him…"

Vlad gave him a flat look. Stared at him until the fussy little man turned away with a disgruntled sniff…and a slight tremor in his hand.

Then he ducked beneath the fragrant vines and faced the sultan. "Your Majesty," he said. It wasn't a respectful tone.

The sultan noticed. He lifted his head, expressionless save the raising of his brows. "Not Your Majesty any longer," he said in Turkish, and Vlad understood every word, because he was fluent now.

Vlad didn't ask what he meant. He waited.

"I've abdicated," Murat said, finally, his gaze steady. "Mehmet is the sultan now, and he readies to leave Edirne."

Vlad was shocked. He hoped it didn't show on his face, and thought he succeeded in masking all emotion.

The sultan's – former sultan's – brows lifted a fraction higher. "You have nothing to say? Your rival will no longer be in the schoolroom with you; do you have no feelings on that?"

214

"No, sir. None."

A subdued smile tugged at one corner of the man's mouth. Or maybe it was just a tic. "I also wished to inform you that your father has been released back to Wallachia."

Oh.

"He's signed a new treaty with us. He swore an oath, on the Bible and the Quran, to be faithful. He paid a tribute of ten-thousand gold ducats, and has agreed to send us five-hundred boys for the Janissary Corps. Do those sound like agreeable terms to you?"

"It is not my place to have an opinion on the matter, sir."

A chuckle that was like the scrape of metal over stone. "Where has the disobedient Vlad Dracula gone? Replaced instead with a mannerly boy of temperance, eh?"

"Sir." The real Vlad, the disobedient dragon's son, was alive and well. But he'd grown patient in his captivity, at the urging of his friend. He'd learn to rake dirt over his furious coals and let them smolder; he trained, and he learned, and he dedicated himself to knowing all that he could about his captors.

And he waited.

Murat studied him, head canted to the side. "It's a shame," he drawled, "that you and my son could never be friends. He could have learned from you – you have something which, despite all his wonderful qualities, he lacks."

"Sir?"

That almost-smile again. "My Mehmet is made of fire. But *you*. You are made of steel."

Behind his back, Vlad's hands curled into fists.

"That will be all. Dismissed."

He did not feel relieved as he walked away; that wasn't possible for him anymore. But something inside him unclenched a fraction. Father was safe. Without Mehmet around, Val would be safe. And someday, they would get to go home. Maybe even in one piece.

~*~

215

Val could draw a bow now. He could nock an arrow and draw the string back to his cheek, hold it there, let out half a breath, and take aim. The *thunk* of the arrow landing in the bullseye filled him with a rush of rare satisfaction.

"Well done," the instructor said behind him.

Val felt himself smile, and was surprised by the fact. Training had never before been a call for smiling.

The arrows waited at his feet, heads sunk in the grass. He plucked up the next and fired again.

When the target was bristling, he turned to ask the instructor about his form – and pulled up short. Vlad stood a few paces behind the old janissary, arms folded, gaze unreadable.

Val swallowed his leaping heart back down, handed his bow off, and went to meet his brother.

There had been whispers around the palace. A court couldn't help but gossip – from dignitaries, to scribes and viziers, to soldiers and servants. Val had even heard the slave boys whispering in the secluded corners of the baths. His hearing was better than that of a human, and so he'd heard the wild speculation: chiefly, that he and Vlad were not full brothers. Vlad, with his pale face, and dark cascading hair, and Slavic bone structure, was believed to be Vlad Dracul's trueborn son. But Val they called a bastard. They didn't know that Mother was golden; that she was a secret; that she'd carried both boys in her womb, and kissed their brows, and sung them to sleep.

The other bit of gossip was that the Wallachian brothers – half-brothers, they all swore – hated one another.

In so many ways, that was the tale that hurt the most. Because Val feared that it was true. On Vlad's side of things, at least.

They'd never argued. Vlad hadn't even been unkind. But he was cold. No smiles, and no touches, no acknowledgement of any kind. It was if he didn't regard them as brothers either – even half would have been better than this cold nothing.

Val had never met anyone as perfectly composed as Vlad Dracula.

"Brother," he greeted quietly, formally, when he stood in front of him.

216

Vlad kept his voice low, out of human reach. "I just talked with the sultan. He's abdicated."

"What?"

"Keep your voice down. Yes, he's stepped down. Old and tired, he said. Mehmet will be sultan now."

A hard shiver stole over him. Vlad's lifted brows told him all he needed to know: yes, Mehmet would be sultan, and that meant he would no longer be a fixture in their lives. A relief to be sure. Mehmet had never behaved aggressively toward Val; quite the opposite. He smiled at him, and sometimes, briefly, would pet his golden hair, grown out now halfway down his back. "Little one," he called him, and his eyes stayed fastened to him for long moments; Val could feel their weight tracing the delicate wings of his collarbones.

But what did any of that *mean*? Being in Mehmet's presence stoked anxiety deep in his gut. Some of that was thanks, no doubt, to the memory of a practice sword connecting with the side of Vlad's head. The awful crack of bone breaking.

But some of it was personal. Disquiet moved over his skin like gooseflesh in the heir's – the *sultan's* – presence. Iskander Bey had squeezed his shoulder and told him that he shouldn't worry on it…but his own eyes had been worried for him.

What sort of sultan would Mehmet be? What would it mean for the treaty? For Father, and for them–

Before he could get lost down that mental trail, Vlad said, "Father's been released. There's a new treaty, and he's going home."

Tears pricked Val's eyes and he blinked them away. "Good," he said unsteadily. "That's good." He didn't dare ask about their own circumstances; he knew better than to hope. It was an almost-crushing relief just to hear that Father was well. In the past two years, Val had tried to visit him, but they'd cuffed Dracul with silver, and so Val had never been able to get within sight of him when he dream-walked. An old trick, Mother had said, and sworn under her breath. A dirty one.

"Father will be negotiating for our release soon. I thought you should know," Vlad said.

"Thank you."

He stayed a moment, and Val thought he might – but then he nodded and turned his back.

No, it wasn't hate. It was worse than that; an absence of feeling altogether.

~*~

Val didn't find Father in his study. That room was empty, so he passed through the hall and made his way to Dracul's bedchamber. He hesitated a moment on the other side of the closed door, listening for voices, and then he passed through.

It was early, just after dark, but his father was already in bed. He sat upright, covers puddled in his lap, staring down at his hands. The silver cuffs had left pink marks on his wrists; they would probably scar.

A single lantern burned on the dresser. Cicero sat in a chair against the wall, statue-still, just beyond the light's reach. If he'd been there physically, Val thought he'd be able to smell the wolf's blended satisfaction and worry. His master was home; but his master was not yet himself.

"Father?" Val said.

Dracul's head lifted. There were new lines on his face. Immortals didn't age the way that humans did, but stress could still carve fissures in their smooth facades. Like rain eating slowly at marble.

A smile broke crooked across his face. "My son. You have no idea how wonderful it is to see you." Tears glittered unshed in his eyes.

Val walked forward to the bed, projected hands suspended over the edge of the feather mattress, useless. "Father – Papa. Are you – you aren't hurt, are you?"

He smiled. "No, no. Only tired. It was a long journey."

Cicero gave a quiet chuff over against the wall, an animal sound of displeasure.

"What about you, my Radu?" He tilted his head. "You've grown."

"I have?" Val looked down at himself with surprise. He knew his hair had grown, and his boots had grown too tight and been replaced. His face was perhaps narrower. But grown? He was still just a slip of a thing. Still Helga's bouquet of flowers. He thought he always would be.

Dracul chuckled. "Of course. That's what boys do." When Val looked at him again, his face fell. "How have they been treating you boys?"

Val swallowed. "We are well-fed. Well-exercised. We can speak Turkish, and we've learned much of geography, and art, and warfare. We've studied Machiavelli, and the Quran. I can use a bow now, Papa. I'm even good at it."

"That's wonderful…but it's not what I asked." His face was pained.

Val took a breath. "We're alright. We are." Though he couldn't keep the despair from his voice. "Vlad. He – sometimes he's willful. They use the crop on him."

"Nothing he can't handle, then." But that wasn't the point.

"He's angry, Father," he admitted. "Blisteringly angry. But he hides it deep, and is cold on the outside."

Dracul sighed. "That's how he is." He shook his head. "I wish I could bring you home. I–" His voice broke, and he cleared his throat.

Cicero stood and went to the pitcher waiting on the dresser to pour a cup of water.

Val's breath lodged in his throat. "Do you mean…" But he knew. He *knew*.

"Radu. I can't rework the negotiations. The treaty only works so long as you're hostages. I have to obey it, or else they'll…"

Kill them.

"We can't come home," Val said, numb.

"I'm sorry, son. But no. Not yet."

~*~

They sent Iskander Bey home.

Vlad sat on his usual pew in the chapel, gaze trained unseeing on the cross. In his two years here, the crawling ivy had never overtaken it. A more romantic soul than him would have called it divine intervention.

Vlad was Roman – half. But he was not romantic. He knew the ivy had been trimmed by the hand of a slave, some boy stolen from his home after his parents were slaughtered.

He heard the scrape of new boots over stone and did not turn.

George settled next to him; the pew creaked. He smelled of soap, and powder, and floral oils. A prince cleaned up and dressed in new finery from his homeland, set to return with a contingent of Ottoman cavalry and terms of lasting peace.

Vlad said, "They trust you, then."

"I've worked hard to ensure that they do."

Vlad turned to him, then. His beard had been oiled and combed; his hair fell in pale sheets down his back. He looked every inch the prince; the persona of hostage had been stripped away.

Vlad snorted. "Will you still do it? Defy them?"

"In all my years here, that's the only thing I've ever been completely sure about. Yes, I will do it. I said that I would."

"People don't always do what they say they will."

"I do," George said, gaze steady. Like he knew what Vlad was trying valiantly not to think. Like he could sense that Vlad's stomach was folding in on itself, pulling tight with an emotion that he didn't dare name *loss*, because he'd been taken from his home, how could this parting feel anything like loss?

"Vlad," George started, voice gentle, and Vlad couldn't stand it.

He jumped to his feet and put three paces between them, his back to the older boy, arms folded tight across his middle. He was afraid if he let go, the horrible thing boiling in his stomach might climb up his throat; might leave his mouth as a wounded sound, or burn his eyes with unthinkable tears.

"Vlad," George said again, and got to his feet, followed him.

Vlad sensed the hand about to land on his shoulder and whirled, teeth bared, growling. His fangs were showing; he meant to be frightening.

But George's expression was almost tender. "I'm sorry I'm leaving you," he said.

"*Leaving me?*" Vlad scoffed. But the sound that left his mouth was more of a sob than a laugh. "Do you think that I care? What are we – friends? No. Do you think this *hurts* me?"

"I know that it does." Calm and gentle. "I would spare you this, if I could, but I have to return to my people. And you have to continue being patient. Yes?"

Vlad looked away and growled. His vision blurred, and he blinked it clear, furiously.

"It's alright to have friends," George said. "And it's alright to miss them."

Vlad flashed his fangs again, and said nothing. It did hurt. It hurt. There were a dozen little ways that George had helped them, tempering the anger of the mullahs and viziers and even the sultan, probably. He'd watched over Val, and he'd known what Mehmet was, the kind of threat he'd posed. And, worst of all, he'd given Vlad hope that he could survive this; that he had the fortitude to learn, and scheme, and wait, and make his move once he was a free man. Not just a friend, but a light in the dark.

Vlad didn't know if he could carry on alone.

"Don't hate your brother," George suggested. "You need him."

"I don't hate him," Vlad said, honesty shaken loose by the rawness of his emotions. "I love him more than anything."

"Then maybe you should tell him that."

"No." This moment now was proof enough that showing weakness – that he needed anyone – could be used against him to ruinous effect.

George sighed. "You are the stubbornest brat I ever met." And then, before Vlad could shift away, George folded him into a strong embrace. "Take care, Vlad," he murmured in his ear. "I'm holding you to your oath to be allies with me when you leave here."

Despite the awful churning in his gut, and the sting of tears in his eyes, Vlad chuckled. "You had better."

~*~

He was still sitting on the pew an hour later when Val found him. He sensed him coming long before his quiet footfalls struck the flagstones.

Val lingered back by the door, smelling of hesitation…and of hurt. The sadness of a little brother spurned for reasons he couldn't understand.

Vlad's hands trembled, and he laced his fingers together where they hung between his knees. His voice was steady, though. "What?"

A beat. "I've been to see Father."

It took every ounce of Vlad's self-control not to ask for specifics.

"He said–" Val faltered. Took a deep, unsteady breath. "He said that we'll be held here as part of the treaty. And that he's taken an oath to not lift so much as a finger against the Ottomans. Not in any way."

"That's generally what a treaty means," Vlad ground out.

"We can't go home," Val whispered. *Melancholy* was too delicate a word for the emotion that colored his voice, small and hushed though it was.

Vlad stood. When he turned, he found Val dashing his sleeve across his cheeks, drying the evidence of a few hasty tears. He was still as soft-hearted as ever, tender as a bruise.

How will you ever survive this world? Vlad wondered. *How will you grow into a man?*

And internally, his own small, childish fear said, *Father, why? How could you?*

To Val he said, "Did you expect him to fight for us?"

Val reared back in surprise. "He's – he's our father."

"And we're his sons. His *Roman* sons. Were we not raised to understand that it's us who serve Wallachia, and not the other way around? He won't risk our whole people just to have us home."

It was the truth. And it tasted vile on his tongue. He wasn't sure he'd even really believed it until this moment, watching Val's lip quiver, hearing the news from him straight-out.

Vlad swallowed a surge of bile and said, "Fathers who sacrifice everything for the sake of their own children belong in fairy stories, Radu." Val flinched; the name had struck him like a blow. "This is reality. Don't be such a baby."

Val's mouth worked silently a moment. Then he drew in a deep breath and shouted. "I'm not a baby! Stop calling me that!" It was the first time he'd ever said such a thing.

Vlad was glad to hear it. *There.* There was the beginning of the spark he knew must lay dormant in the boy. They were of the same blood; there *must* be some inner steel in Val, ready to be coaxed out. "Then stop acting like one," he said.

He moved to brush past him.

A small hand latched onto his wrist and clung hard, blunt nails biting through fabric and into skin.

Vlad could have shaken him off, but he paused instead, turned to him. Was met with a snarl. And tear-bright eyes.

"Why are you so hateful? Doesn't this bother you?"

Yes. I want to howl. I want to snatch up the nearest sword and slaughter everyone here. And when the blade is dulled, I will tear out their throats with fangs and claws.

He said, "I've always been hateful. It runs in the family."

He twisted his wrist away and left his little brother standing, stunned, beneath the waving ivy and the silently judging cross.

~*~

Vlad saw his first impaled man that summer. A traitor. A vizier who'd intended to betray his sultan to Western forces, passing messages. Mehmet wasn't at Edirne, so his men carried out the orders: they impaled the man on a long wooden stake, up his rectum and out through his chest, and mounted his moaning, half-dead personage on the palace walls. A warning to others. An attraction for flies and ravens.

As a very young boy in Sighișoara, he'd watched from the house's second-floor windows as convicted criminals were led to the bank square and publicly hanged. He remembered the way their necks had sometimes snapped, and sometimes not. The last flailing of feet and hands.

This was more violent, more visceral. This was a spectacle. Like something from the gladiatorial pits; death at the whim of a dictator.

The breeze stirred his hair and he pushed it back off his forehead. *I will do this*, he decided. *One day, I will do this to them.*

And so he did.

20

BLOODSTAINS

Autumn, 1444

An evening breeze came in through the open windows of the Despot of Mistra's study. It ruffled the curtains, and the pages of books left open, but Val couldn't feel it against his skin. He sat cross-legged on a span of empty tabletop, watching the sunset ripen over the pine-studded hills and plateaus. The last fingers of light touched the pale stone buildings with the colors of tangerines and early lemons. The mountains lay quietly in the distance, the gentle spines of some sleeping dragon. He wondered if the air smelled like olive trees; like sap; like the water he could hear tumbling in a courtyard fountain.

George Sphrantzes no longer looked on Val as if he were a ghost or an abomination; he didn't speak to him directly very often, but he'd come to accept his presence in his master's study. Tonight, he had news.

"The message is old at this point," he said, waving the bit of unrolled parchment in his hand. "The pope absolved the Hungarian king, Ladislas, of his treaty with the Ottomans. Murat stepped down, and now Mehmet is sultan. Ladislas," he said, dread heavy in his voice, "has declared a new crusade. He and John Hunyadi are marching south to cross the Danube with Vlad Dracul's blessing. They seek Wallachia's aid in their campaign."

Val sat up straight. His breath caught in his throat. "My father? He–" He choked on air, and both men turned to him.

Constantine studied him with open sympathy. Carefully, he said, "Just because they asked for your father's help doesn't mean he gave it."

"He couldn't." Val's lips – his whole face – felt numb. "If he breaks the treaty, they'll…they'll kill us." The last he whispered, hands shaking where they'd knotted together in his lap.

Sphrantzes looked between them, gaze heavy with regret. His eyes dropped to the page. He read, "Prince Vlad Dracul of

225

Wallachia sends his eldest son and heir, Mircea, along with a contingent of cavalry–"

Val couldn't hear the rest over the pounding of his own heart. He dropped his head into his hands and gripped tight; his body must have been doing it too, back in his bed in Edirne, because he felt the rough scrape of the calluses on his fingertips at his temples; the throb of the veins there.

"…Val." Someone had been saying his name. For a while. "Val." Constantine, voice steady, but gentle. "Val, look at me."

He did, but the familiar, kindly face was of no comfort now. "They'll kill us. They *will*." Maybe he should have been fearing for Mircea's chances in battle, or for father should Ladislas and Hunyadi decide his inability to commit more troops was capitally offensive. But he was ten, and selfish, and right now, all he could think about was his body, and Vlad's, impaled on pikes along the sheer white palace walls.

"You're far too valuable to kill," Sphrantzes said, reasonably.

Constantine sighed. "They won't kill you," he said, softer. "George states it bluntly, but he's correct. You and Vlad are valuable."

"Right." His teeth began to chatter. "They'll just burn out our eyes instead." He closed his own then, swallowing the urge to retch as he thought of Stepan and Gregor, the linen covering the ruined, scarred sockets where their eyes had once been. That was worse than death, he thought.

"Maybe not," Constantine said, sounding less certain now. "But Val, you must be prepared for them to threaten such things. They'll let you think they mean to hurt you, even if they don't. You have to be strong."

Strong like Vlad, who'd bow up his back and take the verdict steely-eyed. Who'd spit in the viziers' faces and call them cowards and monsters.

But Val wasn't brave like that.

"What of their chances?" Sphrantzes asked his friend and master. "The sultan is young, and he's had trouble at home." He gestured to Val.

That was true. Amidst his panic, Val tried to grab onto the news he'd brought with him on this evening's dream-walk, that Mehmet had been plagued with all the troubles anyone could expect for a boy sultan. Religious fanatics stirring up unrest in the city; doubting, back-stabbing viziers; push-back from some of the outer territories. And over it all hung the disquiet of a people who didn't understand why Murat had abdicated. Val had seen the former sultan walking in the garden, offering bits of seed to the birds, sitting quietly on benches with his young, Serbian wife, Mara. He'd abdicated because he was tired, Val thought, and because he didn't have the heart or the stomach for the kind of expansion that some members of his court salivated over.

Mehmet was different, though. Mehmet was ambitious, and full of fire.

Mehmet was a *vampire*; bloodlust was a part of him, body and soul.

"My brother means to give him more trouble," Constantine said.

Sphrantzes lifted his brows in question.

"Orhan, the pretender – John is going to release him."

Orhan. Val knew that name. For years, the Greeks of Byzantium had allowed the Ottoman pretender asylum within the city's impenetrable walls. It was a part of the tenuous peace they shared with the Turks: Orhan got to live, and lavishly at that, but he wasn't allowed to leave on his own recognizance, for fear he'd try to start a revolt.

"God," Sphrantzes said, eyes wide. "How could he? The treaty…"

"It appears it's a time for breaking treaties," Constantine said, tone grim. "I'm afraid my brother still holds out some hope that Rome will send aid to the east."

"There's not much chance of that."

"I'm afraid you're right, old friend." He turned to Val again, and Val had calmed himself enough to register the regret in the man's eyes. "Is there anything else you can tell us?" He regretted having to ask, Val knew. Needing information from him, given the circumstances.

227

He shook his head. "No. There was gossip about Iskander Bey, but–"

"Who?"

"Skanderbeg," Sphrantzes said. "That's what his men call him. The Albanian prince sent home with a Turkish cavalry unit." A bare smile touched his mouth. "He betrayed them immediately and swore an oath to spend the rest of his life fighting the Ottomans."

"He was a hostage with us for a while," Val said. "He's been gone a year."

"Doubtless Hunyadi's tried to recruit him, too," Sphrantzes said.

The two men fell into a conversation that didn't exclude Val, per se, but which didn't need him. He was only a boy, after all, and they had serious matters of state to discuss.

He knew he needed to go back, to wake up, go find Vlad and tell him what he'd learned here. Vlad probably wouldn't respond; he might grunt, if Val was lucky, nod his head once. But they were brothers, and their inevitable demise was something he deserved to know.

But he lingered, here in his astral shape. Got up off the table and willed himself through the wall – his body tugged at him, trying to draw him back, but he pushed on, rematerializing out on the balcony.

The sunset had progressed, now kissing the mountains with lavender and indigo, colorless directly overhead. He lifted his arms and watched his sleeves rustle in the breeze…but still, he couldn't feel it. He didn't understand how projection worked in that sense. Maybe he never would. There were no Familiars at the Ottoman court, and no way to learn without admitting aloud what he was.

The scrape of shoes over stone heralded Constantine's arrival a moment before the despot pulled up alongside Val. He leaned forward and rested his forearms along the railing. The wind toyed with the thick dark curls of his hair, swept them back from his face. He looked pensive, melancholy in that way that Val had learned was characteristic.

It was silent a moment between them. Down below in the valley, sheep baaed as they hurried toward their shepherds and the evening meal, bells tolling faintly around their necks. Doves called. A beautiful, tranquil Greek evening.

Constantine gathered a breath and said, "It's an old tradition: hostage-taking. It's not dishonorable. Even Alexander's beloved Hephaestion was a political hostage to begin with." He turned to face Val. "But tradition doesn't make something more bearable, does it?"

Val turned away, swallowing reflexively. "They're…fair to me. I am clothed, and fed, and I've had an education."

"An Ottoman education."

"Yes."

Constantine's sigh was so deep and heartfelt that, for a moment, Val forgot that he was incorporeal and expected the weight of a comforting hand to land on his shoulder. The words had a similar effect, nonetheless: "You are not Hephaestion, I don't think. And no matter how much he studies him, I don't think Mehmet is the Alexander he thinks himself to be." Softer: "It's perfectly alright to wish for home. For family, and for the education and upbringing of your own people. No matter how kindly treated, a hostage is still a hostage, and that is a bitter medicine to swallow, I'm afraid."

Val's chin trembled, and he clenched his jaw tight to stop it.

"If you would take some advice from a man who's next in line to be emperor," Constantine continued, "then I would urge you and your brother to courteously and carefully comport yourselves when you're brought before the sultan. Cruel as it is to say, George is right: you are too valuable to kill. A little sweetness might dissuade them from maiming you, though."

Val looked back to him, to the earnest sadness in his dark eyes. "Do you believe so?"

"I do."

He nodded. "Alright. I can be sweet."

When he slipped back into his body, he opened his eyes to an evening gone nearly full-dark. He sat up and blinked back the grogginess, rubbed a hand down his face. The last bit of color was fading in purple hues beyond the window, and there were only two places where Vlad might be at this time.

He hadn't lied to Constantine: he could be sweet, and almost always was. It was why there were no guards posted at his door, and why none of the ones he encountered on his way out to the garden gave him more than a passing glance. He and Vlad were a part of the household at this point, but it was common to see a janissary lingering just out of reach whenever Vlad was present. To see the guards following him with their eyes; to see the thinly veiled contempt in the gazes of viziers and the higher-ups at court.

Vlad had a presence about him. He'd grown lanky and severe, his gaze arresting. His was not a magnetism generated by beauty, or conviviality. No; it was his stern, constant, prowling threat that sucked all the air out of every room he entered. Only a handful knew that he was a vampire, but everyone could tell that he was a predator.

The gardens lay in shadow, the last pale twilight catching on the metal chasing along arbors and benches, little topiary spires. It seemed another world, heavy with the scent of autumn's first and last flowers. It was still warm, but the air held the promise of an oncoming chill.

Val found his brother in the chapel. The candles had been lit along the makeshift altar. Vlad knelt on the flagstones before it, hands pressed together in his lap, head bowed.

Val hesitated in the doorway.

After a moment, Vlad said, "You know I can tell that you're there, don't you?" Toneless.

Val swallowed and walked in on silent feet. He approached his brother slowly, as he would a wild animal. "I didn't want to disturb your prayers."

Vlad snorted. As Val drew alongside him, he could see his smirk in the glow of the candle flames. "Is that what you think I do in here? Pray?"

"Isn't it?" Val held his breath as he waited. He wanted to believe that of his brother – that when he bowed his head it was to ask for heavenly guidance. He wanted to believe that, under this new cruel façade, Vlad was still a boy who doubted, and wished, and hoped. That they were the same in that way.

Slowly, Vlad's expression relaxed into one of quiet surprise, eyebrows lifting. When he turned away, he shook his head, slightly. "What is it, Radu?"

He'd almost grown used to the name at this point. Its bite wasn't as painful. "I went to see Constantine tonight."

"Constantine Dragases," Vlad said with a snort. "Him again?"

"We're friends."

"What are you hoping to gain from a widower Greek despot, eh?"

Val sighed. "We're *friends*, I said." It was quite possible his brother had no concept of friendship.

Vlad shrugged. "So? What of him?"

"He'd had news of home."

"Oh?" Vlad's tone was casual, bored even. But his spine stiffened, and Val sensed the acceleration of his pulse.

This was the part that hurt to say. That choked him. "The pope dissolved the treaty between the Turks and Hungary. Ladislas and Hunyadi are marching to war."

"You'd think they'd get tired of doing that over and over."

"Father sent Mircea and a cavalry unit with them."

Vlad turned back to him. Even in the meager candlelight, Val could see the blood drain from his face. "No." Not disbelief or fear, but a command. *No, don't tell me that.*

"It's true," Val said, panic tightening around his throat like a vise. "George Sphrantzes read it aloud; the message had come from one of Ladislas's generals. There's a new crusade, and Father has helped with it."

Vlad stared at him a long moment, expressionless, chest heaving as he breathed. His gaze finally shifted to the worn wooden cross hanging on the wall.

They'd been allowed to keep their god, to worship in the way that they chose. A kindness.

"He broke the treaty," Vlad murmured. "He's sentenced us to death." His head snapped around. "Did you ask him why?"

"Why? No, I – I haven't seen him yet. I–"

"It doesn't matter. He's made his choice." He stood and dusted off his knees. "When you do see him next, don't hassle him about it. A prince must protect his people. That's what he's doing. You and I aren't of any consequence. He has Mircea – he has an heir. That's what matters." His voice was terrible: brittle, fragile in a way it never was.

Val reached for him. "Vlad–"

Vlad brushed past him, heading for the door.

Val watched him go. He wanted to call out, to try and offer some kind of comfort. But Vlad would never accept that.

He returned to his room instead, and stared at the stars beyond the window for a long time before sleep finally came.

~*~

In the days that followed, Val waited for a summons. He attended his lessons, tried valiantly to please his sword and archery masters; sparred with the other boys until he was dripping sweat, even in the autumn cool, and presented himself clean and tidy at all mealtimes. But worry lay over him like a funeral shroud.

He kept trying to make eye contact with Vlad, in the fleeting moments that they were together, wanting to offer support and commiseration. But Vlad never looked back.

And when he could, when he was in his bed at night, or when he stole an hour to himself in a quiet corner of the garden, he went dream-walking.

He found Mircea on a bloody hill. The screams of dying men and dying horses indistinguishable from one another. The air filled with the smoke from the crudely cast canon that had laid waste to the enemy. Val was glad he couldn't smell the ash, and the blood, and the shit. He closed his eyes against the sight of it, all that death. And yet it wasn't a victory. Mircea's sword gleamed crimson, his face streaked with dirt. His horse was still under him, but he was blowing and lathered, and almost done.

Val wasn't proud, but he fled. Retreated back to his body, his hiding spot in a corner of the palace wall, lacy strands of ivy trailing over his face. He scrambled to the side and vomited in the crushed rock of the path.

That night, when he laid down to sleep, he went to find his brother again. The post-battle Mircea that sat slumped in front of a dying campfire looked pale and unsteady, his face still dirty. A deep cut marred one brow; it would scar, Val thought.

There were others about, but they were at a further distance, half asleep in their bedrolls, too exhausted to notice a spectral boy pick his way up to the fire and settle on the hard ground beside his brother.

Mircea had always been startle-prone when it came to Val's dream-walking, and tonight was no exception. But tonight, a man now, a warrior, Mircea ripped his dagger from his belt and brandished it – firelight dancing across the freshly-whetted edge – before he realized it was Val beside him.

"Radu," he breathed in relief, and his arm dropped. The knife clattered against a stone and fell out of his hand to land in the dirt. "My God. How did you find me?"

"I found you earlier, too." Val swallowed against the images that tried to overtake his mind.

"You're getting stronger, then." Mircea's face fell. "You saw the battle?"

Val nodded.

Mircea licked at cracked lips. Dirt had worked its way into the creases around his eyes, lines of stress that hadn't been there a year ago. "We lost." He said it matter-of-factly, too tired and battle-sick to try to paint it in a flattering light. "Hunyadi escaped, as did we. Ladislas is dead. They cut his horse out from under him. I saw them take his head."

Val swallowed again. "The crusade failed?"

"Yes." He blinked, and his eyes looked wet. "I'm sorry, Radu. I wanted to bring you home–"

Val couldn't throw his arms around his neck, so he smiled at him, and wished that felt like enough.

~*~

He found his mother in her bedchamber, staring sightlessly into the fire, embroidery hoop forgotten in her lap. Utterly still. He'd never seen her like that, and it frightened him.

"Mama?"

233

She started, head lifting with a gasp, hands clasping the embroidery hoop and lifting it in front of her. A shield — a weapon, more likely. In that first moment, before she recognized him, he saw that her pale eyes were wild, her fangs visible. A growl built in the back of her throat, and then quickly died. A moment of his mother the shieldmaiden, and then her face crumpled, and tears filled her eyes, and she said, "My darling," and reached for him.

He went, though he turned to smoke under her hands.

She wiped her eyes and forced a sound that was meant to be a laugh. "Look how big you're getting," she said, hands hovering over his projection. "Your hair is so long. It's beautiful. *You're* beautiful."

They talked of silly, sweet things long into the night. And when he left, before he faded away, she finally let fall the tears she'd been holding in check the whole time.

Her hands hovered beside his face. She gritted her teeth. "I will get you back," she said. "I *will*."

He wanted to believe her, but he knew better.

~*~

Quiet, well-mannered, fluent in Turkish and a favorite amongst the women of the harem — they liked to braid his golden hair and buss his cheeks and smile into his eyes until he blushed and looked away, which made them laugh — Val heard not just the palace gossip, but the truth behind it. From the servant girls who attended to Murat's Serbian wife, he heard that Murat had left the palace so that he could rouse his own troops in order to run to Mehmet's aid. Not just aid — he crushed the forces that Mehmet had been unable to, shaming his sultan son, all but taking the title back from him.

The day of Mehmet's arrival dawned in creamy pinks and oranges; an autumn storm sky. Clouds built slowly all day, stacking up like gray wolf pelts until it seemed the weight of them would crush the horizon.

Val had trouble eating, belly full of nameless dread. The electricity in the air — dancing tongues of lightning that flirted along the distant tree tops – kept inducing little shivers. Goosebumps that ached and prickled up the back of his neck. He felt restless; he wanted to spar, an urge so alien to him that it sent him into a quiet panic attack beneath the oils and combs of the slaves sent to beautify him for the reception banquet.

It had been years since he'd last seen Mehmet, and it occurred to him now, wincing as tangles were tugged free, that those had been peaceful years. Years in which Vlad suffered the riding crop less; years in which there were no near deaths in the practice yard; years in which Val had started to hope that, maybe, just maybe, if they minded their manners, and learned their Ottoman history, they could go home soon.

But Father had betrayed the treaty.

Mircea's men had died in a field of mud, and blood, and horse shit. All for nothing.

And Mehmet, defeated and shamed, marched home now. He'd been an arrogant, angry boy before. Now…

Val closed his eyes against the threat of anxious tears and prayed feverishly that Vlad wouldn't do anything stupid tonight.

He went down to the great hall in a gold-trimmed blue kaftan and gold silk şalvar, his hair done up in elaborate braids, woven through with jewels and tiny bells that chimed when he walked. His slippers had bells, too – not his usual, functional schoolboy boots, but fine leather slippers lined with cozy fur.

"*Beautiful*," one of the slaves dared to tell him, just a warm whisper in his ear. The mirror proved that to be a true statement.

He fell into step with Vlad along the way, and Val did a double-take.

It wasn't often that Vlad actually looked the part of a prince, with his hair tangled and his sharp cheekbones smudged with dirt from the training yard. He had no affection for finery; he would rather ride, and fight, and work with his hands. The sort of second son born for the battlefield, wrong-footed indoors amongst polite company.

But the slaves had attacked Vlad tonight with their oils, and combs, and abrasive soaps. He gleamed.

Twin braids hugged the curve of his skull, falling loose down the back of his neck, his hair thick and glossy and dark. Like

235

lamp oil in the flickering torchlight. His kaftan was deep red, blood-colored, picked with both gold and silver. His şalvar were white, tucked into buffed black riding boots. A heavy jeweled belt rested on his hips, hung with a ceremonial dagger, its hilt set with a massive ruby.

There was no scrubbing away his scowl, though. "What?" he demanded, hand settling on the dagger hilt in a gesture Val thought was unconscious.

"You look nice."

Vlad snorted.

The great hall, with its ornate tiles and soaring columns, sparkled with torch and lantern light, a rainbow of colored reflections. Low, portable tables had been arranged in a double row down the center of the room, each lined with rugs for sitting. One stood apart, at the head of the room: a royal table for the young sultan and his father who'd rescued him in battle. Incense burned, undercut by the rich, savory smells of the food about to be served; between the tables stood decorative bowers twined with flowering vines, a thousand candles wavering in the breeze from the high windows. All of it like something from a fairy story.

Val stood, staring in quiet wonder, until Vlad took his arm and steered him in the direction a hurrying slave indicated. "Isn't it beautiful?" he asked, leaning into Vlad's side.

"No."

They were seated at a table with the other hostages and the sons of some of the notable members of court. Several of them looked at Vlad with wide eyes, but quickly ducked their heads when Vlad's gaze fell over them.

Oh, brother, Val thought. *Why do you want everyone to be afraid of you?*

The room slowly filled with diners. The regular court, a collection of Ottoman nobles, scribes, viziers, relatives, and shameless hangers-on – same as at any court across the world. Then there were the leaders who'd pledged loyalty to the boy sultan's campaign, a mix of austere tribal lords and Mongols in furs. They'd come from all corners, all willing to pledge fealty to the Turks for the chance to smash the West.

Mehmet was the last to enter the hall; even his father was already seated. A collective hush, and then a turning of heads, a swiveling of bodies. A pointed murmur that moved through the room as a wave. The disgraced sultan entered with head held high, jewels glittering on every part of his person. Every inch royalty, from his crisp white turban, to his gold kaftan and şalvar, to the crust of sapphires on the tops of his boots, and their pointed golden toes. A ring gleamed on every finger.

He'd grown tall and lean in his time away from Edirne, his face angular and handsome. He wore a close-trimmed auburn beard, and the green in his eyes was visible even from a distance – as was the shame. His bearing was arrogant and bored, but Val saw the single line pressed between his brows, the little lines of stress bracketing his mouth.

He was a proud, proud boy, but he was just that: a boy. And now his entire empire knew it; had watched his father go rushing to his rescue.

Val was startled by a low, pulsing growl beside him, and turned to look at his brother. Vlad's jaw was clenched, his hands balled into fists where they rested on the tabletop. Nostrils flared, scenting the air.

"Brother," Val whispered. He laid a hand on his arm. He'd caught Mehmet's scent as well – vampire, male, threat, alpha – but his first inclination had been to duck down beneath the table, not to leap over it and start a brawl. "Please. You mustn't."

Vlad's response was to bare his teeth and issue a real growl, chest heaving, head tipped back as he looked at–

Oh. Mehmet had stopped before their table.

Val tucked himself into his brother's side. The boys across from them ducked their heads low over their empty plates, whites of their eyes showing. It grew quiet again, eerily so, and the loudest sound was Vlad's growl.

There were members of the Ottoman court who knew what the Wallachian brothers were, but in this packed room, the majority thought they were only hostages princes, not immortals who drank the blood of living creatures. Vlad was exposing them. Startled glances came their way. A few guests lifted their heads, searching for the strange animal noise rolling across the polished floors.

"*Vlad.*" Val pinched him. Hard. Right in the soft part of his inner arm.

From above them, a chuckle. Val lifted his head, and the sultan was smiling at him, wide enough to flash his fangs.

His eyes danced. "It's alright, little prince." A purr underlined his voice. "Your brother doesn't frighten me." He extended one ringed hand, palm-up.

What did he...?

Why was he...?

Vlad's hand clamped down on Val's thigh, pinning him in place. "Don't."

Mehmet's smile widened. He wiggled his fingers, gemstones catching the light.

Every eye in the room was fixed on them. If he refused the sultan, in front of everyone, after his father had been labeled a betrayer...it wasn't possible.

But Vlad's fingers dug bruises into his leg.

The sultan knew. He turned his smile on Vlad. "Like father like son?" he asked in Slavic.

Vlad tensed.

Val clapped his hand down over his brother's. "Please, no," he hissed in Romanian. "They'll kill you, Vlad!"

In the silence that followed, Mehmet leaned forward and braced his palm in the center of the table, the boys in front of him flattening themselves to get out of his way. His fangs elongated, and his eyes flashed. "What will it be, golden one?"

He had no choice. Hostages never had a choice.

Slowly, he pried Vlad's fingers loose and stood. Walked with head down and face flaming around the table to join the sultan.

Mehmet extended his hand again, and it was warm and rough when Val slipped his own inside it. The rings were a disguise for the hard calluses at the base of each finger, the half-healed lacerations on his palm. Not just a dazzling sultan, but a warrior, too.

Val gulped against his stuttering pulse and looked up at him through his lashes. Mehmet smiled at him again, no fangs this time, but with a brightness that Val didn't understand. Mehmet looked at him with intent – but he was just a boy, he didn't recognize it.

"Come along with me, little prince," the sultan purred, and drew him up alongside so he could hook their arms together. "You can sit and dine with me. Won't that be an honor?"

"Y-yes, your grace."

Val twisted back, once, to look over his shoulder at his brother.

Vlad stared down at his empty plate, hands curled into claws on the tabletop, chest heaving. He didn't lift his face, not once.

~*~

It was a lavish feast, a fitting celebration of an army returned home victorious. Val, seated at Mehmet's side like an honored guest instead of a hostage, stared down at his fifth course, delicate slices of stuffed quail, seasoned to perfection, and thought of Mircea, dirt-streaked and pale-faced beside his fire. Thought of King Ladislas, his horse cut out from under him, his head taken to the sultan as proof of death.

There would have been a feast in Hungary, if it had been Mehmet's head on a pike. One man's butcher was another man's hero, and so it went, so it had always been.

Val didn't realize his breathing had gone high and quick until he felt a touch on his leg. A light brush of fingers on his thigh that startled him nearly up off his rug.

When he turned to Mehmet, the sultan laughed quietly, green eyes dancing. "You're very nervous tonight."

Val started to deny it, but Mehmet was a vampire; he could sense the truth: Val *was* nervous. He was scared, and stressed, and he wanted to go home, and he worried for his family, and he wanted his brother to love him, and he wanted his mother to laugh again–

A warm brush against his cheek startled him back to the moment at hand. Mehmet cupped his jaw, swept his thumb along the tender skin beneath Val's eye. "Beautiful boys should never look as sad as you do right now." He shifted forward, leaned in a little closer, breath warm across Val's face. "What's the matter, Radu?" Slow, hypnotic sweep of his thumb; low purr of his voice. And he was *looking* at Val, gaze fixed on him. Vlad never paid him notice, never stared into his eyes like this, never...

It was on the tip of his tongue. *My real name is Val. Call me Val.* But he hesitated. Mehmet wasn't family; he wasn't even a friend. He was a sultan — *the enemy* sultan — and why was he stroking Val and calling him beautiful? Why was...

"Shh." Mehmet laid a finger against his lips just before they opened. The ring was warm from his skin. "I asked you a question," he said, so gently, his smile soft. "Aren't you going to answer it?"

Val closed his eyes a moment, swallowed. The sounds of the feast around them blurred together, inconsequential. They might hate him, or think nothing of him, or whisper in his ear that he was lovely to look upon, but it was this man here — this boy — who held his fate in his hands. Literally, now, the calluses scraping lightly at Val's throat as his touch trailed down to fiddle with the collar of his kaftan. Mehmet was at the forefront of all his senses, the heat and scent of him, his intent a low pulsing rhythm that made Val want to fidget in his chair. What did this mean? What did he want? What, what, what. He didn't understand, and he wanted to howl.

"And still he doesn't answer," Mehmet said, lightly mocking. He gave a tug on Val's collar. "He won't even look at me."

Damn it. He wasn't doing this right.

He opened his eyes and took a deep breath, ready to plead for his family, for Vlad, and Mama, and Father, and Mircea, and the people of Wallachia—

But Mehmet's *eyes*. They glowed. His hand circled Val's throat, thumb a gentle, steady presence right in the hollow.

In his panic, grace abandoned him. "Why do you look at me like this?" he blurted, face heating until it must surely catch fire.

Mehmet leaned in even closer; his face was the only thing Val could see, the wild light in his eyes, his own terrified reflection staring back. "Like what?" Just a soft huff, more panther than human.

"M-m-my father broke the treaty. My brother has bested you in hand-to-hand combat."

Mehmet pulled back a fraction, his expression arresting. Brittle. His thumb pressed, just a little, into Val's throat.

"Don't you hate me?"

"Do you think I should?" Voice tighter now, flatter.

"Vlad does."

Another smile, this one humorless. Slowly, Mehmet released him and eased back– he'd been half-falling in order to touch Val. He turned away and reached for his wine. "I am nothing like your brother." A declaration.

Val searched the crowd for Vlad, but when he spotted his table, his brother was gone.

~*~

Mehmet drank. Cup, after cup, after cup of wine. It took quite a lot of spirits to get a vampire drunk, but it was possible, and Mehmet managed. He didn't speak for the rest of the meal, and ate only little, brooding over his ever-full cup, a slave always at the ready to top it off from the pitcher. By the end of the meal, when Mehmet tried to rise, he had to brace both hands on the table, and swayed.

"You will accompany me, Radu," he said, no longer teasing and smiling, but commanding.

Helpless to do anything but comply, Val followed the sultan back to his royal apartments.

It was a long, unsteady journey, Mehmet stopping often to brace a hand against the wall. Sometimes, he muttered under his breath; others he laughed.

When they arrived at his rooms, Val just...stared.

Back home in Tîrgoviște, his parents, and the princess, each enjoyed their own suites, with big four-poster beds draped in furs. His mother had a gold-backed mirror and brush set; a box of

241

jewels that she brought out on feast occasions. But the palace was a new one, constructed at Father's instruction, and it had been built for functionality more than beauty.

This, though, this suite of the sultan's…it defied all expectation of sumptuousness. An antechamber fed into a bedchamber and dressing room, all of it a dazzle of complimentary riches.

A bed heaped with pillows, and draped with silk panels. Great tall wardrobes thrown open to reveal enough clothes to suit a small army. Imported Greek and European furniture: dressing tables with mirrors, sideboards with glittering decanters, chests stuffed so full the lids wouldn't quite close. An archway stood open to the garden, letting in the cool breeze, a wedge of star-studded sky visible beyond the walls, sheer white cliffs that glowed in the moonlight. Mehmet had his own little courtyard in the garden, a bench, and a fountain, and a gnarled apple tree that swayed, the susurrus of leaves like the sound of rain.

A pair of slaves, waiting as they entered, rushed ahead to light the lamps beside the bed, and turn down the coverlet. Movements quick; they smelled of fear.

Mehmet smelled of wine…and of anger.

"Leave us," he ordered, gesturing sloppily to the door.

The slaves had been approaching him, ready to undress him, but they bowed and backed away instead, and fled.

Mehmet followed them, steps laborious, and pulled a key from an inner pocket. He locked the door, and, despite his unsteadiness, slipped the key away somewhere on his person in a blink; Val couldn't follow the movement. Then he turned around and put his back to the door; Val could tell it was all that held him upright.

He reached up and dragged his turban off. Some of the pins caught, and the whole elaborate headpiece began to unravel. He let it fall to the floor, careless, wincing as he reached to smooth his hair with his other hand. It was even redder than his beard, shiny with perfumed oils, thick waves that fell past his shoulders.

"Did you know that vampires can become intoxicated?" he asked, and it took Val a moment to realize the sultan was addressing him.

He drew himself up to attention, bells chiming in his hair. "I did, yes, your grace."

Mehmet smiled with his eyes shut. "And you didn't think to warn me?"

"I...I didn't know you would...would drink so much. Your Majesty." The last was a whisper.

The sultan's smile spread, slow and lazy in the way of a cat who hadn't yet decided to pounce. Head tipped back, his hair unbound, drunk and disheveled, he still felt like a threat to Val. "Of course you didn't. You'd never do such a thing yourself, would you?" He cracked one eye open, a bright slit. "Little golden prince, always so polite. It wouldn't be mannerly to get sloppy drunk, would it?"

Val bit his lip and didn't respond.

"Tell me, Radu: why *are* you so well-behaved?"

So you won't kill me, Val thought. *So you won't hurt my family. Because I'm your captive, and I don't want to be starved, or beaten, or stripped naked and thrown in a cell.*

"Whatever your reasons," Mehmet continued, "your brother doesn't share them." He laughed. Strained. Unhappy. Though his smile remained, a muscle in his cheek twitched. "He's bound and determined to be as rebellious as possible, isn't he? Whether he endangers himself..." His other eye opened, and suddenly, drunk or not, he looked coiled tight as a viper about to strike. "Or his little brother."

Val edged backward a half step.

"He cares nothing for you, does he? Not until someone pays you a compliment, that is."

Another half-step. His heart pounded painfully against his ribs.

"He's jealous, you know. He's ugly as mud, but then there's you. Beautiful as a jewel. He hates it."

Another step. "Vlad's a warrior," he said, voice high and wavering. "He doesn't worry about beauty."

Another laugh. "Everyone worries about that. Trust me." Then he pushed off the door and stalked forward, his steps steady now.

Vampires could get drunk, but it didn't usually last that long.

It was burning off now.

Val backed up again, but the backs of his legs hit the end of the bed.

Mehmet closed the distance between them, his grin wide…manic. He laughed, looming over Val, reddish hair fanning around his handsome face, his eyes sparking. "What are you afraid of, little prince?"

So close – he was so close. Heat, and wine-smell, and a kind of intent Val couldn't put a name to. Was this sumptuous bedchamber to be the scene of his murder? Would Mehmet strangle him? Bite him and drain him? Or would be pluck the ceremonial sword off the wall behind him and run Val through?

Teeth chattering, he said, "Please don't kill me."

"Kill you?" He leaned in even closer, his knees pressing into Val's thighs. "Now what makes you think I'd want to do that?"

Why wouldn't he?

Val took a series of choppy breaths through his mouth. "M-my father. And my brother–"

"Oh, they'll get what's coming to them. Traitors always pay. But." He lifted one jeweled hand that wavered; still drunk; he still reeked of wine. He petted at Val's hair, smoothed it back where the humidity of the close, body-packed room had sent baby-fine pieces twisting up into curls. A bell jangled. "You're not a traitor though, are you, Radu? You're obedient and sweet. Yes?"

I can be sweet, he'd told Constantine. He closed his eyes and whispered, "Yes."

"That's what all your tutors have said: that you're a good boy. That you always mind your manners. Always gracious." The sultan's touch shifted down, a fingertip trailing along the ridge of his cheekbone, and around the curve of his jaw, feather-light. "Always…*lovely*. Look at me, Radu."

He opened his eyes – always obedient, always sweet – and the sultan's face was right in front of his, close enough to count his lashes; close enough to see the glazed hunger in his eyes and finally know that's what it was. The sultan was angry, and ashamed, embarrassed by his failures in battle, and he wanted something, desperately.

My blood, Val thought, himself desperate, trying to lean back.

But then Mehmet's other hand landed on his chest, and smoothed down the front of his body...all the way down, until it cupped around what rested, soft and small, between his legs. He smiled, fangs long. "Undress," he said, an order, "and then you can tend to me."

A memory flooded back, fuzzy from early youth. Going in search of Mother, and following her scent to Father's rooms. No wolves to guard the door – strange. And peeking through the door he'd found his parents, unclothed and intertwined.

When he asked Vlad about it later, his brother had cuffed him across the back of the head. "You idiot, they were fucking."

That, he realized with dawning horror, was what Mehmet wanted.

Val gasped and tried to twist away, but Mehmet caught his shoulder, his grip tight. He wasn't much older, but he was much, much stronger; his fingertips dug in hard, and Val could already feel the bruises forming. His other hand tightened between Val's legs, until pain bloomed, and stars burst behind his eyes. He gagged.

"What's this?" Mehmet said through his teeth. He smelled of anger now, acrid, burning anger that rolled off his skin. "The little prince wants to get away? I thought we just decided you weren't a traitor, Radu? I thought you wanted to save your skin?"

Val drew a tremulous breath; what little he'd eaten threatened to come back up. "P-p-please, your grace..."

"Please *what?*" A snarl.

"*Please don't hurt me.*"

"Hurt you?" His grip eased, but his tone was cruel and mocking. "Why would I want to do that? Do you think I *enjoy* inflicting pain?"

Yes. Yes, Val thought he did.

He smoothed the fine embroidery of Val's kaftan with trembling fingers, lingering at his chest, stroking him through the silk. "I seek only pleasure. That's what you were made for. Beautiful things are meant to be enjoyed."

Val closed his eyes against the prickling of tears. All those times Mehmet had stared at him, the things he'd hissed to Vlad during those awful sparring matches, laughing, wild-eyed. *This* was

245

what it had been leading to. A drunk noble pawing at him; a hostage unable to resist. Nakedness, and fucking; writhing like the horses he'd seen bred back home. He thought of a mare, a stallion's teeth sunk in her withers; remembered the way she'd screamed.

And he was a *boy*. How could the prince...what would he...

The tears slid down his cheeks. He couldn't stop them.

"You'll like it," Mehmet said. "You'll see." His touch pulled back, and he stepped away. Val heard the rustle of cloth and cracked his eyes open.

Through a blurring of tears, he saw that the sultan was undressing, his movements clumsy, fingers still slow from the wine. He tore a button free when he couldn't work it, cursing, the golden circle landing on the tile with a *ping*. He had his back to Val; he didn't think he would flee. And why would he? Obedient. *Sweet*. The tame Wallachian prince who observed every courtesy wouldn't dare deny the Ottoman sultan, would he?

The door to this suite was locked. Maybe Mehmet would drop the key, fumble it like the buttons he kept ripping free. But...

Val blinked to clear his eyes. There lay the garden, its jasmine-scented breeze lifting the bed curtains, cooling his overheated face. If he could get around the bed, he could get out there, and he knew the gardens well, now. Knew all its nooks and hiding spots.

He closed his eyes again, and tried to find some reserve of courage to draw upon. If he did this, if he refused the sultan...

He didn't let himself think. He only knew that he had to run now, while Mehmet's back was turned.

He wiped his tears with his sleeve, took a deep breath, and leapt.

He made it around the bed before Mehmet let out an enraged sound, half-growl, half-scream.

Val screamed in response, and tried to duck – but the sultan snatched him by the back of the kaftan, yanked him up off his feet.

The room spun. His back slammed into the wall, and Mehmet's face shoved into his, teeth bared, veins standing out in his temples. He growled, low and constant, seething.

"Are you running from me?"

"N-no-no, Your Majesty." Val flattened his hands against the plaster of the wall, trying to gain purchase, searching for–

His fingertips brushed cool steel. Mehmet's fists were balled in the front of his kaftan, tearing seams and popping buttons, and he didn't dare turn his head. But he rolled his eyes to the side and just glimpsed what he'd seen in his earlier glance around the room: the sword hanging on the wall. It was well within reach, and hung by flimsy decorative pegs.

"Look at me!" Mehmet shouted in his face, spraying spit.

Val complied. The sultan's eyes were wild. He'd seen bloodlust, and battle fury, had lived his whole life with Vlad's particular brand of low-simmering contempt for everyone and everything, but this...he'd never seen this before. This terrified him.

I can be sweet. Yes, he could, and he had. It was, no doubt, the thing that had spared him the crop thus far. Maybe even what had spared his life. He should be sweet now; should go limp as a doll and let Mehmet use him for whatever pleasure he sought.

But Val was only a boy, and fucking was fine so long as it was something glimpsed through a half-closed door. Here, now, with his captor, with wine-breath, and aggression, and terror, he –

No. He couldn't do it.

What would Vlad do? he thought. And then he closed his hand around the sword's hilt, ripped it from its hooks, and swung it.

The hit landed, and in his shock, Mehmet dropped him.

Val collapsed to the floor; the impact knocked the sword from his hand.

Mehmet stared down at his side, where the dark red of blood was already soaking through his kaftan, a rapidly-spreading stain. But he was still on his feet; he reached to touch the wound, fingering at the silk above it with quiet disbelief.

No! Not a mortal hit. Not even a crippling one. Just enough to stoke his already out of control anger.

Val scrambled to his feet and fled. The sultan wasn't fast enough to catch him this time, and he ducked out through the double doors into the garden.

247

~*~

The moon was waning, but Val could see well in the dark. He moved quick and quiet, keeping low behind the boxwoods, staying to the shadows cast by topiaries and ornamental trees. He could have hidden from a human, but Mehmet could track him by scent. So he went straight for the herbs, and plucked rosemary and lavender and mint, rubbed it over the pulse points at his wrists and throat. Stuffed it into his kaftan.

He tore at his hair, yanking out the bells and casting them into the shrubs. Threw his slippers as far as he could throw them – a decoy, hopefully – and proceeded on bare feet, silent now.

He felt his heartbeat in his *mouth*; if he coughed, he thought it might spill out onto the gravel of the path, black and pulsing. His fear was so overwhelming that he couldn't process it; he was numb now, focused only on hiding, getting away, getting safe. With first light would come the sultan's sobering…and his punishment. They would be killed for sure now – both of them. All this time he'd thought it would be Vlad's petulance that doomed them, but no, it was his own childish fear of sodomy that would do them in. If possible, Vlad would hate him even more.

He envisioned his brother's face as they waited on the top of the wall, as executioners sharpened the long spikes they would be impaled upon.

Congratulations, Vlad's voice said in his head now. *You're still going to get fucked, only with a spear instead of the sultan's cock. Which is worse?*

Tears filled his eyes, and he blinked them away and kept running.

He'd become an expert at dodging guards and nighttime garden-walkers; the gardens were vast, but no obstacle for his regular endurance. Tonight, though, as his adrenaline waned – sustained for too long already – and exhaustion set its hooks in him, he knew he had to stop.

He found a tall apple tree with far-flung branches, and shimmied up it. Rested in the crotch of two wide branches, tucked up and hidden beneath the leaves, and let his flushed face rest against the cool, rough bark.

He breathed through his mouth for long minutes, trying to will his heartbeat slower. The breeze tugged at his loose hair, a gentle sigh through the branches all around him. His cramping muscles unclenched by degrees. Alone, untouched. Alive.

Sleep beckoned, and he let it claim him.

He dream-walked.

His mother sat on her favorite bench in her own garden, the dark close around her, a light shawl all that shielded her from the chill, her hands white-knuckled on its edges. Her bench rested on top of a low hill at the palace's base, and the land sloped down, so that she could see across the moat and toward the moonglow-silvered roofs of the houses in Tîrgoviște.

"Mama?"

In the first moment, when she turned to him, she couldn't hide the grief etched into her face. Loose pieces of hair haloed a countenance drawn tight with deep sadness.

"My darling," she whispered, and held out her hand.

Val settled on the bench beside her, as well he could in his projection form, and she leaned in close, even though his edges smoked and wisped away into the night.

They sat a moment, together in this one small way they could be. Until Val felt tears threaten. He wanted to be real; for his mother to put her arm around him and wipe his tears away with her thumb that smelled of herbs, and kiss his hair. Tell him that she would make it all better.

"Mama?"

Her hands twitched on the edges of her shawl; she wanted to be able to touch, too.

"Have you ever…" It was an impossible thing to ask.

"Have I ever…what?" She sat up straighter. "What is it, darling?"

He would give anything not to reveal this about himself – that he was the kind of boy that men wanted to grope, and fondle, and seek pleasure in. That he was weak, so much weaker than his brothers, warriors both. They were worthy princes, honors to their Roman heritage, and he was only beautiful.

But fear closed around his throat like a fist, and he wanted to know. Needed to. If there was some way to grit his teeth and get through this thing that was being demanded of him.

"Have you – has anyone ever…forced you–" He choked on the words. Saying this to his mother had to be some kind of sin.

She stared at him a long moment, when he couldn't say anything else, and then she understood, eyes flying wide and white, shiny in the moonlight. "Who?" She tried to grab him, his shoulders turning to mist beneath her touch. She growled, but it was a despairing sound. Halfway to a sob. "Val, who? Who – did someone – who would – oh, *love*…"

He was snatched away from her.

Back in his body, his eyes flew open, and in that first moment of disorientation, he knew only that it was still dark, and that he lay hugging a tree branch, and that someone's warm hand rested on his ankle. He gave a shout of surprise and sat up.

It was a small tree, decorative, and the sturdiest branches, one of which Val straddled, hung low enough that Mehmet could stand below and reach to touch him – which he was doing now. The pearlescent light of dawn suffused the misty garden, and by its light, Val could see the black stain of blood on the sultan's kaftan, dry now; no doubt the wound had already healed.

Mehmet's smile was very small, and very determined. The night's drunken lust had hardened in the past few hours; he now stared up at Val with sober surety – but no less hunger. *You will obey*, his gaze said, accompanied by an intangible shove of resolve. *You will come to me, or I will do terrible things to you.* His was the face of a prince who'd been crowned a king too early, who wielded all of the privilege, but carried none of the weight.

He tugged lightly at Val's ankle. "Found you."

Val couldn't speak.

"How about," the sultan continued, the words casual, his voice anything but. "You come down and we'll go have a nice breakfast together. We can pretend that last night never happened."

Do as I say, and I won't punish you for refusing me.

Val closed his eyes and thought of his mother's face, the way it had crumpled, the tears in her eyes. *Oh, love...* But what was he to do?

Being alive...that had to be better than being dead, didn't it?

That was the conclusion he came to, anyway, in all his nine-year-old wisdom.

He swallowed, and nodded. "Yes, Your Majesty."

~*~

Oh, he thought, dazedly. *There's blood.*

Mehmet had stripped off his clothes without ceremony; run his hands over his body, like he was judging a horse at market. Had pinched his nipples until Val had to bite the tip of his own tongue; tugged fruitlessly at his soft cock a few times, growling under his breath. Then he'd put Val on the bed and pressed his face into a silk pillow, hand cupped around the back of his skull, holding him there. He'd used a palmful of fragrant oil to ease the way; Val had jumped, surprised, when he felt it. But a firm smack stilled him.

And then–

He knew he'd cried, because the pillow was wet when he was finally allowed to sit up, but he was proud that he'd been silent, sobs muffled in the silk. And he'd felt something tear; pain like the blinding like of a sunset, overwhelming him; he'd been split open.

He twisted around now, as the sultan sat at his dressing table, ignoring him, and saw fresh red blood on the sheets – his own. Felt more dribbling out from inside him. He reached to touch himself with careful fingertips, trying to assess the damage, and recoiled with a bitten-off cry. It hurt so badly.

Fresh tears clouded his vision.

"If you go crying to your brother about this," Mehmet said lightly, not bothering to turn around, "I'll send his head back to your father in a box."

Of course he couldn't go crying to Vlad – he'd only call him a baby and say he'd invited this on himself for being so soft and pretty.

21

WORSE THAN DEATH

Dawn found Vlad on the back of a horse. A rangy gelding built for speed rather than battle. In the dim glow of a lantern, Vlad tilted at the practice dummies in the stable yard until a host of sleepy grooms arrived for the morning feeding, the animals whickering and stamping. The gelding swiveled his ears, interested in the prospect of food. Vlad steered him away from the barn, out to the open field where they took the hawks hunting. There he leaned low over an already-sweat-damp neck and dug his heels into fleet sides; pushed his mount into a gallop, the wind snatching tears from his eyes.

When the sun unfurled above the tree tops, blood orange, he finally pulled up. Let his tired horse walk with his neck stretched low, catching his breath and occasionally stripping the seeds off a tall stalk of grass with nimble lips.

Vlad was sore from tilting, all his muscles pleasantly exhausted. Sweat glued his shirt to his body, and his breath came deep and labored. But he still carried so much pent up energy that his bones seemed to vibrate.

He was, without question, the worst brother in existence. Worse even than his uncle: Romulus had killed Remus, or at least tried to, and there was some dignity in death. It was clean, at least. What Vlad had allowed to happen to Val, though…

He closed his eyes tight and let the horse's movements sway him side to side in the saddle.

Why couldn't it have been me? If only he'd been the one with the fine features, the soft little face, the sweet, doe-eyed look of innocence. Then perhaps Mehmet would have wanted Vlad, have reached for him across a table. And then, when he was in the sultan's bed, he could have slit his throat and cut the awful immortal heart from his chest.

But Val was sweet. And innocent. Val would never defend himself. Val would cooperate to stay alive.

And now Val had to know that some things were worse than death.

The gelding tossed his head. Vlad's hands had clenched to fists on the reins, and he forced them to relax. He wanted to *kill*. With sword and dagger, but with his fangs and bare hands, too. Wanted to drink deep of his enemy's blood in a visceral urge stronger than lust, or hunger, or homesickness.

His horse came to a halt, ears flicking back and forth, questioning his rider's agitation. Vlad tipped his head back and stared up at the lightening sky. The moon was still out, a wide cheery smile.

He snarled at it. "I *will* kill him," he murmured, a promise to himself, to his family, to God. "I will."

When he returned to the stable, the day had begun in earnest: riders coming and going. Messengers, troops moving between outposts, nobles off hunting, hooded hawks on their gloves. A boisterous group of merchants had arrived with laden wagons of merchandise, shouting directives at harried stable boys. No one paid Vlad any mind. He unsaddled and rubbed down his mount himself; paused afterward to cup water from the fountain in his hands and splash his face and neck, letting it pour down inside his shirt. He stood a moment, after, hands braced on the stone lip, staring down at his wavering reflection, water dripping off his nose, and lashes, and hair. How young he looked, still, though he felt he'd lived a lifetime already.

Just a boy, still. A hostage boy, helpless in the face of everything.

He straightened, turned…and there was Mehmet.

The sultan was dressed for riding in dark leathers and a simple turban, sword belted to his hip. His Grand Vizier, Halil Pasha, flanked him, along with a scribe and a noble whose name Vlad had never bothered to learn.

A growl built in Vlad's chest before he could check the impulse. He *hated* him.

Mehmet turned to him, his grin slow and mocking. "Ah," he said, and Vlad realized he'd taken three long strides toward him, hands balled into fists. "There he is: the prince who can't control his temper."

Vlad let his growl swell; it drew startled glances from the merchants. A pair of stable boys ducked around a wagon.

Mehmet moved toward him, unhurried, unbothered. He clasped his hands behind his back, and let his shoulders fall at a casual angle. Four guards had materialized behind him, lances at the ready to defend their sultan. "Been out riding?" Mehmet asked. "Enjoying my horses? They're exceptional, aren't they?"

"Enjoying my baby brother?" Vlad snapped. Mehmet smelled like oil, and soap, and clean clothes, yes…but he also smelled of spend, and blood, and fear-sweat. And of Val. He hadn't washed *everywhere*. He'd kept the scent of rape on himself, so he could linger over it…or maybe to taunt Vlad.

Eyes widened around them. Halil laid a hand on Mehmet's arm. "Your Majesty–"

Mehmet waved him off and stepped in closer to Vlad, eyes glittering like gems: bright but cold. His voice was a low murmur, just for the two of them. "Can you smell him?" He inhaled, breathing in the scent that lingered on his own body. Showed Vlad his fangs. "He is *exquisite*. Gentle. *Tight*. More beautiful than any girl."

Vlad growled again.

Mehmet chuckled. "Hit me. And see what happens."

He almost did. It was more tempting than anything had ever been in his life. But he checked his swing. Striking the sultan would get him clapped in irons, and beaten to within an inch of his life…probably killed. And of the two of them, he was determined not to die first.

So instead, he said, in low Greek, "I'm going to kill you."

Mehmet laughed in his face. "Lofty aspirations, Wallachian."

"I will," he insisted.

"Hm, maybe so." Mehmet tipped his head to the side. "But first…I think I'll kill your entire family, and take your palace for my own."

He departed with one last smile, turning back to his retinue, confident that he could present Vlad with his back and remain unharmed.

He was right in that, at least. When Vlad eventually put a sword through him, he wanted to be looking the fucker right in the face.

~*~

Val woke in a panic. He hadn't intended to fall asleep. As dawn broke over the palace, slaves had come to assist Mehmet with his morning ablutions. Val had lain in the rumpled bed that reeked of his own blood and Mehmet's seed, clutching a pillow to his chest, hiding beneath the covers. He hurt; he burned. He felt like he choked the tears back one at a time, a struggle that took all his concentration.

"Bring the prince a breakfast tray," Mehmet had ordered, and someone had scurried to comply.

Val's plan had been to lie quietly until Mehmet left, off to do sultan things, and then he would gather his ripped clothes, and the tatters of his dignity, and go back to his own quarters.

He hadn't meant to fall asleep.

He sat up now, too warm beneath the sheets, flinging them off in a haste. Thick, golden sunlight fell in through the iron grills of the garden doors. It was late afternoon. Songbirds trilled, lazy from a day's activity.

"Oh no," he groaned, scrambling to get up. He was still sore, and worse, weak from hunger. He'd slept nearly the whole day away, still naked, still in the sultan's bed.

He got unsteadily to his feet and was reaching for his discarded şalvar when he noticed he wasn't alone. A small slave boy, not much younger than himself, one of Mehmet's eunuchs, sat quietly on a stool, his plain clothes and downcast eyes lending him the air of a sculpture; a servant meant to be useful, but not seen.

Val yelped with fright, and tried to cover his nakedness, snatching the pants to his chest.

"I'm sorry," he said, stupid with fear. His hands and his limbs and his breath trembled. "I'm sorry, I'm sorry, I'm sorry."

The boy lifted his face, but did not meet Val's gaze directly, his own downcast out of respect. "Forgive me, your grace." Voice soft, unobtrusive. "His Imperial Majesty the sultan bid me offer you food and draw you a bath when you woke."

"When I…" Val tried to catch his breath, his head spinning. "I should – my own quarters, I…"

"Shall I fetch you a tray from the kitchens?"

Val sagged back and let the bed hold his weight. What about his studies? His lessons with the other boys? His training and exercise and endless archery lessons?

Deep down, he knew the answers to these questions. Lessons and training were for hostages who would be sent home. Wards turned carefully to allies who could return to their kingdoms and principalities to rule as puppets of the empire.

Meals in bed and slave-drawn baths were the indulgences of mistresses.

Of a ruler's favored pet.

He closed his eyes. His stomach growled. "A tray, please," he whispered.

Val nibbled at fresh pita, still warm from the oven, with hummus, and olive oil, and sipped red wine craftily mixed with blood while the slave boy filled a copper tub set before the coal brazier with hot water. He had no appetite, but the few bites he managed, and the blood-wine, helped to settle his stomach and calm some of his shaking.

"It's ready, your grace," the boy said when he was done, moving to stand with a bowed head beside the tub, a cloth draped over one arm, cake of soap in-hand. A well-trained bath attendant.

"Alright. Thank you." His legs were steadier now, when he stood and crossed the distance, but his fingers stilled on the laces of the shirt he'd pulled down over his head at first opportunity. His bruises from before – the dark shapes Mehmet's hands had pressed into his skin – had all faded, but he didn't want to be naked in front of anyone, not even a slave who wasn't looking.

Why not? a mocking little inner voice asked. Everyone in the whole palace doubtless knew what had happened. Everyone at the feast last night had seen Mehmet single him out, reach for him, take him up to an honored seat at the high table. Val had slept in the sultan's own bed all day. How could anyone *not* know? And what shame was simple nakedness in the face of that?

He felt his face heat regardless, as he slipped the laces free and stepped out of the shirt. A flush that went all the way down his throat, and chest, and made it hard to breathe. He stepped quickly into the water, and then sat, even though it was too hot on the still-tender parts of his body that Mehmet had made use of.

He drew his knees up to his chest, and hugged them, teeth clenched against a pain that had little to do with his physical hurts. Every blink was a chance to replay it. Every distant sound in the hallway left him flinching; Mehmet would return, and when he did...

"Your grace," the slave said, and Val started. "Shall – shall I wash your hair for you?"

"Oh." His heart fluttered, a trapped bird. "Um. Yes, please."

The boy moved slowly, deliberately. And his touch was soft as he moved to kneel beside the tub and urged Val to tip his head back. Val closed his eyes, and the warm water poured carefully along his scalp, the boy's free hand coming up to shield his eyes. He was thorough: wetting, lathering, massaging the soap in and working the tangles free with deft fingers.

For a little while, Val allowed himself to pretend that he was back home in Wallachia; that the fingers in his hair belonged to his mother, or Helga. Someone who loved him, and who was fussing over the knots he'd gained from a day's training and playing. *Whatever shall we do with you?* People who thought he was just a boy, rowdy and intractable like his brothers; people who touched him with love.

But all too soon he was clean, and the water was cold, and it was time to face reality again.

He dried with a length of toweling and the slave held up a blue silk robe that settled sweetly against his chilled skin.

But a robe, no matter how luxurious its gold trim and gold tasseled-ties, did not count as clothes. Not the kind you wore when you were out in the palace attending meals with other hostages. This was a robe for bedchambers. For intimacy.

A robe for a concubine.

"The sultan," the boy sad, halting and red-faced, "wishes you – he wants you to stay." He pointed at the floor with one small finger. "Here. He'll be back by nightfall."

Val swallowed…and swallowed again, trying to push down his queasiness. "What's your name?"

The boy's head jerked up, eyes wide. "M-m-my name, your grace?" Confusion writ large on his face. No one ever asked him that; no one ever cared.

"If you're willing to tell me," Val said. Both their voices were sad, hushed little things; they could barely meet in the space between them. He had the absurd mental image of two mice creeping along the floor of a predator's cave.

The boy studied him a long moment, his face a mask, his scent giving off fear…and curiosity. Finally, just a whisper: "My mother named me Arslan."

"Arslan," Val repeated.

Turkish for *lion*.

~*~

Mehmet returned after sunset, after slaves had lit lanterns and tall taper candles around the room, started a fresh fire in the brazier. The suite glowed with golden light.

Val sat on the padded bench at the foot of the bed, still in his robe, his hair combed and oiled, arranged over one shoulder. Arslan had brought him a supper tray and seen to him: rubbed his skin with fragrant oils, drew careful lines of kohl around his eyes, painted his lips with pigment and oil so they shone. It had felt very much like being a horse groomed for a tourney; all he lacked was a ribbon in his mane.

Slaves attended to Mehmet in the outer room, stripping him of boots and turban, offering wine and carefully sliced wedges of goat cheese and pita. A bath had already been prepared, the copper tub full of clean, steaming water before the fire.

He dismissed them all, and came into the inner room alone. He lingered in the doorway a moment, elbow braced against the wall, cup of wine held in his other hand. He stared; behind him, the outer door closed with a thump.

259

The sultan was beautiful. Val could admit that objectively, though the beauty of men and boys had never inspired anything other than admiration in him. He felt no stirring of want, no niggle of embarrassed interest, like when he watched the kitchen girls at home home tuck loose curls of hair like corkscrews back from their faces, cheeks flushed from the cookfires.

He did not want the sultan to look at him as he was now, green eyes slitted and greedy as a cat's. But. He had no choice, he supposed.

Finally, Mehmet took a long sip of wine and shoved off the doorframe and into the room. He set the cup aside on the dressing table and reached to pluck at the buttons of his plain blue kaftan. "You look comfortable," he said lightly.

Panic welled in Val's throat. *No, no, please no.* But he swallowed it down. The worst had already happened. "I am, your grace."

"Hmm. Certainly a pretty sight to come home to. I've been negotiating with fools all day." He flicked his fingers. "Come. You can attend me."

Not only a concubine, but a servant as well, it seemed.

But this was better. This he could perform with less shame.

Val slid to his feet and went to attend the sultan. He made deft work of buttons and laces. Beneath his silk shirt, Mehmet smelled of horses and sweat…and of last night, still.

He touched Val's chin, startling him, and tipped his head back. Bare-chested, golden and smiling in the candlelight, a work of muscle and sinew in the flickering shadows. "Do you smell it?" he whispered, delighted.

Val didn't answer. He unlaced the sultan's tight riding leathers with flaming cheeks. Mehmet swiveled his hips, leaned into the movement; he was growing hard behind his flies, and Val's fingers grew clumsy with nerves and sweat. He didn't want this. The gorge rose in his throat.

He pushed through, though, and finally the sultan was naked and stepping into the bath, sinking down into the water with a hiss.

Val knew a moment's reprieve; nothing untoward would happen now, while the sultan bathed. Freedom for a spell, at least.

260

But then Mehmet said, "Wash my back."

He did, slow and uncertain at first, but he took up the soap and the cloth and applied himself to the task. Recalling Arslan: "Do...do you want me to wash your hair?"

Mehmet hummed and tipped his head back, eyes shut, expectant and trusting.

Val wet it first, using the pitcher at the base of the tub; the reddish curls turned black when wet. He worked up a lather between his hands, and applied it as he would to himself, fingertips working in circles, massaging the sultan's scalp.

Mehmet let out a quiet purr and went boneless, shoulders slumping against the edge of the tub. "You're very good at that," he said after a while, voice low and rich with pleasure. "You'd make an excellent slave."

Val stilled.

Mehmet chuckled. "Rest assured. I know you are a prince, and a prince you shall stay. I'm only making an observation."

Val resumed his work, worrying snarls loose with his fingertips.

"I saw your brother today." Light, airy.

Val kept working; forced himself not to react.

"He was coming in from a ride. Lathered one of my nicer geldings." He *tsk*ed. "He was his usual gloomy, uninspiring self. I've never seen someone with *such* a stick shoved up his ass. His constant expression is that of someone with the most terrible stomach cramps." He tipped his head. "To the left, just behind my ear – yes, there." A deep sigh; he slipped down a little farther in the soapy water that was, nevertheless, clear enough for Val to make out the sultan's hardening cock beneath the water. It had begun to curl up toward his stomach; threatened to breach the surface.

"I must tell you, Radu," Mehmet continued, eyes still shut, legs stretched out as far as the tub would allow. "And I don't say this to hurt you – far from it. If anything, I wish to spare your feelings. It'll be easier if you begin to adjust to this idea now, while you're young. Hurts carried into manhood can be crippling, you know.

"Anyway, your brother. He didn't ask after you. Not even once." He cracked one eye open, green as spruce needles, calculating. Its weight pinned Val in place, his hands sunk in the sultan's hair. "Vlad didn't ask after you," he repeated, slower. Trying to press the point home. "I know you love your brother, but he doesn't return that sentiment. I've seen you worry after him, trying your best to be a good brother to him. You're heartbreakingly sweet, aren't you? But it would be best, for your sake, if you gave up on him. He will never feel the same. He will never love you as he should. You'll only get yourself hurt trying to save him."

Val dropped his head; he couldn't look at him anymore, stared instead down at the surface of the water. Droplets splashed down, rippling its surface, and he realized he was crying. Silent, relentless tears that poured down his face; it was like someone had upended cups down his cheeks.

Mehmet sat up, and took Val's wrists gently in his hands, lowering them out of his hair and to the water. "Radu," he said, softly. "I'm sorry. I shouldn't have told you."

Val pulled in a shuddering breath through his mouth and tasted salt. He closed his eyes…but he couldn't stem the flow of tears. They had built for so long, for so many reasons. This was merely the tipping point.

"There, it's alright," Mehmet said. His hands slid up Val's arms, over the bunched, damp-edged sleeves of his robe. Up his shoulders, down over his collarbones, their sharp shapes beneath the silk. Down his chest, his belly, to the ties at his waist. An expert flick of his wrist and the robe fell open. The chill air of the bedchamber whispered over Val's skin, teasing his nipples to points.

He gasped and opened his eyes as Mehmet's warm, callused hand moved over the bare skin of stomach. "Here," the sultan murmured, and with his free hand took hold of Val's wrist again. Drew him down, pulled his hand beneath the water. Guided his fingers right where he wanted them. "Let me show you something."

Simple touch seemed to content him at first, his eyes fluttering shut, his mouth falling open on a deep groan. But Val's hand was small, and inexpert, and eventually Mehmet pushed the loose robe off his shoulders and pulled him into the bath with him, to sit in his lap.

At least, Val thought to himself, he knew what to expect now.

22

AND SO HE DID

A pattern developed. All of Val's things – what meager possessions he had been allowed to accumulate here at the palace – were shifted into the sultan's suite. His had his own small chamber, one that adjoined, with his own small bed and washstand and gilt-edged mirror; more often than not, though, he slept with the sultan, in his massive four-poster. He didn't attend Mehmet as a slave would – Arslan and the other boys still took care of that – but sometimes, if he was feeling playful, Mehmet would dismiss the boys and beckon for Val; have him slip a few buttons and unknot a few laces; put his hands on the skin he found beneath.

Val studied with a private tutor now, Mehmet's own, a mullah who, to Val's surprise, seemed pleased by his gentle curiosity and impeccable manners. He complimented him, sometimes: "Yes, that's right;" "very good;" "your Turkish is flawless." He hated himself for it, but he clung to those compliments.

Mehmet had compliments of his own. "You're learning quickly." "Yes, like that." "Such a gorgeous boy."

He worried. In the cool dark hours, once Mehmet had rolled over and begun to snore, after Val had snuffed all the candles and slid back beneath the covers, all the things he kept carefully lidded during the day pried loose and unspooled within him like dark streamers.

What of Stepan and Gregor, who clutched at his arms and asked him to describe things for them?

What of his family back home, Mother with her tears, and Mircea with his haunted, battle-weary look? Father in his study, poring over maps and treaties, his back against a wall like it hadn't been since Rome.

Most of all he worried for Vlad. Logically, he knew he'd had no choice: Mehmet would never have accepted "no" for an answer. He would have pursued him, tortured him, until Val finally broke; finally gave him what he wanted. But still, he was haunted by the knowledge that it had taken only one night. Vlad would have lasted longer. Vlad would have died on a stake, choking on his own blood, hurling invectives to his last breath. And Val had given in, lay here now, in the sultan's bed, watching his bare chest rise and fall as he slept.

He'd abandoned his older brother. And it didn't matter if Mehmet said that Vlad didn't ask for him, and didn't love him: they were family. They were supposed to stick together.

One day, Val knew with certainty, Vlad would finally snap. The last of his limited patience would run out and he would do something atrocious and unforgivable. Val wanted, desperately, not to be the cause of it.

~*~

Mehmet brought him gifts.

Candlelight caught on the sapphire's many facets, dazzling flashes as the pendant rotated slowly on the end of its chain.

"Do you like it? I picked it to match your eyes." With his free hand, Mehmet cupped his chin and tipped his face up, smiling down at him with what had a become familiar expression, part-ownership, part-feral want, carefully hidden behind a screen of smugness.

"It's lovely," Val said, even though his eyes were much lighter than the gem, a clear blue, the pale, freshwater color of his mother's Nordic people.

Mehmet fastened it around his neck, and his hands lingered afterward, combing through his hair, sweeping it back off his face. "You should grow it out longer." It wasn't a suggestion. He laced his fingers together at Val's nap, and pressed with the whole of both hands. A signal: Val went down to his knees, the necklace heavy and cold at the center of his chest.

The sultan wore only a robe, fresh from the bath and still-warm. Val's hands found the ties and undid them. His eyes closed as he leaned forward…and Mehmet's hands tightened on the back of his head.

"No. Look at me."

And so he did.

~*~

The slaves treated him like nobility. He *was* nobility, but they'd always handled him with considerate indifference. Now, though, they bowed and trembled and touched him with gentle reverence, the same way they did Mehmet. Arslan was the only one that Val could draw any kind of true response from.

"What do they say?"

It was late morning, and the hot water in the copper tub went a long way toward soothing Val's sore muscles. He sat forward, his legs drawn up to his chest, his growing hair falling over his knees in wet mermaid waves. Behind him, Arslan paused, soapy cloth pressed to the top of his spine.

He resumed a moment later. "What does who say?"

"Everyone." Val let the slow, circular motion of the cloth push him forward on every pass, the water lapping at the sides of the tub. "The palace gossips. What do they say of me?"

A telling pause. "They don't talk of you," Arslan said softly. Val had never heard him speak at normal volume.

Val turned his head a fraction. Over his shoulder, he could just see part of Arslan's face, the way his brows were drawn together, the corner of his mouth turned down. "They don't call me a whore?" he pressed. He didn't know why he was asking; the truth could only hurt – not as badly as when Mehmet forced his way inside him. But. Still. "That I'm going to hell?"

Arslan sat back on his heels and applied more soap to the cloth. He sighed. "It isn't my place to repeat such things, your grace." He could be killed for doing so.

Properly chastened, Val faced forward again, gaze going toward the shifting apple branches beyond the open doors in the courtyard. "You're right. I'm sorry."

Arslan scrubbed at his back, careful over the tender bite mark Mehmet had left on the point of his shoulder. After a long moment, he said, so soft, "They do not speak of you, your grace, but of the sultan. Taking a boy as a lover is forbidden by our holy book. It is shameful."

Val rolled the words over in his mind, traced their shapes, marveling at the weight of them. "A lover?" he asked, voice catching. "Is that what I am?" He wore the sultan's sapphire around his neck; wore the marks of his teeth and fingers, the dark bruises left by the driving of his hips.

Arslan's hand stilled. Water droplets fell into the bath, loud as hammer blows in the silence of held breath. "I think," he said, finally, "that you are a slave. Just as I am."

Val closed his eyes and rested his forehead on his knees.

"I'm sorry, your grace. I shouldn't say such things."

"No. I'm glad you did." He swallowed, and it felt as if the chain at the back of his neck bit into his skin, the stone too heavy to hold. "It's nice to have company."

~*~

The days bled together; a routine developed. Mehmet was pleased; Val could tell he was when he left his chambers that morning, thumb swiping across Val's still-slick lower lip. He bent down to kiss him before he left, tongue flicking slow and sly into Val's mouth. He was pleased, and he wasn't worried about Val trying to get away or "run crying" to anyone.

Val dressed, and went, at last, in search of his brother, Arslan in tow, a dutiful eunuch chaperone.

The scent was easy enough to pick up in the garden, the familiar notes stirring both longing and embarrassment in the pit of Val's stomach. He ached for boyhood, for the shared bed, and the cold nights keeping warm under heaps of furs. Vlad had never been sweet – that wasn't in his nature, all the most violent parts of his blended Roman and Viking heritage coming to the fore – but he'd been accepting. He'd loved Val, in his own way. It was love that Val missed more than anything, more than home and Helga's cooking and the bravery of their wolves. He missed being loved; now he was only desired.

And now, he was no longer desired from afar. He'd bathed, but he carried the sultan inside him now, and on every piece of hand-picked clothing; in the jewel around his throat and the

267

delicate gold circlet set in his hair. He was no longer a boy, but a possession, and he knew he reeked of it.

Vlad was in the training yard, crossing swords with a janissary in steel and leather gauntlets and greaves. Vlad, by contrast, wore only breeches and a shirt; a cut in his sleeve and a drying line of blood marked a hit won by his opponent, but he was otherwise unharmed, moving impossibly fast as he dove into his next strike.

Val took up a place against the wall, waiting, Arslan nervous beside him.

Vlad could smell him, no doubt. But he finished his bout, pressing the taller, yet weaker, janissary back until he finally knocked the man's sword away and held him at bay, tip of his own sword pressed to his opponent's throat.

"I yield," he said, hands lifted. His Turkish was rough, accented; he'd come recently from somewhere farther east, Russia maybe.

Vlad stepped back, chest heaving as he caught his breath, ghost of a smile flitting across his mouth. He was straight-faced, though, when he turned to Val. His jaws and brows set at disapproving angles. He ambled a few steps closer and produced a cloth from his waistband that he used to wipe down his blade. His gaze dropped. "The sultan's favorite plaything," he said, and it wasn't a greeting.

Val had been expecting as much – he'd expected worse. But it stung all the same. He drew himself upright and said, with as much dignity as possible, "Brother. I wish to speak with you. Will you walk with me?"

Vlad chuckled. "And be seen in your company? So I can lose my hands?"

"You're my *brother*," Val said, growing desperate. "Mehmet – no one thinks that you…" He gritted his teeth, and Vlad laughed again. An ugly sound, mocking and cold. As flat as his dark eyes.

"I have no choice, do I?" Vlad's gaze flicked up, and had Val not already stood against a wall he would have staggered back beneath the force of it. "I will walk with you, yes." He glanced toward Arslan. "Is this your chaperone?"

Val laid a hand on the boy's shoulder, and felt him flinch beneath it. "This is Arslan."

Vlad snorted. "Don't get sentimental, *brother*." Mocking, again. "Someone like Mehmet has no attachment to slaves. Neither should you if you wish to remain his mistress."

Val took a deep breath. Vlad was baiting him, that was all. He stepped away from the wall and forced a smile. "Thank you. I thought we could go through the garden."

Vlad dropped his practice sword in a barrel full of others and shrugged, falling into step. Arslan followed them, silent but watchful.

Vlad smelled of fresh sweat, and horses. Himself. Clean, outdoor smells of exertion. He didn't smell like a lover; like a kept pet. Val found that he'd started to drift toward him, and corrected course, walking straight ahead from the stables to the start of a garden path.

When it became apparent that Vlad wouldn't speak first, Val said, "How have you fared these past weeks?"

Vlad said, "Better than your ass, I'd wager."

Val bit back a shocked sound and stared resolutely forward as the path curved and ducked beneath a vine-covered arbor. In a quiet voice, sheltered by the shade of vines: "I didn't ask for this."

Vlad didn't respond.

"I had thought…thought that we might be able to come to some sort of understanding, the two of us," Val admitted. "It's true that I'm…" He couldn't say it. "And I have his favor. I could curry favor for you if you would only–"

"Spread myself and bend over?"

"If you would only behave yourself!" Val shouted.

Belatedly, he realized that he'd come to a halt, and that several doves had been startled into flight by his outburst. A duo of gardeners looked over, curious…concerned once they spotted the source of the disturbance. A few weeks before, Val would have thought they hurriedly ducked their heads to avoid drawing Vlad's attention. But maybe, now, they didn't want to make eye contact with the sultan's boy whore.

Val stared at a topiary shaped like an eagle in flight and blinked back the burn of threatening tears. He took a few

269

steadying breaths. When he spoke, he was surprised by the evenness of his tone. "I am trying," he said quietly, "to help you, brother. I can't change what's happened. This is – this is what I have to do now. But if you can learn to be even a little conciliatory, to bite your tongue, and attend your lessons, then perhaps I could soften Mehmet toward you. Over time. I'm trying to help you, Vlad."

When he dared to look his way, Vlad was sneering at him. His eyes flashed in the sunlight, *cold.* "I don't want any help bought on your back, Radu." That name; the sting of it. "Keep me out of your bedroom games." And he turned and walked away, shoulders set.

Val watched him go, lungs hitching and stuttering inside his chest. *He hates me,* he thought. He'd known it for a long time now, but somehow the evidence always hurt like a fresh wound.

"Your grace?" Arslan asked.

He hates me…and maybe I should hate him, too.

"It's alright, Arslan," he sighed. "Let's go back. I don't want to be late for my lessons."

~*~

Mehmet was passionately obsessed with Alexander the Great. His upbringing in Macedon, his childhood exploits; his parents, and his friendships, and his purported bisexuality. His valor in battle, his golden beauty, his conquest and expansion. As weeks bled into months, and Val was kept on as concubine and bedwarmer, and, more and more often, listening ear, the sultan began to speak more freely in the evenings. After he'd ravished Val, when the candles burned low, he picked up the cup of wine on the bedside table and propped up against the pillows. Waxed lyrical about his hero, gesturing with his hands, voice warming to that of an excited young man.

"We are kindred spirits," he said, lifting his cup, smile bittersweet. "Or, we would be, if we'd lived in the same age."

Val, lying on his side, arms around a pillow, tried to shift his hips in a way that didn't aggravate the bruises there. "You admire him greatly."

Mehmet's gaze flashed down to his, hazy with pleasure and wine. "What's not to admire? The most valiant, inventive, inspiring warrior in all of history. A man would be a fool *not* to admire him."

Val knew well not to needle his master. He'd been slapped once, across the face, for making what he'd meant to be an innocent remark; a moment of weakness, feeling sorry for himself. Mehmet bore the faintest of scars along the crest of one shoulder, the place where, during his duel with Vlad years before, the bone had shattered, and portions of it had come through the skin. Just a silver line, but as Val knelt on the cool tiles beside the bath, he'd passed a fingertip along the mark and known a moment's deep satisfaction; Vlad had inflicted that wound. Every time Mehmet saw it in the mirror, he'd be forced to think of the Wallachian prince he'd been unable to best in the ring.

Mehmet had stilled; the story he'd been telling had cut off mid-sentence. "What is it?" A warning in his voice, one that Val had been too absorbed to heed.

"This." He traced the scar again. "This is from my brother. When he bested you."

Mehmet had caught his wrist and half-dragged him into the tub. His other hand had cracked against his cheek. Hard enough that he saw stars; hard enough that a red mark lingered there for hours.

He hadn't made a mistake like that since. But. Sometimes he tested his boundaries. Times like now, when his ass was sore and his throat ached and he knew that he couldn't get away. Moments when Mehmet compared himself to a man who'd never mistreated a hostage.

"Alexander had golden hair, though," he murmured, pressing the words into the pillow.

Mehmet heard him, though. There was no getting around vampire hearing. He stilled, and a little of the color drained from his face. "Yes." Voice flat. "He was." He reached with his free hand to push his hair back, the sweaty tangles that kept falling forward over his face. His rings caught the light; Val knew the texture of each of those rings intimately. "Do you wish I was golden, then? Like Alexander? Like *you*?"

271

"You're very handsome," Val said, by rote.

Mehmet bared his teeth in a semblance of a smile. "Ah, handsome. But handsome isn't beautiful."

"Handsome is a kind of beautiful." Val clutched his pillow tighter.

Mehmet chuckled. "It's not the same thing, pet. You're far too clever not to know that."

"Beautiful is for pets," Val amended. "Handsome is for kings. For sultans."

His brittle smile softened, truer now. "Yes, I suppose you're right." He drained off his wine and slid down to lie against the pillows. When he reached for Val, Val went willingly, knowing that he must. He let the sultan pull him up flush to his side, his arm around him, so that Val's face lay in the hollow of his scarred shoulder. "I frustrate myself sometimes," he admitted. "Wanting to be Alexander."

Val hummed a neutral sound.

"It's only—" His hand tightened on Val's waist; Val could feel the energy running through him. Some of it was vampirism, but mostly it was true passion. "There's been no one like him since. There were the Romans. Your people, I suppose." He chuckled, and this time the tightening of his hand was possessive, taunting ages and emperors past. *Oh, mighty Rome, now I have you in my bed, my teeth marks in your neck.* "They accomplished the impossible. But nothing was quite so impossible as Alexander, was it?"

Val kept silent, his thoughts unspoken. Chief among them: Mehmet was in love with Alexander. Or at least the idea of him. But a Roman golden boy would suffice for the time being.

~*~

The young sultan loved Alexander, yes, and Greece. But he talked of Rome, too. Rum, he called it in his own language. Val had been raised as both Roman and Romanian, with Spartan warrior and equestrian training, and lessons in Hellenistic culture from his father's homeland. Mehmet had read widely, and knew much, but when he drank and dreamed aloud, he combined the city of Rome, seat of the ancient empire, and the city of Constantinople, the new, eastern seat of an empire that had been winnowed down to one fortified city; one last bastion of the old ways, ruled by a Greek emperor. John, elder brother of Constantine Dragases, whom Val called friend.

It was six months after becoming the sultan's concubine that Val realized Mehmet meant to sack Byzantium.

He stood at the washbasin, braiding his hair over one shoulder in the mirror there. "Get the slave boy to do that," Mehmet had said, but Val was enjoying doing this one small thing for himself. It felt almost like having a bit of control.

He'd reached the last inch of braidable hair and set about tying it with a strip of leather. His reflection stared back at him, sleepy-eyed, disinterested. Mehmet had been talking for nearly an hour about Rome as he leafed through his own notes on the subject, spread out on the table amid a platter of grapes and a cup and pitcher of wine.

"I mean to take it," he said, and Val turned to him, flicking his completed braid over his shoulder.

"What?" He'd found that, slowly, some of his deference was wearing thin at the edges. When he was tired, or feeling especially desperate, he slipped; addressed the sultan in a more familiar way – a familiarity he loathed, truth told.

Sometimes Mehmet noticed it, but he didn't tonight, his gaze nothing but proud. "Constantinople. I'm going to take it. This" – he gestured to the room around them, the palace – "is my father's palace. I mean to have my own, and I'll build it on top of the last remaining jewel of Greece."

Val had grown so numb in the past few months, inured to his new daily routines, that the sudden swell of panic surprised him. The wash of heat and cold, the prickling of his skin, the tightness in his chest. He worked hard to breathe normally, and to keep his face blank. "That – that's your goal?"

"No. That's my *plan*." He cocked his head to the side, expression almost fond. "Have you even been listening to me, Radu? Or did I tire you too thoroughly for that? Come." He cleared a space on the table, in front of the chair that faced his own. "Sit."

273

Val obeyed. He always did.

"You see," Mehmet said, voice laced with excitement, eyes fever-bright, "I am, essentially, the heir to Rum."

Val stared at him.

"You are, undoubtedly, a descendent of the original founders. And therefore Mars," he added, resigned. "But! Your father was never king. Your uncle was. And *I'm* your uncle's designated heir." He held his arms out to the side. *Behold, it is I.*

"But…" Val said carefully. "Uncle isn't the king of anything anymore. He hasn't been for centuries."

Mehmet flapped a dismissive hand. "No matter–"

"But–" Val bit his tongue. Too far; he'd gone too far.

Mehmet drew upright in his chair, jaw clenching. "Romulus chose *me*." He thumped his palm to his own chest. "Two vampire nephews right in front of him, and a half-breed, no less, and he came to my father to ask for *me*." Pride, yes, but also: desperation. Val was seeing it more and more, the way it peeked through the cracks when Mehmet was tired, or drunk, lulled by the sense of safety and acceptance his bed, and obedient bedmate, provided.

He was very young. It was easy to forget, sometimes, but Val could see it now, youth spurring cruelty. He ducked down low, trying to look even smaller, more defenseless.

Mehmet put both hands on the table and leaned forward. His fangs descended a fraction, far enough to catch the candlelight. "Have you ever stopped to ask yourself why? Why your uncle would rather turn a human than leave his riches to his own flesh and blood?"

What riches? Val wondered. Romulus held no titles, or lands. He didn't even have any Familiars, to Val's knowledge.

"Maybe," the sultan continued, voice knife-edged, "he knew there was no hope for greatness from a violent idiot and a little whore. He wanted an heir who could reclaim his old empire. Well." A harsh laugh. "That's me, little prince. I will take back the empire. It will be *mine*. And it starts with the Red Apple of Byzantium."

~*~

Val had been afraid to dream-walk purposefully, afraid that if Mehmet stirred in the night he might find Val's lifeless body somehow suspicious; that Val himself might murmur in his sleep, betraying the conversation he was having in his astral shape. Mehmet knew that he was a vampire; knew the texture of every patch of his skin; knew the sounds he made when he was entered, when he pressed his face into the mattress and tried to pass pain off as pleasure. He knew his family, knew more about them than anyone outside of it ever had.

But he didn't know that Val could dream-walk, and that was a secret he would guard with his life. It was his lone hope in a sea of unending despondency. He hadn't risked revealing it, but tonight…tonight he had to.

When the room was dark, and Mehmet was snoring, Val rolled over so his back was to the sultan, closed his eyes, and went walking.

He found Constantine in the darkened bedchamber of his quiet palace at Mistra, moonlight filtering through an open window. The despot lay on his back, one arm flung aside on the empty pillow beside him; the place where a wife would lie if he could find one. Dark curly hair framed his head on the pillow, a halo of shadow.

Val stood a long, indecisive moment, not wanting to wake him. He himself could no longer sleep peacefully, but he didn't want to take such a gift from another, knowing its worth.

In the end, he didn't have to. Constantine shifted, the bedclothes rustling, and cracked his eyes open. When his sleepy gaze landed on Val, he bolted upright with a gasp, reaching with one hand to dash the grit from his eyes, and with the other toward a sheathed dagger that lay on the night table.

That was new.

"I'm sorry, your grace," Val rushed to say. "I didn't mean to wake you."

The despot froze. "Val?"

"Yes, your grace."

"Oh." He let out a deep breath. "Christ." A sleep-roughened chuckle. "I'm sorry, you startled me."

"*I'm* sorry," Val said. "I wouldn't have bothered you now, while you're sleeping. It's only – I have unfortunate news."

A beat. "Hold on a moment." He had human eyes; Val watched him fumble across the night table for a candle. Wished he could reach out with corporeal fingers and take it from the man, help him flip back his covers and slide down out of bed.

"I'm sorry," he said again, miserable.

"No, no, don't be." Constantine crossed slowly to the hearth and knelt to light his candle on the smoldering coals there. When he stood, flame cupped behind one hand, the light glinted off his eyes, alert now, troubled. He walked up to Val, sat down on the large chest at the end of his bed, so they were on eye level. "What's the matter, son?"

Val took a breath to steady himself. It was immense, what he'd come to tell. Impossible and unimaginable. "Mehmet," he said, and the name brought a foul taste to the back of his tongue. "He – he's been dreaming. Talking." Deep exhalation. "Your grace, he's set his sights on Byzantium. He means to march on Constantinople and take it for his own."

Constantine's brows jumped, but his face remained otherwise calm, light from the candleflame dancing over it. "He's ambitious."

"He's *insane*," Val blurted out before he could help it. He'd been stuffing all his emotions down deep, willing himself not to feel any particular way about his current situation. If he allowed himself to actively hate it...he knew there was no coming back from that. He'd go mad. But here now, alone in the company of a true friend...it all came spilling out. "He's terrible, and violent, and he thinks he can make himself a Roman emperor, just because he wants it. He talks publicly about glory for the Ottomans, but he just wants to style himself as Alexander and conquer the whole damn world!"

He was panting by the end, arms flung wide. Constantine's gaze moved down, flicking toward the join of shoulder and neck that had been exposed by the slow slide of his night shirt. Too late, Val remembered the sultan's fangs there, the sharp sting of a bite as passion overtook him. He reached to tug the shirt back over the mark, but the damage was done.

When Constantine met Val's gaze again, his own was almost wounded. "Val." His voice sounded like a sore throat; like an ache. "What has happened?"

Val felt a tremor start, bone-deep. Tiny little quakes that would spread out and out until his hands shook if he didn't gain control of them. "Only what I told you. That Mehmet means to sack—"

"*Val.* I don't care about that. What has the sultan done *to you?*"

Pride warred with shame. And with yearning – he wanted badly to tell someone, a childish need for comfort. Vlad had always told him not to act like a baby, but…but…

He took a shattered breath, and then another. *Nothing* died on his tongue. A dozen other protests formed, but he couldn't voice them. He felt the burn of tears, and wondered why he was forever crying in front of this man, who had much greater worries than the emotions of a Wallachian child who couldn't manage to keep himself out of a sultan's bed.

"Son—"

"It's my fault." Val closed his eyes, fighting the tears back, unable to face the sympathy on the man's face. "I could have…could have refused…or…"

Constantine sighed. "It is *not* your fault," he said patiently, and when Val cracked his eyes open, he was surprised to find that it wasn't sympathy, but anger on the despot's face. Hardening his jaw, throwing the tendons on his throat into stark relief. "There's nothing you could have done to stop it." His hand tightened around the candlestick in his hand until the flame wavered. "It is the job of men to stop that sort of thing from happening. And apparently there is a shortage of those among the Ottomans."

A shudder moved through him, and he bared his teeth. But then he took another breath and calmed visibly. Another sigh. He shook his head. "Emperors, and kings, and sultans will do as they want, though." And here came the sympathy. "I'm so sorry, Val. I wish I could…" He trailed off. There was nothing he could do, and they both knew it.

"I didn't mean to tell you," Val said. "I only came to warn you of Mehmet's plans to take your brother's city."

"He can't take the city. No one can breach its walls." Dismissive, certain. "But you…" His eyes widened. "Val, does he know you can do this? That you can visit someone outside of the palace this way?"

"No."

"You mustn't tell him. You would be punished." He looked like he wanted to say more, but cut off, visibly biting back the words. "Val," he said, helplessly, "I'm sorry."

"I know, you've said." Val scraped up a smile. "Thank you, but I'll be alright."

They stared at one another a long moment, the despot clearly at a loss.

"I should return," Val said at last. "May — may I still visit you? When I'm able?"

"Of *course*."

"Thank you." Val shut his eyes and slipped away. When he opened them again, it was to the darkness of Mehmet's bedchamber.

The sultan still snored behind him.

Val lie awake for a long time, silent tears soaking his pillow.

23

THE GUILT AND THE GRIEF

December, 1447

Word had come the summer before that Wallachia had signed a new treaty with the Ottomans, and that the brothers had been officially spared. Murat had been the one to inform Vlad, brought before the old sultan while the new one stood off to the side, lip curled in derision, trying and failing to catch Vlad's gaze. Vlad paid him no mind; he knew what everyone at court knew: that Mehmet was merely a figurehead at this point in time. He could give commands, and storm his way through the palace, shouting at slaves and commandeering women and boys of his choosing, but Murat was the real power behind the empire now, as he'd been before. The only true influence Mehmet practiced was that acted out in his bedchamber, and that he did, according to gossip, frequently and wildly.

Vlad tried – and often failed – not to think of his little brother. He caught glimpses of him, sometimes, though he tried not to. Val was growing tall, and willowy; waif-like at certain angles, with his sheets of rippling golden hair and delicate features. But some glimpses hinted at the steel edges beneath his porcelain veneer. He shared Vlad's blood, after all. There was a warrior in there, under his pretty façade. One that would no doubt never be allowed to see the light of day, dripping in fine silks and even finer jewels, his blue eyes smudged with kohl at Mehmet's pleasure.

The guilt and the grief would cripple Vlad if he allowed himself to feel them keenly. And so he tamped it all down, buried it deep. But he let the hatred fester. He trained, and he studied, and he crafted himself into the perfect knight; into an avenging warrior with his sights set on only one prize. And the hatred kept festering, kept growing. He hated everyone; it was a hatred that lived within him day and night, galvanizing him.

And then.

December arrived.

And with it…word from home.

Vlad was in the training yard, breath pluming like smoke in the chill, his opponent flat in the dirt, when a messenger came for him. "The sultan wants an audience."

He didn't bother cleaning himself. He went, sweaty and dusty, to Murat's audience chamber.

The former sultan was alone, save a single witness. A vizier, of some sort. Vlad didn't care to know the man's name. He observed only the barest courtesies, half-bowing, and then waiting, hands clenched into fists at his sides.

Murat made him wait a long moment, though a speculative light came into his eyes, his head tilting to the side. Then he turned to his underling and murmured something behind his hand. The man bowed and then rushed out of the room. He returned a moment later leading…

Leading a Romanian noble. A boyar, dressed in traditional garb, dusty and filthy from the road, mustache more gray than brown, hairline receding. His gaze fell on Vlad with intent, and after a moment's staring, Vlad realized he recognized him as one of the nobles most loyal to his father. His former chancellor.

"Cazan," he said on a gasp.

"Your grace." The boyar came to stand before Vlad and went to one knee. He carried a bundle under his arm: a long, narrow shape that was obviously a sword, wrapped in layers of cloth. With bent head, the man said, "I come – I come with – with terrible news." His voice was shattered. When he lifted his head again, Vlad saw the lines of strain and exhaustion on it, the dirt caked into the creases. He hadn't even bothered to wash himself before requesting an audience.

Vlad had lived in a state of numb fury for so long – and now, suddenly, his heart lurched and his palms began to sweat. "What news?"

"Your father. And your brother," Cazan said haltingly. His eyes shone with checked tears. "They are dead."

Vlad let the words fall over him. Took them in, processed them. Dead. Father and Mircea. And Father a vampire. Father, who was Remus…purported dead before. Perhaps he…

"How?" he asked, and he could hear the calmness in his voice, could watch Cazan startle in response to it.

Cazan gathered himself a moment, through a series of deep breaths.

"I need to know all of it," Vlad prompted. "Everything that happened." So he could make sense of it.

"Perhaps," Murat suggested, "your friend would like to refresh himself first."

"No," Cazan said, "no. I am fine."

But a slave did bring a folding chair, and he settled into his gratefully. Vlad had to catch his arm and guide him to his seat when his legs wobbled and gave out.

"Your grace," he said when he could, panting. "It began with John Hunyadi."

The resentment, and the scheming, had begun, Cazan presumed, during the war council at Dobriya the summer before. The White Knight of Hungary was detained; Mircea had blamed him, personally, for the devastating battlefield losses of the Christian causes. He'd argued for Hunyadi's arrest, trial, and execution. The rest of the council had disagreed, and let him go, but Hunyadi left that council nursing a massive grudge against House Dracul.

A grudge that sharpened his ambitions of leadership to something barbed and weaponized. He wanted the Hungarian throne for himself, and to get it, he needed an ally in Wallachia – one he wouldn't find in Dracul, and his son and heir, Mircea. And so he backed Vladislav II of the Dânești clan, at the time living in Brasov. And he launched a blistering propaganda campaign against Vlad Dracul.

"They met together last month," Cazan said, face flushed with high emotion. "Hunyadi crossed the Carpathians. He was headed for Tîrgoviște!"

"Did my father close the gates to him?"

"Yes, of course. But." He winced. "There was a revolt amongst the boyars."

"Which boyars?"

"Those aligned with the Dânești. It was – it was most of them, your grace. Your father and brother were not in the palace at the time. They had some of their most trusted guards with them, but..."

The wolves. Their faces flashed through Vlad's mind: Cicero, Caesar, Ioan, Vasile. Fenrir would have been with Mother, in the palace; he was her wolf.

"Your father," Cazan continued, "told me that he and your brother Mircea were separated in the melee. He lost sight of him, but, one of his guards was able to help him get away...and he ran to me.

"He was scratched and bleeding, his clothes torn. I could tell he'd been running through the forest on foot. And his eyes – they were wild, like a spooked horse. Something terrible had happened, I knew. His grace gave me two tokens, and he told me to get them to you, through whatever means necessary. 'Should anything happen to Mircea,' he said, 'then Wallachia belongs to Vlad.'" Cazan took another series of breaths, blinking against tears. "He told me what had happened in Tîrgovişte, and I begged him to allow me to hide him. I have an old cellar beneath the stables; no one could have found him! But he would not risk my safety, he said. All of the Wallachian nobility had turned against him. And so he fled again, through the forests.

"I could not leave him to make his way on his own, though. I gathered some of my men – my best fighters – and we followed. He'd left a path of footprints in the soft earth, and broken branches to mark the way.

"We caught up to him. But..." He shuddered, and closed his eyes.

Vlad wanted to shake him. *Just say it!*

"Your grace." The man's voice cracked. "The enemy was upon him, men in Vladislav's armor. They had a hunting hound with them, something massive and hairy – it looked like a wolf! And...and..."

"*What?*"

"They had cut his heart from his body. One of the soldiers held it. It steamed, fresh and hot. It..." He choked a moment, coughs that tried to disguise sobs.

Vlad didn't care. Someone could have swung a sword at his neck, and he wouldn't have noticed.

His heart. They'd cut out his *heart*.

Vlad lurched forward and grabbed Cazan by both shoulders. He did shake him this time, hard, and the man gasped.

"Your grace—"

Vlad growled, and the boyar went silent. "You're sure? The heart? They took the heart out? You saw it with your own eyes?"

Cazan gaped at him a moment – whether in response to his tone or his growl, Vlad didn't know or care – but finally swallowed. "Y-yes, your grace. I saw. And they – they *burned* it."

Six long years had passed since that awful day at Gallipoli; six years of Ottoman captivity. Vlad had long since lost hope that his father would manage to bring him home – or so he'd told himself. The Ottomans might kill him for Dracul's treaty-breaking, or they might keep him until he was a grown man, numb, a usable puppet.

But he found now, as he was unable to draw breath into his lungs, that hope had lingered. A tiny scrap of it, lodged deep between his ribs. So long as Father was alive, there was a chance for freedom.

He thought of a tiny pyre, just big enough for a heart, and something in him…broke.

He turned around, and vomited on the pristine floor tiles.

He hadn't had breakfast yet, and so it was only bile. He wiped his mouth with the back of a shaking hand and said, "Where is he?"

"Your grace?"

"My father. *Where is he?*"

"He is – buried, your grace. After – they left him, and I couldn't…I left strict instructions with my men to see that his body was properly wrapped and carried to the chapel near my home. He'll have a proper Christian burial, I assure you. I myself rode straight here. To deliver the news – and these."

Vlad turned back, and Cazan was unwrapping the sword he'd brought. It was Dracul's Toledo blade, given to him by emperor Sigismund at Nuremburg in 1431 – the year of Vlad's birth.

"There is also this," Cazan said, and from a pocket on his person produced a gold collar engraved with a dragon. "They belong to you now. You are the reigning Prince of Wallachia."

Vlad couldn't bring himself to touch either item. "My brother is the heir. Where is he?"

Pale and shivering, Cazan answered carefully. "I do not know, your grace. But I know that his survival is – unlikely."

~*~

Word of Mircea arrived a few hours later in the form of a Wallachian messenger on a blown horse. The heir was dead. Tortured. Mutilated. And buried alive, face-down in a deep, deep hole.

Vlad was, in fact, the Prince of Wallachia.

Vladislav II of the Dânești clan had claimed the title as well.

~*~

A bitter evening, wind sighing through the open sides of the folly that was the palace chapel, candle flames wavering, guttering, but staying, stubborn as the man who knelt in front of them. Vlad held the gold collar, running his thumb over the dragon emblem again and again, tracing its sinuous body with his thumbnail.

The man who'd been Remus, a pagan, the son of a god, had, in the end, been a member of a holy Christian order. Vlad Dracul. Alive for over two thousand years…dead at last. At the hands of a petty Romanian clansman.

He closed his hands around the collar until his knuckles went white; he felt the soft metal start to give; he could break it, if he wished.

A soft step behind him. A whiff of perfumed vampire. "Vlad," Val said, and his voice was a wreck.

Vlad didn't turn around; he didn't trust himself not to reach for his brother. He laid the collar on the altar in front of him, lest he snap it in half.

"Vlad," Val repeated, and walked up the aisle. He knelt down beside him, an arm's length away. He was shaking. Under his perfume, and the unwelcome taint of Mehmet, he smelled also of tangible grief. A sharp odor, like fear sweat. "Mehmet said – is it true? Father? And Mircea?"

Vlad nodded toward the collar, candlelight making the dragon seem alive, writhing. His voice was flat when he spoke. "I had it from Cazan. Dânești men cut Father down, and then took his heart. Burned it."

Val whimpered.

"They had a wolf. That must be how they..." Subdued him. Long enough to deliver a fatal blow. Father hadn't seen any fighting in a long time, grown soft and comfortable at home in the palace. "Vladislav is staking his claim."

"Mircea..." Val breathed through his mouth, quick, hitched little breaths that rattled in his throat. "He was...buried alive? Maybe he's..."

"I don't know. I have no idea how resilient a half-breed is."

It was silent a moment, save the whistling of the wind in the eaves. Vlad was painfully aware of his brother beside him; distress poured off him in waves and Vlad's fingers curled against his thighs.

Val started to cry, quietly.

And Vlad turned to him, finally.

Val wasn't dressed for the weather. In stark contrast to Vlad's wool breeches and tunic and oilskin, he was wore deep blue silk, a kaftan left open halfway down to his navel, bare skin blue-tinged in the cold. His hair had been left down, wavy over his shoulders, a cold circlet on his head to match the gold rings on his fingers and the fine chain around his neck. White silk șalvar and soft slippers. Indoor clothes. The clothes of an expensive royal plaything...not those of a warrior prince.

Tears ran unchecked down his face, glistening like crystal. A bite mark on his neck peeked out from behind gilt hair.

Vlad could envision it all too distinctly: Mehmet holding him down, sinking his fangs into a tender patch of skin, using him.

He thought he might be sick again.

Instead, he swallowed hard and said, "Valerian."

His brother's head snatched up, red-rimmed eyes flying wide.

"There may no longer be love between us." Val's mouth opened on a silent, anguished sound of protest, his chin quivering. "But I promise you this, brother. I *will* reclaim our home. I will find out if Mircea is truly dead, and I will have revenge on everyone who did this."

Val wiped his eyes with delicate fingertips. "How?"

"I don't know yet." He faced the candles again. One stuttered and went out in the next draft. He sighed. "Somehow. I'll appeal to Murat, I don't...I don't know." He dug his hands into his legs, felt the bite of his own nails through his breeches. If it weren't for the fabric, he would have drawn blood.

Val shifted closer, silk rustling. "Vlad..."

Vlad didn't know what he meant to say, only that he could no longer keep his distance. Not now. Not with half their family dead.

He reached out, quick enough that Val tried to duck back – but then he relaxed when he realized Vlad was merely putting an arm around his shoulders, and drawing him in. Val came willingly, then, tucking in close, his head on Vlad's shoulder. He breathed in shuddering gasps, his slight ribcage pressing against Vlad's. Delicate as a flower stem.

Vlad held his brother, and tipped his head back, gaze going to the weathered wooden cross that hung above the altar.

God help me, he prayed. *Help me kill them all.*

~*~

He was called before Murat again the next morning. Clean-faced from his morning ablutions, surprised, he followed the slave sent to fetch him back to the old sultan's audience chamber.

The vast space had been heated with coal braziers, and they did a remarkable job of pushing back the chill. Murat sat swaddled in furs, a great mink thrown across his lap, as tidy and imperious as ever. "Good morning," he greeted.

Vlad didn't bow. He came to stand in front of the man, hands linked behind his back, waiting. He'd allowed himself to grieve, silent and dry-eyed, in the chapel last night, while Val sobbed quietly into his shoulder, soaking his jacket. He let the fury and sadness sweep through him like a tide…and then forced it away. There was no time for that now. Emotion would serve no purpose.

"You seem very composed," Murat observed, "for a man who's been informed that his father and brother were brutally murdered by a pretender to the throne."

"Shall I weep, Your Majesty?"

The old sultan chuckled. "My, but you are full of hate. No, I don't think weeping suits you. But I think you should like to take action, no?"

Behind his back, Vlad clenched his hands together, tight, until he felt his nails score his skin.

"I think you want the heads of the men who killed your family." A pause. The old fox was waiting, dropping little gaps, seeing if Vlad would barrel his way into them, red-faced and shouting. "I think you want *blood.*" His brows jumped on the last word. *Yes, I know what you are. I know what you drink.*

Chin tilted upward, as coldly as he could manage, Vlad said, "And yet here I stand, Your Majesty. A prisoner. Unable to do anything."

"So you do." A long moment passed, the man's gaze calculating. "You are still made of steel, I think." Almost a note of approval in his voice. "Now, your brother is—"

"My brother is a child and a whore."

Murat was silent a beat, but he said nothing more of Val. Good. It was better if he thought the boy was of no threat or importance. Whores got to live, while warriors were so frequently tested – for honor, for sport, for wickedness.

"Your father," he said at last, "was, I think, an honorable man. So are you, in your own way. That is why I'm sending you home."

Vlad fought valiantly to keep from reacting to that statement. His nails bit through skin, and blood pearled against his fingertips. He bit down hard on the inside of his cheek, and a fang nicked the tender flesh.

"Nothing to say?"

"I don't see how such a thing is possible, Your Majesty." But his blood *sang.* Home. Revenge.

"Hmm."

Coals hissed in the braziers. Cold wind whistled up high, at the edges of the window shutters.

In a low, even voice, Murat said, "I know who your father is, child."

Vlad bristled. "You—"

A weathered, jeweled hand lifted, waving him to silence. "Did you forget who made my son immortal? I know of Romulus. And of Remus, who calls himself Vlad Dracul. *Called*," he amended. "If what his former chancellor says is true, then his heart has been destroyed, and there is no hope of his regeneration."

Vlad clenched his jaw against a curse.

"You may be immortal, but you are young. This is the way of the world, Vlad: strong men rule until stronger men come to cut them down and supplant them. One man's god is another man's devil.

"Your father lived a very long time, but he was killed by another man's puppet. You shall have your revenge, and may it bring you peace. But only if you allow me to grant you the opportunity."

"I…don't understand."

"I mean to free you. Completely. I will give you armor, and weapons, and a horse. Grant you your own cavalry regiment, and send you north with Mustafa Hassan and his infantrymen at your disposal. You will kill Vladislav, and take back Wallachia. It's a vassal state of my empire, and I shall choose who sits on its throne. I choose you, Dracula, if you are man enough to set aside your hatred of me and take up this mantle."

Help me kill them all, he'd prayed last night, while his brother cried.

God had a grand sense of humor, it seemed. Sometimes he sent you exactly what you wanted as a gift from someone else you wanted to kill.

For the first time in his nearly seven years of captivity, Vlad went to his knees. "Yes, Your Majesty. I will accept."

~*~

Vlad was taken to meet with Mustafa Hassan, first, a competent military commander indifferent to Vlad. He was marching north anyway; he could spare men to help Vlad retake Tîrgovişte.

Vlad didn't care. If those foot soldiers could help him accomplish his goal, that was all he needed.

Then he met the captain – destined to be his second in command – of the cavalry unit he was to take.

The first surprise was that the man was a janissary, and not a true Turk. The second was that he bore the dark, almond eyes, glossy black hair, and high cheekbones of someone born much farther to the east than Adrianople.

His name was Malik Bey, and the long scar at the outer edge of his left brow proved he'd seen battle.

"Vlad Dracula," Vlad introduced himself. "Prince of Wallachia."

"I know who you are," Malik said in perfect Turkish, and clasped Vlad's forearm in greeting. His voice was even, calm. Polite. Outwardly, he seemed disinterested. This was just another boy prince set to give him orders.

But Vlad sensed a certain interest in the man; the subtlest hint of curiosity. Janissaries fought valiantly and loyally for their Ottoman masters – but that didn't always mean they wanted to.

"I hear we have a coup to plan."

Vlad smiled, and he couldn't remember the last time he'd done such a thing. "Yes. We do."

<u>24</u>

THE CAMPAIGN

All that winter, Vlad spent his days running drills with his new cavalry, poring over maps, talking of strategy, honing his already-strong body into something beastly. The few glimpses Val caught of him on the palace grounds were shocking. His legs were still long, but no one could call him "lanky" now. Broad shoulders, thick arms, a trimly muscled waist: Vlad looked every inch the young warrior, his countenance ferocious; the sort of thing grown men would stagger back from.

Val grew as well. The sleeves of his kaftans became too short and his entire wardrobe was replaced. In the mirror, he could see the changes, the way baby softness was slowly fading into the long lines and sharp angles of adolescence. His face narrowed; he looked almost elfin. And he looked nothing like a warrior – which was what he needed to be if he had any hope of being sent back home with his brother.

When winter broke, and the mountain passes were clear, Vlad would head for Tîrgovişte with Murat's blessing and manpower. Val meant to go with him.

Thus began his slow, careful campaign to win Mehmet over to the idea.

Val sat back on his heels, catching his breath, his hands still braced on the sultan's open thighs.

Mehmet slumped back against the wall, hands twitching weakly where they lay on the cushions of the bench where he was sitting. His chest heaved, flushed where it was visible beneath his unlaced shirt. He breathed through an open mouth, lips still shaped around his last, deep groan, his eyes shut, his lashes dark fans on pinkened cheeks. If pressed at knifepoint, Val would admit that ecstasy was very becoming on the sultan.

"Your Majesty." His voice sounded as raw as his throat felt. "I have a request." He'd planned this carefully, waiting until Mehmet was well-satisfied; that was when he was at his most generous. He moved his fingertips in little circles, a delicate massage.

Mehmet cracked one eye open. "A request?" Curious, but still languid. Malleable. He cupped Val's chin in one weak hand, traced a thumb over his shiny lower lip. "Ask and ye shall receive, beautiful one."

My freedom, Val thought, wildly. But that was folly. He had to start small, and build up to it.

He forced a smile, lowered his lashes to a discreet angle, and said, "I was only thinking that it's been a very long time since I've had any training like I used to. I haven't sparred in *such* a long time."

Mehmet seemed to return to himself a little, lifting his head up from the wall, gaze clearing. He flicked a lazy, though disbelieving smile. "You want to *spar*?"

"I should like to, yes," he said, demure and hesitant. "I was in training to become a knight at one time. Before…"

Mehmet stilled; he held his breath and his thumb froze a moment, before pressing into the center of Val's lower lip. When Val lifted a pleading gaze to him, he exhaled on a quiet laugh. "A knight? *That's* what you want?" He fingered a lock of golden hair. "Why would you waste such beauty on a battlefield when you can be comfortable here?"

Will I not ever be allowed to be a man? Val wanted to scream. *Can I have not one scrap of honor? Only your whore, and whores don't wield swords.*

He took a measured breath and fought to keep his voice low and soft. "You flatter me. It's only…"

Mehmet sat forward, one elbow braced on his knee, the other hand winding into Val's hair. Their faces were very close together now, close enough to kiss if Mehmet hadn't minded the taste of his own come. "Only what?" Sultry, almost sweet, but Val had to tread so, so carefully.

Val wet his lips, and Mehmet's gaze followed the quick pass of his tongue. "It's only that I want to be…useful." A muscle

291

leaped in Mehmet's jaw. "All the other boys at court are being groomed for leadership and I...want to do my part. For your empire."

Mehmet held his gaze a long, tense moment. Then he laughed and sat back, petting lazily over Val's head. "You do your part plenty, Radu. Don't worry over that."

~*~

Well, that was that, Val thought bitterly. So much for trying.

But a few days later, Arslan toted in a hamper that threatened to buckle his knees, setting it down gratefully with a sound of shifting metal from inside.

"What is this?" Val asked, climbing off the divan where he'd been reading.

"A gift for you. The sultan had it all specially made."

Val settled on his knees on the carpet, folded back the lid and found–

Armor. Lightweight, beautifully crafted steel, padded with red leather.

And beneath that, a sword.

Val sucked in a breath. He stared at it a long moment, resting there on a bed of silk, drinking in its long, clean lines and its elegant cross-guard and hilt, worked with gold and tiny sapphires. It was too fine a weapon for a common soldier; the sort of thing a king – or a sultan – carried both during battle, and ceremonies. Deadly, functional, but a beautiful showpiece, too, designed to project an image of power and opulence. No one wanted to be subjugated by a pauper; they wanted the jewels and the flashing of gold.

"This can't be mine," Val murmured, not daring to touch it. His hand opened and closed in the empty air above it.

Arslan made a strange sound – when Val lifted his head, he found that the boy was *laughing*. He'd never heard such a thing from him before. When he did, his eyes danced, and his smile broke white and straight across his face.

"What?"

292

"Of course it's for you," the slave said. "It was commissioned just for you. For your size. See? It's too small for a regular soldier."

Finally, breath held, Val reached in and pulled the sword out. Sunlight winked down the length of it, blinding. When he held it upright in front of him, distorted reflection staring back, wide-eyed, he saw that Arslan was right: it was a short sword, narrow and light. Built for a boy who was not quite a man.

"Why did he have this made for me?"

Arslan shrugged. "He said to bring it to you. That you would know why."

Because he'd asked to spar.

Val shivered…and for the first time in a long time, not from fear or pain.

~*~

The next day, Mehmet turned up just after lunch dressed in simple, worn clothes, his own sword on his hip. He grinned rakishly. "You wanted to practice, oh great golden knight?"

Val raced to throw on his own humble clothes and gather up his new sword, its jewel-studded scabbard belted tight around his slim waist.

They didn't go to the regular training yard where the other boys at court practiced. Instead, a short walk from Mehmet's chambers found them in a circular, hedge-lined room in his own private area of the garden, shaded with grape-laden bowers and cherry trees, the footing a loose, small gravel that crunched underfoot. A water jug and ladle waited, as well as an array of other weapons, laid out on layers of leather and silk on one of the decorative benches.

"It's just us?" Val asked, apprehension blooming sudden and tight in his belly. He didn't know why he was worried; they were alone together all the time. He slept in the man's bed, gave of his body every night. But unease crawled across his skin, itchy as a rash.

Mehmet crossed to the bench and reached for a set of leather bracers there. "The privilege of being a sultan: privacy. Here, come help me with these."

Val went to do up the complicated laces on the bracers, Mehmet holding out each forearm in turn.

"You know," he mused, as Val's fingers made quick work of the task, "when you first mentioned this, I admit that I was offended. Here I've been heaping you with luxuries, and yet you wanted to spar. You were bathing in rose oil, wearing all the most lavish silks and jewels, living like a prince for the first time in your life, and yet you wanted to get sweaty and dirty in the training yard. What was I to make of that?"

Val wisely didn't answer.

"But then I thought about it a little more," Mehmet continued, "and I decided it sounded like a fun way to spend the afternoon. Treaty negotiations have been giving me a headache all week." Val finished, stepped back, and the sultan flexed his hand into a fist, smiling down at the way the leather bracer tightened against his wrist. "Let's have a go, then."

They stripped off their scabbards and set them aside on the bench; faced off from one another in the center of the circle. Val's sword was light, yes, but he could feel keenly, already, what months of being a lapdog had earned him; his arms quivered, the muscles soft and weak. He would tire quickly, he realized, and struggle on his follow-through.

Damn. Perhaps this had been a poor idea after all.

But no. He had to get stronger so that he could be of use to Vlad. The only way to improve upon weakness was to work.

Mehmet, by contrast, looked fit and lithe, balanced on the balls of his feet, sword held casually, as if it weighed nothing. It was a larger blade than Val's, longer and heftier.

Val's was no match for it.

It was the same here as it was in all other areas.

"Ready?" Mehmet asked, grinning. He waved the tip of his sword through the air, a showy little twirl.

Val took a breath and let it out hard through his mouth. "Ready."

In all the ways that swordsmanship was like dancing, Val excelled. Light on his feet, quick, agile, downright graceful. He could remember his proper footwork, and keep his balance effortlessly, focusing on his opponent and not his own steps.

But his swings didn't have as much power as other boys; bigger boys. His blocks were less steady. Quickness would get him by at first, but once he tired…

No. He had to practice. Had to improve.

They circled one another, gravel crunching, feinting and feeling one another out. Val had never sparred with Mehmet before, and he moved differently than Vlad and the boys back home, more like the other hostages.

Then Mehmet moved in, one long step, and moved to strike. It was slow, almost gentle. Like he was aiming at a child. He laughed as Val blocked it with his new blade, the steel chiming like bells.

"Good. Now you move into me," Mehmet said, backing away, giving Val leave to advance.

Val hesitated, worrying his lip with his teeth, sword held suspended in a defensive position, still. Swing at the sultan? That seemed…ill-advised. Shit, this was a terrible idea. He should have found a pair of practice swords and begged Arslan to go to the training yard with him.

(He hadn't because he'd feared that the sight of a eunuch slave holding a sword might result in one more impaled body on the palace walls.)

"You wanted to spar," Mehmet prodded. "So come on."

So he did. A timid swing that Mehmet batted away without effort.

"That was pathetic. Put your weight behind it next time."

He tried again, more forcefully, and Mehmet laughed when he met his blade with a block. "Better! We'll work on it."

It wasn't like any lesson he'd had from a swordmaster back home, nor the ones he'd had here, in previous years, before his irrevocable change of status. Mehmet was relaxed and cheerful, not barking orders and smacking at Val's shoulders and shins with the flat of his blade the way he was used to. In that sense, it was almost…fun. He began to feel lighter; found himself smiling. For

295

a few precious minutes, they were no longer master and slave, not sultan and hostage, but two boys playing.

Val knew something like joy.

For a time.

But then.

Tired, sweating, his blood thrumming, Val lost himself. He lunged in, too close, too wild, his tiredness making him sluggish, clumsy. He went a half-step too far, and when he tried to correct, he reached too far. His brand new sword, sharp-edged, struck Mehmet's arm. Tore cloth, drew blood.

For a breathless second, all was still. Val gaped, sword still extended, wavering.

An accident. But.

A fun afternoon of practice between two young men. But.

Val *felt* the growl that built in Mehmet's chest, the leashed thunder of it reverberating through the air between them. When he looked to Mehmet's face, he saw slitted pupils and lowered brows, extended fangs.

An automatic reaction, his instincts told him. A vampire, especially a dominant one, a leader of men, would react with immediate violence if his blood was drawn.

But Val remembered that first night, the heft of the unfamiliar sword in his hand, the blooming of bright blood on Mehmet's rich feastday kaftan. Remembered the growl, remembered running, remembered the rough bark of the tree he clung to all night. And then he finally relented, and his face was pressed into the pillow, and rough hands shoved his legs apart, and, and–

Terror unfolded inside him, a spark to powder. Violent, painful. And with it, anger.

Mehmet lifted his sword and took a retaliatory swing at him – clumsy, something Val was meant to duck and roll away from, come up stammering an apology.

But Val braced his feet and parried. Steel met steel not with the soft chime of bells, but with the clang and screech of a true battle.

Mehmet growled again, his eyes wide with disbelief. "What are – are you – do you *defy me*?"

Val felt his own fangs grow long in his mouth; felt something come alive inside him, some well of strength previously untapped. He was slender, and golden – but he was Vlad's brother, and Remus's son, and he was destined for something besides whoredom.

He growled back. "*Yes.*"

And then, suddenly, they were fighting for real. Wild swings that crashed together with shrill sounds; panting, growling, lunging, sliding on the gravel when they tried to brace their feet.

In the back of his mind, Val knew they were making too much noise. Someone would hear, even if it was just a pair of curious gardeners, and come to see what was happening. Once they realized that the sultan's pet had lost his mind, guards would be called, and the best Val could hope for would be a good clubbing on the back of the head from a spear butt.

But Val had never felt like this. Had never been rippling with energy and aggression, bloodlust roaring like a second pulse in his ears. He wanted to set his teeth in Mehmet's neck, and *destroy* him. His growl was low and constant, a rippling echo like thunder.

Am I beautiful now? he thought wildly. *Your pet has fangs after all.*

Mehmet swung high, and Val blocked it – only for Mehmet to kick him in the stomach and send him sprawling back across the ground. His head smacked against the gravel, and stars pinwheeled across his field of vision.

Damn it! No matter how strong he felt now, Mehmet was still stronger, and by far the more experienced fighter. He'd let his emotions get the best of him, all his pent-up rage and grief. And he couldn't stem it now, not even to save his own life.

He tried to scramble to his feet, but Mehmet was on top of him, his knee pinning him at the sternum, free hand grabbing his wrist and slamming it to the ground. His other hand held his sword aloft, ready to strike. The sultan was all fangs and snarls, his face contorted into something inhuman. A long string of saliva slid down one fang, dangling into the air between him.

Val *hated* him.

He roared. He'd never conjured that sound up out of his chest before; it emptied his lungs and left him breathless, gasping.

Mehmet roared back, and brought his sword down.

~*~

Val opened his eyes sometime later. Not a killing blow, then. A hard smack with the flat of the blade. His head ached, dull and insistent across his forehead, temples, and behind his eyes.

His vision cleared slowly, and proved what he already knew from scent: he lay on a couch in the antechamber of Mehmet's suite. Sun hung in fat, slanted beams from the windows: late afternoon. Hours had passed.

A pitcher of pale white wine and a cup rested on the table beside him, and when he was able, he rolled over and reached for it. That was when he saw it.

A narrow silver band around his wrist. Narrow, yes, but solid. And trailing from it, a length of silver chain. It slid across the tile with a sound like a hiss as he pulled his hand to his face and squinted blearily at the cuff. There was no clasp, no way for him to unlatch it. He flicked it with the tip of his tongue – yes, solid silver.

His stomach lurched, and suddenly he was wide awake.

He sat up and swung his legs over the side of the couch, so his bare feet hit the cool tiles. His other wrist bore a matching cuff, trailing chain, and when he looked down to identify the cool weight puddled in his lap, he found another chain…one that led up to the collar around his throat. When he swallowed, his Adam's apple rubbed against it. The chains were hooked to rings set in the wall, brand new, the plaster around them chipped.

Val took a series of deep breaths. The important thing was not to panic.

"I thought you were dead," a timid voice whispered, and Val looked across the room with a start.

Arslan sat tucked in a corner, knees to his chest, arms wrapped around them. Shivers wracked his thin frame, so the hems of his loose pants fluttered against the tiles.

"I'm not dead," Val said, and slumped back against the wall. He felt drained, and that was only partially because of the fight earlier, and the subsequent concussion. "But I wish that I was."

Arslan peeked out from between his knees, face drawn and pale. "You shouldn't wish for such a thing."

"No?" A laugh escaped him, humorless and dark. His voice sounded wrong, deeper, maybe, but also hopeless. "I am a prince who's become a whore. Your sultan sodomizes me nightly. Even if I managed to make it home, my family would disown me – what little family remains, that is. Father is dead. Mircea is dead. Vlad hates me. And now this." He lifted both hands and let them flop back, the chains rattling. "Who wouldn't wish for death in my place, Arslan?"

The boy stared at him a long moment. And then he got to his feet and *stomped* over, slipper heels striking the tiles with sharp *pat-pat-pat* noises. He came to stand right in front of Val, hands on his hips, shaking now not with fear, but with anger. Little thunderstorms burst in his eyes.

Val wanted to laugh, but he knew it wouldn't be appreciated.

"You don't get to wish for death," the slave snapped at him. "You – you're still a man. They didn't take your manhood like they did mine. I can never have children. I will never be strong and powerful like you will. I'm not even a woman – a woman could be useful! I'm just – just – just a thing!"

"Arslan–"

"I know what you are." And here the boy looked apprehensive again. "I know that it's blood in the cup I bring you, same as the sultan, and your brother. I know that you…" He swallowed and leaned back, remembering himself.

"Does that mean you're afraid of me?"

"N-no."

Val sighed. "Forgive me, Arslan. None of this is your fault."

Arslan studied him a moment. "He'll set you free eventually, you know. No one ever keeps princes. Not forever."

"My brother is on his way to take Wallachia back."

"Still."

Val leaned forward with a groan and dropped his face into his hands. "Not forever. But for a very, very long time." Right now, immortality didn't feel tangible. It seemed he'd lived most of his life away from home, a prisoner – and he had. *Eventually* held no comfort for him now.

It was silent a spell, one in which Arslan's breaths grew uneven and hitched. Tears clogged his voice when he finally spoke. "Forgive me, your grace. I shouldn't have spoken out of turn. I–"

"Shh, it's alright." When Val lifted his head, the boy threw his arms around his neck and pressed his heated, tear-stained face just behind his ear.

Val felt a strange sort of tenderness. He felt protective. "It will be fine," he assured, rubbing Arslan's back, the prominent bumps of his spine beneath his kaftan. "I'll kiss up to Mehmet and make things right with him. You'll see."

Footsteps in the hallway beyond.

Arslan sprang back and put a respectable distance between the two of them, retreating to the other side of the table.

Mehmet entered in a whirl of scents: oil and soap from the communal bathhouse, the smell of women, several of them, and the musk of sex. He slammed the door open and marched into the room, head up, shoulders back. Partaking of his harem had obviously not quieted the rage that still burned in him, reduced now to a low, sustainable simmer.

He very pointedly didn't look at Val, going instead to the side table and the collection of bottles there. "Get out," he said, flat, as he uncorked a bottle with his teeth and poured a more than generous cup of dark red wine.

Arslan sent Val an apologetic look and then retreated, pulling the outer door shut behind him.

Then they were alone.

Mehmet drained off his wine in a few swallows, head tipped back, then poured a second cup. After, he turned and leaned a hip against the table, finally lifting hooded eyes to meet Val's gaze.

In the beat before the sultan spoke, Val felt an odd stirring. Somewhere deep, up under his ribs, where it was warm and well-protected. It was…it was resolve. Only a small kernel of it, but hard and bright as burnished steel. It rearranged his insides to make room for itself, pushed out some of his awful, desperate prey drive. He was chained to the wall with silver, a slave in all the ways that counted, but he had a *fight* brewing inside him, the long-range, patient kind. He couldn't let it out now, no. But someday. It could wait. *He* could wait. And maybe Mehmet would beat him, would doubtless ravish him, but Val found that he wasn't afraid the way he'd been up to this point.

He lifted his chin.

Mehmet took another swallow of wine and then set the cup aside, eyes never straying from Val's face. "I expected cowering."

Val didn't respond.

"You know, Radu, when I was in the baths, I managed to convince myself that I'd overreacted before. I thought maybe what you needed was some lenience and a chance to prove that you will still obey me. But now I stand here and look at you, and I am *furious* all over again." His hand curled to a fist in demonstration.

Val said, "You've chained me with silver." His voice was eerily calm, composed in a whole new way. Mehmet noticed, if the way he lifted his brows was any indication. "And you would punish me still? Is your masculinity really so fragile?"

Mehmet took two strides forward and slapped Val across the face with an open hand. It snapped his head to the side. He felt a jeweled ring open a cut along his eyebrow. He gritted his teeth and faced the sultan, refusing to flinch. "I'm sorry, Your Majesty," he said without an ounce of sincerity. "I shall endeavor to behave myself from now on."

Mehmet bared his teeth and lifted his hand to strike again – but checked the motion, hand hovering in the air. He grinned. "You're goading me. You've never done that before."

"I don't know what you're talking about."

The slap fell. The crack of it echoed off the walls. Val's skin throbbed; he could feel the bruise forming.

Mehmet took hold of his chin, fingers digging in, and leaned into his face, so close that Val went cross-eyed trying to look at him. "You have not even begun to imagine all the ways in which I can make you miserable," he seethed. "You know *nothing* of pain."

It was hard to speak with his jaw clenched so tightly, but he managed to say, "Just kill me."

For a moment, he thought that might happen. And he wanted it, cowardly though it was. He didn't want the pain that would attend the killing, but to finally be free...that was fine. That was good.

But Mehmet released him and stepped back. His expression shuttered. "Why did you ask to spar? And don't lie to me."

"I wanted to build my strength up, and refamiliarize myself with a sword."

"*Why?*"

"So that I could return to Wallachia with Vlad."

He thought Mehmet would strike him again – his face contorted terribly, red and screwed-up, a fit of childish emotion – but he refrained, and returned to the side table to fetch his wine. "You thought I would allow that?" he asked over the rim of his cup.

Val shrugged, and the chain attached to his collar swayed. "I thought it was worth a try. I thought I could manipulate you into it."

"You thought..." His eyes widened, face going blank with disbelief, and he drained his cup. He set it down and reached for the bottle again. "I had no idea you were this willful," he murmured. "I've underestimated you, clearly."

He walked in close again, and raised the cup to Val's lips, pressing the sticky rim between them. Val opened his throat and drank, obedient in this small thing. Swallow after swallow, and he immediately felt the throbbing in his head ease.

Mehmet gave him half and sipped at the rest himself, sitting on the edge of the table so they were on eye level with one another. In an eerily calm voice, in control of his vast temper now, he said, "Do you think me stupid?"

It was defeat, and not bravery, that gave Val the courage to speak the truth. "I think you're lustful, and unhappy, and spoiled."

Mehmet stared. Then he laughed, sharp and hollow. "The two of you really are brothers, aren't you?"

"No one ever seems to think that. Palace gossip has it that we're half-brothers."

"You certainly look it. But that *rebellion*," he said the word like a curse, "is certainly an inherited trait. Perhaps from your father. He never could adhere to a treaty."

Father had rebelled when he saw no other choice. But it was Mother who'd passed along her temper. Val kept such knowledge to himself, saying a quiet prayer that, against all odds, she was still alive.

"You might be beautiful, but you aren't stupid," Mehmet continued. "So you already know that you could never go back with your brother."

"Like I said. It was worth a try."

"My, but I hate you like this."

"Then why not let me go?"

A cruel smile. "Come now, I just paid a compliment to your wits. You know why you must stay. You are leverage against your brother."

"Vlad hates me."

"He acts as if he does, yes, but he doesn't. He wouldn't hate me so if he actually hated you. So you will stay here, and be a good little boy, so Vlad Dracula knows to uphold his part of the bargain." Another smile, this one satisfied. "You are here for the duration, little golden Radu." He stood and paced back toward the side table for a refill. "You should be grateful," he said over his shoulder. "You still have all your limbs, and both your eyes. Comfortable accommodations and the sultan's favor." He spread a hand across his own chest in demonstration. Tilted his head. "It would be wise of you to *keep* my favor."

Yes, keep it. Until he was able to get loose, to run home. Stay on Mehmet's good side, gain his trust, gain his freedom…

That little bead of resolve inside him gathered mass, weighty as a stone in the pit of his stomach.

He thought of Vlad, of the riding crop slapping his head, his shoulders, the backs of his knees. His willfulness and sullenness in the face of all his teachers. *That* was resolve. The kind of thing that got men through captivity. It was only his body that had been hurt – and it was a strong body at that. An immortal one.

What was a little pain and a little time to a vampire if it would, in the long run, get him what he wanted?

Val decided something. He wet his lips. "Alright. Let's make a bargain, then."

"A bargain?" Mehmet's laugh turned slowly disbelieving, and then faded away altogether as he took in Val's seriousness. "Alright," he said, quieter, "what sort of bargain?"

"I'll be obedient," he said. "I'll pleasure you." It was only a physical sacrifice, after all. What did it matter? "And you will train me to be a proper prince."

It was a risk. He could be killed on the spot.

But Mehmet smiled, slow and nasty. "You're terrible," he said.

And Val knew, though abuse awaited him, that he could do this. That it was worth it.

And that, even in this small way, he'd won.

25

RUMOR HAS IT

Somewhere on the Road

Malik snapped several twigs in half and fed them into the fire. Then he sat down on the felled log opposite Vlad's, elbows resting on his knees. Thus far in their march, Vlad had never seen the man look tired. He woke before dawn, without prompt; rose from his bedroll without all the usual griping and stretching and blinking. Just popped to his feet, bundled up his bedroll, and went to rouse his men. He never yawned. Never complained.

If he hadn't been able to tell differently, Vlad might have thought he was an immortal.

"The horses are secure," he informed Vlad. "Watches have been posted."

"Good. What of Mustafa's men?"

"Sleeping." He gave a little grunt that Vlad had learned was a one-note laugh. "Gambling."

Vlad snorted. "Will they be ready if we're ambushed, you think?" Vlad dangled the line as an opening – an invitation to criticize the foot-soldiers together.

But Malik said only, "Yes."

Vlad nodded and reached for his saddlebag, which waited at his feet. From his carefully rationed allotment of food, he chose a piece of flat bread and some dried goat meat. A cloth-wrapped bottle of dark wine lingered at the bottom, but he wouldn't break into that yet. He wanted to be sharp. Sometime later, when the others were asleep, he would move silent and careful to the horse lines, and take a little blood from his mount.

Malik dipped into his own rations, and they ate in silence for a time, the fire crackling between them.

They'd crossed the Danube two days ago, and it was now that their travel had to become stealthy. For the first weeks, marching out from Edirne in a wide column that occupied the whole road, travelers and merchants had quickly moved to the shoulder, heads bowed in deference to the emperor's Janissary Corp in their fluttering crimson capes. Road dust kicked up from hooves and boots had hung over them like a cloud; Vlad had tasted it every time he'd opened his mouth to issue a command. They'd made good time on well-traveled roadways; an ideal trip.

But the river marked the boundary. Vassal state of the Ottomans or not, the Romanian-held lands of Wallachia were under Vladislav's control. If any of his men spotted janissaries, or worse, Vlad himself, on the move, they'd raise the alarm. When Vlad arrived in Tîrgovişte, he wanted it to be a surprise for his nemesis.

As he chewed the tough jerky, and stared into the hypnotic dance of the flames, he realized he hadn't had so much time to stew in his own thoughts since he was first taken captive all those years ago.

At Edirne, his days had been full. Schooling all day, in groups and with private tutors who, despite his insolence, had been forced to grudgingly admit that he was clever. Then it was riding, dueling, archery practice, and dancing lessons. Of all the crimes the Ottomans had committed against him, no one could claim that hadn't given him a proper knight's foundation. He was only seventeen, but he'd been prepared for this moment – for this war for his homeland.

But he'd been *busy* then. His thoughts only his own in the twilight moments before exhausted sleep claimed him, or in his quiet visits to the chapel. Now, save a few commands, and consultations of the map with Malik, he was plagued with the quiet. The creak of saddle leather, the clink of armor, the clop of hooves, and the background din of soldiers' voices. As they moved slow and steady toward Tîrgovişte, he was left to his own imaginings. And there was only one thing he *could* imagine: death.

He imagined his father as Cazan had described him: ragged and breathless, writhing on the ground in the jaws of a wolf. Dying alone. Imagined the red, wet knives of the men who'd known they had to cut his heart from his body. How had Vladislav known? How had he acquired a wolf?

He imagined Mircea, sputtering around a mouthful of dirt, weak and bleeding out. His last vision had been of darkness. How quickly had the earth they'd heaped on him crushed his chest? Or could he still be alive? Asleep? Like a true vampire?

He imagined his mother, their household wolves. Cut down screaming, blood spraying across walls, soaking into the cracks of the paving stones.

He imagined the ways in which he would kill Vladislav. Personal, painful. He would drag it out and make it hurt; he would know the fear in his eyes before his soul left his body.

Every dream, every blink, visions of death played out behind his eyelids.

If he allowed himself to analyze this, he would be appalled.

"...Vlad."

"Hm? What?" He lifted his gaze from the fire – the flames had branded his vision, a flickering white afterglow lingering – and found Malik staring at him, the beginnings of a frown notching his brows together. The firelight shadowed his scar so it looked deeper, almost sinister in the dark.

"I asked about your father," Malik said.

Vlad clenched his hand into a fist; the piece of jerky in it snapped in half and fell to the underbrush.

"You think of him often." It wasn't a question.

"He was killed violently, and we march now to avenge that death. Of course I do."

Malik was unphased. "Many men hate their fathers. Or at least resent them. You could march to avenge him, and still not think of him at all."

Vlad tilted his head in bare acknowledgement. "Alright. I'll grant you that."

"What sort of man was he?"

He hadn't expected this. Hadn't expected this emotionless, methodical cavalryman, sent to war at his sultan and emperor's whim, to care what sort of Romanian whose land he was sent to help retrieve.

Malik Bey, Vlad was beginning to think, was no ordinary cavalryman.

"Do you truly wish to know?" Vlad asked. "Or are you toying with me?"

Vlad's tone, his glare, paired with his position of command, would have cowed most. But Malik, smooth-faced and unperturbed, said, "I truly wish to know."

Vlad sighed. He wasn't used to putting such things into words. In his seven years of captivity, he'd rarely had a chance to express himself with any meaning.

"Father is…" He caught himself. "*Was.*" Though a part of him wouldn't believe it until he'd touched the cold, rotting body with his own hands. "A kind man. Far kinder than me. More like Va…my brother. Radu." He'd almost slipped; almost spoken Val's real name. A name didn't mean anything, in the grand scheme of the world, but Val was a pawn and a whore. If his true name was all that he still held as his own, then Vlad would help him keep it secret.

"You think yourself cruel?"

"I know I'm cruel."

Malik looked like he almost smiled. It could have been a trick of the firelight. "You are honest."

"What point is there in being otherwise?"

Quiet a beat. And then Malik said, "May I tell you what I think?"

"You're awfully talkative tonight." When the man's expression didn't change, Vlad rolled his eyes. "But, yes, you may tell me. Though I don't have any idea what you find so important you've finally deigned to speak to me as a man."

He ignored the jab. "I think," he said, "that the cruel man is the one who takes pleasure in the pain of others. Vengeance isn't cruelty. Not by itself. Not when it's justified."

Vlad studied him a long moment, searching for a lie. He found none, though he conceded that he didn't know the man well. Not at all, really.

"And what if I do enjoy violence?"

Malik shrugged with one shoulder and dropped his gaze to the fire, reflective. "We all learn to, at some point. Tenderness will drive you mad if you let it, and some joy, even that kind of joy…it helps."

Vlad nibbled on his flatbread. "You make an excellent point, Malik Bey." And, strangely, he felt lighter for a time, as they sat by the fire. He'd been carrying his burdens for so long, and alone, that he'd forgotten the relief of a spare set of shoulders.

~*~

Tîrgovişte was not the sort of sprawling metropolis in which a man could hide an invading army – even one so small as Vlad's. The second they left the cover the of the trees, they'd be made, and then they'd be fighting Vladislav's people in the streets. A dangerous, bloody, foolish plan if ever there had been one.

Vlad left his infantry under cover of forest. "I'll send a messenger for you, and when I do, come double time, understood?"

"Yes, your grace."

His foot soldiers were loyal first to the empire, and second to Mustafa, but the long march, and Vlad's unfailing straightness in the saddle, his mastery of their language, and his brusque manner had gone a long way toward winning them over.

His cavalry he split into twos and threes, and had them enter the city from different angles, at different times. Their armor he had them pack away in their saddle bags, or cover with dull cloaks they'd bought off a passing merchant three days back. Duck your heads, he told them, and round your shoulders. Look like merchants, or weary travelers, and keep your swords hidden.

It was a thin ruse, but it was the best he could concoct on short notice.

"A smart plan, your grace," Malik said placidly beside him, as they rode side-by-side down a narrow, twisting roadway between high, tile-roofed houses.

"It'll be smart if it works," Vlad said. "Keep a sharp eye. He could have spies in those upper apartments."

His tone was sharp, but inwardly, it wasn't fear making his heart pound against his ribs.

He was home.

The palace alone at Edirne was finer and busier than the entirety of the city. But it was Romanian being spoken by the two women hanging wash out on a line strung between second-story windows. And these narrow streets brought back a hundred memories of boyhood; of lessons finished early, and of traveling singers and trapeze artists, of piping hot street food that burned his fingers, of his friends' laughter, and Val's little hand clutching at his sleeve.

He hadn't felt this way in an age, and it took him long minutes of peering at Tîrgovişte from beneath the hood of his cloak to name the sensation: happiness.

But as it so often was, happiness was fleeting.

He smelled rot just before they reached the city square, and he knew what he would find there before they rounded the corner.

Father had been a lenient prince, all things considered, but public hangings had been carried out to demonstrate the cost of lawlessness. The gibbet stood where it always had, in the bank yard that abutted the garrison house. And it was occupied.

Three weather-blackened corpses dangled from the ends of fraying ropes. They'd been dead a long time, had long since swelled, and burst, and then dried out to husks. Featureless now, their clothes tattered streamers that played in the wind. A few flies buzzed, but there wasn't much left for them. The crows, Vlad well knew, had gotten the lion's share of the meat.

"They're up there for treason," a voice said, down and to his left, and he turned his head to find a bent old crone wrapped in a scarf, the ends clutched tight in one gnarled hand just beneath her throat. She'd spoken in Romanian, and the sound of it from an unfamiliar throat – from anyone who wasn't Val – nearly startled a delighted laugh from him.

He composed himself and replied in the same language. "What do you mean, treason?"

She squinted up at him. He had the impression that, had he been standing on foot beside her, she might have thwacked him on the arm for his stupidity. "For being loyal to the old prince."

A sensation like a band around his chest, squeezing tight. Happiness had long fled; his old friend rage was back to stay. "The old prince? Vlad Dracul, you mean?"

She nodded. "Him, yes. Most of the boyars and the rich ones went over to the *new prince*." Her tone told him what she thought of him. "But there were a few who were saying they didn't want Vladislav, that it wasn't right, what he did."

Vlad fought to keep his voice even and disinterested. "What happened there?" When she peered up at him, he said, "I've been away for a time. I've only heard bits and pieces of the story, and who's to know if any of it's true." What did the peasants think, he wondered.

She nodded again, seeming satisfied. "Well, there was a great scene up at the palace, I heard. I didn't see it, mind, but my grandson did. He's in the garrison," she said proudly. "He said it was a great tangle of people there, spilling out of the gate and across the moat – the bridge was down, you see. He reckons someone from the inside was working with the Dânești." This she whispered. "It was them, and the palace guard, and a great heap of boyars and their household guards, all fighting. And dogs, too. Great big ones that looked like wolves.

"The old prince, Dracul, got away somehow. But the Dânești and the boyars got hold of the son. The heir. The garrison and the palace guard, you could tell they were trying to get him free, but there were too many. And so many were injured, or dead by that point. They buried that poor boy alive, they say." She spat on the ground, wrinkled face screwed up with disgust. "The devil take Vladislav, and I don't care if he knows I said it."

"What would he do if he knew you had?" Vlad asked.

She paled. "Sir, I–"

He waved her silent. "Your sentiment is safe with me. I feel the same. But tell me, Mother. Vladislav has wanted Wallachia for a time. Why move now? Who helped him?"

She looked carefully side to side, searching for eavesdroppers. Then she stepped in close, a hand braced on the shoulder of Vlad's horse, and whispered, "I heard it was that John Hunyadi from Hungary. Vladislav is only his puppet, you see." She mimed operating a marionette with her free hand. "But you didn't hear that from me."

"No, ma'am, of course not." He flipped her a coin from the pouch at his belt: a Turkish coin that she peered at closely. She turned a gaping look up at him afterward.

He brought a finger to his lips. "I'll keep your secrets if you'll keep mine."

"Oh. Oh, yes, sir."

"Rumor has it the old prince had another heir, yes?"

A slow, sly grin transformed her face. She'd been pretty as a girl, he could tell. "Yes, sir," she said, surer now. "Rumor also has it that Vladislav is away right now, seeing to business to the north."

Vlad felt his brows jump. "He's not at the palace?"

"No, sir." She bobbed a curtsy and moved on, quick for her age.

When Vlad turned back to Malik, the janissary looked at him with something that might have been mistaken for admiration. "That was cleverly done."

"Do things cleverly, or don't do them at all. Come on. We need to find the others."

It took longer than Vlad would have liked — now that he knew Vladislav was away, that they stood a chance, he wanted to move right away — to find the rest of the cavalry unit, but find them they did. Slow and methodical, he passed the message along. Be at the palace gates at midday. Vlad would make sure the bridge was down.

Then he took Malik, and they headed out of the city and up the hill, toward the home he hadn't seen in seven years.

~*~

"Will your father's guards have turned against you?" Malik asked as they neared the gate. It was, unsurprisingly, shut, the bridge pulled up. A man in helm and mail, a spear propped on his shoulder, left the guard tower and signaled them.

They pulled their horses up to a halt. "Anyone still loyal to my father is either dead, or rotting in chains in the dungeon. These at the gate — they'll belong wholly to Vladislav."

The guard walked closer, face set in a scowl.

"What do you mean to do?"

"Just listen. And play along."

"Ho!" the guard hailed, raising a gloved hand. As if they hadn't already halted. "State your names and your business." His accent was Transylvanian; not even one of Vladislav's then, but Hunyadi's.

Vlad left his hood in place, shielding his features from full view, but he reached for the clasp of his cloak. "Easy," he said, when the guard twitched and took his spear in both hands. Vlad affected a Turkish accent, made his Romanian clumsy and thick. "I am Iskander Bey, and this is Malik Bey." He opened his cloak to allow a glimpse of his clothes, the plain, but very fine kaftan and sash over his riding leathers. He wore the ornamental dagger with the rubies in the hilt. He knew he looked a foreigner, down to the curved toes of his boots in the stirrups. "We are cavalry captains in the Janissary Corps of the Ottoman Empire, sent as envoys from His Imperial Majesty Mehmet, son of Murat."

The man frowned. "Janissary Corps?" He hedged backward a step, though. He knew what the Corps was. Everyone all the way to England did.

Malik opened his own cloak, showing the crimson cape beneath, and the unmistakable cavalry uniform of his office. He pushed his hood back as well, and there'd be no mistaking him for a rival Romanian lord. "We are a small host, only the two of us, and didn't wish to attract undue attention on the road," he explained in his own halting Romanian. That part, at least, was no act.

"Word reached Adrianople that there is a new prince in power here," Vlad said. "One who has not agreed to proper peace terms with His Majesty yet. We bring the sultan's demands." From his saddlebag he produced a scroll, sealed with a blob of red wax and Murat's personal seal. The missive inside was written in Slavic, in a scribe's elegant hand, but it did not offer peace terms. Instead, it was a message to Vladislav from Murat himself, informing him that, effective immediately, Vlad Dracula was the prince of Wallachia, and that Vladislav was a pretender, and fugitive.

The guard reached to take the scroll, and Vlad pulled it out of reach. "We have orders to hand it to the prince himself. Or his second in command. Not to a gate crew."

The man made a face, but withdrew, chin lifted to an imperious angle. "Wait here." He headed back for the gatehouse, where two of his comrades were now peering out the door at the riders.

"I'm not sure this will work," Malik said quietly.

Vlad tipped a covert glance toward the sky. It was midday, or only a hair shy of it. "It doesn't have to work for very long. Only until the gate's open."

"Hmm."

Let him doubt. Vlad's first approach was trickery – if that failed, he'd bash his way into the gatehouse, kill all the guards, and open the damn gate himself.

The first guard returned with two of his fellows in tow. It was one of the new ones who spoke, his hand extended. "If you'll let us look at the missive–"

"What part," Vlad said, slowly, forcefully, "of 'only the prince or his second in command' did your idiot friend not understand? This isn't a birthday congratulations. It's an official treaty document from the sultan. It is not going to touch your hands, underling. Now open the gate and let us speak to your master. Or have you forgotten who owns Wallachia?"

All three men glared savagely at him, grinding their teeth, no doubt wanting to pull him down off his horse.

But, finally, the speaker gave a jerky nod and turned back toward the gatehouse, hand half-cupped around his mouth. "Lower the bridge!"

Careful to keep his expression haughty and shuttered, he darted a glance toward Malik, whose gaze was likewise surprised, his face carefully blank.

Groaning, creaking, rattling, the gate lifted, and the bridge began to lower. Straining to hear over these sounds, Vlad could detect hoofbeats, many sets, moving at a steady trot up the hill.

He gathered his reins and tried to make the motion look casual. "Be ready," he muttered.

The moment the first row of riders crested the last hill, the guards would know something was wrong. Vlad needed to be on the other side of that bridge when that happened, whether or not he had backup.

It lowered, lowered, lowered…

He tightened his calves, and his mount danced.

The hoofbeats drew closer; a vibration he could feel through his own horse, through the ground.

The bridge landed with a thump and a puff of dust.

The riders crested the hill.

"Go!" Vlad put his heels in his horse and the gelding lunged forward. He dropped the reins, and reached back beneath his cloak to pull free his bow, already strung, ready, a curved little short bow perfect for the task. With his other hand he drew an arrow from the quiver hidden between his shoulders.

The guards ran for the gatehouse, shouting, waving their arms, as the Turkish cavalry unit arrived in a great swirl of dust and three sharp blasts of a horn.

Vlad's mount crossed the bridge, and he turned in the saddle to take the shot. He got off two – two of the guards fell face-down in the dirt.

And then he was across.

He dropped his bow and drew his sword – his father's sword, the finely-crafted Toledo blade from the emperor.

He took the arm off of one guard. The head from another.

"Close the–" an interior guard shouted, and Vlad cut him down with a vicious strike across his throat, blood spraying.

"Keep the gate open!" he bellowed. "If you value your life, keep it open, damn you!"

He looked over his shoulder and saw Malik strike down another guard.

Those left threw down their spears and fled for the stable.

The cavalry arrived at the edge of the bridge, and began to thunder across unchecked, dust swirling.

They were in.

~*~

Pandemonium erupted in the main yard, the kind that reverberated through the stable, the training yard, and the gardens…but the kind of a people who knew they'd been conquered. Vlad's cavalry poured in, and immediately he appointed riders to secure the gatehouses and apprehend what guards they could. Doubtless some had slunk off to bolt holes, and he'd have to execute them later. But for now, he had a palace to retake.

315

Vlad dismounted and handed his reins to one of his men. He sent a rider back to their camp to summon the foot soldiers. "Malik, with me."

Sword in hand, he made his way toward the palace.

~*~

There was something almost therapeutic in the way his father's old blade could cut a man into pieces. Not just any men, either, but Vladislav's lackeys. Every scream, every slice – he imagined it as some tiny vindication for Father. For Mircea, face-down in a hole somewhere.

He sent men around to other doors, the one that led into the kitchens, the one that let out into his mother's lavish gardens.

But he himself went in through the massive front doors, straight into the great hall, with its long feast tables and its unlit iron chandeliers.

Men came to apprehend him, swords gleaming.

Vlad cut them down, Malik at his side. The janissary stood beside him, back-to-back, both their blades dripping blood down onto the stones.

Vlad cocked his head, listening. Running footsteps, up above. He tested the air, but the scents of wolf were faint…as was the scent of his mother. If anything had happened to her…

"This way." He led Malik to the stairwell.

It was like a dream. The same stone steps he'd tread as a boy, worn from years of boots and slippers. The curved walls, the iron sconces that held torches, the windows that looked out on the gardens, the grounds, and toward the Tîrgoviște rooftops beyond. How many times had Fenrir thrown him over his shoulder like a sack of turnips and carried him down these stairs, laughing uproariously all the way? How many times had he pelted down, ducking under the arms of amused wolves and startled maids, hell-bent for a day in town with his friends? He'd been away from this place for seven years, but it was the same; he was a boy again, sprinting, legs burning pleasantly.

But the scents were wrong. Instead of Helga's honeycakes, it was blood he smelled; and dirt, and filth, and humans he hated.

A pair of guards met them at the top of the stairs, and they fell like young trees beneath sharp axes. Vlad wasn't even sweating.

He heard the creak of a door, caught a whiff of scent—

A familiar round face peeked out of a room, and stared at him, wide-eyed with surprise, as he moved toward her, armored and bloody and furious.

His face was changed, longer, thinner, his hair tied back in a regal way, his clothes Turkish and strange. But her nostrils flared, and then she knew him, and her face crumpled.

"Master Vladimir," Helga cried, stepping out into the hallway, tears glittering as they spilled down her cheeks. "You've come home."

~*~

It was almost painfully easy to secure the castle. Vladislav had obviously taken his best men – if they even existed – with him, and left only a skeleton crew behind to guard the palace. What had he to fear, after all? Hunyadi was on his side, his rival was dead, and as far as he knew, Vlad was still learning arithmetic in Edirne. Or so he thought. The first of what Vlad hoped would be two fatal mistakes – the second of which would be underestimating Vlad himself.

Vlad left none alive, and his foot soldiers arrived in time to take over at the gate and to search the rest of the grounds for any cowards who might have fled.

Helga crushed him to her ample breast and burst into wet, noisy sobs, clutching at his cloak and kaftan. "Master Vladimir," she said, over and over, until he'd patted her shoulders and eased her back.

He offered over his lace handkerchief, and after she'd blown her nose and wiped her eyes on it, she composed herself once more. "I didn't mean to get you all wet and make such a scene, your grace," she said, patting at the damp silk over his heart. "It's only that it's such a shock to see you, such a happy shock! When things here have been so terrible. Ever since…" She bit her lip to stop it from trembling, and shook her head.

"I know about Father, and Mircea." He cleared his throat, but that didn't help the roughness of his voice. "But what of my mother?" He knew fear then, cold and sharp in his belly, when he'd been nothing but angry while killing the men downstairs.

Helga sighed. "The princess," she said, meaning Father's true wife, and Mircea's mother. "Didn't take the news about His Grace Mircea very well. And then Vladislav, he…well, gods bless her, she got away from him, and she leapt out of a window. One in your father's old study. She's dead."

He ground his teeth. "I asked after Mother." He had no love, nor even affection for the princess. But still it seemed an unfitting end. Father would not have wept – he'd never loved the woman – but he would have been outraged.

Helga nodded. "She is well. She is grief-stricken." A grief that echoed in Helga's voice. Her mistress's mate was dead, and she grieved alongside her. She managed a smile, tremulous, but warm. "She will be glad to see you. To see the man you've become."

"Take me to her."

When Father was alive – when Vlad was still a boy in the palace – Mother had held her own suite of rooms on the second floor of the palace, overlooking the gardens, with shelves loaded with her favorite books, and tables where she could display cut flowers and herbs by the windows; as airy as could be found in a stone building, full of light, redolent with the scent of fresh, growing things.

But now, Helga led him up to one of the high turret rooms, four floors from the ground below. A room where he and Val had played as boys, kicking up dust as they scuffled, reading books in the light that came through tall, thin windows. *Oh, Mama*, he thought as they climbed the stairs.

"Did Vladislav send her up here? I'll–"

"No," Helga said, holding a candle to light the dim stairwell. Even during the day, the passages up here afforded little light. "You know your mother: lovely as spring roses. With that flaxen hair, and that delicate face. Vladislav rounded up the whole household on that first day; they'd a wolf – I smelled it on them. But they never brought him in here. So no one save us wolves knew what your mother was – nor who she was to the master. It was your mother's idea: we dressed her up as a maid, and we drew a frightful birthmark on her with charcoal and crushed flower petals. Put padding under her clothes so she'd be lumpy and unlovely. He never looked at her twice."

She paused a moment, and looked back over her shoulder at Vlad, expression grave. "'Twas undignified, I know, considering what she was to your father." Mates trumped marriage for immortals. Every time. "But it spared her Vladislav's lust."

Vlad nodded and motioned for her to continue. Inwardly, he thanked God. Perhaps he'd become a religious man after all.

They arrived, finally, at the door at the top of the stairs. Heavy wood. He'd wondered at it as a boy, but now he knew: it was to keep something locked inside. In this case, it was a blessing.

Helga knocked. "My lady," she began.

But it swung inward, and there she was. Eira wore a maid's costume: simple brown dress, apron, and cap, golden hair tucked away. She looked too thin, hollow-cheeked and wan, with dark circles under her eyes that marked long, sleepless nights.

She'd scented him, of course. "Vlad," she whispered, hands braced on the door and its frame, white-knuckled.

"Mama."

She lunged at him, and he caught her.

~*~

With her kerchief unwound, Eira's hair spilled in riotous golden curls down her back, each strand a different hue, sunlight from the small window glinting off the thick mass of it, brighter than any metal. She stood looking down at the palace grounds below, little lines of tension at the corners of her eyes. *I'm beautiful,* she'd told him once before, without any pride. *That is a good thing, because it means that the people around me always underestimate my mind…and my sword.* She studied the movements of his troops now with keen eyes; he could almost hear her thoughts, the calculations and questions forming.

319

He'd forgotten, at times, as a boy, that she was a shieldmaiden. Seeing her now, with older eyes, he didn't think he'd ever forget again.

She looked so much like Val in that moment.

"How many do you have?" she asked, turning to look at him. Her eyes shone like polished blue glass in the sunlight, hard and ready.

"Two-hundred-and-fifty foot. One hundred cavalry."

"That won't be enough."

He sighed. "I know. But it's what I have."

"Then we shall make use of them." She paused, tilted her head. "*You* shall make use of them." Then her expression softened. "You look like a man, now. And so much like your father."

He inclined his head in thanks, but found he couldn't speak. Not about Father. Not even about himself.

"You have the castle," she said. "How do you intend to keep it?"

"By any means that I can."

A knock sounded at the door, and Helga poked her head inside. "Your grace." She winced in apology. "One of your men wishes to see you."

Vlad knew who it was by scent. He nodded. "Let him in."

She stepped in, pushing the door wide, and Malik entered behind her.

"Sir." His gaze darted to the window, to Eira, resplendent even in a maid's simple dress, and then hastily back again. Vlad stepped in front of his mother, a physical barrier, and he thought he heard Eira breathe a laugh behind him. He knew what she must look like to a mortal: young and beautiful, certainly not Vlad's own mother. And she wasn't the princess.

"What?" Vlad snapped.

Malik straightened another fraction, heels clicking together comically. "The palace grounds are secure, your grace, and we've raised the bridge and closed the gate."

"Good. Find a scribe and tell him I wish to dictate a letter to Vladislav as soon as possible."

320

"Yes, your grace." He stole one last, covert glance at Eira over Vlad's shoulder, and then quit the room.

Helga shut the door behind him with a thump and a sour expression that seemed to say *good riddance.*

Eira let her laughter bubble out, and Vlad ached hearing it. She'd smelled of tears when he'd come in the room, long-dried, but her skin tainted by the salt of them. She'd loved Mircea, even if he wasn't her son — if only because he was loved by his father and brothers. And Father…Papa…he'd been her soulmate. Her grief was a fourth presence, a shadow lurking at the edges of the room.

"Your new captain?" she guessed as he turned to her, her eyes dancing like old times — even if they were shadowed.

"Yes."

"Does he know what you are? What *we* are?"

"Perhaps. He's clever. But I haven't told him outright."

"Do you trust him?"

Vlad considered.

"He's Turkish."

"No, Mother. He's a janissary, fighting for the Ottomans. But he is most definitely not Turkish."

Expression thoughtful, she moved away from the window to sit at the foot of the narrow bed that occupied most of the room. She folded her hands in her lap. "How complete is the sultan's support of your campaign here?"

He understood the question. Propped a shoulder against the edge of the window and let some of the tension bleed out of him. "Depends on which sultan you ask," he admitted with a sigh, finally letting his doubt come through in his voice. He might be a man, one on a sultan-sent mission, one hell-bent on revenge…but this was his mother, and he was only seventeen; a boy to her, and always her son and baby.

"Murat abdicated several years ago," he said, and saw her brows lift in surprise. "It's not something widely known outside the Empire, I don't suppose, because the heir — the new sultan," he said, scowling, "Mehmet, is so terrible at ruling. Their decisions are not always unified. Murat is old and tired, and he wants nothing to do with warmongering anymore. He's content with the lands they already hold, I think. He's the one who gave me Malik Bey and what forces I brought with me here. He wants me to retake Wallachia and rule as Father's rightful heir. To know that Wallachia is still a vassal state, and, more importantly, a barrier between Hunyadi and the Ottoman lands.

"Mehmet, on the other hand." His voice grew dark. "Is an expansionist and an egomaniac. He wants glory, and lands, and–" He bit his tongue on his next words: *innocent little boys.* "He sees himself as Romulus's heir, and I supposed he is, since Uncle's the one who turned him."

Eira made a quiet sound of shock, but her brows slanted downward, enraged. "I *knew* that bastard was up to something when he started coming here. You're sure of it? He's Mehmet's sire?"

"I tasted his blood. I'm sure of it. And then the fool bragged about it."

She shook her head, lips pressed into a thin, pale line. "He stopped coming, right after the three of you were taken. He made one last visit, the night after we received the note from the sultan. He wanted to…to *console* me. To *share in my grief.*" She looked up at Vlad, defiant, hands balled into fists in her lap. "I kicked him in the bollocks and sent him packing."

He managed a smile at the thought.

"Vladimir, I had no idea," she whispered, voice breaking. "I didn't know that he–"

He waved her to silence. A lump was rising in his throat, and he couldn't do this now, here, in the daylight, when there were things to learn and men to command. "It's been done for a long time. Now, we have to fight." The next question had him shrinking down into his own collar, terrified of the answer. "Mother…what of the wolves?"

~*~

Helga led him down. She knew the way well. Down the long hallway past the kitchens, and the storerooms, through the heavy door that marked a staircase that spiraled down, down, down beneath the palace, the way marked with sputtering torches. She carried a lantern, its meager light reaching out in tentative fingers to probe at the gloom – unable to penetrate it.

Vlad could see well enough, the rough shape of things, the edges of shadows left untouched by the crackling torches. And his nose alone could have guided him: it smelled of wolf down here. Angry, tired, miserable wolf.

They reached the dungeon, and Helga paused, pulling the lantern in tight to her chest, drawing in a shaky breath. "I…" she started.

Vlad laid a hand on her shoulder, and she turned to him. "It's alright," he told her, as gently as possible. "I'll turn them loose." He took the keys – taken off a dead guard – from her unresisting hand, and stalked forward between the rows of empty cells.

They were kept together, at the very back of the cold stone room, chained by both hands a good ten feet apart.

"To hell with you," Fenrir spoke first, and Vlad heard the sound of someone spitting on the ground. They both smelled frightened, but defiant. "You bas…" He trailed off.

Vlad was close enough that the he could see the shapes of the two wolves, the lines of their faces: thin, sallow, but stern. Their arms up above their heads, the lines of the chains.

Close enough to scent one another.

"Gods," Fenrir breathed.

And then Cicero: "Your…your grace?"

Vlad couldn't speak, his throat aching. He rushed to them in turn, opening their cells, and then their cuffs. Fenrir first, and then Cicero. He fell to his knees in front of Cicero, his father's most loyal Familiar. The wolf was far too thin, dirty, and he was missing an eye, his arms heavily scarred.

Cicero bowed his head, shaking. "Your grace. Oh, heaven bless us, you've returned. *Prince Vlad.*"

Vlad pressed his forehead to his, skin-to-skin, close enough to scent without barriers.

Vlad felt tears sting his eyes, and closed them tight.

Cicero sobbed. "Your grace."

"I'm here, I'm here."

It was a long moment before he could stand and lead them up to the light.

~*~

Vlad had a boyhood memory – he'd been five, maybe six – of playing with a set of hand-carved wooden animals on the rug in his father's study, light from the hearth flickering over his hands, and the carefully-wrought horses, and cows, and the more exotic creatures. An elephant; a bear; a giraffe. And a set of wolves, more detailed than the others, their tails streaming behind them, legs extended in a graceful lope, jaws open, tiny teeth sharp to his fingertips. The eyes had been painted: rings of gold and blue set in deep black.

Father had stood at his desk, sighing, rubbing at his temples, talking over treaties with his wolf captains.

Among the household wolves, Fenrir was notoriously upbeat. The massive, jolly uncle figure always up for a game of tag or hide-and-seek, endlessly affectionate with his masters and the young princes alike.

By contrast, Father's wolves were stern. And in the case of Cicero, alpha of his small pack, severe, even.

But that day, with Mircea at a lesson and Val napping, Vlad had been the only child in attendance, out of the way and silent, playing quite contentedly by himself.

Someone had knelt down across from him, suddenly, with a creak of tall boots and a rustle of a cloak, a sudden rush of comforting wolf-scent. Cicero. He extended one hand, its wrist laced up tight in a leather bracer, sword-calluses marking his skin. But on his palm, a freshly-carved wooden animal. A fantasy creature: a sinuous dragon, painted green and red, with fiery eyes. His face, strangely gentle.

"Here, your grace," he'd said, softly. "To go with the others."

Vlad wondered, now, if that dragon, so precise and clever in its design, still lurked at the bottom of the hope chest in his old room, hidden away in a velvet pouch alongside other useless childhood treasures: toys, a striated pebble, a bright red feather.

The man – the werewolf – who'd made the dragon looked half-made himself, now, hunched over a steaming bowl of stew at the long plank table in the palace kitchen. Vlad tried and failed to tear his gaze from the ruined eye. The lid was closed, and sunken; the eye itself was obviously gone. But the blood had been allowed to run down his face and dry. No one had attempted any sort of medicinal arts to help with pain, or cleanliness. Vlad suspected that it was only a wolf's healing abilities that had kept him alive and free of infection.

Across from him, Fenrir sat as a shadow of his former self, thin in a way he'd never been, the knobs of elbows and knees visible beneath threadbare clothes, his massive shoulders too spare, squared off like a picture frame. His beard lay in tangles on his chest, his hair knotted on his shoulders.

Helga sat beside him, working at the snarls with a comb and a little pot of oil, clucking her tongue and muttering, brows drawn together, hiding her relief and fear and grief behind mothering, the way she always had. Fenrir was weak, and furious, and he mourned the loss of Father and Mircea, doubtless, but he was not broken.

No, that was Cicero.

The wolf nibbled at his food, dunking bits of fresh bread into the broth and studying them for long moments before finally taking a bite. He was a man lost. Completely defeated.

Vlad wanted to get him alone, to ask him about Father. But Malik arrived, suddenly, with a scribe in tow, one of the Turkish ones brought from Edirne. He came armed with quill and parchment.

"A scribe, as requested, your grace," Malik said, falling into parade rest at the door. Clearly, he didn't intend to excuse himself. And he looked at the wolves with undisguised curiosity.

Vlad took a measured breath. "Yes, thank you." To the scribe, who'd settled at the end of the table farthest from the smelly former prisoners: "I wish to send a letter to Vladislav. Prepare to take dictation."

"Yes, your grace." The man settled, arranged his things, dipped the quill into ink.

Vlad could have written his own letter, but that wasn't done. Princes didn't sully their hands with scribe business, and he meant to be a prince. So.

"Dearest Father-Killer and Traitor," he began.

Fenrir paused in his eating, brows lifted. Malik resettled his feet at the door. But the scribe wrote immediately, in flawless, elegant Slavic.

"I reach out to you now," Vlad continued, "not as your countryman, but as the future deliverer of your death."

"Ooh, that's good," Fenrir said.

"I write to you from your own stronghold in Tîrgovişte," Vlad continued, "which is in fact *my* palace. Just as it was my father's, before you murdered him. Know that you will answer for that. You and every turncoat boyar who helped with the execution."

The scribe paused, quill hovering above the parchment.

Around him, silence. Helga had stopped combing; Fenrir had stopped eating; he was aware of Cicero's one-eyed gaze against the side of his head.

"Was that unclear?" Vlad asked.

"No, your grace." The scribe resumed writing.

"By order of His Imperial Majesty, the Sultan of the Ottomans, I, Prince Vlad Dracula, do hereby assert my claim over Wallachia as its rightful leader. From this point forward, you, Vladislav II, are a murderer and war criminal, sentenced to death. Should you choose to return to Tîrgovişte, know that your life is forfeit. You may prepare now for your public execution."

The scribe finished off the letter with a few last scratches of his quill, and then silence reigned.

"Will that be all?" the scribe finally asked, hesitant.

"Yes. Have it sent to him. I'm sure he can be found beneath the same rock under which John Hunyadi is currently hiding." He went to lend his signature, and his ring for the wax seal. After, the scribe secured the missive and left to see about sending it, bobbing a quick, but deep bow on his way.

When he was gone, Vlad turned back to his people, all too aware of Malik's presence, still lingering silent by the door.

Fenrir and Cicero had left off eating, and stared at him. Helga paused in her combing, frazzled lock of her husband's red hair held in one hand.

"You're gaping," he informed them.

Fenrir blinked, and then laughed, low and hearty, if a little rusty from disuse.

Helga gave a wobbly smile. "It's so good to have you home, your grace. A proper prince and head of the household pack."

Is that what he was now? The head of his household?

He let out a deep breath, and hoped it sounded steady to the keen ears around him. Turned to Cicero. "When you're finished eating, I'd like an audience with you in Father's old study."

The wolf nodded, resolve setting his features in a way that improved his look of exhaustion. He'd always been someone who needed a task, a purpose. "I'm ready now, your grace."

Vlad shook his head. "No. Finish your meal." He felt a smile tug at his mouth. "That's an order."

"Yes, sir." The wolf resumed eating, this time with something like enthusiasm.

~*~

The study was still the study, only now the hearths were heaped with old ashes, and the desk was cluttered with sticky wine cups, greasy half-eaten bits of trencher, and a clutter of messages, maps, and melted candle stumps. The paperwork Vlad pushed aside to sort through later, on the off chance he might glean something useful. The rest of the clutter he dumped out the window once he'd opened the shutters.

He stood a long moment behind his father's chair, his hand on the back of it. The only times he'd ever sat here as a boy had been in Father's lap. He drummed his fingertips on the smooth leather, and little metal studs that bordered the wooden frame. It was just a chair, but it had brought him up short and rendered him momentarily stupid, awash with memory, with useless emotion.

"He would be proud of you," Cicero spoke, voice hushed. Reverent.

Vlad found that he couldn't have possibly been here, in his father's sacred space, with anyone beside the centuries-faithful wolf. He had to be strong for Mother; had to be forceful for Fen and Helga. But Cicero had known and loved Remus Vlad Dracul better than anyone, and Vlad felt his foundations waver; felt tears burn his sinuses, and clog his throat.

He gripped the chair back until his knuckles popped, and swallowed hard, swallowed it all down. He lifted his head and saw Cicero looking thin and frail in the chair on the other side of the desk, his black, tangled beard and his wild hair. He'd always been upright, and clean-shaven, impeccably turned out in house colors and fine jewels and furs. A proud, proud, beloved Familiar. Reduced to a wretch, a shivering prisoner. But he gazed at Vlad with his one remaining eye as if he was a savior. As if this trembling boy of seventeen was his whole hope for the future.

Vlad wet his lips. "If I sit here, then…" His voice shook, all his doubt and grief bleeding through. "Then that's it. He's really dead." He'd never shown such emotion in all his days as a hostage; he'd thought he'd lost the ability to.

"Oh, son," Cicero said, achingly. "He's already dead. And he wouldn't want anyone else to sit there but you."

Vlad pulled the chair back and all but fell into it. "Tell me what happened."

Cicero didn't need to ask for clarification. He linked his hands together in his lap and took a deep breath. "There had been rumblings. Some of the boyars came for audiences, asking your father to align with Vladislav. He said, and was correct, that he himself was not the enemy of Hunyadi and the rest of Romania. What did they hope to achieve by appealing to him? But we knew." He shook his head. "There was unrest. They wanted a war with the Turks. And they didn't – forgive me, your grace, they weren't worried about you or your brother, not the way Dracul was." His look was entreating. "He was your father, and he loved you, and he wanted to bring you home."

"But he couldn't. He caved to pressure."

Cicero bowed his head. "We prepared. But. It was an ambush on the road. Vladislav's troops…there were many. And five wolves. And a *mage*."

Five wolves, he'd started to exclaim, but was brought up short on *mage*. The word hit his brain like a spiked mace, scattering all other thoughts.

"A mage? You're sure?"

"A woman," Cicero said, nodding. "With pale hair. She held fire the way a man holds a weapon." He cupped his hand around an imaginary flame. "I...have never seen anything like it."

Neither had Vlad, though his parents had described mage powers to him in detail. They'd spoken of them with shudders, and head shakes. *Not natural*, Mother always said. *They're not like wolves or vampires – we rely on our sight, and sense of smell, our strength and speed and our wits. But mages manipulate the natural world; they are not a part of it. They're not predators...they're tricksters.* She'd thrown a joke about Loki in there somewhere, but her eyes had been distant and fearful.

"She was powerful," Cicero said, and in those simple words Vlad could see what had happened: the leaping flames, the wolves crashing out of the woods, the screaming humans armed with swords and spears. "And we fought. We tried to get your father and brother inside the gates, but." He drew a shuddering breath, head bowing. "I was struck a blow in the face, and I was knocked unconscious. When I came to..." His hands tightened to fists in his lap, and Vlad had the impression it was an effort not to reach for his ruined eye. "They had captured Fen," he said. "The others, Caesar..." He shrank down into himself, shoulders slumping.

"I'm sorry," Vlad murmured.

"As am I."

"Only the two of you survived? No others?"

"Fen says Vali got away. But he hasn't come back. Perhaps just a father's hope."

"Perhaps." Vlad would ride out and try to find him, though; see if there was a scent trail to follow. Locate the body, if nothing else, for a proper Norse pyre – if there was anything left to burn.

He took a deep breath, hands braced on the desk. The words he needed to say now scraped at his throat like broken glass, but he had to get them out. "Cicero, there's something I have to do. When Vladislav receives word, he'll march back, and we'll have a battle on our hands. But before then, I have to..."

Another breath; his lungs were tight. "I won't ask this of you, not after all you've been through–"

"Ask me." The wolf lifted his head, sorrow giving way to resolve, gaze hardening. "Ask me anything, your grace."

Vlad hesitated. It didn't seem fair – even if life wasn't, if nothing was, it seemed that a prince should offer what fairness he could, when he was able.

"Anything," Cicero repeated. "I am yours."

He knew then, the sunlight catching in Cicero's dark eye, that his father was dead, but he intended to go and see for himself anyway.

~*~

Cazan had spoken truthfully. The grave was in the churchyard, just as he'd described. Vlad knelt and pressed his ear to the earth; a scattering of delicate grass stems already grew there, covering the freshly tilled patch of dirt. He could detect no heartbeat, no sign of life. He breathed deep and smelled decay and dirt and rot.

He smelled death.

In a shallow, unmarked grave beside it, he dug up a jar full of ashes. He dipped a finger in and set a few specks on his tongue: charred, but still recognizable as heart meat. As his father.

Cicero whined softly, a lupine sound in the back of his throat.

Vlad smoothed the dirt back into the now-empty hole and tucked the jar away in his saddlebag. He gathered his reins. "Where is Mircea?"

~*~

It was a place Vlad recognized, a quiet glen screened from the road by pines and holly bushes. It smelled of fall: of turning leaves, and tree sap, ripening berries...

He refused to acknowledge the last scent. The telling one.

"Your grace," Cicero said, quiet and careful.

Vlad ignored him. He unslung the shovel from the back of his saddle and began to dig.

Malik had offered to send men with him, to help with the digging. But Vlad had refused. Even Cicero's gaze on him was almost too much to bear.

So he dug alone. Until, despite the cool of the afternoon, the sweat began to pour down his body, soaking through the layers of confining fabric. He stripped off his kaftan, and his shirt; tied his hair back with a strip of leather. Dug, and dug, growling at Cicero when he tried to help, first with words – "you're too weak" – and then with only with sounds, deep and desperate in his chest. And then he couldn't even do that, could only dig, not protesting when Cicero shifted and put his great wolfen forepaws to use, dragging up dirt with his claws.

Vlad's fingers touched something hard, finally, smoother than rock. "Wait," he said, and Cicero halted, up to his wolf shoulders in the pit they'd dug.

Hand shaking, Vlad drew out a bone. Human. From the upper arm.

His brother was bones.

He kept digging.

Cicero whined again, and leaned toward Vlad, prodding at him with his large wet nose.

Vlad waved him away. "No. I'm going to do this."

He dug Mircea up, down to every little knuckle and toe bone, laid him out in the best order he could manage on the length of burlap he'd brought along, intending to use it for a litter if…but no. Mircea was – had been – a half-breed. He hadn't survived the suffocation.

He wiped the skull clean with a bit of cloth, only to smudge it again when he traced the empty eye sockets with dirt-caked fingertips. "Hello, brother." He set it down gently, and then sat back on his heels, hands braced on his now-filthy riding leathers.

Cicero came to curl up beside him, leaning into his side, warm, and solid, his fur soft against Vlad's bare skin.

Vlad smoothed a hand down his head and neck, laced dirty fingers in his ruff.

He had to bury it. The awful, dark, choking bundle of anguish trying to claw its way up his throat. If he let it out, if he acknowledged it – there was no coming back from that. Not ever.

He closed his eyes, and thought of bodies on spikes along a palace wall. Thought of boy princes with burned-out eyes. Thought of the scent of sex on his little brother. The taste of blood; the sound a man made when he died.

Kill them, kill them, kill them all.

"Alright." He opened his eyes. "Let's go home."

~*~

Taking over a palace was, to put it bluntly, a lot of work. He dictated a dozen messages, ones to inform surrounding nobles of said takeover, ones to request audiences, and one he took special joy in: a renunciation of Vladislav and all his prince-killing boyar cronies that he sent off to John Hunyadi. That one began *I will kill your man, you know.*

"Quite savage, your grace," Malik said, voice bland, brows lifting in a way that might have been approving.

"I intend to be the most savage prince any of these fools have ever seen."

Then it was getting the household in order. He had several of his men round up all the servants and inspected them. All of them were holdovers from his father's days, all of them frightened, shaking, but dissolving quickly into shock when he informed them of his identity.

"You served my father loyally for years. Are you prepared to serve me as well?"

A chorus of "yes, your grace," and a round of bows and curtsies.

Vladislav had left a single steward behind, a middle-aged man in a ripped coat and the kind of dignity born of terrified defiance. He was, Vlad thought, the easiest sort of person to break. Two of Vlad's men held him up by the arms, though he didn't struggle, and he met Vlad's gaze bravely when Vlad came to stand in front of him.

"Is there anything useful you might tell me of your master?" Vlad asked.

The steward spit on the floor at Vlad's feet. Several droplets spattered across his dirty boots. "Turkish swine."

The soldiers tightened their hold, but Vlad stayed them with a gesture. He smiled at the steward. "In your time in the dungeon before your execution, I ask you to think on this: you're the one who helped a man bent on selling this entire principality to the Hungarian throne. So who's really the turncoat between us?" He tapped the man in the chest with one finger. "If anything important comes to mind, send for me. Otherwise, make your peace with God."

He retired then to his father's – to *his* – study, and began sorting through the stacks of paper chaff that Vladislav had left behind. Some of it was scrolls, others dashed-off notes on parchment scraps. He found several journals, half-full, the handwriting so slovenly it was nearly indecipherable. He wondered if Vladislav had written any of it himself, or if it was the work of the steward currently being chained up in the dungeon.

"Tell me about him," he said, distracted, squinting at what appeared to be a list of either favorite dishes, or an order for the chefs on their way to market.

Eira sat beside him in a second chair, chin propped on her hands, touching the paper Vlad passed her with only the tips of her fingers, nose wrinkled delicately, as if she didn't want to touch the same parchment that Vladislav had touched. "He is both small and narrow minded," she said. "I didn't know such a thing was possible, but now I know better."

Vlad snorted as he paged through one of the journals. "I know what kind of man he is." He had a sack of bones and a jar of heart ashes to tell him that much. "I mean what is his routine; what are his habits. I want to know how best to manipulate him when I finally get him in front of me."

Eira scoffed. "You might be a man now, but you've been a hostage all these years, my son, and not among Romanians. You'd do well to listen." Like all her reprimands from his youth, her voice was light, her words strong. She had a way about her.

He sighed. "Yes, fine. Tell me what I should know, then."

She nodded. "He is—"

A knock sounded at the door, and it swung inward before he could inquire. *That* was something he'd need to address soon.

The intruder proved to be Helga, bearing a tray of bread, fresh soft cheese, grapes, wine, and, by its scent, blood. She carried it in with the gait he remembered from childhood, her hips swaying beneath her skirts and tidy apron, her face set with motherly concern. He felt a boy again, for a moment.

"You need to eat something to keep your strength up, your grace, my lady. It's getting late, and you can't stay up all night on an empty stomach."

Vlad turned to the window as she set the tray on the edge of the desk and began unloading platters and cups in front of them. The sun had slipped below the tree line, the sky a dusky rose. There was hardly any light left in the room; he hadn't even realized he'd been squinting to read.

"Yes, well, thank you." He eyed the two small cups of blood as Eira moved to light the room's candles. "This smells like wolf blood, Helga."

"It is. Fresh from my Fenny."

"Helga—"

"You've been on the march, sir, and haven't taken a bite all day besides. And if you'll pardon me saying so, you didn't smell a thing like a wolf when you got here. I'm guessing those lousy Turks don't even have wolves to feed you from, and—"

"*Helga.*"

She froze, hand hovering beside a platter of cheese and fruit. Not just grapes, he saw now, but figs, too. The last of the year that had been crushed into jam.

"Fen can't afford to give any blood now," he said, firm, trying not to sound cruel. Cruelty rolled naturally off his tongue; he scowled the way other boys smiled. It frightened him, if he was honest. "There are horses in the stable, and cattle in the field. I need not for blood."

She studied him a moment. Swallowed. "With all due respect, your grace—"

"Fen's blood," he said, even firmer, so that she straightened up with a tiny yelp, clutching the tray to her chest, "stays inside his veins until he's stronger. Mother and I shall be just fine until then."

She bobbed a quick curtsy. "Yes, your grace." Eyes downcast: "Also, I ought to tell you, that fellow with the scar, the one with the Far East look about him, wants to see you."

He nodded. "Send him up, please. Thank you, Helga."

She hurried from the room, looking much smaller than she had when she'd entered.

When she was gone, Eira resumed her seat, candlelight flickering around the room now. She sat upright, head lifted, disapproving. "That was harsh."

"It needed to be. You know how she is: she loves mothering everyone. If I don't put my foot down, she'll continue to bring us Fen's blood."

"Vlad," she said, serious and low, "it's a Familiar's honor to provide for his or her vampire—"

"I'm not her vampire," he said, turning to her.

Her gaze was narrow, sharp, lips pressed together.

For a moment, a half a heartbeat, he knew a boy's uncertainty.

But he wasn't a boy anymore – he hadn't been since the day he woke in silver cuffs in a janissary tent, bound for Edirne. "I'm not," he insisted.

"You're right. She is mine. And you are my son."

"Who is now the prince of Wallachia, and who can make his own decisions. I won't risk the health of *your* Familiar for the sake of a little rich blood. I've grown used to going without wolf blood. I can make do now. I will not be a boy on apron strings anymore, not while I'm trying to secure our home."

She stared at him a long beat, then finally nodded and turned her attention toward the food, plucking up a bundle of grapes. "You need your own Familiar," she said, quietly. "Cicero will offer. He would not bind himself to me."

"I have no need of a Familiar."

"Don't say that."

"I don't–"

"*Don't say that.*" She turned to him again, eyes flashing. "You are a man now, and a prince, and I can't imagine what you've lived through at the Ottoman court. But you are young, and I've lived a long, long time. Do not disparage the idea of a loyal Familiar. I couldn't have survived this long without mine. If Cicero offers, don't dismiss him lightly. He will offer out of love and loyalty, and I believe you'll need all the allies you can get."

He was angry; angry at her; angrier than he should have been. But he felt a wry smile lift one corner of his mouth. "You speak boldly, Mother."

"Well, someone has to. You might be the most savage prince that ever lived," she said, throwing his earlier proclamation back at him, "but that just means you're more likely to need someone to help you see reason."

A knock sounded at the half-open door. Malik.

"Come in." To Eira: "I thank you for your counsel." He turned to face the cavalry captain as he entered.

Malik still wore his armor, even carried his armored turban beneath his arm, the long white and red tail of it swaying against his legs, layered over the hem of his kaftan. "Your grace," he said, ducking his head briefly in greeting. In that moment, Vlad saw his lashes flicker, and knew he'd stolen a glance at Eira.

Vlad drummed his fingers on the desk. He'd end up having to do something about this...curiosity. "What is it?"

Malik straightened, admirably unphased by Vlad's tone. "The troops have all been settled, your grace. I took the liberty of forming up groups for guard duty and scheduled shifts. The rest are stationed in the barracks beyond the stable."

"The horses?"

"Happily eating, your grace. There were plenty of grain stores, and the hay is set to be reaped next week, the stable boys said."

"Very good."

"All the messengers have been sent as well."

"Yes. Thank you, Malik." A clear dismissal.

He lingered, unmoving...save his eyes, which shifted to the desk, to the food laid out...to the cups of blood.

"Something else you needed?" Vlad asked.

Malik's gaze lifted again. "I only wanted to ask, your grace, if your earlier errand was successful."

Ashes in a jar. Bones laid out on burlap.

He knew a sudden, visceral urge to leap over the desk and attack the janissary with hands and fangs, to taste human blood.

He said, coldly, "No, it was not. Anything *else?*"

Malik hesitated, and for a moment, his face showed doubt. He smoothed it quickly away and said, "Shall I lodge in the barracks with the men?"

"No. There's a captain's suite at the end of the hallway. Take it." Vlad waved toward the door.

Finally, the man bowed and took his leave.

"Does he know what you are?" Eira asked.

"I'm beginning to suspect that he does." He frowned to himself. "I haven't told him, but someone back in Edirne might have. God knows what Murat is up to."

~*~

Though his body was exhausted, Vlad's mind was too awake to seek his bed. That was what he told himself; in truth, as he yawned into his shoulder, he knew that what he dreaded most was going back to his old room. Lying on the old pillows, staring up at the old ceiling, and knowing that this wasn't the homecoming he'd dreamed of. Everything was different; almost everyone was dead. He needed to be strong, as unbendable as the steel Murat had claimed him to be, and he didn't think he could slide beneath his old furs and blankets and manage.

"He's already opened his vein," Eira said, nudging one of the blood cups toward him. "Don't let it go to waste."

He scowled at her, but her responding look was implacable.

He drained the cup in one swallow, and the blood hit his stomach like the richest wine. He'd forgotten wolf blood, the way it fizzed, the way it tasted like every kind of delicious fruit all at once, and something darker, and richer, too.

Breathless, he said, "Happy?"

"No. And I don't suspect I will be for a long time." She turned back to the list in front of her. It was nonsense, all of it was; Vladislav was a raging idiot. "You should get some rest."

Vlad sighed and pushed the journal in front of him to the side, massaging his tired eyes with fingers that still bore traces of grave dirt caked beneath the nails. "It's been hours," he said, "and you haven't asked about him yet."

"Asked about who?" But she sat up stiff and straight in her chair, tension stealing through her. Her eyes moved back and forth, too quick; she was no longer reading, but fighting to keep her breaths even, chest hitching unsteadily.

Vlad thought it would be a kindness to allow her this evasion. To say that she was right, and kiss her head, and go off to sleep in his boyhood bed, searching for traces of his brother's scent in the pillows.

But savage did not mean lenient. If he intended to do the impossible, to hold this palace, this principality, to earn its eventual independence from the Ottomans, then he had to learn to live as a hard man. Compromise only begat more compromise; he could not shrink from the unpleasant just to spare tears — no one had spared his tears, nor Val's.

He did soften his voice, though. "You know who I mean, Mother. Val. I had thought you'd ask about him right away." A thought dawned. "Or have you been keeping contact with him yourself?"

She took a trembling breath in through her mouth. Shook her head. "No. He — it's been some time since he came to see me. I had wondered…" She turned to him, unshed tears glittering like jewels in her blue eyes. "You do not smell of him."

"I hadn't much contact with him before my departure. Our paths within the palace diverged some months ago." Two years, to be precise. His brother had been the plaything of that serpent for *two years*.

She blinked against the tears, gaze narrowing. "What does that mean, Vlad?"

He resisted the urge to fidget. Savage or not, she was still his mother, and her gaze could still stop a cavalry charge when she wanted it to. "Valerian is…better liked at court than me."

"And yet here you sit, free and at the command of your own troops. What aren't you telling me? What are—" Her eyes went wide. "Oh, gods. Something he said to me, the last time I saw him, he…" Fresh tears welled. "Vlad, what has…?"

His chest ached. "Murat's son, Mehmet, the true sultan. He took a liking to Val. He has…a taste for boys."

Eira sagged forward on a deep exhale, as if the words had driven all the air from her lungs.

"Val had no choice. To refuse him–"

"Would have meant death," she murmured.

"I know him to be cruel. I can't imagine that he is kind. But Val is alive. Dripping with jewels." He smiled, bitter and brittle. "He makes quite the mistress."

She groaned, bending forward, hands pressed to her middle as if she might be sick. "Oh, my baby. My sweet little baby." Tears rolled down her cheeks, and pattered down onto the parchment below. "He asked me – oh, gods, he asked me if I'd ever been forced. If a man had ever…I tried to ask him what he meant, to ask if he was well. But he turned to smoke."

Vlad watched her cry, helpless. It didn't matter how many guards he'd slaughtered, how many gatemen; how many furious messages he'd dictated and sent. None of that rage mattered if his little brother had been raped for two years.

"Mother." He laid a hand on her shoulder, and she leaned into it, though she didn't look at him. "Mother, I'll get him back, I swear to you. And I'll take Mehmet's head from his shoulders myself. He will *pay* for what he's done. I promise you."

She reached to cover his hand with her own. "I know, I know." Sniffed hard. "But there's no undoing what's already been done." She lifted her wet face, eyes red, lashes spiked. "You can kill all you like, but that will never heal your brother's wounds." She touched her own chest. "They don't make a salve for those kinds of hurts."

"Then what would you have me do?" he whispered.

"Kill anyway. Kill all of them. That's all you *can* do."

<u>26</u>

FIGHT OR FLIGHT

Vlad slept for three days in the big chair at his father's old desk, knees drawn up at awkward angles, waking with the dawn with a crick in his neck and an aching back. During the day, he traveled into the city, Malik and heavily armed guards flanking him, to talk with shopkeepers and the heads of households. Hearing stories, asking for loyalty.

One thing became apparent: all but only a small handful of boyars had joined Vladislav's and Hunyadi's efforts to depose Vlad Dracul.

"They'll have to be dealt with," Vlad told Malik, and earned only a nod in response.

No word came from Hunyadi or Vladislav, nor did Vlad's scouts see any sign of them.

Under the cloudless autumn sky, Vlad felt the pressure of a thunderstorm, a gathering darkness along the horizon, not seen, but weighing on his bones all the same.

On the fourth night, his eyelids heavy, as he finally pushed aside his half-drunk cup of cow's blood and prepared to settle down for a fitful nap, a shadowy figure pushed open the door and lingered in the threshold, limned in torchlight from the hallway beyond.

Vlad knew him by scent.

"Come, Cicero," he called with a gesture, voice heavy with fatigue and dissatisfaction. "You know that you are always welcome counsel."

The wolf entered, but did not sit. He remained standing opposite Vlad, hands at his sides, face set in lines of resolution. He had shaved since last Vlad had seen him, so the clean, angular lines of his jaw were visible, his hair washed and tied back in the front, left to fall across his shoulders behind. Someone, Helga no doubt, had fashioned a patch of black cloth for his ruined eye. In fresh clothes, with color back in his cheeks, he looked the Dacian warrior that he was again, and no longer a sad prisoner.

It was silent between them at first, candle flames and edges of pages dancing in the breeze from the open window.

"Your father named me after a Roman," Cicero said, finally.

Vlad managed a faint smile. He'd always liked this story. "Marcus Tullius Cicero. The greatest orator in history."

"He said it was because I argued my case so prettily." Alone, half-starved, Remus had been spending his days in a mountain cave, subsisting off rats, berries, and rainwater, in the high hills of what had once been the Dacian territory, but which had been occupied by Roman commanders. A pack of wolves had found him, their initial aggression turning to uncertainty once they'd sniffed out what he was. Three of that pack had been werewolves, and had shifted with seeming difficulty. At the time, only Cicero had been able to speak, a half-garbled language supplemented with gestures and whines. He hadn't shifted in nearly a decade. An exchange had been made: learning and civilization in exchange for blood to keep strong. It had been years before true trust had grown between them, and by then it had been love, and Cicero had agreed readily to a binding.

"He said that Rome would never have existed as it is remembered today if not for the kindness of a wolf," Cicero said, eyes downcast, pain writ clear across his face.

"Father always loved wolves. He impressed upon us the importance of that bond. The naturalness of a Familiar's relationship with his vampire."

"He was my first and only master. I didn't expect..." His hands curled to fists. "I didn't know how badly it would hurt. When the binding was severed." He reached to touch the side of his head. "It felt like something burst. Here." Touched his heart. "And here."

"Grief is a good thing," Vlad said, and knew he sounded flat. "It means that it was a binding of respect and love, and not one of slavery."

He took a deep breath. "Your grace..."

Vlad closed his eyes a moment. He knew what was coming. *If Cicero offers, don't dismiss him lightly. He will offer out of love and loyalty, and I believe you'll need all the allies you can get*, his mother had said.

He opened his eyes.

"Your grace," Cicero said again, sinking down slowly into the chair now, so they were face-to-face across the desk. "If you should want to – if you would allow me to – it would be the highest honor to bind myself to you now."

The thought terrified him. To have a Familiar was not merely to have a bodyguard. His parents had taught him that. A Familiar was a vampire's sworn protector, his packmate, his primary source of blood, and his unfailing confidante and best friend. In return, the vampire provided support, comfort, camaraderie, and protection. It was a symbiotic relationship that benefitted both parties. It was like a marriage, one bound by blood and a psychic pull neither side could resist, once established.

A binding could only be broken by the death of one party, as Vlad understood it.

"This is not a light thing you're asking for," Vlad said, leaning forward, bracing his elbows on the desk.

Cicero's shoulders slumped as he exhaled. "I know that I am" – his fingers twitched on the edge of the desk – "disfigured. I–"

"*Cicero.*"

The wolf lifted his head, eye glimmering.

Vlad said, "You are the most honorable and fearsome man I have ever met. The honor would be mine. But you served my father for centuries. I wouldn't make a servant of you so soon, not until you're sure it's what you want."

Cicero cocked his head, earnest, younger somehow. "Your – *Vlad*. My pack is dead. I want now only to be useful. To avenge your father, and to serve you. And…" His breath hitched. "I've grown used to being loved," he whispered. "I am weak."

No, I am, Vlad thought. He was seventeen, and in too deep, and completely overwhelmed, without a father or a mentor on which to lean for advice, working in service of a family he hated, a family that had made a whore of his brother. How easy, how tempting to accept.

He wanted to be savage, to be a prince, to kill and avenge, and rescue Val. But he was, to his shame, overwhelmed. Did that make him horrible? To lean on someone who deserved freedom?

"What will make you happy?" Vlad asked.

Relief touched Cicero's face. "To serve you, your grace."

Vlad stood. "Come with me, then, old friend."

~*~

Now, finally, he stood in the center of his old bedchamber. It had been made ready for him days ago; fresh candles, clean linens, a thorough dusting and airing out. He crossed to the washstand and found a fresh bit of toweling laid over the edge of the bowl; the ewer held clean water, still faintly warm when he tested it with his fingertips. The maids prepared this place for him every night, though he hadn't used it yet.

By all accounts, they should be in his father's old suite. He knew that Helga had seen to it personally that every trace of Vladislav had been scrubbed from that room, that lemon juice and cinnamon, and mint had been used to wipe away his scent. And he was the reigning prince now; the finest set of rooms should have been his own.

Perhaps he would graduate there, eventually. But now, this, tonight...this was his binding. It needed to happen in a place that was purely his. He needed Cicero to understand that he wasn't binding himself to the Prince of Wallachia – but to Vlad. To a very angry boy bent on killing a good many people.

Vlad turned and went to sit on the edge of the big four-poster bed. His feet didn't quite touch the ground, so he rested his heels on the edge of the bedframe instead.

Something in Cicero had changed since Vlad had accepted his offer. He projected calmness now, his expression soft and kind as he moved to sit beside Vlad. Close, but not crowding.

Vlad realized, to his surprise and embarrassment, that his palms were sweating. He wiped them on the legs of his pants. His voice came out rough, and he'd never felt so keenly like a boy playing at being a man.

"I know how this works. But...I've never done it. Obviously."

Cicero huffed a soft laugh, his smile fond. "It's alright; it won't be hard. You start – offer me your wrist. I'll go under first.

343

Then." He reached to pull his hair over one shoulder, exposing his throat on the near side. "Come find me."

Vlad wet his lips. "But what if — what if I can't do it? Val's the dream-walker, not me."

Cicero shook his head slightly. "You can. This is ancient, Vlad. This is how it's supposed to be." He reached to place a careful hand on the top of Vlad's head, and it had an immediate grounding affect. Even with one eye, his gaze was quietly earnest. "I won't let you get lost in the fog. Trust me on that."

"I do trust you." One of the only ones he trusted now.

Vlad brought his own wrist to his mouth and stared at it a moment, breath hitching. No going back after this. His fangs elongated in his mouth and he bit hard, punched through the skin.

When he offered the bleeding wound, Cicero took his arm into two reverent hands and lifted it to his face. Breathed the scent in, once, deep, eyes closed, and fastened his mouth to the open vein.

No one had ever fed from Vlad before, so he wasn't anticipating the shock of it. A sensation like the prickling of his skin just before a thunderstorm. A wash of heat chased by cold, pleasurable little ripples.

He lost himself to it, for a moment. Was this what George had felt, all those years ago in the chapel at Edirne? The drug-like calm?

But no, a binding went both ways. He shook off his stupor.

Cicero was still too thin, undoubtedly weak, but his pulse throbbed, strong and visible in the side of his throat, a tempting stretch of clean, unmarked skin. Living blood, so rare, a feast he always denied himself. And here, wolf blood, offered freely, out of loyalty and love.

He couldn't help the sound he made as he leaned in and bit, a low, pleased growl.

Cicero responded, a muffled huff of breath, encouraging.

And then the blood hit Vlad's tongue.

He drank. Velvet, lush; no wine had ever tasted so sweet. Necessary, too perfect to be illicit; the taste of it was *right*.

At first he only drank, and for the first time in so, so long he felt whole. Cradled in the dark, a part of something bigger and stronger than himself.

But then he found that he stood on an empty plain, stars bright above him in a moonless sky, a twilight fog swirling up from the ground, wrapping around him close as a blanket. A wolf stalked out of the shadows toward him, through the mist, a great shaggy brown beast with only one golden eye. He came up to Vlad, tongue out, tail wagging. Pressed his head into Vlad's outstretched palm.

Hello, old friend, Vlad thought. *I promise I'll be the best master I know how to be.*

A bright flash.

He shut his eyes against it, and when he opened them he lay on his side on the bed, face still tucked into Cicero's throat, blood in his mouth, and Cicero lay boneless half-atop him, warm and pliant.

Vlad retracted his fangs and licked the wound closed, then carefully withdrew.

Cicero lay with his eye half-closed, dazed, blood smeared on his lower lip. It was harder on the wolf; the wolf had to open his mind and let his master in, bind himself to another living being.

Looking at him, Vlad was filled with peace. And with sorrow – he didn't want to be responsible for anyone's death, or heartbreak, or sacrifice. He didn't deserve it.

He licked his own wound shut and got up on unsteady legs to walk to the ewer and basin.

Cicero whimpered, empty hands opening and closing on the counterpane.

"Shh, shh." Vlad returned with a wet cloth and knelt on the bed again; gently wiped the blood from Cicero's mouth and neck, dabbed the sweat that had gathered at his temples. He dropped the cloth to the rug, heedless of the wet patch it would leave, and settled back down, arms going around Cicero, pulling the larger body against his own, so the wolf's face was tucked into the hollow of his throat, where his pulse and scent where strongest. Cicero's fingers curled into the fabric of his shirt, and he let out a deep, tired sigh, breath tickling at Vlad's skin.

345

I have a Familiar, he thought, and closed his eyes. He was asleep long before the candles guttered out.

~*~

Vlad woke early the next morning, when the dawn was gray, incredibly well-rested, wolf fur tickling his nose. Cicero had shifted sometime during the night, and now lay curled up in a ball at Vlad's head, his face tucked in close enough that hot wolf breath ruffled Vlad's hair on each exhale.

He cracked his good eye open when Vlad pushed up on an elbow.

"It's fine. Go back to sleep."

The wolf made a protesting sound, but happily flopped over into the warm patch Vlad left behind when he got to his feet.

Silvery light filtered through the gap in the shutters as Vlad stretched and yawned his way to the basin, where he splashed his face with last night's stale water. Chin and lashes dripping, he walked barefoot out into the hall, down across the cool stones to the window that waited at the far end, where a slender figure in a simple dress stood gazing out at the first rays of the sunrise.

"Mother," he greeted, propping his elbows on the window ledge.

"You smell like a wolf."

"Hmm. Yes."

"Sleep well?"

"Like the dead." He sighed. "You were right."

"Of course I was."

"You don't have to be smug about it."

"I'm going to be, though."

This particular window afforded a view of the gardens, the palace wall, and, beyond, a wedge of rolling pastureland that climbed up and up in hills shaped like the humped folds of a quilt, all of it silver and gilt-edged, light spanning the horizon in bold fingertips. The scene looked like something from a painting.

"I've been thinking," she said.

"That's typically what people do when they gaze out of windows at sunrise."

"Where does your attitude come from? Your father was always such a sweet man."

"From you."

She snorted. "Unfortunately, you're right." She sighed. "I've been thinking about my place here."

In an instant, all his loose-limbed contentedness evaporated. He straightened. "What? Mother, you know that you—"

She silenced him with a hand. She turned to him, and that was when he saw that her dress was – unconventional. The bodice was supported by a tightly-laced leather corset, worn on the outside, one designed to cover and support her breasts, rather than flaunt their curves. The skirt was split down the middle, revealing a man's breeches and riding boots worn beneath. Bracers pretty enough to be decorative encased her wrists, but were certainly functional. Her hair was braided tight, out of the way.

"With the exception of Cicero, Fenrir, and Helga, all of your men think your father was married to the princess. They don't know who I am – nor who I am *to you*. For all my faults, I certainly don't look my age." Bitter smile. "They will think I am your lover."

His stomach turned, and he made a face.

"They will. Rumors can't hurt me – I'm only a mistress. *Was* only a mistress."

"Mother—"

"No, listen. I loved your father dearly, but I was of little practical use to him. You are a man, and I respect that, but you are also short on men at the moment." She lifted her chin. "I am tired of being a pretty girl kept in a tower. I want to fight. I *can* fight. Let me serve you in that way."

He stared at her, helpless.

Her voice cracked. "I don't want to be left behind anymore, Vlad, locked up in my own skirts, weeping over my family. What good are an immortal's powers if I never use them? Let me fight with you. Let me help you get Val back. Please."

What could he say? "They'll know you're a woman."

She smiled, grim. "Let them know. I'm not worried about *that.*"

The sound reached both of them at the same time, faint, but growing closer, and they turned to the window. Nothing but a smudge against the coming dawn, a lone rider approached from the city, hoofbeats a sharp tattoo against the hard-packed ground of the road.

"A messenger," Eira said.

Vlad drew himself upright and pushed his shoulders back. "Well, let's see which coward finally decided to reply to me." And he went to fetch his boots.

~*~

"'My dear Lord Dracula,'" Vlad read aloud for the room to hear. "'Allow me first to offer my deep and sincere condolences on the loss of your father, and of your brother. They were men of scant honor, but doubtless you loved them.

"'If your letter is to be believed, then it would appear that you've taken control of the palace at Tîrgoviște. I commend your cunning and bravery; it is no mean feat, especially given that you are only a boy of seventeen. But I must inform you that, here and now, such foolishness ends. Being that I am of far superior arms and number, a trained veteran to your green youth, it would be extremely ill-advised for you to pursue the course on which you've set yourself.

"'You are hereby ordered to present yourself to me as soon as possible, so that you may explain your actions – this vile, ungentlemanly usurpation of power – and so that you may explain what you have done with the governor of Transylvania, His Grace John Hunyadi.'"

The parchment quivered in his grip before he forced his hands to still. The study was silent save the call of birds beyond the open window, and the snapping of the fire on the grate.

Cicero, teeth bared throughout the reading, went now blank-faced with surprise. "Your grace...did the letter not *come* from John Hunyadi?"

"It's signed by the Transylvanian vice-governor, Nicolae Ocna," Vlad said, passing the letter to his Familiar.

"Obviously, you can't go to meet with him," Eira said. "It's a trap."

"Obviously," Vlad echoed. "But what the hell's happened to Hunyadi?" He looked at the surrounding faces in turn. "Do any of you know?"

Fenrir shrugged. "I've been in the dungeon, lad."

Leave it to Fen not to lean on formality; it was refreshing, given all the titles thrown at him lately.

"We've heard nothing here," Eira said. She looked startled, disturbed.

"The lad," Fenrir said. "The messenger."

Vlad said, "Right." He shouted toward the door, "Malik Bey!"

The door opened and the janissary entered, polished and composed as ever. "Yes, your grace?"

"Bring the boy. The messenger. I wish to question him."

Malik nodded and withdrew.

Vlad listened to his footsteps retreat down the hall, and then said, "If Hunyadi is dead—"

"He's not," Eira said. "He's too clever for that."

"We only know that he's stubborn and wicked," Vlad said. "And a coward who manages to slip out of large-scale battles unharmed. His cleverness has not been tested."

"Don't underestimate him," his mother warned, and he shot her a look. *Don't undermine me, Mother.*

She was, as expected, unimpressed.

"If he is in fact missing," Cicero said, passing the letter back, "we couldn't know for how long. None of us were a part of Vladislav's retinue."

"Yes, and thank God for that."

The wolf gave him a brief half-smile.

Malik returned, a foot soldier in tow, one that pushed the messenger boy forward into the room ahead of him.

Vlad had been surprised, at first, to find that the figure who'd galloped up to the gates bearing the vice-governor's seal had been only about fourteen. But then he'd seen the logic behind it: Vlad had promised death…for quite a few men. Nicolae Ocna doubtless hoped he'd be less likely to kill a child.

But it offered a boon for Vlad as well: a man might have lied or resisted questioning. This boy was already white-faced with terror, and Vlad hadn't even spoke to him yet.

"You may wait outside," he informed the soldier, adopting an indolent posture in his chair, the sort of thing, he realized with disgust, that Mehmet would do. An elbow braced, his weight shifted. *I don't care about you*, that pose said to others. Cruel princes slouched, did they not? "Malik, bring the boy forward."

The janissary clamped a hand on his shoulder and propelled him right up to the desk. The boy, Vlad noted, flicked glances to either side, looking at Cicero, at Fenrir, even at Eira, and the surface of the desk, but not straight at Vlad. He'd been told, then, of Vlad's promised killings. Probably that he was insane, as well; princes didn't just go around promising murder. Politics was a delicate art, one built upon lies and civility.

"Boy," Vlad said, and the boy in question jumped beneath Malik's hand. "Who is your master?"

His mouth opened, but no sound left it.

"To whom do you report? Are you the governor's, or the vice-governor's?"

"I–I–I–" His gaze had fixed to Cicero, to the patch over his eye.

Plainly, this would not work. The boy was frightened – but not properly. Not in a *helpful* way.

Vlad thought of his little brother, dripping jewels on the garden path, little chin raised up as he clung to his last scraps of pride, pleading angrily. *If you'd only behave.* Val had not broken; Val had ten times this boy's courage.

The indolent prince could only inspire stuttering. Hadn't he wanted to be savage anyway?

Vlad drew himself upright in his chair, hands braced on the carved ends of its arms, spine straight, and looked down the long line of his nose, though, sitting, he was no taller than the boy. In his coldest, most commanding voice, he said, "Stop stuttering, you fool, and look at me."

The stuttering stopped.

"*Look at me* if you wish to keep your eyes in your head."

Vlad heard Fenrir make the softest sound of protest in the back of his throat, but no one else said a word.

The boy's mouth shut with a click of his teeth, and his eyes came straight to Vlad's face, and didn't stray again. So pale, even his lips looked white; not just scared anymore, but terrified past the point of shaking. So scared that he'd decided obedience was the only way to come out alive.

Just as Val had decided in Mehmet's bed.

No more posturing. Vlad said, simply, "If you wish to live, and retain all of your limbs, you will answer the questions I'm about to ask you quickly and honestly. Do not stutter, and *do not* lie to me."

He swallowed with obvious difficulty. "Yes, your grace."

"Who is your master?"

"The vice governor. Nicolae Ocna, your grace."

"Where is the governor?"

The boy began to tremble, but his gaze stayed fixed. "I don't know, your grace. No one knows."

Vlad frowned. "He disappeared?"

"Yes, your grace."

"When? Under what circumstances?"

"He'd marched north, to meet the enemy. I don't know everything; my master didn't tell me. But I heard it said between the governors that it was expected to be a small skirmish. But his grace did not return, nor none of his men, and no message has been sent. That was a month ago."

Vlad lifted his brows, surprised. "And Nicolae thinks *I've* done something to Hunyadi?"

"He believes so, yes."

Vlad found himself smirking. "And why is that?"

"He said..." And here the boy hesitated.

"Speak."

"He said – he said you were possessed of a rare evil. Beg pardon, your grace. He said you'd been tainted by the Turks, and that you were cunning and ruthless, like them. And that you'd want petty revenge."

Vlad linked his hands together in his lap, elbows still braced on the chair arms. "That's what he said, eh?"

"Yes, your grace."

Vlad gestured. "Take him away."

Malik asked a question with his brows, and Vlad shook his head. No, he wouldn't have the boy killed; better to reuse him than to waste one of his own men on the errand back to Transylvania.

Malik took the boy back to the door, handed him off to the soldier, but stayed in the room. Vlad decided to allow it.

"This is fortuitous," Vlad said. "Without his puppet master at the helm, Vladislav should be easily routed."

"But where did Hunyadi *go?*" Cicero wondered aloud. "An army can't simply vanish into thin air."

"Ha," Fenrir said. "Perhaps a strigă got them. There's monsters in these mountains, you know." He winked and laughed at his own joke.

"It wasn't the Ottomans," Vlad said. "There would have been much celebration in Edirne, and a message would have been sent here." He looked to Malik, and the janissary nodded in agreement.

"The question then becomes," Eira said, "who hates him more than *you*, Vlad?"

~*~

Their answer came a week later, in the form of a letter signed by the Serbian prince George Brankovic.

"His sons were at court," Vlad said, tone mild with surprise. Stepan and Gregor; he remembered them clinging to Val's sleeves, shuffling along slowly, white strips of linen bound around their heads to hide the ugly scars. "Just before Val and I arrived, they tried to send word to their father. The slave told on them, and Murat had their eyes burned out with hot pokers."

Cicero growled quietly.

Vlad folded the letter and tucked it into his belt. The messenger had arrived while he was inspecting the palace grounds, his Familiar at his side, and he'd read it as they strolled between the barracks and the stable, headed back for the study to inform the others.

Fall had descended in earnest and it was a cold day, with clouds building up over the peaks, pushed along by a sharp wind. It would rain by nightfall.

Vlad found the weather bracing. The heat made men languid and slow; the cold kept them sharp and alert. And right now, Vlad needed every one of his too-few men to be at his best.

For his own part, he felt jittery. At night, Cicero had taken to bedding down with him, most often in his wolf shape, spread lengthwise across the foot of the bed, or tucked into a deceptively small knot at the small of Vlad's back. Sometimes in his man shape, his deep, even breaths and the familiar smell of him lulling Vlad to sleep. He never stayed asleep, though; woke often in the small hours, drenched in sweat, launched from a nightmare. The dreams were always different, but one theme carried throughout: he wasn't the one in danger, and was instead made to watch, helpless, as his family was killed, tortured, raped. Mircea screaming through a mouthful of grave dirt. Father watching his own heart cut from his body. And Val, always Val, with his pretty blue eyes burned to gaping holes, or hanged by a heavy gold chain studded with sapphires, or with Mehmet looming behind him, taking him, grinning at Vlad with a bloody mouth over the boy's shoulder.

Last night he'd awakened to the light of the full moon spilling through the window, through the shutters he'd left open. Shirt glued to his skin, hair clinging to his damp face, covers twisted around his waist. Cicero, in human form, had rolled toward him, and flung an arm across his chest at some point, doubtless trying to keep him still. He was awake, eyes wide and dark in the moonlight, watching, wolfish.

Vlad had rolled away and climbed out of bed; gone to the window and leaned on the ledge, letting the chill night breeze rush across his skin, and cool it. Behind him, he heard Cicero slip from beneath the covers and come to stand a pace behind him. He didn't press, and his scent was calm; he let Vlad mull it over, ready to come closer if it was asked of him, or away, too, if that was what Vlad wanted. He knew that; he'd known it before, watching Cicero with Father, but now he knew it with certainty, bone-deep.

The moon-gilded hills of home glowed silver below, the city's tile rooftops gleaming. One of those clear, crystalline nights, cold enough that, had they been mortal, they would have already caught their death sleeping without a fire and with the window open like this.

Vlad had admitted, quietly, "It was never supposed to be me here. I was the second son. I was supposed to be the warrior, not the leader. And now I have to be both."

Cicero was silent a moment, then said, "I bore great affection for your half-brother, and he was both brave and intelligent. But truth told, I think you're better suited for the job, Vlad." It was always *your grace* in the daylight, in front of the others. He liked hearing his name in the dark, when he felt uncertain.

"But I'm so *angry.*" He folded his hands into fists and rested his chin on them. "I'm furious. All the time."

A little quaver in Cicero's breathing. A show of nerves. "Your father was kind, and tried always, even when it was difficult, to be cheerful. And now he is dead. I think – I think maybe anger is the right way to feel now."

Vlad glanced back over his shoulder; Cicero looked almost a ghost, in his white shirt, skin washed pale by the moon. "And you. You're angry?"

"I am *enraged.*"

"Good. Now we just have to keep our wits about us."

Now, their boots crunching over stone and winter-ready grass, Vlad chewed at his lip and thought over the contents of Brankovic's letter.

Cicero touched him on the arm, and he lifted his head to find Malik Bey striding toward them, expression one of subdued determination. Too soft for the mortal to hear, Cicero said, "Do you trust this man, your grace?"

"Do *you?*" Vlad asked.

"He seems earnest," Cicero said. "He doesn't smell nervous, the way treacherous men always do. But he *is* human."

"Yes," Vlad sighed. "But he's all we have, I'm afraid." Malik was near, and Vlad drew to a halt to wait, letting the janissary take the last steps to close the distance. "Captain," he greeted.

Malik bowed. "Your grace. I saw that a messenger had come."

"And you, what, rushed over here to interrogate me about it?"

The man blinked, and looked almost startled. "I thought there might be important news."

"As it happens, there is." Then he waited.

A long moment.

"Your grace. If I am to be of service to you in your fight to hold Wallachia, then keeping me informed can only be helpful to you."

Vlad showed his teeth; it wasn't a smile. "Yes, well. That would be helpful, wouldn't it?"

The breeze stirred up a handful of errant leaves, and dust.

Malik's brows lowered, a sign of real emotion. He'd been so calm, so unflappable throughout, and Vlad had to know what lay beneath that façade. Murat might have sent him here, and he might have the empire's goodwill for the moment, but Vlad had seen curiosity in Malik; the curiosity of a traitor? Or someone who wanted to get out from under the sultan's thumb just as badly as Vlad?

"Is that what you want?" he pressed. "To be of service to me?"

Malik frowned. "That is my duty, your grace."

"Yes. Duty. Always important."

Cicero cleared his throat, a polite, *get on with it, your grace.*

Vlad sighed, but it was just as well. Malik plainly wasn't going to step wrong now, here, and for a moment there, he'd been – almost – having fun. He wasn't sure he was ready to examine that.

"The message," he said in a normal tone, resuming his walk. Both men fell into step on either side of him. "Came from the prince of Serbia. His sons, the princes at court alongside my brother and myself, you know."

A stolen glance revealed that Malik raised his brows. Doubtless he'd never laid eyes upon the boys; who knew if he'd even heard of them.

"He managed to surprise Hunyadi, and the Albanian prince, the one they call Skanderbeg as well, and has taken them captive."

Skanderbeg. George Castrioti. The name had leapt off the page, and Vlad's pulse had stuttered. He remembered a kind smile when there were none, an exposed throat, an offer of freely given blood. A hand extended, and an offer of an alliance. He remembered a lesson on patience. And hope. George Castrioti had offered him hope.

He understood wanting vengeance for lost sons – he *understood*. But Castrioti was a force for Slavic Europe. A force for resistance to the mighty empire, and Vlad could have cheerfully strangled Brankovic.

"Why has he done such a thing?"

"Apparently, he's displeased with Hunyadi's seeking of personal glory, and the way he's been using the rest of Eastern Europe for his own gain, casting us aside when it profits him, bullying us. He refenced my father. Hunyadi's support of Vladislav after my father risked our lives to support him." He found that he had to take a steadying breath. "So he wants to coerce a marriage. Hunyadi's son Matthias will wed Brankovic's daughter. Or else he shall remain in irons."

Malik ground to a halt, and Vlad stopped as well, as the men turned to face him, brows raised up to the edge of his turban. "For a marriage?"

Vlad felt a smile tug at his lips. "Apparently. Brankovic's family has suffered greatly during the course of Hunyadi's ill-advised crusades. Revenge is understandable, though I suppose, all things given, he lacks the will to kill the man and go to war over it. More's the pity.

"But." He resumed walking and the others followed. "I should like to see Geor – Skanderbeg," he corrected, "freed. I'll draft a letter to Brankovic, promising cooperation and alliance in exchange for the Albanian's release."

"Will he honor that request?" Cicero asked.

"Not likely. But I have to make it anyway." For the sake of the boy who'd befriended him in enemy hands.

"This doesn't solve the issue of the vice governor," Cicero said.

Vlad sighed. "Yes, I know. I've already written to him. I will not leave here. That way lies a trap, and I don't intend to fall into it."

"Where is Vladislav?" Malik asked.

"Off warmongering somewhere. We're lucky, in that."

They passed the practice yard, where foot soldiers practiced with spears, their friends and fellow soldiers watching, encouraging them with shouts and jeers.

Cicero and Malik drew breath at the same time, and Vlad silenced them with a wave. He knew what they were going to say. "If Hunyadi agrees to the marriage, and is freed, doubtless he will join up with Vladislav and they will march here. And yes, I already know that, as good as these Turkish troops are, we lack the numbers to defend ourselves." He frowned into the middle distance, imagination taking hold, showing him a palace with walls tumbled by sappers, black smoke billowing from the towers. "This place isn't home to either of them," he said, quietly. "They won't think twice about razing it to get me out. We can't face them," he admitted, shame a terrible lump in his throat.

His men were silent a moment, and then Cicero touched his arm, two fingers hooked into the crook of his elbow, and pulled him to a halt so they faced one another. Vlad spared a moment to think that Malik must be surprised by the gesture. Subjects, even captains and confidantes, didn't assume such familiarity with their princes. And only a Familiar dared touched a vampire in this way. Had Malik understood the existence of immortals, this would have served as all the proof he needed.

Cicero's eye sparkled amber in the sunlight, a smile threatening. He looked so different than he had in those first days; happy again, hopeful, and it had little to do with a shave and a bath and clean clothes.

"You're right, your grace," he said, "we can't hold the palace with just your men. But what if it was more than that? What if it was the whole city?"

"What?"

"You haven't addressed your people yet." Cicero waved toward the wall, toward Tîrgoviște beyond it. "You are their prince's son; they would be on your side. They would help!"

For a moment, he thought–

But no. Practicality won out. "They are farmers and tailors. Wives and children. They can't fight for me."

"There are sons, too, plenty of them."

"Your grace." Malik stepped around to stand beside the wolf. "That woman in the square on your first day. He's right: the people do remember you, and they want you leading them."

"Go into the city," Cicero said. "Address your subjects. Tell them what's happening, and make an appeal to them."

"I…" He wanted to kick himself. For faltering. Princes didn't falter. Didn't utter half-sentences. Not savage ones, anyway.

He took a breath and started again. "I should address them. Yes. That's what a leader does. But. A battle needs weapons. Needs money, and trained men. A battle needs the support of boyars, and I have no nobles on my side; not after they cut my father's heart from his body."

Both of them looked chastened.

Vlad put a hand on Cicero's shoulder. "It's a good idea, though, old friend. We'll see it done."

The wolf flicked him a small smile.

~*~

They cheered him.

A messenger had been sent ahead, to cut down the desiccated corpses from the gibbet and to stand atop the platform, shouting in Romanian. Vlad had sent Cicero to do this, a figure the people would recognize from Dracul's retinue; one of their own, a friend. *Vlad Dracula, the Son of the Dragon, is your prince now, come to protect his people from Vladislav's unsavory forces. Make ready, because the prince rides in an hour to address you all in the town square.*

And even with only an hour's preparation, they did make ready. They came out in droves, waving streamers made from old quilts and cleaning cloths. They lined the streets, and cheered when he approached on his roan charger, children jumping and waving their arms, fathers putting them up on shoulders so that they could see him better.

He wore red. A cobbled-together ensemble that was half-Turkish, half-Romanian, and wholly his own. Not a boy dressed up in his father's shadow, nor a conquering foreigner from the east.

His cavalry, turned out in gleaming mail and polished helms, cleared a path to the square, to the freshly cleared gibbet, and his people called to him the whole way. Vlad lifted a gloved hand in greeting, unable to smile or even to call back, stunned stupid by this reaction. He'd never anticipated it, not in his wildest dreams.

When he reached the gibbet, Cicero stepped forward to take his horse, and Vlad slid down to the ground breathing heavily through his mouth. He might be panicking.

The nearness and scent of his wolf helped. As did the hand Cicero laid on his shoulder, the two of them tucked out of sight behind the horse. "They already love you," he said with an encouraging smile, and a little shake. "All you have to do is love them back."

Vlad nodded. Swallowed a swell of nausea. "Right."

Then he climbed up on the platform and faced his people.

He could have done this other ways. Could have held an audience in the great hall at the palace, asked the citizens to walk and ride up the long hill to the gate, and file across the bridge. Could have sent messengers around to each and every house. Could have sent Cicero or Malik to speak in his stead. But this, addressing them directly, on their turf – this had been the right choice; he knew that now, looking at the sea of smiling, hopeful faces, listening to the shouts of his name. Young women batted lashes and waggled fingertips at him. Young men threw back their shoulders and stood at attention, proud, wanting to impress in a different way. Old women wrung their hands and turned their eyes heavenward, murmuring prayers of thanks.

For a moment, he was frozen, terrified in a way that he'd never been. No enemy had ever frightened him; but this, making people rally behind him, cheer for him – he'd never been the lovable brother. That was Val, miles away in a sultan's bed.

They already love you. Cicero's words echoed through his mind. *All you have to do is love them back.*

He took a deep breath, and willed the fear away. Savage. He must be savage, even in his love and defense of his people.

"Tîrgovişte," he called. Loud, authoritative. His voice bounced off the building walls around him.

All fell silent as one.

He continued, and the words formed one after the next, until they were effortless, and he knew this was what he needed to say. "I shall not introduce myself, because you all know who I am. My father, Vlad Dracul, a distinguished knight, a man of battle – and of learning – loved this city better than any in the world. He raised my brothers and me here. He died here, deep in these forests, cut down by the knives of a usurper and a pretender. And by the very nobles who claim themselves to be loyal Wallachians."

Boos, hisses, jeers.

"They robbed you of a prince and an heir, and for what? For the goodwill of John Hunyadi, a Hungarian who doesn't know you, or care for you. Who doesn't understand what it's like to live on the borderlands. To give your wealth and your young boys to the Ottomans. Hunyadi would use this place as a pathway to the east, never caring if war comes here, to your doorstep.

"It's Hunyadi's wish to consolidate all of Romania, and absorb it into Hungary. To drag you into his kingdom. To take you from one master, and force you to be subjugated by another."

Raucous sounds of disapproval.

Below him, Malik pressed his shoulder back against the edge of the platform, and tipped a questioning look up to Vlad. Yes, Vlad was prince, but under Murat's authority, wielding an army of Turkish soldiers.

Vlad didn't care. The words became a tide inside him, and he couldn't stop them.

"But I grew up here," he continued. "I bought bread from you, and watched traveling performers in these streets. I played and hunted with your boys. And I sat beside my father each time a new treaty came to his desk, and the Ottomans twisted his arm for just a few more sons, and just a few more gold ducats. More raids, more taking.

"That's what Hunyadi wants to do: take. Someone is always taking from us."

A collective shout. He saw red faces, open mouths, feverish eyes. He had them.

And he was one of them.

"Well I say it's time to end that," he said.

A roar. A din of overlapping voices like waves slapping at rocks. Is this what drowning sailors heard? This rushing in their ears?

"We are Wallachia," he said, shouted. "And we will no longer belong to anyone but ourselves! Join with me. Help me hold our lands, and I shall be the prince you deserve!"

They loved him, Cicero had said, and their love was deafening.

~*~

Vlad couldn't stop shaking.

"Darling, it will be alright," Eira said. She hovered a few paces away, a cup of wine mixed with blood ready to offer, should he want it. She hadn't tried to approach him again since he'd growled at her.

He felt bad for doing so, but it had been a reflex. Night had fallen, and still he reeled.

He'd spoken today of a free Wallachia, and here he was, granted leadership of this land by the very empire he'd sworn today to shake off. He'd said impossible, stupid things today. He supposed all kinds of love had the potential to make fools of men.

"Vlad," Cicero said, low and soothing. "You should come to bed. Rest. It will seem easier in the morning."

Vlad stopped in his pacing before the fireplace, and thrust a hand toward the shuttered window. "What will seem easier? The fact that I just scorned the very people guarding this palace? Or the fact that, the moment he's free, Hunyadi's going to march down here and kill us all?"

Cicero, stripped down to breeches and a simple shirt, hair unbound, folded his arms and sent him a very unimpressed look with his good eye. "You should talk to your men. Most of them aren't even Turkish by birth. Who's to say they won't support you?"

"And what if they do? Then Mehmet will march to put me down, my whore brother in tow."

"*Vlad,*" Eira snapped. "*Do not* call him that."

In the silence that followed, the flames crackled loudly on the hearth. A log shifted with a thump and a flare of sparks.

Cicero and Fenrir looked between mother and son, waiting. She was his mother, but he was a prince.

Vlad turned around and folded his arms across the mantlepiece, rested his forehead on them and peered down into the flames, though their heat was uncomfortable against his face. "Forgive me, Mama."

She approached then, and set the cup by his elbow. Put her hand against the back of his neck, the vulnerable stretch of it exposed by his pulled-down collar and his tied-up hair.

"If Sultan Murat were here before me now," she said, "then I would tear his throat out with my fangs and enjoy it. But I'll grant you the man isn't a fool. He sent you here to secure Wallachia, and you took an important step toward that today. He knows your people are no fans of his. You said what you had to. Write to him, let him think you're rabblerousing to defeat Hunyadi, and then later, when you're stronger, when you can, you can see about throwing off the Ottoman yoke."

He rolled his head so he could peer at her over his forearm. "You make a terrible amount of sense, Mother."

She smiled. "Of course I do. You don't think your father loved me just for my hair, do you?"

"Your captain's coming," Fenrir said, tone suddenly hostile, and a moment later a knock sounded at the door.

Vlad sighed and straightened, half-turned, one hand still on the mantle. "Come in, Malik."

He did so, looking a touch unnerved. He hadn't announced his presence after all.

Fenrir bristled in a way that Vlad could feel, and he sent the big wolf a quelling glance.

"Your grace," Malik said, "I have the list of names you requested. The boys in the city old enough and willing to fight."

"Very good. You may place it on the desk."

His footfalls echoed in the loaded silence as he moved to comply. And then he lingered. "Your grace."

"Yes?" Vlad turned to face him, and as he did, he noticed the way the firelight touched the wolves' eyes. A bright gleam, completely inhuman. He was grateful to have the fire at his back, to have his own face in shadow. A part of him wanted to know what Malik saw when he looked at him, but another, larger part of him already knew.

Malik stood as unruffled as ever, calm as a frozen lake in winter. But he smelled nervy. "Your speech today," he said, the words slow. "It was…very rousing. Effective, your grace."

"Thank you, Malik. Will that be all?"

"Yes, your grace." He took his leave with a bow.

When he was gone, and his footfalls had faded, Fenrir let out a deep breath. "That one knows. He doesn't know what, but he knows something."

"Yes, well, I can't kill him just yet, not while we need his men." Vlad tipped his head. "Though, eventually, I think I might have to."

~*~

He woke to howling.

Despite all his restless doubt and worry – and probably because of three cups of wine – Vlad had managed to not only fall asleep, but stay asleep. So the howl dragged him out of the depths, launching him into sudden, frantic wakefulness. He opened his eyes to a room made dark by closed shutters, close and cold, humid body heat trapped beneath the blankets and furs heaped over him, and Cicero beside him.

The wolf had been sleeping on his back, one arm flung up over his head. The most restful Vlad had seen him since their reunion. He jerked awake now, and grabbed wildly for Vlad, finding his arm, holding tight. He pulled a little, an instinct. *Stay here so I can protect you.*

Vlad shook him off and slipped from bed. The fire had burned down to coals, and the stones felt like ice under his bare feet. He didn't care. He rushed to the window and threw back the shutters, letting in a gust of sharp autumn air, deeply cold and scented with leaf mold from the forest.

Another howl. A second. A third. They could have been regular wolves, hunting a stag by moonlight. But they were close; they sounded right outside the walls. And Vlad didn't believe in coincidences.

"Get dressed." He went to his wardrobe. "We'll take Fen and handle it ourselves. Maybe it's nothing."

Vlad felt alert, anxious, but it was nothing compared to the energy rolling off his Familiar as he tugged on breeches and opened up the chest at the foot of the bed. Cicero vibrated; palpable emotion that warred between nervous and excited and furious, none of it comparing to the choking sense of responsibility. Vlad felt his presence, a weight at the back of his mind, the assurance of protection, and devotion, and unconditional, animal love.

With quick, though reverent movements, Cicero drew his pelt from the chest and unfurled it. Slung it over his shoulders and did the clasp; pulled the hood up over his head.

It was an old, old tradition, wolves wearing their pelts to battle. He'd asked Cicero about it when he was only four or five, curious. Wolves could shift and fight without it; they didn't need it. It was, in essence, just a bit of old dead skin and hair. It was to honor the wolf that birthed them into immortality, Cicero had explained.

It also looked damned unnerving.

Vlad buckled his father's sword to his hip. "Ready?"

They didn't have to get Fen, it turned out; he met them on the stairwell, his own pelt a rusty red that nearly matched his hair. He looked monstrous in the dim half-light of moon and shadows. Vlad caught a faint glimmer of metal in his hand – his massive battle axe.

"Vlad." He sounded eager.

"I know, I know, lead the way."

There were guards posted, soldiers who'd think nothing of a few howling wolves. They went out through the kitchens to avoid them, slipping silently out through Eira's gardens.

The howling had stopped. Vlad had time to spot a long line of shadow – of rope – trailing down from the outer wall, and then he smelled them.

He'd always liked the scent of wolves; each unique, but all bearing a certain earthy warmth, a musk, a hint of pine needles and forest, tree sap caught in fur. But *these* – these wolves had tracked and helped to kill his father, a phenomenon he still couldn't comprehend. And so this scent now, not of natural wolves, but of werewolves, lifted all the small hairs at the back of his neck.

He growled, and his own wolves answered it.

"They're here," Vlad said as they fell into a triangular formation, blades ready. "Can you scent them? Is it them?"

Cicero's growl deepened, low and vicious. His voice wasn't quite human anymore. "It's them. I'm going to *gut* them."

Three on three. Vlad liked those odds. And there was no need to go hunting; their prey came to them.

A hedge rustled, and a gray-brown blur leaped over a line of boxwoods, wet fangs flashing ivory in the moonlight. They'd climbed over as humans, and then shifted.

Vlad side-stepped, and brought his sword up in a short, forceful swing.

He missed. *Damn it!*

Fur brushed his cheek as the wolf sailed past him…and landed just behind Cicero. Vlad turned in time to see fangs sink through thin cloth and then flesh, just above the top of Cicero's boot. He raised his sword for another strike.

Cicero yelped, and whirled, dropped his sword, and shifted.

"No!" Vlad shouted, but it was too late, and the two wolves fell to the ground in a seething, growling tangle. Impossible to attack without hurting or killing his own Familiar.

Footsteps.

Vlad spun, muscles bunched, ready. "Stay on your feet!" he called to Fenrir. "That axe will do far more damage than your fangs."

Fen chuckled, and the axe sang as he twirled it expertly; Vlad could feel the breeze it made as the edge sliced through the

365

air. "Don't you worry, young prince. I can keep my wits about me."

Vlad snorted. "When have you ever?"

And then a man stood up, just on the other side of the hedge.

Vlad had an impression of dark, snarled hair, a dirty face, and a strong body clothed in rags. Then Fenrir roared and leaped at him, axe already swinging.

Strong, but fast, it turned out; the strange wolf danced back, and Fen gave chase, laughing wildly.

"Crazy fool," Vlad muttered, and turned, knowing what would happen now.

It did, predictably.

Vlad sensed him, scented him, before he'd gone a quarter of a revolution, and he blocked the swing of his opponent's sword with his own. The blades came together with a shining sound like the ringing of a bell.

The third wolf was broad, and tangled, and dirt-smeared, but his moth-eaten clothes were finer. A uniform, one from an age Vlad didn't recognize right away. Slavic bone structure, and fixed, sightless eyes. A puppet.

That didn't mean he couldn't fight, though.

Vlad spun, and ducked, angled his next swing at the wolf's wrist, wanting to take off his sword hand.

The wolf parried, and then advanced.

Vlad met him, and looked for his next opening.

He could still hear Cicero tussling with the wolf who'd bitten him; heard Fenrir shouting, too loud, determined to wake the whole palace, apparently. But his focus narrowed to his own fight, to his footwork, and the strength of his arms, and on everything every sword master had taught him in his seventeen years.

He blocked, and parried, and he kept stepping back, retreating beneath his larger opponent's swings. He clenched his teeth and snarled, hands white-knuckled on his sword, fingers numb with the effort. Relentless, emotionless, the wolf kept attacking.

What if he lost?

The idea formed as his boots skidded on pebbles and his sweat-slick grip shifted. All his training, all his hatred, all his big talk of savagery and revenge – what if that all boiled down to this moment, here and now? He was still young, still untested on the battlefield. And he was a vampire, yes, but this was a wolf, and a wolf would know how to kill a vampire.

Just like he'd known how to kill Father...

An image filled his mind: Father held down. The knife. The blood...rivers of it.

He heard another yelp. Cicero.

If he and the family wolves died here, now, Val would be the only one left. A sultan's plaything, but alive. Which was worse? He–

He caught the scent the same time his opponent did.

No, Val wouldn't be the last one.

His opponent reared back, surprised, but not quickly enough.

A flash, as Eira drove her sword between two of the wolf's ribs. A sound like a sigh; she'd punctured his lung.

With one hard swing, Vlad took the creature's sword arm off just above the wrist; his blade clattered to the ground. And then Vlad ran him through, a clean stab, right into the heart. The body shuddered, and toppled. Vlad held his sword tight, and it pulled out as the wolf fell back, a gush of blood and gore following.

"Mother." Acknowledgement and recrimination in one.

She'd laced her leather corset on over her nightgown, the scalloped white hem of which fluttered around her booted calves. She lifted her brows. "You get up in the middle of the night to fight invading wolves and you don't tell me?"

"Ha!" Fenrir exclaimed, drawing their attention.

His opponent lay at his feet, destroyed by the axe.

"Cicero," Vlad said, and went to his Familiar.

Cicero, still in wolf form, struggled to his feet, limping on his back left, the limb the other wolf had bit. But his opponent was down – was gutted, Vlad saw, just as promised – and Cicero greeted him with a lupine smile and a lick when Vlad scratched at his ears.

"It's alright," he soothed, voice shaky. His hand came away wet with blood. "Shift back so we can see to you," he said, a gentle order.

Cicero ducked his head, as if to comply.

And then Vlad smelled smoke.

He looked up.

Fire bloomed a half dozen yards ahead of him.

"Fuck," he murmured. The wolves had been a distraction. This was the real threat.

She stepped out of a tall column of flames, the fire skirting all around her, skimming over pale skin, and rich blue dress, but never touching her, never burning.

Young, pretty, smirking. Ageless.

When she spoke, it was with an accent he couldn't place, though her Romanian was flawless in a technical sense.

"Now, now, down, boys," she said, and the two wolves froze. Vlad could hear their hearts beating, but they didn't move, didn't twitch.

Mages could do this, Father had told him once. Command humans, wolves, sometimes even vampires. They could control them.

The woman walked forward, flame sweeping out behind her like a cape. Past Cicero and Fenrir, who in their right minds would have torn her to pieces. "You too, Mother-dear." She snapped her fingers, and Eira went oddly placid and still, arms falling to her sides.

She smiled, flashing teeth, as she strolled up to Vlad, unhurried. "And here he is," she drawled. "The Prince of Wallachia." She stopped a pace away from him and folded her arms, cocked her head. "Bit scrawnier than I anticipated. Not as handsome as I'd hoped."

He'd never met a mage, and her scent repulsed him. Ash, and death, and unnatural things; fire, and the scent of the air just before a thunderstorm.

He growled, and showed her his teeth in kind – fangs extended. If she wanted to compare, then let her see what she was dealing with.

She laughed. "Just a little boy after all." She raised her hand in an unmistakable gesture; he didn't have any experience with women, but he recognized *come hither* for what it was.

Vlad stood his ground; lifted his sword in a two-handed grip.

She frowned. Repeated the gesture, more forcefully.

Vlad lowered his head and rolled his shoulders; made ready for an attack. "Who is your master?" he asked.

She stepped in closer with a huffy sigh. "Oh, honestly, this is just—"

Vlad touched the very tip of his sword to her breastbone, the froth of laces and silk that covered her heart. The red of the blood on his blade glimmered in the moonlight. He said, "Who sent you?"

Her lashes fluttered, and her mouth worked. Beneath the ash-and-fire stink of her, he caught the first notes of fear, of sweat gathering across her skin. She was afraid. Wolves, vampires, humans – she could control others at will, and obviously did. But she couldn't control him.

"Magic not working?" he asked.

Her gaze narrowed. "You shouldn't be able to do this."

"You have *no idea* what I'm capable of. I'll only ask one more time: who sent you?"

She burst into flames.

The fire sprang up from nothing, engulfing her head to toe, and it rushed toward Vlad, a curl of it like a great tongue, straight for his eyes.

He didn't think about what he was doing; he simply reacted. He reached through the fire, a fast grab, and gripped her by the throat. The fire burned him – bright, blinding pain on the skin of his hand, scorching his shirt, eating away at flesh – but then it cut off with a puff of thick, acrid smoke. His hand was a red, blistered mess, but the sinews still worked; he was still able to squeeze until the mage choked, coughing and fighting for air.

Vlad dragged her in close, toes of her fine shoes fishtailing in the pebbles at their feet. Close enough to see her eyes bug, to see her face go dark with suffocation.

He peeled his lips off his fangs, long and sharp. Snarled. *"Who sent you?"*

She made a few croaking sounds, and he loosened his grip the barest fraction. "R-R-Rom-ulus," she stuttered.

Romulus. Ah, Uncle.

He squeezed *tight*, and her neck broke with a pop. Her head sagged.

He dropped her to the path, and the others came back to life around him, shaking their heads, bewildered.

Cicero shifted back to his man shape, and stumbled immediately to one knee, his other leg torn and bloody.

"Your grace," a voice said, behind him, and Vlad sighed. Turned.

Malik Bey stood just outside the kitchen door, a lantern held aloft, highlighting a face made wild, for the first that Vlad had seen, with unchecked emotion. Shock, and terror, and disbelief.

This was it, then.

Vlad wiped his blade on the sleeve of his shirt, the one that wasn't burned, and sheathed it. Held up his ruined hand for the janissary to see. "Malik Bey," he said, and his voice sounded heavy, the way the words felt in his mouth. "May I formally present my mother, Eira, Viking shieldmaiden from the Norse lands. Her Familiar, Fenrir. My Familiar, Cicero. Werewolves. And myself." He gave a mocking little bow, best as he was able in his current state. "Vlad Dracula: the vampire prince of Wallachia."

~*~

"It'll heal on its own," Vlad said through his teeth, resolutely not flinching under Eira's ministrations. It *hurt*.

"Healing isn't the same as healing well," she chided, dabbing at his burned and blistered skin with a warm, wet cloth. Helga stood beside her, a bundle of herbs picked fresh from the pots in the kitchen window ledges ready and waiting; the scent filled the room, covering the stink of blood and dead skin coming off his ruined hand.

He sat in a chair by the fire in his father's – in his own – study, the glow of flames and of the candles lined up along the mantle giving his mother light by which to clean his wounds. Fenrir stood beside the closed door, listening, keeping watch. Cicero, after a lot of protesting, had been pushed down into a chair beside Vlad; his leg had bled all over the floor. Vlad had insisted he be seen to first, an insistence that had left Cicero whining in distress; he wanted his master seen to, cared for; he could have bled to death, happily waiting. Vlad had stood over him, holding him by the scruff with his good hand, rubbing soothing circles with his fingertips until the Familiar pressed his forehead into Vlad's stomach and subsided with quiet, protesting chuffs.

Now it was Vlad's turn, and the bandaged Cicero watched Eira's hands, unblinking, his shoulder pressed to Vlad's.

Malik stood in the center of the room, admirably calm for a man who was, clearly, dumbfounded.

Vlad looked at him, finally; he needed a distraction, if nothing else. "You still haven't said anything."

"I'm thinking, your grace."

"In my experience," Eira said as she worked, "that doesn't do much good with men. They still do whatever stupid thing they set out to do in the first place."

Malik's gaze went to her, eyes brimming with questions.

"You've been thinking the whole time," Vlad said. "Mostly, you've been thinking my mother must be my mistress, because she doesn't look old enough to have a son my age. And also because the princess, my father's wife, is dead."

Malik looked back at Vlad, the shadows on his cheeks seeming darker – a blush. "I – forgive me, but yes, your grace. I've been thinking exactly that."

Eira sighed as she stepped back and set the cloth down, reaching for the herbs and grease and mortar and pestle Helga offered her. "Honestly, Vlad, don't toy with the man."

"Is that an order?"

"It's a suggestion, from someone much older than you." She began to grind a handful of herbs in the mortar. "Curiosity," she said to Malik, "is only natural – and so are we."

Malik took a shallow breath. "Vampires? There...there are stories..."

"That our kind sleep in coffins and burn in the sunlight," Vlad said. "That we turn to smoke, and fly, and abduct young women."

"That you drink blood."

"We *do* do that," Eira said. "But only to survive, and mostly from our wolves."

"Mostly," Vlad emphasized with a grin, and Malik's throat worked as he swallowed. He sobered. "We can go about in the daylight, as you can plainly see. And we can eat garlic, and go into churches – I was raised Eastern Orthodox, and I pray to the Christian God. I can neither turn to smoke, nor to a bat. But we are strong, and we are immortal." He hitched up straighter in his chair, feeling defiant. "My father was not only Vlad Dracul of Wallachia, but also Remus, son of Mars, co-founder of Rome."

Malik's gaze went wide. His mouth worked, but he could not speak.

"Your sultan?" Vlad continued. "Mehmet? He's a vampire as well. Not bred, as I was, born of two vampire parents, but turned. Turned by my uncle, Romulus, who is still very much alive and, apparently, sending mages and wolves to attack me.

"The woman? With her fire? That was a mage. Learn the word – learn to fear it. They're far more dangerous than any other immortal."

"I-immortal."

"Immortal," Vlad repeated. "Wolves, mages, vampires. That's what we are. We can be killed – but not easily. And if not." He shrugged. "So now you know."

Malik's mouth fell open, a rare show of discomposure, and he took a series of slow, deep breaths. Then he closed his lips, nodded to himself. "What you said in the city square today." He sent Vlad a pointed, questioning look.

This was the big question. The one that could have his own men turning on him.

Vlad took a deep breath, and heard the other immortals in the room do the same. His mother hesitated, poultice ready, but not wanting to intrude.

What was this truth after the mind-bending reveal of what they really were?

372

He said, "I'm here with the sultan's blessing. I know this.

"But the Ottomans have been my captors. My tormentors. The entire reason why my father fell into conflict with the neighboring princes. And they–" His voice caught, emotion rising, and he swallowed it down. "*Mehmet.* Has disgraced my brother in every way imaginable. He's *hurt* him. I know you belong to the sultan, but make no mistake: when I'm able to, when I have the means, I will forsake my alliance with him in a heartbeat. And if I can, I will wash this land clean of his influence."

He lifted his chin. "What do you think of that, captain?"

Silence.

Vlad stared at the janissary. He didn't have his father's power for persuasion, nor Val's sweet, pretty looks. He could only hope that honesty was a kind of weapon in and of itself.

And if all else failed, he could kill Malik Bey and make it look like an accident.

Finally, Malik spoke, and the words were not what Vlad had expected. "I do not remember my family," he said. "I was taken from my mother's breast, and nursed by a slave woman. I don't remember my mother's smile. My father's laugh. I don't know if I had any brothers or sisters. I don't know which god my family worshipped; what their home looked like; what they ate, and how they fit into their community. I was handed a spear when I was old enough to hold it, and told how to pray, and who to serve, and how to fit into the place I'd been given. I don't remember my name – my real name, that my mother gave me the day of my birth; I hope she kissed my forehead. I hope she loved me.

"I was raised a janissary, Prince Dracula," he said. "And I am a slave. I would like, very much, to serve a man who might change that."

Slowly, Vlad sat up straighter in his chair.

"A man who doesn't want glory," he continued. "Who doesn't want to take over the world just because he can. Anyone can make slaves of the people he conquers; it is another thing entirely to serve a peasant people and to be loved for offering them freedom.

"There were rumors amongst us in Edirne: that the heir – and now sultan – wasn't quite human. We spoke of his appetites, though we dared not make accusations. And I thought, 'Who could stop such a creature? Who could halt his ceaseless, violent progress?' It would take another such creature. One who is also a man of worth.

"I don't know what you are – not completely. But I will fight for you. Whatever happens, whatever your orders from the sultan, you shall have me as an ally." And he bowed deeply, his fist to his chest.

Eira stood with her tools held in limp hands, eyes wide. She looked at Vlad, brows raised.

All three wolves looked likewise stunned.

Vlad eased to his feet, pushing up with his uninjured hand, aware of a dozen aches and pains he hadn't known before he'd sat. "I will know if you're lying," he said.

Malik tipped his head back, his throat exposed, his gaze clear. "Then it's a good thing I am not."

Vlad tested the air. The man smelled nervous – but a normal amount, considering what he'd just been told. Good old-fashioned fear for one's safety, and not the acrid stink of deception and guilt.

Vlad found that he believed him.

He extended a hand. "I'll hold you to what you've said tonight."

Malik clasped his hand with his own. "Yes, your grace."

~*~

"You should drink."

Vlad looked down at his bandaged hand, curling his fingers. A tiny movement that brought great pain. Eira had wanted to wrap the whole thing up, like a club, but he'd told her to leave his fingers free so he could use them – even though doing so left him breathless. The pain made it difficult to sleep. He sat by the hearth in his bedchamber, examining his ruined flesh by the firelight, replaying the night's events in his mind. Beyond the window, dawn crept across the horizon on slow, silver feet.

"I will do no such thing," he said. Exhaustion took the bite out of the words.

Cicero snorted and dropped a heavy fur over his shoulders.

With his good hand, Vlad reached to pull it tighter, pressed his face into it and inhaled. An old, old wolf fur, musty with age; he imagined he could still smell his brother on it.

Cicero limped over to the other chair and eased down into it with a wince.

"Look at you – you can barely walk," Vlad said. "I should be the one taking care of you."

Cicero settled in, his smile small, tired, but true. "That isn't the way this arrangement works."

"It should be," Vlad insisted. "Familiar's aren't slaves. They shouldn't have to serve if they're hurt or sick."

Cicero tipped his head, expression soft, fond…sad. "Did your mother teach you that?"

"You know she did. Don't be coy. And she's right."

Cicero held up a hand. "Not coy, just…you were away from home for a long time." Among enemies. Away from Eira's life lessons, and her relentless, ironic gentleness.

"That's irrelevant," Vlad said. "I am the same person I was always going to be."

"Only a little angrier, I should think," his Familiar said, gently.

Vlad slumped back in his chair, fur pulled tight around his shoulders. "You're very old and wise. I'm in no mood for it today."

Cicero chuckled, and then sobered. "If that mage truly was sent by your uncle–"

"Then we have more than Vladislav to contend with." A fresh wave of exhaustion crashed over him. He fought it, blinking, curling his fingers so the pain would keep him alert. "I think," he said, "that things will get much worse before they get better."

"Unfortunately, that's usually the case."

~*~

Hunyadi's son Matthias married the Serbian princess. The Hungarian was free.

375

As the weather grew colder, Vlad's small force at Tîrgoviște began preparing in earnest. He drilled his troops, and his troops in turn began training the boys who willingly joined his tiny army. Some were strong – blacksmith apprentices and farm boys with wide shoulders and thick arms. But most were too young, or too sickly, or so old they weren't boys at all, but ragtag fathers and husbands in need of a job. All of them had spirit – but spirit wouldn't hold a palace.

They began stockpiling: hay and grain for the horses, carted up from the city in wagons pulled by oxen. Craftsmen made arrows, barrels of them. And there were barrels of wine, and ale, and casks of cured meats and pickled vegetables and fruits.

"Will the walls hold?" Malik asked one day, as Vlad stood atop them, bitter wind tugging at his clothes and hair.

"Unless they have sappers or siege towers, yes."

But his heart thudded too hard in his chest, and anxiety crawled across his skin like insects.

It wasn't enough. Vladislav was coming, and he was only seventeen, and he had too few troops, and no allies in the region, and–

A hand landed on his shoulder, light, unobtrusive. Malik's face, when Vlad turned to look at it, was unusually kind. "What?"

"I just wanted to say, your grace, speaking as someone with – forgive me – a fair amount of war experience more than you – that there is no shame in standing down, if that's what it comes to."

Mother had told him the same thing. Doubtless Father would agree, given his record of surrender and appeasement. Logically, he knew that there was honor in retreating, in surrendering, especially when it was done to prevent one's people from being slaughtered.

But his jaw tightened, and his pulse elevated another notch. "This seat is my birthright. Those are my people down there." He motioned to the city, the glazing of shiny frost on the rooftops. "I can't..." He trailed off. The weight of it crushed him.

Malik squeezed once, comforting, and let go. "Just an observation, your grace. We are with you."

376

Three days before Christmas, the scout arrived. A wild-eyed boy atop a winded, lathered horse. "An army, your grace!" he shouted, hysterical, as he slipped to the ground and nearly fell. "Thousands!"

Vlad went to the top of the wall, but of course he couldn't see them yet. They were still miles away.

Eira joined him, dressed for battle – or for travel.

The awful tug in his guts told him he'd already made his choice.

"Mama," he said, helpless, turning to her, and she touched his face. Cupped his cheek in one small, strong hand.

"Oh, baby. I know," she murmured. "It's alright."

"I should fight. I *promised* to."

"Darling." She smoothed his hair. "They are too many. We can't win."

"Are you telling me to flee?" Shame made his stomach hurt.

"I'm telling you to *live*. This isn't the time for your fight. Be patient – you have forever."

But it *was* fleeing. And it shamed him, badly.

He took his troops, and what was left of his family, and he bid a momentary adieu to his childhood home.

He paused, at the crest of the last hill, and looked back, though he knew he shouldn't. There was the city, and above it, perched pale and regal on the hill, the palace that he hadn't been able to hold.

His heart clenched.

I'll come back, he promised, and hoped it was a vow that he could keep.

27

TUCKED TAIL

"And so he returns," Murat said from his favored chair, his audience chamber warmed with coal braziers, lit by dozens upon dozens of candles. "Not as a conquering hero, but with drooping ears and a tucked tail. You failed."

An accusation would have been easier to swallow – he could have argued his case against it. But a simple statement of fact, such as this, settled across the back of his neck, heavy as a yoke. He clenched his hands together behind his back, nails digging into his palms. "I had but a small number of men. Vladislav's numbers were superior."

"Yes, and yet you didn't stay and test them against your own. Knowing you, and your penchant for…futile violence. I expected rashness, rather than retreat."

"Sorry to have disappointed you."

Murat waved. He looked bored. "I overestimated you, it would seem. You are, after all, just a boy, and clearly not ready for leadership."

Vlad opened his mouth and drew in a deep, fast breath; he felt his fangs against his lip. The former sultan's attendants lifted their brows in some alarm.

He checked himself. Swallowed, forced his shoulders to relax. "If I had more men–"

"No." Murat snapped his fingers and a pair of slaves stepped forward behind Vlad. "You may stay." The *for now* was silent, but very much felt. "I will figure out what to do with the new prince of Wallachia. Until then, what remains of your belongings and retinue have been stowed away in guest quarters. You may follow the slaves."

He bowed and did so. Furious. Shamed.

In the end, there hadn't been much choice in returning to the Ottoman capital. Without any allies in the immediate area, fleeing from Vladislav's forces, with all of his own forces belonging to Murat…they'd turned up on the palace doorstep only hours ago.

Vlad had never known such self-loathing.

The slaves both carried lanterns, and they led him out a side door and onto the grounds, all the usual beauty of the gardens muted and pruned back for winter.

A shadow peeled away from the trunk of a pear tree and fell into step beside Vlad, so quiet the slaves didn't notice. Cicero.

Vlad wanted to scold him – he'd left the wolf with strict instructions to stay with their possessions and rooms, though he should have known his Familiar would want to keep close watch on him.

Soft enough just for Vlad to hear, he said, "Was your brother there?"

"No." And he hadn't expected him to be. "Neither was his master."

But Val's scent was here. Faint traces in the corridors, on the shrubs they walked past, here.

"They'll want to keep us apart, I'm sure," Vlad said. "And for his own safety, I can't be seen seeking him out."

"But your mother…"

Vlad sighed. "That will be a problem."

~*~

"What's happening?" Val asked, and Arslan stilled behind him.

When Val tried to turn his head, the slave corrected him with a gentle touch of fingertips at his temple, and resumed brushing out Val's hair. It had grown long; sleek and flaxen, it held waves when the weather was damp, but could be smoothed into submission with a boar-bristle brush and a small dollop of oil. This was part of their now-normal morning routine, his and Arslan's. After a great amount of obedience, and true effort in bed, Val had been able to request the slave as his own.

Something about that day after the failed duel, waking to find himself in chains, had hardened Val's resolve. He no longer cried; no longer pressed tears into his pillow and choked back pained cries. But he wasn't afraid of the sultan in the same way, either. He requested things; he negotiated. *"You're growing bold,"* Mehmet had said with clear disapproval, but then Val had taken his cock into his throat, down to the root, and Mehmet hadn't punished that boldness.

So two months before, Val had risen from bed, shaken his gold hair back over his shoulder, and said, *"I wish to have a slave of my own."*

Mehmet had reached for the cup on his night table and laughed.

"I'm quite serious." He still wore the cuffs, and a new collar, less noticeable, had been designed for him: delicate silver, with a sapphire set in its center, dampening his psychic abilities. *"Concubines have servants. Am I not a concubine?"*

"You do make a very good case."

He'd picked Arslan, and doubtless the boy's status as a eunuch was the only reason Mehmet had allowed it. His was the only company Val enjoyed; treasured, even, in this palace full of men who would rather pretend he was a bit of ornamentation in the corner than acknowledge their young sultan's blasphemous proclivities. No one but Arslan spoke to him (Mehmet did, but, well...that was rarely a conversation). He'd enjoyed visiting the harem when he was younger, but he'd grown tall, willowy – starting to look like a proper little man now, and he was uncut; feminine company had been denied him.

"Arslan," he said now, watching the boy's face in the mirror. "What is happening in the palace? I can feel the energy; it's a hum, like a beehive in spring."

A notch formed between Arslan's black brows, and he studiously continued brushing. "I don't know. I'm only a slave, your grace."

"Only a slave," Val chided gently. "The slaves are the source of all the best gossip. Come. What do you know?"

Arslan pressed his lips together until they paled at the edges, holding his breath. Finally he let it out in a rush, with a defeated little groan. "I'm not supposed to tell you. The sultan *forbade* it." But his loyalty did not lie with the sultan. "But your brother is returned."

"*What?*" Val leaped up from the low bench he was seated upon, whirling to face his slave. "Vlad's here? When? Last night? Why? He was—"

"Please," Arslan said, ducking his head, clutching the hairbrush to his chest. Anxiety coursed through him, made him shake. "Please, your grace—"

"Hush." Val moved around the bench and knelt down before him, took his small, smooth hands into his own, setting the brush aside. "I won't betray you, not to anyone, I promise. You know this."

Arslan looked up through his lashes, dark eyes slick with tears.

"I need to know," Val said. "Why is my brother back here again?"

"It's — it's only rumors, but, some of the other boys were saying, they overheard last night, that he — that he couldn't hold Wallachia. He had to flee."

"Flee?" Val felt his brows scale his forehead. "Vlad? *Flee?*" Nothing had ever sounded so preposterous.

He gripped Arslan's shoulders. "What of the others? Were there survivors from the palace there? Our family?"

"I don't know, your grace. I don't know anything else, only that he's here, and he brought a retinue."

"A retinue? Maybe…" His pulse fluttered, fast and too-light, making him dizzy.

"Your grace, I don't know."

"I know, I know, it's alright." He rubbed the boy's arms soothingly a moment and then stood. The room swayed as if he'd been drinking. "I have to go see him." His belly clenched and nausea rolled within him, but he had to. He took a deep breath and imagined he could smell his brother in the palace, rooms and rooms away.

"But, your grace, you have archery practice."

"You're right. Damn it." He put his hands on his hips and breathed through his mouth. He really thought he might pass out. "Alright then, braid my hair, let's hurry." He dropped back onto the bench and presented his back, and Arslan's nimble fingers went right to work.

He braided Val's long hair into a simple plait that hung straight down his back, and then laid out his clothes: finely-crafted, but muted kaftan and şalvar, all of it in shades of blue, boots, belt, leather bracers, gloves. He was starting to have calluses on his hands again, signs of training. The fancy sword had been taken away, but a practice blade awaited him in the training yard, along with a bow, a quiver bristling with arrows, and an array of targets. An arms master that gave him private lessons in proper form and battle tactics.

A proper prince, Val had said, when he and Mehmet had bargained, and so far, the sultan had upheld his end of the agreement.

As had Val. His thighs still felt weak from this morning's activities.

When he was ready, he paused, and looked to the mirror, trying to see himself through a stranger's eyes – no, through a brother's. A brother who knew his shame, and who hated him for it.

He'd grown taller; his legs longer, his face a little narrower; bone structure sharp like the facets of a cut gemstone. He looked like his mother. He looked, despite the plain colors of his clothes, like a kept thing, with soft skin, and long lashes, and a collar that looked more like jewelry than a restraint.

He sighed, and went out, Arslan trailing dutifully along behind him.

The whole long walk to the practice yard, Val tested the air, straining to catch a whiff. He thought he did, once, but it was a cold day, and the wind was blowing, and the smell was swept away from him.

His training yard was a private one, used by Mehmet himself. Once he became sultan, he refused to spar with the hostages at court, preferring instead to work with private archers and sword-masters, pitting himself against trusted janissary opponents when he needed to work with another.

The archery master waited for Val, seated on a bench, restringing a bow. He glanced up without much interest – but Val detected the man's usual flare of tension. His shoulders rose and locked up; his fingers fumbled over their familiar task. No one on the grounds was frightened of Val – but they were frightened of what might happen to them if they mishandled him.

The first day, the man had said, *"You're late."* And he had been; Mehmet had been feeling…amorous that morning.

Val had kicked his chin up, looked the man in the face, and said, *"I am not. Which one of us is the prince anyway?"*

That hadn't been a kind thing to say. Kindness grew more and more difficult.

Today, the man said nothing, just stood and passed Val the freshly-strung bow. "Whenever you're ready, your grace."

"Thank you. I'm ready now."

The lesson began.

He'd improved immensely in the last few weeks. Just three or four years ago, he'd finally gained the ability to properly draw and fire; his arrows even made it all the way to the targets. But the shots were always wide; a good many landed in the dirt beside the target. Anger, hatred, and resolve had steadied his hand in a way that love and careful instruction never had. He felt determined now; this was a way to reclaim his status as a prince, his masculinity. Becoming a warrior was the only way to ensure that, one day, when the time eventually came, he would possess the means to escape…and keep escaping.

When the target was bristling with arrows, his instructor said, grudgingly, "Well done."

"Thank you." Val lowered the bow, arms shaking from the effort of drawing it again and again.

The man got a speculative look, eyes cutting at him sideways. "I've noticed." Oh no. "That you always shoot better when the sultan isn't here."

Val swallowed. That was true, and it was intentional. He didn't want Mehmet knowing how skilled he'd become.

"He asks for reports after every lesson, you know."

Damn.

Val nodded and handed the bow back. "Yes, well–"

A scent reached him; it moved through his senses with the force of a lightning strike. He turned in a circle, searching wildly, heart hammering.

There. In an upper window overlooking this courtyard, bright hair covered by a scarf, but her face unmistakable.

His mother.

"Your grace—" the instructor began, but Val was already sprinting away.

He knew the palace now, better than he remembered the palace of home, and he knew which door to go through, startling a pair of guards who knew better than to reprimand him. Up a set of cut stone stairs that spiraled around twice, and into a hallway set with wide, arched windows that let in white winter sunlight.

Eira waited there, hands clasped together in front of her, shaking, tears bright on her cheeks. She opened her arms and he barreled into them.

She wrapped him up tight, too tight to let him breathe properly, one hand on his back and one cupping his head. "Oh," she murmured, voice full of cracks. "Oh, my precious boy. My Valerian. Darling."

"Mama." He pressed his face into her neck, sniffling, tears clouding his own eyes, seeking out her scent and warmth. "Mama, is it really you? You're really here?"

"I'm here. I'm here, I'm here, I'm here."

Her scent – or maybe the sprint up all those stairs – turned him dizzy and languid, the muscles in his legs weak. He swayed, and she swayed with him, turned it into a back-and-forth shift, like when he was small enough for her to hold, and she'd rock him in her lap after a nightmare.

"*How* are you here?" he asked. "Father..."

She sighed. "It's a very long story."

"Yes," said a too-loud male voice behind her, "and she hasn't even told you the best part yet."

When Val pulled back, Mama was smiling. He peeked over her shoulder and there was–

"Fen!"

The big Viking wolf laughed. "My little prince, all grown up!"

Val disentangled from his mother so he could throw himself at her Familiar, and Fenrir caught him with his same old effortless strength, swinging him up and around, so he felt like he was flying.

~*~

Val found them a secluded bench tucked away in a hedge-lined corner of the garden, beneath a trellis loaded with winter grapes. Eira sat near to him, hip-to-hip, one of his hands held between both of hers, fingertips tracing the soft skin on his knuckles.

She didn't bring up the obvious: the fact that he must smell like another man's pleasure.

Fen stood guard, arms folded, his back to them, but Val knew he was listening intently. The idea of Fen hearing any of his shame, big, hulking, hyper-masculine man that he was, put a knot in his belly. So, when Eira looked up at him, eyes full of questions, he spoke first.

"Mama, tell me what happened."

Somehow, it was worse than he'd expected.

Until the part of the story when Vlad showed up. Excitement fluttered in his chest like a bird as he listened to her describe Vlad's assault on the palace guards, how he'd cut down Vladislav's men. How he'd ridden into the city to the cheers of the people of Tîrgovişte.

But as was always the case, good things couldn't last.

"We were too few," she lamented. "Our enemies too powerful." She shook her head. "And he is still just a boy, after all."

"Like me."

She squeezed his hand, and he lifted his head to see her small, sad smile. "No. Not like you."

"But–"

"Vlad is exceedingly intelligent. A natural born leader. But he doesn't know how to bend – and in that way, he is still very much a boy. You, though, know how to give ground."

"To *bend*," he said, self-mocking. "Yes, I'm very flexible."

She reached with one hand to touch his face, gentle fingertips along his cheek. "Oh, darling. I'm so–"

"Please don't say you're sorry. It isn't your fault. There's nothing you could have done." He tried to smile; it wobbled.

385

Her touched firmed, palm cupped around his jaw. "I'm your mother, which means I can apologize for whatever I want to whenever I want to. And…gods, I can't – it breaks my heart, Val."

"I'm sorry." He tried to turn away.

"Don't *you* apologize. It isn't your fault either," she said fiercely. "The world should be a better place."

"But it isn't."

"Parts of it are." She smoothed a wisp of hair behind his ear. "We're going to take you with us." This she said like a declaration, firmly.

He turned back to her. "What?"

"We can't stay. We're not welcome here, not really. Now that Vlad has failed to hold Wallachia, and given the way he and the sultan hate one another, it simply isn't possible. Not that we'd want to anyway," she tacked on, expression souring. "We can't stay in this place. And neither can you."

How long had he dreamed of leaving? Dream-walking was made nearly impossible by the silver on his wrists and throat, but he still dreamed regularly, as mortals did. Dreams in which he managed to scale the smooth palace walls and drop down, undetected, into the fragrant pine forests around it. Dreams in which he stole a horse from the stables, and rode past guards too shocked to bar the gates. Dreams in which Father, and Mircea, very much alive, laid siege to Edirne, eyes blazing, swords flashing, rescuing him in a feat of valor not seen since the old days.

But that was all fantasy.

"Mama, I *can't* leave."

A spark flared in her eyes, wild, beyond reason. A glimmer of the true fear and desperation she kept so well hidden. "Val, you have to. I don't know what he's told you, or promised you." She clasped his shoulders, fingertips digging in hard. "But it's all lies. He's manipulating you, he–"

"Mama," he said again, gentler this time. "I know. I'm not a little boy anymore. I know exactly what's happening, and why it's wrong."

"Then–"

"I'm leverage."

She blinked at him.

He sighed. "I'm the way he keeps Vlad in check. Mehmet is…" Volatile. Vain. Spoiled. "Not stupid. He talks as if Vlad is beneath his notice, but he *does* fear him. He knows that Vlad is stronger than him in every way that counts. He knows that Vlad is smart, and angry, and that he can best him, man-to-man. Vlad may be here on his doorstep, begging asylum, but he knows that Vlad will someday be a threat. He can't kill him, because they might need him. All that's left is to manipulate him, and he needs me for that. Even if you stole me away in the middle of the night, Mehmet would send men to give chase. He has endless, endless waves of men to throw at the things that he wants."

She blinked again, this time in an effort to push back fresh tears. Her smile trembled. "When did you get so clever?"

"Mama—"

"I know, I know. You've always been clever. You're just growing up." She slipped her arm around his shoulders and pulled him in close, urged his head down onto her shoulder, where she was warm, and smelled of home. "I'm so sorry," she murmured. "Gods, I…Valerian. *Baby.* I'm so sorry."

"I know. But it's alright. If I'm to live forever, then I supposed I'll have to endure some unpleasantness."

She breathed a hollow chuckle. "That's one way of putting it."

A growl split the peace of their garden nook, low and threatening.

Val straightened, and Eira's hand tightened on his shoulder.

A familiar, richly-dressed figure stood just beyond the half-drawn curtain of winter ivy. Hands linked behind his back, posture deceptively casual; his head was cocked at an angle Val knew well by this point – a dangerous one.

A fresh kind of terror stirred in Val's belly, one akin to the blood-chilling terror of that first night of Mehmet's…attentions. After the feast, when he'd stabbed the sultan, and fled into the garden. Fear of the unknown. He'd grown used to Mehmet's tempers, his slaps, his passions, his requests. He'd studied the man as he studied languages and arithmetic and politics; learned every gesture and slow blink, as he would with a difficult horse.

But Fenrir was massive, and angry, and growling. And Mother was…she was leverage *against Val*.

He swallowed the lump forming in his throat. "Fen," he said, levering as much authority into his voice as he could muster. "Stand down."

The growl cut off; Fenrir stilled, poised on his toes. He was huge, yes, but he could be quick when he needed to be. Val felt that faint ripple of energy through the air, a subtle pulse, the kind that usually preceded a wolf shifting to his four-legged form.

"Fenrir!"

Mehmet laughed. "Oh, no. By all means – let's see what he intends to do to me, hm?"

Eira's hand tightened as she stood, the movement elegant, soundless; her fingertips biting through silk into Val's skin. He had the sense she was trying to hold him in place, keep him at her side.

"Fenrir," she said, quiet, authoritative. An inflection rarely heard from her, an unmistakable order as a master. "Come."

Slowly, with great reluctance, Fenrir backed away from the sultan. Joined the two of them at the bench; sat on it, even, head bowed, ashamed, and leashed.

Val realized he was breathing rapidly through his mouth and pressed his lips together, forced his lungs to slow.

Mehmet took three steps forward, so he blocked the entrance to the alcove, booted feet splayed apart on the crushed-rock path. A sultan, but he stood like an indolent heir, still.

"Your instructor said you fled from your lesson," he said. "I thought I might find you consorting with our guests."

Val started to respond, but Eira dug her nails into the join of his neck and shoulder.

"Not consorting," she said coolly. "Visiting with his mother."

Mehmet's brows lifted. "Mother? Pardon me, but…" His gave moved down her figure, bold and assessing, "you hardly look old enough to have sons. Tell me." He prowled a few steps deeper, so he was only two arm lengths' away from them. "Do the people of Wallachia know that you're the boys' mother? And not Vlad Dracul's late wife?"

She snorted. "You think to intimidate me with old truths? Do your own people know that you yourself are immortal?"

Something passed across Mehmet's face, a brief flash of an emotion that he quickly tamped down.

"You have no Familiars," Eira continued. "No immortal allies. You were turned and not born – how sure are you that, should the truth slip out, your people will support you when they know that you drink blood to stay alive?"

Again, the sultan didn't answer.

"Will they accept you for what you are? Or will they call you a demon? There's a distinct history of mobs overtaking monarchs in this world. If they turn against you, will they cut you down? They *can* kill you, you know, as my mate was killed."

A faint, insincere smile finally touched his mouth. "Or perhaps I'll just kill you now."

Her hand tightened another fraction, silencing Val before he could speak. She smiled, and it was wide, and it showed her fangs, and it wasn't only sincere, but wicked. "I know who made you. I know his strengths – and his weaknesses. And I am far, far older than you, little boy. I could snap you in half."

"Then it seems we're at an impasse."

"So it would seem."

The moment stretched out, drawn tight as a bowstring wound one too many times. Ready to snap.

Slowly, Val reached up and removed his mother's hand from his shoulder. He stepped in front of her, and of Fen, putting himself between his family, and the man who owned him.

"If I come with you now, will you leave her alone?" he asked, evenly. He'd learned to control his voice, to stuff all of his emotions down deep to a place where they couldn't cut him so. "She has nothing you want. She doesn't matter to you."

"*Val,*" Eira said, soft, but deeply pained.

His stomach clenched, and his pulse fluttered, and his hands curled into fists. But he did not turn back to her. He couldn't – not if he meant to keep her alive.

"Please, your grace," he said, tipping his head back a fraction, showing his throat – his obedience. "*Please.*"

Fenrir whimpered.

Mehmet smiled. "Well. Since you asked so nicely." He held out his hand.

Val slid his own into it, and went with him, the eyes of his people like hot brands pressed to his back.

This was the way it had to be.

~*~

Vlad and his entourage occupied a series of rooms much finer than any he'd enjoyed during his stay here as a hostage. Sumptuous furnishings, gilt-edged mirrors and thick rugs, coal braziers to keep out the chill of winter. Beds heaped with quilts and furs, and food brought on trays by timid slaves. He'd been offered his choice of female or male companionship, shaking young things with downcast eyes. He'd refused.

"We can't stay," he said to Cicero. He sat slumped over his room's desk, idly paging through a Latin text, an invisible noose tightening slowly, inexorably around his neck as the minutes ticked past. He didn't believe in premonitions as a general rule, but something was coming. He could feel it.

"I didn't figure we would," his wolf responded calmly.

Vlad twisted around in his chair and lifted his brows in question.

Cicero shrugged. He sat at the foot of the bed, sharpening his falx with a whetstone. The weapon gleamed as if new, though its shape suggested a primitive sort of wickedness. One of those little reminders of just how very old Cicero was.

Like the moments when the sun had caught Father's profile just so, when his hair was swept back from his face, and Vlad had seen the Palatine Hill around him, the modest wooden villages and stone walls that had been Rome at its birth; the Tiber, gleaming like a serpent, and a basket of babies washed up amid the reeds.

"You and the sultan are enemies, I'd say. This was never a long-term plan."

"No," Vlad agreed, propping an elbow on the back of the chair. "I supposed I'll have to flee again. I can be the Prince Who Ran Away. Retreating can be my legacy."

"Vlad," Cicero chided gently. "You're young yet. That won't be your legacy."

He snorted.

Rapid footfalls in the hallway preceded the door swinging open. Eira came in red-faced and furious, dashing at the tears on her cheeks with quick movements. Fenrir followed, outwardly somber.

"Mother," Vlad started, and then caught a sharp whiff of Val's scent as she paced across the floor, skirt swirling around her calves.

He stood. *"Mother.* You went to see him? We discussed this."

She rounded on him, eyes flashing. "He's my son, Vlad. He's just as much my son as you are, and he's–" She cut off with a choked sound and resumed pacing, wiping at her face again. "We can't leave him here. We *can't.*"

Vlad wouldn't allow himself to think of his brother. Of the things that he did, the way that he lived, in order to stay alive. He could not, or he'd take up his sword and go charging out of this room, ready to face Mehmet one final time.

He swallowed down every expression of sympathy, and kept his voice calm. Reasonable. "And what did Val say when you spoke to him?"

She took an aggressive step toward him, chin lifting. He thought she might strike him. "What?"

He wanted to shrink back, to give – she was his mother, who'd nursed, and raised, and loved him…

But this was bigger than family bonds now.

"I assume you told Val that you wanted to take him with us when we left. What did he say to that?"

She breathed harshly through her nose, face going slowly red. But then she turned away from him, and banded her arms across her middle. Shoulders slumping as if in pain.

The room was silent a long moment save the ragged sound of Eira's breathing. Then she took a final breath and said, "He said to leave him here. That he was leverage against us. He can't leave, and we shouldn't try to help him."

A surge of pride in his brother. Delicate to look at, but strong inside. "He's right, and you know he is."

She didn't answer.

A knock sounded at the door, and Cicero went to answer it, falx still in his hand.

To his credit, the slave boy on the other side didn't reel back in shock at sight of the weapon, though his gaze did touch upon it. He then looked to Vlad. "His majesty wishes to speak with you, your grace."

"Which one?"

~*~

Murat.

He didn't leave Vlad in suspense. "You cannot stay here," he said, offhand, accepting a jewel-studded cup from a tray-bearing slave. "I'm sure you know this."

He did, but he ground his back teeth anyway. "Your Majesty, if this is about Mehmet and me—"

The former sultan cut him off with a wave. "It is not." The slave still stood at his side, and Vlad noticed now that the tray also held a roll of parchment. Murat reached for this now, and unrolled it leisurely. He sipped his wine. Waited, intentionally, to set Vlad on edge.

Vlad could wait, too, and was careful to keep his expression neutral, his hands folded behind his back.

Finally, Murat set aside his cup and began to speak. "I have here in my hands a letter from Vladislav, the man who drove you out of Wallachia, and co-signed by the governor of Transylvania, the Hungarian John Hunyadi. It reads, quote, 'I wished to inform you as to the stability of my rule here in Wallachia, a rule which intends to work alongside you, Your Majesty, and your great empire in order to achieve peace throughout the Romanian lands. I should also like you to know of the treachery of your puppet Vlad Dracula, who, I have it straight from witnesses' mouths, gave a traitorous speech in the town square of Tîrgoviște, in which he promised to free the people from your tyranny. He promised to turn on you, fight you, and push you out of Wallachia altogether.

He is a violent, petulant boy, Vlad Dracula, and he wants only violence, and never peace. I'm afraid you have misplaced your trust in him, Sultan Murat.'"

He set aside the letter and leveled his gaze at Vlad, heavy, implacable. There would be no arguing his case, Vlad saw in his expression. The decision had already been made.

"Do you deny that you did such a thing?" Murat asked.

"No, Your Majesty. I said it."

"Do you have an explanation?"

Would it matter? No. The axe was already poised and ready to fall.

So with the same stubborn spirit that had earned him daily beatings as a schoolboy in this palace, Vlad thrust out his chin and said, "I said it because I meant it."

Murat stared at him a long, still moment. Not bothered, not angry, but watchful. Calculating. Finally, he nodded. "So I thought. Your stay here has come to an end, then. You will be escorted back to your rooms where you will gather your things and what people belong to you, and you will leave the city of Edirne tonight. Understood?"

"Understood." Vlad gave a short bow and turned to leave, though his heart was pounding.

"Vlad Dracula," Murat called, and Vlad paused, glanced back over his shoulder.

It would be the last time he ever laid eyes on the old sultan.

And to his surprise, emotion glittered in the man's eyes. Carefully checked – but he gave off the faintest hint of fear.

"I don't know what your uncle is planning," Murat said, quietly. "But the older I grow, the more and more I begin to think that it isn't something sanctioned by any god of any king. Take care of yourself, your grace."

Shock froze Vlad in place for a moment.

On his walk back to his rooms, he found that, though hatred was a living spirit inside him, he hated the old sultan a little less, and pitied him a little more.

No one was surprised when he relayed the news.

Silent, crystal tears slipped down Eira's cheeks, and she clenched her jaw tight against the crushing guilt and rage that having to leave Val behind brought. But she wiped her face and said, "I think I know somewhere that we can go. Someone who will help us."

Which was how Vlad Dracula was forced to leave his little brother behind a second time, and how he ended up completing his Romanian education and knighthood training in the principality of Moldavia, alongside the pretend cousin who would become his best mortal friend…who would become Stephen the Great.

<u>28</u>

THROAT-CUTTER

Winter of 1451-2
The March Home

Prince Radu Dracula of Wallachia currently carried his title because he was the son of a prince, and had been told that he would someday rule as one, when the appropriate time came to place him on the throne in his homeland, a dutiful ally to the Ottoman Empire.

This was his official title. To the slaves and guards and janissary captains, he was Prince Radu. They accepted small orders from him, so long as they did not conflict with orders given by their sultan, and they bowed and saluted him as was proper for his station. He was, officially, no longer a hostage, but an advisor and confidante of their sultan, Mehmet.

Everyone had to know that he was also the sultan's lover, though none made mention of it in his presence. Sometimes, his vampiric senses pricked, he could pick out bits of gossip. Mehmet was possessive, outwardly affectionate, and did not try to conceal their relationship. For his own part, Prince Radu had learned that he rather liked...messing with the men around him. If he could make them uncomfortable, petty though it was, it brought him a small, guilty sort of joy.

In his own mind, however, he was still Valerian. Val. His true name was his most closely guarded secret outside his immortality. He carried it close in his heart, letting it warm him on the coldest of nights, when the Greek wind whipped at the sides of the tent, and bent the flames in the braziers double.

He wasn't proud of any of the things that he'd done, but he was proud that he'd survived. That he'd learned to be a real prince, and a knight; learned how to manipulate, and succeed, even.

He was sixteen, and he figured that, if he could stay alive, he had the rest of forever to try and heal the scars on his soul; to carve himself out a life that was good, and gentle.

Until then, he was clever, and beautiful, and he would use those things to his advantage.

He still wore silver: a thin, solid band around his throat that rested along his collarbones. Too tight to pull off over his head, studded with three small sapphire chips so that it looked like a decoration, and not a dog collar to keep him obedient. It sapped a little of his preternatural strength, enough that he was more dependent on blood, and it was a tether he could not break should Mehmet see fit to lock him away for some infraction. For a time, when he was younger, the silver had dulled his psychic abilities as well. But he'd practiced. And practiced, and practiced, and he'd learned how to dream-walk while wearing it.

Which was why he sat now in the private study of Constantine Dragases Palaiologos, Emperor of the Romans, at the Palace of Blachernae.

The emperor himself, sworn in after his brother John's death in 1448, wore a few more sun lines around his eyes, and streaks of silver in his black curly hair, but his face was still kind. That of a friend.

"I appreciate your concern, Val. And your attempts to warn me. But I feel I made the right decision. And, honestly, this city has stood – and resisted most siege attempts – for seventeen-hundred years. I'm not too worried about young Mehmet accomplishing the impossible."

Val, cross-legged on a tabletop, tossed his long braid over his shoulder. Impatience bled through in his voice. "But he's building a palace – a fortress! A massive one, just on the other side of the Bosphorus. He's already clearing the forest and hauling lumber. Do you know what he's calling it? The Throat-Cutter."

Constantine shrugged. "I don't own the land on the other side of the Strait. He can build as many fortresses there as he likes."

"You're not taking this seriously."

"On the contrary. But, forgive me, I'm a bit older and more experienced than you. I don't think it's time to panic just yet."

Val bit back a frustrated growl.

"Besides," Constantine continued. "I'm up to my neck in this thrice-damned religious war."

Val took a breath and resettled – he wasn't going to convince the emperor of anything today. He found a smile. "Which side is winning at the moment?"

"Certainly not me. I've been declared a heretic by the Orthodox and Catholic leaders. That's what I get for trying to broker an accord between them – I'm a bloody heretic! Those fools. Our economy is in crisis, your sultan's building fortresses called Throat-Cutter across the Strait, but oh no, the Schism between one faction of Christianity and another is our greatest problem. God." He slumped back in his chair and massaged his forehead, smoothing the furrow between his brows. "I hate them all. What idiots."

"Civil wars can topple entire empires," Val observed.

"So I've told them. But rather than listen to reason – they both worship the same God, carry the same cross, share the same enemies beyond our walls – they would just as soon paint me a villain and bicker with one another endlessly until our entire religious system breaks down into chaos. Why is there no tolerance? Why can't people just let things go?" He threw up his arms in supplication.

Val shook his head.

Constantine aimed a forefinger at him. "Men are categorically allergic to peace," he said. "They ought to be content with happy wives, and healthy children, and enough coin to eat their fill, but they aren't. They never have been, and they never will be, and I will *never* understand it." He raked both hands through his hair, curls springing up in the wake of his fingers. He looked tired, his shoulders slumped beneath his burdens. He was a widower, and childless, and though he had close friends and advisors, Val knew him to be a lonely man. He could relate.

The emperor said, "I don't even have a preference myself. If I thought it would help, I would gladly convert and order the whole city to observe the Catholic faith. But this is an Orthodox city. I might very well be dragged from this palace and stoned to death in the street." He chuckled hollowly. "You don't know of any peaceful religions, do you?"

"My mother still worships the old gods."

"The Roman ones? Jupiter? And Mars?"

"Er, no. The Norse ones."

"Norse? Now there's an idea. We'll erect a great statue of — what's the most important one?"

"Odin."

"A great statue of Odin right in front of St. Sophia. Invite the pope to witness it." He grinned. "The old codger would have an apoplexy on the spot." When he laughed, Val joined him.

Then he sobered. "I'm sorry, son. I don't mean to go on about my problems when…" He trailed off.

"You're allowed to complain, and I like to listen, when I can. I'm your friend just as you are mine. It goes both ways."

The emperor smiled. "Yes, I suppose it does. So I will now stop complaining, and allow you to do so."

Val shook his head. He'd already done what he'd come here to do — warn of the new fortress, of Mehmet's vigorous response to Constantine's last letter claiming that Byzantium and the Roman people would no longer pay for Orhan the pretender to live in luxury within the city walls. His brother had threatened the same thing, once. But that was when Murat had been emperor; his son took such threats as calls to arms.

Instead of rehashing any of that, Val said, "I don't think my brother believes in peace."

Constantine frowned. "He was run out of Wallachia, wasn't he?"

"And then Edirne." Val had dream-walked to visit his mother in Moldavia, where Vlad was said to be thriving under Romanian tutelage, enjoying the friendship of Prince Stephen, a year younger and of a boisterous, fun-loving disposition. "But he's always been serious, even as a very young boy. I think my earliest memory is of him frowning." A fleeting smile, a flash of fond memory. "But after our capture, he became angry. Furious. He wants revenge." Another smile, this one bitter. "He certainly wouldn't be trying to find a peace between the Catholics and Orthodox worshippers."

"He's young yet." Consoling. "And revenge is a young man's game. He'll mellow over time."

"You're optimistic."

"I try to be."

A tug on Val's toe startled him upright. It was easy to forget, in friendly company like this, that he was here only in spirit, a vaporous projection. The tug came again, a pinch of slim fingers, insistent.

He sighed. "I'm sorry, Your Majesty, but I must leave you now."

"I'm sorry you have to. You're always thoughtful company, Val."

He smiled, grateful for the man's kindness and patience, his attention, when he'd never been obliged to give it.

"Until next time," Val said, waved, and returned to his body.

He opened his eyes to the cream canvas ceiling of Mehmet's campaign tent, head cushioned on a pile of furs.

Arslan's face popped into view above his, narrow, finely-drawn, wide-eyed and worried.

"Your grace," he hissed. The tug at Val's toe had come from him. He reached now to gently shake Val's shoulder. "He's coming!"

Val blinked a few times and sat up. "Thank you, Arslan." The room swayed around him, and he waved at the boy, who quickly scurried to the sideboard to grab a cup of wine mixed with blood.

Val shut his eyes a moment, and pressed a hand to the side of his head. He'd been gone longer this time; he was weaker, shaky, dizzy. The damned silver collar turned his magic into a physical weakness.

He heard the tent flap open; agitated, booted footsteps across the hard-packed ground. He cracked his eyes and saw Mehmet, fine clothes coated with a layer of dust from the road, face set in a scowl, striding toward the sideboard, where Arslan was already pouring a second cup of blood and wine for him.

Just as Val had grown tall, and willowy, and leanly muscled, the sultan had grown into a proper warrior: broad-shouldered, strong, imposing. His face had gone from pretty to handsome; he'd gained a greater degree of control over his expressions, so that he looked stern, and inscrutable, rather than angry all the time.

At least, in front of others. He let his guard down in his own private tent, around Val.

He drained his cup and reached to refill it himself, since Arslan was kneeling down on the pallet at Val's hip, offering him his own cup.

"Thank you, my dear," Val said with a tired smile. His hand shook, and he raised the drink to his mouth, fangs already long in anticipation.

"Don't use pet names with the boy," Mehmet said. He went to his desk and slumped down in the ornate folding chair in front of it; Mehmet the half-Greek had employed Greek furniture for this expedition. "You coddle him too much."

Val took a restorative sip of wine, and some of the shaking began to subside. "I've found that a little kindness and familiarity goes much farther than treating a person like property and barking orders at them."

"Hmph. It never worked for you."

"You're a wealth of comedy, Your Majesty."

Mehmet hooked a leg over the arm of the chair. "What are you still doing in bed anyway?"

Val had projected a polished image of himself into Constantine's study, kaftan buttoned up to his chin, hair braided, boots polished. In reality, he was naked, hair tangled over his shoulders, covers pooled around his waist. He glanced down and saw fading marks on his chest, the impressions of teeth.

"You tired me out this morning," he said, and sipped more wine. "Arslan, will you—"

But the boy was already in motion, fetching his robe and slippers from his trunk, a brush clenched in one hand.

"What's got you out of sorts?" Val asked, standing as his slave returned. He wobbled a little; incentive to drain his cup and let the blood do its work. It was warm and fresh, horse blood, but it didn't work as quickly or effectively as wolf blood would have.

Mehmet blew out a breath. "The janissaries want an increase in salary. Have *demanded* one. Can you believe such a thing?"

"I can, actually." He slid his arms through the sleeves Arslan offered to him, the silk cool and lovely against his bare skin. When he had the robe belted, he went to sit in the chair opposite the sultan, and Arslan set to work on his hair with a gentle, deft touch. "They're your crack troops. The rest of the army is just boys with sticks. The janissaries are the ones who keep you alive and win you battles. They deserve to be paid handsomely for that."

Not to mention, he didn't add, *they're essentially slaves*. He thought they deserved some recompense for the displacement. He himself had learned to feel nothing but enjoyment when it came to rich fabrics, and dazzling jewels, and hot baths in copper tubs.

"I hate it when you speak logically," Mehmet muttered into his cup. "I should have your mouth sewn shut."

Val sent him a sharp smile. "Ah. But then how would I suck your royal cock?"

"Stop talking."

"No. Someone has to offer you council, and you've frightened all your own people away."

"I've done no such thing."

"Darling, you impaled a man yesterday morning before breakfast."

A smile plucked at the corners of the sultan's mouth. "You might have a point there."

"I always have a point. You'd be lost without me."

Mehmet hummed an agreeing sound and sat upright. It was then that Val noticed there was a large set of building plans laid out on the desk between them, all of it labeled carefully in a precise hand.

Mehmet tapped the edge of the paper. "What do you think of the fortress?"

The blood and wine turned over in Val's belly. He fought to keep his expression one of vague interest as he sat forward and scanned the architect's drawings. "It's…"

"Beautiful," Mehmet said. "I know."

Val would have gone with *terrifying*.

"Incredible progress is already being made. It should be finished by spring."

"Spring?" Val nearly choked on the word. That sort of speed in building was unheard of.

"I'm sparing no expense. Not in materials, nor in manpower. This fortress will be the place from which I launch my assault."

Val felt dizzy again, and this time it had nothing to do with dream-walking. "You're serious, then. About laying siege to Constantinople."

His brows went up. "You thought I wasn't?"

"Well, no." He'd just hoped that one of the many viziers who had the sultan's ear would have pointed out the sheer folly of the notion by now. "It's only that I don't understand why you're so fixated on this."

"Fixated?" His tone, edged with offense, carried a warning. Val could be bold, could speak his mind most of the time...but only because Mehmet allowed it. "You're beautiful, but I know you're not stupid. You know that the only way to rule effectively is through shows of strength. Giving your people an outside enemy to conquer so they don't turn their malaise and dissatisfaction on their king. Taking Rum expands my empire, it rallies my people, and it hamstrings the Westerners who'd see me dead."

Val swallowed – with difficulty, because his throat had gone dry. A cup set down at his elbow; Arslan, sensing his need, bringing him more wine. The boy was a blessing.

"Constantinople is un-sackable," Val argued. "You know this. Those sea walls, the boom across the channel – no one's breached its perimeter since the Fourth Crusade. And those were Crusaders themselves, who could at least claim the element of surprise. That's *one sack* in the city's history, Mehmet; only one since *300 B.C.*"

"Then I'll go down in history, won't I?"

Val threw up his hands. "How many times have we had this same conversation?"

"We have this conversation only because I allow it. You're foolish to keep seeking it out." He aimed a finger at Val, voice hard now. "Leave it, Radu."

Val picked up his cup and drowned a sudden swell of rage with sweet red wine. In moments like this, he allowed himself a familiar fantasy: a blade in his hands, Mehmet's blood on the carpet. At times, he managed to convince himself that they were friends of a sort. Almost equals. That, maybe, as he grew older, and the sultan's touch began to kindle a physical desire beneath his skin, that he'd developed a softness for the man.

But then there were moments like now. When he knew an urge to violence so intense he thought it might choke him. Moments when he remembered that he was related to Vlad after all, and that he wanted to crack Mehmet's skull against the edge of a table like a fresh egg.

He drained his cup and dabbed at his lips with his fingers. Arslan resumed brushing his hair, long, sure strokes to bring out its shine. "When do we break camp?" he asked, to change the subject, and quiet the rage inside him.

"An hour. Will that give you time to beautify yourself?"

"Barely." Val turned his head to the side, glancing across the lavish tent. Mehmet loved it when he acted prissy. Easier to pretend he was a woman then, he supposed.

As expected, the sultan chuckled, and pushed to his feet. He moved around the desk, and Val tensed, hands balling into fists in his lap.

Mehmet cupped his chin and turned his head back and up, so they faced one another. Ran his thumb over Val's wine-stained lower lip, expression cycling from admiration, to lust...to something harder.

"Don't test me, Radu. That never ends well."

Gently, Val took the tip of his thumb between his teeth.

Mehmet grinned, and leaned down to kiss him, quickly, before he withdrew. "Wear the blue coat I got you," he said over his shoulder as he left the tent.

Val gave a little wave of his fingers to signal he'd heard.

Arslan began separating his hair into bunches for an elaborate braid.

Val sighed. "God. I *hate* blue."

~*~

Returning to Edirne didn't feel like a homecoming – his heart didn't fill with gladness, because this was the place where he lived, but not his home – but Val relaxed when he was within the familiar palace walls again. It would be nice to sleep in a real bed again, and not to march constantly, forever saddle-sore and covered in road dust.

It was morning, bitterly cold, steam rising off the thick crust of frost that coated the grass. Val wore his hair loose to cover his ears, a thick, dark brown fur made of bear pelt wrapped around his shoulders and neck. He felt well-rested and energized today; Mehmet had been paying visits to his wives since their return, taking them gifts, fulfilling his husbandly duties toward producing an heir. It had given Val time to himself, dinners eaten alone, long, uninterrupted baths; a bit of reading by candlelight before bed. Sleeping, blessed, all by his lonesome, stretching out his arms and legs to the far reaches of the mattress.

Today, he was to supervise a new batch of young janissaries, singling out the ones best suited for Mehmet's personal corps of guards. Mehmet would of course have the final say-so, but Val felt something like pride to have been given this responsibility.

He felt pride where he could.

"Gentlemen," he called as he paced along behind the tidy row of potential recruits. "Today you will demonstrate your proficiency with the bow, with the spear, and with the sword. You will–"

"A moment, your grace!" Grand Vizier Halil Pasha's wheedling voice called across the practice grounds, and Val bit back an unhappy sound.

He turned to meet the man's approach, already frowning, and froze.

Wolf.

He smelled a wolf.

The Grand Vizier walked toward him with his usual short strides, his gait impeded by the length, thickness, and weight of embroidery on his kaftan and overcoat. Behind him marched a line of able-bodied young janissary recruits.

Once, they'd belonged to the far reaches of the world. Val spotted black skin, and brown. The almond eyes of the Orient, and round blue eyes. Hair a finer gold than his own.

One of them was a wolf.

He took a deep breath, to be sure, and, yes, he was positive. There was no concealing the distinctive musk of a werewolf, even when he walked on two legs instead of four. He picked him out of the line: a clean-shaven boy with pale skin and dark hair, slighter of build than some of the others, but that would make no difference on the battlefield. Wolves were ungodly strong.

Halil Pasha finally drew to a halt in front of Val, puffing and red-faced from his walk through the cold. "These recruits are to be considered for the sultan's private guard," he said, motioning toward them with a limp hand. He pressed the fingers to the base of his throat afterward, over his visibly fluttering pulse. "Test them with the others."

Val's fangs elongated a fraction in his mouth. With Halil Pasha, the honorific "your grace" was used sparingly, only when absolutely necessary. And he gave orders as if Val were a slave boy.

"Of course," Val said, tone chilly. He smiled, and let the man see his fangs.

As hoped, Halil Pasha took a hasty step back, scowling. "They're green. Test them rigorously."

"Of course," Val repeated.

The Grand Vizier turned to the recruits. The wolf boy stood staring down at the toes of his boots, lashes flickering against his cheeks as he blinked. Tears? A reaction to the biting cold? He smelled of nervousness and stress.

"This is Prince Radu," Halil Pasha told the boys. "He is a knight, and an expert marksman." Ah, a rare compliment. "He is beloved of the sultan as if he were his brother." *Brother, yes*, Val thought. *That's a lovely word for it.* "You would do well to impress him today."

He departed with a warning glance thrown over his shoulder at Val – though what he was warning against Val had no idea. The man liked to sound in charge of things.

"Alright, you lot," Val said, clapping his hands together. "Fall in line with the others."

They moved to do so. And as they filed past, Val saw the wolf boy's nostrils flare. He'd caught the scent of vampire. He darted a quick glance up at Val as he passed, sideways and furtive. Amber eyes.

For the first time since he'd arrived in Edirne, there was a wolf inside the palace walls. Val didn't intend to let him slip away.

~*~

All of his recruits were green – but they were athletic, sharp, and eager to please. Archery would take some time to master, but many were already proficient with spear and blade. And they followed orders quickly and without backtalk.

Val was impressed.

And then there was the wolf.

The boy was by far the least capable with the weaponry. He tried gamely, and was clearly strong, but he lacked a natural born fighter's grace and ease.

Val finally called for a break when the sun was at its zenith and the day had warmed a fraction. The recruits had long since stripped off cloaks and kaftans, and their bare arms steamed in the afternoon light.

The wolf sat apart from the others, on one of the low benches against the palace wall, waiting his turn to seek the water pails and ladles currently being mobbed by the others.

Val took his own waterskin and went to sit beside the boy.

He startled violently, and nearly fell off the bench.

"Easy," Val said, chuckling, and offered the skin. "I only came to offer you a drink."

The boy regarded him a long, unblinking moment, body poised, tense, on the edge of the bench. Fear-sweat bloomed, immediate and pungent. With his eyes wide, it was easy to see that his pupils had narrowed to a shape less than human. Val bet that, if he were to touch the boy's neck, he would feel the prickle of hair emerging along his ruff.

He shook the waterskin. "Here. You must be thirsty."

Slowly, as cautious as a fawn, and not the wolf that he actually was, the boy took the skin with a soft "thank you." His accent was thick. He hesitated, skin poised at his lips, but when he finally drank, he did so desperately, eyes closing, throat working as he gulped all of the chilled water down. He splashed some onto his shirtfront, his skin, and didn't seem to care.

Finally, he lowered it with a gasp, and his eyes widened again. "Oh. I. I'm sorry." He wiped his mouth with the back of his hand and he looked sheepishly down at the now-empty skin. "I didn't mean to–"

"It's alright," Val assured. "There's no shortage of water here. The wells are deep. Would you like some more?"

"No. No, no, I'm sorry, your grace." He passed the skin back with shaking hands.

"What's your name?" Val asked.

The boy ducked his head, a frightened sort of deference. "Nestor, your grace. Or, um, rather, Iskander."

"Nestor-Iskander, then. And where are you from? Your accent is familiar."

Flatly, he said, "I am a janissary of His Majesty's–"

"No, dear. Where are you *from*?"

A whisper: "Russia, your grace."

"Ah! I thought that was it," Val said, in Russian. "I speak many languages, and that is one of them. Though I worry my accent isn't very good. What do you think?"

Nestor lifted his head, expression broken open by surprise. "You speak Russian?" he asked in that language, and the words came much easier in his native tongue. "But you are…"

"What? You thought me Turkish? With this hair?" He tossed it over one shoulder with a chuckle. "I'm Romanian, originally. I always wanted to travel to Russia someday. I've heard it's beautiful."

Nestor snorted. "Right now it's nothing but snow. Up to your neck in places." He touched his own in indication. He brightened. "Romania? I was trained in artillery with a unit in Moldavia before I came here. That's where I was…" And he dimmed. "Taken."

Val frowned. "How does a Russian end up in Moldavia?" Inwardly, his heart pounded. Last he'd heard, Vlad was in Moldavia.

"I was in the employ of a group of monks. Studying with them, training to join their order someday. We encountered a checkpoint on the road, and." He shrugged, and looked down at his dusty boots.

"So you are literate."

"Quite."

"Which languages can you read and write?"

"Russian, of course. Also Slavic, Romanian, French, and Turkish – though that isn't very strong yet."

An idea began to form in Val's mind.

But first…

He lowered his voice, so soft that even the most enterprising of mortal eavesdroppers wouldn't be able to hear them. "Nestor. Do you know what you are?"

Nestor stilled. Slowly, he lifted his head, and the fear was back, all the blood drained from his face. "Your grace?"

"It's alright," Val assured. "If you do, then surely you can tell what I am. Can't you?"

His gaze darted, out to the yard, across the resting soldiers, finally back to Val. He wet his lips. "I…"

"You're not frightened of me, are you?" The idea disappointed him. He'd missed the company of Familiars desperately. This boy wasn't Fenrir, huge and boisterous and unbeatable, nor Cicero, stern and protective. But there was a comfort in being near a wolf, an instinctual quieting.

Nestor swallowed with obvious difficulty. "No. No, your grace, I'm not frightened. It's only that – I've never met a…anyone like you."

"But you have heard of us, yes?"

He nodded. "My parents told me stories, when I was very young. They were both…the same as me."

"They were wolves?"

"Yes."

"So you were born instead of turned?" His voice lifted on the end, and he reined it in. But this was exciting! "That is a rare thing, Nestor."

"So they said." He fidgeted, looking uncomfortable. "The village where we lived…the people there…when they found out…"

"Oh," Val said, understanding, heart twinging with sympathy.

"They thought it witchcraft. A curse of some sort. My parents tried to explain to them, but they'd seen me shift, and they…" He drew a ragged breath, blinking hard. "My parents were killed. The monks took me in."

"Oh, my dear. I'm so sorry." He wanted to lay a comforting hand on the boy's shoulder, but wasn't sure it would be read as reassuring.

Nestor wiped quickly, ashamedly, at his eyes, and lifted his head, offered a smile. "And now I'm here."

"And now you're here," Val echoed. "I'm sorry for that too."

The other recruits, a few of them sitting or lying on the grass, stretching their muscles, suddenly all snapped to attention. They got to their feet and lined up, ramrod-straight and correct.

The sultan had arrived at the practice field.

"Wait here," Val instructed Nestor, and went to meet his lover.

Mehmet was flanked, as usual, by a pair of janissary guards. He'd left Halil Pasha behind, thankfully. He stood with his arms tucked behind his back, head tilted back, testing the air with his nose.

"What is that fascinating smell?" he asked. "I smell a lot of sweaty humans, and…something else." He cocked a brow, inviting an explanation.

Val had to phrase this very carefully. "Will you walk with me a moment?" he asked, smoothing his face into something pleasant and inviting.

Mehmet nodded, and motioned for his guards to stay put. They set off across the practice yard, side-by-side.

"Is it a familiar smell?" Val asked.

"No. Well…not exactly."

"Remember when my brother was here? Briefly? And he brought his household?" *And you threatened to kill my mother in the garden.*

409

"No, that…Wait." He ground to a halt, and turned to face Val fully. "It's a *wolf*, isn't it?" His eyes sparkled with excitement. "Did my people manage to accidently capture one of the beasts?"

"Now. Darling." Val held up a staying hand that Mehmet's gaze went right to, an immediate questioning of Val's boldness. He pressed on anyway. "It would be helpful to adjust the way you think of wolves in general. And perhaps this one in particular. They're not beasts – they're immortals just like you and I."

Mehmet snorted. "They're nothing like you and I. What is it they're called?"

Val withheld a sigh. "Familiars."

"They're *servants* for beings like us. That's the very definition of a beast."

Val let his displeasure show.

"Are you lecturing me?"

"Never." He inclined his head. "Though I might advise a bit more subtlety in situations such as this."

"You." Mehmet pointed at him. "Have grown spoiled." There was no threat to his words, though. "Alright, show me this wolf," he said, walking again. "I suspect he'll make one of our better warriors."

Val fell into step beside him with a wince. "Actually, I'm not so sure. This one appears to be more of a scholar."

"*What?*"

"He was abysmal with the weapons." Val decided to leave off the bit about artillery training. Mehmet had plenty of foot soldiers to blow up with his fragile canons, and his plan required Nestor to be very much in one piece. "And he says that he was training to be a monk in Russia, before joining your troops. He's literate, and speaks several languages. I think he might be of better use off the battlefield."

Mehmet was silent a moment as they walked, dry winter grass crunching beneath their boots. Finally, he said, "Wolves can *read?*"

"As I said: they're not beasts. Being a Familiar doesn't mean they have any less capacity for the arts, or research, or higher levels of reasoning."

His expression grew thoughtful.

"Did my uncle not tell you any of this?" Val asked, exasperated. "He's traveled the world. He's had innumerable encounters with wolves." And, according to Mother, had sent three of his own to their deaths at Tîrgoviște, along with a mage whose neck Vlad had broken personally. He still shuddered, overcome with wonder, when he thought about the fact that his brother could somehow resist a mage's powers of compulsion. He'd reached *through her fire*, and killed her with his bare hand.

"He didn't exactly stick around to mentor me," Mehmet said, defensive. "And Father would never..." He faltered.

"Buy you any pet wolves?"

"You've just insisted they aren't beasts!"

"They're not. That was a test. Now, here he is. He's very nervous, so don't try to frighten him."

"I'll do what I like," Mehmet said, but lightly, which meant he was most likely to obey Val's wishes for the moment.

They arrived at the bench, and Nestor looked up at the two of them like a cornered pup, bristling with dread, eyes wide, pupils tiny pinpricks.

"It's alright," Val said. "This is Sultan Mehmet, and—"

Nestor slid off the bench and went to his knees. And prostrated himself before the sultan.

"Oh, dear," Val sighed.

Mehmet chuckled. "You should try this sometime, Radu. It pleases me."

"I please you plenty," Val muttered. To the boy: "Nestor-Iskander, please sit up."

The boy did so, hands braced on his thighs, terrified.

"I've been telling the sultan about your skills and recommending that he employ you as a scribe rather than a soldier."

"Have you now?" Mehmet said.

"He'd be wasted as a soldier," Val said. "And you could use a scribe who wasn't so mired in the muck of court intrigue." He lifted a single brow, inviting Mehmet to think otherwise.

The sultan's frown melted slowly from disapproving...to thoughtful. "An unbiased scribe."

"Yes."

"The idea has merit." His gaze slid to Nestor. "But what of him being a wolf?"

The boy's shoulders slumped as he tried to burrow down into his shirt collar. "I – I'm sorry, Your Majesty–"

"A rather meek wolf, as you can plainly see," Val said. "Nestor, you can tell that the sultan is also unique, can't you?"

He nodded.

"It would be an honor to be of service to him."

"A tremendous honor, your grace."

Val turned away from the young wolf, catching Mehmet's elbow, towing him away a step. He was the only one who dared touch him so casually, and Val suspected that was one of the reasons the Turkish nobles at court hated him so.

"Something for you to consider," he said with a shrug, feigning casual. "A trusted scribe. A way to keep the only wolf in the palace close."

A furrow had formed between Mehmet's brows. He really was considering. "Yes," he mused. "It's not a bad idea."

"Until then," Val said lightly, moving on, "I thought I'd have the best candidates demonstrate for you."

It was true what the Grand Vizier had said: Val was an excellent marksman. And he was a decent swordsman at this point, his vampiric strength making up for his lack of the sheer mass needed by the most fearsome of armored warriors.

But his greatest weapon, Val was coming to learn, was his ability to manipulate those more powerful than him.

<u>29</u>

PRINCE WITHOUT A PALACE

Brasov, Transylvania
1452

The sun set early in the mountains, the peaks throwing jagged shadows over the close-set Baroque style buildings around the cobbled city square, the February chill creeping in through the cracks in shutters and the gaps under doors.

In the great room of a second-floor apartment, Vlad Dracula sat slumped down in a chair before the fire, staring unseeing into the flames. A fur had been draped across his shoulders; it carried Cicero's scent in the places where his skin had touched it. The wolf sat at the table several paces away, studying maps by candlelight with his one eye. The others were all downstairs, in the apartment below, the occasional rising swell of a voice coming up through the floorboards. Vlad could have made out the words if he'd wanted to – he didn't.

"We'll have to move again soon," Cicero said with obvious regret. "There were men watching you in the market today."

Always someone watching. They were always moving – fleeing. He was the Cowardly Prince Who Fled.

It had been his mother's idea to seek asylum with Prince Bogdan II, ruler of Moldavia. "If anyone asks," Eira had said, "Bogdan is your uncle." A truly baffling explanation; almost as baffling as the way Mother and Bogdan had greeted one another like old friends.

It had taken a long time to settle in the palace there. To accept the idea that he wasn't on the run. That he was neither a puppet nor a prisoner. He woke each morning in a sumptuous bed, was brought a breakfast tray by a servant, and took his morning meal while Cicero looked on like a stern matron, ensuring he ate everything on his plate. The wolf offered his vein afterward, and Vlad would drink until his belly was warm, and full, and then doze some more, in that hazy, aroused post-drink state,

413

sun falling in through the window, Cicero resting a comforting hand on his head.

Then it was time to dress and be off for his lessons.

That had been the strangest part: being a student again.

He wasn't responsible for anything save learning, and training, and those things he did beneath the watchful eyes of quiet-voiced monks and Moldavian sword masters. No one struck him with a crop, nor reminded him of his place. No one cuffed him, or denied him food, and no vengeful heirs challenged him to unfair duels with sharp blades. He learned of the Ottoman Empire not as its ally, but as a Romanian – as someone studying the enemy. It was a proper Romanian education he had now, the one that had been cut short when he'd been taken from his father in Gallipoli.

And Vlad flourished.

His family, his pack, was safe, and he didn't allow himself to think *for now*. It was selfish, he knew, but he didn't worry about the future. About what would happen if Bogdan grew weary of him, or no longer wished to harbor a fugitive. He threw himself at his studies and his training – at being a young prince, being a boy. Just a boy. One who cracked the occasional smile.

A boy with a friend.

~*~

Vlad handed his blade off to one of the squires in attendance and accepted a cup of water from one of the others. The summer sun beat down on the practice grounds, reflecting off the white sand with glaring brightness. The water was cool, straight from the well, and he gulped it down greedily, short of breath afterward.

His body ached in a good way, tired and sore from rigorous exercise. He'd always been a competent duelist, and a brutal fighter, but he could feel himself improving day by day; quicker, stronger, more patient when he needed to be, more confident as his skills sharpened.

Stephen slumped back against the wall beside him, accepting a cup from the squire and pressing its cool side to his forehead. "Christ, man," he said with a breathless laugh. "If that's how the Ottomans teach all their boys how to fight, no wonder they're in charge of half of Europe these days."

Slowly, over time, Vlad was finding that mentions of his former captors didn't fill him with an immediate, blinding rage. He merely grimaced now, and wiped his forehead with his shirtsleeve. "Don't give them all the credit. Some of it's just natural talent."

"Oh, sure, sure." Stephen laughed again. He was *always* laughing.

The Moldavian heir was of a height with Vlad, and a ferocious swordsman in his own right, but that was where the similarities ended. He was broad, and more obviously, heavily muscled than Vlad. Square-jawed, and golden-skinned, his hair fell past in his shoulders in a bright mane of riotous bronze curls. A young lion, confident, proud, but friendly, his smiles easy. The energy that propelled him through his days was a happy one; it radiated out of him, in every joke, or tease, or gallant bow to a passing maid that had her blushing and giggling.

Vlad had wanted to hate him for that at the beginning. What kind of a prince smiled so much? What reason did he have to do so? And, petty though it was of him, he'd felt skinny, and sallow, and ugly beside the other boy. He'd never cared about his looks – how could he when his own little brother looked like an actual angel, and had always drawn the stares of every man, woman, and child?

But Stephen had drawn him out of his black depression, relentlessly cheerful. One night, Mother said, "You're so handsome when you smile," and he'd blushed, and grumbled, and turned his back to her quiet, pleased laughter.

The squires refilled their water cups and then retreated across the yard. Vlad could sense Stephen's anticipation before the boy spoke; it raised the fine hairs on the back of his own neck.

"So," Stephen whispered when they were alone, "I know about the strength, and the speed, and the healing, but – does it actually help you learn faster?"

Vlad sent him a narrow-eyed glance. Bogdan and his son both knew about immortals. Had already known – at least,

Bogdan had, thanks to a friendship with Father. By the time Stephen had finally asked Vlad outright, only a month ago, they'd been such friends that Vlad hadn't been able to lie.

He regretted sharing the knowledge, though.

"What do you think?" he asked.

Stephen rolled his eyes. "I think anyone with magical powers is, technically, cheating."

That startled a laugh out of Vlad. "Shall I tie one hand behind my back and have us go again?"

Stephen lifted his head in a theatrical display of mock-haughtiness. Vlad had told him once that he looked French when he did that, and so he kept doing it, just to get a chuckle out of him. "No," he said loftily, "I think you should share."

Vlad's laughter died away. They'd had this conversation several times now, and each time, Stephen grew less teasing, and more sincere. "It's not the gift you think it is," he said quietly. The squires were a distance away, at the well, but he didn't want anyone overhearing.

Stephen let his head thump softly back against the wall. "Or is it just that you want to be special?" he said, and all hints of teasing melted off his face, leaving him curious – hurt.

Anger flared: quick, hot, immediate. He'd been trying hard to control those sorts of reactions. The people here weren't his enemies. He couldn't use violence to solve all his problems – his failure at Tîrgovişte had proved that.

He took a steadying breath and said, "I can't believe you would actually want my life. It's anything but special."

Stephen's gaze dropped, and his lips pursed, chagrined.

"My kind can die," Vlad continued, managing to keep his tone soft, almost apologetic. "We might be harder to kill, but that just means we have longer to feel pain. It hurts when someone cracks open your ribcage to get to your heart, Stephen."

"I know."

"The way they did to my father."

"I know!" Not a shout, but loud enough to have the squires glancing over, startled.

Stephen huffed a breath and shook his head. "Forgive me, cousin." It was a lie they'd slid into easily, a blood relation.

Oftentimes, Vlad wished it was the truth, that he was just a mortal boy, unencumbered by the legacy of a long-since-fallen kingdom. "I don't envy your trials. You know this." He offered a small smile. "It's just that it sounds like a fantasy sometimes."

Vlad sighed. "That's what everyone who doesn't have to live forever thinks."

A figure approached from across the courtyard. Malik Bey, dressed now as a Romanian at court, though he still favored scarlet – it was Vlad's family color, after all, and Malik had gone down on one knee and pledged himself to House Dracula.

"Your grace," he said now, pulling to a halt in front of Vlad. He'd always stood tall and correct, but there was a lightness in his posture now that hadn't been there when he'd been a janissary. Stealing him away the night they left Edirne had been a risk, but one Vlad was glad of. The man got on well with Cicero, and had become something of Vlad's left hand – the position a mage would have occupied if he'd had one. Or been able to stomach the thought of one.

"Your graces," he amended, including Stephen in his address. "The prince wishes to see you in his study. He's had word from his brother."

~*~

That had been June. The June before, in 1450, Vlad and Stephen had fought beneath Prince Bogdan's banner together, crushing the invading Polish army at Crasna. Two triumphant young princes hailed as heroes by the Moldavians. Cheers, and flower garlands.

Followed by a cozy winter reading by firelight. And a lazy summer rich with horseback riding, and hunting, and training, and growing into his own skin.

In October of 1451, Prince Bogdan was murdered by his own brother.

It had been four months since that horrible day. Four months of fleeing. Hunyadi had their scent, and they couldn't stop anywhere for long; no one wanted to take them in; betrayal was a constant worry.

A prince without a palace. Without an ally. Without anything.

Vlad stared into the flames. They were dying, the last flickering tongues, deep orange. The firewood basket sat empty by the hearth. Someone would have to venture out and buy more; another chance to be recognized, to be reported, targeted.

The stairs creaked, and he heard the weight of footfalls. Vlad didn't turn; Cicero was on guard.

And, truthfully, he didn't care anymore. Let a villain come. Let them try to kill him. He relished the thought of a real fight, rather than all this damned *fleeing*.

But it was only Stephen. Vlad caught his scent, and the other prince walked past Cicero unimpeded, coming to kneel down beside Vlad's chair and grip his arm with shaking fingers.

He stank of fear. His voice came out desperate. "Vlad." His hand tightened on Vlad's arm until Vlad turned his head to meet his panicked gaze.

"Vlad. There's men in the alley. Five of them, all dressed in black. I saw a flash – they have knives." His voice wobbled, but didn't break. He was working hard to sound brave, but the months of flight and hiding and the assassination attempts were getting to him.

"Vlad!"

Oh. He'd just been sitting there.

But emotion surged. Adrenaline flooded his veins in a sudden, warm rush.

He stood, and crossed to the window. "This alley?" he asked as he opened the shutters and looked out through the frost-rimed glass. He could feel the cold coming in through the cracks, sharp enough to make his teeth ache.

That emotion – it was *anticipation*. He sought his own reflection in the glass, and realized he was smiling, fangs long and sharp.

Five man-shaped shadows slunk along the wall of the alley down below.

"Well," Vlad said, turning the window latch, his voice more beast than man. "I wouldn't want to keep them waiting."

"Vlad, what are you…"

He pushed up the window, letting in a blast of frigid air.

"Vlad, no!" Stephen made a grab at his arm that he avoided.

He thought he heard Cicero sigh somewhere behind him, but he climbed up onto the sill and leapt out into the night before the wolf could protest.

It was a short fall, but long enough for the wind to whip at his clothes and hair, for the cold to make his eyes tear, for the bottom to drop out of his stomach in that way that meant he was about to do something wild and dangerous.

Then he landed, light on the balls of his feet, like a housecat, perfectly balanced and ready to strike. And then he smelled men – smelled flesh, and *blood*. And he *roared*.

The would-be assassins whirled to face him, gasping. He could see well enough, with vampire eyes, to make out their shocked expressions.

A light thump beside him announced Cicero's arrival, already shifted into wolf form. He gave a lupine snort of disapproval.

"You know you want to kill something, too," Vlad said, and attacked.

To their credit, the assassins recovered quickly from their surprise. Knives flashed, and Vlad heard the rasp of a sword leaving a scabbard; the moonlight glinted down its length. A short sword, designed for one-handed use. This wasn't a battle, but a dead-of-night killing.

Well. They *thought* it wasn't a battle.

Vlad was weaponless, but he didn't care. A part of him relished the fact.

There were five opponents, and they split up, two moving around on Cicero's side, three on Vlad's. Confident his wolf could handle himself, Vlad put his back to Cicero and turned to meet the man with the sword.

That was doubtless what the enemy wanted him to do: focus on the largest, most obvious threat, leaving his sides exposed to the other two – and their knives. He had no idea if they knew what he was, but that didn't matter. Vampire-savvy or not, they weren't prepared for *him*.

419

The swordsman moved in quick and close, a short jab; a killer and not a showy knight, aiming at Vlad's arm with a blow meant to disable. Vlad ducked down low. A curse above him. He felt the other two closing in, meaning to hem him in from above. They'd fall on him then, all together.

He tucked and rolled to the right, fast, and used his shoulder to ram one of the knife-wielding assassins in the knee. The man grunted and flailed out with his blade, trying to catch Vlad with it even as he fell. Vlad dodged the blow – clumsy as it was – and elbowed the man in the groin. Kept rolling, and popped back up to his feet in a lithe flex of back and hips.

The man he'd tripped regained his feet – but not as quickly as Vlad. Vlad kicked him in the back, hard, high, right in the kidney. He felt something give beneath the sole of his boot, and the man collapsed with a choked-off shout.

Vlad registered a flash – the short sword coming at his face – and put his hand up. He *caught* the blade. It bit deep, deep into his palm. It hit bone. The pain was bright, and sudden, and he gritted his teeth against it – but knowledge helped him contain it. Knowledge that he could live through this kind of injury, heal from it, fight with it. He was immortal, and these people weren't. They could hack him to pieces, and he could still throttle them.

Blood poured down his arm, into his sleeve, hot and thick. But he grinned. And he reached up with his other hand, and yanked the sword out of the man's grip.

The assassin cursed, but reached for the knife at his belt.

The second one closed in as well.

Vlad moved his hands down to the pommel, blood making his grip slippery and inexpert. His hand felt on fire. He needed to get his mouth on the wound to staunch the blood flow, but there was no time for that now.

The third assassin dragged himself to his feet, limping, teeth gritted – shiny in the gloaming. A rib or two was broken, but he would attempt to finish the job he'd been hired to do.

Vlad braced his feet, and met them.

His first swing, with all his strength behind it, severed an arm. The shock of blade-on-bone moved up his arms like a thunderclap, one he absorbed as he prepared for another swing, ears filled with screams.

Another strike. Sharp smell of blood that wasn't his own.

He was aware of other sounds beyond his personal fight: Cicero snarling, men grunting, cursing. A door opened, flung back on his hinges, and he smelled his people: Fen, and Mother, and Malik, and Stephen.

He took off the last assassin's head with two forceful strikes, and the thump of it hitting the cobbles was the last note of the fight.

Vlad shifted his pilfered sword to his good hand and brought the wounded one up to his face. In the moonlight, he could see shiny blood glimmering over bone. He put his tongue to the wound and lapped it thoroughly.

Cicero shifted back to his two-legged form, clothes settling around him with the customary puff of vapor; it was old magic, stuff Vlad didn't really understand, but had accepted all his life.

Stephen, white-faced in the moonlight, jumped and yelped, still not used to the sight of a wolf becoming a man.

Malik knelt and pulled the hood back from the face of one of the assassins. "Not Turks," he said, frowning.

"No," Vlad agreed, swallowing a last mouthful of his own blood. "Hunyadi's this time."

Eira went from corpse to corpse, searching through their pockets for letters, coins, anything of value to them.

Helga lingered at the open door, hand worrying the neckline of her dress.

Fen bent down and picked up the decapitated head by its dark hair, standing to hold it up to the moon, scowling at it. "You should have left one alive so we could question him."

"I was trying to stay alive, Fen," Vlad said, breathless. Damn, he was tired, the exhaustion only now setting in. He hadn't fed in two days, and he needed to rectify that, as Cicero was always insisting.

As if summoned, his Familiar stepped in front of him, scowling, the effect no less sinister with only one eye.

Vlad turned away–

And Cicero caught his chin in his hand.

421

"Bold," Vlad said.

"You're tired," his wolf said. "You need to *drink*, Vlad."

Fenrir threw the head at the wall, and it bounced off with a nasty, meaty splat. "Bah!" he shouted. "Let them come! I'll kill them all!"

"Fen!" Mother and Helga said together.

"What?" he demanded, turning to them with open arms.

"Vlad—" Cicero started again.

He inhaled. Smell of more men. Many more.

The immortals turned as a unit, facing the mouth of the alley. Faint lick of torchlight against the wall, moving closer. *Many* torches.

"More," Vlad said, and licked his lips. Why feed from his Familiar when he could feast on men?

But Cicero grabbed his arm.

Mother said, "We have to leave. *Now.*"

And still he fled. Always fleeing.

<u>30</u>

AN ACCORD

The estate belonged to a man who was an ally – but grudgingly so. Someone loyal to Stephen's father, but who knew better than to share such opinions publicly. He had given them momentary shelter, a chance to rest a moment behind the safety of his high estate walls and screens of planted cypress trees. But Vlad had never seen him wear an expression like the one he wore now, as he rushed across the pebbled courtyard where he and Stephen sparred.

Vlad stepped back, lowering his blade. Stephen did likewise, but slowly. Sweat streamed down his face, cheeks flushed from exertion. Vlad had been pushing him harder lately, using more of his real strength, pressing his advantages. It was no time for gentle lessons; time for learning how to be brutal and unforgiving.

Stephen lifted his brows in question, and Vlad nodded toward the boyar rushing toward him, the graying man puffing from the effort. Why hadn't he sent a servant after them? Why did he look chalk-pale with obvious nerves?

"Your grace," the man said breathlessly when he finally reached them. He addressed Vlad. He winced and grabbed at his side, panting. "Your grace – John Hunyadi is here."

Vlad lifted his sword with a snarl.

The boyar's eyes went wide and he stumbled back a step. "No, no. He wants to talk to you. Your grace, he wants *peace.*"

~*~

"Your grace," the boyar puffed beside him, jogging in his attempt to keep up with the long walking strides Vlad took down the gallery toward the man's study. "Perhaps – perhaps you would like – to freshen up?"

He'd gone charging off straight from the practice field, Stephen right at his heels. He wore only the sweat-damp, open-throated shirt, breeches, and boots he'd taken to wearing while sparring. He still carried his sword — though, that wasn't an accident.

"No," he snapped. He wanted to meet Hunyadi while his blood was up, while his muscles were warm and primed for fighting. He didn't want to have a civil breaking of bread with this man. He wanted his head.

As they neared the closed door of the study, Cicero peeled away from the wall and fell in at Vlad's side, jaw locked, brow furrowed.

"You've seen him?" Vlad asked.

"Yes. He doesn't look it, but he's nervous."

Vlad growled softly under his breath. "He should be."

"Your grace," the boyar pleaded behind him. "Please don't do anything rash. Peace for Romania would be a blessing from God himself."

Vlad whirled on the man, and he stumbled to a halt, nearly cowering. "God isn't here though, is he? Only me. And the man who killed my family. I shall do with him as I like."

Stephen looked shocked, but said nothing.

Vlad turned back to the door. Cicero opened it for him, and he stepped inside.

The study, like the entirety of the estate, was practical, but comfortable, and crafted of fine materials. A large room, with a polished desk positioned in front of the mullioned windows, natural light spilling in diamonds across its surface, and the Turkish rugs that covered the floor.

The governor of Transylvania sat in a padded leather chair with a high back like a throne, a place for a guest of honor directly across from the desk. He held a cup of wine, and several of his own servants stood ranged behind him, two soldiers, and one a steward, his clothes rich, his air scholarly.

Hunyadi himself looked to have changed little since Vlad had last seen him, as a boy. Thick through the shoulders and middle, but strong, solid. A warrior's body, even if not a very tall one. He wore his hair long and curled on his shoulders, the points of his thick mustache tipped up at the ends with a smoothing of oil. He held his cup carelessly, his appearance casual. Unconcerned.

But Vlad could sense the restless nerves buzzing under his skin. It tainted the air; human skin smelled different when its wearer was afraid of something, and that scent filled the study now.

Vlad stood a moment, once he was inside the room, breathing in that odor, feeling the weight of its advantage.

Hunyadi's gaze moved down him and then back up, catching on the sword. He lifted his brows. "Did my arrival interrupt your training?" he asked mildly.

Vlad moved to the desk and sat down behind it, laid his sword on its polished surface, right hand still curled around the grip. Stephen and Cicero moved to stand to either side of him, flanking him. "No," he said, and met the man's stare with a relentless one of his own. "But it seemed wasteful to bathe before subjecting myself to the company of pigs."

A grin tugged at Hunyadi's mouth. "I heard you had a temper. It seems the rumors were true."

"This is not my temper."

"That's true," Stephen chimed in. Vlad could sense his anxiety, but his voice came calm and airy. "This is Vlad in a happy mood, your grace."

Vlad bit down on the impulse to smile. Instead, he enjoyed Hunyadi's baffled expression and said, tone icy, "My gracious host tells me you want to talk of peace."

"He's correct. Yes, that's why I'm here."

"Peace on what terms?"

Hunyadi cast a discreet glance around the room, touching on all of its inhabitants.

Vlad turned to their boyar host. "Leave us."

The man looked glad to do so, closing the door behind him.

Hunyadi took a bolder glance. At Stephen. At Cicero. Pointed.

"Doubtless you know of Stephen, son of the late Prince Bogdan of Moldavia," Vlad said. "My cousin and ally. Cicero is my chief advisor. He goes where I go, and hears what I hear. Make your case, governor."

"My case? You're wise to listen, but I admit that I'm surprised you would. Considering."

425

Vlad slid his free hand down the length of his sword. It was his father's Toledo blade, rather than a blunted practice sword. Sharp enough to split a hair, gleaming in the sunlight like the scales of a serpent. Ready to strike.

"Hmm. Considering," he said. "Considering the fact that you murdered my father? My brother? Backed Prince Bogdan's killer? Sent assassins after us again and again?"

"I'm sure you understand–" Hunyadi started.

"My brother," Vlad continued, voice getting colder, darker, louder. "Was beaten, and dragged, and stabbed, and buried face-down while he was still breathing. I found his grave. I dug his bones up myself, by hand.

"My father fled on foot. Cut down by a mob of men. And *wolves*." He stressed the word and watched Hunyadi's eyes widen. Did he know that werewolves had been employed? Or had that been part of Romulus's machinations? "They butchered him. Cut his heart from his body."

Vlad felt Cicero's hand land on his shoulder and squeeze, bracing and loving.

"And that sniveling coward Vladislav. Who had not a single legitimate claim to the princedom. Your puppet. You backed him because he was spineless. Because he would do your bidding. Because he would act out your butchery and pave the way for you in Wallachia. The people of Romania faced the same threat, and yet, rather than unite them, you chose to pit them against one another, to slaughter them, so that you could take these three principalities for Hungary. You styled yourself a crusader, someone fighting against the Ottoman invasion of the west. And all you wanted was power for yourself. Explain to me, *your grace*, why I should listen to a *fucking* word you have to say."

Cicero's fingers tightened again, still supportive, grieving, caring.

Hunyadi took a breath and let it out slowly through his nose, nostrils flaring. He dipped his head. "That's...fair."

"You're damn right it is," Stephen said, to Vlad's surprise. "How dare you show your face here, after you tried to kill us?"

426

Hunyadi sighed. He put his hands on the edge of the desk, fingers spread wide, the gemstones in his rings winking in the light. "Son…"

Vlad growled. Not in a human sense – a proper vampire growl.

Hunyadi's people stepped forward, the soldiers reaching for the daggers at their hips. The man himself gaped, open-mouthed.

"Do not," Vlad said, the growl pulsing through his voice, "call me *son*."

Hunyadi stared at him…and then looked away. "Alright."

"I hate you," Vlad said. "I've fantasized about killing you for a long time now."

But Hunyadi wasn't the only one he hated.

"So plead your case," Vlad continued. "Tell me why I should make peace with the man who murdered my family."

Silence.

Hunyadi's attendants looked worried.

The governor studied Vlad a long moment, jaw working side to side. "You're honest," he finally said.

"Apparently, that's not fashionable among the nobility."

"No, it's not." Another pause, this one thoughtful. Hunyadi's anxiety seemed to lessen, his scent settling. "Flattery clearly won't work, so I think I'll have to be frank with you, Dracula."

Hunyadi's steward leaned in, as if to whisper advice, and the governor waved him back.

Vlad felt his anger boiling inside him, churning in his gut like a sour dinner. Fantasies came to him, one after the next: lifting his blade and sweeping the governor's head from his neck; launching himself across the desk and sinking his fangs into the man's throat, drinking and drinking until he was a desiccated husk, and Vlad had taken every drop of life from his body; stabbing him, again and again, until the blood ran out of him, spilling all over the fine carpet like wine from a ruptured skin. His hand began to ache from gripping the sword; the blade vibrated, faintly, rattling against the wood.

Hunyadi's brows pinched together, and his jaw worked a moment before he spoke. "I didn't wield the blade myself, but I suspect that makes no difference here. Yes, I'm responsible for your father's death. And your brother's. They were not crimes of passion, but calculated political moves. I needed Dracul's troops, and free access to the Danube for my campaigns. Time and again I gave your father the chance to join me in my fight against the Ottomans, but he either refused, or delayed, or contributed a mere handful of men to the cause. Vlad was impeding my war efforts, and so I had him removed, and replaced him with a dull-witted lackey whom I knew I could control."

When Vlad spoke, his voice vibrated with the catlike harmonics of a vampire. Everyone in the room save Cicero and Stephen visibly recoiled from the sound. "My father had a treaty with the Ottomans. If he'd broken it, my brother and I would have been killed for his disobedience."

Hunyadi cocked his head. "The leader of a people must always make sacrifices. Your father chose you – and sacrificed his people. I made a different choice."

"Of course you did, because we were someone else's sons. Where was *your son*? Your Matthias? Home safe in Hungary? In Transylvania?" He didn't realize he'd risen from his chair until Cicero gently pressed him back down into it. He breathed in short, sharp bursts, chest heaving.

He had to be calm. Had to be.

He closed his eyes a moment, and took a sequence of deep, measured breaths. Slowly, the adrenaline bled out of him. The rage stayed, though, cold, and hard, and relentless.

When Vlad opened his eyes again, he was met with Hunyadi's patient gaze – though he could hear the rabbit-fast kicking of the man's heart.

"Fine," Vlad said, and his voice was normal again. "It was political. Am I to assume that's why you're here now?"

A chagrined little smile that twitched his mustache. "Vladislav is no longer…amenable to our original plan."

"How sad for you."

Hunyadi sighed. "Vladislav has been growing friendlier with the Turks over the past year. Now he's being vocal about it. He says he sees wisdom in allying ourselves with them. Stop all this

428

constant warring, and just agree to their terms. He wants to be a good little vassal."

"It's a smart move, really. The Ottomans are far superior in number, arms, and wealth. Standing against them is a hopeless cause. Even a 'dull-witted puppet' can see that."

"All true," Hunyadi said. "But is that what *you* would do?"

"What does that matter? I'm nothing but a refugee."

"I'm curious. Indulge me."

Cicero's fingertips danced against Vlad's collarbone. A warning to be careful.

Vlad didn't need it. He knew exactly where Hunyadi was going with this. This whole scenario had begun, alarmingly, to resemble the day Murat had given him his father's blade and told him to take his rightful place as prince. Hunyadi was no different from the old sultan. Just another powerful, heartless man who'd butchered families and made use of marionettes to get what he wanted. He meant to use Vlad, appealing to his unrelenting hatred, dangling an empty promise of power.

Whatever the man proposed, agreeing to it would be seen as a sign of acceptance for what had been done to Father and Mircea.

Vlad stared fixedly at the sword in front of him, eyes tracing its familiar lines again and again. "What would I do?" he asked, just a whisper. "I would very much like to kill you now, leap out of this window behind me, and run off into the forest never to be seen again."

Hunyadi's men laid hands on their weapons, and Cicero growled. They paused, surprised all over again.

"But," Vlad continued, "nothing would give me more satisfaction in this world that cleaving Sultan Mehmet's head from his neck. And so you can see that I have a difficult choice between the two."

Mildly, Hunyadi said, "I have these men here, and more in the chamber beyond. You couldn't kill me now."

"You have *no idea* what I'm capable of," Vlad said, and for the first time he saw the gleam of true fear in the man's eyes.

Cicero growled again, a deep rumble in his chest, to drive the point home.

Vlad looked at the governor across from him, the Hungarian devil who'd manipulated and badgered his family since before Vlad himself was born. He saw a brutal, loveless man hellbent on battle, damn the consequences. He could talk of "people" all he wanted, but Hunyadi wanted glory, influence, and wealth.

But when he blinked, he saw his brother. The skin of Val's throat marred by bruises and fang prints. His neck weighed down by jeweled chains. His skin musky with a rapist's spent passion.

He blew out a breath. "Mehmet has my brother, still. If you're suggested an alliance between us, then I'm listening."

A slow smile broke across the governor's face. "I spent months as a prisoner alongside your old friend Skanderbeg. He spoke highly of–"

Vlad waved a hand to silence him. Swallowed the lump in his throat. *Be patient*, he heard George's voice in his head. *You have to learn to be patient.* "It's not possible to flatter me. Tell me your proposition."

Hunyadi sat forward, eager. "I've already got men lined up to help you dispatch Vladislav. I want you to be prince in Wallachia, Vlad. And in exchange, I want free access to the Danube. I can also guarantee that together we'll win back Moldavia for your cousin," he said with a nod toward Stephen. "And together, a unified Hungary and Romania will have one last proper crusade. If the pope won't help us, then to hell with him. But we will finally have the manpower, and the cooperation, to drive the Ottomans out of our lands for good. The Ottomans march even now on Constantinople, and Mehmet means to try and sack the city. Now is no time for old feuds and grudges. We have to stand together, Vlad, or fall one-by-one beneath the enemy."

Put that like, Vlad didn't suppose he really had a choice to make after all.

~*~

Hours later, when the deal had been hammered out and parchments had been signed, sealed, and sent, after Vlad had forced himself to shake the hand of the man who'd seen his father killed, he sat in his temporary bedchamber, the sword across his knees, staring at the blinding flare of moonlight down its length.

"I don't understand how you aren't furious with me," he murmured.

Eira finished lighting the tall tapers on the mantlepiece and blew out the tinder she'd used to do so. She came to sit beside him, her split skirts rustling. Her hands twitched before settling together in her lap, like she'd wanted to touch him, but couldn't, because of the sword.

"Nothing we do will bring your father back," she said quietly. "We have to look after ourselves. And your brother."

"And what of Wallachia?" he asked, already knowing the answer.

Her expression hardened. "Wallachia is yours by birthright. It always has been. You'll be doing right to defend it."

"And John Hunyadi?"

"We'll use him. For now," she said, tone ominous. She leaned down to kiss his forehead, and whispered, "But we will have our revenge, darling. Don't worry." She pulled back with a smile that didn't touch her eyes. "Get some sleep. We ride tomorrow."

Back home, to a palace that would be his for a second time.

He nodded and she left the room, murmuring something low to Cicero, who stood at the door.

When she was gone, and the door was shut, Cicero went to the sideboard and poured a cup of wine; Vlad could smell its sweetness. The wolf brought it to him, and held it before his face, close enough to be tempting.

"Here," he said, voice gentle. He'd been so, so gentle with Vlad all afternoon and evening, a hand on him at almost all times, face drawn with lines of sympathy. "Drink this, and then you need to feed." He tilted the cup a fraction, so moonlight silvered the inside of his wrist, the veins there dark and inviting.

Vlad took the cup without much interest. "My mother left the room, you know, and yet I'm still being mothered."

Cicero snorted. "Because you're twice as difficult to mother as anyone I've ever met. Drink your wine."

Vlad did, grudgingly, admitting to himself that its taste and tartness and warmth was immediately soothing. Cicero took the empty cup after, and offered his wrist.

Vlad stared at it a moment, the sinuous tracks of the veins, breathing over them. His fangs descended in automatic anticipation, but he didn't bite. Not yet. "Can I tell you something?"

"You can tell me anything," came the immediate response.

Vlad sighed.

"Vlad," his wolf urged.

He closed his eyes and pressed his forehead into Cicero's open hand. "I hate myself," he whispered. "I should have killed him. But I'm weak. I want revenge on Mehmet…even if it means consorting with the enemy. *Another* enemy."

Cicero stroked his hair with his free hand. "Friends are few," Cicero said, and his voice become reflective; the words sounded like old wisdom, something he'd heard elsewhere and was repeating now. "Pack is family, and family is love. Family is trust. You can help others, and let them help you, without trusting."

"Hmm," Vlad hummed. "Not exactly helpful."

The wolf chuckled, and his voice was his own again, rough and familiar, a touch uncertain, but warm. "Allying ourselves with Hunyadi in order to defeat the Ottomans and rescue Prince Val…that's not weak."

"It feels like it is."

"Sometimes things aren't the way they feel." Another pass of his callused hand across Vlad's head, down his unbound hair, to his shoulder. A squeeze. "Drink now, come on."

He took the wolf's wrist in his hand and bared his fangs, and bit. As the blood filled his mouth, his thoughts shifted to his brother. He wondered where he was now, if he had access to blood. If he was strong, and healthy.

He suspected that, even if Val had been able to dream-walk, Vlad was the last person he would want to come and visit.

31

HEADSMAN

"My scouts have sketched it for me," Constantine said, tone aiming for disinterested, but ending up grim instead. "It's...impressive."

Val bit back a sigh. He loved these visits – really he did – but he didn't have much time, and pacing along the wall top while the waves crashed below with a dull roar, pennants snapping in the breeze, wasn't the best use of these few stolen minutes. "Yes. I told you about the plans," he reminded, as gently as possible. "We're marching there now."

"We?" the emperor asked, tilting his head Val's direction.

He did sigh this time. "I'm a part of his retinue, remember? Advisor. Ally." He left off *lover*. "I'm closer to him than anyone." In more ways than one. "I listen to his obsessive rhetoric on the topic near-constantly. Constantine." He halted, which forced his friend to do the same, and turned to face him. "He's coming here. He's having cannons cast from bronze. He's..." His breath hitched as his anxiety swelled. "I've tried to discourage him the best I know how, but I can't stop him."

Constantine smiled at him. Softly, sadly. "I know you're trying. That's kind of you."

No! he wanted to scream. He wasn't being kind! He was helpless, and stupid, and without scruples. He sucked cock to stay alive, and he had to watch his captor march steadily westward, unchecked, nothing but a spectator to his conquest. He wasn't trying. He was *terrified*, and he couldn't seem to impress the emperor with the seriousness of the situation.

He opened his mouth to respond–

And opened his eyes back in his body. Damn it.

Val sat up, fighting the usual post-walking wave of dizziness. A moment later, the tent flap opened, and Mehmet stalked in, brow crimped and gaze indrawn with thought. He let the flap fall shut and headed toward the war table at the center of the tent, but paused, finally noticing Val.

He blinked, and his frown deepened. "Sleeping in the middle of the day? How industrious of you."

Val scrubbed a hand across his eyes, working the grit from between his lashes. He could only have been unconscious for a half hour or so, but dream-walking left him as disoriented and groggy as a full night's sleep. He'd first slipped out of his body while sitting cross-legged in the center of the rug, not wanting to truly stretch out in bed, instead ready to leap back to full awareness. But he'd obviously fallen over, and had awakened on his side.

He got unsteadily to his feet, stifling a yawn. His limbs felt heavy, and his heart raced, as if he'd just awakened from a nightmare. He was getting bolder and bolder, doing this during the day, in stolen snatches of time. Arslan had been sent to carry a message, and there hadn't even been anyone to warn him of Mehmet's return.

One day, the sultan would catch him at it, hear him mumbling, lift a lid and see that his eyes had rolled back. He didn't like to think about the punishment that would follow.

"You keep me awake most nights, so I have to steal rest when I can," Val quipped as he joined the sultan at the table. He passed a finger along the delicate collar at his throat, and suppressed another, nastier comment about the silver he was forced to wear. "What's got you so pensive?" He sidled up close, shifted his weight so their hips bumped together. Usually, he liked to do that when there were viziers and generals around, enjoying the way it made them all squirm and divert their gazes. But mostly he did it because it was important that Mehmet think him smitten.

"Scouts encountered an engineer this morning," Mehmet said, distracted, as he pulled out a roll of parchment and smoothed it across the table, over a map. It was a sequence of drawings, notes made in messy Greek beside each. "He said the emperor, the fool, declined to use his talents. We have guns...but *these* guns..." He laughed, low and delighted.

With a chill, Val realized what he was looking at – read the numbers for what they were: measurements. Impossibly huge measurements.

"This is a cannon," he said, voice flat with shock...and horror.

Mehmet chuckled. "It's the largest cannon ever cast. And it's going to be mine."

"Greedy," Val said, teasing. But inside he was numb. His eyes traced the plans. God, it was massive. The kind that could penetrate walls. "You want everything."

"As well you know," Mehmet said, leaning into the pressure of Val's hip, brushing their shoulders together. "Care to help me celebrate?" He turned his head, so his warm breath gusted across Val's ear. "Where's your insufferable little slave? Are we alone?"

"Oh, Arslan!" Val whirled away, a different kind of fear coursing through him. "He should have been back by now. My mare lost a shoe, and I sent him to ask the blacksmith–"

The tent flap opened, and the bottom fell out of Val's stomach. He knew his mistake right away.

Nestor-Iskander held Arslan around the waist with one arm, keeping him upright, supporting most of the boy's weight. Arslan limped on one leg, expression dazed, his face mottled with bruises that were still red and new, but which would darken over the next few hours. A split lip, a drop of blood on his chin. Ripped, dirt-smudged clothes.

But the worst was the smell: the scent of sweat, and fear, and sex.

Val choked on a whimper, and rushed to them.

"Arslan! Oh, sweetheart. Here. My God. Oh, what happened to you? Who did this?" He cupped the boy's chin in the gentlest of touches, mirroring Arslan's wince. He ghosted his hands over his shoulders, his arms, tears burning his eyes.

He looked to Nestor. Firmer, teeth clenched: "*Who did this?*"

Arslan coughed weakly, and clutched at his ribs. "It's...it's alright, your grace. It's...my fault. I shouldn't have–"

Val took his chin again; the boy winced but he held on, forcing eye contact. "It is *not* your fault," Val said. "I should never have sent you alone down to the horse lines. I–" He took a ragged breath, fighting sharp pain in his chest. This poor sweet boy. So much already taken from him – his autonomy, his masculinity. And now his dignity. And his innocence.

Tears spilled down Arslan's bruised cheeks, silent but steady, and he dropped his gaze, ashamed.

Val looked to Nestor. "Who?" he demanded.

The scribe bit his lip.

"Please, no," Arslan sniffled.

"Hush." Val put his arms around him and pulled him away from Nestor, into his own grip, tucked his face into his throat with a hand at the back of his head. "Who, Nestor? I want their names."

Again, the scribe hesitated.

"They won't hurt you in retaliation," Val said. "They won't hurt anyone ever again."

Arslan looked up, eyes wide.

Val heard footsteps behind him.

Mehmet. He'd completely forgotten about Mehmet. Damn it.

He straightened and turned, finding the sultan behind him, arms folded, expression more curious than anything else. "It looks like someone ravished your slave."

Val set his jaw.

Then Mehmet said, "What are you going to do about it?"

~*~

A warm day. The heat intensified the pungent stink of latrines, of unwashed soldiers on the march, of horse manure ripening in the sun. Even a tidy camp, such as this one, reeked.

Val strode with his sword at his hip, boots kicking up puffs of dust. Long strides, his shadow bobbing along head of him.

Mehmet walked beside him, and a foursome of janissaries tailed them.

The sultan hummed quietly to himself, unbothered.

Val *seethed*.

He held his jaw clenched tight, breathing harshly through his nose, despite the stench. His hands tightened into fists at his sides, over and over, fingers itching to claw, to scrape, to hurt. His fangs were descended; if he spoke to anyone, they would be clearly visible.

He didn't care.

He'd left Arslan in Nestor-Iskander's care. The scribe had found him by the picket lines, he'd said, and known right away that Val would want to see him for himself. He'd been right; just as he'd been right that Val would want to mete out punishment once he knew the perpetrators' names. In the months since becoming Mehmet's most trusted scribe, Nestor had grown fond of Arslan – as did everyone who interacted with the boy. Sweet, and lovely to look upon, shy, unfailingly proper – except when he was alone with Val and Val asked him to speak his mind. He was slender, finer-boned than other boys his age, because he'd been castrated.

Val was no fool. He knew the way eunuchs were used here amongst the Ottomans. They guarded the women, and they serviced the men – Mehmet had at least a dozen, hand-picked from conquered towns, young men kept in a sort of forever boyhood, with smooth cheeks, and delicate limbs. Val found the whole business disgusting – but he had his own problems. His own backside to guard, as it were. He couldn't control the things Mehmet did outside of the bed and tents and rooms they shared.

But this.

This.

Arslan was *his.* Val had Mehmet's word that he'd never try to touch him.

Val tightened his thighs around Mehmet's hips, enjoying the way his pace stuttered, and his eyes and mouth opened with surprise just before Val flipped them over, and surprised him some more. He put one hand on the sultan's throat, and with the other pulled the knife from beneath the pillow where he'd stashed it before, pressed its tip to the delicate skin just beneath Mehmet's eye.

Mehmet panted, half from his interrupted exertion, half from shock. Voice admirably steady: "I'll put you over my knee and beat you 'til you bleed for this."

Val growled at him, a proper vampire growl. His hair fell around them, a golden curtain closing them in together, face-to-face. Inside him, he felt Mehmet begin to flag. "Fine. I don't care. But I'll have your word on one thing."

"If you wanted more jewels, all you had to—"

Val pressed in with the knife; a tiny bead of blood welled, and Mehmet's frantic gaze flicked between the knife and Val's face. Val could feel the silver pulling at his energy – always pulling, always making him weak – but even then, fresh from feeding, he was as strong as Mehmet. Maybe stronger.

"Arslan," he said.

Mehmet wet his lips. "Your little eunuch? What about him?"

"I've seen your eyes. Following him. Covetous. You will not touch him."

Mehmet's gaze tightened. His hips shifted a fraction, a bare flexing of his spine.

Val tightened his grip: on the knife, on his hips, on his throat.

"You want something to fuck, is that it? Instead of always taking it?"

"He is a child. A little boy who had his pants pulled down and his balls cut off. He won't suffer your lust – not anyone's. You do whatever you want to me, but don't touch him. He's mine – you gave him to me. And I won't have him used for that."

Mehmet studied him an endless moment. "You're serious."

"Deadly serious."

It turned out the sultan enjoyed a bit of an even match in bed, a true fight like they hadn't had since Val had stabbed him that first night. Val hadn't been able to leave the bed the next morning, Arslan helping him sit upright and bringing him breakfast and blood on a tray. Watching him with outward worry, nibbling at his lip while Val nibbled at flatbread on back teeth that felt loose against his tongue.

But Mehmet had given his word about Arslan, and so far, he'd kept it.

No one else would dare lay a finger on Arslan – Val's property. Mehmet's property, by default. And, worried about the impending siege, trying desperately to make Constantine see reason, Val had grown lax. He'd been sending the boy to run errands, take messages, assuming he was safe.

But a war camp was a war camp, after all.

Soldiers bowed their heads in deference as they passed. A few went down on their knees. They turned between two tents, and then two more, moving away from the more orderly rows where soldiers camped, and toward the workmen and camp followers, the modest tents crowded together at haphazard angles, a maze of human and animal filth; and wide-eyed craftsmen and whores, startled to see the sultan and his pet prince in their midst.

Not too startled, surely, because janissaries had been dispatched a half hour ago. A group of uniformed, armored men with crested helms, shiny and out of place in the midst of the blacksmith's yard. Two tents had been set up, open-sided, and a moveable forge assembled in a patch of trampled grass. A few horses on pickets, waiting to be shod, shifted nervously a short distance away, snorting. They could smell fear, just as Val could, as they entered the yard and saw the rapists.

There were four of them. Two blacksmith apprentices, and two of their friends. Sturdy, thickset men in their twenties. Strong, heavily muscled from physical labor.

Four against one. Brutes against a delicate boy.

One sported a swelling eye – Arslan had admitted, haltingly, that he'd kicked one of them as they tried to hold him down.

Val felt light-headed, and forced himself to take a deep breath. He'd ground to a halt, staring, fuming, aching inside.

Beside him, Mehmet said, "Well. This is your show. Run it how you see fit."

Val couldn't believe Mehmet had let him get this far, and now he was handing the reins over fully?

He turned his head and searched his lover's face.

Mehmet lifted his brows. "They need to be put down. They laid hands on something that belongs to their royalty. But this is your slave. This is your punishment to mete out, my dear."

He'd never punished anyone in his life.

He'd rarely ever raised his voice.

(Holding a knife to Mehmet's eye didn't count. Of that he was sure.)

Val took a deep breath and walked toward the accused. He didn't have to interrogate them – he could smell Arslan on them. But he found himself speaking anyway.

"The slave you raped," he said, voice surprisingly even. "Did you know who his master was?"

The men looked down at the ground; shuffled on their knees.

439

"I am *speaking to you. Look at me.* Did you know who his master was?"

They tipped their heads back, seeking his face with reluctance, shrinking down into their coat collars.

A crowd of onlookers began to gather, motion and murmurs at the edges of Val's awareness.

"Had you," Val continued, beginning to pace a tight line in front of them now, "seen him around camp? Fetching water? Carrying a letter for me? Did you notice his fine clothes, and the jewels around his neck? Did you think to yourselves, 'He must belong to a wealthy master? To a *prince*, even?'"

He turned a slow circle, hand on the pommel of his sword, and met the gazes of those around him. Faces full of shock, of worry, of anticipation.

He turned back to the captives. "A whole camp full of whores." A sweep of his arm to the gathering crowd, still growing, their whispers getting louder. "But no. The four of you decided to have a go at my personal slave. You took from me. From your sultan. What do you have to say for yourselves?"

Silence. Even from the crowd; Val could sense them straining to hear the answer.

The one with the injured eye finally licked his lips. "It – he – it wasn't rape, your grace. He wanted it."

Mehmet had dispatched janissaries right away, and in the time before a breathless messenger returned to tell them the criminals had been found, Val had eased Arslan's ruined clothes from his wrecked, trembling body and ordered a bath drawn. A pair of Mehmet's slaves had seen to him, and Val had bit his lip until he tasted blood, cataloguing the scratches, scrapes, and bruises on the boy's skin.

"He wanted it," he said in a flat voice, and the murmurs started up again, a ripple moving through the onlookers like a wave. "He wanted you. You fat, smelly louts. To take turns at him."

The other three had the grace to duck their heads once more.

The speaker shivered. "I – I – but he–"

Val pulled his sword and swung.

A chorus of low shouts from the spectators.

The blade caught the man in the side of the neck. It was a sharp, well-made weapon, and Val's swing had been powerful. But still – swords weren't made for taking off heads.

Blood spurted, splashing across the face of the man beside the speaker. The blow severed the spine, killed him instantly, but the head fell sideways, connected to the body by a stretch of muscle and skin.

Somewhere in the back of his mind, Val was screaming.

He swung again, and the head rolled across the grass.

He couldn't breathe.

"Your grace," one of the janissaries said. None of them had flinched. "If you'd like for one of us to–"

"No. Line them up. I'll do it."

His arms ached afterward. Blood on his blade, on his hands, on his clothes. He wet his lips and tasted it there, too, hot and salty. He could kneel down, in the puddle on the grass, and drink straight from the stumps of their headless necks.

He turned instead to face the crowd, and they shrank back, though their gazes stayed fixed on him, fascinated. "This" – he gestured with his sword – "is what happens when you touch something that doesn't belong to you! This is a lesson!" He turned his sword on them, aimed its bloody point at his audience. "Learn it well!"

It grew fuzzy after that. He walked away, and everyone let him go. He was aware of his legs and his lungs working, the weight of his sword in his hand.

He walked right out of camp, and no one stopped him. Into the trees, the shade and pine-scented cover of the forest, away from all the stink, and the flies, and the tightly-packed humanity. The gentle chuckle of a stream drew him, and when he reached it, he knelt on its bank, sword falling from numb fingers to a cushion of moss.

Val stared down into the clear water, its bed of smooth, brown rocks. His distorted, broken reflection stared back, just clear enough to make out the pattern of droplets and spatters on his face. Blood, gore, chunks that he didn't want to think about.

441

He leaned down and braced his hands on the moss, stuck his face in the water. It was shockingly cold, its source some deep underground spring, cool beneath the soil. It trickled past him, washing away the blood, the sweat, the tears.

Could I drown? he wondered. If he breathed in now, and let the water fill his lungs, could he die like this? It wouldn't be so bad. In the cool, and the dark. Alone.

Or would he pass out, and eventually expel the water, all his immortal powers pushing him toward life and health, like always?

He finally sat back on his heels with a gasp, water streaming down his face, his throat, onto his clothes. His hair stuck to his cheeks, and he reached to push it back, pausing when he saw the blood still on his hands, caked in under his nails.

The killing had happened so quickly – how had he gotten so thoroughly coated?

He washed his hands in the stream, doing the best he could without soap, scrubbing beneath the nails and between each finger.

He waited for his gorge to rise, but it didn't.

Waited for shakes that never came.

He felt…nothing.

When his hands were clean, he reached for his sword and washed it as well, using water and a clump of pulled-up moss. He noticed a nick along one edge: a place where bone had proven stronger than steel.

There was nothing to do for his clothes. He'd have to bathe and then burn them later.

Footsteps approached from behind, not trying to be stealthy. Mehmet.

"I'm impressed," he said as he drew up behind Val. His shadow fell across the creek, blotting out Val's reflection in the water.

Val's heart throbbed in his chest. One strong beat, where before it had felt like there was nothing. He was *aware* of the organ, suddenly. One painful contraction. Followed by another, and another, and another.

Mehmet walked closer, right up beside him, to the edge of the stream. "That sword will need to be seen to."

Val tilted it in his lap, so it caught the light.

"Is that the first time you've killed a man with your own two hands?"

"You know it is." His voice came out a gravelly scrape of sound, like the edge of a door grating across a floor.

"Hmm. You did well. Stronger than I expected, actually. And I'm surprised you got through all four without handing it off to one of the janissaries."

His heart pounded, and his skin prickled, and he thought of Arslan, his bruises and bloodied lip. Thought of himself at age ten, fingernails digging into the bark of a tree limb, trying to stay small and hidden. Thought of drool-damp silk against his mouth, hands digging into his hips, sharp burning pain in a place he'd never even touched himself before.

He turned his head so he looked up at Mehmet.

The sultan looked down at him with mild interest, brows raised. "Are you finished?"

Val climbed to his feet and sheathed his sword. The sun beat on his back as they walked back to the tent, until sweat trickled between his shoulder blades.

But chills rippled up and down his arms the whole way.

~*~

When Mehmet reached to touch him that night, Val refused, ducking and shrugging away. Mehmet glared at him, but left him be. He went, flanked by guards, into the torch-smudged night, and Val knew he would seek to spend his passion elsewhere – Val was glad of it.

He went to the small tent that abutted the royal one, the tiny, but private place he'd given to Arslan, and found his slave bundled up in blankets, sweet-smelling and clean and pampered as any prince.

Nestor sat on the edge of his makeshift bed; Val caught his sad, sympathetic expression before he whirled around to face him...only to relax when he saw who it was.

"Thank you, Nestor," Val said quietly, and the scribe took it for the dismissal it was, patting Arslan on the shoulder before taking his leave of them.

Val moved to take his place. Reached slowly to brush Arslan's shiny black hair off his forehead, tuck it behind his ears. The boy flinched, but looked up at Val, gaze trusting.

Fresh tears welled up in his eyes. "I'm sorry."

"No, no, hush that," Val murmured, stroking his face. "You have nothing to be sorry for."

Arslan closed his eyes, and the tears slid down his cheeks.

Val climbed up onto the pallet fully, and stretched out beside him. Arslan came unresisting when Val gathered him into his arms, bundled him in against his chest. Val himself was slender, but Arslan felt like a bundle of twigs, breakable and tiny. Tremors coursed through his body, and he pressed his tear-stained face into Val's throat.

"*I'm* sorry," Val whispered. "This should never have happened to you."

Mehmet's words came back to him, spoken on their walk back to camp earlier. *'I think you've made your point about people touching your things.'*

'He's not a thing. He's a boy.'

'He's only three years younger than you. And he's a slave. This is commonplace – it isn't as if he never expected to be fucked at least a time or two.'

Val's hands curled into fists, gripping Arslan's robe tight, and he forced himself to relax his hold. He stroked the boy's back instead, the fragile line of his spine through the silk.

"I promise you," he vowed, "that nothing like that will ever happen again. I won't let it."

Arslan whimpered and squirmed in closer, but he didn't say he believed Val. How could he?

~*~

The camp never truly slept – guards always patrolling, soldiers always staying up to drink, or find whores, or tell ghost stories by the firelight – but the aimless chatter of it became a discernable heartbeat about an hour before dawn. When people stirred with purpose, ready to begin the arduous process of breaking camp and moving on.

Val woke then, in the pitch black, all the candle stumps burned down. He could see. Somewhat. Arslan slept against him, body finally limp, no longer trembling, warm and still. He clung loosely to Val's clothes, face turned toward him, utterly trusting.

A trust he didn't deserve after he'd sent the boy off on his own, totally vulnerable.

Val pulled away from him slowly, careful not to wake him, and slipped next door into the sultan's lavish tent.

Mehmet was awake, and bore the look of a man who hadn't slept for very long, eyes shadowed, his hair mussed, a silk robe open over his naked chest. He sat at his war table, sipping something from a gold cup. His two preferred slaves bustled about behind him, making up a sleeping pallet that didn't look at all slept in, bundling clothes into trunks and pulling out fresh garments for the day ahead.

Val plucked an orange from a bowl on a side table and went to occupy his usual chair. No one else ever sat in it; it boasted the print of his own narrow backside, and no one else's, on the crushed velvet seat.

Mehmet acknowledged him with a low hum that was half a purr. He smelled like sex and male sweat.

Val peeled the orange in long, satisfying strips, enjoying the sharp scent of citrus. He very purposely didn't think of anything; his mind felt brittle and fragile as old glass this morning.

"How's your pet?" Mehmet asked.

Val popped an orange wedge into his mouth, bright burst of sunshine on his tongue. "It isn't like that."

"Of course it isn't like *that*. I wouldn't allow it," the sultan said, light and matter-of-fact. He sighed and lifted his head, finally, gaze that of an adult exhausted with a child's antics. "The boy will heal, Radu. Have one of mine braid your hair for you until he can attend you again. But right now we have to focus on bigger things."

"The war," Val said flatly.

Mehmet didn't seem to notice his tone, nodding and dropping his gaze back to his map. "We'll reach the fortress today. From there we'll…"

Val listened with half an ear as the sultan launched into his assault plans. He would need to know these things so he could relay them to Constantine. But thought of the emperor sent him off down another mental path.

He'd spent so long trying to convince Mehmet this was folly, if only to spare the people of Constantinople – and his friend, Constantine – the horrors of a protracted, impossible war. But perhaps he'd been going about this all wrong.

Perhaps he should have been helping Mehmet. If he could get to the city – not just as a projection, but as a flesh-and-blood person…

If he could earn enough trust to be sent beyond the walls, perhaps for the sake of a diplomatic mission…

Val set his orange aside, licked his fingers, and sat forward. "Might I make a suggestion?" he asked, reaching toward the map.

Mehmet's brows lifted. "Of course."

And as Val began to talk, the sultan smiled.

32

IMPOSSIBLE

Mehmet's suite of rooms at the Throat-Cutter – finished early, while the outer walls and towers were still being built – were sprawling and lavish. The building as a whole was a practical military installation, but Mehmet wanted to sleep in his usual style for their short stay here, before they marched down to Galata, and the inevitable skirmish that would take place across the Strait. Val had his own room, all to himself, save for the nights when Mehmet wanted his company – which was often. Still. It was as comfortable and lavish as the sultan's own quarters, and that was where Val headed now, Halil Pasha huffing and puffing to keep pace with his long legs.

"I thought," the furious Grand Vizier hissed, voice low though they were alone, "that I could at least depend on you to echo my reasoning. And here you are encouraging his delusions!"

Val halted and turned to face the man, surprised to see that, at some point in the last few years, he'd grown a good head taller than him. He had to look downward now to meet his gaze. "I'm sorry. Were you under the impression that you and I are allies in some way?"

The Grand Vizier bit his lip, visibly holding back a retort. He lowered his voice again; Val wouldn't have been able to hear it if not for vampiric hearing. "This siege is a fool's errand. It can't be done! And he'll die throwing himself against those walls. Then where will the Empire be? Who will take control? His sons are mere babes at the teat!"

Val shrugged.

"You're encouraging him!"

"On the contrary. I'm his favorite whore. I have no influence."

He fumed. "You have his ear—"

"I have his cock," Val corrected.

The Grand Vizier's face purpled with impressive speed. "You can't – can't just *say* that!"

"Why not?" Val shrugged. "It's the truth. I'm only trying to be honest."

The vizier stood up on his toes and thrust his face into Val's, flecks of spit landing on Val's cheeks as he spoke. A low, furious whisper, veins standing out along his temples. "You are an *abomination*. A filthy temptress with a cock swinging between your legs – and you're *not even human*. You've enchanted him, haven't you? Bent him to your sick perversions? You're a creature born of no god, and you'll drive him, and our whole empire, into ruin to satisfy your lust." Chest heaving when he was done, body vibrating with barely checked fury.

Val held his gaze, unblinking, until the man's ankles began to shake and he lowered back down, flat-footed on the stones. And then Val chased him, ducking low, hair swinging forward. He opened his mouth and activated that untouchable muscle in his jaw, that tiny flex, so that his fangs descended, long and proud, so they gleamed in the afternoon sunlight that spilled through the window, unmistakable.

"On the contrary." He let the growl come into his voice, a low purr that ribbed every word. "My father was born of a very particular god. And if you're so curious about what's between my legs, you could always ask to see it. Or grab a handful for yourself." He made an exaggerated lunge with his own hand, straight for the vizier's crotch.

The man jumped back with a yelp, and Val pushed out a laugh. "You're the one who sent that letter," Val reminded, as Halil Pasha whirled around and went charging back down the corridor. "You wrote to Emperor Constantine and told him to release Orhan! To send the Hungarians! To send all of them!" He chased him around the corner with another loud, braying laugh, and then he was gone.

Val snapped his jaw shut, retracted his fangs; the aftereffect of forced laughter tasted like bile on his tongue, and he swallowed it down.

He whirled and continued on his way.

Nestor and Arslan waited for him, as instructed, in his bedchamber. Arslan sat on a low stool, polishing Val's spare boots, but Nestor-Iskander sat uneasily on the trunk at the foot of the bed, and leaped to his feet when Val entered.

Arslan looked up with a small smile for Val, silently laughing at Nestor's nervousness.

"Sit down, sit down," Val said with a wave, and shut the door. He pressed his ear to it a moment, listening, but could detect nothing out in the hallway. "Arslan, stop working, come sit."

Both boys settled on the trunk and Val pulled out the bench at his dressing table and sat across from them. Energy coursed through him, and he wanted to pace – but he also didn't want to make them anxious. And he wanted to be looking at their faces, to really press his point home and judge their reluctance for himself.

"Alright, you two." Serious glance between them. "I trust this is a given. But. You know what I am, don't you? What I really am?"

Arslan's eyes got big, and he bit at his lip, but he nodded.

Nestor's eyes got even bigger. "Oh. Um. I. Your grace…"

"You've suspected, at least? Or there's been gossip?"

The Russian scribe blushed. "A little, your grace."

Arslan turned to him. "It's not like the stories," he said with uncharacteristic boldness. "He's not evil. He's not a demon." Almost scolding.

"I know that," Nestor huffed. But he looked at Val with uncertainty. "I know that you drink…I've seen it put into cups, and I…" He gulped.

Val chuckled in spite of himself. No one around here was frightened of him; this boy's nerves were refreshing, actually. "Here, look." He lifted his lip with his thumb and pushed his fangs out again.

Nestor startled.

Arslan snorted a quiet laugh.

Val dropped his hand. "Lots of creatures have fangs," he said primly. "Wolves, and bears, and foxes, and even bats. It's how they eat. Well…in my case. Drink."

Nestor swallowed with obvious difficulty. "But you eat food. I've seen you."

"Yes. I need both to survive. Arslan's right: it's not like in the stories." He held out his hand. "I'm real, I'm alive. I'm warm. I'm not the undead."

Nestor looked at his hand a long second before he took a breath and squared his shoulders, like he was preparing to go into battle.

"It's a good thing you told me about all your languages," Val said, "because you'd make a terrible soldier."

Nestor frowned, and reached to lay his hand over the back of Val's.

"See? Warm," Val said, and withdrew. "You should also know that your sultan is a vampire as well."

Nestor's brows jumped.

Arslan said, "He's not my sultan."

"Hush, you," Val said. "But, listen. The reason I speak of it now, is that I need to explain something to you. I need you to understand it because I'm going to get you both away from here."

They started to protest, together, and Val held up a hand. "No. I can handle this life. My future is already set here, but I won't have you two suffer similar fates. I can't..." He took a tight breath, and his gaze strayed to Arslan, memories of his bruises and his terror flooding back, painful. "Let me protect you," he said, softly, and Arslan looked away with guilt. "Let me, please."

And he told them of his dream-walking.

He explained it in limited terms, to protect them, should they ever be questioned about it – and to protect himself. He left out Constantine, and any specific destinations.

"In the chaos of the coming battle," he said, "I think I can get you both away. But I'll need your secrecy, and your cooperation."

Arslan nodded straight away, though his big gold lion's eyes brimmed with sadness. He'd grown attached, Val knew, just as he knew it would pain him to no longer see the boy's sweet face once he was gone. But he was determined now.

Nestor looked less convinced. He fidgeted, knocking his boots together at the ankles. "It sounds...forgive me, but it sounds impossible."

"So does everything, at first. For instance, I've just told you I can send my mind across continents."

A shaky breath. A nod. "What would happen to you? If the sultan knew you'd helped us escape?"

Val offered a smile. "You let me worry about that. There's nothing he can throw at me that I can't take."

~*~

Constantine picked his head up – he'd been sitting with his chin in his hand, gaze growing distant as a cardinal wheedled at him about the Schism yet again – and noticed Val standing at the back of the room. He nudged George Sphrantzes with his elbow and flapped a hand at the cardinal and his retinue. "That's enough, Paul. No more for now. Leave us."

The cardinal let out an aborted sound of frustration, a bitten-back protest he thought better of, and jerked to his feet. His retinue, all of the gilded church set, stood and together they trooped out of the room, surly-faced as a bunch of wet nurses with ill-tempered charges.

None of them noticed Val because he didn't allow them to.

Sphrantzes blew out a relieved breath when they were gone. "You should pop in more often," he told Val. "How about every time those pompous windbags show their faces?"

"I'd like nothing more, sir," Val said, gliding forward and projecting himself down into one of the vacated chairs, legs crossed at the knee so that the candlelight flashed off his polished boots. "But my own windbag keeps me busy, I'm afraid."

Sphrantzes snorted in disgust – disgust and solidarity. Val found that he appreciated it.

"We thank you for the interruption," Constantine said. "But I'm assuming you're here on business."

"Now, that stings," Val said, and meant it.

Constantine smiled, soft and chagrined. "I know. I'm sorry. I'm always glad for your company."

It shouldn't have warmed him – it was a pathetic thing, really, someone enjoying his presence, spectral though it may have

451

been. But, well, Val was a pathetic thing himself. So he smiled and was thankful.

"No, you're right. There's business to be discussed." Arslan was watching the door for him, but he didn't have any idea how long it would be before Mehmet came knocking. "I came to tell you that we've arrived at the fortress, and it's full speed ahead on the battle plans. Mehmet intends to conquer all the lands between here and the Bosporus, and likely will either capture the people there, or put them to the sword to send you a message." He was a little appalled by his matter-of-fact tone. He'd grown jaded with Mehmet's practices at this point.

Sphrantzes swore, but Constantine stroked his beard and took a measured breath.

"I have to, by all outward appearances, support the sultan."

"Of course."

"But I will help you when I can, coming here and giving you information."

Sphrantzes said, "Doesn't Mehmet know that sacking this city is impossible?"

Val felt a bitter smile touch his mouth. "*Impossible* is the theme of the day, don't you know?"

~*~

Val stood – or gave the impression that he did – beside the emperor on a dangerous little ledge that ran around the topmost dome of the St. Sophia cathedral; one of the highest points in all of Constantinople. Hands shading their eyes, for all the good it did Val, they could just make out the bustle of activity six miles away, across the deep-water inlet of the Golden Horn, up the rise toward the site of Mehmet's Throat-Cutter.

Below them, heat mirages shimmered in the narrow, twisting streets and alleys of the city, a deep-baked summer heat that Val could neither feel nor smell, but which he imagined. Back in his bedchamber, those six miles distant, doubtless his unconscious body sweated through his clothes.

"The walls have gone up quickly," Constantine said with deceptive mildness. He rested his hand on a thin metal railing, the breeze tugging at his curls, and the long lines of his royal tunic. He turned to Val. "How is this possible?"

I warned you, Val wanted to say. *I told you he could accomplish this.* Instead, he said, "The Ottoman Empire is vast, densely populated, and diverse. Mehmet pays well, and he punishes severely. His workers are motivated, and there are plenty of them."

Constantine wiped a hand down his face, and he looked exhausted. "Meanwhile, we've slowly bled dry. The religious divide is crippling us."

As was the city's economic downswing, one which seemed to be a lasting condition, and not a momentary trend.

"I've sent missives," Constantine said. "He's building that fortress on land that doesn't belong to him. This is a breach of our treaty."

"The treaty hangs by a thread," Val said, as gently as possible. "Threatening to turn Orhan loose again…"

Constantine groaned. "We underestimated Mehmet. When his father died, all of Europe rejoiced. Mehmet was young, and we'd all heard the stories that his head was turned by, well…" He trialed off, and Val looked away from his pointed glance.

Constantine had never come outright and asked Val about his relationship with the sultan. Val wasn't going to start offering that story up freely now.

"You thought," he said, "that the threat of Orhan's existence, him free to rally a force of his own and challenge for the throne, would distract Mehmet for a time. I'm telling you" – as he'd told him before – "that Mehmet thinks he's the second coming of Alexander. Nothing will keep him from attempting to take this city. Believe me, I've tried."

"I know, I know."

"He'll try to draw you out. He likes that – playing games. He'll do something to provoke you."

"I won't respond to it."

"You *can't*."

"Val," the emperor said. "Have you ever thought of…can you not slip away? At night? It's only that you're so close now."

He gestured toward the distant activity, a bustle like a disturbed ant hill. "If you could get away from Mehmet…"

Val shook his head. "No. No, that won't…no." A bare smile. "But I appreciate the sentiment."

~*~

The next morning, Mehmet's eyes had that glazed, feverish look to them after they'd looked at the map. A runner came to tell him about the latest fortress developments, and Nestor came to give a quiet word to Val about Arslan: he was up and nibbling on flatbread and honey for breakfast.

Val felt lighter. Comparatively. A faint nausea still tinged his belly, but that was normal by now; he wasn't sure what he'd do without that sensation, truth told.

"Have our horses saddled," Mehmet said to one of his slaves. "And gather our clothes. We're going riding."

"Riding where?" Val asked with raised brows.

"You'll see." He sounded far too pleased with himself.

An hour later saw them riding up to the tiny square of one of the little farming villages that lay between the Throat-Cutter and the outpost of Galata, just across the straight from Constantinople. Ottoman soldiers lined both cross streets – no more than dirt footpaths – that met at the square, and at the center, a huddle of village men, farmers in roughspun with falling-apart shoes. They ranged in age from barely ten, to barely alive, white-haired and stooped. Val thought it might be the entirety of the village's male population.

He reined his horse up and turned a dark look toward Mehmet. "What is this?"

Mehmet smiled at him. "A bit of sport. Come, Radu." He slid out of the saddle and tossed his reins to the soldier who'd stepped up to hold the stallion's bridle.

Val's chestnut mare fidgeted beneath him, and he laid a quelling hand on her neck.

"Radu," Mehmet called over his shoulder, sing-song – he never liked to shout or scowl at him in front of witnesses.

With a bitten back groan, Val dismounted and handed his reins off; followed the sultan the short distance to the knot of men.

Mehmet's janissary guards fell in around the two of them as a physical barrier – not that any of the villagers seemed wont to launch an attack. They all cowered, big-eyed, shaking, fathers held the shoulders of young sons, keeping them tucked in tight against their bodies, as if they could spare them. Most were rough-featured, but a few of the teenagers bore softer profiles, almost pretty under the dirt of farm work.

Val's breakfast curdled in his stomach.

Mehmet stepped forward, janissaries clearing a path with gauntleted hands and upheld spears. He leaned in to expect the most beautiful of the boys, the one with a cap of tight black curls and big amber eyes. He was maybe fourteen or fifteen, with an elfin face and thin, shaking shoulders.

Mehmet smiled to himself. "Yes, this one."

Two soldiers reached in and seized the boy by the arms.

"No!" A man – his father; he had the same eyes – shouted, trying to shove forward through the crowd. His friends held him back, though he clawed and scrabbled to get loose. "No! Please! He's my only son!" Tears shone in his eyes.

"You're spirited," Mehmet told him. He jerked his head to another pair of soldiers. "He'll make a good slave. Put him in irons."

"No!"

The boy began to cry as he was led away, and a clanking set of chains and cuffs was hauled from a saddlebag for his father.

"That one," Mehmet said, pointing out another boy, who was grabbed and pulled from another pleading father. He turned to Val. "I'll give you your pick, Radu. Any of the rest to replace your boy who was damaged."

Val clenched his hands until his nails bit into his palms. "No. Arslan is all I need."

Mehmet shrugged. "Suit yourself." And went back to his sorting.

Three other young ones joined the first two, and the able-bodied fathers and husbands were shackled and smacked into submission with spear butts.

Val was just starting to wonder where the women were hiding when the door of a homely little cottage flew wide, and a plump woman in a white apron came flying out, skirt flaring all around her, face red and wet with tears.

"No!" she cried. "No, my baby—"

A soldier tripped her with the end of a spear, and she collapsed in a pitiful sprawl, sobbing.

Mehmet turned to the captain of his janissary guard. "Take these back. Keep the men chained. The boys will be castrated. Kill the rest here."

Val rode ahead, grinding his teeth together, body drawn so tight he ached. His mare danced beneath him, and though he patted her, he couldn't calm himself.

Mehmet caught up to him, probably much to the relief of the two guards who'd felt the need to flank Val, wide-eyed and worried; having their noble charges split up left them on-edge.

"Do you like any of them?" Mehmet asked when he'd reined in close beside Val, tone unworried, and conversational. "I'll share them with you, if you like."

Val tossed him a look, not daring to speak for fear of what he'd say.

Mehmet shrugged, the movement exaggerated thanks to the quick pace of his horse. "I can be generous."

Val faced forward, and said nothing.

Back at camp, he waited until he'd taken his evening meal, and blood, and refused a second invitation to join the sultan in sampling his fresh prizes. When he was alone, he posted Arslan as watch, and went dream-walking into the city.

Emperor Constantine stared morosely into a cup of wine.

Val approached his chair slowly, the only sound the crackle of the fire; the flames provided the only light, leaping long across the floor, bathing Constantine's feet, and the Turkish rug, and casting strange shadows. Still, the emperor didn't startle when Val said, "Where's George?"

456

Constantine heaved a hard sigh and drained his cup. "George is with his wife and children. I sent him away. He was fretting over me."

"Oh." Val hesitated. "Should I go?"

"No." He lifted his head, finally, and offered a tired smile. "I would be grateful of your company."

Val moved to sit on the edge of the table, near the emperor's elbow. "You've heard about what happened today, I take it."

"You did say that he would try to provoke me."

"He wants to draw you out into battle. Beyond the safety of the walls." He pressed a warning into his words.

Constantine shook his head. "That sort of blustering is a young man's folly." Another smile, this one miserable. "I don't know if we can hold out against him forever. I won't pretend such confidence. But he'll have to come over or through these walls to take Constantinople from me. This I promise."

"Good." Val knew a moment's fleeting relief. At this point, he would take such small boons as favors.

32

THAT WAS WINTER

The city of Constantinople occupied a triangular jut of land shaped like a horn, flanked at its very tip, and its northern and southern sides by water. To the north: the Golden Horn, a deep-water inlet where the Roman fleet was docked, fed by the Bosporus Strait. And to the south: the Sea of Marmara. A Mediterranean city, with a coastal clime, but a blended one. In the year 324, the Roman Emperor Constantine the Great established himself there, in what was then Byzantium, renaming the city after himself and declaring it the new capital. A Greek city made Roman, it became the heart of western culture, politics, and religion. It served as the seat of the Greek Orthodox church, and it housed the remnants of the Library at Alexandria. A gilded, thriving city, bursting beauty from every crevice, teeming with life, and language. The soaring grandiosity of St. Sophia inspired the entire nation of Russia to adopt Greek Orthodoxy as its official religion. Just one of the legacies left by what had once been the richest city in the world.

But none of this was the city's true claim to fame. No, that honor belonged to its sheer impregnability, to Constantinople's Theodosian Walls.

An ingeniously designed double layer of protection, with a moat, a low wall, then an outer wall, a terrace, and a soaring inner wall, the barrier had protected the city from all but one landside attack, that of the Fourth Crusaders in 1204. On the sea side, the walls went straight up, and up, and up, and there was no design of man that could scale them, topple them, or break through them.

Val rode near the head of the endless columns of armored soldiers. When he twisted around in his saddle, he was nearly blinded by the glint of sunlight off the metal of helms, and breastplates, and spear-tips. The army *breathed*; a regular rhythm of clinking mail, and stomping footfalls, and creaking saddles. The column stretched back, regular, disciplined. *Impossible.* That word came to him again. Yes, the idea of sacking Constantinople was impossible – but so was Mehmet's army.

Val turned away, his heartbeat quick and shallow, and as they rounded the next bend in the road, waves thrashing along the coastline just beyond this strip of forest, the trees parted in front of him, and he had his first glimpse of the sea walls.

A cheer went up amongst the men.

Val swallowed…and swallowed and swallowed, trying to contain his tripping pulse.

In his mind, he'd imagined the army falling on a quaking city, one crouched at the shore, half-swallowed by waves. But here now, seeing it in person, Constantinople towered. Pennants thin as threads from this distance snapped along the high, crenelated walls; the waves barely skimmed the rocks upon which they stood, proud and mocking, daring weak mortals to take a run at her.

Val let out a breath and thought, *he'll fail. He has to.*

Beside him, Mehmet's heart beat like a drum, excitement dancing around him like sparks. "Don't worry," he said, puffing out his chest, misreading Val's anxiety. "The battle won't last long. And then we'll be on top of those walls. I'll hand-feed you dates and fuck you sweet in a room that overlooks the sea."

"Poetic," Val said dryly. His stomach lurched.

"Hmm," Mehmet hummed in agreement. When Val glanced over, the sultan's gaze was pinned to their view of the wall, his look faraway – dreamy. "This will be my triumph, Radu," he murmured.

Val swallowed again, and kept on, and on.

~*~

They had wintered in Edirne. Once Mehmet was satisfied with the progress of his fortress, they'd decamped back to the capital last year, to spend the cold months in the palace, warming themselves in front of coal braziers and enjoying all the comforts of royalty.

Mehmet saw to his wives, and entertained the dignitaries visiting from the east. Held lavish feasts where the wine flowed freely, enough to intoxicate even a vampire.

459

Val trained. He stripped down to the waist and threw himself at jousting dummies and any opponent who would have him, skin steaming, hands numb around the grip of his sword from the cold. He took his mare galloping, bareback, holding himself to her with the strength of his thighs and his core muscles. He weighted the ends of poles with water buckets, and carried them across his shoulders; ran along the palace walls, enjoying the burn in his lungs and his legs. He was still lean, but he bore a sleek suit of clear-cut muscle now, strong and sculpted.

He started to feel like a man that winter – the man he would need to be to turn the tide of war when spring came.

And it was also the winter in which he first noticed that something wasn't quite right with Mehmet.

Arslan had come to fetch him from the communal baths – up to his ears in the steaming water, all his muscles unknotting, not caring that some of the high Ottoman officials kept shooting him badly disguised appreciative looks. He was beautiful; let them stare. Warm and pleasantly loose-limbed from the heat, wrapped in a silk robe and a fur, he followed his slave back to Mehmet's suite, humming quietly to himself, a hint of desire stirring low in his belly. He'd long since stopped berating himself for his arousal.

In the sultan's antechamber, slaves were clearing away the remnants of a meal and tidying the sideboard and its array of gold and silver decanters. Val handed his fur off to one of them and proceeded into the sitting room, where more slaves were lighting candles, past the crackling fire and on into the bedchamber, where the space was warmed by the glow of candles and the heat of two coal braziers.

Mehmet sat on the edge of his bed, hands on his knees, rubbing at them and wincing to himself.

Val slouched into view with an affected step, canting his hips at an angle he knew emphasized the narrowness of his waist. "Here I was coming to scold you for having me pulled out of the bath, but it appears you're the one who needs a good soak. What's wrong with your knees?"

"Nothing." Mehmet sat upright, but not without obvious effort, a note of strain in his voice. "It's only the cold air. Makes my joints ache."

460

"It's gout," Val said, matter-of-fact, and went to pour a cup of wine.

"What? Impossible."

Val took a measured sip as he turned back to the bed, and moved to stand just beyond the sultan's reach. He cast a glance toward the slaves – the last of which lit the final taper and saw himself out of the room with a bow, pulling the door shut after him – and then back to his master. Gaze narrowing, studying. Mehmet still looked young, was still strong, still bore a look of robust health.

But he was…fleshier, than he had been. A little softness along his jaw, and around his waist.

"Gout," he said, again, pronunciation crisp. "It's a malady that affects the joints of–"

"I know what it is," Mehmet snapped, color blooming in his cheeks. He left off rubbing his knees, though his brows stayed pinched together. "I meant it isn't possible that I have it. Not after I was…turned." The last he merely breathed, a whisper. Still a superstitious human, despite his powers.

"Hmm," Val murmured. "And the cold shouldn't bother you either." Inwardly, his thoughts raced. Mehmet was right; this *was* impossible. But Father had always said Romulus couldn't turn a person properly. Val had never understood what that meant, but he thought that was what he saw now. That wrongness. "Did you know that my uncle has never had a proper heir?"

"What?" He frowned, and touched his own chest. "No, that's why–"

"Excluding you, of course. You're his heir *now*. But my uncle is very old, you know. *Very* old. I wonder why he never had an heir before now. Do you wonder, too?"

"No." His frown deepened to a scowl. "Give me that." He reached for the wine.

Val took one last sip before handing it over. "I just think it's interesting, is all. We have no way of knowing how potent Uncle's blood is – whether it would prevent against normal human sicknesses."

Mehmet downed the wine in a few long swallows, breathless afterward, hand shaking as he set the cup aside on the bedside table. "Enough chattering," he decreed. "People have been talking at me all day, and I don't need it from you, too."

"Of course, Your Majesty," Val said, and Mehmet didn't seem to notice his mocking tone.

He patted one thigh. "Come here, I'm afraid you'll have to do most of the work tonight."

"Don't I always?"

And Val tucked all his questions about Romulus's blood, and Mehmet's health, away in a safe place in his mind, where he could ruminate over them properly later.

~*~

It should have been a restful winter…but it wasn't.

The sultan didn't know how to rest.

Near the end of November, Mehmet dragged Val from bed one morning and told him to dress for riding.

Val loved riding, but the command chafed at him, as did the earliness of the hour. "There's frost on the ground outside," he complained, peering through the window at the dawn-silvered morning.

"It won't be there by the time you get your ridiculous hair braided. Come on."

They dressed warmly, and rode with a full honor guard to Didimotkon, not far from Edirne. They sat astride their horses in the square, waiting, and finally a bedraggled group of men in chains was led out for the sultan's inspection. One was younger than the others, his features fine even beneath a layer of sweat and dirt, and Val watched Mehmet's gaze settle on him a long moment. Too long.

"Your Majesty," the captain of the local guard said, and bowed deeply to the sultan. "I present to you the blockade runner, and criminal, Antonio Rizzo, and his crew."

Val tensed, and his mare shifted beneath him uneasily. He'd heard Mehmet give orders to the skeleton crew they'd left at the Throat-Cutter, to set up a blockade at the head of the strait, and toll every Latin merchant who attempted to pass through. This man, Rizzo, head held high despite the iron collar around his neck, had attempted to outrun the sultan's ships, and avoid the toll. Doubtless he was one of the few brave ones attempting to take grain into Constantinople. Last he'd visited Constantine, the emperor had been massaging his temples, stressed, fearing a famine in his city.

Mehmet swung down out of his saddle, and two janissaries fell in beside him, spears raised and ready. He ignored them, and passed down the line of captives, inspecting each one. He stood longest before the boy; twitched a smile and reached with a jeweled hand to chuck the boy under the chin.

"The captain's clerk, Your Majesty," the captain of the guard said.

Mehmet motioned over his shoulder, and more janissaries stepped forward. The boy was unhooked from the others, and led toward one of the spare horses they'd brought. He would be cut and go to the seraglio, same as all the boy captives Mehmet took a fancy to.

Then Mehmet paced back to the captain, Rizzo. The man stared him in the eye.

"Bold," Mehmet told him.

The captain spoke with a raspy voice, his throat doubtless dry. "I figure I'm already good as dead. Boldness won't hurt me now," he said in Latin.

Mehmet grinned. "No, no, you're right." He stepped back, and nodded to the guard captain. "Kill his men. Make an example of the good captain here."

Later, as they rode out of the city, the clerk in tow, Val twisted around in his saddle to look back. He didn't want to, but he felt compelled to do so; to show some sign of respect to the man who'd defied the sultan.

Antonio Rizzo had been impaled on a long wooden spike, and mounted on the walls. Still alive – sunlight glimmered off the blood that dripped down the spike – but the crows waited, already cawing in anticipation.

"Go with God," Val murmured, and faced forward again.

~*~

Val woke most nights, in the small hours, to the sound of feverish mumbling, and wandered out into the antechamber to find Mehmet poring over a map, or a scroll, or some dusty old book, eyes glassy, hands trembling, a cup of wine at hand.

The first few times, Val tried to tow him back to bed, but Mehmet bared his teeth, and growled, and swatted him away.

"How can you rule an empire if you don't get some sleep?" Val tried to reason.

Mehmet shook his head, and his attention went back to his scroll, woeful. "I'm having dreams. Dreams where I'm Alexander...I want to make him proud, Radu..."

Some nights he sketched; designs for walls, for armor, for weapons, all frustratingly fantastic, none of them able to be made by his architects or weaponsmiths. He sketched what he remembered of Constantinople's walls and battlements, with shocking accuracy. Val felt a jolt when he looked on them, at the precise lines of ink, neatly labeled.

"This is my life's work, taking this city," he murmured, like a mantra. "My life's work." Then he tipped his head back, gaze both beseeching, and unseeing. Lost in his own fantasies. "Do you think my people recognize the kind of achievement this will be?" he asked Val, and clutched at the edge of his robe.

Val reached to gently, but firmly, dislodge his fingers. "I guess you won't know until it's done, will you?"

Mehmet blinked at him a moment. He didn't smell of wine, and hadn't been drinking, but he looked intoxicated. Then he sat upright with a jerk, and awareness returned to his gaze. He fumbled across the desk, and its wealth of half-open scrolls.

"Wait," he said, "wait, wait, wait..."

"Yes, I'm waiting."

His hand closed over a particular scroll with a small shout of triumph. "I've been reading about the emperor Nero."

"Dangerous topic," Val said mildly.

"Did you know," Mehmet pressed on, heedless of the jibe, "that Nero dressed as a commoner and went out amongst the Romans? He asked them about their emperor, to see what they said of him?"

"I thought Alexander was your hero, and he was Greek, dear."

"But *I* am Roman." Frantic, spray of spittle. "My sire is Roman, and I am the heir to the empire, and I–"

"Yes, yes," Val said. "Where is this going?"

Mehmet grabbed his robe again, knuckles white. "I want to do that. To disguise myself and go out among my people."

"That's...a terrible idea."

"No, listen–"

"It was a terrible idea when Nero did it, too. What will you do if you find out they loathe you? Or if they recognize you?"

Mehmet didn't answer, turning away. "You shall come too."

"I don't remember asking to come."

"Too bad."

It was too late then, too close to dawn, and Val hoped Mehmet would forget it, but of course, he didn't. The next night, he was presented with rough-spun, dirt-smeared clothes, a cloak with a hood, and dark paint for his face.

"Really?" Val asked, pinching the cloak between thumb and forefinger. It *smelled*.

"Put it on," Mehmet ordered, his own face unrecognizable. "We're leaving."

They went without an escort of the usual honor guards and janissaries, just two men, cloaked, dirt-streaked and unremarkable, shoulders intentionally stooped. Val wasn't proud of the fact that he held to Mehmet's elbow, his heart fluttering like a trapped bird in his chest. They were the most dangerous creatures on the streets of Edirne that night, but it didn't feel like it. Without the safety of palace walls, and guards, and the deference of bowing slaves and court members alike, the city felt like a jungle, beasts round every corner.

One night they came across a group of stumbling, drunken youths, and Mehmet had whispered, "Let's hunt."

"No."

But he'd put his arms around the young man Mehmet shoved toward him, warm, and sweaty, and his pulse so, so tempting, and he'd sunk his fangs into his neck. Live blood, intoxicating, dizzying. Mehmet had pulled him in a night-black alley behind a shop, after, and fucked him up against a wall, a handful of cooling blood used to ease the way.

Val woke the next morning with a pounding head, and couldn't eat any food, sick to his stomach over what he'd done. He was the puppet of a monster, but he couldn't allow himself to become one as well.

He tried to refuse, after that, but there was always some threat, some elegantly-dropped hint about his brother. And so Val went, and he hated it, and one night Mehmet was recognized, and the sultan stabbed the man to death right there in the street, so that word would not get out.

"Have you learned anything?" Val asked, tone cutting, as he pushed back his hood and went to wash his face at the basin by the window. They were back in the palace now, in the royal apartments, and he wanted the scent of the street off of himself. "Is this little experiment finally over?"

Mehmet didn't seem to hear the disdain in his voice. He sank down on the edge of the bed, gaze fixed on the middle distance. "They are…not in agreement."

"About you?" Val snorted and wiped his face with a length of toweling. "Did you expect them to be? A ruled people are never in agreement about their ruler." Except for the fact that most of them *hated* that ruler; they just disagreed on the reasons why.

"They want me to take Rum. Some of them do. It will be a victory for not just me, but our entire people. But…" He shook his head. "They think me a heretic." He blinked and his gaze focused, lifted to Val. "They know that we are lovers, Radu."

Val bit back his kneejerk response – it would only get him slapped. He said, "It's not as if you're subtle about it, dear." He gestured to the room around them. "We're together nearly every night. I'm by your side always. And," he dared to say, "you keep collecting young boys and stashing them with your harem. What did you *want* people to think?"

"It's none of their business."

"You're their sultan. Everything you do is their business."

Mehmet growled quietly, and glanced away.

Val dampened a cloth and went to stand in front of him. Took his chin in-hand and began to wipe the dirt from his face.

"Did you think they'd call you Alexander?" he asked. "You're only a hero in your own mind, Mehmet."

The sultan reached up, a sudden burst of speed, and caught Val's wrist. He turned a glowing, furious look up at him. "That's a bold thing for you to say."

"Hmm, yes. Shall you impale me? As you did Captain Rizzo?"

Mehmet struck out, a vicious slap aimed for Val's face.

But now it was Val's turn to catch his wrist, to hold him off. His heart beat wildly in his chest, frightened by his own daring, but he kept his face smooth, his voice serene. "If you want your people to think of you differently, perhaps you should behave differently."

They held a moment, tense; Val's pulse beat in his ears as if someone was knocking on the bedchamber door.

And then Mehmet released him, and a smile broke across his face, and Val's knees went weak with relief.

"You're always honest with me, aren't you, Radu?"

"I make every effort to be, yes." Val resumed cleaning the sultan's face, and he allowed it this time.

Mehmet sighed. "No one else is."

"Then it's a good thing you have me, then."

"Yes. A very good thing."

~*~

Val rose before dawn the next morning, left the sultan snoring, dressed simply, and went out for a walk in the gardens.

A sharply cold, but still morning, all the garden's delights rimed with hoary white frost. Steam issue from the rooftop vents in the bath houses, and from the seraglio; bright crystal stalactites dripped off the spouts and edges of frozen fountains, water chiming lightly as it began to thaw and trickle, gleaming as the first pale light washed across the palace grounds.

Val could enjoy none of its beauty. Though pulsing with energy, healthy and strong from last night's feast of live blood, sickness and shame weighed heavy in his belly. He'd killed a man last night; an innocent commoner. Did he have a family?

Children? His blood gave Val strength, an indulgence taken by a spoiled, rich prince. That's what he was, wasn't he? Even if he wore a choking silver collar of ownership, even if his fate was not his own, he was still a pampered royal pet.

Lost in the troubling reflection of his own culpability in Mehmet's overused power, he nearly tripped over the neat little figure sitting on a curved iron bench along the path.

He pulled up short, embarrassed by his own startlement, and glanced down to find a plump, gray-bearded man smoking a hookah pipe, expression serene.

The man wore a costly, richly-embroidered kaftan of purple silk with ivory buttons, peacocks stitched along the hem. White şalvar, and gold slippers, and a snowy turban set with a jeweled peacock brooch above his round, sun-lined, pleasant face.

"Good morning," he said.

Val glanced at the man's hookah, and noted, absurdly, that someone must have carried it out here for him, because it looked too heavy for its owner. "Good morning," he echoed, and started to move on.

But the man said, "You look tired, child."

He couldn't have; he didn't *feel* tired — not in a physical sense. But he could feel the tightness in his own jaw, and wondered how haunted his eyes looked.

"You wouldn't be interested in sitting for a spell and keeping an old man company, would you?" The man smiled, revealing small, tobacco-stained teeth, surprisingly intact for a mortal of his advanced years.

"I…" Val started to refuse, but couldn't. In all his years at court, no one had ever invited him to do anything. No one save Mehmet, and that was never really an offer. Everyone knew who he was, and *what* he was to their sultan, and they shunned him on principle. "Why not," he said, voice flat to his own ears, and sat down on the bench.

The man smiled around the stem of his pipe, and hummed a pleased note as he puffed. "Isn't the frost lovely? And once it melts, I think we'll have a fine, clear day ahead of us."

Val made a quiet, agreeing sound. He didn't know what this was, or what this man might want.

"Spring will be here soon," he said, "and then I suppose the sultan will march for Constantinople."

"I suppose," Val said.

"You will accompany him, I should think?"

Val's skin prickled beneath his clothes. "I accompany the sultan always."

"The two of you share an admirable closeness."

Val turned to look at him, frowning. "Envious?" he asked, levering venom into the word.

The man chuckled, unperturbed, staring at the frozen fountain in front of them. "Oh, no. I have friends aplenty."

Val snorted.

"But I admit that this isn't my first morning sitting out here in the cold. I've been trying to catch an audience with you, Prince Radu." His gaze slid over, then, sharp as steel, intensely clever, but not unfriendly.

Val's stomach rolled, though. Here was the proposition. He couldn't think of anything bolder than a man making a pass at something that belonged to the sultan. "Why?" he asked through his teeth.

"Why do you think I might wish to speak with you?"

Val lifted his lip, a silent snarl, the pressure of a true growl building in his throat.

"Not *that*, dear boy. Lower your hackles."

Val felt his face go blank with shock.

The man turned away, and puffed on his pipe. In perfect Romanian, he said, "My servant is waiting on the other side of the hedge behind us. He'll guard us, but still, I'm sure we don't have much time. I'll speak plainly. They don't dare say it, but there are a number of those at court who dislike the sultan's plan to lay siege to Constantinople."

Another shock: just the boldness that had led this man to say such a thing out loud. "Halil Pasha, I should say," Val said, voice faint with a mounting anxiety.

The man nodded. "Oh, yes, the Grand Vizier hates this plan. But there are others, too. The Grand Vizier's friends. Me, for instance."

Val let out a short, sharp breath, steam pluming. "Who *are* you?"

"That's not important," the man said with a wave. "What's important is that you know there are those of us who – if we were able – would argue against this war. And" – his gaze returned, full of unexpected sympathy – "who regret the things that have happened to you, Radu."

Val sat perfectly still a moment, unable to breathe.

"I fear," the man said, glancing away, mercifully, when Val began to shake, "that the problem with monarchs is that they can't be checked. Whatever his breeding, whichever god he prays to – a king is a king, his word is law, and we all serve at his pleasure. Even when those pleasures are cruel...and unrequited."

Val finally managed to suck in a ragged breath. The words, the simple truth of them, spoken to him by a man who was obviously of some import among the Ottoman court, landed like physical blows. His chest ached. "Why are you telling me this?" he asked the ground between his boots, vision swimming.

"Oh. Well. I'm a doddering old fool who likes to hear myself talk." He chuckled. "Usually I inflict my little speeches upon my sons and grandsons, but they are otherwise occupied this morning. Just a doddering old fool...who is an Ottoman Turk first. And a subject of Sultan Mehmet second."

Val lifted his head so fast it left him dizzy, and he gripped the edge of the bench to keep from falling.

But the man's face gave nothing away. "We are, by nature, a temperate and godly people. We love our families; we pray faithfully. But we obey our sultan."

A human stepped around the hedge, and Val tensed – but it was only the man's servant, who bent to pick up the hookah.

The richly dressed man stood with a groan and obvious effort, his knees and spine cracking in the cold morning. He turned to Val, and smiled, eyes glittering with things unsaid, gaze wily as a fox's. "May God keep the sultan safe on his travels to Constantinople. May he guide his sword, and raise him up victorious." He gave a short bow, and said, in an entirely different tone, "I will pray for you, Prince Radu." A whisper: "Good luck." And he winked, and turned away.

Val sat for a very long time, shaking, as the sun warmed the garden, and thawed the fountain, contemplating the vastness that lay between tyrants and the peoples they ruled.

~*~

Mehmet spent his winter dreaming of a siege, but not everyone in his court thought this was a good idea.

"What do you think of Halil Pasha?" Mehmet asked one night, apropos of nothing.

Val marked his place in his book with a finger, and lifted his head. It was a bitter night, wind and stinging rain lashing at the walls beyond the antechamber, and Val sat curled up beneath a heap of furs, reading by candlelight. Mehmet was at his sketches again, murmuring almost constantly under his breath. Val had been waiting for a question, but not this one.

"Halil was a loyal Grand Vizier to your father," he said. "And now to you."

Mehmet sent him an unimpressed look. "You think he undermines me."

"I think he does so because he genuinely cares about you, your family, and the empire at large. Not because he's a rat bastard – though no one would love to call him that more than me."

Mehmet shook his head, but a smile tipped up the corners of his mouth. "Go and fetch the guards," he told the slave currently refilling the brazier. "Tell them they're to bring Halil Pasha to me here, now."

"Really?" Val asked when the boy had scampered off to follow orders. "Right now?"

"Why not now? Everyone always knows just which sweet lies to tell during the middle of the day. It's after bedtime that you find out what someone really thinks."

The guards took longer than Val expected. Mehmet had gotten to his feet and was pacing the length of the room when they finally arrived, a trembling Grand Vizier between them.

Halil carried a large golden salver, heaped with coins that gleamed in the candlelight, the tray rattling as he shook. He set it on the table, careful not to impede on any of the maps and scrolls there, and then got down on his knees and prostrated before Mehmet.

"Good evening, Your Majesty," he said, and his voice shook, too.

Mehmet looked at the guards, at Val, at the man splayed out before him on the floor tiles, lip curling. "What is this?"

"For-forgive me, Your Majesty," Halil said to the floor, "but it is customary when a noble is summoned before his master at an unusual hour that he not arrive empty-handed. I have brought you—"

"Sit up," Mehmet ordered, and the Vizier did so, his lip trembling, his face bloodless with fear. "Do you think I don't have gold aplenty?"

"I – I – I—"

Mehmet tucked his hands together behind his back and continued pacing. "Tell me, Grand Vizier. What do you think of my plan to take Constantinople?"

Halil gaped at him. Then he turned to Val.

"Mind your sultan," Val snapped.

Mehmet turned around, grinning. "Yes, Halil, mind your sultan. Well? What do you think?"

"Your Majesty—"

"Answer the question!"

"I think it's reckless," the man said in a rush, gulping air. "Ambitious, yes, because no one save crusaders have ever accomplished such a thing. But it is dangerous, and yes, it is reckless." He swallowed, and tears stood in his eyes. "Would you throw all of your army at it, even if they died and failed?"

"Yes," Mehmet said, without hesitation. "This isn't about an army, Halil. It's about our future. As Ottomans. As leaders of the world."

Halil bowed his head.

"My father," Mehmet continued, "was a great man. But a weak one, ultimately. He got tired – of war, of having to choose what was most important. I know no such fatigue. The most important thing in the world is to take Rum. That's what a leader must do: choose what is most important. Would you argue against me?"

"I…no, Your Majesty."

"Will you refuse to serve as Grand Vizier if I continue to plan the siege on Byzantium?"

"No, Your Majesty. I am loyal to you always, in all things."

Mehmet's smile was tight, and toothless. He turned to Val. "Do you hear that, Radu? In all things Halil is loyal to me."

When Halil glanced toward Val, quickly, touched with revulsion, Mehmet stepped in close to him and snapped his fingers, drawing his attention.

"Loyal to me," he repeated, voice low, and silky. Val knew that tone well, and it sent goosebumps rippling down his arms. "And I am the sultan; you obey *me*, and Radu is none of your concern. Yes?"

Halil swallowed. "Yes, Your Majesty."

Mehmet turned and walked back to the table. Reached with deliberate slowness out to the salver, and picked up a handful of gleaming coins. Then he spun and threw them at his Grand Vizier.

Halil scrambled to shield his head with his arms, crying out in alarm. But most of the coins clattered harmlessly across the floor. A few tipped up on their sides, and rolled until they hit the wall.

"I don't want your gifts," Mehmet said. "I want the city. Will you help me take it? Or will you keep gossiping about me?"

Halil lowered his arms slowly, wobbling where he knelt, tongue flicking over dry lips. He swallowed, and made a visible effort to gather himself. "I will help you take it, Your Majesty."

Mehmet nodded, and motioned to the guards, who stepped forward. "Take him away, I'm tired of him."

Halil moved as if to prostrate again, then thought better of it, and let the guards escort him out.

When they were alone, Mehmet turned to Val, hand resting on the tabletop. "He's been wanting to broker a peace treaty with the Romans, you know."

"I've been in your presence when he's urged it," Val said. He didn't say that Halil Pasha had come to him on more than one occasion now, begging Val to help him sway the sultan. "He's not a young man anymore. And war is expensive, and stressful, and gets people killed."

"War is progress," Mehmet countered. "You have to conquer people before you can shape them into what you want."

Val held his gaze, and his hands tightened into fists in his lap. He thought of the taste of salt tears, and the roughness of tree bark under small fingers. Thought of a young sultan's face tipped back, bathed in early light, eyes shining like a panther's.

"Yes," he said mildly, and his face felt stiff. "I suppose conquering really is the only way."

Whatever Val's expression was doing, Mehmet turned away from it with a smile, humming softly under his breath, pleased.

The problem with his plan, Val thought, but didn't say, was that sometimes people didn't *stay* conquered.

~*~

Val could see the effects of the wind that tunneled down the aisle, blown in through the open doors of St. Sophia as the cardinals led their overwrought procession toward the altar. The Romans around him pulled their cloaks in tighter around hunched shoulders; breathed warm air into their cupped hands. A child wiped his running nose on his sleeve, and an old woman's teeth chattered. Val couldn't feel the cold, though, nor smell the incense, nor the beeswax candles, nor the press of bodies, all those overlapping human scents.

Beside him, Constantine managed to whisper without moving his lips too noticeably. "I imagine it must be bittersweet to sit through a service like this."

"More like unfamiliar," Val whispered back. He'd shielded himself from the view of anyone besides the emperor, but he enjoyed the little thrill of feeling like a little boy sharing secrets in church. "I was brought up Orthodox. I've never sat through a Catholic service before."

"Really? But your father…the Order of the Dragon…that's a Catholic institution, is it not? They're crusaders."

"I have no idea what sort of institution it is. All very hush-hush. Father never talked about it with us. I always liked to imagine there were brown robes, and iron masks, and lots of chanting in old crypts."

Constantine disguised a low chuckle with a clearing of his throat. "That is quite the picture."

"Isn't it?"

They lapsed into silence once again.

Someone pulled the heavy doors shut, and the head cardinal, clothed in gold and crimson, began to speak in Latin.

Val didn't listen; instead let his gaze wander out across the congregation, noting their somber faces. Today, this ceremony, marked the official union of the churches in Constantinople. No more Schism, no more war between the two factions of Christians within the city walls.

From the top of this very cathedral, you could see Mehmet's impossible fortress, a slumbering dragon, waiting only for the spring thaw, and then it would strike. This union of church and church was necessary.

But Val didn't know that it would be enough.

~*~

That was winter.

And now it was spring, and they were settling in the Throat Cutter.

And Val was very, very afraid that he couldn't save Constantinople.

But he would try.

33

BATTALION

They camped in a lightly-forested plain at a midpoint between the Throat-Cutter and the Bosporus, Constantinople drawing all eyes like a beacon. Enough timber to be cleared and used as firewood, and enough grass for the horses. An ideal location.

Night had fallen by the time the royal tent was habitable, and Val sank gratefully into a chair with a cup of mixed wine and blood.

"Don't get too comfortable," Mehmet told him, accepting his own cup, and perching on the chair opposite. Slaves still bustled about, dressing the bed, and unfolding nightshirts, but the table was set up, and Mehmet reached immediately for a rolled parchment.

"Why ever not?" Val asked on a sigh. His first sip hit his tongue too richly, and he suppressed a grimace.

"We need to talk of your battalion."

Val choked and set his cup down. "My *what?*"

"Battalion." Mehmet unrolled the parchment and weighted it at either end with their heavy gold cups. On it, a scribe had drawn a diagram of army companies, names labeled in an elegant hand. "Here. These are your men. I'm giving you a company of janissaries, and the rest are shock troops. You'll be behind one of the gun crews, on the land wall side, and you'll be intercepting whatever Roman forces come out to attack the guns. We'll undoubtedly lose some of Orban's big ones to explosion, but they can't risk a true shot. You will—"

"*Mehmet.*" Val had been trying to catch his attention for the entirety of his explanation, growing frantic. When the sultan lifted his head, Val said, "Why in heaven's name are you putting me in charge of an entire battalion?"

Mehmet blinked at him a moment, surprised by the question. Then he grinned. "It's high time you earned your keep, Radu. You're a knight, with all the training and education of a proper prince. Everyone here" – a sweeping gesture seemed to indicate the entire camp – "is well-acquainted with you. How could I ask them to fight while you sit in total comfort inside a tent? You're a prince, yes, as I said, and you should act the part. You will lead a battalion for me. I think you'll do quite well with it."

It was Val's turn to blink, blank-faced a moment, before that grin made sense. "Oh," he said, unpleasant prickling sensation crawling across his skin. When he swallowed, he felt his silver collar press at his throat. "I see."

Mehmet's smile froze; doubt touched his eyes. "You do?"

"Yes. You think if I lead troops into battle, I won't look quite so much like your favorite concubine."

The sultan's expression hardened. "That isn't what I said."

"But it's what you meant." Val reached for his cup, and drained it off, though his stomach rolled at first. The parchment rolled, too, satisfyingly; it snapped up with a crisp sound, hiding the battalion from view. "Your men are loyal, but they do talk, you know. You can have as many wives as you want, but everyone knows who shares your bed every night. What better way to make me look more like a man, and a valuable one at that, than to put a sword in my hand and throw me at your enemy."

Mehmet stared at him a moment, uncharacteristically closed-off and hard to read, then eased back in his chair. "Yes," he said after a moment, "they do talk. It's unavoidable, I'm afraid. But I am their sultan, and they obey me. You, on the other hand." He pointed at Val. "You are foreign, and golden, and my favorite besides, yes. Do you think their talking bothers me? Or does it bother you?"

Again, Val was struck by the sense of being wrong-footed. He was too tired, he guessed, from the day's long march.

"I don't care what they think," he said, aiming for haughty, offering a little wave for emphasis. "They aren't *my* people, after all."

"No? And who are your people?"

Val found he couldn't look at his face, that satisfied upward tick at the corners of his mouth, so he didn't; let his gaze land somewhere along the canvas wall of the tent. He shrugged. "Who could know? I've been nothing but a bedwarmer my entire life."

"And a talented one at that," Mehmet agreed easily. Sometimes he was led to provocation with the slightest comment, and sometimes, like now, he was maddeningly calm. "But, as I've said, you're also a knight, and a scholar trained in the art of ruling."

"Which I will never do."

"I have to put *someone* on your brother's throne after I kill him. It might as well be an actual Wallachian prince."

Val looked back to him, unbidden, and felt his lips part. Shock pushed the breath out of him. "What?"

Mehmet lifted his cup. "What exactly did you think I intended to do with you?"

A dozen possibilities came to mind, none of them worth speaking aloud.

"Vlad was supposed to go and be a good little vassal," Mehmet said, finally, rolling his eyes. "But, as usual, he fucked everything up. That leaves you, my golden one. You're intelligent, crafty, loyal, and beautiful enough to make anyone fall in love with you. You'll do far better than your brother could ever hope to. So, yes, you will rule someday. You will rule *for me.*" The last he stressed heavily. "So it's time you gained a reputation for something besides lolling about and eating fruit lasciviously, don't you think?"

"Yes," Val said faintly. "I suppose you're right."

"Besides," Mehmet added, winking, "I shall so enjoy throwing a Western prince at the walls of Constantinople."

The truth, at last.

Val caught the eye of one of the slaves. "More wine, please," he requested through a dry throat.

Mehmet chuckled.

~*~

The next morning, Arslan dressed him in armor, and Val emerged from his tent to find two janissaries awaiting him, his mare already saddled, pawing at the ground impatiently.

"We're to take you to your men, your grace," one of the janissaries informed him.

"Alright." He couldn't seem to swallow, hands shaking as he took the reins and swung up into the saddle. His mare danced beneath him, reading his nerves, and he couldn't soothe her as he normally did, with a few strokes along her arched neck.

The janissaries walked just ahead of him on foot, so that he was forced to keep a tight rein not to run them over, and led him through a camp bustling with activity. The sun flirted along the tree tops, its first rosy blush painting the undulating line of the Theodosian walls in stripes of ivory and crimson, so that it already looked blood-drenched. Val didn't need to ask where they were going: he saw the men, arranged already, with sharp-tipped lances, in perfect company formation; and, ahead of them, the gun.

It was an ugly, unwieldy war machine. Cast of bronze, and drug all the way from Edirne on overtaxed wagons pulled by teams of mules, horses, oxen, and men, it dwarfed the regular Ottoman cannons, at least five times the size of the typical guns. Its designer, Orban, had gone first to Constantine, and, when denied a commission, had come all the way to the palace at Edirne, where Mehmet had gladly heaped gold upon his head.

Val's breakfast curdled in his stomach as he laid eyes upon the beastly thing now. It had been propped up on boulders and wooden blocks, a team of operators bustling about, fussing with the preparation. If the thing blew — and there was every chance it would — it would kill anyone within a dozen yards of it, and the shrapnel would reach farther.

But if it didn't blow. And if its massive ball reached its target of the wall...

Val swallowed and closed his eyes a moment, willing his stomach to settle.

"Your grace."

His horse pulled up, and he opened his eyes to find his core knot of janissaries standing at attention, awaiting instruction.

"I shall so enjoy throwing a Western prince at the walls of Constantinople."

Mehmet had kissed him that morning, only minutes ago; shoved his tongue into his mouth, and nipped his lower lip until

Val tasted his own blood. Heated and thrilled for battle. *Make me proud, Radu.*

Val looked up at the walls, and watched the colors shift and bleed like the patterns of sand at a river bottom, as the sun climbed, higher every moment. He saw the snapping pennants, and the archers along the wall-top, and the men in polished helmets awaiting their siege towers.

I am *Radu*, he thought. *If I ride against that wall, and put Roman blood on my sword, then I am Prince Radu, and not Valerian at all.*

He cleared his throat. "Gentlemen. The most pressing matter is to protect the gun," he said, projecting his voice.

A murmur of assent went up from them all. They looked up at him, most of them blank-faced in a way that he read as careful; but a few sneered. Probably they thought he couldn't see.

He was, after all, a hostage. A Western prince, and not of their blood, nor did he worship their god. And he shared the sultan's bed; bore the marks of his teeth even now on his throat. A foreigner, and, worse, a whore. Doubtless they hated him.

Just as the archers waiting along the wall hated him. They didn't know his name, or his lineage, nor care how many times the sultan had fucked him. He was merely an enemy captain, leading a host against them, standing on the wrong side of a gun built to blast their walls to bits.

It struck him, then; left him breathless. He was a villain on both sides of this war.

34

SIEGE

The smoke of the cannons blotted out the sun, the stink acrid in Val's lungs. He dodged the flashing silver blade that fell through the haze toward him, turned it away with his own sword, and brought his leg up; kicked the Roman soldier hard in the hip, and sent him sprawling. Before he could gather himself, Val clapped him hard on the side of the helm with the flat of his blade; it rang like a gong, and the soldier lay still.

"Fall back!" Val shouted to his troops. "Fall back, and make way for the siege towers!" He could already hear the creak and groan of their approach somewhere behind him, the huffing breaths of the men who pushed them. "Fall back!"

Another Roman came barreling toward him, and he side-stepped him easily. Drove him to his knees with another well-placed kick, and left him unconscious, but not dead. He'd found that if he stayed hydrated, and well-fed, he could use his superior physical strength to great advantage; he didn't have to spill blood, only show a good example for his men, and exert himself appropriately.

Though why he bothered, he couldn't really say. Most days he wished that he wouldn't wake up at all, and could lie quietly in some sort of coma until the siege at last ended.

It had to end at some point, didn't it?

The siege towers rumbled up, slip-sliding on ground gone muddy from the soaking-in of blood. The city walls had been cracked in a dozen places; gaps showed through, giving glimpses of the inner walls, and the moats. Sappers had dug beneath and set fires, collapsing small portions at intervals. Still, the city remained unconquered.

Thankfully.

He dream-walked when he could, going to provide an increasingly-harried Constantine with intelligence on troop movements and numbers. He'd given advance warning of Mehmet's – admittedly – ingenious plan to subvert the boom that stretched across the mouth of the Golden Horn. On that visit, as on all his others since being handed control of a battalion, Val had been careful to project an image of himself in his usual foppish finery, silk, and soft slippers, and jewels, without a bit of armor in sight.

"He's taking them *overland?*" Constantine had asked, brows at his hairline.

"His carpenters have built a series of – of tracks," he said, still not quite believing it himself. "There are wheels, and ropes, and pulleys, and – yes, suffice to say he's in the process of moving the majority of his fleet up through the pass and plans to drop them into your harbor."

He'd told them about it, and still Mehmet had succeeded. He had too many men, so many that no amount of naval battles, ships lost to cannon shot and Greek fire, could dim their chances.

The Romans fell back, too, fleeing to the berms they'd built up at the base of the wall, where they could duck down, and take some water, and catch their breath before they launched their inevitable assaults upon the siege towers, while their fellows on the wall-top poured Greek fire on their Ottoman assailants.

A runner appeared, a skinny, breathless boy, bearing a bucket of water and a ladle. It was warm, and fetid-tasting, but Val forced himself to drink deep, droplets running down his chin and throat, over the silver collar that dragged at his energy, always. "I need blood," he told the boy, who nodded, and scampered away.

"Your grace, take from me," one of his foot soldiers said, appearing beside him, and pushed up his sleeve to offer a sweaty, dirt-smeared wrist.

Ordinarily, he would have resisted, but he couldn't afford to, now. He caught the soldier's wrist in his hand and brought it to his mouth; bit fast, and hard, and sure, and drank a small amount of blood. It hit him like a drug, fairly vibrating through his veins, and he let go before he latched on for good, licking his lips clean.

The soldier looked glassy-eyed and dazed. "Go." Vlad gave his shoulder a shove. "Fall in."

With a low, resonant thump, the siege towers landed against the wall, and a new kind of battle began.

Val had strict orders not to go harrying up the ladders to the top of a tower until the defenders on the wall had been completely overrun, and there was no chance Val would end up with a face full of Greek fire. "Afraid I'll damage my pretty face?" Val had asked, flipping his hair.

Mehmet had not taken that as a joke. "It's an order, Radu."

And, truthfully, Val wanted nothing to do with that kind of death. So he'd obeyed, waiting, biding his time for the moment when the wall was won, and he could get over it, and never come back out.

His men rallied around the great wheeled base of the tower, swords and lances lifting to engage with the Roman soldiers – dirty and bloody and exhausted – who came running, screaming, to meet them from the wall's shadow. Above, the would-be-wall-takers screamed; Val smelled hot oil, and scorched flesh.

He parried a stroke aimed for his head, ducked, spun, and struck.

The boiling oil hit the wooden base of the tower, and sent up a rolling cloud of steam. It wafted in front of him, veiling the man he fought. But Val could still hear him, and smell him; feel him. He struck again, two quick strikes, and when the cloud passed, he saw that he'd killed the Roman, his throat red and open.

He turned to meet the next attacker, thrumming with energy from the blood he'd taken; he felt too big and too strong for his skin, restless even as he cut down the next man.

It was so *easy*. That was what frightened him, the ease with which he cut men down. The way he almost…almost *enjoyed* it. Men died too quickly; and he was so much stronger, in every sense. He–

The discordant shouts from above, the hisses and curses of men being burned by boiling oil, changed, suddenly. A high, collective scream of panic.

Val tipped his head back just in time to see the brilliant-white gout of Greek fire, and to hear the sizzle and crack of the tower's joints giving way.

"Fuck," he murmured, and tried to run, as the whole thing came crashing down.

Pain blossomed, swift and overwhelming, and then it was black.

~*~

Val woke slowly, one eye at a time, to a splitting headache, and the royal tent swimming around him.

Arslan's face popped into view first, expression plainly relieved. "Your grace, are you well?"

He was dragged back, eyes going wide, and then Mehmet hovered over him. "Do you have any wits left?"

Val closed his eyes with a groan. "Fuck off." His mouth and throat felt desert-dry; it hurt to swallow, and his eyes ached, so badly he thought they might burst.

Mehmet chuckled. "He'll live."

He did, unfortunately, and a few hours later, shadows long across the floor, muted evening light coming in through the open tent flap, he managed to sit upright, with Arslan's help. He'd drunk a full cup of fresh horse blood, and his headache had dulled to a low pounding, keeping time with his pulse. When he reached back along his head, he found a sizable lump, and the crustiness of dried blood.

Mehmet awaited him at the table, and he hobbled there, and all but fell into a chair. When Mehmet slid a cup of wine toward him, he accepted it gladly.

"What happened?"

"What do you remember?"

He winced. He didn't want to remember. "Greek fire. It destroyed the tower."

"Yes, and then it collapsed on top of you. Killed five mortals," Mehmet said, absently, plucking grapes from a gold dish and popping them one-by-one into his mouth. "You were lucky."

"No. I'm a vampire." Val closed his eyes and rested his head against a folded hand.

"Your men are worried – asking after you. And impressed, besides. No one else beneath the debris survived."

"Hooray."

484

"This is a good thing," Mehmet said, patient, as if speaking to a child. "Your reputation will be—"

"I don't *care* about my reputation." After this statement, nearly shouted, it was silent so long that he finally cracked his eyes open a fraction.

Mehmet sighed, his expression disappointed. "We've been over this. A good showing here cements your strengths as a future prince of—"

"*I don't care.*"

A withering look, and then the sultan stood. "You're in a terrible mood. Pardon me if I seek company elsewhere tonight."

Val glared him out of the tent, and then closed his eyes again. When he did, he replayed the last weeks over in his mind, grisly images of hacked limbs, and ruptured bellies; of men dying on his sword. *Roman* men. People who should have been *his*.

Alone save for the slaves, he put his head down on the table and dream-walked.

To his credit, Constantine was not cowering in his palace; he stood on the ramparts, along the top of the inner wall, cloak flapping in the breeze, surveying his barely-holding defenses, and the ruin of the siege towers they'd managed to destroy.

Also to his credit: he didn't startle when Val appeared beside him. Not at first, anyway. But when he turned his head, his ready, exhausted smile fell from his face, and he gasped. "Val. What's happened?"

Val looked down at himself, at the projection he'd created, and swore. Tired and still disoriented, he hadn't bothered to conjure any sort of glamour, and had appeared in his current condition: barefoot, clad only in loose white şalvar, his torso wound with bandages, the skin that showed mottled with healing purple bruises. When he lifted his head again, he saw Constantine make an aborted reach for him with one gloved hand.

"Was this—" His brows drew together. "Was this Mehmet?" he asked in a low hiss. "Has he beaten you? Did he—"

"No, no. I'm fine. And I'm healing. Vampire, after all," Val said with an attempt at a smile.

"But you're injured! How?"

Val attempted to smile, but knew he only gritted his teeth. "Don't make me tell you. Please."

Constantine's gaze shifted over him, and then the panic melted into pain. "You've been fighting."

Val let his grimace fall away, blank-faced with exhaustion. "As any good puppet should."

Constantine studied him a long moment, eyes touching every scrape and hurt, before he turned away, mouth pursed, shaking his head. "I'm sorry."

"I've slayed your men," Val said. "I'm sorry. I…" His stomach was a yawning chasm, guilt and hunger and self-loathing. "I shouldn't be here. Shouldn't bother you—"

"*No,*" Constantine said, forceful, facing him again. Gentler: "Do not apologize to me. Not for anything. There are men who don't want to fight on both sides of this war, trust me." He blew out a breath that left his shoulders slumping. "I only regret that I can't help you. Don't ever apologize for coming here, or for seeking my company." Small, self-deprecating smile. "Such little comfort that it is."

Val reached for him, his hand turning to smoke, throat clogged with tears.

"I know," Constantine murmured, and moved his own hand, so that, had Val been here in the flesh, he would have been patting the back of it. "I know, son."

<u>35</u>

THE EMPEROR

Lightning split the sky overhead, jagged white tongues fracturing along the undersides of the clouds. Val was grateful, for once, that he wasn't here in his physical form, and that he couldn't feel the rain.

The people of Constantinople were parading the holy relics. For luck. For a divine blessing. A great statue of the Virgin Mary rode atop a wooden cart, its wheels catching and bogging down in the mud as men tried to push and force it along.

Your grace, a voice whispered, inside his head. Not his voice – it was Arslan, calling to him, from the place where his unconscious body rested.

A gust of wind caught the rain, driving it sideways. Citizens blinked, and shielded their faces with their hands, cowering as thunder crashed overhead.

Then, horror of horrors, the cart tipped. People shouted, and reached, and flailed – but the Virgin Mary tumbled down to the mud. And broke.

"Shit," Val breathed.

Your grace.

The wailing was immediate, panicked and high-pitched. Lightning struck somewhere above, the high peaked gable of a roof, with a shower of sparks, a burst of flame, and a roar of thunder.

"Do not panic!" George Sphrantzes shouted, but no one paid him any heed, and his own eyes were wild and white-rimmed as he instructed his men to run see to the fire.

Your grace, please, wake up!

Val felt a touch on his shoulder; someone shook his body, back in the tent, where he'd sought physical shelter from the storm. He didn't have long; Arslan wouldn't be calling to him this urgently if it wasn't important.

But he searched for Constantine with his eyes, and found the emperor's fine clothes streaked with mud, sodden from the rain, expression horrified. Val wanted to go to him. "Constantine!" he called. "Please, I have to talk to you," he said as he approached, drawing the emperor's gaze. "I have to tell you about Mehmet. You have to surrender!"

"Val," the emperor said, shell-shocked and helpless, his curls plastered to his forehead. "What are you saying? I can't surrender." He gestured to the tableau before them, the blasphemous disaster. "I have tried to rally my people, to—" He gestured again, and sounded choked. "I can't abandon them, or our cause. It's the right one." His gaze burned.

Val gulped. "But I can…"

Constantine reached, as if to lay a hand on his shoulder, and pulled back with a frown before he sent Val's limb to smoke. "You can't," he said, sparing a moment's gentleness.

"But…" It was selfishness, he knew – look at these people, their terror and despair – but he didn't care about saving them right then. Nor the city. Mehmet would win, he now knew; victory for the Romans was, and had always been, a futile hope. But Constantine was his friend; he could save him. Get hands on him, turn him, making him a strong immortal and maybe they could…

"Val!" A voice from the other side, but a shriek this time, high and loud; it hurt his ears, because he'd heard it not just mentally, but physically. He opened his eyes, already panicking.

He lay curled on his side in the center of the bed, just as he'd been earlier, when he first lied down to go for this particular walk. A stolen moment, on this dark and stormy day, Mehmet fervent, and wound-up, and hounding all his generals about what he called "the inevitable victory." Rain beat down on the canvas of the roof; it had covered the sound of an approaching party – or, maybe not. Arslan *had* been trying to wake him for a while.

The boy scurried back from the bed now, face pale, eyes huge. He scuttled back to lean against a stack of trunks, shoulders hunched, trying to appear small.

Val pushed upright, shaky and drained-feeling, and ran his gaze over the source of Arslan's fear: the dripping-wet men standing on the rug before him.

It was Mehmet, and a full coterie of janissary guards. Grand Vizier Halil Pasha, especially bedraggled, his soggy wet turban trying to come unwound. All of them, even the guards, wore dumbstruck expressions.

Val reached with unsteady fingers to tuck his hair back over his shoulder. "Well. You all look terrible." He aimed for biting, but it only sounded tired.

Mehmet took a breath, and drew himself more upright, gaze hardening, growing suspicious. "What were you doing just now?"

Val eased his way to the edge of the bed, joints and jaw aching in that way that Mehmet always complained of these days, and swung his slipper-clad feet down off the edge, onto the rug. "What are you talking about? And you're ruining the carpet."

Mehmet ignored him, and stalked up to him, reached out and caught Val's chin in his hand, tipped it back. Val tried to twist away, but the sultan's fingers bit into his jaw; not hard enough to bruise, but close.

Over his shoulder, Val saw Halil's face twist up with thinly veiled disgust.

"What were you doing?" Mehmet repeated, gaze narrow, and sparking. "You were muttering to yourself when I walked in."

Val's heart raced; he tried to force it slower, to take a few deep breaths. If he smelled of fear, no lie could save him here. "It was a nightmare. The storm. Nothing important."

Mehmet's thumb pressed into the soft place just beneath the point of his chin. "No. It sounded like you were having a conversation. You said 'Constantine.'"

Oh no. Val took a few shallow breaths through his mouth, terribly conscious of the stares fixed on him, and the thumb digging into tender skin. "We're at war with him, no? It would make sense that I had nightmares about the man." He attempted a laugh.

Mehmet shifted his hand to Val's throat and that forceful thumb landed on his Adam's apple, and applied pressure. His laugh choked off.

"You were talking with him," Mehmet said, voice hardening a fraction. "*Pleading* with him. 'Please, I have to talk to you,' you said. 'I have to tell you about Mehmet.'" He leaned in close, hot, wine-sour breath wafting across Val's face.

489

"It's funny," he said, corner of his mouth hitching up in a smile that didn't begin to touch his eyes. "We've had so many hopeful soldiers make their way to our camp here, wanting to lend me their assistance, to work themselves into my good graces. Craftsmen, and artisans, and warriors. Scribes, and monks, and mullahs, and prophets. And one man, who's just come this past week, who is a mage."

Every muscle in Val's body seized. He tried to sit upright, a surge of adrenaline burning through his exhaustion, but Mehemet's hand tightened, and held him fast, right above the tight silver collar that marked him as property.

A *mage*. Val had never met one; they were the rarest of Familiars, and Father had always spoken ill of them – manipulative and twisty, he'd called them, untrustworthy – but he knew that they had a smell. "Like a forest on fire," Mother had said, lips pressed. He hadn't scented fire – well, but maybe he wouldn't, between the campfires, and cookfires, and the greasy, rancid funeral pyres they'd been forced to use, because the stinking corpses kept piling up, drawing flies, rats, and foxes. Perhaps he'd scented one, and hadn't known; perhaps one had walked right past him, knowing exactly what he was, and that he'd been subjugated by a master, smirking at his circumstances.

"This mage," Mehmet continued, "has proved an excellent source of information on those like us. Like you and me." He shifted his hand side to side, a gentle shake that left Val grinding his teeth. "For instance: did you know that some of us have mental abilities? Psychic, really, beyond human comprehension." He dropped his voice at the last, a whisper, just for the two of them.

Dread opened up like a chasm in Val's belly.

"Did you know that some vampires are capable of projecting their consciousness and an image of themselves across vast distances? That they can converse with others, have entire conversations, across oceans, and over city walls?" Something dangerous flared in his eyes. "They call it *dream-walking*."

No. No, no, no.

"Your Majesty–" Val began.

Mehmet's hand tightened. Hard, hard, cutting off his air, and then eased back. "Are you a dream-walker, Radu?"

He didn't dare swallow. Blink. Flinch. Croaking through a dry throat, he said, "No." And then waited, forcibly blank-faced, for the slap to come.

Instead, Mehmet released him, and turned to face his entourage. "Leave us."

They did so, with quick bows, even Halil Pasha, who bit his lip as it to keep from saying something. When they were gone, and the tent flap had fallen in place, the rain a steady hiss like a great serpent above and around them, Mehmet turned to Arslan.

"Come here."

Val had known fear moments before, but the sight of Mehmet's gaze trained on Arslan – that was terror.

"Wait!" He scrambled up onto his knees, and reached out.

Mehmet turned back to him, his gaze a warning, but one Val ignored.

"You promised never to touch him. You *promised*," Val said, and growled.

Mehmet's brows flew up to the edge of his soaked turban, and his mouth opened, agape for one long moment. And then he composed himself. "I did, didn't I? And what would you do if I went back on that promise?" he drawled.

Val's hands curled into fists. He let the growl bleed in heavier, a low, angry purr that pulsed through the tent. "I would stop you." He could do it, too; he was faster, leaner, stronger these days. He was purebred, and fueled by hate, and he could overpower this pitiful, glutted, turned creature before him.

And Mehmet *knew it*. Val caught a faint whiff of unease before he chuckled and said, "How much damage do you think you could do before my guards came rushing in here? Is it worth the risk?"

"Do not lay a *finger* on Arslan."

Mehmet kept his gaze trained on Val. "Come here, boy," he called, beckoning.

Arslan came, quiet and shaken as a mouse. When he got close enough, Mehmet rested a hand on his shoulder.

Val started to rise from the bed, one foot planted on the rug, fists hovering at his sides, growling, teeth bared.

491

"Arslan," Mehmet said, voice warm, in the way that it so often could be, "don't be worried." He never looked away from Val. "Tell me, child. What is it your master does when he lies down and sleeps for long stretches? It's funny: I always seem to find him half-awake, groggy, and sluggish. He rests so *very much*. What is he doing?"

"I...I, he..."

"You can tell me. Nothing will happen to you – so long as you're honest."

Arslan sniffled.

Val looked to him then, and let his growl fall away. Tears glimmered on the boy's lashes, and Val's chest ached.

Val took a deep breath, and looked back to Mehmet, kicking his chin up. He braced his feet, one on the edge of the bed, the other on the ground; gathered his uneven, post-walking strength. "Alright, yes, fine: I'm a dream-walker. I have been since I was four-years-old."

Mehmet patted Arslan's shoulder. "That'll be all, boy. Go on now." He folded his arms, and a triumphant glow flared to life in his eyes. "I knew it."

"You didn't even know such a thing existed until someone told you. Since when, tonight?"

"I have always known there was something suspicious about you," Mehmet snapped. "Always tired, always sleeping. I've never entered a campaign tent that you weren't dragging yourself up from bed, haggard as a crone. That collar is not the only reason." He stepped forward, reaching for Val's throat again.

And Val slapped his hand away.

The slap of skin-against-skin cracked like the meeting of blades.

Neither moved, after. Val didn't breathe.

And then he leapt off the bed and paced a wide circle around the edge of the rug, putting distance between them, growling a warning.

Mehmet spun, facing him. "You've been visiting the emperor, haven't you? Constantine Dragases. You've been speaking with him, plotting with him. Telling him of me? That's what you said. That's what you were muttering in your sleep." The last he spit, words coming faster and faster, as fury took hold of him. His eyes blazed. "You've been conspiring this whole time, haven't you, you little whore? Telling him of our plans, helping him. *Helping my enemy!*"

He lunged, swiping out with one hand like an enraged bear. Val danced back out of reach.

"I met him when I was four," Val growled in return. "He's been my friend for most of my life. Long before your father wrapped me in chains and gave me over to you as a plaything."

Mehmet lunged again, a contained roar tumbling from his open mouth, his fangs descending. "You witch! You fucking traitor!"

"Traitor?" Val backed up until his shoulder collided with the bed post. Trapped. "Traitor?" he repeated, and barked a laugh. "Do you think I was ever on your side? *Ever?* After everything?" His heart beat so fast he thought he'd faint, but he couldn't, not now, and he lifted his hands, felt his own fangs prick his lower lip. Furious. Ready. "Yes, I helped Constantine when I could, when he would let me. "I'm a *Roman*, you stupid fucker. The only true Roman in this tent. And I would give my life to see the Emperor of Rome drive his sword through your tainted heart."

He'd never said anything like that before. Never spoken the truth that lived in his soul, as dark as any of Vlad's mutterings, tended like a campfire deep in his heart. After, there was a moment of utter, stunned silence.

And then Mehmet struck.

Val ducked beneath his arms, lunged forward, and caught the sultan by the throat. He dug in with his fingertips, and smelled blood, as his momentum toppled them backward onto the rug.

Val landed on top, a knee in Mehmet's ribs, and all the air rushed out of Mehmet's lungs on a gusty exhale as his back landed against the floor. The look of him, eyes white-rimmed in momentary panic, thin lines of blood on his neck where Val's nails had scored him, ignited something predatory in Val. Words abandoned him. He snarled. He lifted a hand, intent on clawing open the sultan's face with it. He wanted to ruin him, to kill him, to bend his head and feast on the blood that poured out of him.

And then something caught Val in the temple, and white stars bloomed across his field of vision. He crumpled, boneless, and through a terrible ringing in his head he realized that someone had struck him, and that he'd toppled off to the side, where he now lay, stunned.

He blinked past the pain and whirling starbursts, and saw that the janissaries had returned; two helped Mehmet to his feet, and the rest aimed their spearpoints at Val.

Mehmet pressed a shaking hand to the marks on his neck, expression dazed. "Fetch – fetch chains," he said. "The heavy silver ones. The blacksmith has them." He heaved a deep breath. "Prince Radu has taken leave of his senses."

This was planned, then. Confront Val, work him to violence – and then take command from him, chain him.

One of the janissaries went running to do as bid.

Another stepped forward, reversed his spear, and brought the butt down toward Val's face.

Pain, and then darkness.

When he woke, he was choking.

His eyes flew wide, and he spluttered. A familiar weight on his tongue, heat and salt and musk, something pressing at the back of his throat.

He was on the bed, the edge of it, on his side, with Mehmet's cock in his mouth. The fingers of one ringed hand were wound tight in his hair, holding him steady while Mehmet fucked into his mouth, fast and rough.

Val had become damn near professional at this over the past few years, but now, being forced, lying awkwardly like this, without a chance to ease into it – he gagged, and felt the sting of bile coming up his throat.

Mehmet pulled out with a sharp, angry sound. "You're awake."

Val gasped for breath, and only got to inhale once before he was being manhandled across the bed, flipped over onto his belly. Cold, hard weights bit into his neck and both wrists, tension pulling tight. He wore a new collar, and cuffs, thick chains connecting them, rendering him helpless. Pain bloomed in his head, and his ribs, and arms, places where he'd been struck with spear butts. And cool air touched his bare legs and backside; he'd been stripped from the waist down, and knew what for, as Mehmet hoisted him roughly up to his knees, his face pressed down into the pillow.

He gritted his teeth, and braced himself for it.

But the pain was still awful when Mehmet forced his way in dry, without opening him up first.

It took him several tries, short, sharp jabs of his hips, working in just a little more each time, grunting to himself; he smelled thrilled.

Val bit the pillow and squeezed his eyes shut, and didn't scream. It hurt, it hurt, it hurt.

Mehmet shoved in the last little way, and started moving straight off, drawing back, and slamming forward. The hot wetness Val felt, that began to slick the way, was his own blood.

"You…belong…to…me." Mehmet punctuated each word with a thrust.

Tears burned Val's eyes. The pain was terrible, but worse was the ache of having been found out. Of having failed. Dream-walking was his one secret, his only means of escaping this man. And now that had been stripped away from him.

For the first time since he was a boy, he cried into his pillow as the Ottoman sultan fucked him bloody.

~*~

Dawn brought clear skies, and a flurry of activity as Mehmet's slaves rushed in to bathe, groom, and ready their sultan for the day's assault.

Val didn't stir. He heard the bustling about, and kept his eyes shut, sinking down deep into his battered, throbbing body. Wearing so much silver, he hadn't healed overnight as he should have, and everything from his feet to his eyelids, and everything in between ached fiercely. Including his heart.

He'd been defeated last night, completely, in every way that a man could be conquered.

When he was dressed, Mehmet walked over to the side of the bed, and Val barely managed not to flinch away from his touch when he smoothed Val's hair along the crown of his head. "Good morning, my beauty," he sang softly.

Val bit down on the end of his tongue to keep from shuddering.

When he didn't stir, Mehmet laid his hand on the side of his head, and said, "I know you're awake, Radu."

Val opened his eyes. He was weak, again, as he'd been as a boy. He could heal from almost any wound inflicted, but his body felt now like one big bruise, and he quailed from the thought of any more hurts. He couldn't take it now. Maybe tomorrow, or the next day, maybe when he had the strength to sit upright. But not now.

Mehmet smiled down at him, a warm and friendly smile, pleased, loving, even. He did love Val, and that was the worst thing of all.

He was dressed in all his battle finery, functional armor plates and lengths of mail draped with gold-embroidered silk and linen. His turban was snow-white, its center set with a massive ruby to mark his wealth and authority, and the slaves had drawn crisp lines of black kohl around his eyes, so that he would look foreign, and fierce, and beautiful to his Greco-Roman enemies.

"Today will be my victory," he said. "I can feel it. And my new mage, Timothée, has predicted it. I ride forth."

Val didn't respond.

"Sit up and give me a proper send-off."

Val's body didn't want to cooperate; neither did his heart, but he dragged himself upright, supporting his weight on shaking arms. He saw blue, finger-shaped bruises all down the lengths of them, places where Mehmet had gripped him, and held him down. He'd lost count of how many times it had been; blessedly, he'd passed out at some point.

Mehmet hooked a finger beneath his chin and drew him forward the last inch. Kissed him hard, and forced his tongue between his lips. Looked triumphant when he pulled back.

After, Val subsided back to the pillows, and closed his eyes again, listening to the guards come to collect their sultan, the clink and jangle of armor and gear, the raucous shouts. Mehmet's army was tired, but they could scent victory, and it compelled them to greater action.

After a while, Arslan crept up to the edge of the bed. "Your grace, you should take breakfast."

Val cracked an eye open. "Did he hurt you last night?"

The boy shook his head, lower lip trembling. "No. Only you."

"Good." And he fell back into a deep, unrestful sleep.

Arslan woke him again, later, and managed to get him to his feet, and to wrap him up in his robe. The cuffs and chains and collar made it too difficult to dress properly, but Arslan persisted, fidgeting with the heavy silk until Val was at least covered, sitting barefoot at the table with tea and honey-drizzled flatbread. "Eat," he said, and Val did eat. He drank the horse blood brought to him in a cup.

Once some of his strength had returned, Val finally became aware of a low roar. Like the ceaseless crashing of the ocean, but louder. The din of battle, he realized.

"What's happening?" he asked.

As if summoned, the tent flap lifted, and in walked Nestor-Iskander, his scribe's satchel draped over one shoulder, his boots dusty from his walk through camp.

"Nestor," Val said, when Arslan didn't answer, "what's happening out there?" His heart lurched in his chest, and began a painful gait.

He dumped his gear out onto the table, and without looking up, said, "Battle."

"I know that. What's happening in the battle?"

He shook his head, and bit his lip, and began sorting out his quills.

Val got unsteadily to his feet. "Nestor," he said sharply, voice cracking. "*What is happening?*"

He finally stilled, and lifted his head, lip still caught between his teeth. He whined softly, in the back of his throat, a wolfish noise. "I think – I don't know, we're too far away, and no one would say – but I think they've finally breached the wall. The *inner* wall," he stressed, when Val began to protest.

"They're inside the city," he said, and his lips went numb.

His whole everything was numb. It didn't matter, he told himself. He didn't care, didn't feel it. He was numb.

Except that wasn't true at all.

He turned away from the table, and his legs nearly gave out. So he turned back, and snatched up the cup, drained the last few drops of blood. "I need—"

"Here." Nestor held out his hand, and Val put the cup into it. He set it on the table, and pulled a sharp little blade from his kit; cut his wrist, clean and quick, and let the blood run down into the cup. "Is that enough?"

"Yes, thank you, that's plenty." Val wanted to stammer out his thanks, as intense and true as it was, but the scent of fresh wolf blood hit him like a slap, and he could only take the cup and drain it down.

The burst of strength it gave him was immediate. His shaking eased, and his head cleared, and his legs straightened.

He went to the center of the rug, and sat down on it cross-legged, his chains clinking together.

"Your grace?" Arslan asked, worry in his voice.

"I won't be gone long," Val said, folding his hands in his lap and closing his eyes. "But I have to see…"

He pushed himself down, and up, and dream-walked into Constantinople.

Into chaos and blood.

A beam of sunlight pierced the patchy cloud cover, and fell, like a spotlight from heaven, on the armored figure atop the white charger, his blade glinting as he drew it. Ornate armor, and a rippling golden cloak emblazoned with the two-headed eagle of Byzantium.

Constantine. And all around him, Ottoman soldiers, weapons raised, screaming, energized by the impossible gap in the wall; fevered with impending victory.

The walls were breached, at long last. Constantinople could not stand.

Val didn't care. His astral projection took off at a run, flowing through Ottomans, leaping over fallen bodies and great chunks of blasted wall, quick as smoke. He had only one goal, now

– now that all his good intentions had failed so spectacularly: save the emperor.

Save his friend.

He burst through the last line of soldiers with a great smoky surge, spiraling and coalescing with a dramatic curl of mist. He heard startled shouts, and cries of alarm. Someone screamed that he was a demon.

He threw up his arms, and Constantine's horse half-reared, eyes rolling. Constantine wrestled him back down with a few tugs of the reins, and turned his head aside. The emperor's face was red and slick with sweat, his eyes nearly as wild as those of his horse. He was terrified, but he wasn't fleeing, even though he should have been.

"Val–" he started.

"Go!" Val shouted at him. "Go! The city is all but fallen. You have to run!"

A sword cleaved right through Val's projection, turning his shoulder, and chest, and hip to smoke. The man who'd done it shouted, and then lunged forward through him.

"Constantine!" Val screamed. "Run! Run, please!"

Constantine turned his attention to his attacker, wheeling his horse, bringing his sword down in a swift, vicious arc. The Ottoman ducked the first blow, and struck next at the horse. The stallion danced sideways, well-trained despite its fear, and Constantine's next blow hit home, carving a line of blood down the man's neck, nearly taking his head off. He fell, gurgling, blood fountaining from his open vein and from his mouth.

The emperor's personal guards rushed forward, blades drawn, and engaged with the enemy. They were vastly outnumbered; they would all be slain. But they could buy their lord some time – *if he would run.*

Val got closer. He felt his pulse in his throat, and pain at his back, his ribs; someone was kicking at his body, it must be.

"Constantine–" he started again, a catch in his voice.

Constantine looked down at him, and for a moment, a stolen moment between just the two of them, as men screamed, and crossed swords, and died around them, his face softened. His mouth turned down at the corners with sadness.

499

"Valerian," he said, "I can't abandon my people, son. I won't. If my city falls, I shall fall with it, but I mean to fight until that happens."

"But – *please*." Val's vision blurred as his eyes filled with tears. He felt a sharp pain in his ribs, and his breath caught. "Constantine, please, run away. *Run to me*, and I can save you. I can *turn* you, I can–"

"No, no," he said, gently. "I love you as if you were my own, you know that. But what you want isn't possible. My place is here."

"But–"

"Look after yourself, Val. I have every faith that you were born for great things." And so, saying, the emperor turned his horse, and re-entered the fray.

Val went to his knees, boneless, weak. He felt the pull of his body – someone was hurting him, and bound in silver, already weak, he couldn't maintain the projection for much longer.

"But, please…" he whispered, tears spilling over, pouring down his cheeks. "Please…"

Constantine swung with wicked precision, hacking and slicing from his saddle. But Ottomans poured in through the gap in the wall, wave upon wave, trampling one another in their haste, screaming like banshees. There were too many. They swarmed the emperor; hamstrung his horse and toppled him from the saddle.

Val watched it all in helpless horror, sobbing, gasping for breath. He saw polished armor, a flash of gold cloak, the glimmer of a sword.

"Please," he said again, an airless whisper.

And then everything spun, and he slammed back into his body, just as someone kicked him viciously in the ribs.

He opened his eyes to find that he lay on his side, curled into himself, sobbing brokenly, aching in a dozen places as if he'd been beaten – because he had been. As he twisted his head and glanced up, he saw three janissaries swarm forward, shouting brusque orders, pushing off the seven regular foot soldiers who'd been laying into him.

"Leave off! He belongs to the sultan, you idiot!" one of them shouted.

The soldiers scattered.

"Your grace," another janissary said, and dropped to a crouch beside Val's head. "Here, I'll help you up. Are you hurt?"

Val ignored him. The sobs wracked his body, and no amount of physical pain, no boot strikes in yesterday's bruises, could rival the pain that howled inside his head. He kept his eyes open until they stung, not wanting to blink, knowing that if he did, he'd see the white stallion falling with a scream, see Constantine toppling into the hands of men with swords.

"Your grace? Your grace!"

Hands under his arms, fingers digging in, lifting him up. His head lolled. He couldn't breathe. Tears and mucus clogged his sinuses.

He was propped up on his knees amidst cursing and grumbling.

"Insane," someone muttered.

"Sultan beat the wits out of him, finally," another said.

Val pitched forward against their hold and vomited onto the rug. It was only watery bile he brought up, his stomach empty; his head throbbing with pain that felt like grief, even if it was only dehydration, hunger, and the healing of physical wounds.

Through the hazy wash of tears, he registered the janissaries parting, and a slender, dark-skinned figure knelt before him. His own sweet Arslan.

"Here, your grace," he murmured, and a cool, soft, damp cloth began to bathe Val's face, slender fingers cupping his chin to hold him still. "It was only another nightmare," the boy slave soothed, lying for him. "I have some water for you." A cup was pressed to his lips.

Val could swallow only a little, and then turned his head away, coughing.

Arslan, in a rare show of bravery, addressed the janissaries: "If you could give him some space, please. And guard the tent, perhaps." And, seeing as how he was the personal slave of a prince, the janissaries listened.

Val heard their footfalls leave the tent, and the rustle of the flap opening and falling shut.

"Your grace," Arslan said when they were gone, and his hands landed light as butterflies on Val's shoulders, cajoling. He urged him away from the mess he'd left on the rug, over so he could slump against the side of the sea chest, and prop his forehead in one shaking hand.

"The soldiers," Arslan said, apologetic. "They came bursting into the tent – there was all this commotion outside. I tried to stop them – I knew you were dream-walking." It was then Val managed to blink his vision halfway clear and see that Arslan had a fresh bruise coming up on one cheek where he'd been smacked aside. "Where did you go, your grace?"

Val tried to reach for the boy's face, but the weight of cuff and chain proved too heavy for his arm in that moment. He slumped deeper into his cupped hand, instead. "Beyond the breach," he said, his voice wet and choked. "They finally breached the wall, did you know?"

Arslan's dark brows were knit together with concern, and he looked at Val with such pity that he couldn't bear to meet his gaze. "Yes. Everyone outside was shouting about it. That's how the soldiers got in; no one was paying them any attention."

"Ah. What better way to celebrate than to rape a pretty prince, eh?"

Arslan made a small, distressed sound. "No, your grace, they were only – bragging. Saying how they'd taken the Roman city. They came to mock you."

"You'd be surprised how quickly mocking a chained-up man turns to raping one." He tipped his head to the side, and caught the boy's stricken look. "What am I talking about: no, you wouldn't. You know, don't you, my sweet one?"

"Why did you do it?" Arslan said. "After what happened last time, why did you risk it?" He sounded on the verge of tears.

Val sighed, and all the bruises along his ribs pulled. "Because I needed to warn my friend. To do something besides..." He shifted, and his chains rattled. "But all I did was watch him fall. Ineffectual to the last. I don't know if he..."

He did know, but he couldn't think of that now.

When he said no more, Arslan eventually rose and went to fetch a bowl of water, and a cloth. Val didn't resist as the boy cleaned his face more thoroughly, and managed to sip the wine he brought him. He couldn't nibble the flatbread, despite Arslan's begging. His stomach was too tender.

The silhouettes of running men flashed past the tent on all sides, and the camp beyond the canvas walls was alive with shouts, and celebrations, and the occasional scuffle as all manner of discipline broke apart amid the joy of victory.

Heartsick, overcome by exhaustion, Val eventually put his head down on the sea chest and dozed.

When he woke, night had fallen, and Arslan had lit the lanterns, and the big coal brazier in the center of the tent; Val lifted his head and felt a lap rug slip down off his shoulders where the boy had draped it over him.

Nestor-Iskander had joined them as well. He sat at the sultan's wide table, bent over a piece of parchment, writing furiously, slinging ink as he dipped his quill again and again.

A commotion still raged beyond the tent walls, but its pitch had changed; Val could hear a steady cheering.

Val cleared his throat and smacked his lips, trying to unglue his tongue from the roof of his mouth. "What's happening?" he croaked.

Arslan paced back and forth in front of the brazier. "The sultan is returning. He's riding back into camp."

"What?" That was ridiculous. A conquering monarch would immediately install himself in the finest rooms of the palace, and send slaves and soldiers to fetch his things. He wouldn't come back himself.

Arslan shook his head.

"He sent a messenger ahead," Nestor said without pausing in his task. "He's bringing you a *gift*."

Val leapt to his feet.

Tried to. It was more a lurching, stumbling, flailing attempt, and he ended up with both hands pressed flat to the chest, breathing harshly through his mouth. Everything in him screamed for him to run, but his chains shivered together, and he couldn't. All he could do was–

The tent flap lifted, and a janissary stepped in, spear propped on his shoulder. He held the way open for Mehmet, who swaggering in with a delighted air, every inch the conqueror.

—wait.

"Oh, good, you're awake," he said, strolling forward. His armor was smudged, dusty; a few curled auburn locks had fallen loose of his turban. His grin dominated his face.

But Val's gaze went straight to the sack he carried. The one stained dark on the bottom. The one that, when Mehmet halted in front of him, began to drip down onto the rug.

It reeked of blood.

Mehmet chuckled. "Prince Radu, I come forth victorious, and I bring you a gift."

Val wanted to look away, but he couldn't turn his head. He started up a low, frantic chant. "No, no, no, no—"

Mehmet upended the bag without ceremony. A human head fell out, and landed with a wet sound on top of the chest, inches from Val's face. It rolled once, and fetched up against his wrist, face-up. Death had a way of distorting features, but he knew that nose, and those open, sightless eyes. The silky black curls on his head.

Constantine XI Dragases Palaiologos. Emperor of Constantinople.

"No, no, no, no—" The chant became a wail, a high, keening sound that burned his throat. He had no more tears, but he choked, and hissed, and howled over the head of the man he'd met as a boy of four, learning how to walk in his dreams for the first time.

Mehmet chuckled again, so, *so* pleased with himself. He crouched down beside Val, and caught a handful of hair in one dirty, gloved fist, pulled tight. The pain didn't register. There was only the dead face staring up at Val, and the white flash of teeth in his periphery, the feral grin of his tormentor.

"I've brought you your emperor, Radu," Mehmet said. "So that you can finally meet him, face-to-face, in the flesh." He breathed hotly in Val's ear. "His head is mine, his palace is mine, his *city* is mine. I have walked through his holy houses, and touched your people's relics with my own hands. The Roman

Empire is *mine*. As are you." He leaned in close, so his lips were against Val's ear. "Never forget that."

"No," Val managed through chattering teeth. "I won't forget it."

36

TURNING

He fell asleep again, at some point, curled up on the rug like a dog, and when he woke next it was morning, and the head was gone. Fresh tears burned his eyes, but he didn't ask after it. Constantine was dead; there was nothing he could do, and carrying around a skull seemed...too delusional, even for him. Nestor would tell him later that it had been returned to the city – that he'd seen to it personally. So that what Romans remained in the city might be able to bury their emperor.

A useless mercy.

They'd moved their camp inside the city walls by this time, filling up the streets with a whole army of Ottomans and their things.

Val stood at a window in the Palace of Blachernae, hand braced on the ledge, gazing out across the city. Black smoke rose from a dozen different fires; he heard the din of humanity as a low roar, louder than the waves that slapped against the sea wall, and the occasional shriek or shout that rose above the others. In the nearest streets, he could see the detritus of the initial invasion: bits of torn cloth – ladies' dresses, mostly; there'd been rape in the streets, and the houses, and in every alley. Bits of broken crockery, forgotten tokens that had spilled from thieves' pockets, gold coins glinting in the late sunlight.

"Those cultureless fools," Mehmet said behind him. He was sorting through crates of books that had been brought to him, heavy tomes with illuminated pages and jewel-encrusted covers, many of them damaged during the ransacking. "The way they tore this place apart like fucking jackals..." He *tsk*ed.

Val didn't turn away from the window. The chains were gone, as were the heavy silver cuffs and collar he'd worn in the tent, but his slender collar remained, the one that looked like jewelry, but was always pulling at him, draining his energy and his mental gifts. He wouldn't have cared if the chains were still there. He didn't care about anything.

"You wanted Rome," he said, flatly, "and apparently so did your men."

"I wanted to lay claim to it, not raze the fucking place! Those idiots raped every woman and girl, even the elderly ones, and they've stolen uncountable valuables! Pulled down the relics in St. Sophia…damn them! This isn't how you conquer a place!"

Perhaps, if he hadn't fallen asleep staring at the head of one of his oldest friends last night, Val would have howled with laughter at the irony. That the man who'd raped a boy hiding in a tree would find fault with his own men for doing the same…

"Radu."

He finally turned. Mehmet was frowning at the stacks of books, but he was overall in a good mood, exuding productive energy and a scent of clean sweat.

But something else, too. Now that Val took the time to notice it, he detected something…something *off* about the sultan's scent. As he watched, Mehmet rubbed absently at a wrist – one thicker than it had been a few years ago, fleshier.

"Come help me sort these," Mehmet said. "My joints ache so."

"Must be all that conquering," Val quipped without any emotion, and walked forward toward the books. "Or gout. You should eat less."

"Watch it," Mehmet said, and they set to work.

~*~

That evening, Val plead an upset stomach, locked himself in his quarters, and sent the guards after his two favorite slaves. "To comfort and attend me," he said.

He didn't have to name them; his preference was well-known at this point. A few minutes later, Arslan turned up, Nestor in tow. The Russian wolf was, technically, the sultan's scribe, but that was a formality. Everyone knew he was a particular favorite of the Wallachian prince.

Arslan led the way, while Nestor ensured the door was soundly shut. "Your grace," the boy said, hurrying forward, expression worried. "They said you were ill. What can I do?"

Val sat upright. "I'm not ill." Not physically, anyway. "But there is something you can do for me. Both of you. You can let me help you escape."

~*~

They didn't like it. Of course they didn't.

"Your grace," Nestor said, panting he was so anxious. He stank of nerves.

"Nestor-Iskander." Val squeezed his shoulder. "You are not bound." He shifted his hand up, so he cupped the side of the boy's neck, thumb pressed over his galloping pulse; not a threat, but a way to ground him, and the young wolf leaned into the touch, eyelids fluttering. "You are no one's Familiar. You are strong, and swift, and if you flee, you can outpace any man, outlast any horse. The sultan owns you as a king owns a servant, but he does not own you as a vampire owns a wolf. Do you understand?"

He nodded, throat jumping under Val's thumb as he swallowed. But said, "He'll hunt us down, though. He'll never allow this."

"How will he hunt you?" Val countered, gently. "With dogs? With men? He and I are the only two immortals in his empire – at least that he knows of. He will be furious, yes, but not forever. Forgive me, dear, but you aren't that important. Not to him, anyway. But I want you safe. Both of you."

Arslan cried openly, but silently, shiny tears tracking down his face.

"Arslan, darling," Val said, turning to him.

The slave threw himself at Val, wound both thin arms tight around his waist, buried his wet face in Val's chest. "I want to stay with you," he choked out. "Please... *Val*, please. I don't want to be sent away."

Val had thought his heart shattered past the point of breaking any further after yesterday, but that proved untrue; those shards were ground now to dust by the boy's tearful pleas.

"My sweet boy," he murmured, rubbing Arslan's back, his own voice threatening to crack. "I would keep you with me always, if I could. But it isn't safe for you here."

Would the wider world be safer? For a slender, beautiful eunuch with big brown eyes? No. But being a eunuch wouldn't matter so much after tonight, after Val was done with him.

"But – but where would we go?" he asked, miserable.

Val lifted his head, and saw that Nestor's expression had firmed to one of resolve. "Russia," he said, and his accent thickened, just on one word. "Out deep, in the wilds. Siberia. Where it's only wolves – real wolves – and reindeer herders."

"Yes," Val said, grateful, "that'll do nicely."

"But I'm only…" Arslan tipped his head back, looking up at Val with tear-filled eyes, jaw quivering. "I'm only…me."

Val cupped his face in one hand, gentle and careful. "No, my darling. You aren't 'only' anything. And tonight, when you leave here, you'll be stronger than any man who would do you harm."

He stared a moment – and then his eyes widened in sudden comprehension. "Your grace."

"I would call it a gift," Val said, "but I don't honestly know if it is. It hasn't kept me from my own fate. But," he rushed to add, "it's kept me alive. And whole." Physically. "It will give you the strength and resilience necessary to survive anywhere. In that sense it is a gift. Will you let me give it to you?"

The boy deliberated a long moment – and Val let him. It was no small decision, this. He'd been born to it, and knew nothing else. But forever was a massive weight to lay across someone's shoulders. There were those he'd seen, had known, for whom death had been a final, welcome escape. Sometimes he thought – no, more than sometimes – that he himself would like to close his eyes and never have to see any of this again. He thought of the day he'd slain Arslan's rapists; that moment when he'd wanted to put his face in the water and breathe it into his lungs.

He pushed Arslan gently back and sat on the edge of his bed. Folded his hands in his lap. And waited.

Arslan chewed on his lower lip a long moment, gaze trained on the toes of his slippers – gold-embroidered, delicate, meant for household attendance, not riding…not escaping. Val would have to stuff rags into a pair of his own boots to pad the toes to give him.

If he agreed to the plan.

Val would never force either of his young charges to do anything. He knew the taste of forced compliance too well for that.

Eyes still downcast, Arslan said. "Would I have to…drink, as you do, your grace?"

"Yes."

He let out a shaky breath. "Could I not be what Nestor-Iskander is instead?" His gaze flicked up, desperately hopeful.

Val had never seen a wolf made, but one night, as a boy hungry for ghost stories, Fenrir had told him of his own turning. Of the sharp knife, and the sound a dying wolf made.

He shook his head. "I have not the means to turn you into a wolf. Nor should you like the process, I don't think."

Nestor shuddered hard, and shook his head.

"This is the best way," Val said. "The only way. Meaning no disrespect to Nestor, vampires are the kings of the immortals. I would like that for you – a bit of power."

Another rattled breath…but Arslan nodded. "Alright. I'll do it." His face creased, as if with pain. "But I don't want to leave you."

Val made himself smile. "Don't worry about me. I'll be fine."

Arslan and Nestor traded a look, knowing it was a lie.

"When the sultan finds out you've helped us escape…" Nestor said, and left the rest dangling.

Val's breath hitched in his lungs, painfully sharp fear. But he frowned and said, "The sultan isn't the conqueror he thinks he is. One day, he will learn that."

~*~

Turning required an exchange of blood. Back and forth, and back again, recycling it, strengthening the power of the process. It was intimate. Val had never done it before, though he'd been told what to expect. But hearing and doing were never the same thing.

Val situated himself against the ornate, carved headboard of his bed, and pulled Arslan down to sit cradled in his lap. The boy trembled head-to-toe, hard shivers that left his teeth clacking together, but he tipped his head back and exposed his throat, completely trusting.

"It's alright," Val murmured against the warm skin of his neck, and kissed him there. "It's alright, I've got you." He opened his mouth, and touched with just the tips of his fangs, breathed over the spot, humid, preparing.

Arslan looped an arm around his neck. Loose at first, tentative, and then tight, fingertips digging into Val's shoulder.

Val bit.

Living blood.

He'd had it, a few times, from his family's wolves. But most often the blood was spilled into cups. To drink blood straight from the vein was an intoxicating temptation. Headier than wine, than hallucinogens; it hit his own blood like lightning, streaking through his veins, flooding him with a breathtaking shock of energy. A sense of invincibility. A predatory urge in the back of his mind, something insidious and instinctual: drain him. A holdover, from the days of his father and uncle nursing from wolf's milk. *Drain.* Feast and eliminate a potential enemy all in one.

But this was his dear sweet Arslan, and aside from that one, frightening flicker, he was never in danger of over-drinking.

He took slow, gentle sips, and then pulled back to bite his own wrist, and press it to the boy's trembling lips. "Drink, darling."

He did.

They went back and forth. Arslan stopped shivering, and began to drink with more fervor, gripping Val's neck tight with one hand, and his wrist with the other, his body warm in Val's lap. Arousal stirred, a natural reaction, and Val could smell it on the boy as well. But they ignored it, and pressed on, drink for drink.

Nestor stood with his back to the door, a barrier that wouldn't be very effective if someone tried to force his way in. When Val glimpsed his face, briefly, he noted a stricken expression. It couldn't be helped.

And then...

Arslan's scent changed.

Slow-blooming, like the opening of a new spring flower, his scent shifted from boy to vampire. A hint at first, and then a flood of scent, and Val felt something like satisfaction, a rich swell of positive emotions.

He pulled back, and licked the wound clean, clotting the blood. When he lifted his head, Arslan stared up at him with heavy-lidded eyes, gaze wondrous for all that it was exhausted.

"I feel…"

"Hush," Val said, feeling his own energy flagging. "Rest a bit." He stretched out on the bed, Arslan cradled to his chest, and cast one last, tired, fading look toward the door.

"I'll keep watch," Nestor said gently.

They slept.

Val woke to a moonless dark, able to pick out shadows, the shapes of furniture, and the faint glow of Nestor's eyes. He sat on the floor, leaning back against the door, but rose smoothly when he realized Val was awake.

"Your grace?" he whispered.

"Yes," Val said, just to acknowledge him. He pushed up on an elbow and touched Arslan's face, which woke him immediately. His scent marked him as a young, healthy vampire. Val felt a little groggy, but otherwise unharmed. "How do you feel?"

Arslan took a breath and sat up. Lifted his hands and stared down at them. His vision would be sharper; Val had no idea how dull a human's sight was, only that he could see clearer and farther than his mortal companions.

"I feel…" He lifted his head, and grinned, teeth flashing in the dark. "Oh, your grace, I feel wonderful!"

Val chuckled. "Good. Up you get. Make sure your legs are steady."

Within a few minutes, Arslan was leaping in place, steady as the young soldier he might have been if not for castration.

"I'm afraid," Val said with regret, perching on the edge of the bed, "that the turning can't rectify everything."

Arslan paused. "It can't grow my…parts…back, you mean." He flushed, afterward.

Val chuckled, though sadly. "It might. Who's to say? I'm not an expert. But don't count on it, my dear. That's a very old, well-healed wound. Connections can be healed, fresh, bloody injuries. But something like that..." He shook his head, and wished he knew more about his own kind. His parents had been loving, had educated him well – but that had only been his boyhood, and they'd been firmly rooted in the human world. Human history, and the ways of human nobles.

That raised another point he wanted to make. "Arslan," he said, and the boy – the vampire – came to sit beside him, close, their sides pressed together. Val had always found him comforting, but the effect was greater now, knowing they were of the same kind; he supposed his own scent would be a new, welcome comfort as well, for Arslan's newly heightened senses. "There are things I must tell you."

And he shared all that he could think of; told him what to expect of his own abilities, about his need for blood, and the best ways to attain it, and control his own appetites. "Wolf blood is the strongest, and wolves are the easiest to feed from; they're stronger than men, and can spare the blood. If the two of you can stay together, it would be mutually beneficial." He glanced between them, and they nodded in understanding.

He warned them of mages, and of the possibility that Arslan could develop psychic gifts in the weeks and months to come. "I was four when I first began to dream-walk. It could take some time, and it might never happen, but don't rule out the idea of it."

And then it was time to bid them farewell.

A lump rose in Val's throat. He choked it down, but his voice cracked.

Arslan looped arms around his neck, and a moment later Nestor crowded in on the other side, an arm around each of them.

Val closed his eyes, and breathed them in. They'd been the only sort of pack he'd had these past years, alone, without family or ally. Bright spots in the bleak gray of his existence.

"I will miss you so," he said, "but you must do this. For me."

Arslan cried some more, and Val's own vision blurred.

513

He ensured they were well-stocked and well-dressed, and put them out the window. Watched as they jumped down to the balcony below, and then found handholds in the ancient stone edifice of the palace. Watched until they were slipping over the garden wall.

Arslan lifted one last wave.

Val waved back, imagining he could smell their sadness from where he stood at the window.

And then they went over, never spotted by the guards, and they were gone.

And Val was alone, in more ways than one.

<u>37</u>

PRINCE OF WALLACHIA

Vlad III, known as Vlad Dracula, second son to Prince Vlad II Dracul of Wallachia, knelt on the cold flagstones of a Hungarian cathedral and opened his mouth to receive his first communion. The priest set the wafer carefully on his tongue, but showed no signs of recoiling from the tips of Vlad's fangs, which he felt were visible now, in this moment of conversion, as his heart beat just a hair too quickly against his ribs. On his right hand, he felt the weight and coolness of his new signet ring – his father's before him, saved from the old prince's body before he was cremated and interred. The seal was of the ouroboros dragon and the cross, the mark of the Order of the Dragon.

The priest dipped his thumb into a golden bowl of lamb's blood, and drew the red cross of St. George on Vlad's upturned forehead. In Latin, he asked, *"Do you Vlad, son of Vlad Dracul, so swear your allegiance to the Crusader cause, as your father did before you?"*

Vlad answered in Latin as well, *"I do."*

Today, Vlad became a Catholic, just as his father had, but it was no normal conversion. Not merely a matter of prayer and confession and kneeling in front of the right kind of holy man. No, this was a commitment to the hushed and sacred Order of the Dragon, an exclusive order established in 1408. Dedicated to the resistance – and the defeat – of the Ottoman threat to Eastern Europe.

An Order that hadn't accomplished much of anything in the last fifty years. His own father, a member as well as an ancient vampire of legend, had caved, and quibbled, and now occupied a box as nothing more than ashes. Beginning with its founder, Sigismund of Hungary, the Order had been an exclusive club, one full of brave warriors, without question. But ineffectual ones, ultimately.

Vlad meant to change that.

Word had come in June, only a week after the fall, borne by a runner on a half-dead horse: Mehmet had taken Constantinople.

515

Mehmet the Conqueror, the spreaders of the story were calling him. With the aid of massive bronze guns, an inexhaustible supply of troops, and a dozen ingenious schemes, he'd broken through the Theodosian land walls and laid waste to the last defenders of the Roman Empire. The tales of cruelty, of rape, of the burning of holy relics, of the castration, slaughter, and enslavement of the Roman people...they didn't just turn Vlad's stomach. They *enraged* him.

His rage never really went away, though. It lived dormant in his veins, waiting for the next provocation. He felt it now, like fire under his skin, a sustainable, banked blaze that fueled every thought, and every goal.

In the months that followed, word came steadily from the rag-wrapped refugees who filtered into the Romanian provinces, Greeks and Romans fleeing the city, and the destruction wrought by the Ottomans. With them they brought tales of killings, cuttings, and impalements, each story more sordid than the last. Vlad had known of Mehmet's proclivities, had watched his own baby brother become a plaything, but the stories of lords' sons being taken as concubines angered him the most.

"*Rise, Vlad Dracula,*" the priest said, "*as a Crusader of the realm.*"

Vlad got to his feet, hands curling into fists, signet ring biting into his skin. He bowed his head in thanks to the priest.

"Go forth, my son," he said in Romanian, speaking the language of Vlad's birth. "Go forth and save us."

"I will." But he needed a throne, first. Hunyadi had promised him one, and the rest of Romania had long-since grown wary of Vladislav's friendliness with the Turks in Wallachia.

It was time to go home.

~*~

Vlad recaptured his father's seat, the princely palace in Tîrgovişte, for himself in the summer of 1456. A summer in which a strange light appeared in the sky, a falling golden star that streaked across the underbelly of the heavens, drawing word of sightings from every corner of the world. A portent some said. A sign of good fortune…or maybe a curse.

Vlad didn't believe in such foolishness. He believed in blood, and force, and the lessons of Machiavelli that he'd learned during his studies in Moldavia: an eye for an eye.

The boyars of his homeland had helped the Ottomans slay his father and brother, and he would have an eye as payment.

His ascension had begun in January.

On the thirteenth, Hunyadi, wrapped in furs to keep the chill out of his old joints, gathered a council of such Eastern lords as were willing to fight. They gathered at Hunedoara: Vlad, Hunyadi's sons, Pope Calixtus III's ligate, Juan Cardinal de Carvajal, and John of Capistrano. The last was an anomaly. Seventy years of age, and a Minorite Franciscan monk besides, St. John of Capistrano looked every inch a skeletal old invalid, with sunken eyes, and deep-set wrinkles, and tremulous hands. His voice wavered when he spoke – but that was only age, and not fear, because he was all of conviction. "God wills it that we chase the Turks out of Europe," he'd said, and had offered a force of peasant crusaders.

Vlad had bitten back a dark laugh; what could this man and his rabble offer to their cause? But he was passionate, and passion wasn't something to laugh at.

The meeting was held because of Belgrade. Word had come down in fits and snatches, through secret channels, from deserters, and Ottoman court insiders, the way that all information did, that Sultan Mehmet intended to sack Belgrade, and from there proceed to claim Serbia, Hungary, and the Romanian territories for his own. No longer vassal states, but truly absorbed lands of his empire. He was insatiable.

Each man in attendance was given a task. Vlad had the responsibility of staying in Sibiu, where he'd been living since brokering a peace with Hunyadi, and from there guard the Transylvanian passes from invasion. He also had orders to retake his father's throne when the time was ripe. "Kill Vladislav, and install yourself," Hunyadi instructed. "But only once the mountain passes are secure."

Stephen, Vlad's ersatz cousin and constant companion, had similar orders. He was to stop any potential march by the enemy into his homeland of Moldavia. And, once that was accomplished, slay the usurper Petru III Aaron and reclaim his father's seat as Prince of Moldavia.

Mehmet's forces began assembling in June. Ships docking at the river delta; gunsmiths beginning work in Kruševac on more of Mehmet's bloodthirsty cannons, the same kind that had broken Constantinople.

Movement came later in the month.

Hunyadi sent requests to the West, to the pope, to Italy, and the rest of the continent, asking for aid.

No response came. It never did. Europe had long since abandoned its own east.

The Conqueror came up the Danube. The scourge of Rome, the breaker of walls...the taker of brothers. He came.

Hold fast, Hunyadi's letter to Vlad read, when he opened it on horseback, mountain wind threatening to tear the paper from his hand, Cicero on one side, and Malik on the other. *Whatever happens, hold fast, and if I can't break him, then by God, it's up to you.*

"He only has Capistrano's peasant soldiers," Cicero said grimly.

"He has his own men," Vlad said, folding the parchment, tucking it into his belt. "His professionals. And he has motive, besides."

It turned out that motive was a hell of a thing, when the forces clashed at Belgrade.

~*~

Val watched from the deck of the sultan's private ship, anchored out in deep water, well away from the fighting. He shaded his eyes with his hand, and he watched, breathless with excitement, as, on the shore, a bloodied Mehmet was put into a boat and rowed back out.

He'd failed.

He'd *failed.*

Up on the hill, the fortress of Belgrade sat unmolested, Hungarian flag snapping in the breeze, and, below it, the flag of House Hunyadi.

The governor of Transylvania had turned back the Conqueror.

Val had watched as Ottomans swarmed the shore, steel glinting bright in the sunlight. Had watched, stomach heavy with dread, as they'd pierced the city's walls and entered its streets. He'd stared fixedly up at the fortress, waiting to watch it fall, to watch its banners struck. But that hadn't happened. No, in fact, Ottomans had begun to fall back, bit by bit.

The guns were mounted on the ships in the river, and they'd been engaged by Hungarian vessels. Two cannons exploded, in the way they were always wont to, and the ships had gone up in bright orange flames, men screaming and leaping overboard. And without the guns on the ground, there was no way to pierce the fortress walls.

Impatient, face going red with rage, Mehmet had ordered himself rowed to shore. "I'll show them how it's done," he averred.

But now here he came, back again. Even more furious than before, and smelling of fresh blood – his own.

It took three men to get him up over the rail and onto the deck; partly because it was awkward hauling dead weight up on ropes, but also because Mehmet was far from lean these days.

"Put me down, I can stand!" he bellowed at his attendants.

They pulled their hands back, slowly, and Mehmet collapsed and went to his knees.

"Ah! Damn it!"

The wound was in his thigh, Val saw, deep, and bleeding freely. Val frowned; it should have begun to repair itself by now.

Mehmet lifted his gaze and found Val. Save the spots of hectic color on his cheeks, the flush of fury, the rest of his face was bloodless and pale. Sweat gleamed on his brow, and he squinted from the pain. "What are you staring at?" he snapped. "Hoping I'll bleed to death?"

Yes, Val thought. "Gentlemen," he said smoothly to the poor attendants. "Run ahead of us and prepare the sultan's cabin,

519

and tell the captain to make ready for a departure. I can only assume that, not having taken the city, we'll be leaving shortly?"

Mehmet growled – a true vampire growl – but didn't argue, which meant that, yes, they were done here.

"Send the signal to the other ships," Val said, going to the sultan's side and bending down to pull one of his arms over his shoulders. "Have the ground troops fall back. Pull anchor and let's be done with this."

"Yes, your grace," the men chorused with a bow, and went to follow orders.

"Come along," Val said, towing Mehmet forward.

He grumbled, but allowed Val to help him, which proved the seriousness of his wound.

Belowdecks, a pair of slaves hovered in the doorway of the cabin, bearing clean linen; a pitcher of steaming water waited on the small, bolted-in desk. "Leave us, please," Val said, and they gladly fled, leaving the linen on the berth.

"Fuck you," Mehmet said without any real meaning as Val eased him down onto the edge of the berth. "Get me some wine."

"It will only make the bleeding worse," Val said, picking up the linen and bowl of water, and kneeling down to better inspect the wound.

Janissaries and soldiers wore şalvar of a heavy weave into battle, but the sultan's were fine silk. Thin, easily penetrated. Val pulled apart the fabric, and it split the rest of the way, revealing a meaty thigh that had been cut clear to the bone, blood still pumping with each beat of Mehmet's heart.

"This is deep," Val murmured, pressing the cloth to the wound to staunch the flow.

"Of course it is. I was stabbed!"

"It shouldn't still be bleeding."

Mehmet paused a moment; blood soaked through the white linen, bright crimson. "Don't just sit there," he finally blustered, fear sharpening his voice. "Do something."

"I am." Val kept pressure, and slowly, the bleeding slowed; became a gentle seep.

Pity, he thought. But he went to fetch a salve, and some herbs for disinfecting. He wouldn't have to stitch the gash, but he could hasten its healing.

"What do you mean 'it shouldn't still be bleeding'?" Mehmet asked, when his back was turned. Note of fear in his voice.

Val was careful; kept picking through packets of herbs, movements slow. Kept his voice light. "Only that the artery was missed. Vampires begin to heal rapidly; the wound should have clotted by now."

Mehmet was silent a moment, and then snorted. "What do you know?"

"Nothing much," Val said lightly, and returned to him, supplies in hand.

It had been three years since Val turned his young slave and helped him escape with Nestor-Iskander. It had filled his heart with gladness to know that he'd removed them from Mehmet's grasp, that they were, hopefully, living quietly in Siberia now, safe from harm, free of another man's ownership.

But Mehmet's wrath had been terrible. First had come a flogging, and then, when his back was raw and bleeding, he'd been pressed down onto it, and ravished. Like all of Mehmet's tempers, it had only lasted a night, and he'd been sweet the next morning, hand-feeding Val breakfast, telling him of the new suit of armor he was having commissioned for him. His most beautiful possession; his lovely prince.

He'd cupped Val's chin in his hand, rings warm from his skin against Val's jaw. "Why do you insist on testing me? Is it fun for you?"

The only fun Val had had in years had been today, watching Mehmet's men fall back. Knowing that somewhere beyond the defiant flags flying above the unconquered fortress, across mountains and green hills, Vlad waited. And someday, perhaps, they might even see one another again.

~*~

521

News of victory at Belgrade arrived to Vlad via runner the night before his own forces moved on Tîrgovişte.

"Very good," he said, humming with satisfaction. He dashed out a reply personally and handed it back to the boy. "Send your lord my congratulations. Head over to the cookfires and get some supper. You can sleep here, and depart at first light. We're making our move, then."

"Yes, your grace." The boy was exhausted, and streaked with road dirt, but he bowed deeply, and flashed a true smile.

Vlad settled back down on his makeshift seat of a felled log, leaning into the shoulder that Cicero pressed to his.

"It's miraculous," the wolf said, voice colored with awe. "How did they manage?"

"The fortress at Belgrade has sturdy walls. And they couldn't get the guns on land, Hunyadi wrote," Vlad said, accepting the bit of roasted hare that Fenrir extended toward him across the fire on a stick.

"What of Val?" Fen asked, hopeful. "Do you think he was with Mehmet?"

Vlad snorted as he bit into the meat, and spoke around a mouthful, grease running down his chin. "He's the bastard's favorite paramour. Of course he was."

Fen made a face. "Vlad, you can't think—"

"I think my brother is a whore, and a traitor. He's a vampire; he can dream-walk. Why has he not come to us?" He gestured to the forest around them, its edges bathed in flickering firelight. "He does not care. He's in league with my enemy, and he *doesn't care.*"

Fen's frown deepened. "I don't think that's fair."

Fenrir had been Eira's bound Familiar for centuries, him and Helga both, and by the time Vlad was old enough to be aware of his surroundings, Fen's scent had been ingrained in his consciousness. There was Mother, and Father, and then the wolves. Fenrir had never, admittedly, been his favorite, but his boisterous laugh and his constant smiles had been a comfort. His presence like a warm quilt on a cold night.

But right then, in that moment, Vlad wanted to leap across the fire and strike him.

He swallowed the urge, but he met the wolf's stare levelly. Challenging. His voice came out low, half a growl. "We sit here in a rough camp, ready to take a throne that should have been mine years ago — that shouldn't be mine at all, because Father should still be alive — and you want to talk of fairness?"

"Vlad," Cicero said quietly.

Fenrir blinked and ducked his head over his dinner, firelight making his face as red as his beard.

"My brother is a traitor," Vlad said with finality. "My mother loves him, and she will talk of him, but I don't want to hear a word about him from the rest of you."

Nods all around.

Cicero stared at him glumly, expression putting a twist in Vlad's belly.

He swallowed down the last of his small meal and stood. "I'm turning in." He didn't want to, but he knew he needed to try and snatch at least a few hours' sleep before tomorrow. He retreated to the shadows, where a squire had already laid out his bedroll. He lied down on the hard ground, using a saddle bag for a makeshift pillow, and forced himself to close his eyes.

His thoughts raced. They'd laid out the plan methodically, and gone over it a dozen times, moving little wooden figures across maps on a table. But he kept running scenarios in his head, playing it out. Especially the moment he finally got to cross swords with Vladislav. That might not happen, Mother had cautioned; Vladislav was a coward, and likely would send his men, waiting until he had no choice but to surrender himself.

But that's what Vlad wanted most. Man-to-man combat. A chance to slay the pretender who'd killed his father. A familiar fantasy, one he'd enacted in dreams — waking and sleeping — a hundred times by now. And for the moment — the possibility of it, at least — to be so close…his palms tingled, and his lungs ached, and he reached to rub the spot between his brows, where a furrow of tension had developed.

A few minutes later, he heard the soft padding of pawed feet, and Cicero, in wolf form, curled up against his back with a gentle *whuff* of warm breath. *Go to sleep, you dumb boy,* that breath plainly said.

Vlad unclenched his muscles, breathed in the scent of his wolf, and eventually drifted off.

~*~

The hour before dawn saw a low, thick mist rolling across the ground; strangely, it made the landscape brighter, though visibility was painfully low.

Eira left first, on horseback, in armor, hair in braids, looking every inch the shieldmaiden she was. The three wolves, in four-legged form, stood ready beside her mount, bristling with energy and intent.

"Don't forget–" Vlad started.

Eira stepped in close, and took his face in both her hands, smiling up at him. "I won't forget. Stop fretting, dear. This will work." She tugged him down so she could kiss his forehead, a forceful smack of lips, and then went to her horse.

Cicero looked at him, and whined.

"Look after Mother," Vlad admonished.

The wolf nodded, and followed the others as they departed into the dark and the gloom.

An hour later saw Vlad seated on his own bay charger, armor plates and mail weighing pleasantly on his body. Malik rode beside him, and a mounted messenger, should he have need of one. The rest of his force was on foot, well-equipped, despite the rag-tag nature of their assemblage.

Vlad led them down out of the foothills and they reached the last crest of the road above Tîrgoviște just as dawn broke silver over the mountaintops. The city would just be coming awake, its butchers, bakers, and field workers heading to their day's work. The height of summer, and the windows would be open, the lines strung up and ready for the wash; children would come scampering out barefoot soon, shooed away by mothers intent on scrubbing floors and mending clothes in their gossip circles.

"I want to be very clear about something," Vlad said, addressing his men. "The common people of this city are not to be harmed. Defend yourselves, and our cause, should they take up arms against us in the traitor's name, but we are here to fight

Vladislav's forces, make no mistake. As for the prince-killer, he is mine. Any man who cuts him down before I can get to him will be executed. Understood?"

"Yes, your grace!" they chorused. The thrill of battle-to-come glinted in their eyes, a feverish excitement.

"You know the plan," he said, and wheeled his horse. "We fall to it now."

The messenger trotted ahead, Malik beside him, dry dust kicked up by the horses' hooves. Then the men, and in their center, Vlad, tall in the saddle, charger prancing every other step.

When they reached the edges of town, a group of farmers with picks and hoes propped on their shoulders came to a halt, mouths falling open in shock.

At the head of the line, Malik called out in Romanian: "Prince Vlad Dracula rides forth! Back to claim his father's lands! To free his people from the tyranny of the pretender Vladislav! Make way for Vlad!"

Heads turned. Whispers started up, a low susurrus like rain on a tiled rooftop.

"Your deliverer! Vlad is returned!"

They cheered him.

Vlad didn't delude himself; he saw clean faces, and mended clothes, and round-cheeked children. It was summer, and the harvest had been good, and Vladislav had not starved these people like the villain of a story designed to frighten little ones. These people cheered because they remembered his father, and the horrible fate visited upon him by usurpers, and because the world loved stories of sons come to avenge their fathers.

Vladislav had, however, rolled over and showed his belly to the Ottomans. Doubtless these families had lost sons to the janissaries – and to Sultan Mehmet's appetites. They'd given over portions of their crop, and their coin, and some of the daughters had been raped or taken as the wives of Ottoman soldiers.

Vlad did not wave to them – not yet. Because he hadn't done anything for these people. Hadn't proven himself to them. But he sat tall in the saddle, and loosened his reins a notch, let his horse prance and chew at the bit a little. The big bay gelding was not anxious – but excited. As was Vlad.

His group reached the center of the city, the cobbled square in front of the bank, where a gibbet awaited treasonous necks. Vlad reined up and regarded it a moment, letting the press of the wondrous crowd fade to background noise. That simple wooden arm, its platform, and its trap doors.

Sultan Mehmet impaled his enemies on long spears of sharpened wood. Just as his father had before him; just as Vlad had seen during his time in Edirne.

A hanging was a terrible thing to witness, but an impalement…

The clear cry of a horn reached his ears.

He turned his horse, and Malik reined in beside him.

The horn sounded again, three long, foreboding blasts, the sound carried on the wind all the way from the palace. An old horn, Viking made, his mother's.

And then came the howling. Three separate voices, because even Helga had shifted to four legs today. A triangular pattern, ahead, and to either side.

"Wolves!" someone in the crowd shouted. "Wolves in the daylight!"

Mama, Vlad thought, hands tightening on his reins. *Be careful.*

The horn meant she'd played her part: slain the guards and opened the drawbridge. Up ahead, high on the hill, Vlad saw a cloud of dust rise, and the sun winked off the metal of armor and the tips of spears. Vladislav was sending his men to meet the foe.

It was the wolves' job to fall in behind them, spook their horses, and chase them down into Tîrgovişte.

One last wolf howl, not the mournful cry of cold nights and full moons, but a deep-throated, almost joyous call to arms: Cicero. Vlad knew his voice. The chase was on.

Vlad climbed down off his horse and drew his sword – his father's Toledo blade. He marched to the head of his men, all of them in a tight phalanx, just as they'd practiced.

"Make ready," he ordered. "If they're wearing Vladislav's colors, cut them all down. I'm not interested in taking prisoners."

They bellowed an assent, thrilled and boiling with energy. He could smell their adrenaline.

526

The troops came down on foot, only their captain mounted, their plate and mail gleaming in the sun. They came quickly, running, and Vlad could scent his wolves; these men weren't so much charging at him, as fleeing what came from behind.

The captain's gaze fixed on Vlad, and he must have recognized him, the way his eyes sprang wide, a clear ring of white around the brown irises. Then he lifted his sword, and spurred his horse.

Vlad stood his ground. And waited, and waited, and waited. Sunlight flared along the sharp edge of the captain's blade.

At the last second, Vlad stepped sideways, and ducked, just low and quick enough to miss the swing aimed at his head. He braced his foot, and rose in a lightning fast arc, his own blade swinging, and caught the captain just above the knee, at the gap between the top of his boot, and the bottom edge of his mail skirt.

It was a hard blow, and the sword was nearly ripped from his hands. Vlad heard the captain grunt, and smelled blood; he tightened his hands on his blade and dodged backward, barely avoiding being trod upon by the horse's back hooves.

The horse leapt into the phalanx of Vlad's men, head tossing, bit tugging cruelly at its mouth as its rider fought to stay in the saddle while his leg gushed blood.

Vlad turned away to meet the furious rush of a foot soldier.

The fighting was fast, and brutal, and bloody. Vladislav's men were well-trained, but they'd been spooked, and grew only more frightened in the face of Vlad's superior strength, speed, and maneuvering. He took a man's arm off at the elbow, and spun before his companion could deliver a strike to the back of Vlad's neck; drove his sword through the man's throat amidst a spray of hot blood. Vlad licked it from his lips and whirled to meet another foe.

You are not better than mortal men, Mother had always said, trying to keep him humble. But in that moment, he was. The enemies around him moved as if their boots were weighted; their limbs grew tired, and their attacks became defenses, and they weren't strong enough to stop Vlad's swings, his vampiric strength.

In the midst of it, he shouted orders to his own men, and sent a dozen up the hill to help his mother hold the palace gate.

Finally, it was over.

Vlad stood, chest heaving, skin wet and prickling beneath his clothes and armor, surveying the carnage around him. He applauded his own efficiency; he hadn't wasted his strokes, had killed as quickly and directly as possible. Still, there was blood, and limbs. And he was glad to see that his men had followed orders: there were no prisoners.

Malik approached him, wiping his sword on the edge of his cloak. Blood dappled his face, but Vlad could tell that it wasn't his own. "There will be more soldiers at the palace. This wasn't all of them," he said, gesturing to the bodies."

"I know," Vlad said, turning his gaze that direction. "To his eyes, we are few, and he thought this would take care of us. But I don't have to defeat his whole army, Malik. Only him."

~*~

By the time they reached the palace, not only had Eira, the wolves, and the dozen mercenary soldiers managed to gain control of the gate and drawbridge, but the men Vlad had sent around the long way this morning had arrived to back them up. Vladislav's men filled the bailey, but the odds were nearly even, and they looked and smelled nervous.

Vladislav himself awaited them, flanked by guards, his armor spotless, and hastily put on, it seemed. He stank of fear.

But he lifted his chin and said, "Vlad Dracula. What you have done here today is treasonous. This is a vassal state of Sultan Mehmet, of the Ottoman Empire, and you—"

"Shut up." Vlad unsheathed his sword, its blade wiped clean of blood, glinting in the sunlight. He pointed its tip at Vladislav. "Do you recognize this blade? It was my father's, Vlad Dracul's, and he had it on his person the day your dogs cut him to shreds and tore the beating heart out of his body."

A low growl sounded behind him: Mother. Her pain and fury was a palpable thing, staining the air.

"I use it now to challenge you," Vlad said, "in single combat. If you slay me, my men will leave. If I slay you, this palace, and this seat, is mine. As it rightfully should be."

An advisor leaned in to whisper in Vladislav's ear, but the pretend prince waved him away. He gulped, throat spasming. "And if I don't accept your challenge?"

"I'll slaughter everyone here anyway," Vlad said, and bared his teeth, showing his elongated fangs. "And feast on them."

The wolves began to snarl, then, snapping and slavering.

"What shall it be?" Vlad asked.

Vladislav drew his sword.

Vlad charged him.

Men scattered, pages, and squires, and advisors scrambling to get out of the way.

Vladislav parried Vlad's first strike, and met the next, steel clashing together with a sound like bells. He gritted his teeth, and Vlad saw sweat on his brow.

Vladislav was not a prince who spent much time in the training yard.

"You could surrender," Vlad said, pushing back, using his arms to push their crossed blades toward his enemy's face.

Vladislav grunted, and retreated a step.

Vlad *shoved* forward, and Vladislav stumbled back, and nearly fell. He got his sword up, just barely, to block Vlad's next attack.

"You're not even a man," he huffed between ragged breaths. "You're some hellspawn wearing a man's skin like a suit."

Vlad chuckled. "Oh, but I'm a man of God, christened in his holy house. I have taken the Blood and the Body into my own." Three quick strikes. The last Vladislav could not turn away, and the edge of Vlad's blade opened his glove, and his hand beneath it, blood sparkling like jewels.

Red-faced, winded, grimacing in pain, Vladislav lifted his sword again–

Vlad batted it away with his own. He put all of his strength into the swing, and the other man's sword went spinning away, landing in the dirt a yard away. Vlad used the momentum for a counter swing, and sliced Vladislav's injured hand off at the wrist.

Vladislav yelled. Blood spurted, and he fell to his knees, clutching at the gory stump.

Vlad saw guards try to move forward, wanting to protect their master, and the wolves moved in, growling savagely, hackles raised, Eira leading them, her own bloodied blade held before her.

"Oh, God, oh God!" Vladislav gasped, as his blood poured down onto the dirt, and tears tracked down his face.

Vlad put the tip of his sword beneath the man's chin, and tipped his head back. "Look at me."

He did, through a sheen of tears, his jaw quivering. He was a pitiful sight, slumped there, dying slowly of blood loss. Vlad searched his heart for sympathy, but found none.

He thought of Father. Of Mircea, dying cold, and crushed, beneath the earth. Thought of his mother's tears, and of his brother the whore slave.

He took a breath. "I think," he said evenly, "that there have always been two sides to everything. Always battles, always men set against each other. So it is now, with us, and the man who holds my brother. You chose the wrong side, Vladislav."

Then he raised his sword, and took the man's head off with one clean stroke.

It toppled to the dirt, and rolled a ways. The body fell over, and landed with a soft thump.

Silence, save the rippling of the banners along the bailey walls above them.

Vlad lifted his head, and met stare after stare after stare. He turned to Malik. "Seize his men. Kill them all. I have no place in my household for traitors."

He went inside to inspect his palace.

~*~

His first night back in his father's palace, in the home where he'd studied, and slept, and played as a boy, it seemed somehow fitting that his little brother came to visit.

Once the last of Vladislav's ilk had been put to the sword, and a messenger had been dispatched to John Hunyadi with the news of victory, Vlad inspected the larders and allotted enough meat, bread, wine, and summer fruit to feast the brave men who'd helped him reclaim his rightful seat. He sat through the merriment for a while, but slipped away while the festivities were still in full swing. He went up to his father's old study, and promptly shoved a stack of books and parchments off the desk and to the floor. The room was as cluttered and dusty and haphazard as it had been the last time he'd taken it over from Vladislav. Servants had scurried to light the candles, dozens of them, in iron candelabras and on silver sticks, their light flickering against the walls, and over the floor. But no one had attempted to set the place to rights. To clear up the signs of its last tenant. Perhaps that was expecting too much.

"His things?" Cicero asked, coming in behind him.

Vlad reached for a candle. "Help me get them into the fireplace. I'm going to burn them."

Cicero came up beside him, and plucked the candlestick from his hand with careful gentleness. "You should feed, first, and get some sleep. It's been a long day, and this can wait until tomorrow."

"I–" Vlad began, chest suddenly tight.

And a silky-smooth voice sounded behind them. "As delicate as ever, I see."

Vlad whirled.

Val quirked one eyebrow and offered a small smile. "Hello, brother."

He'd grown up since Vlad saw him last. A man, now, one much prettier than Vlad himself, their father's strong bone structure softened by their mother's golden hair, and freshwater eyes. He wore silk, gold, and red, and blue, with white şalvar, and gilt-edged slippers, his hair braided elaborately, a jewel-studded silver collar on his throat, tight enough that it couldn't be lifted off over his head.

He looked like a spoiled court brat, but Vlad saw the breadth of his shoulders, the narrowness of his waist, and the way the fabric shifted over a honed warrior's body when he tipped his hips to the side. Not *only* a spoiled brat, then.

Cicero gasped. "Valerian." A hushed whisper; wonder, or dread, or perhaps both.

531

Val's gaze shifted to the wolf, and his smile deepened, though was somehow sadder for it. "Cicero," he greeted softly, voice going boyish. "I was afraid that—" He cut off and swallowed with obvious effort. "You've bound yourself to a new master, I see."

Cicero lifted his head, proud. "And gladly."

Val glanced back to Vlad. "Father's wolf, and Father's blade, and now Father's palace." Vlad opened his mouth, a scathing retort ready on his tongue, but Val said, "As it should be." He tipped his head, and the candlelight caught a glimmer of wetness in his eyes. "It's good to see you again, Vlad." And even if he wasn't really here in body, he was in spirit, and those were real tears forming.

For a moment, Vlad felt exactly as he had upon walking into this room, but for an entirely different reason. His chest squeezed, and his breath came short, and he wanted to sit down; to take the burden off his weary feet, and maybe rest his head on something for a while. Tired, and rattled, and as full of rage as ever, but so weighted down by it that he didn't know what to do. He didn't want to strangle his little brother, though, or burn anything.

But whatever he felt, he had no idea how to channel it.

So he said, "What are you doing here, Radu?"

Val's expression shattered.

But then he smoothed it over, put on a face that was bland, bored almost. He cleared his throat, and then his voice came out prim, and sharp, and arrogant. "I've come to give you a warning, if you're not too stubborn to hear it. Sultan Mehmet is furious after his defeat at Belgrade. And now that you and Stephen have managed to roust princes who were deferential to the Ottoman cause, he will be incandescent with rage. He'll come for you, brother. He means to have your seat."

Vlad snorted. "The 'Ottoman cause.' He wants only to rape, and pillage, and cast his shadow over everything."

"Yes." Val smiled tightly and humorlessly. "He's very ambitious."

"So am I. Run tell your master that I will be ready for him, when he's done licking his wounds. I mean to be the last thing he sees before he departs this earth forever."

Val bowed, deep, grave, and mocking. "Very well." His face twitched, and nearly broke. "Give my love to Mother." He vanished with a small curl of white smoke.

It was silent a moment.

"What?" Vlad growled. "I can tell you want to say something."

"No, your grace," Cicero said. "But come. Feed and rest."

Tired now in spirit, as well as body, Vlad let himself be led from the room.

~*~

Vlad was twenty-five-years-old, and a great falling light had been seen in the sky, burning orange and trailing tails of fire. A good sign, because he had slain his enemy, and a small council of boyars had come together – grudgingly, he thought – to elect him officially. His official title, adopted in the vein of the princes who'd come before him, was Prince Vlad, son of Vlad the Great, sovereign and ruler of Ungro-Wallachia and of the duchies of Amlaş and Făgăraş.

John Hunyadi died that month, carried away by the plague that swept all of Eastern Europe. His son Matthias took up the mantle of governor of Belgrade, and leader of Transylvania in his stead, and it was to him that Vlad reached out, as well as the mayors of Brasov and Sibiu. It was important to establish correspondence, Eira told him; she stood at his side in the study, his constant advisor in those early days. Politicking was not his strong suit, but it was a necessary part of princedom. He built alliances, and tried to foment a revolt amongst the receptive boyars along the Moldavian border, to aid Stephen's cause there against the man who'd slain his father. They traded letters as often as they could, the two of them, bound by their youth spent together in the schoolroom and training grounds, and by the bitter loss of sons made princes too early, thanks to murdered fathers.

Val's warning about Mehmet haunted him. He felt something like guilt every time he remembered that scene in the study, the look on his brother's face when he'd called him Radu. That had been a cruelty, even for him.

But mostly, he fretted over the Ottomans.

And come they did, though not with spears and swords. Shortly after Stephen was confirmed in Moldavia, a delegation arrived, prim and proper, led into the great hall in front of Vlad by Malik, formerly Bey, who Vlad could see received more than one shocked look.

The head delegate, a thin, reedy man clothed in burgundy and white, his black turban small and tightly wrapped, stepped forward with a bow. "Vlad Dracula," he said, in flawless Slavic. "Congratulations from my sultan, Mehmet, on retaking your ancestral seat."

"Please give him my thanks," Vlad answered in Turkish, and thought the man looked caught between pleased and surprised when he straightened.

"I shall also be happy to convey your agreement to terms of peace," the man said glibly. "There is a customary treaty already in place between the Empire and Wallachia. The sultan expects that you shall assent to it as graciously as your father did before you."

Vlad pushed a humorless smile across his face. Whatever it looked like, it caused the delegate to take a half-step back. "Two-thousand gold ducats and free passage through Wallachia?"

"As well as a pilgrimage to the capital to pay homage."

Vlad snorted. "He can have his gold and access." He motioned, and two of his men stepped forward, lugging the chest between them. It held newly minted coins, his own face on one side, and the falling star of his summer of ascension on the other, for luck. "But I won't be making any pilgrimage. Not even if I currently lack sons to be kidnapped and taken as hostage."

The man regarded him a long, cool moment, then finally nodded. "Yes. Fine. You will need to sign this." He produced a parchment, and Vlad's scribe hurried forward with portable writing table, ink, and quill.

It pained him in every sense to sign the treaty, but he was no fool. Right now, he lacked the manpower to halt a true invasion. *Patience*, he heard Iskander Bey say in the back of his mind, an old mantra from an old friend. *You must be patient.*

So he signed, and set about the business of ruling his small country.

Vladislav was dead, but Vlad wasn't content. An eye for an eye. But there were others who had wronged him. Others who'd helped in the murder of his family.

Within days of his installation, the boyars began to come to pay their respects; they brought gifts of wine, and jeweled belts, and ornamental daggers. They bowed, and curtsied, and smiled painfully at him; poured forth effusive praise, and promises of loyalty, and wishes for his good health and long reign. And all of it was a farce. These were the people who'd chased Father through the forest like hounds after a fox.

But he waited, patient.

His most immediate concern was fortifying his lands. He wanted walls, as high, and smooth, and foreboding as those at the palace in Edirne. Tîrgoviște was the beating heart of Wallachia, its center of commerce, and culture, and politics, but the rest of his lands' keeps and castles were either sad timber lodgings, or crumbling to dust, left too long in disrepair. If he was to stand against Mehmet, he would need multiple fortresses, places where he and his men could overnight safely as he traveled about, defending and inspecting his kingdom.

He started in Bucharest, taking the sleepy necklace of modest pastoral residences and walling it; building it up. He wanted it to rival Tîrgoviște in every sense.

He rode with his builders and architects, Malik and Cicero, and often his mother, alongside him, into the mountains, and drew up plans for towers and keeps, impenetrable holdfasts that he would staff with troops when he wasn't in residence, places that could serve as stumbling blocks to invaders, and places from which messengers could bear news of attack to wherever Vlad was staying at the moment.

It was at one of these mountain fortresses that an epiphany struck.

It was an old castle, tumbled down to rubble, perched near the Hungarian border. Vlad's steward, a dour but efficient little man named Florin, speculated that it had been built a century ago, by one of the Basarab princes, and had served as an observation

535

outpost for Castle Bran, just across the way in Transylvania. An ideal location, strategically, in the foothills of the Făgăraş range, near Curtea-de-Argeş.

Here, he thought, was an opportunity.

For the most part, the boyars still loyal to Vladislav – and, to a lesser degree, their Ottoman vassal lords – had bowed and scraped and pretended loyalty to Vlad. But there had been one, early, right after he was crowned, who'd styled himself Albu the Great, one of Vlad Dracul's old opponents. He'd attempted to organize a revolt, one that Cicero had brought him word of, while spying on four legs. Vlad had personally led the ambush against the man, his wolves, and Malik, and a few trusted household guards at his side.

~*~

Vlad paced the length of the Turkish carpet in the central room of Albu's sumptuous house. The fire crackled in the grate, but not loudly enough to drown out the sounds of frightened, frantic breathing. Albu and his entire family knelt on the carpet, heads bowed, shaking with terror. They'd all watched Cicero shift back to his two-legged form, and Fen, still a wolf, sat on his haunches, smiling at them with all his gleaming ivory teeth.

Vlad glanced at Eira, just to take her measure in this moment; her expression surprised him, though maybe it shouldn't have. It was closed off, her face smooth, her mouth colorless and immobile. Her eyes, though, burned with a kind of focused, cold hatred that Vlad had only ever seen in the mirror.

He'd wondered, occasionally, where his great capacity for anger came from, because his father had been a gentle soul, all things told. He'd worried that it was a trait he shared with his uncle Romulus. But he saw now, with startling clarity, that his rage was his mother's. She'd given it to Vlad, and given Val her beauty, and sweetness, and creativity. It wasn't an even parceling of gifts, but Vlad would take it; he needed all the rage he could get.

He knew, then, what he needed to do here. What he had to.

He halted and turned to face his captives, hands loose at his sides. Calmness descended. "Albu," he said, "if you're brave

536

enough to raise a revolt against me, then you can be brave enough to look me in the eye."

Albu lifted his head, shaking, his eyes wide. He met Vlad's gaze, though his shoulders slumped another fraction.

"Why do you want to overthrow me?" Vlad asked.

The boyar hesitated. He licked his lips, and glanced toward Cicero, who had moved to stand beside Vlad, the hood of his pelt pushed back, but no less wild for it. There were twigs caught in his hair.

"I would have an honest answer," Vlad prompted.

"Because – because you are not a man. You are not a natural, mortal, Christian man. You are–" He looked to Cicero again, to Fen, and back to Vlad, miserable and terrified. "Life is good. Vladislav brought us peace with the Ottomans. Life is good, and you will ruin that. Your grace," he tacked on at the end, ducking his head once more.

"Peace," Vlad echoed. "Peace for people like *you*, you mean. For rich boyars, who do not need to give their sons and daughters over to Mehmet's lust and soldiery."

Albu lifted his head once more.

"Peace always has a price," Vlad said. "Vladislav's was other people's children. Mine will be the blood of traitors like you."

Vlad impaled his first man that night. Albu and his family.

"Let them see," he said to Cicero. "Let Wallachia see what the sultan will do to them."

"Right now, it's what you are doing," his wolf said, evenly, staring steadily at him.

"What I'm doing to my enemies. An eye for an eye, Cicero. A scar for a scar. A knife for a knife. That's how I mean to rule this land."

And that was how he did.

~*~

It was Easter, and boyars unfurled blankets, and unpacked portable feasts on the shaggy, wildflower-studded fields that lay just below the ruins of the old castle in the foothills of the Făgăraș. They had been invited, by the prince himself, to enjoy the warm weather. All the boyars who feigned loyalty. Who'd gladly helped to kill the prince's father, Dracul. They brought their wives, and children, their heirs, these nobles who had wanted to join in with Albu.

They stood when Vlad strode into their midst, all in crimson and sable and fine, dyed-red leather.

"Happy Easter," he called, and the wind carried his voice through the field, loud, but not merry. "Welcome to the site of what will someday soon be one of my great fortresses."

There were cheers. A smattering of applause.

Someone, a wife, turning to look for her wayward child, finally saw the soldiers moving into place. She touched her husband's arm, and pointed, and then others looked. And then they all noticed. Wallachian foot soldiers in full armor, spears braced on their shoulders, swords belted at their hips.

The happy chattering shifted in tone; grew distressed, worried.

"My men have brought stone, and mortar, and timbers," Vlad continued. "And you, my loyal boyars, will be the manpower."

They all turned to him, wearing faces of shock, and horror. Disbelief.

"Roll up your sleeves, ladies and gentlemen. You're going to build me a castle. And after, if you can still stand, you may fall on your knees and beg me to spare your miserable, traitorous lives."

~*~

None survived that Easter of forced labor. The boyars who'd killed his family were dead; the few who didn't collapse were impaled.

An eye for an eye.

After, Castle Dracula stood proudly silhouetted against the clear spring sky, a testament to the patience of Vlad Dracula.

Of Vlad *Tepes*. The Impaler.

38

THE CONQUEROR

*Istanbul, capital of the Ottoman Empire
(formerly Constantinople)
1461*

Mehmet had a new favored scribe, a fair-faced boy whose name Val refused to learn; he would have no more intimacies with slaves or servants, he'd decided, and also, he could tell by scent that Mehmet was fucking this boy, and he didn't really want anything to do with that. Every night Mehmet went to someone else's bed, it gave Val a chance to catch a few hours of actual sleep.

The scribe sat today at the sultan's big war table, as Mehmet and Timothée the mage paced unhurriedly around the wide, marble-floored chamber, plotting a course for invasion.

"It will require toppling the pillars of European civilization," Timothée cautioned. "Rome is the real prize; take the Vatican, seize the pope, and then France, Germany, and Britain will wish to negotiate."

"I don't want to negotiate."

"Yes, but that's how it begins. And then you can topple them one-by-one."

"Yes, yes," Mehmet mused, rubbing at his beard. He stood staring down at his largest map, other hand kneading at his lower back. He'd gone from thick to almost fat by this point; he huffed when he rode or walked long distances, and he groaned when he stood, complained always of aching joints and a sore back.

Gout, Val kept saying, just to needle him. But he'd gotten a taste of his blood during a vigorous night's fucking, and he'd nearly vomited from the taste. This wasn't gout. Whatever it was, something was wrong. Something about the vampire blood was breaking down, going rancid. He'd never heard of such a thing – a foul turning. He laid awake some nights, worrying that it was a family curse, wondering if maybe poor Arslan was out there somewhere, going through the same thing.

"But first we must get through the east," Mehmet said, motioning to the map. "Hungary, Romania, Serbia." He frowned.

Timothée flapped a dismissive gesture. "That won't be difficult."

Val barely restrained a snort.

That he didn't like the mage was a given. That Mehmet actually respected and listened to the man was a shock. Then again, Timothée appealed to Mehmet's vanity at every turn.

Val had found him unlikely. In his mind, he'd imagined mages to be tall, rail-thin fellows with long, pointed beards and stormy eyes. There might have been black cloaks, and long fingernails, and rolling trails of smoke involved, too. Childish wonderings. The reality was far more ordinary. Timothée, no surname to speak of, was French, and short, and a bit round in the middle. He had thinning salt-and-pepper hair, kept short, and a matching beard. Small eyes that looked like glass beads, and a ready laugh, and a face lined from smiling. He looked like someone's grandfather, which didn't make much sense to Val, since mages were immortals. Where was the ageless, smooth, sophisticated enchanter he'd expected?

He did stink like a campfire, though. And could conjure modest balls of flames in his hands. And talked often of the wife and son he'd left behind in France. Val was sick of hearing about "little Philippe."

Mehmet lifted an unimpressed look. "Have you forgotten what I told you of Belgrade?"

Val's stomach tightened with remembered excitement, just like it did every time Mehmet was forced to mention the disaster at Belgrade.

"John Hunyadi is dead, is he not? You shall take more men the next time, and be better prepared."

"Hmph."

Timothée stepped in closer to the table, voice lowering, growing serious. "Your Majesty, we stand now in the Palace at Blachernae. In a city that you took from the Romans. You conquered *Constantinople*. What is Belgrade in comparison to that?"

Mehmet pursed his lips, not considering – he'd considered all of this before, at length, rambling about it to Val as he took him angrily from behind. But he was flattered. He had always been so easy to flatter.

Val was an expert at it, by now. And save the times he'd pushed Mehmet to the point of rape and brutality, he knew when he could flex his contrariness. Not that he had to, but because it was one small thing he could control.

"Forgive me," he drawled, "but you're both forgetting one very important factor in all of this." He made a lazy gesture toward the map, leaned back in his chair, one leg kicked up over the arm.

Mehmet shot him a glare.

Timothée turned to him with his usual pleasantly bland smile, his eyes hard and bright as polished stone. Val knew the mage hated him, though he hadn't figured out why yet. He didn't think, though, that it was for any of the reasons the rest of the court did.

"And what is that?" he asked, hands folded together primly before him.

Val lifted a finger. "My brother."

Mehmet's jaw clenched, muscle leaping in his cheek.

Timothée's bland smile tightened a fraction. "That would be Vlad Dracula, yes? The Prince of Wallachia?"

"That's him, yes." Val couldn't keep a hint of proud smugness from his voice.

He realized his mistake when he saw bright malice flare to life in the mage's eyes. "His kingdom is small," Timothée said, "and he is a violent, ill-tempered ruler. Purported to have a taste for the blood of his subjects."

Val let his feet fall to the floor, and sat up straight in his chair. "Vlad doesn't feed from humans."

The mage cocked his head. "Then why does he kill so many of them?"

It would take hours to properly explain Vlad, and his regimented sense of justice and revenge, his intense, long-burning anger, hot and relentless as dragon fire. And to explain that it was a patient, calculated, controlled rage. He didn't kill in fits of temper, like Mehmet was prone to do. He weighed the morality of everything, and once set on a course, could not be swayed from it.

"Because they're not loyal to him," he said, simply.

Timothée *tsk*ed and turned away. "A trivial concern," he told Mehmet. "We'll route him, and be about our business."

But Mehmet had crossed swords with Vlad as a boy, had seen that incandescently cold rage up close, face-to-face, and he didn't look so ready to dismiss him. "I will have his head," he said at last, going to back to stroking his beard, "but it will be a true fight."

He stepped back from the table, suddenly, with a sigh. "Enough of this. My eyes are swimming." He rubbed them briskly a moment, with a pained sound.

"Very well, Your Majesty," Timothée said. "There are other things we might do." He lifted his brows, and Val realized he'd missed something, when Mehmet said, "Ah, you're right. Has he been talkative?"

"Not so far, but I haven't inquired yet today."

"Hmm."

"What?" Val said, skin prickling with unease.

"Come along, Radu," Mehmet said, as he and the mage headed for the door. "This will be educational for you."

"Christ," Val muttered under his breath, but got to his feet and followed.

In the hallway, the usual janissary guards fell into step, and their party skirted the gardens from the inside, going away from the throne room, and the feast hall, and all the public areas where members of the court gathered, and instead to a darker, less beautiful, less royal part of the palace.

Since his conquest of the city, Mehmet had been expanding, improving, even, upon the old Palace of Blachernae, but here was an area he had not touched, and one it looked like even Constantine hadn't inhabited. Old, weathered stones, gone soft as cloth to the touch, and floors untidy from a lack of use; dust, and leaves, and rugs that needed beating.

A guard opened a door for them, revealing a staircase, and the scent of blood struck Val: old *and* fresh. And then he knew where they were going.

The dungeon.

He'd never seen it before, but there could be no other name for whatever lay at the bottom of this staircase, scented with mold, and damp, iron long rusted from the salt air of Constantinople.

Istanbul, now.

Someone came up to meet them with a lantern, and led them on, until they finally arrived in a long, narrow chamber that struck Val as mirroring a stable: an arched stone ceiling, with thin, high windows at the top, no bigger than a handspan, to prevent escape. A central aisle, and to either side, tables, and racks, and places where old manacles dangled from the walls. It was too deep to see all of it, shadows looming at the end. But shafts of light fell in through the windows, slanted bars of it, and there were torches, and candles, and more lanterns.

Enough to see the man chained on his back to a table.

And the scent of blood, viscera, and excrement was so strong that Val cupped a hand over his nose and mouth. He retched quietly, once, and then managed to swallow his gorge before he brought up his lunch.

"Who is that?" he asked, voice muffled by his hand.

It was Timothée who answered him, sounding delighted. "One of your brother's allies. Mihály Szilágy."

Val did not know him, but as he walked slowly closer, seemingly pulled against his will, he noted the man's Slavic features, now twisted up with pain. A young man, built as a warrior. Val noticed, too, the bloody stumps that had once been fingers and toes; the long red stripes where the flesh had been cut from his torso.

One of the torturers gave a report to Mehmet in Turkish: "He's said nothing still, Your Majesty. Only curses us, and calls down God's wrath upon us."

Mehmet waved the man aside, and stepped up close to the table, leaned over it, so that his face hovered above Szilágy's. The contrast between them, the clean, well-dressed, perfumed sultan, and the sweaty, grimy, bloody prisoner, hit Val's breastbone like a shove.

"Why will you not talk?" Mehmet asked, congenial, almost smiling. "Surely you must know by now that you will die here. I won't release you back to your masters, so that they may punish you for revealing their secrets. I wouldn't do such a thing to a man."

Szilágy's hands flexed, the blood catching the lantern-light. Val saw a flash of white bone, where a finger used to be.

"Tell me what Vlad Dracula is planning. He sends messengers to tell me of his loyalty, but he is not loyal, is he? He's planning to move against me, yes?"

It was silent a moment, save the harsh, wet sound of Szilágy's breathing. The man's jaw and lips worked, like he was gathering the strength to speak.

Only he didn't. He spit in Mehmet's face instead.

The sultan reared back, and wiped at his offended cheek.

Val let out a low groan. *Brave idiot*, he thought.

Cold fury settled over Mehmet like a mantle, one he'd worn often, though not well. Blind rage was a better fit for him. He reached out a hand. "Give me the saw, I'll do it myself."

Val turned away, and walked for the stairs.

"Leaving?" Timothée asked, high and mocking.

Val didn't answer; he couldn't. He'd seen Mehmet cut a man in half before, watched entrails fall out onto the floor while the victim still screamed. He didn't need to see it again.

Please, Val prayed silently to whichever gods might be listening, *give my brother the strength to kill him*.

39

CRUSADE

"You *agree?*" The monk was a small, soft-handed fellow, who nevertheless had managed to look at home aboard the mule that had brought him to Tîrgoviște. He'd been to Bucharest first, he said, chasing after Vlad, sending runners, pleading for an audience. Vlad had scoffed, initially, at the idea that the pope would send a holy man to treat with *him*. But here the man sat, bearing sealed documents from Pope Pius himself, talking of a crusade.

"Of course, I agree," Vlad said with a shrug. Cicero made a sound beside him that might have been a laugh. "Am I not the Eastern prince with the most outspoken hatred of Mehmet?"

"Oh. Yes. Well. You are." The man tugged at his sleeves and shifted in his chair. He didn't look nervous, though, exactly; nor did he smell it. Eager, maybe. "It's only that so many of your allies have refused involvement."

"I'm aware."

The years since Vlad had taken his father's throne had brought unexpected changes.

First, John Hunyadi died. No more than a month after his victory at Belgrade, a plague swept the region, and the old governor fell to it, carried off by fever and delirium. His son, Matthias, had taken his throne and governorship, ruling over Hungary, and Transylvania, respectably. He was a shrewd leader, but a convivial one, and Vlad found that, though he didn't exactly call him friend, he did like the man, and approved of him. And he shared Vlad's loathing of the Ottomans – even if he was less vitriolic about it.

But then there was the matter of Stephen. Matthias had, during the summer of revolutions, allowed safe passage for the Moldavian prince that Stephen had defeated, and Stephen still harbored a grudge. One so strong that he had, at the Congress of Mantua a year before, declined to join in a crusade effort, wanting nothing to do with aligning himself with Matthias. He'd agreed to a treaty with the Ottomans, instead.

Vlad wasn't sure if he could forgive his friend for that.

The Congress itself had been pointless. Save Holy Roman Emperor Frederick III, and the pope himself, no one wanted a crusade. Peace was easier, and it did not matter that Mehmet was currently trying to conquer the lands along the Danube, cutting off the river, and thereby access to the Black Sea, from Eastern Europe. Frederick had offered funding, and manpower, but the lords of Moldavia, Serbia, and even Skanderbeg, in Albania, had declined to take up the cross. Matthias remained undecided; he would do what suited him, Vlad knew.

And Vlad, well, he hadn't been invited to the Congress, but he'd made no secret of his leanings. He wanted Mehmet to rot slowly on a spike outside the window of his palace.

"The pope really means to declare a crusade?" he asked.

The monk nodded. "He does." And then he reached into the saddlebag he'd wedged into his chair beside him, lifted the flap, and drew out a bundle wrapped in rough cloth. This he unfolded, and revealed snowy linen, a field of white...and a red cross.

Vlad's lungs, and heart, and gut tightened a moment, a full-body clench. A thrill.

"Vlad Dracula," the monk said, adopting a formal tone. "The pope means for you to slay the dragon. If you will."

Beside him, Vlad felt Cicero shiver, and sensed the racing of his heart.

Malik murmured something low and wordless under his breath.

"A crusade," Vlad said, and smiled. "I accept."

~*~

"Vlad," Eira said later, coming into his bedchamber without knocking. "I want to talk to you about something."

Vlad hung his cloak up in his armoire and turned to her with lifted brows. *So, talk.*

She sent an unsubtle glance toward Cicero, who sat perched in the window ledge, on the cushion there, reading by candlelight.

He lifted his head, and slowly closed his book, looking between them, nonplussed, but no doubt picking up on the tension Eira had brought with her into the room.

"Really, Mother?" Vlad asked. "Anything you have to say, you can say in front of Cicero."

She tipped her head. "Would you say anything to me in front of Fenrir and Helga?"

Vlad worked his jaw a moment, biting back the *no* that formed on his tongue. *That's different*, he wanted to tell her. *This is Cicero.* He didn't think she would appreciate the distinction, no matter how he explained it, so he turned to his wolf.

Cicero was already unfolding himself from the ledge, leaving his book behind. "I'll go," he said easily, though he radiated curiosity. He gave Eira a deferential bob of his head on the way out, and closed the door.

"What?" Vlad said, and could hear that his tone was short.

She lifted her brows, a mild reproach, and moved to take Cicero's seat, legs crossing primly.

He gave an internal groan. When she played the lady, it was because she was about to say something he didn't want to hear. "What, Mama?" he asked, though softer this time, and sat down on the chest at the foot of his bed.

She smoothed her skirt, and folded her hands together. "*Mother.*"

"Oh, fine. I'll just say it straight out: you need to take a wife, Vlad."

Of all the things he'd expected her to say, *that* wasn't one of them. "I need to take a *what?*"

"A wife," she said, exasperated. "Princes have wives, and they have heirs. You have neither, and people are beginning to talk."

"So let them talk."

"Vlad—"

"No." He stood up, startling himself with the suddenness of it, rippling with energy, now. He started to pace, needing to move. "If it's the sense of propriety that bothers you, we can

547

pretend that you're my wife. You're with me all the time anyway, and you look like a young woman, still. The only ones who know you're my mother would never tell a soul that you are."

"Am I to put on a charade?" she asked, affronted. "Sleep in your bedchamber? Kiss you? And act like–"

"You said so yourself: it would only be a charade. Do you take me for incestuous?"

"No, of course not, but I don't think your mind is–"

He rounded on her. "Mehmet butchered Mihály yesterday!"

She fell silent, face pale and drawn, though she did not tremble, and she did not shrink from him.

"*That* was what was in the missive that arrived earlier today. He sawed him in half while he was still alive, because he would not give up information about me." His chest ached, and he took deep, sharp breaths. "And that was only after he tortured him."

"You impale your enemies," she bit back. "And they are still breathing when you do it."

He felt vicious, suddenly, hungry, and desperate, and clawing. "*I do.*" He bent forward at the waist, and leaned into her face. "And if you expect me to feel remorse, then I don't, and if that makes me the monster that he is, so be it. We are at war, Mother. We have been at war my entire life. He has taken Smederevo, and pushed the despot out of Morea, and knocks now at the door of Belgrade. Did you think he would be satisfied with Constantinople?" A growl built deep in his chest, rolled out through his voice. "He will *never* be satisfied. And every other prince and king and protector is handing over all his gold, and hiding behind his women's skirts, and *appeasing* the bastard! I don't mean to do that, Mother! Do you understand? I will not fall to my knees for the man who nightly rapes your other son!"

Mention of Val brought a sudden, brilliant rush of tears to her eyes. But she stared at him, unflinching.

And Vlad realized he was only inches from her, fangs long and bared, growling constantly.

He pulled back with an explosive breath and moved away from her. Reached to massage the knot at the back of his neck, a near-constant affliction these days. Quieter, he said, "Mama, you don't understand. I have done what good I can for Wallachia, but

I'm not here to leave a legacy. To carry on a dynasty. I don't need a wife, or an heir. The only thing I care about is killing Mehmet."

When he looked at her again, she'd blinked her tears away. She sighed. "My darling. We are immortals. We *have* to plan for dynasties. We have to think beyond blind rage and grief, even when that's all we care about." Softer: "I'm only trying to look after you."

"I know. But my answer stands. Talk to me about a wife if I survive this."

40

GIURGIU

Vlad received a missive from Matthias Hunyadi that read: *May the sun shine upon your health and good fortune.* It was a pre-arranged code between them, one that meant the Ottomans had intercepted one of their messages.

"Well," Vlad said, folding the parchment. "They're onto us." He felt a grin threaten. "At least, they think they are."

"Beg pardon, your grace?" the vizier in front of him said, brow furrowing. Mehmet had sent a special delegation, fronted by the bey of Nicopolis, Hamza Pasha, who waited now upon Vlad's answer to an agreement proposed by the sultan. Matthias's letter had arrived in the midst of the negotiations, and had Vlad believed such things possible, he would have called the timing poetic.

"Nothing," Vlad said, refocusing on the man. "So, let us review. Mehmet wishes to meet, face-to-face, in Constantinople, so that we may negotiate the terms he's laid here." He gestured to the parchments strewn across his desk.

"Yes, your grace."

"Though he's asking for thirty-thousand gold ducats, and no less than five-hundred boys for his Janissary Corp. Yes?"

"Correct. But numbers are, after all, negotiable."

"Of course." A dagger lay on the desk, in plain view, and when Vlad traced his fingers idly along the desk's edge toward it, Hamza's eyes followed the movement, throat bobbing as he swallowed. Sometimes he loved having a reputation. "Hmm. I would rather start negotiations now. Here." He snapped his fingers to get his scribe's attention. "Draft a missive to the sultan, from Hamza Pasha himself. Tell him that I will meet, but that I won't come to Istanbul. It must be a point between our thrones, respectively. Somewhere along the river would be amenable. But be sure to emphasize that I am most willing to bargain with him. It shall be a pleasure to see him in person once again."

"Yes, your grace." The quill began to scratch.

"As for you," he said to Hamza. "Malik, put him in irons. Him and his entire party."

The vizier's eyes flew wide. "Your grace—"

"And confiscate all their baggage. I need their clothes."

~*~

"There's a very good chance we'll all die," Malik said, matter-of-factly.

Vlad adjusted his turban, tucked a stray piece of hair back into it. "That's what makes it a good plan: it's too crazy for anyone to expect it."

"You're not wrong on that," Cicero said.

They marched forward, surrounded on all sides by Vlad's best mercenaries, and trailed by cavalry, all of them dressed rather haphazardly in Turkish garb. Ahead, the fortress gates awaited his trickery.

Giurgiu was an island fortress, built out into the Danube river; built by Vlad's father, in fact, at his personal expense. It had been in Ottoman hands since '47, which was exactly why Vlad, writing as Hamza Pasha, had suggested it. His mother might think him foolish for being so hell-bent on revenge, but he wasn't stupid, and never had been. He knew that he was outmanned in every sense of the word. He would have to outsmart Mehmet.

He walked now, his own sword fitted into a pilfered Turkish sheath at his hip, to the barred gates of the fortress, dressed as his own enemy, and approached the captain of the guards on duty there.

"Ho, there!" the captain called, raising a hand to stop them. He cast a critical look across Vlad; gaze flickered briefly to Cicero's eye patch, conspicuous with his hair bound and secured in a tight crimson turban. "We're awaiting Vlad Dracula's party. Where have you come from?"

They *had been* expecting Vlad's party. Bits of the costumes they all wore had been plucked from the corpses of the would-be ambushers that Vlad and his men had killed several miles back down the road.

Vlad, dressed in Hamza Pasha's finest kaftan and armor, lifted his chin to a regal angle and spoke in perfect Turkish. "Dracula knows about the ambush. His party re-routed, and they're approaching now from the other direction. I need to send a message to the sultan. I need more men."

"More…men?" He glanced all the way down the line, toward the stamping horses of the cavalry. "But…"

"Open the damn gate, you fool."

The captain hesitated a moment longer, but then he turned and barked a command, and there came the thumping of the big double gates being unbarred from the other side.

Malik whistled softly, just for Vlad to hear, impressed.

Cicero barely suppressed a chuckle.

The gates swung open.

The men started forward, a steady march, that quickly dissolved into a dash, boots kicking up dust.

The guard captain went goggle-eyed. "Oh–"

Vlad drew his sword and opened the man's throat with one clean slice. "Thank you," he told the toppling body, before he went to join his men. "But I'll be taking back my father's castle, now."

~*~

Vlad carved a path through the defenders that threw themselves at him. He turned blades aside with his own as if they were feathers, hacked through limbs as if they belonged to training dummies. Men screamed, and fell, and blood ran thick down his sword, and across the stones of the courtyard.

From the first, the battle for the fortress had felt like a victory; there were men here, strong and well-trained, but there weren't enough of them. Not as many as would have accompanied the sultan, had he deigned to come.

"Vlad!" Cicero called.

Vlad took a man's hand, and spun as the Ottoman fell to his knees, screaming, clutching at the stump, seeking out his wolf. Cicero stood partway up a flight of stone steps that led to an upper gallery – and an entrance into the fortress's royal apartments. Vlad had never been here, but his father had talked often of the place when he was a boy, and he knew where Cicero wanted to lead him.

He ducked a swing aimed at his head, caught the soldier just under the ribs with a vicious slice, and went to join Cicero.

Two Ottomans waited at the top of the stairs, the only ones guarding the entrance to the apartments, it seemed. The battle was chaos, enemies dressed as one another, nearly impossible to tell friend from foe. But these two at the top of the stairs had seen Vlad fighting, no doubt, and they paled and braced themselves, visibly, as Vlad urged Cicero aside and started up toward them.

They came at him together, swords slashing from opposite angles, clean bright steel flashing in the sunlight. He caught one with his own blade, and the other with his gloved hand. And then he *shoved*.

Bloodlust and adrenaline roared in his veins, the promise of victory, and they toppled backward to land on the stones. Vlad wrenched the sword in his hand free, and tossed it away. Stepped on that man's throat, and crushed his windpipe with his boot. The other he disarmed with a deft flick of his own sword, and then drove the point through his eye.

The bodies stilled beneath him.

"You shouldn't take such chances," Cicero said, panting, as he joined him.

"It wasn't a chance," Vlad said, and kept moving.

The door to the apartment gave under one kick, and there he found a silk-dressed, sniveling official of some sort, attempting to hide beneath a couch.

Cicero took the lead this time, dragging him out by the collar with a vicious, wolfish snarl, and throwing him down on the rug at Vlad's feet.

Vlad laid his bloodied sword against his throat. "Where's your sultan?"

The man whimpered, and tried to shrink down into himself.

Vlad pressed harder with the sword, and reached with his free hand to pull the turban from his own head, dark hair spilling loose down his shoulders. There could be no mistaking who he was, now. "Where is he?"

"A-asia Minor, your grace," the man stuttered, breathing through his mouth, tears streaking down his face. "He thought – forgive me, he said you'd be killed on the road. You weren't supposed to…" He trailed off, his teeth chattering.

"He's off on another campaign, then," Vlad said, speaking more to Cicero than to this man. "I wasn't ever supposed to enter the fortress alive, so what was the sense in him coming all this way?"

He slew the official with one efficient stroke.

Vlad nodded. "I think he'll come now."

~*~

"Your *brother*," Mehmet hissed, and flecks of spit struck Val's face. He'd burst into Val's bedchamber a moment before, and, when Val had lifted his head from the book he'd been reading, taken him by the throat, dragged him off the bed, and pinned him up against the wall.

"Yes, I have a brother," he said mildly, and swallowed against the press of Mehmet's hand at his Adam's apple.

Mehmet bared his teeth and growled.

Val sighed, and feigned boredom, though his belly clenched with excitement. "What's he done now?" Whatever it was, if it made Mehmet this angry, Val was glad of it.

Mehmet snarled, but at least turned loose of him and stalked away – stumped away. His joints must have been hurting him especially tonight, because he lacked all grace.

He fetched up against a table, leaned heavily against it. "That bastard," he said over his shoulder, still growling, "has taken Giurgiu!"

It took a moment for Val to remember where that was. And then he had to bite back a laugh. He barely managed to suppress his grin. "I believe my father built that fortress."

"He doesn't even have enough men to pull off something like that!" Mehmet shouted.

Val shrugged. "So? He's Vlad."

Mehmet seethed.

"Perhaps," Val suggested. "You'd finally like to face him for yourself, rather than send wave after wave of men for him to slaughter."

The sultan glared at him, and Val knew that, in this small way, he'd won something. Not a war, but a skirmish.

"Pack your things," Mehmet said, gathered himself, and stormed for the door. "And prepare your princely raiment, Radu! You'll be a prince before the year is out."

Or, Val thought viciously, *you'll be another trophy in the Impaler's courtyard.*

41

FANGS LONG AND SHARP

The Campaign of 1462

Vlad routed Ottoman forces up and down the Danube, freeing the waterways for trade and travel into and out of Romania. He put every Turk to the sword – or he impaled them, grisly warnings above gates and along wall-tops.

The pox came with the late summer heat, and his men died, and fell sick. They sheltered in the cool of stream-fed mountain forests, and his wolves hunted fresh game, and Eira spent nearly as much time trying to comfort the afflicted as she did training with her sword, sparring with Malik, when the wolves refused to raise a hand toward her, even in the name of preparedness.

And then, finally, Mehmet came. He brought to bear such a force that two vampires, and three wolves were not enough to tip the scales in their favor. So they began a protracted retreat, fighting, killing, engaging their enemy, but all the time falling back, back.

But not quietly. And Vlad hadn't given up, yet.

~*~

Vlad knelt at the water's edge and inhaled, smelling the taint of human waste in the water; the enemy was upwind. He stood, and accepted the unlit torch that Cicero handed him. Eira was there, too, and Fen, and Malik, and five other of his most-trusted and fearsome warriors. Night lay black and starless over this patch of forest; owls called, low and somber, and small, slinking creatures moved through the underbrush, watching them.

"Don't linger," he reminded everyone. "Kill if you can, but do not allow yourselves to get mired in a fight. This is about destruction, and fear."

Murmurs of assent.

He looked at his mother, her hair tightly braided, three lines of blue painted like claw marks over each eye, bleeding down her cheeks. Before he could say anything, she lifted blue brows and said, "Going to tell me to stay behind again?"

He'd done it several times now, and she'd nearly slapped him once, and outright refused to listen at every occasion.

"Be careful, Mother," he said, and bowed his head to her.

She snorted, and rolled her eyes, quick flashes in the dark. Then she came forward, put her small but deadly hands on his shoulders, and stood up on her toes to kiss his cheek. "You, too, my darling." She pulled back, and smiled, her fangs long and sharp. "And good luck."

~*~

"God, I hate campaigning," Val muttered, sinking down into a chair.

This particular campaign was nothing like that of Constantinople, where there had been a fixed camp, one allowed to sprawl and grow over time, the campaign tents homes of a sort, to return to each night, and the battles fought on the same land, and on the same ship, every day. But here, now, Vlad continued a slow retreat, without ever conceding that he'd been defeated. He led them deeper and deeper into the mountains, deeper into his own lands, toward Tîrgovişte, Val had realized. And he harried them constantly. A third of Mehmet's men had come down with pox in the last fortnight, and eventually, the torturers had gotten hold of a few strange soldiers, and learned they were in fact Wallachian. Vlad had sent his own dying men to infect Mehmet's forces.

Val nearly grinned every time he thought of it.

The night was dark, and close now, cool mountain breezes chasing away the day's dry heat, the stars all hiding. Breath of moisture in the air, as it if might rain; a weight that Val could feel pressing down on his shoulders.

Slaves had put up the royal tent hastily, without installing half its usual finery; wagons had been abandoned miles back, and so Val would content himself with dozing in this chair, since a bed would not be made ready.

Mehmet wore dark smudges beneath both eyes, so deep they looked like bruises, but he paced. He'd been drinking blood from some of the baggage horses, and even, Val suspected, from his slaves, and so his gait was strong and quick, with only the occasional wince or sign of a limp.

"How is he managing this?" he wondered aloud.

It was rhetorical, but Val wanted to answer anyway. "Because he's Vlad."

Mehmet growled.

Timothée, absently twirling the wine in his cup, turned to Val, brows drawing downward. "Why do you keep saying that? 'Because he's Vlad' isn't an answer to anything."

Val was too tired to laugh, so he settled for a smirk instead. "My brother defies all explanation. If you'd ever met him, you'd know that. Why is he able to keep ahead of us? Why has he not surrendered? Why can our spies not catch sight of him? Any other man would have been thrice defeated by now. But he's Vlad." He shrugged. "Don't overthink it." He threw the mage a wink just to watch him frown and turn away in disgust.

"I for one–" Timothée began.

And was cut off by the clear, forlorn howl of a wolf. A wolf that was very close.

Val sat bolt upright in his chair before he could check his reaction; gooseflesh broke out like a rash across all of his skin, even his scalp, which prickled fiercely. He knew that howl. Fenrir! Mother was here.

Vlad was here.

"These fucking mountains," Mehmet swore. "And their fucking wildlife."

Timothée, though, knew it was no ordinary wolf, as another howl, a different one, shivered through the night air from the other side of camp. "Your Majesty–" he started, setting his cup down.

The low din of normal camp sounds erupted all at once into chaos. Shouts, screams, the thunder of hooves.

A janissary burst into the tent, more rattled than Val had ever seen one of the elite soldiers. "Your Majesty! We must get you to safety!"

"What's happening?" Mehmet demanded, already reaching for the sword he'd discarded earlier.

For the moment, no one gave notice of Val, and he took advantage of it. The tent, ill-staked amid the exhaustion and hurry of the march, showed a loose bit of canvas along the ground. Val slipped out of his chair, rolled beneath it, and stood up amidst a camp that had fallen to madness.

There were horses everywhere, running, and shying, and trampling tents and campfires. Riderless horses – the picket lines had been cut. Loose horses would have been chaos enough, but all of them were terrified, because half the camp appeared to be ablaze. Val saw bright orange flames licking up from collapsing tents, a dozen different sources of fire, its light catching on horseshoes as horses reared, glinting off the animals' rolling eyes; illuminating the thick clouds of smoke that billowed up from the burning canvas.

Val heard a shout, and ducked aside just as a rider galloped past. He twisted in time to catch sight of an armored man in the saddle, mouth open in something like a smile. The soldier carried a lit torch that he tossed onto the royal tent, and then spurred his mount on into the melee of human and horseflesh.

Another howl, right in the middle of camp this time, followed by screams – of men and horses.

The oil from the torch paved the way for the flames, and the roof of the royal tent caught fire with a soft *whump* sound. Mehmet, and Timothée, and a host of shouting guards stumbled out of it.

Val ran.

He turned toward the sound of the wolf, and took off as quickly as he could, shoving between panicked bodies, stepping out of the way of a bolting horse.

Ahead lay a tent that had become a bonfire, gouts of flame leaping straight up, and its glow hell-red. A wolf stood there, lifting its head from the throat of a fallen man, jaws dripping blood. A great, red wolf. And behind it, horse held firmly in check, a rider. Erect and slender, hair in a crown of braids, face painted with blue stripes.

"Fen!" Val cried. "Mother!"

Above the tumult, he heard Eira shout, "Val!" But then she wheeled her horse, and raised her blade to meet the soldier rushing at her with a lance.

Something heavy and warm collided with Val's shoulder, and he staggered forward, barely managing not to go face-first into the fire. With a snarl, Fen lunged between him, and whatever had hit him. He turned to see a figure standing with hands raised; a figure on fire.

No. It was Timothée, and he *held* fire, a bright crackling ball in each palm.

"Fen, no!" Val shouted.

The wolf was already in motion, springing off from the ground, snarling, jaws open.

Timothée reached as if to meet him, and the fire shot forward, a blinding draft of it, straight at Fenrir's face.

Val didn't decide to move; suddenly he was leaping, growling, full of hate. He heard Fen yelp, but he caught the mage around the waist, and tackled him to the ground. A quick burst of heat and pain, burning through his clothes, but then the fire went out, and Val cocked back a fist, and punched the stunned mage right in the eye.

He put all his strength behind it, and Timothée managed only a weak *oof* before his head fell back, and he lost consciousness.

Val stood, panting, and turned to search for Fen.

The wolf was rubbing a paw across his singed snout, but he snorted, and blinked up at Val, unharmed.

"You're alright?"

He sneezed in the affirmative. Then turned to seek out his mistress – currently surrounded on all sides by soldiers. Val smelled horse blood, and saw shining wounds on her mount's flanks. His heart leapt. If they couldn't topple her from the saddle, they'd cut the horse out from under her, and then have her at their mercy. She was a valiant fighter – even now she spun her horse in tight pirouettes, forcing her attackers to dodge and weave, and she slashed down with her blade, drawing shouts of pain from her opponents – but the soldiers had lances, and she couldn't charge through, not without killing her horse, and then she'd be on foot.

Fen ran to her, snapping, frightening the men. He gave her an opening, just enough, and then she heeled her mount through the line – and straight into an oncoming knot of janissaries. Armored, armed, and, in the midst of all the panic, calm and ready for battle.

A sword lay beside the body of the soldier Fen had killed, gleaming in the firelight. Val snatched it up, and went to defend his mother.

~*~

Vlad pulled his sword from the neck of an Ottoman soldier – the man fell over, choking on his own blood, sword falling from a now-limp hand – and spurred his gray stallion forward. He was a new acquisition, one Vlad liked better every day. A big animal, smoke-colored, with fat dapples on his flanks and a thick, black mane and tail. Beautiful, but thought cruel by his previous master. He did have a temper, but he and Vlad got on well, and it had been easy to train him to bite and kick for battle.

Vlad touched him lightly with the rowels of his spurs, now, far back behind the girth, and the stallion – he'd named him Steel – kicked out with both hind legs as he leapt over a fallen soldier. A scream told Vlad the kick had connected with the enemies behind them.

But it was time to leave.

In the initial minutes of the raid, they'd managed to loose all the Ottoman horses, fire more than half the tents, trample, maim, kill, and destroy any semblance of order. But the generals were finally whipping their men to attention, arming them; bucket brigades were assembling to douse the fires; and the janissaries were on the march, as professional as always.

Cicero appeared at his side, four-legged, falling into stride beside the horse. Ahead, Malik rode into view, sword bloody, shining in the firelight.

"We can't stay longer," he said as Vlad reined in alongside him.

"I know. Where's Eira?"

Fenrir howled, and they wheeled in that direction, riding two abreast, slashing at the lances and swords that reached for them, Cicero running ahead, snarling and terrible, sending Ottomans scattering. Men on horseback they knew how to engage, but the wolves frightened them near-senseless.

When they reached them, Fenrir and Eira were facing what looked like a whole company of janissaries.

But they weren't alone. Vlad hesitated a moment, confused, when he saw the lean figure crossing swords with a janissary, gold hair loose and gleaming in the firelight, flash of metal around his throat.

Val. Defending Mother.

Vlad hadn't ever watched him fight, not as a man grown, and for a moment, he sat, staring, dumbstruck. Because Val was *good.*

Val was more slender, and less obviously muscled than Vlad himself, but he was still a vampire, and still strong, and he was a quick, fluid sort of fighter, always moving, dancing, almost. The janissaries didn't seem to know what to think about the fact that he'd turned on them, but that wouldn't last.

Vlad heeled Steel forward, and they crashed into the janissary line from behind. Shouts, and the crunch of armor collapsing, and the snap of bone. Enough chaos for Vlad to catch his mother's eye, and motion for her to retreat.

Val, she mouthed, eyes darting to him.

Vlad shook his head.

She glared at him, long and hard, furious, but then she wheeled her horse and was away, Fenrir following her.

Malik joined him, and Cicero, and they pushed through the line, and then loose, pounding out of the camp, and into the dark of the forest.

~*~

They rendezvoused at the appointed place, a clearing on a rise a half-mile from the Ottoman camp. Vlad slid from the saddle and loosened his girth so Steel could catch his breath; let his reins out so the horse could drink from the trickling little creek that burbled to life amid the rocks here.

Eira left her horse in Helga's care and stalked toward him, eyes fairly blazing. "You left him," she accused, voice laced with a growl.

"So did you," he said, stopping her with a hand on her shoulder. She trembled beneath his palm. "We had to leave him. Once we kill Mehmet, we'll bring him back. Mother, I *swear*."

She turned away from him. "When we kill Mehmet. You keep saying that."

"We'll do it."

Cicero shifted back to his two-legged form, and pushed back the hood of his pelt. "They suffered losses tonight." He sounded proud, still breathless from running.

"They did," Vlad agreed. But he couldn't smile. "But not enough."

Because now they would retreat again. Every day, they fell back farther toward Tîrgovişte, and there, Vlad knew, would be the last stand.

~*~

A slave offered Timothée a cold, damp cloth, wetted from the creek, and the mage pressed it gingerly to his swollen eye with a hiss.

"What do you mean, you were attacked?" Mehmet demanded for the second time.

They were arranged on a patch of damp ground, a safe distance from the charred and smoking remains of the royal tent. Dawn streaked the sky with deep lavender and rich pink.

Val accepted the cup of water offered to him, and tried not to stare at the mage. The janissaries he'd attacked had kept quiet out of professionalism, and by virtue of being no more than servants. But Timothée had no such constraints, and no love for Val, either.

563

"I'm not sure," Timothée said. "The wolf was leaping at me, but I had my fire directed at him…something crashed into me, and I blacked out. But there was so much chaos. Men and horses everywhere…" He shook his head, and then winced when it jostled his eye.

Mehmet turned to Val. "And where were you?"

"Trying not to get trampled, thank you very much," Val said with his best haughty sniff.

Mehmet glared at him, but when Val only glared back, he turned away, calling for one of his viziers.

Val relaxed, sinking back against the tree trunk behind him, letting it hold his weight. His arms and shoulders ached pleasantly from the exercise of fighting, but he couldn't revel in that soreness now, not while he was remembering his mother's face, and that brief glimpse of Vlad, furious and bone-chilling atop his gray stallion, like a figure straight from Richard's Crusade.

Had Vlad seen him? Did he still hate him?

Lost in his own wonderings, it took him a moment to realize Timothée was staring at him with his good eye. "What?"

"That was your mother, wasn't it? And her wolf?"

His pulse leapt. He fought to keep his face slack. "Who are you talking about?"

Timothée's lips compressed into a grim, flat smile. "I heard you. 'Fen.' And 'Mother.' She looks like you, though I didn't expect her to be a warrior. I also find it surprising that she left you here, without any attempt at rescue."

Val lunged to his feet, staggering a step when his tired knees tried to give out. He leaned down into the mage's space, and caught him by the collar of his silk, European-style jacket. "Don't you ever–" he started, snarling, and then bit back the rest of the words when Timothée laughed.

"Just as I suspected," he said, unperturbed by Val's grip on him, or the sight of his bared fangs. "You're the son she doesn't care about. The *spare*."

"*Shut up.*"

"Or what? You'll black my other eye? It's time to admit it, Radu. Whatever you used to be to your family, you're nothing now but the sultan's whore. Perhaps it's time to stop fighting that truth, and learn to embrace it."

Rage boiled up, and Val knew what he wanted to do. Envisioned lunging, biting, sinking his fangs deep and draining this witch dry. Drinking in all his magic blood; would it taste like ashes? Would it burn his stomach? He wanted to claw at him, that same awful violent urge he'd felt the night he'd admitted that he was a dream-walker to Mehmet. *That* night had been this man's doing. Val's one escape, and it had been turned against him because of *this creature.*

But he remembered the spear butts, and the chains, and the brutality of Mehmet's body against his own.

He released Timothée with a low roar and stalked away, shaking.

The mage laughed again, like he'd won something. "Just think: someday you'll be prince."

Val slumped against the tree and turned around, exhausted all over again, heart-weary. "Why do you care? You're French. You have no reason to take a side in this war."

He cocked his head, gaze going serious. "My dear fool. This here." He gestured to the ruined camp. "Is not the war. Not the real one. The entire world is up for grabs. Some will lead, and others of us will align ourselves with the leaders with the best chance of winning. That's what I'm doing here now."

Val tried to digest that, but couldn't. He had a dozen questions, none of which he trusted Timothée to answer truthfully.

He turned away.

Around them, the camp slowly began to right itself as the sun finally crested the horizon.

42

THE FOREST OF THE IMPALED

Vlad stood at the main gate of Tîrgovişte, staring down the road that led to the southeast, heat mirages shivering above the packed brown dirt. Late summer, and a dry spell. Sweat rolled unheeded down his temples, and down his torso, gluing his clothes to his skin. Though they'd harried, and sickened, and killed, and fought to the last, Vlad's army was a ruin, and Mehmet was still coming.

Behind him, the city hunkered down and prepared for invasion. He heard common folk shouting to one another, fastening shutters, gathering children. A baby cried. Many were hitching carts and wagons to horses and mules, preparing to head deeper into the hills, to caves and monasteries, where they might seek shelter from the Ottoman monolith that couldn't be stopped.

He couldn't explain it, but Vlad still didn't feel that he'd failed, even though something close to panic tightened his throat. *Patience*, he thought, and glanced down at the ring on his hand. His father's. The sign of the Dragon Order.

Poor Father. He'd tried. He'd wanted to be a good prince, to protect his people, and his family.

No, a voice whispered in the back of Vlad's mind, one fraught with rage and childhood pain. *He didn't try to get you back. He didn't care about you.*

Father had tried. But trying didn't count for much when you were dead in the ground. When your heir was buried alive. When your enemy raped your youngest, your baby, and turned him into a sad puppet.

Trying would not slay a dragon.

Beside him, voice soft, hesitant, Cicero said, "What are you thinking?"

When Vlad turned his head to look at his wolf, he found Cicero staring levelly at him, with his good eye, full of faith, and affection, and unwavering loyalty.

"I'm thinking that no one has ever had such a loyal Familiar. Thank you, old friend, for everything."

Cicero's brows lifted, and his mouth opened on a sound of surprise. "Vlad." *Don't say goodbye*, his face silently pleaded. *Don't say we're finished.*

"Go and see if you can find me some woodsmen," Vlad said. "We need to fell some trees. A great many trees."

~*~

Mehmet sent a Familiar, first.

A scout spotted a small party, only three. An old man, the boy said. With a beard, and strange clothes.

Fen had described him already, after the night raid; he'd carried the red flecks of burns across his cheeks and nose for days before they'd finally healed, and complained of blurry eyesight. Even his great red brows had been singed. "An unimpressive fellow. Gray-bearded and slight. I'd know him again in an instant."

The boy described him as such, and when Vlad glanced over at Fenrir, he found his eyes big, and going glassy with the urge to shift.

"You think it's him?"

"*Yes.*" More a growl than a word.

Vlad stood, and called for his armor.

He took Cicero, Fenrir, and Malik with him, though his troops, those still standing and mostly whole after these brutal months of campaign, asked to come. But no. He would not take a company to do a job he could do himself.

"Stay here. Guard the city."

Cicero fretted. "Last time…" he said, face pained, remembering the mage that Romulus had sent during Vlad's first, failed attempt at rulership. When the wolves had frozen, minds going blank, as the mage had forced her way into their minds, and tampered with their free will.

Vlad cupped the side of his neck. "I won't make you come with me. But I *will* protect you from him. I promise."

Cicero closed his eyes, ashamed, and whimpered softly in the back of his throat, an injured sound. "I'm the Familiar. *I'm* supposed to protect *you*."

Vlad leaned in, and pressed their foreheads together. "We protect each other."

Cicero tried to protest again.

"I'm not your master," Vlad said. "We're pack, and when one member stumbles, the others pick up the slack. I have you," he swore. "I have you."

They went out on horseback, all of them, and rode a quarter mile, through Vlad's new forest, to meet the enemy. When they arrived, the mage and his party sat still in the saddle, horses reined up, their gazes affixed to the spectacle that Vlad had prepared for the sultan. The only sound was the caw and croak of ravens, and the occasional whimper, when the birds pecked at something that wasn't quite dead yet.

Vlad knew the mage straight off; could smell him, the stink of char. He took immense satisfaction at the sight of the man – gray, and lined, and unimpressive as Fen had said, yes – with his head tipped back, his eyes wide, his mouth open.

Vlad halted his horse, and the others did so a half-pace behind him. They stayed mounted, though, when he swung down out of his saddle, and left Steel with a quick pat to the neck.

"Where's your sultan?" Vlad called in Turkish.

The man blinked, and dropped his gaze, hastily trying to school his features. His smile fell short of blandly pleasant, though. "My Lord Dracula. It seems I have the advantage of you. My name is Timothée." He executed a short bow from horseback.

"I didn't ask what your name is. Where is Mehmet? What sort of sultan sends three men to face a foe?"

The mage chuckled, tightly. "Rest assured, he lies only ten miles or so behind me. He will come. But he's sent me to make one last bid for peace."

"Peace."

Slowly, awkwardly, the man climbed down from the saddle. He was even less impressive on foot, short, and plump, and grandfatherly. If he hadn't reeked of smoke and singed hair, nothing about him would have projected a threat.

But as it was, all of Vlad's hackles were raised as Timothée walked toward him, and stopped only an arm's length away, hands folded together in front of him. He smiled up at Vlad, truer this time, skin around his eyes crinkling. He projected confidence, now, unaccounted for. And Vlad felt a *push*. Gentle, exploratory; another mind trying to nudge against his own.

"My," he murmured. "You really are savage, aren't you? The stories have been impressive, but…" His gaze flicked up, over Vlad's head, touching the tips of the spears that cast long shadows across the road. "Seeing it in person is an entirely different experience." He focused on Vlad once more, their gazes locked, and pushed again, harder this time.

Vlad felt it like a chill rippling across his skin, but nothing more. "There's nothing you can say that will foster a peace. Peace was never a consideration when I was a boy, and hit over the head; when I was stolen from my father. The chance for peace died with my brother's virginity."

Timothée flinched at the word.

"Go back to your master. Tell him to come back himself, and we can treat with steel." He rested a hand on the hilt of his sword. "I have nothing else to discuss with you." He started to turn.

Timothée conjured a palmful of fire. All pretense of a smile fell from his face. "Surrender to me, and it will be easier for you." He sent another push – a shove – at Vlad's mind, struggling, clawing to get inside it, to bend him.

Vlad's grip tightened on his sword. "You shouldn't have come."

~*~

"We march," Mehmet said, after three days had passed, and Timothée had not returned. "He was useless anyway."

But Val saw the spark of fear in his eyes.

They broke camp, and horses were saddled. The force that readied was not the force that had struck at Belgrade at the outset of this campaign; more than half sick, a third dead, those still healthy only so in the loosest of terms. When he gazed across them, Val didn't see crack troops in gleaming steel; he saw limping, dirty, exhausted soldiers worn nearly to the bone, their helms dented, their armor patched, their clothes tattered.

For his own part, he knew an excited nervousness that left him reeling, sick to his stomach. The last time he'd been on this road, he'd been astride his favorite pony, trying to keep up with Vlad and his leggy gelding, Father and Cicero riding at the head of their small party, bound for Gallipoli, and a doomed meeting with Sultan Murat. It had been so long ago...but he knew these trees, the scents of sap, and cold mountain water; knew the sigh of the wind in the branches, and the red of the dust on the road.

This was home.

And he rode back to it now wearing a silver collar on his throat, and the brand of ownership on his soul.

"With me, Radu."

Val didn't have to ask why. With Vlad childless, Val was technically his brother's heir. What better statement than to ride into Wallachia as a conqueror, with the Wallachian heir by your side?

Caught between hope and despair, Val couldn't keep relaxed in the saddle, and his mare fidgeted and danced the whole way.

Until...

Four miles out from Tîrgovişte, Val smelled them.

They rounded a slow bend in the road, passed a screen of trees, and then he *saw* them.

Tall, pointed-tipped wooden stakes lined the road ahead, two and three deep on either side, packed in close together, their shadows lying long across the ground. And on each spike: a body.

Their company halted a moment. Val heard Mehmet's breath leave his lungs in a short, sharp gust beside him.

He held his own breath against the stench. The stink of putrid corpses rotting in the sun, bloating, and bursting, and spilling. Ravens dove and wheeled and cawed, feasting, a black cloud of them hovering above the grisly spikes.

Val's stomach tightened, but he didn't look away. "Vlad the Impaler," he murmured.

Mehmet growled, and spurred his horse. "Keep going." He smelled like sweat, and fear, though. And the horses didn't like the gory spectacle any better than the humans.

Val's mare balked, and he had to stroke her neck and whisper endearments until she calmed enough to heel forward.

Mehmet wrestled with his stallion, spurring him again and again, sawing at the reins when the beast tried to rear.

The army followed along as softly and silently as any army had ever moved. Awed. Frightened. They'd been to war, and they'd seen unspeakable things – but no one living had ever seen a thing like this.

Val guessed the bodies had been hanging about a week, faces blackened, great chunks of flesh eaten away by the birds. Still, there were flies, heavy droning clouds of them. And the heat mirages shimmered up from the road, baking skin to leather, worsening the stink.

But as they rode, the corpses became fresher. Still mostly intact. One even had its eyes.

And, here, it was easier to tell, from clothes and faces, that these were Ottoman dead. Prisoners of war.

Mehmet pulled to a stop, suddenly, gasping, and Val followed his gaze.

Timothée the mage. Mouth open in a silent scream, blood still wet on his lips. A raven landed on his graying head and reached down to pluck out a beady eye with one quick peck.

Val searched the other faces. He recognized envoys and viziers sent to treat with Vlad. Generals, and janissary captains. Everyone who'd gone missing, everyone presumed dead, they were all here.

And they were still a mile from the city walls, and the impaled stretched on and on, unending.

Val's breath rattled in lungs gone empty and reverent as a cathedral. He waited for the fear, for the revulsion – but it wouldn't come.

And then...

Slowly, gaze haunted, Mehmet turned his horse around.

Val started in his saddle. "What are you doing?"

571

Mehmet stared off down the road, back the way they'd come, past the ravaged bodies of his own men. A heartbeat passed, and then another. Very quietly, the sultan said, "Retreating."

Val looked toward Tîrgovişte.

Retreating.

Home.

Retreating.

He smiled. It took him a long moment, his face aching, to realize that's what he was doing. Then he wheeled his mare and followed.

The order went down the line: turn back, fall in, we're leaving. Soldiers complied with relieved sighs.

Retreating.

The most beautiful word he'd ever heard.

43

KING OF ROME

Romulus came three days later.

As the bodies still stood watch from their pikes, bloated and black with flies, a runner came pelting into the throne room to report a lone rider. "Handsome and princely," the boy struggled to say between gasps for breath. "He looks – forgive me, your grace, but he looks a little like you."

Vlad tossed him a coin and sent him away.

"Leave, everyone," he said, motioning to the advisors and scribes who'd been urging him to send another half-dozen missives to allies and foes alike. "All save Malik and Cicero and Fenrir, out."

They obliged, seeming relieved to be out of his presence.

"Helga, take my mother up to her chambers, please."

"Yes, your grace."

Eira stood up, affronted. "I am not your wife, Vlad. You can't just send me away because I'm a woman, and–" She fell silent when he looked at her. He wasn't sure what sort of face he was making to cause that, but he was glad of it for the moment.

"It's Romulus, Mother."

She swallowed. "I know."

"I'm going to ask him about Valerian."

Her eyes widened, and sparkled, though no tears actually formed.

"I don't want you to have to listen to that. Mama," he added, softly, pleading.

She glanced away, blinking rapidly. "Fine." Heaved a breath. And then sent him a scowl. "Don't you dare let him leave this hall alive."

"I won't," he promised.

They waited.

Fenrir couldn't hold still. He paced the length of the throne room, booted footfalls ringing on the stones. He wanted to shift,

Vlad could tell, and maybe he would need to. But Vlad wanted them all man-shaped, at least to begin.

"You defeated his heir," Malik said, stating the obvious. "Is he coming to chastise you? Or to take you under his wing?"

Vlad sat up taller in his seat, surprised, and glanced up toward his advisor. "You think he wants to repair our relationship?"

Malik shrugged. "He wanted an heir badly enough to turn an Ottoman prince. That prince has failed, and you're the one who stopped him. And his own blood besides."

"An heir to what, though?" Cicero said. "We understand Mehmet's motives – he styles himself the next Alexander. But what is it that Romulus wants?"

Vlad took a deep breath; he found a tremor in his lungs, a little hitch of nerves. He tamped it down. "We'll find out, I suppose."

Vlad heard him long before two guards escorted him into the chamber. Heard the rhythm of his footfalls, and the low murmur of his voice as he attempted to engage his escorts in conversation. Scented his blood, and his skin, and the fact that he was a relative, blood-family. Loathed.

Vlad steeled himself.

And still he growled when his uncle finally came into view.

The guards broke away, and took up posts at the door, blank-faced.

Romulus paused just inside the heavy wooden doors, visibly rocking back on his heels. "Hello, nephew," he said after a moment, and continued forward. He came to a lazy halt, a pace too close to Vlad's throne for politeness. Smiled. "It's good to see you again. To see you as a man."

For one terrible moment, Vlad was a boy again. Young, and beardless, propped on an elbow in the bed he shared with his brother, watching Val's eyes shift beneath his closed lids, lashes fluttering as he dream-walked. Uncle was here, and Mother had gone running down to be at Father's side, and Vlad wished, so vehemently, that he could walk with his brother; that he could see what he saw, hear what he heard, and protect him from things he couldn't yet understand, and shouldn't have to bear–

Vlad gave himself a mental shake. *To see you as a man.* Romulus wanted him to go back to the past. To feel small, and weak, and captive.

But a forest of Ottoman dead along the roadside spoke to his manhood. And Romulus was one blood relative who could not sway him.

"You haven't changed, though," Vlad said. "Landless, wifeless, crownless. Just as always."

Romulus laughed, loudly, his head thrown back, his eyes dancing when he leveled them on Vlad next. "Oh, Vlad, you're charmingly terrible." He grinned with all his teeth, positively beamed. But Vlad caught a whiff of disquiet; something unhappy in his scent. "I could have used you in the Rome of my day. So many lickspittles, all liars and traitors, but not you. You're honest, even when you shouldn't be. I like that. Insults are easier suffered than the knives of conspirators."

Vlad gestured toward the door. "Those men you rode past on your way in. Do you think insults killed them?"

Another laugh, this a soft chuckle, and the smile dimmed. "I could tell nothing of their faces." He composed himself, properly somber. "Who were they?"

"Don't play ignorant. You know who they are. Ottomans. Enemies. And," Vlad said with sudden relish, "one French mage. Sadly, he had a quick death; I impaled him myself." He lifted a hand, and flexed his fingers to demonstrate.

"How proud you must be." But something flickered in his eyes, almost like fear.

"What of you? Are you proud, Uncle? Of me? Or of your heir?"

The last of Romulus's good humor seemed to melt away. He stared forward, stony-faced, and shifted his stance so that he stood with heels together, hands folded before him. "My heir–" he began.

"Tucked tail and ran," Vlad continued. "I killed his men, and he fled before me. Some heir that is. Some choice you made."

Romulus lifted his brows. "Are you finished?" When Vlad kept silent, he said, "Yes, Mehmet is my heir, and yes, I'm proud. He's done wonderfully. He conquered Constantinople. Whereas you have…" He spread his hands to indicate the throne room. It was no great soaring space like some, but it was grand enough by far for Vlad. "This," his uncle said, dripping contempt. "I chose Mehmet because he is ambitious. Because he has a thirst for greatness. And I knew that you would always be happy grubbing in the mud of some backwater territory. Just like your father."

Vlad pulled the dagger from its sheath on his thigh, and threw it.

Romulus dodged it – but barely – and it clattered to the stones of the floor.

"That" – Vlad stabbed a finger toward the door, toward the spectacle that had sent Mehmet running – "isn't anything like what my father would have done. What do you want, Uncle? Someone to conquer the world for you? You picked the wrong warrior."

Romulus inclined his head a fraction. "Perhaps I did."

"Close the doors," Vlad said to the guards at the door, and they complied.

Romulus lifted a hand, though, and they paused. "A moment, nephew. If you'll allow my advisors to join us."

Vlad stood. "No."

"Really?" Romulus asked, as the heavy doors thumped shut, and Vlad descended the dais, already reaching for the sword that Cicero offered him. "You're going to execute me?" He sounded both bored and amused.

"No." Fenrir pulled another sword, and offered its hilt to Romulus with a glare and a low growl. "I'm going to duel you."

He scoffed.

Vlad drew his father's Toledo blade with the hiss of steel on leather. "Let's see what the King of Rome is really made of."

Romulus stared at him.

"That's your great secret, isn't it? The truth? You might have been a king, but you were never a warrior, and a poor vampire on top of it. You always need someone else to get blood on their hands for you."

Romulus opened his mouth, and his fangs descended. He reached for the sword, and drew it.

The wolves stepped back, and they circled one another; Vlad's pulse leaped in anticipation; he felt at home like this, pacing, sizing up his opponent. He didn't truly live in his own skin until he was about to throw himself teeth-first into a fight.

"I'll give you the first strike," Vlad offered. "Elders first."

Romulus lowered his head and growled, a deep, awful, inhuman sound, like a tiger in the gladiator pits of Rome.

Vlad answered with a *roar*.

Romulus charged.

Vlad braced his feet, raised his blade, and met the stroke. The swords came together with a cymbal crash that echoed off the stone walls.

Romulus was strong.

Vlad was stronger.

He'd taken his uncle's measure the moment he walked into the room; had judged his pace, and his movements, watched the way his clothes had fit, and evaluated the level of muscle beneath the fine silk and wool.

Romulus parried his stroke like someone who knew how sparring worked, but who'd had very little real experience with it. It was an unfair fight, to be sure, and Vlad was going to make every use of it.

When their blades slid apart, he launched an attack of quick, flurried strikes, connecting each time, forcing Romulus back step after step after step.

The blades crossed, and Vlad's slid down, and managed to nick the back of Romulus's hand.

Romulus spun away, a full retreat, and brought his hand to his mouth to lick the wound. He coughed a laugh, panting. "Well done, nephew." He lifted his sword in a kind of salute. "I yield. Let us have a cup of wine and toast your superior swordsmanship."

"No."

His eyes widened, and showed the first real flash of fear. "Vlad—"

Vlad charged again.

Romulus barely got his sword up in time, but it was an unsteady, one-handed grip. Vlad caught the blade with his own, a forceful stroke, and sent the borrowed weapon spinning off and away, landing on the floor with a crash.

Romulus put both empty hands up, palms-out, one bleeding freely. "Vlad! Vlad, no!"

Vlad swung.

Romulus screamed, and fell back. Blood sprayed out, a hot flashing arc of it; Vlad caught some on his lips, and licked it away as he went to his knees, kneeling over his uncle's chest, blade pressed to his throat. One of Romulus's arms lay flung out beside him, gushing blood, barely connected at the elbow; bone visible, meat and muscle severed.

He made an inarticulate, animal sound of pain, that cut off abruptly when Vlad pressed in closer with the edge of his blade. He breathed in ragged gasps, throat leaping, tears streaming from his eyes.

"V-v-vlad," he pleaded. "Nephew – *son*. Please. We're family! You, and Val, and I – we're the only ones left! The last sons of Rome!"

Vlad had imagined this moment at least a dozen times. Had envisioned himself attacking his uncle, slaying him, taking revenge for his father, and Mircea, and Val, and the heartbreak of his mother. And of Fen, and Helga, who'd loved father, too. And poor Cicero, who'd been his most devoted wolf. He'd thought that if he got the chance to put Romulus on his back, and drive a sword through his throat, that he would be a snarling, furious, raging beast, more animal than man. A blood-drinking, dirty-handed vampire beyond words or reason.

But here he was, the bastard completely at his mercy. And he felt only calm, and cold, and certain, and the words came easy.

"Stop your sniveling," he ordered. "I want to know why you tried to kill Father while you were king."

Romulus sucked in a few deep, trembling breaths, but calmed himself. His free hand landed on Vlad's thigh, and squeezed, tight, fingertips digging in. But it was a sad attempt at fighting back. "What?"

"Father. Why did you try to kill him? He didn't want to rule, he said. You were king uncontested."

Romulus panted a moment, hot, humid breath rushing up into Vlad's face. "You – you think," he finally gritted out, face tight with pain, "you know what it was like. You believed – his stories."

"*Why?*"

Romulus tightened his hand. Gripped hard. "Because" – he snarled, and the pain left his face, replaced by hate – "he was *weak.*"

He bucked Vlad off of him, as forcefully as any horse. And Vlad was so shocked that he could do nothing to prevent it.

He held onto his sword, though, and managed to tuck and roll, springing back up to a fight-ready crouch several lengths away. He braced himself with a growl, ready to leap back to his feet and reengage.

But he couldn't believe what he was seeing.

Romulus sat up. He left behind a slick puddle of blood on the floor, but his arm, nearly severed, reknit before Vlad's eyes. He heard the crack of bone growing, saw muscle and flesh regrow. One last pop, and Romulus flexed his fingers, and rotated his wrist. Healed.

"Your father," he said, as they both climbed to their feet, "was an aimless idiot. We were immortals! Stronger, and more capable than *anyone.* But he didn't want to rule. He wanted to *waste* our abilities. To drink, and caper, and fuck women, and *go adventuring.*" He stalked toward Vlad as he said this, spitting and hissing like a great cat. "He could have helped me! He could have been with me when I was attacked! And then, all these centuries later, *he* wants to rule. Not when I needed him, no, but on his own! And not even as himself. As *Vlad Dracul.*"

Vlad backed away, circling, trying to reconcile what he'd seen. Vampires could heal from seemingly mortal wounds. He himself had survived a fractured skull as a boy; but he'd lain with the wound for days, needing George Castrioti's blood to give him strength, and to help the bone mend. As long as you left the heart mostly intact, beating inside the chest, a vampire could live. Mother had even told a story of a vampire she'd known once, in another century, who'd been decapitated, and when the neck was pressed back to the shoulders, and wolf blood poured into the wound, and into his mouth, the head had reattached.

But all of it took time. And more often than not, the vampire went into a deep coma, healing while he slept, only waking again when a wolf called to him.

Romulus's arm had healed in a matter of minutes.

The two wolves had shifted, and circled them now, snarling, hackles raised.

"No," Vlad told them, staying them with a hand. "No. I have this."

Romulus laughed, giving a showy twirl with his sword. "Do you?"

"How did you do that?" Vlad kept moving, and motioned toward his arm.

"Ah, nephew. I can do all sorts of things." He attacked.

Vlad held his ground, and met him.

Their blades crashed together again, again, again. Romulus was no faster, and he felt no stronger. But he'd *healed*.

"I am not," Romulus said, panting, but holding his own, "the same as the others. I'm not just a vampire. I'm the son of a *god*."

Vlad had never known if he believed that – that Mars was real, and actually a god, and actually his grandfather.

"I have the same blood," he said, parrying.

"Diluted. That whore your father–" He cut off with a startled yell, as Fenrir's fangs sank into the meat of his calf.

Fen was a big wolf, with big teeth, and he tore a huge bloody chunk of meat free.

Romulus turned his head, searching for the source of the pain.

Vlad drove his sword through his throat.

Romulus made an awful gurgling sound, spitting blood, but he didn't fall this time. He attempted to swing at Vlad with his own blade.

Vlad caught it, yanked it free, and threw it away, all while pushing his own sword deeper, deeper. The hilt butted up against flesh, and his uncle's head was nearly severed; his windpipe, his spine, no doubt.

But he buckled slowly, still scrabbling with his hands.

Vlad felt the first stirrings of panic. He pushed his uncle down, and knelt on his chest. The wolves rushed in, taking his arms in their teeth, growling, holding him in place.

"What are you?" Vlad demanded, and the panic bled into his voice. How could this be happening? How was it possible?

Blood poured out of Romulus's mouth, red and thick. He couldn't speak without a throat, but his eyes sparked, and he mouthed the words clearly. *I told you: I'm a god.*

Vlad growled. "Gods can die." He ripped his sword free with a fountain of blood, and brought it down.

It took three swings, impossibly. After, he stood and kicked the head away, so it went rolling halfway across the throne room.

The body continued to spasm, and the wolves stepped on it with their paws, pinning it in place.

Vlad wiped his face with the back of his hand, clearing the blood from his eyes and mouth. His uncle's blood. It tasted dark, and vile, and so much more volatile than what he'd tasted the day he'd bit Mehmet as a boy. Mehmet had been an infection, but this was the source. The font of the evil.

He spat on the ground, and drove his sword straight down into Romulus's heart.

Finally, he lay still.

~*~

"He's not dead," Eira said. She strode boldly across the floor, heedless of the blood that stained the trailing hem of her skirt. When she reached the body, she knelt beside it, sniffing, lip curling in distaste.

"He will be," Vlad said, hand resting on the pommel of his sword where it jutted upward, still embedded. "If I can actually cut his heart out." He glanced down at the body and frowned; already, the flesh was trying to heal around his sword, the heart repairing itself.

Cicero, human-shaped again, came back to them with the head, fingers threaded through the thick curly hair. The features had gone slack, the eyes shut, and the stump of the neck so longer

581

bled. But Romulus didn't look dead; asleep, only, and almost peaceful. Cicero held the head out away from himself, face caught in a snarl. "How did he heal himself? I've never seen anything like it."

Eira stood, dusting off her skirt, brow knit. "I have," she said, grimly.

"What?" Vlad and Cicero asked together.

"The old gods," she said. "All the pagan ones. I haven't met them all, none, actually, save one, once, when I was a girl. I've had this theory, ever since. That they aren't gods, maybe, not really. But they aren't like regular vampires either."

Vlad glanced down at his uncle's headless body. "Can they be killed?"

"Your father was," she said, in a soft voice. "Romulus isn't a god – only the son of one. I think you can kill him." But there was a note of hesitance there.

"Mother?" he prompted.

She sighed, and sent him a look that was almost pleading. "I hate him. More than anyone, you know I do. But we know no one like him. No one else with this power."

With a lurch, he realized what she was suggesting. "You want to keep him."

"Preserve him," she corrected. "And I don't *want* to. But I wonder if his strength" – she gestured to the head Cicero held – "is something we could learn from. You're only one more generation removed from Mars than him, Vlad. It's worth trying to figure out the secrets in his blood."

"Where has my vengeful, Viking mother gone?"

"Nowhere," she said, lifting her chin in a challenge. "But she's tired of fighting, and she's grown wiser, in her old age." Softer: "I've lost too much, Vlad. Remus, and Val–" She bit her lip until it turned white. "I understand the violence in you, my son, because it lives in me, too. But I think maybe this is a time when mercy is the wiser choice."

"Mercy," he echoed. That was her name, after all. His merciful mother. "Sometimes death is a mercy."

"I agree. Is it one he deserves?"

He felt his brows go up. "Perhaps a mercy for the rest of us, so we can live without the threat of him."

She nodded. "I'll leave it up to you, then."

Vlad looked down at the body again, still but warm, its skin still flush with life. He'd never seen anything like this.

Was it worth something?

Worth keeping?

He searched his heart for some scrap of love. This was his blood relative; his father's twin. And a figure of legend as well, even among humans.

But there was no love. Only pragmatism.

He lifted his head to search out Cicero's gaze, and found his wolf watching him, unjudging, curious.

He nodded. "I won't keep him here."

"No," Eira agreed. "Put him away to sleep. And hide him. Bury him deep."

"Yes. Very deep."

~*~

The stood over the body, still, when a sharp rap sounded at the throne room doors; they creaked open a moment later to admit a guard whose face had gone pale with shock. "You grace," he gasped, bracing a hand against the heavy wood. "Your uncle brought men with him – only two. The advisors he mentioned."

"Yes?" Vlad said, impatient.

"You should – forgive me, your grace, but you should come see for yourself."

Eira stayed with the body, and Fen beside her; Vlad didn't think he could have moved her with any urging. He, Cicero, and Malik went to see these advisors.

Two cloaked and hooded men waited in the courtyard, at the foot of the wide stone stairs that led up to the palace's entryway. They weaved a little on their feet, shoulders tipping to the side, the front, the back. Subtle movements, that might have just been the wind tugging at their clothes – but was not.

The wind blew their scent into Vlad's face: vampire. But the faint hint of blood that usually accompanied his own kind was deepened, darkened. A rusty, rancid smell.

Cicero growled immediately, a low, constant rumble.

Three palace guards stood in a loose ring around the strange vamps, swords drawn. They darted worried glances toward Vlad, who waved them back.

He still held his own sword, and brandished it as he approached. "Your master is dead," he said, bluntly, voice echoing off the stone façade of the palace. "Show your faces. Hand over any weapons you carry."

They didn't move.

He growled at them. "Show yourselves, or I'll cut you down where you stand."

Slowly, both heads lifted, hoods slipping back a fraction.

Vlad had seen his uncle's body do something truly astounding only minutes before, but he wasn't ready for the sight that greeted him. Two different faces, one dark, and one pale, but the same expression. The same gaze.

Eyes bright with fever, glassy, unfocused, sunk deep in shadowed sockets, the whites etched with red veins. Mouths half-open, slack, fangs showing. No awareness; no spark of life or intellect.

Together, they began to growl: a breathy, hissing sound, without the usual depth and threat.

"What *are* they?" Malik asked, and his voice shook.

They moved together, a sudden lunge.

Vlad cut the first down, and his guards closed in on the other. It batted them away, snatched one's sword, heedless of the way it cut its hand, its blood running thick and black…like that of something already dead.

Vlad pulled his sword from the open, sucking wound on the first creature's neck, and spun to stab the other through the heart. The vampire fell with an ugly, gurgling sound, clawing at his face as he chased it to the ground and drew his dagger, scratching his cheeks and throat with long, ragged nails like claws.

Cicero drew his falx and took both its arms.

584

It screamed, loud, awful, wordless. A sound that held nothing of civilized language.

"Gods," Cicero murmured, awed, frightened.

Vlad cut it open, and cracked the ribcage with his bare hands; black, clotted blood. It stank of putrefaction. The heart, when he ripped it free, was shriveled, blackened, barely beating.

"It's dead," Cicero said. "Isn't it? It has to be. It…"

Vlad brought his thumb to his mouth, and flicked his tongue against it, tasting. He spat on the ground, afterward. "Not dead. Turned by my uncle. He sired this thing."

Silence a moment, wind snatching merrily at the flags hung above the door.

And then it hit him.

Romulus had turned these things; men made not into vampires, but into things without minds or souls. Immortality in exchange for…absence.

Would this, then, happen to Mehmet?

And if it did…what of Val?

He hunted for the answer in his own mind all that night, as they burned the two corpses, but he could see no easy solution. Not now. He had to deal with Romulus first. And then, finally, it would be time to rescue his little brother.

~*~

He left the next day, before dawn. He took Cicero, and Malik, and three trusted native Wallachian soldiers, his best mercenaries. He left Eira behind to sit the throne, her wolves at her sides.

"When they ask, tell them I'm going to the Holy Land like all the other Crusaders."

But he didn't go there, no. And only his party knew where he eventually lowered his decapitated uncle into a deep hole, and covered him with earth, and stone, and left him to gather moss.

44

DOWNFALL

Decisiveness, Vlad had long since learned, was a trait often called for in kings and princes and sultans, but rarely ever admired. Smallfolk loved a brave leader…but his fellow leaders never did.

Reckless, vicious, dangerous, without reason – these were the things said about him. Accusations he could see now in the eyes of the man who sat before him; who slowly rose, the silk of his robes of office rustling together.

"Vlad," Matthias Hunyadi, now Corvinus, said, tone that which he would use on a wayward child. "You know this isn't something I wish to do, old friend. But you must see reason."

"Reason?" Vlad bristled. "You didn't care about *reason* when you were all cowering inside your castles, letting me face Mehmet alone." He looked at Matthias, and at Stephen, the traitor, standing with hands folded, and brow pinched in disapproval. "I sent the Conqueror running back to his lair to lick his wounds. Not you, not anyone else. You should be toasting me. And here you point lances at me instead."

He and Cicero stood alone, surrounded on all sides by Matthias's men-at-arms, a ring of spear-points hemming them in. This was to have been a celebration, a meeting between friends. Instead, it was an ambush.

Cicero growled, low and unmistakably lupine. Several of the soldiers gaped, but they didn't waver, or lower their weapons.

Vlad put a hand on his arm, and the growl cut off.

Matthias had noticed it, though, his head cocked to the side. "So the rumors are true, then. Stephen told me" – Stephen ducked his head – "but I didn't quite believe. What *are* you, Vlad? What besides a warmonger?"

"I am the only thing standing between you and something much, much worse than me," he snarled in answer. When no one responded to this, he said, "Fine. If this is a lecture instead of a feast, I won't prolong it."

He turned to go.

The spears shifted in, closer, tighter.

"Vlad," Matthias said behind him, voice heavy with something like regret. "You're not leaving. You're under arrest."

~*~

A moment's stirring was all the warning Vlad got before Cicero's good eye flew open, and he tried to launch himself upright, hands lifting, fingers already trying to shift to wolf claws.

Vlad was ready, pinning him down by the shoulders, keeping his head in his lap where it had been resting while he was unconscious. "Shh, it's alright, it's just me."

Cicero's eye darted wildly another moment, and then finally settled on Vlad's face, and recognition dawned. He subsided with a gusty sigh. "What happened?"

"Well, let's see," he said, dryly. "You flung yourself in front of me, and tried to attack an entire regiment of guards. Got stabbed. Got hit over the head. They were about to kill you before I surrendered us both. And now here we are, locked in a tower."

"What? No!" He lurched upright, swaying, and Vlad had to catch his shoulders to keep him from toppling over. He scanned their surroundings, frantic, panting.

All told, it was a tower, yes, but a lavish one. The solar where they now sat was furnished with two four-poster beds, a long table and chairs, and a massive fireplace, flames crackling merrily. Wardrobes, and tables loaded with cups and pitchers and jars lined the walls. Fine tapestries, and heavy shutters could be used to seal the windows that now stood open, flooding the chamber with light slatted by the heavy silver bars anchored in the ledges.

But Cicero twisted around to look at him with horror blooming across his face. "Vlad. Why did you surrender?"

"Because they were going to kill you."

The wolf groaned and looked away. "You should have let them."

Vlad had stood, spear-tips pressed all down his back, pricking through his clothes, drawing blood. He could have fought them; could have survived the injury and blood loss. But he would have eventually passed out, and then need to be revived. Would Mother have come when she heard the news? Would she have been able to?

And in the meantime, Cicero would be dead. And that was unconscionable.

"No," he said, and put his hand on Cicero's shoulder. "I don't regret it."

But he had no idea how they would get out of this place.

~*~

Val couldn't stop shaking.

When a soldier took his mare by the bridle, he slid gratefully to the pebbled ground of the palace courtyard, and his knees nearly buckled. A cloudy day, rain rolling in from the west, and it cast his childhood home – the palace at Tîrgoviște – in a sinister light. Her towers and crenels stood proud, casting no shadows, the color of dirty teeth against the gray of the sky. He shivered, and attempted to look princely.

Three weeks ago, Mehmet had come to Val's bed in an unusually good mood. Val had paused in the act of unbraiding his hair, and really scrutinized the sultan. "What are you smiling about?"

Mehmet had climbed up onto the bed, grinning with all his teeth, revealing the one in the back that was beginning to rot. Val had been so busy thinking that vampires shouldn't have rotten teeth, and wondering what would fail Mehmet next, that he hadn't heard him at first.

Mehmet had sighed. "Are you listening? I said you're going to be a prince."

"I already am a prince." But his pulse had picked up, and worry had blossomed like a flower.

"A prince with a *throne*. Your brother's been deposed."

The story went like this: in the aftermath of Mehmet's unprecedented retreat, the other lords of Eastern Europe had put their heads together and discussed what was to be done with Vlad. Because, fearless though his resistance had been, it had also been reckless. Vlad had killed hundreds of prisoners, those impaled along the roadside, in what had become known as his "forest." To do such a thing, to execute so many, without a hostage negotiation, without consulting with anyone…smacked, some said, of dishonor. And now, in the wake of his defeat, Mehmet was far less reasonable than he had been, and less willing to allow his vassal states any sort of leeway.

The choice, as the princes saw it, was simple: make peace with Mehmet, or face invasion and subjugation. What was Vlad's pride, and Vlad's throne, worth in the face of impending destruction?

It was Matthias Corvinus, old John Hunyadi's son, who'd invited Vlad to his castle, and sprung a trap upon him. But Stephen the Great had helped. All of Vlad's allies had agreed to this imprisonment, and so now Vlad was shut up in a tower, like a princess in a children's story.

And Val was to be Prince of Wallachia in his stead. Mehmet's faithful puppet.

According to Corvinus, who'd already arranged a journey to Tîrgoviște to congratulate Val on his ascension, he held only two prisoners: Vlad, and his faithful servant, the one-eyed man named Cicero. Val found some comfort in knowing that his brother had his bonded wolf by his side. But it begged the question: where had Mother, and Fen, and Helga gone?

Were they here, still?

"Gather up the household," Val said when the steward greeted him in the throne room. "I wish to inspect them, and introduce myself."

"At once, your grace." The man spoke politely, and hurried to do as bid, but Val didn't miss the contempt in his gaze. Val might be Vlad's little brother, and a true Wallachian, but he had a reputation as a sultan's bedwarmer. Vlad was the hero who'd turned away Mehmet, and Val was his pet.

He would find no love here. Unless Mother…

But he wouldn't hope.

A servant brought him a cup of wine, which he thanked him kindly for, trying to be warm, smiling; not that it mattered – the boy scurried away again. Val sighed, and took a sip, and contemplated his father's, and most recently, brother's throne.

It was spare, straight-backed. Just a heavy chair, really, with a bit of gold embellishment at the edges. The seat itself was dark in the center, from the rubbing of backsides, a shallow little depression worn into the wood.

He didn't want to sit there. Not for anything.

"Your grace?" The steward was back with the household.

Val turned to inspect them. Cooks, maids, household guards, runners and page boys. But not his mother nor her wolves.

The loss of them hit him like a blow. But he drew himself upright, pasted on a smile, and gave them his best, most solicitous welcome speech, thanking them in advance for their loyal service and hard work, sparing some words for Father and Vlad, offering condolences for the loss of previous masters.

One of the cooks took one of the runner boys by the shoulder – her son, no doubt – and pulled him close to her skirt. Away from their new prince, most notorious for lying with a man.

Val dismissed them with a barely held-together smile, and then dismissed the steward, who looked concerned to see him striding for the stairwell unattended. Let him be concerned; this was his palace now.

He breathed deep, and caught the faint flickers of scent on his way up. A place where Vlad had pressed his hand, here; a corner where Cicero's cloak had brushed, there. He detected Eira, and Helga, and Fenrir. But they were old scents, little more than memories.

He went to her bedchamber, anyway, the one with the prime view of the gardens. The bed was there, neatly made, its drapes tied back to the posts. But any signs of habitation were gone. Her jewelry box, her hairbrush, and bottles of imported scent; the wardrobe stood empty.

His heart sank.

The windows were open, letting in a fresh breeze, and the light falling through caught on something on the desk, small and bright. Val crossed the chamber slowly, and when he reached for the thing, his heart didn't sink, but clench, tight and painful. It was his bell. Small, unremarkable, and dented, threaded onto a silver chain. Warm from the sun, he imagined it had been in her hand;

that she'd placed it in his palm and folded his fingers around it, like she had when he was a boy.

He put the chain around his neck, dropped the bell down beneath his shirt, and left the room. Nothing waited for him here.

~*~

Val feasted Matthias Corvinus and his men in the throne room when they came.

John Hunyadi's son was a handsome man, with thick, glossy dark hair that fell to his shoulders, gently curling, a proud nose, strong jaw, and an easy, straight smile. He embraced Val like a brother, kissed him on both cheeks, and waved forward a pair of servants bearing a long, narrow box. Matthias flipped back the lid and revealed a blade, simple by design, strong, beautifully crafted. An efficient, high-quality weapon. A *warrior's* weapon.

"For you," he said. "As a gesture of goodwill, and our new alliance."

Val took it slowly from its bed of velvet, surprised by the heft of it. He lifted it toward the light of the flickering chandeliers, peering down the length of it, and finding it perfectly straight.

"I thank you for the gift," he said, trying for awe, afraid he sounded as jaded as he felt. Gifts were never given freely.

Matthias beamed. "A sword needs a name. What shall you call her?"

He felt the tiny weight of the bell, resting against his breastbone. Thought of Mama, and her sweet smiles, and her sharp sword.

"I think...I think I shall call it Mercy."

~*~

After the meal, Matthias wished to talk privately of alliances, so they repaired to the study.

Val spent too long a moment staring at his father's old chair – Vlad's, most recently – smelling them on it, and Cicero, too, where he'd leaned against its arm, a dutiful Familiar. Finally, he settled into it, feeling like a fraud, acutely aware that his backside was too narrow to fits its depression.

Matthias slouched down in the chair opposite the desk, relaxed, and refilled both their cups from a flagon of fresh wine without asking. "I do apologize about your brother, Radu. Unfortunate business." He made a show of grimacing, shaking his head, gaze properly tinged with sadness. "But I'm sure you understand." He lifted a searching glance to Val. "Vlad would make a better general than he does a prince. His bravery and bloodthirstiness are commendable, but he's going to get everyone in the region killed by that Conqueror of yours."

"Vlad has always been forceful."

"Forceful! Ha! There's an understatement." He chuckled as he sipped his wine. "It took fifty of my best men to subdue him. And that was only after we threatened to run through that friend of his." His mouth puckered with distaste. "Whatever he is."

"Cicero," Val said, and felt a cold numbness begin to steal over him. He'd been faking interest and enthusiasm all night, but now an active hostility cooled his temper further. "His advisor."

"Cicero? Named for Marcus Tullius?" Matthias snorted, eyes gleaming. "Tell me, though, truthfully: what sort of creature makes a sound like that? That *growling*."

Val pushed an attempt at a smile across his lips. "I have no idea what you mean. But that was cowardly to threaten a mere steward."

Matthias's brows went up. "It was the only way to clap silver manacles on your brother. A mere steward? No. If I suspected such things, I'd say they were more than likely lovers."

Val checked his own growl. But he couldn't maintain the smile. "Cicero is a most devoted Familiar."

Matthias didn't seem to notice the stress he put on the word. Why should he? But he narrowed his gaze and said, "While we're on the topic, I do wonder. You and your brother and your people – you must admit you don't strike outsiders as normal."

"I supposed that depends upon your definition of normal."

"Oh, come now, Radu." Matthias set his cup aside and leaned forward, arms folded over the desk. A spark in his gaze, one Val didn't particularly like. "Don't take it as an insult – it certainly isn't meant as one. Truly, normal could be taken as an insult, when unique is as exceptionally beautiful as you."

"Beg pardon?"

"You are beautiful. You must know that. There's a reason you were Mehmet's favorite."

In that moment, Val understood with perfect clarity how Vlad was able to justify impaling people. He swallowed down a surge of bile, and said, "Are you propositioning me?"

"Don't play coy." Matthias reached across the desk, intending to lay his hand over Val's. "You are—"

Val pulled his hand back, and Matthias's froze, hovering in mid-air.

Val stood. "It grows late, your grace, and you're clearly too tired to be thinking clearly. I'll summon a servant to show you to your quarters for the evening."

Matthias sat back, cleared his throat, fiddled with his embroidered jacket. "Yes. Um. Very well, thank you."

No gift was ever given freely, after all.

Val sat at his window for a long time, that night; he watched dawn break slowly over Tîrgoviște, bright stripes of color you could only see in mountainous climes. His reflection stared back at him, pale and ghostly in the glass, an impression of a narrow, smooth face, and big glittering eyes, and long, moon-silvered hair.

His beauty had always been his curse. He'd hoped that, at least, Vlad's sallow and charmless countenance might spare him the world's evil. But he languished now in a tower, shut up, just as Val had always been.

You're not better than mortals, his mother had always said. No. Maybe, they were in fact worse. And perhaps captivity was their just punishment for it.

~*~

It was night. Vlad sat up in bed, reading by candlelight, pretending he hadn't read the same line again and again. There was no sense letting his mind languish, though his body was imprisoned, but his hate had become a physical presence inside him, and it drowned out his usual enjoyment in learning.

593

Cicero dozed fitfully, stretched out at the foot of the bed in his wolf shape, ear flicking occasional in response to some sound coming in through the open windows.

"Hello, brother."

Vlad lifted his head and found Val standing beyond the foot of the bed, hands folded before him, as unassuming as he'd ever looked. It took Vlad a moment to realize that he wore no jewels, and that, instead of his usual Ottoman garments, was clad now in the dark red finery of a proper Hungarian noble.

"It's true, then," Vlad said, setting his book aside. "They put you on my throne."

Val dipped his head, gaze somber. "I promise you, I didn't want it. I simply went where I was told."

"Like a good little slave."

"Vlad," he sighed, and moved around the bed so he stood beside him. "I don't want to fight anymore."

"How can I fight with someone who isn't here?"

He frowned, pain flaring, briefly, in his gaze. He shook his head. "I…" He sighed, and started again. "You know why they're holding you. I'm sure they've told you. They've told me that they're letting you cool your heels until they've repaired relations with Mehmet. That this is only temporary."

"But I've been dream-walking," he said, urgency stealing into his voice. "Vlad, they're going to assassinate you."

Cicero's head lifted, and swiveled toward Val; he whimpered in question.

"What do you mean?" Vlad said. "Who is?" He wanted to discount such a statement, mainly because it was coming from Val – an Ottoman puppet. But he'd been leery of such a thing these long months he'd been imprisoned. It made a horrible sort of sense.

Val shook his head again, growing visibly more frantic. "Matthias won't do it himself – that would reflect poorly on him. But everyone's decided you're too great a liability. There's a group of displaced boyars amassing support – those who fled before you impaled all their friends. They've been living in Transylvania and Moldavia, hating you all this time. Matthias has agreed to secretly fund and arm them, and to allow them passage here, up to this very tower; he's going to turn a blind eye while they butcher you." The last he said with a tremor in his voice, wringing his hands. "Vlad, they know how to kill you; I've heard Matthias talk of cutting out your heart. You–"

Vlad cut him off with a wave. "If that happens, I can handle myself."

"No you can't!" Val burst out, shouting. His eyes widened, like he'd surprised himself, but he pressed on. "Vlad, you let yourself be taken in the first place. If fifty men with swords and spears and armor pour in here, and threaten Cicero again–"

The wolf shifted, a man again, kneeling on the counterpane and glancing back and forth between them. "Vlad won't surrender to save me again," he told Val. And to Vlad: "You *won't*."

Vlad sighed. "Even if you're telling the truth, Radu–"

"I am!"

"*Even if you were*, I won't fall so easily to a pack of angry bumpkins. They're more likely to stab each other than actually land a blow on me."

"God." Val tipped his head back, and blinked, and when he faced forward again, tears sparkled in his eyes. "Are you really going to be this stubborn? You'd risk dying rather than listen to me?"

"Yes."

"But *why*?"

"Because I don't trust you."

A ragged, anguished sound tore out of Val's throat, and then he vanished.

Cicero turned to him. "Vlad." An accusation.

"Do you think those tears were real? He's spent most of his life in Mehmet's bed. Why should I believe anything he says?"

"Because he's your brother. And he loves you."

"No. I don't believe that."

Cicero whimpered, but didn't argue further.

~*~

Of Val's regrets, only one felt like something he could, and should have been able to prevent. Constantine's death. He replayed it in his head: the horse falling, Constantine spilling from the saddle. And the head, face twisted, neck dripping gore, haunted his dreams. A lifelong friend reduced to a bloody trophy. He could argue with himself about all of Mehmet's attentions, about having to fight against Romans in a siege. He hadn't had a choice; he'd been forced. But he should have saved his friend, and he knew it.

He wouldn't see the same thing happen to Vlad.

He left at nightfall, alone, cloaked in dark rags. It was a week of travel, keeping off the roads, avoiding patrols, dream-walking ahead to scout the best paths. All in black, he slipped onto the grounds of Corvinus Castle like a wraith. There were guards stationed at Vlad's prison tower. Val left them unconscious, and took their keys, and let himself into his brother's prison with his very last shreds of hope clutched round him like armor.

Cicero leaped up with a growl, and Vlad, reading by the fire, surged to his feet, reaching for a sword that wasn't there.

"Shh," Val said, shutting the door behind him and pulling back his hood. He could sense the air change when they both caught his scent. "It's me."

"Radu," Vlad said flatly. That name would never stop pricking like a barb.

"Dress warmly," Val said. "I've come to rescue you."

They stared at him.

"You're here in person," Vlad said, without inflection. "You came in through the door."

"Yes, because I'm actually here. Like I said: to rescue you."

"I'm not a maiden in a tower to be rescued."

"Well," Val said, patience wearing thin. He crossed the floor to peer out the window, searching for signs of having been spotted. He saw a few lanterns bobbing along in the dark, heading this way. "You are in a tower, I might point out, and seeing as you're unwed, you may well be a maiden. So." He went to the heavy chest at the foot of the bed.

But when he tried to lift the lid, Cicero's hands came down on top of it, stopping him, and when he lifted his head, he met the wolf's one-eyed stare.

"Valerian, what's happening?"

He sighed, and tried not to let his mounting panic get the best of him. "It's as I told the great lout a month ago: Matthias has funded a group of angry boyar assassins. They're on their way here now, to kill you both. I'm here to get you away."

Cicero's look drew inward, considering; he at least was taking Val seriously. "How did you get past the guards?"

"I might be a whore, but I'm properly trained. I knocked them out, gagged, and bound them. But we don't have much time. Help me." He was allowed to lift the lid of the trunk this time…

Only to have it slammed nearly on his fingers. Vlad strode over, and forced it down again.

Val whirled on him. "Are you really this petty? Or just stupid?" he bit out. "I'm here to help you. They will *kill you*, Vlad. Just as they did Father and Mircea. You might be strong, but you can't survive having your heart cut out and burned."

Vlad stared back at him, implacable. "Why should I believe you?"

"This again? Really?"

"You might be my brother," Vlad said, in that iron tone that Val knew was immovable. "But blood relation doesn't mean anything. Romulus orchestrated this entire mess, and he's our uncle. Forgive me, *brother*, but I don't trust you, and *I never will*."

It shouldn't have hurt. He'd heard it before, had known it would be hurled at him again. But hearing it now, close enough to feel Vlad's breath on his face for the first time in years, close enough to touch, to grab his brother, and seek shelter in a loving embrace – it cracked something inside him. Val felt a splintering behind his ribs, like a crust of ice shattering on the surface of a lake.

Whatever broke, it fractured the panic, too. Calm flooded through him. Certainty.

"What happened to Mother?" he asked, and his tone, the levelness of it, surprised them, because they lifted their brows.

"I left her at Tîrgovişte when I came here."

"She was gone when I arrived. She left this." He fished the bell out of his shirt, and let it dangle outside of his clothing.

"Your bell," Vlad said, expression smoothing again.

"I think she left it for me. I hope, wherever she is, that she's somewhere safe."

Vlad growled. "You're lying."

"No." He was tired. So tired. "I'm not. I never do, really, except to stay alive, sometimes, when Mehmet's fucking me into the mattress and trying to choke me to death. I lie then, so he doesn't kill me."

Cicero turned his face away. An opening.

"You know," Val continued, "the worst part is that I still love you. You will always be my big brother, and I'll always want to please you." He offered a smile. "But you won't let me help you, will you?"

Vlad stared at him a long moment. Val thought he almost – but, no. There was no love there. He supposed there never had been. "No," Vlad said, finally. "I won't accept help from a sultan's whore."

"As I thought."

Val sighed.

And flicked a dagger free from his belt, and drove it between Vlad's ribs.

He made a gasping, punched-out sound, and went to his knees.

Cicero turned alarmed, already snarling, scenting blood, eye glowing.

Val was ready. Cicero shifted as he leaped, springing over his fallen master, and Val caught him with both hands, by the ruff and by jaw. He forced his mouth shut, and threw him, hard as he could, toward the fireplace. His head cracked against the mantle, and he fell to the floor, unconscious.

Vlad had been shut up here for too long, without exercise, without practice, and though he'd been doubtless feeding from Cicero, he'd gone soft in his captivity. Just soft enough.

Val drew his sword, the blade he'd named Mercy, for that's what this was. "I'm sorry, Vlad. I love you." And he buried his blade in his brother's shoulder, slicing down to his ribs, just shy of his heart.

~*~

The blood loss was immediate and devastating. No less than a mortal wound could have done it. Vlad slipped into a coma, the deep, restorative vampire sleep that would heal him – but keep him under until a wolf used blood and old Latin words to wake him.

Val worked quickly. He bundled his sleeping brother in cloaks, and, with some effort, hefted him up over his shoulder. Fled the way that he'd come.

In the months that followed, his flight would be a blur in his memory. Heart beating wildly, hands slippery with Vlad's blood, the stink of it deep in his nose. Somehow, he got off the grounds, and got back to his horse.

He heard a long, horrible, mournful howl go up, when he was miles away. Cicero.

He rode through the night, and as the warmth of morning drew perspiration from his skin, he tamped the last shovelful in place. An island grave, in the shadow of a church.

He swam back across the lake, and lay, dripping and exhausted, on the bank, until the sun had dried his clothes. When he could manage, he dragged himself back into the saddle, and set off through the swaying shadows of the trees.

He was done, now. With ruling, and with serving, and with being a creature alive on this earth.

He had only one thing left to do, and then he would crawl deep into a dark cave, and stop eating, and give himself over to the endless peace of an unending sleep.

One thing. And then he could die.

45

VALERIAN

A heavyset sultan, plump, jowly, richly-dressed, a jeweled ring on each sausage-thick finger, made his ponderous way belowdecks on his royal galley. It was to be a short voyage, but his joints ached so, and he could bear neither standing nor sobriety. He groaned with every step, leaning heavily upon the cane he'd taken to carrying, its head shaped like a horse, gilded, ruby-encrusted. A flock of attendants, slaves as fluttery as birds, hovered above and below, ineffectual small hands reaching out to catch him should he fall. He would crush them, if he did.

Finally, he reached his private cabin, draped in silk, richly-appointed, scented with incense. He waved the boys away, impatiently, all but his favorite: a eunuch boy from Serbia, blue-eyed and golden-haired, mouse-quiet, with a tendency to blush and cry when Mehmet pulled him into his lap. He'd been well-trained, at this point, and went to fetch a cup of wine as Mehmet eased down to sit on the edge of the wide berth with a groan.

Alone, just the two of them, that was when the wardrobe door creaked open, and a figure dressed in black stepped out into the cabin.

Compared to the last few years of his life, sneaking onboard this galley had been child's play. Hooded, wrapped all in black clothing, no one had noticed him in the pre-dawn gloom. Even if not for his nose, he would have known Mehmet's cabin by the finery. Then it had only been a matter of waiting.

The eunuch boy made a small sound of distress, and dropped the cup. Wine splashed across the boards, catching the candlelight in jewel-bright arcs.

"Leave us," Val told the boy, and nodded toward the door. "Tell no one," he added, catching him by the arm as he fled.

"It's fine," Mehmet said with a wave. "Go on. Radu's an old friend. This is merely one of his games."

The boy mumbled an agreement and was gone.

600

Mehmet sat calmly, or appeared to. Val could sense the leaping of his heart, and the sudden quickness of his breath; something in his lungs rattled, low and wet.

"Radu," he said, and only a faint tremor of alarm betrayed his tone.

Val moved to the door, and barred it.

"You look well."

Val whipped off his cloak, and hung it from the peg beside the door, leaving himself clad in black breeches, knee boots, and black velvet tunic, belted with gold and rubies. "You don't," he said, moving to stand opposite the sultan. "You've gotten fat, and old. You grunt like a hog when you move."

Mehmet chuckled, though his pulse beat like a war drum, the loudest sound in the cabin. "Acerbic as ever. I guess ruling suits you."

"You know very well that I rule no longer."

That earned the hint of a mocking smile. "No, you don't, do you? You Dracula brothers are terrible princes, both of you."

"Says the man who put us on thrones."

A sharp grin. "Clearly, I'm a poor judge of character."

"Yes," Val agreed. "You tend to underestimate the people around you. Vastly."

The grin lingered a moment longer…and then faded, when Val said nothing else.

It was funny, he reflected, now that he was standing here, how calm he felt. The moment he'd set foot on the deck of the ship, he'd known a sense of peace. Deeper, colder, more right than the peace he'd known after burying his brother. He'd felt a hint of it then, and in the moments he'd fought with Vlad and Cicero, a tantalizing caress of it, but now it was solidified. Had had time to galvanize, diamond-bright, and just as hard. It was a cold clear-headedness that allowed him to think quickly, and feel little. Perhaps this was how it had been for Vlad, sometimes.

"I've heard," Mehmet began, with that particular air of someone trying to break an awkward silence, "that Vlad's own people killed him. Spurned boyars armed with torches and pitchforks – a regular mob. But there are rumors, too, that you killed him. Something about a vengeful wolf combing the countryside, calling for *your* blood, Radu."

"Valerian."

"What?"

"My real name is Valerian. I would hear you use it before I kill you."

A high, thin laugh. "What?" he repeated.

Val lunged.

Mehmet tried to lift his hands, tried to heave his ponderous bulk from the berth, tried to shout for one of his men. But he was, in fact, old, and fat, and slow. And Val was lean, and strong, and looked no more than twenty-some-odd, and was the grandson of Mars, God of War, besides.

Val batted his hand away, clapped his own hand over his mouth, and toppled him back to the bed, straddling his bulky hips and pinning him in place. "Hold still," he ordered, and reached for the vial he'd tucked into his belt. He uncorked it with his teeth, and pulled his hand off Mehmet's mouth – only to grip his jaw, force it open, and pour the vial's contents down the sultan's throat.

Mehmet spluttered, and Val felt the quick burn of a few droplets against his wrist. But it was nothing. Pain, shame, fear – all of it had abandoned him, and there was only certainty, and only his own strength, as he held the choking sultan down.

Mehmet finally swallowed, and heaved a deep, gasping breath. Eyes bugging, hands scrabbling ineffectually at the one Val pressed to his throat.

"Burns, doesn't it?" Val said, conversational. "That's silver shavings, mixed into wine. Give it a moment to take affect: you'll grow sleepy, and heavy, and want nothing more than to take a nap. You'll feel very disconnected from all your strength – from the things that make you a vampire. That's how I felt, wearing your collar, and chains every day."

Mehmet wheezed, and bucked feebly beneath him.

"Here's something that should spark memory, though. Remember our first night together?" Val ripped the silver dagger free from his hip, and drove it into Mehmet's heart.

The sultan lurched, and made an awful, breathless sound of pain. Blood spilled out of his mouth, a trickle that ran down toward the coverlet. But he was still alive. Could still feel.

"Stay there," Val said, and got to his feet.

Mehmet stayed – of course. He didn't move, save to breathe in short, sharp jerks, panting, groaning.

"Now," Val continued. He pushed up Mehmet's kaftan, bunched it up around his waist. "This is just like old times. Like our first time. Remember, lover? Remember how I stabbed you with your own sword? I spent the whole night in the garden after that." He undid the laces of Mehmet's şalvar – white silk stretched to their limit by his bulk – and tugged them roughly down. "And then you found me, and you took me back to your chamber, and you fucked me dry. I bled, remember? Just as you're bleeding now."

He unsheathed his sword.

"Ra-Ra-Ra-du–"

"Nuh-uh," Val sang. "What did I tell you my name was?" He lined up the tip of his sword.

Mehmet's face – colorless, bathed in sweat – was a mask of terror, mouth working, eyes white-rimmed.

"Say it," Val said, almost sweetly.

He wheezed a moment. Then, finally, "Valerian." And then: "*Please.*"

Val took a moment to look at him, sprawled out, half-naked, pitiful. Whatever gifts Romulus had given him decaying, leaving him aging, and ruined, and in pain. This was the man who'd tormented him. Broken him.

He gathered himself. "That's right," he said. "My name is Valerian. And today is the day *I* fuck *you.*"

He slammed his sword home.

~*~

An hour later, he dragged himself up into the little boat he'd left anchored just off shore, a wet satchel weighted with a heart slung over his shoulders. Mehmet would steal no more boys' innocence. Never again.

He lay there a long moment, staring up at the blue cloudless sky, the boat rocking gently beneath him, the lap of the water echoing the pulse that drummed steadily inside his ears.

"It's over," he murmured.

There was no peace. But a quiet emptiness that was almost as good.

Three days later, Cicero ran him down in a patch of sun-dappled forest. Val was underfed, and tired, and he didn't bother fighting. The wolf had a human with him, the man Malik with the Asian eyes, who'd been servant of Vlad. They'd raised a small army. Humans loyal to Vlad.

"Kill me," he said, and offered his throat. "I'm done."

They put silver chains on him instead.

46

I PROMISE YOU, BROTHER

Blackmere Manor
Present Day

First there was nothing, and then there was black. Stars wheeling. The cool touch of wind on his face.

He'd fallen out of the vision – out of the past – and this was the astral plane in its pure form. He'd tried to explain it to Vlad once, when they were boys, but then there had been no describing the endless, echoing dark, and its constellations, its orange pinpricks like torches, trying to guide him to others with supernatural abilities. Then, in 1439, he'd had no frame of reference for how vast it was. But now, after centuries spent stalking others, after sort-of watching the new Star Wars movie while he projected himself onto Mia's couch while he really watched her, the television's blue light playing across her beautiful face…now he knew that the other plane was like the vastness of space. This was what astronauts saw, he supposed.

And then he felt his body tugging, calling him back, and he returned to it with a sense of grimacing, because this was going to hurt.

And it did. Physical awareness returned, and he felt like he'd drank bottle after bottle of wine, shaking and weak as a new foal, short of breath, aching all over. He cracked sleep-crusted eyes and saw that night had fallen; it had taken hours, showing Vlad. *Seeing* Vlad. Because he hadn't known before what it had been like in his brother's head back then, but he knew now, and he didn't think his world would ever be the same.

A lamp had been left burning, before, because Vlad must have known it would take hours, this dream-walk. Val saw that his palm, too-white, shaking, was still pressed Vlad's forehead and he pulled it off with difficulty.

Vlad's eyes opened. That was all he did for a moment, while Val tucked his trembling hand into his own chest and took several unsteady breaths, fighting a swoon. He needed food, and sleep.

Vlad blinked at him.

"So," Val said, voice a rough scrape. "Now you know. Now *I* know."

Silence lay between them a moment, heavy.

And then Vlad lunged.

Val tried to shrink away, or shield himself, but he was too weak.

And then it didn't matter, because Vlad caught him by the neck with one strong hand and reeled him in, pressed their foreheads together.

"*Valerian*," he said, voice choked, and oh, Val wasn't ready for that. For the weight and acknowledgement in his name. The way Vlad was saying that he *knew* him. Tears filled his eyes, and he closed them.

"I promise you, brother," Vlad said, "that nothing like that will ever happen again. Believe me."

Oh *no*. A strangled sound tried to claw its way up Val's throat, and he gritted his teeth against it. He couldn't stop the tears, though. "I – you don't–"

Vlad gathered him close, into his heat, and strength, and his implacable resolution. "I will make it right," he said. From anyone else, that would have been a stupid boast.

But from Vlad…

Val almost let himself believe it.

"It's alright," Vlad said, softer, and stroked his back.

Val gave up all pretense and slumped forward, allowing himself the comfort he craved. They were men now, instead of boys, but he still fit under Vlad's chin, and it was still a safe place there.

~*~

About five minutes after Val fell into an exhausted sleep, Vlad sensed someone coming down the hall toward his quarters.

Several someones, in fact, and as these modern humans said: just no.

He climbed out of bed as quickly and carefully as possible. Val clutched at the blankets, but didn't wake, hiding his face in a pillow. He didn't look grown to Vlad in that moment; he looked four, tear-stained and fresh from a nightmare.

He went to the door and had it open just as the man on the other side was lifting his hand to knock.

It was a black-clad military officer of some sort, one of the ones with a radio and a gun on his belt, his hair shaved close on the sides of his head. He was a large, mean-looking man, and he was flanked by two others of his kind, but he shrank back from Vlad, face paling.

"Sir," he said, and his throat jumped as he swallowed. "Your grace."

"What?" Vlad snapped.

"Oh. Um. Well. Sir…your grace, I mean–"

"*What?*"

"Your brother," the man said in a rush. "He's not in his cell. And Dr. Talbot said you took him out. That he's with you."

Vlad folded his arms and propped his shoulder against the doorjamb. "And what of it?"

His expression clearly said *please don't make me say it.* "Dr. Talbot said…Dr. Talbot said he can't be allowed loose in the house. He has to go back, sir." The poor man shivered. "Right away, he said, sir."

"Hmm. Is that an order?"

The man darted glances to his companions, who refused to make eye contact with either him or Vlad, wanting to stay out of it. "Um," he finally said. "Yes, I believe so, sir." He winced. "I'm sorry. But yes, it is."

Vlad started at him a long moment. "My brother," he said, pronouncing carefully, "was filthy. He hadn't seen a bar of soap in months."

The man looked confused.

"He's half-starved. I can count all of his ribs."

"S-sir?" The man's brows were climbing. What he wouldn't say was this: *you electrocuted him. Why do you care?*

"If I return my brother to his cell, then I expect him to be afforded all the best meals and chances to bathe and properly groom himself." It wasn't a request.

The man studied his face, trying to be sure. Then jerked a nod. "Yes, sir, of course."

"I will return him there in the morning. Tonight he sleeps in a real bed. Send someone with a dinner tray."

If the man intended to protest, he didn't get the chance before Vlad shut the door in his face.

When he turned back to the bed, he saw that Val was still lying down, pillow clutched to his chest, but that his eyes were open. Because the soldier at the door had awakened him with his idiotic insistence that Val be put back in his cell. Dr. Talbot's orders…let Dr. Talbot see how well he liked "his grace" when Vlad was–

"Brother," Val said, and Vlad realized he was growling, a constant low rumble deep in his throat. "Are you thinking violent thoughts?" His tone was joking, but his voice was a jagged ruin, as if he'd been screaming. As if the things he'd relived through memory while dream-walking had manifested themselves physically.

Vlad cut off his growl forcibly and took a deep breath. "Yes," he admitted. "Some."

"Well take a break from it. Violence is exhausting."

"Hmph," Vlad muttered, but he went to sit on the edge of the bed. He made a conscious effort to soften his voice. "You should get some more sleep. I told that idiot to bring up food."

"If he doesn't, will you impale him?"

Vlad growled again – but it was only for show, because Val laughed at his own joke, and even weak and hoarse, it was the best sound Vlad had heard since he'd been awakened.

Val quieted, settling into the pillows with a soft hum, eyes closing.

A thought occurred. "When you escaped your cell," Vlad said, frowning to himself. "You were in Talbot's office – you broke Treadwell's jaw. You could have killed Talbot."

Val hummed again.

"Why didn't you? Did you spare him for his daughter's sake?"

"Mostly." His eyes opened to slits. "No one deserves to have their father killed. And also…"

"What?"

His eyes opened a little wider, very blue, very young-looking. "Uncle," he said, just a haunted whisper. "He's really awake?"

"No, not yet. We would know. But his curse is awake. And I think someone's looking for him. Someone wants him awake." He felt the stirrings of old rage, still hot under his skin.

For the world, it had been nearly six-hundred years.

For him, it had been less than a month.

"Who would want to wake him up?" Val whispered.

"Someone stupid. Or someone ambitious. Someone who wants him to take over the world…or wants to use him to do it for himself."

"That's…terrifying." Then his eyes sprang wide open and he pushed himself up unsteadily on one arm. Vlad made a reflexive reach to steady him. "Vlad," he said, voice shaking. "The mage – the Necromancer – is it him? Is he the one starting all this?"

Vlad had wondered as much. "If he is, he'll regret it."

~*~

A dinner tray did indeed arrive, and it wasn't the prepackaged, microwaved fare Val usually enjoyed in his cell. No, this was freshly prepared by hand in the manor's kitchen, the same food that Vlad, and Talbot, and Treadwell, and all the mortals in the mansion ate. Roasted chicken, and rice, and steamed vegetables, and a cup of pig's blood alongside a dish of something soft, and chocolate-smelling.

"What is this?" he asked, prodding it with his spoon. It wiggled.

"Pudding," Vlad said, like the idea of such a thing was beneath him. Sour enough to have Val biting back a laugh. "It's dessert."

It was delicious, is what it was. Val ate every bite of it first thing, and then licked the dish before taking a more civilized approach with his chicken.

When his belly wasn't so empty, he slumped back against the headboard and ate more slowly, sipping blood in between. "Alright, oh patient one, tell me of your elaborate plan."

Vlad stood at the window, arms folded across his chest, staring out through the parted curtains at the moonlight lying across the lawn. It shouldn't have, considering all that had happened since their reunion – Val set down his cup and reached to gently touch the wound that lay beneath his shirt, still angry-red in the mirror and healing slowly from the inside out – but the sight of him there, immovable as ever, was a comfort.

As if he sensed these thoughts, Vlad's gaze slid over to him. "What?"

Val smiled. "You're a warrior in every century, aren't you?"

His brows lifted.

Val explained: "Now. In this century: they have no shortage of soldiers. Weapons – weapons we never could have dreamed of. Don't take this the wrong way, brother, but they don't need you. They want you, yes. But. But you could...you could be something different. You could" – he thought of Nikita Baskin and Sasha Kashnikov, holed up in a rundown New York apartment, working mundane, mortal jobs – "be whatever you wanted to be. But you are a warrior."

Vlad stared at him, outwardly unimpressed with his logic. "It's what I was born for."

Val sighed. "Of course it is."

"And I'm the one who buried Romulus. I stand the greatest chance of killing him."

"You couldn't kill him then," Val reasoned, but not unkindly.

"I *didn't* kill him. There's a distinction." Vlad's lip curled. It could have been a snarl, but Val knew it to be a smirk. "And, as you said: they have weapons we never could have dreamed of."

"Ah. Going to drop a bomb on him, are you?"

"Among other things."

Val couldn't help but smile. He was the same as always, and he was glad for it. "Tell me your plan," he prompted for the second time.

So Vlad did. In usual Vlad Dracula fashion, it wasn't a bad plan at all.

47

ARRIVAL

Fulk took a sequence of deep breaths which did nothing to calm the rage boiling inside him. He hadn't snapped at anyone in a *very* long time. He'd always found it a bit shameful – losing his composure in front of others. In front of mortals, especially. It damaged his credibility as a man. *See, he's just an animal after all*, the darted glances suggested.

But right now, he was dangerously close to erupting in the middle of Dr. Talbot's office.

He chose not to address the terror coursing through his veins and instead focused on the blistering fury. He planted both hands on Talbot's desk and leaned low over it, growling in the back of his throat. "You did *what?*"

"You're acting as if I've invited him," the doctor countered, adjusting his glasses. "I merely told him that his visit would be appreciated after he insisted on dropping by personally. We do need him to recast his tracking spell on Prince Valerian, after all."

"Trust me when I tell you that you don't want him here."

"He's already been here."

"*When?*" Fulk's voice was more growl than pronunciation now.

"Before you and the baroness arrived. Give me some credit, my lord. I knew there was bad blood between you and Mr. Price. I knew better than to have the two of you in the same room."

Fulk could imagine it: letting the wolf peek through; leaning across the desk, too fast for the doctor to duck away; taking Talbot by the throat and digging in with nails, with claws; the blood, the scream, the–

He snarled and spun away, chest heaving.

Talbot said something, but it was muffled by the blood roaring in Fulk's ears. Whatever it was, it wasn't important.

He remembered a moment, centuries before, before Annabel, before he'd betrayed his vampire master. A moment in the evening, in the duke's study, opening and reading aloud his master's daily correspondence by the light of a few candles and the fire in the grate.

One letter stood out from the rest, sealed with red wax pressed with the dragon and cross signet ring that belonged to Vlad Tepes of Wallachia. It had come a long way, and bore the scuffs and rips of travel; a smear or two of what Fulk could tell was blood.

It was written in painstaking Latin. It smelled of an alpha male wolf.

I send this missive to the few powerful Western vampire lords of which I know, at the suggestion of what remains of my pack. It is with much grief that I tell you that my master – Vladimir by his mother's tongue, and Vladislav by his father's, Vlad Dracula, Prince of Wallachia, is given over to the immortal sleep. Though he is not dead, I am ashamed to admit that I cannot find his resting place. His brother, the traitor Valerian, also called Radu, is responsible for the grievous injury done to my master. I have captured Valerian, bound him with silver, and sought answers to my questions as to his brother's whereabouts. He will not answer, even under torture. I have entrusted the care of the prisoner now to a group of monks, and taken my leave of civilized life. The enemy is nigh, and I must go. Should any brave crusaders remain who wish to take up my master's mantle, I leave evidence of Valerian's whereabouts. You may contact my mortal companion Malik Bey should you wish to assist my search for Vlad.

A hand-drawn map accompanied the letter. All of it was signed by a wolf named Cicero of Wallachia.

Fulk stared at it a long moment. Finally, he said, "We had word that Dracula was indeed dead. Killed by his brother."

Over by the fire, Liam swirled the wine in his cup and chuckled. "Come now. Brother killing brother? Who would do such a thing?"

Fulk heaved a sigh. "Their uncle, for one."

"Yes," Liam said, smile stretching. "That *was* the joke. Thank you for explaining and taking all the fun out of it, my dear idiot."

"Quiet, both of you," the duke said, waving a dismissive hand. "Throw that nonsense on the fire, Strange. I have no use for it."

"But, your grace—"

"Vlad Dracula is an overeager fool. He tried to take on the might of the Ottoman Empire – Mehmet the Conqueror! Who sacked Constantinople! What sort of half-wit attempts such a thing?"

A brave one, Fulk thought to himself. *Or a furious one.* He said, "He won, though."

"Won? Pah! He turned back one march. And now he's asleep. How is that winning? On the fire it goes, I don't care."

Fulk did cross the room to the fire, and he did throw in the letter…but he crumpled the map in his hand and pocketed it.

When he turned his head, Liam grinned at him with all his teeth, but the mage said nothing to give him away.

It was one of thousands of moments that Fulk wanted to pull out of his head and play on a screen for the good doctor. He wanted to show him Liam's quiet cunning, his insincere smiles. Fulk had long since decided that Dr. Talbot was an idiot, and possibly a madman, and definitely more egotistical than was healthy…but he didn't believe the man evil.

Liam, though…

He took another sequence of deep breaths and turned back around, features schooled into a mask that was almost polite. "The girl. The one who escaped. She's his daughter."

Talbot didn't blink. "Yes, I know. Mr. Price and his wife donated sperm and eggs respectively, and the children were incubated by surrogates, and raised in our New York lab."

Of course. Because mage mothers had a hard time carrying children to term. Using their powers drained valuable nutrients from the fetus – and the reverse could be true as well.

And also…

"What the fuck," Fulk deadpanned. "You bred your own mages."

"We've tried to, yes."

"How many?"

"A dozen survived past birth." His expression clouded. "The Russian vampire killed one at the New York lab. A boy. Only ten-years-old."

Fulk couldn't say he blamed Nikita Baskin one bit, child or no.

614

He shook his head to clear it. "None of this explains why Liam is coming here."

"Haven't you figured that out yet? Our crusader will need a mage, and the girl escaped."

Oh.

Oh.

~*~

It was the middle of the night, and there was nothing to see beyond the helicopter's windows save layered shadows and the occasional pinging red light of a cell tower.

Mia had spent the day in a private jet flying across the country, meeting the oncoming night. From the tarmac, she'd been none-too-gently bundled into a dark-green military helicopter and told it would only be "about ten minutes" until they reached their destination.

Treadwell had tried to make small talk on the plane. She'd asked about Val, and he'd clammed right up, scowling. That was fine; she would get answers from her father, then.

She had a list of things to be angry about: the fact that she hadn't had a chance to tell her mother goodbye, or pack a bag, or give her horse one last big hug. The idea of being taken in and of itself; abducted by people who weren't acting according to any sort of law. The fact that she was about to be forced into her father's presence again, when he was the last person on earth she wanted to see right now.

But clothes could be bought, phone calls to Mom could be made, and who knew, maybe it would prove cathartic to shout at her dad in person.

The untenable thing, for her, was Val's situation.

After all, she was a girl living on borrowed time; why not go out with a bang doing something for someone who had a chance to live a better life – or several lives, as it were.

A net of yellow lights appeared just ahead, and Mia hitched herself up against the seat, straining to see out the window. A city, she thought; that was the only thing that would explain that many lights all clustered together.

The helicopter slowed, and she clutched at the hard-plastic edge of her seat as the machine tipped sideways and swept out in a wide turn. The beginning of their descent, then.

"We're here," Treadwell shouted at her over the constant thump of the rotors.

No shit. And then every other thought flew out of her head, because it wasn't a city…it was a single house.

Not a celebrity mansion. Not a new-construction nightmare of clashing styles. This, its thousand windows blazing, its glass-walled conservatory lit up like an incandescent bulb, belonged to an age of landed gentry that had never existed in this country. The palatial estate of royalty. It had wings, and peaks, and leaded glass, and gas lampposts illuminating pathways and soaring stone staircases that led to gardens, and fountains, and a stable built to match.

In her awe, she forgot a little of her hatred for Major Treadwell. "What is this place?"

"Blackmere Manor, home of the Baron Strange of Blackmere. Unofficially. Officially: the Virginia branch of the Ingraham Institute of Medical Technology."

~*~

Fulk left the meeting with Talbot feeling like a shaken can of soda. Faintly, far above the manor, through layers of stone and steel, he heard the chop of helo blades – Talbot's daughter arriving, then. He and Anna had discussed it, and they'd agreed that Anna be on hand to welcome her. To sniff out her intentions…and offer her a friendly face if necessary. If Valerian could be believed –

So lost in his own thoughts, he didn't see Dracula until he'd nearly run smack into him. He pulled up short at the last minute.

Vlad, of course, didn't move. Merely drew to a halt, one unimpressed eyebrow raised. "You've come from Talbot," he said.

Fulk took a deep, somewhat steadying breath, and noted that Vlad smelled of his brother, and of soap, and that he was on his way up from the dungeon. "And you've come from your brother. I heard you took him upstairs."

Vlad grunted and headed for the elevator.

Fulk fell into step alongside him.

When they were safely in the car, and the doors had closed – two nervous interns waved them off and insisted they could catch the next ride; Fulk didn't blame them – Vlad said, "I need to ask you about the Necromancer."

Fulk growled.

Vlad chuckled.

Fulk was a half-head taller than the vampire, so he had to look down and not just over as he checked with sudden fascination to see what his face was doing. Vlad's smile wasn't exactly friendly or comforting, but it was a smile nonetheless.

"You still hate him after all this time?"

Fulk said, "If I put Mehmet the Conqueror in front of you right now, would you still hate him?"

It was Vlad's turn to growl.

"So now we understand one another," Fulk said. "Liam Price is, to put it bluntly, a motherfucker. He's never helped anyone willingly in his life – everything he's ever done has been self-serving. He will exploit a person's every weakness to get exactly what he wants." He swallowed hard, trying to choke down the grief and rage that rose in his throat. "His wife is Annabel's sister."

"Hmm." Fulk detected one quick vibration of interest from him. "Can he really raise the dead?"

"I've seen him do it. And I wish I hadn't." He turned his head so he could gauge the vampire's next reaction. "Talbot and his crew expect Liam to become your mage. To go into battle with you."

Vlad's lip curled. "I don't want or need a mage. I've never liked them."

Fulk felt an answering smirk tug at his mouth. "On that we are agreed. But you might not have a choice in the matter."

"Let me ask you something, le Strange." He turned his head, so they faced one another, his eyes very dark and flat under the overhead elevator lights. "This place, and these people, need me. Do you think for one second that *I* need *them*?"

He...hadn't thought of it that way before. "Huh."

"I would ask you to trust me," Vlad continued, "but I know that you won't. One thing, though."

The elevator slowed.

"Your wife seems to bear some affection for my brother. Do you share that affection?"

"...I'm not sure."

"Think on it." Then the doors opened and he stepped out into the library.

~*~

From a rooftop landing pad, Mia traveled with her escort in an elevator that dropped them three floors down and opened onto a long hallway lit with wall sconces, tiled with black and white checks. Tall, mullioned windows let in the night, bracketed by clusters of toile-printed armchairs. Light glowed at either end of the hall; in one direction lay the warm, exotic environs of the conservatory. In the other, the rest of the manor house.

Even this, just a place to pass through, to maybe stop and read a book beside a rain-streaked window, was awash in simple splendor.

"You get used to it," Treadwell said at her side, but she didn't believe that at all. He was an artless man, after all.

"This way." He took her elbow in a gentle grip and attempted to steer her toward the main house.

She pulled away – quietly, but firmly – and walked at his side without touching. She thought the woman, Ramirez, smirked.

The hall fed into another, this one floored with polished hardwoods. Doors opened along one wall, leading into dim parlors with dainty furniture. It turned out to be a sequence of connected hallways, each larger than the last, until they finally reached a soaring entryway. Galleries for the two floors above looked down on the tile floors, a massive skylight at the top of the atrium softly lit by electric light.

Mia came to a stop, head tipped all the way back as she stared. She probably looked like an idiot, but she didn't care. She'd never been inside something like this before. It was like the Biltmore Estate, but *bigger*. And that she'd only ever seen in photos.

"It's crazy, right?"

Mia dropped her head and saw a young woman in cutoffs and biker boots walking down the grand staircase toward her. Everything about her seemed incongruous with their surroundings. And yet...not.

"It's beautiful," she countered.

"I think it is," the girl said, arriving at the foot of the stairs with a clack of bootheels. "My husband hates it, but that's just the bad memories talking, I'm convinced."

"Your husband – you *live here?*"

"Kinda sorta." The girl reached Mia and stuck out her hand. "I'm Annabel le Strange. Your welcome wagon."

Mia accepted her shake with some hesitation. This girl seemed friendly, and her smile was wide, and her accent was hopelessly Southern. But Mia had been brought here against her will. And somehow, Annabel must know and work with her father. "Mia Talbot."

"I know."

"Oh. Yeah."

Annabel chuckled. But then she leaned in. Close. Closer than was comfortable. When Mia tried to draw back, a hand darted out and landed on her shoulder, much stronger than it looked.

"Your man's downstairs," she whispered. "Play along during dinner and I'll see if I can get you down to see him."

Annabel squeezed her shoulder and pulled back with a smile that said, *Work with me.*

And then Dad called, "Mia!" across the cavernous expanse, voice echoing, and she didn't have a chance to respond.

Annabel stepped back, and Mia resisted the urge to grab for her hand and pull her back in. Whether to beg more information of her, or use her as a shield against her father, she wasn't sure.

As it was, Edwin had a clear line to her, as he came hustling over the patterned tiles, wringing his hands together in outward excitement of some kind. He wore a dress shirt and slacks under a white lab coat; various ID badges and keycards hung from lanyards and retractable spools. His hair was grayer than she remembered, his glasses of a new style; his face more lined, pale from being cooped up indoors.

His smile was edged with hesitation, and at least she had that; at least he was nervous to come face-to-face with her.

Mia drew herself upright and folded her arms. Let him come all the way up to her and open his arms in a clear invitation for a hug.

She stared at him. "Would you like," she said, slow and clear, "to explain to me why these two thugs showed up at my place of business and kidnapped me? Dragged me here? Would you like to tell me what sort of crime I've committed that things like jurisdiction don't matter?"

His face fell. He dropped his arms. "Mia, please, let's not do this—"

"Oh, we are so doing this."

He sighed. "As I explained to you over the phone, there is an experimental drug—"

"*I don't want to hear about your drug,*" she hissed. "I told you I didn't want to take it, and you sent *military* people to collect me! Do you understand that that isn't a normal reaction?"

Slowly, his expression hardened. "Very well. I was going to try to appeal to your higher sense of reasoning, but given your current emotional state, I see that won't work. Let me put it to you bluntly, Mia: you are my daughter. You might not believe it – in fact, I'm sure you don't – but I do love you."

She made a disbelieving sound in her throat, and he spoke over her.

"I love you," he repeated, "and I would do anything to see you safe and healthy. Anything. You're sick – you're dying—" His voice wavered with emotion. "And I have the means to make you well. You can dig in your heels out of some sense of misplaced pride. Maybe you need to. But I will do whatever it takes to give you this injection. It's going to save your life."

A pretty speech. An astounding possibility.

If she let herself, she could fall into the fantasy: a miracle cure that could make her strong, and healthy. One that could save the world. No one need ever suffer from an incurable disease again.

But she said, "What about side effects?"

"What?"

"Side effects. You know: those things they list off on drug commercials? May cause migraines, rashes, face swelling, suicidal thoughts, explosive diarrhea, and *death*?"

He sighed again, but something sparked in his eyes. Hope, maybe. "If it will ease your mind, I'd be happy to take you to my lab and walk you through the process. You might also like to speak to drug recipients. Both Major Treadwell and Sergeant Ramirez take the serum daily."

She hadn't expected *that*. She glanced toward both of them in turn, searching for outward signs of injury and illness. They still looked cool, capable, and unfriendly as before – though Treadwell had a little notch pressed between his brows. Some kind of stress.

But she remembered Val's warning. Screamed at her, tight with panic. She couldn't lose sight of what was really happening here.

She took a deep breath. "I don't care about the injections. I want to talk about Val."

There was a collective intake of breath around her. A stiffening of posture.

Her father frowned. "Mia, we can't–"

"He came to see me. For weeks. Don't try to pretend that wasn't real. And that's why I'm really here, isn't it? It's not about a cure; it's about me consorting with your prisoner."

The frown deepened into an outright scowl. "Prince Valerian is most dangerous. He's manipulative, and ruthless."

"Right, right."

Dad started to respond, face a pinched red mess –

And a low, accented voice said, "Is this the girl my brother's been talking to?"

A hard chill skittered up Mia's spine.

She turned, already knowing who it was – *Vlad*, the name echoed like a death knell in the back of her mind. She envisioned him as a boy, sullen and sallow, like Val had shown her…

But the figure striding into the room was a man. Long, dark hair streaming down over broad shoulders. Contoured with sleek muscle; his clothes clung to him.

The cool, unknowable light in his eyes made her want to take a step back. He didn't glare, didn't snarl. He *stared*.

He looked nothing like his beautiful brother.

Dad's expression went through a series of quick changes that would have been comical in another moment, among other company. "Ah, your grace, excellent timing, as always. My daughter's just arrived. This is Mia.

"And Mia." He sighed. "I'm sure you already know who this is. Vlad Dracula of Wallachia. Prince." He said the last crisply. *Be polite*, that word meant. *Don't embarrass me in front of royalty.*

She said, "Hello, Vlad."

He didn't respond. Just stared. Studied her, she realized, from the crown of her head to the toes of her paddock boots. His expression never changed.

She shivered again.

"Dinner should be ready soon," Dad said, catching her attention, and she couldn't believe this. How was it happening? How could he think that she would want to sit and have dinner with him when–

"Dr. Talbot," Annabel interrupted smoothly. "I was thinking Mia might like to freshen up. Change her clothes, maybe, if she wants. I was going to take her up to her room before dinner." She was smiling, and very polite, but it was a statement and not a request.

"Oh," Dad said. "Oh, um, yes. Of course. That's fine. Do you–"

"I know which room." Annabel looped her arm through Mia's. "Come on up."

Dazed, Mia followed.

It was a wide, ornate staircase; the risers had been sized for a man's stride, and Mia felt a little dizzy by the time they were halfway up. They hit a landing, one that fed forks off to the left and right.

Annabel towed her to the left and whispered, "I'm guessing you didn't bring a bag with you?"

Anger flared again. "No." She looked down at her dusty barn outfit of breeches and t-shirt; she'd polished her boots not long ago, but they looked obscenely dirty against the crushed red velvet carpet runner.

"Don't worry." Annabel patted the back of her hand in a gesture at once familiar and out of place. It was a grandmotherly gesture; no one in this generation did that sort of thing. "We'll find you something."

The top of their climb found them along a gallery with a spectacular view of both the ceiling and the floor far below. And a series of narrow, wood-paneled hallways that Annabel navigated with ease. An outfit of spare workout gear was located in a closet, and then Mia was led to "her" room.

She had to pause in the doorway and take it all in.

There was a theme, and that was burgundy. Heavy velvet drapes, and an elaborate counterpane with matching pillows. Burgundy woven into the rich weave of the rugs, and patterned into soft florals in the wallpaper.

The bed was a monstrous, heavy four-poster thing, with drapes held back by golden cords. Angels were carved into the headboard, the legs, angels reflected in the overwrought lines of the matching dressing table and dresser. Through a half-open door, she caught a glimpse of an adjoining bathroom with a claw-foot tub.

"This is…"

"Yeah." Annabel urged her to the side with a little shooing motion and shut the door. "The man who commissioned this place had *very* rich tastes. I'm not sure if this is the original stuff, and they just cleaned it up, or if someone spent a shit-ton of money on eBay trying to find furniture out of some old mansion basement somewhere."

Mia turned to look at the girl beside her, and knew her face was full of questions.

Annabel's smile was wry. "It's crazy, I know."

Mia could tell she wasn't just talking about the décor. She set the borrowed clothes aside on the dressing table and sat down on its matching stool. "What's going on here?" An emptiness seemed to swell in the pit of her stomach, a vacuum that was an act of self-preservation, a place to put all the panic, and doubt, and hurt where it couldn't mess with her head.

Annabel held up a finger, tilted her head. Listening. She sniffed the air, nostrils flaring delicately. Then she nodded and went to sit cross-legged on the end of the bed. She held onto her ankles, young and comfortable in her own skin.

But something...something was just a little bit *off* about her. Nothing wrong, nothing threatening. Something *other*, though.

But Mia wasn't afraid.

Annabel said, "Did Val tell you what he was?"

"A vampire? Yeah."

"Do you believe him?"

A loaded question. A heavy gaze leveled at her.

What sort of person admitted to believing such a thing? But she did believe. "Yes."

Annabel studied her a moment, eerily similar to Vlad in that respect. Then she nodded. Her tone was matter-of-fact. "My husband Fulk is the Baron Strange of Blackmere. He's a British lord, he's seven-hundred-and-fifty years old, and he's a werewolf. So am I."

Her back was sore and tired from the long flight; she needed to eat; her head spun lazily, a constant dizziness that left her imagining her tumor creeping slowly larger and larger as the minutes ticked past. But she sat up ramrod straight. She was in love with a vampire who could visit her in the form of smoke. And the girl sitting opposite was a werewolf. And she wanted to understand.

"Tell me," she said, and Annabel did.

She told her in blunt, Southern-accented tones about the Institute, about what it was doing here, and about why it wanted to use her husband's manor house. About the Romanian vampire brothers her father had been using to conduct experiments on humans like Major Treadwell and Sergeant Ramirez. About meeting Val – "your Val," she said, smile going soft and affectionate – in the subbasement that was really a dungeon. About taking him a cat that he named Poppy, and Frappuccinos, and giving him someone to talk to. About, briefly, the ways that wolves and vampires had enjoyed symbiotic relationships throughout history, since the founders of Rome had washed up on a reed-choked riverbank and been nursed by a she-wolf.

It was so much. All of it. *So much.*

But she believed it, somehow. "He's not evil," she said, quietly.

Annabel smiled. "No, I don't think he is, either." She sat forward. "And this is interesting. Since Vlad woke up, we've all assumed he hated his brother. Because, well." She shrugged. "I mean, look at the guy. But something's going on. He brought Val up out of the dungeon today. He gave him a *bath*."

Mia's pulse kicked at her ribs, high and fast in her temples. "He did?" She kept seeing Val in her mind's eye as he'd last appeared to her, in tattered clothes, his hair in greasy clumps, gaunt and filthy. He'd been so neglected for so long… "Does that mean–"

"I don't know." Excitement sparked in Annabel's eyes. "But I think it might. Mia." And here she grew serious. "You're not the only guest coming to dinner tonight. There's someone else." She bit her lip and looked even younger, uncertain for the first time in the past few minutes.

"Who? Frankenstein's monster?" Mia tried to joke. It fell flat.

"I wish," Annabel said, without a trace of a smile. "It's an old acquaintance of my husband. A mage named Liam. They used to work together, bound to serve the same master."

Mia frowned. She was still struggling to understand the whole vampire-mage-wolf thing that Annabel had explained. "Is Dad just collecting people with supernatural powers?"

"More or less. Liam is–" She shuddered. "Look, I don't want to tell you anything about your dad that will make you even angrier with him…" But her face said that she was dying to tell someone this and be understood. Almost pleading.

Mia had a horrible realization. Val wasn't the only prisoner here.

"You and your husband aren't hospitable hosts, are you?"

Annabel hesitated a moment, then shook her head. "No. Fulk keeps telling me to leave, to sneak out on my own – he's the one they really want. He woke Vlad up, and they don't know how many other of the Old Guard they might be able to discover and need awakened."

"So Val was right. Vlad really was sleeping?"

Annabel nodded. "Checks and balances. It takes a mage to turn a wolf, and a wolf to wake a vampire. Keeps things evened out." She sighed and glanced toward the closed bedroom door. "Vlad says there's a war coming. Someone – we don't know who – is trying to wake his uncle up. There's some old, dark magic that's been popping up in the Middle East. Romulus's magic. Turnings gone bad. People that aren't people anymore.

"Mia, your dad is trying to put together a superhuman army to put down that threat. That's not a bad thing. But. The way he's doing it…Liam has kids. Young ones. Ones who were born from surrogates and raised like lab experiments."

"Are you serious?" She felt faint, and it wasn't because of the tumor.

"I met one of them. A girl." She shook her head. "She got away, though, so now we're back to square one."

"And now the father – this Liam – is coming."

"Vlad needs a mage. Or, your dad thinks so, anyway. He wants to do it very traditionally. I think he thinks there's some magic in that."

Mia slumped down on the stool and tried to wrap her head around all of this. She couldn't.

"I'm sorry. I know it's a lot to take in."

"Yeah."

"Do you love him?"

Mia lifted her head in surprise. "What?"

Annabel's expression had gone soft. "Val. You're in love with him, right?"

Mia sighed. "Against probably anyone's advice. Yeah." She shrugged, but this was something of which she was sure. On the flight over, she'd wondered if that kind of panic would set in – a crisis of heart and soul. Did she really love him? Or was that just a convenient fancy for a sick, lonely girl? But no. Her conviction hadn't wavered. It was the only part of this nightmare she didn't even have to think about.

Annabel smiled. "Good. I just wanted to make sure."

She sent the other woman a questioning glance.

Annabel held up her index finger. "I like Val. He tries to be this smarmy bad boy prince type, but he's a sweetheart. He's had a shit life, and he needs more people to love him. And." A second finger. "In my experience, knowing where your heart lies makes this sort of thing easier."

"This sort of thing?"

"I don't know *what's* going to happen, but *something* is about to *go off*. Get ready."

Mia took a deep breath. "Yeah. Okay."

48

DINNER

When Annabel left her alone, she went to explore the decadent bathroom. It was all sparkling and new, designed after historically lavish bathing rooms from a century ago. Someone – Annabel? Dad? – had laid out everything she could need on the marble countertop: lavender-scented soap, shampoo, a hairbrush and toothbrush, hair ties, disposable women's razors, and a stack of fluffy towels. A basket offered moisturizers and lip balm.

"It's like a hotel," she murmured, quietly horrified. And then she noticed the terrycloth robe hung up on the back of the door.

Someone wanted her to be comfortable. To feel welcome.

That was how hostages grew content with their situation, she thought.

But for the moment, she would take advantage of the hospitality. She took her time showering, and then blew out her hair with the dryer she found under the sink. She lingered in front of the mirror a moment, smoothing a fingertip along one freshly-moisturized cheek.

She looked tired – that was unavoidable. But she didn't think she looked sick...did she? Her skin was clear, bridge of her nose dusted with a few pale freckles from the sun. She had lines branching out from the corners of her eyes, faint, but present; souvenirs from too many horse show days in the blazing sun.

She wondered what Val thought of her. What he'd think of her in person, close enough to touch. That sort of thing had never mattered to her before, but now, stomach sinking, she realized that it did. A little, anyway. He was beautiful, and she loved him, and she wanted him to think she was beautiful too.

She turned away from her reflection with a sigh and pulled on the borrowed clothes.

Annabel came to collect her for dinner a few minutes later. "I'm sorry in advance," she said as they headed for the grand staircase. "This is going to be *awkward*."

Downstairs, scientists in sneakers and white lab coats still moved about, but the candles in the heavy standing candelabras had been lit; the juxtaposition of modern science and historic grandeur was jarring.

"I can't get over this place," she murmured.

Annabel said, "Just wait." And then they reached the dining room.

As she had in the bedroom, Mia felt herself grinding to a halt.

Three crystal chandeliers hung suspended over a table that could have comfortably seated the entire court of a small nation. Light reflected off its polished surface – and the wealth of white china, cut crystal, and gleaming silver of flatware. Candles flickered on silver sticks. White roses floated in big glass bowls. A tablescape fit for a king.

Or...a prince. The Prince of Wallachia, who stood at the head of the table, hand resting on the back of an ornate, carved chair.

Mia took a deep breath and continued into the room.

Vlad wasn't the only occupant. Her father was there, and a forgettable man in a suit. And a man whose eyes went straight to Annabel – her husband, Mia figured.

He was worth a second look. Tall and lean, pale, his face all sharp lines and bright blue eyes. Regal, like Val, but harsher, more withdrawn. He wore his hair in a thick black braid that hung over one shoulder and reached nearly the center of his chest. His clothes, she noted, red leather and black cotton, belonged on a mannequin at Hot Topic. He pulled it off, though.

Annabel leaned in to whisper, "That's Fulk." The warmth in her tone left no question as to their relationship.

"He's hot," Mia whispered back, and felt herself smile for the first time in hours.

Annabel smothered a giggle with her hand.

"You're here, wonderful," Dad said, and Mia felt her smile drop away. "Here, Mia." He pulled out a chair for her. "You can sit–"

"She will sit by me," Vlad said.

Mia hadn't realized there was noise in the room: side conversations, the movement of staff as they rolled in carts loaded with food, a bartender preparing drinks at a sideboard. But everything went dead silent after Vlad spoke. Everyone froze. Everyone stared.

"I…" Dad started, and trailed off.

Solemn and deliberate, Vlad stepped around the corner of the table and pulled out the chair beside his own. He waited behind it, expectant, hands on its carved back.

For a moment, she was terrified. She'd read just enough about Vlad Tepes online to know that she should be frightened of him. The rumors, passed down from Italian monks, and other leaders of the time, like Matthias Corvinus, linked him with everything from baby eating to by-proxy rape. The sight of him in the flesh only furthered that impression.

But she took a deep breath and recalled the image Val had shown her, of Vlad as a boy, with dark circles under his eyes and copper highlights in his sun-bronzed hair. Whatever else he was, Vlad was Val's brother, and for that link alone, she owed him the benefit of the doubt. At least a little.

"Alright," she said, and moved to take the seat he'd offered. When she was settled, he scooted her in so she could reach the table, and only when he stepped back and took his own chair did she finally exhale.

She thought that was when everyone exhaled, because then there was a flurry of movement. The staff resumed passing out drinks and wheeling in trays. Dad sat down beside her. Fulk took the chair opposite her, on Vlad's other side, Annabel next to him.

A waiter put a brimming glass of white wine down in front of Mia and she reached for it immediately, only spilling a few drops over the rim as her hand shook.

"You've met the baroness, and His Grace Vlad Tepes. Mia, this is the Baron Strange of Blackmere," Dad said, because in the midst of this insanity, he thought formal introductions were important. "He owns this lovely house."

She met the baron's – Fulk's – stare over the top of her glass. "Congrats on the giant mansion," she said, tone flat with…with exhaustion, and disbelief of a kind she didn't know how to classify. "And on being a werewolf, I guess." She hoped he could read her gaze: *Who's side are you on in this? Please don't agree with my psycho dad.*

He stared a moment longer, then inclined his head in a polite nod, eyes almost seeming to flash. Maybe it was just a trick of light refracting off crystal, but she didn't think so. "Pleasure to meet you," he said, and even if she couldn't read his tone all that well, she could tell that something was there. Something heavy.

Annabel sent the tiniest of smiles across the table, and then dropped her head over her plate.

"We've been doing incredible work here," Dad said, and launched into an over-detailed description of all he hoped to accomplish with vampire research.

A salad landed on the charger before her. Caesar...with tomatoes, for some reason.

Mia took a deep breath that did nothing to soothe her nerves.

"...and the potential applications..." Dad continued.

"Why you?"

Vlad's voice wasn't loud, or even especially deep, but it resonated. He had the voice of someone used to getting exactly what he wanted. It cut through the tension, and in a way, it was a relief.

"What?" Mia asked, turning to look at him.

There was nothing human about the way he regarded her, and so she could ascribe no human emotion to his gaze. Not judgement, or disappointment, or disapproval. Just an animal assessment that made her want to squirm in her chair.

"My brother can dream-walk almost anywhere, and talk to almost anyone. Why did he choose you?"

Someone on the other side of the table, Annabel probably, made a quiet noise of shock.

Mia lowered her fork, salad untouched. "I don't know," she said, truthfully. "The first time, I don't think he meant to. He asked where he was, and who I was." She remembered him peering at her bookshelf, golden and lovely, and her chest ached. "I guess when I told him my name, he knew who I was right off. I don't know why he kept coming back. You'd have to ask him."

His expression shifted, lips pressing together. "Hm. You smelled like horses when you came in."

That was right: vampire, after all. She swallowed. "I work at a training facility in Colorado. I ride every day."

A hand reached over her shoulder and lifted away her untouched salad, replacing it with a steak and steamed broccoli.

Vlad turned his attention to his own steak, reaching for his utensils. "Val is an excellent horseman."

"Yes, he told me."

"You don't agree with your father's experiments here."

"I…" The only sound besides their voices was the scrape of silver on china as he carved off a large bite of steak. She looked at the two werewolves across from her, but they were of no help. Annabel had leaned into her husband, so their shoulders touched. "No," Mia said, back to Vlad. "I don't. I get that he's working toward some breakthroughs, but this is completely unethical in all aspects."

"Mia," Dad said, and she whirled on him.

"You're keeping a man prisoner in the basement."

Levelly, he said, "He's not a man, dear. He's a vampire."

The words hit her like a slap.

A quiet huff of agitated breath across from her proved that Fulk felt the same way. "That's how he justifies his ethics problem, you see," Fulk said, his accent giving the words an extra bite. "He chooses not to see us as humans. As people. And no one cares what you do to an animal, do they?"

"That's – that's not at all what I meant!" her dad protested. "It's just – I only meant that – Prince Valerian is a criminal!" His voice went shrill, trying to convince them all.

Vlad reached for his wine and said, "My brother was locked up for killing me. But I'm not dead, am I?"

"Well…" Dad said, helpless.

"When we are finished eating," Vlad said with finality, "I will take you to see him."

Mia's stomach flipped, and she reached for her silverware.

~*~

Mia couldn't decide if her father was frightened of Vlad, or merely trying to butter him up to encourage his cooperation. Probably both.

For her own part, she settled on thoroughly intimidated, but unwilling to show it. (Or, okay, unwilling to show *too much* of it.) But she wasn't afraid. Not really. Maybe she should have been. But she'd spent her life studying animals, and nothing about Vlad's tone, or posture, or hard to read glances suggested that he intended to harm her.

After dinner, he led her through a stunning library and into a sleek, modern elevator. When the doors slid shut, closing them in together, their reflections stared back at them: strange at best. Her, tired and wilting, and him, implacable and steely.

It was silent a long, tense moment, as the car started its descent. Then Vlad said, "My brother's life has been...difficult."

"That seems like a massive understatement."

He snorted and it sounded like agreement. "Your father—" he started.

"Is an asshole," she finished. "I'm not here for Dad, or for me. I'm here for Val." She turned to face him, rather than the reflected image of him, and thought he might be holding back a smile.

He took his time in returning her glance. "He cares for you," he said. "That much I gleaned the last time I spoke with him. And that means he trusts you."

A fluttering in her chest.

"I neither know you, nor care for you. And I don't trust you," he said, flatly, and the fluttering died down. "But you don't smell like a liar."

She swallowed. "That's something you can smell?"

"Sometimes." He faced forward again with an air of dismissal, but said, "If you love my brother, you'll do as I say when I say it."

She bristled.

"Hush, child. You don't know what I know. Or what I'm planning. If you love him, you won't hurt him."

She forced a deep, slow breath. "I would *never* hurt him."

The elevator arrived with a quiet ding. Just before the doors slid open, he said, "Good."

~*~

Vlad had put him back in the cell, but he'd left off the cuffs, and collar, and chains. The bars were silver, but there were gaps, and through those, Val could feel it when she arrived.

He was lounging back on his cot, one leg drawn up, arm resting along his knee, contemplating his freshly clean fingernails, when the faintest vibration shivered down the walls. A helicopter landing all the way up on the roof.

He sat bolt upright, that shiver moving under his skin. People came and went – soldiers, staff, scientists flown down from the New York location. An arrival wasn't unusual.

But Vlad had said Mia was coming.

He waited like that, even when his back grew sore from holding the position. He inhaled deeply, testing the air, searching for the tiniest scent, the smallest sound. Straining, really, his heart beating butterfly-fast in his throat.

It could have been minutes, or hours. He convinced himself that he could sense her presence, though he had no idea what she smelled like; didn't know the unique rhythm of her heartbeat. So he only imagined he could hear her footfalls through all those layers of steel, and stone, and floorboards.

But then.

Then...

Unmistakable thrum of the elevator. It went up and down dozens of times a day, maybe even hundreds. But *this* time, drawn tight with inspiration, Val let the sound draw a quiet gasp from him.

He waited, barely breathing.

And then footfalls moved overhead, through subbasement one. Two sets. One heavy and purposeful, the other light and uncertain.

God. God, could it...

The outer door opened with a hiss of the lock. And then...

Then he caught her scent.

An unfamiliar female, lavender from the bath soap upstairs, clean underneath. Ripe. Warm. But also nervous. And also sick.

"Oh," he said aloud, when he detected the tumor, that awful festering thing that didn't belong in her beautiful head. His eyes burned, and his heart hammered, and he swayed on his cot. "*Oh, Mia.*"

He tried to stand as the barred door creaked open, but his knees gave out. Still weak, but also shivering with a kind of excitement too acute to name. He was terrified. He wanted to cry. He wanted to touch her.

The only thing louder than the thump of her pulse was his own. He gripped the edge of the cot hard, until his knuckles cracked, and then Vlad stepped into view.

And then...there she was.

He closed his eyes a moment, wanting to stamp the sight of her into his mind, in case this was a hallucination. If she wasn't really here, he wanted to tuck her away between the pages of his sweetest fantasies, and pretend this was really happening.

Someone had given her black workout gear to wear, clinging black pants and a zippered jacket with a high collar. The dark washed her out a little, highlighted the shadows under her eyes. Her hair, normally pulled back under her helmet, fell in dark gold waves over both shoulders; it looked soft.

He opened his mouth, breathing through it, trying to taste her presence. She burrowed up into his sinuses and set his head to spinning.

He wet his lips and felt that his fangs had extended. "Vlad." His voice was a cracked, shaky semblance of calm. "Am I dreaming?"

Vlad made an impatient sound. "Open your eyes, stupid."

He smiled – because that was his big brother alright – and he did open his eyes, and Mia was still there, staring at him with wide eyes and parted lips. She couldn't believe it either.

Vlad, face set in a way that suggested he thought they were both idiots, unlocked the cell door with the key and held it open. "You have half an hour," he told Mia, "and then I'll return. Otherwise, your father will become problematic."

"Okay," she said faintly, but didn't move.

Vlad gave a sweeping gesture of invitation. "You're not frightened, are you?"

"No—"

"No," Val said, because she wasn't. She smelled the way he felt: completely overwhelmed.

Vlad looked between them, unimpressed, then turned and walked away, cell door left open.

They were alone. And they were only ten feet apart. No bars, no cuffs, no thousands of miles and incorporeal forms. They...

They started moving at the same time. Val lurched up from his cot and Mia staggered forward. He saw tears fill her eyes, bright like crystal, and then they crashed together.

There were so many things he wanted to do, ways in which he wanted to touch her – brush her with careful, worshipful fingertips like the priceless piece of art she was. But that would have to come later, when he was less desperate, when he wasn't choking on her scent for the very first time. He wrapped both arms around her and crushed her to his chest; felt her arms slip around his waist, vise-tight, hands digging into the back of his shirt. She pressed her face, hot, soft skin, into his throat with a gasp.

Val dropped his face into hair, panting, and an embarrassing sound like a groan built in his throat, worked its way past his lips.

He hunched his shoulders, shielding her, hiding her away. They weren't close enough; he wasn't sure they could be. "You're here," he murmured into the top of her head. Clutched her shoulders, pressed his fingers to her neck to feel the heat there, to know that she was real, her pulse flying under his touch. "You're here, you're here."

"Val," she said, like a sigh, breath hot across his collarbone.

He wanted to say so much. Everything. An abundance of gratitude, disbelief, and regret that she was here at all. The words gathered in his throat, too many, too fast, a logjam.

They could wait, he decided. He kissed her crown, and breathed her in, and basked in the pressure of her heart pounding against his.

49

THE NECROMANCER

He'd shown her, briefly, through his projection, what he really looked like. Not the graceful, gleaming prince who'd lounged around her apartment, but his true body, trapped in a cell. Filthy, bedraggled, painfully thin. This version of him, the one holding her, the one whose shirt collar she pressed her nose into, was a few pounds heavier than that wraith she'd seen back at the barn, and he was clean; he smelled of the same lavender soap she'd used. But she could feel the press of his ribs through his shirt; the tiny tremors that wracked his frame.

Her arms tightened around him when she felt his knees try to give out for the third time. He should have felt lithe, and strong – impossibly strong, he was a vampire. But instead, he felt fragile; nothing but brittle bones held together by sheer force of will. As the initial shock and joy faded, as her pulse slowed to something only quietly frantic, she realized they couldn't keep standing here like this – Val couldn't, anyway.

"Hey," she said, pulling back far enough to look up into his face. He was slower to retreat, his eyes still closed, lashes long and dark on his sunken cheeks. He breathed through his mouth, slow and shaky. "Let's sit down, okay?"

His eyes opened, and they were so blue in person. Full of an emotion she didn't dare name. "You're here," he said again. It was all he'd said. And then: "Oh, darling, you're *here*."

It had seemed too good to be true on her end, an achingly sweet fiction.

She hadn't stopped to consider that it had been the same for him.

"I am." She reached up to touch his face, the sharp plane of his cheek cool beneath her hand. "Let's sit down before you fall."

He blinked a few times. "There's only the cot." Then he grinned, and his fangs were long and sharp. "Trying to get me into bed already?"

She laughed, but it wasn't for the joke. Joy filled her, swelling impossibly bigger on each breath. "Sure, we'll go with that. Come on, easy does it."

She managed to walk him backward the few steps to the cot and get him eased down onto it, his back to the wall. She ended up going, too, though, because he hooked an arm around her waist and, even thin though he was, there was no shaking him off. Not that she wanted to – no, all she wanted in that moment was to fold her legs up and settle in against his side, one hand on his chest, the other at the back of his neck, on the warm skin up under his hair.

He tipped his head back, and the harsh light from the caged overhead bulbs slid down the sharp line of his nose, his lips, his chin; carved shadows in the hollow of his throat.

He was beautiful. Even like this. Maybe especially – because he was real, and his chest rose and fell under her hand, and if she leaned in closer, she could…

He tipped his head a little to the side, so he could look at her. "A hot bath, and a visit from a beautiful lady," he said, voice rough. "It *has* been a remarkable day." He attempted to smile…but it crumbled. His breath caught, and his lashes flickered. He whispered something low and pained in another language.

Mia bundled him in close as best she could; cupped the back of his head and drew him down so they were cheek-to-cheek, close enough that his quiet, hiccupping little sobs were buried against her neck.

All she could say was, "I'm here." Over and over, a mantra. She held him, and shushed him, and hoped it was enough.

~*~

Fulk threw down his entire glass of port in one go and then poured another as he was trying not to choke. Of all the things that could be effectively chugged, port wasn't one of them.

Behind him, Dr. Talbot paced back and forth across the Aubusson carpet, no doubt wringing his hands. Fulk's skin prickled, hackles raised, in response to the doctor's fretting. The energy in the room made him want to growl. He just barely restrained himself.

"You can't really think he'd hurt her, doc," Annabel said. She had that charming Southern way of calling a person an idiot while making it sound consoling. "Val's crazy about her."

"And what, Lady Strange," he snapped, uncharacteristically severe, "would be at all relieving about *that*?"

Fulk turned around and leaned back against the ornate sideboard, wineglass held in one hand, aiming a finger toward the man with the other. "I don't like your tone."

Talbot's already flushed face colored further. "My daughter is alone with a madman! My tone is understandable."

"Not alone. Vlad's with them," Annabel pointed out.

Fulk sent her a look.

She shrugged.

"Two madmen!" Talbot threw up his hands. "Wonderful!"

"So I'm a madman?" Vlad asked, tone mild. Fulk had heard and scented that he was approaching, and it was worth holding his tongue to watch Talbot yelp and spin to face him.

"You, uh, no, I–" Talbot sputtered.

Vlad paced slowly into the room, hands clasped behind his back. Relaxed, unconcerned. Every blink and every step was a threat. "No, it's true," he said mildly, coming to the sideboard beside Fulk and picking up a clean glass. He poured himself a Scotch, and the normal, comfortable way he handled the decanter was one of those strange moments that kept sucker-punching Fulk: those Vlad-the-Impaler-is-just-a-man moments.

Not just a man. A vampire. A vicious one, at that. But one who slept, and ate, and who liked Scotch, apparently.

Vlad took a sip and lifted his brows at Fulk over the rim of the glass.

Fulk shrugged and looked away, back toward Talbot – who was starting to turn purple with a combination of fear and anger.

"It's true," Vlad continued, mirroring Fulk's pose against the table. "I've been called a madman by many." He didn't seem bothered by it. "A monster. A murderer. Warlord. Blood-drinker. Eater of the dead. What do you think, Doctor? Did you wake up a madman to fight your war for you?"

Fulk paused with his glass pressed to his lip, watching.

Talbot's face went slowly blank. "I – of course I don't think that."

This was the problem, and had been since his birth: People underestimated Vlad's intelligence. No one could reconcile the idea of a person accused of such cruelty as being razor-sharp, but he was. Fulk didn't think he'd met anyone as calculating in his life. But the difference between Vlad and every scheming Cassius that had ever lived was that Vlad always took the most direct route. Because he could, morals and obstacles be damned.

Staring unblinking at Talbot, Vlad said, "You seem frightened."

"Do I? I'm only worried for my daughter's safety."

"Hmm." Another sip of Scotch, and then Vlad set the glass aside. "Do you want to know what I think?"

Fulk did. A quick glance at Anna proved she did, too.

But.

Fulk felt it as a low pulse deep in the center of himself. The tolling of a bell. He'd felt it recently, only a few weeks before, the day they'd brought the redheaded girl into the manor. Anna liked to joke that it was their internal alarm system, but it wasn't much of a joke if it was true – and it was. Whenever a mage got close enough to sense, something went off inside him like a depth charge. *Danger*, his wolf growled, and raised its hackles.

Vlad must have felt it, too, because he tipped his head back and looked up at the ceiling.

A moment later, the faint thump of helicopter rotors drifted down from the roof; the building shuddered, quiet, in a way that humans couldn't detect, when the Blackhawk touched down on the pad.

Fulk's stomach clenched hard. He growled, an unhappy rumble he couldn't help, one that Anna automatically echoed. "Liam."

Vlad's nostrils flared as he inhaled. "It seems your necromancer has arrived, Dr. Talbot," he said, gaze dropping. "Let's see if he lives up to expectation."

Talbot began to wring his hands. "Yes. Well, he's very agreeable, as I'm sure you will see. A very respectful man, he..."

His voice faded into the periphery. Fulk strained for the sound of an elevator, for footfalls, but all he could hear was the rush of blood in his ears, strong like the tide, drowning out everything else. Air turned thick in his lungs, hard to push, hard to pull in; his chest ached, and his stomach cramped, and—

A small, warm hand touched his neck, and he jerked his head down, vision swimming.

Annabel looked up at him with the softest smile. "There he is. It's alright, baby."

He growled again, and spoke through his teeth. "It is *never* alright when it's about him." Every time he blinked, he saw Anna the way she'd been *that day*: lifeless, limp, bloody. Dead. In that last moment, before he plunged the knife in, he'd searched for a rapidly-fading pulse, and hadn't been able to find it. It was the wolf that had brought her back, howling and clawing. The wolf and the demon had brought his wild girl back to him, made her whole, made her immortal.

But it was Liam who'd—

"Fulk." She shifted her hand, up his jaw, over his cheek. He raised his own and covered hers with it, held her to him. "Do you want to shift? Will that make it easier?"

It would. They could go down to four legs and leave the manor, go running through the dark woods, until the smell of pine forest and the thrill of the chase had crowded out all his fear and hate.

But he said, "No," with a deep sigh. "He'll know I'm avoiding him." And appearing weak in front of him was anathema.

Anna urged him down, until their foreheads touched, so that all he could see, and smell, and feel was her. "It's not like it was then, baby," she murmured. "We're both so much stronger now."

She was. Physically, at least – she'd always been stronger than him mentally, emotionally. And what was he now? Not a man, nor a wolf, but a tool that allowed itself to be used.

"Fulk," she said again, stern this time, and a smile ghosted across his lips.

"You're right." He kissed her, once, then pulled back. "We'll be fine."

"That's what I keep telling you." She rapped her knuckles lightly against his forehead. *You idiot.* Her smile was fond.

"Strange," Vlad said, and Fulk glanced over.

The vampire's face was doing something odd. It took Fulk a moment to realize that he was *smiling.* Faint, but definitive, amused even.

"Leave this to me," he said, a murmur too low for Talbot to make out. "Just stand there and try not to look terrified."

"I'm not terrified," he huffed.

"Mmhm."

Make that intelligent and a smartass.

A tech in a lab coat came barreling into the room, wild-eyed and out of breath. "Dr. – Dr. Talbot – they sent – sent me to tell you–"

"That Mr. Price is on his way down?" Talbot seemed relieved to have a distraction from his immortal company. "Yes, I know. Have him brought here, please, and ask the kitchen to send in a plate of refreshments. Is his wife with him?"

The young man wheezed and nodded.

"Very good. Thank you, Brandon."

The tech took a few furtive glances at Vlad, and then Fulk and Anna, and retreated with an air of gratitude.

"Humans were not so frightened all the time in my days," Vlad said, and Fulk bit back a sudden, unexpected laugh.

"Don't take this the wrong way, but, uh, they're kinda afraid of you, chief," Anna said.

Vlad snorted. "Ridiculous. They haven't seen me do anything."

"You *did* almost cut your brother in half."

Fulk thought he looked vaguely pleased, the weirdo.

And then two nameless soldiers in black led Liam and Lily Price into the room, and all other thoughts flew out of Fulk's head.

They were the sort of couple that even humans paused to notice, simply because they were striking. Tall, and slender, both redheads. Lily's hair was a pale red, heavily threaded with orange, and her eyes were like Annabel's: deep green, flecked with gold. Liam had blue eyes – cold eyes. And his hair was the russet of an

Irish setter, just as his daughter's had been. He'd worn it to his shoulders in the past, but now had trimmed it so it fell in a soft, curled tumble to just below his ears. His nose was still crooked, smile still sharper than the point of his chin.

Fulk nearly choked on the growl that tried to build in his throat. Annabel moved to stand beside him, and hooked their arms together; leaned into him, her temple pressed to his shoulder. A united front.

"Liam. Lily," Dr. Talbot greeted warmly, "I'm so glad to see you both again." Under his wide smile and reaching handshake, the man reeked of nerves. A scent just perceptible beneath the campfire stench of the two mages.

Liam had always been charming. He reached now to clasp the doctor's hand between both of his, a friendly press to accompany his smile. "Doctor. A pleasure as always." He released Talbot's hand slowly, righting himself, smile slipping into a look of concern. "Though I do wish it was under better circumstances."

"Yes, as do I." Talbot bowed elaborately in Lily's direction, and she acknowledged him with a nod. Her expression was calm, but she didn't smile. The lifeless sister, Fulk had always thought; it was as if the fire she wielded sucked all the strong feeling out of her, until she could be nothing but serene. "We have much to discuss concerning–"

Talbot broke off suddenly, and Fulk realized too late – distracted, sinuses flooded with mage-stink – that there was a third newcomer to the room, one lingering beyond the magical couple, hanging back in the shadows of the threshold.

He smelled...

He smelled like a graveyard.

Fulk and Annabel growled together, and beside them, Vlad let out a low pulsing snarl of his own.

"Ah." Liam's gaze lifted over Talbot's head and came straight to Fulk, eyes twinkling as he smiled. "You've noticed that we brought a friend."

Fulk pushed Annabel back behind him, though she protested; felt her nails score his forearm as she tried to claw her way around him. He lowered his head, felt his wolf press up close beneath his skin, ready to shift. His voice was a growl. "That thing's not alive."

Liam chuckled. "I assure you he is. Very much so. I watched the flesh knit itself together over his bones myself."

"What did you do?"

Liam cocked his head, smile smug, and, somehow, pitying. *Oh, Fulk*, it seemed to say. *As stupid as ever.* "I already told you: I made a friend. A very valuable one, I can assure you. Now if you'll lower your hackles and act like a civilized person, I can explain—"

Two things happened at once.

Vlad stalked forward, hands curled into claws, snarling like a jungle cat.

And the dead man slid out of the shadows to stand in front of Liam, shoulders angled for a fight, balanced up on his toes. He was dressed all in black, a hood pulled up over his head so that only the end of his nose and the scar on his chin were visible. He held a knife in one hand, and its edge caught the firelight in a wicked flash.

The fire itself rested in Liam's palm, conjured with a thought.

Vlad...hesitated.

"Hello, my lord Dracula," Liam said. "It's *quite* the honor, though I assure you that my friend here will put that knife to good use if you attempt to come any closer."

Vlad grinned, and his fangs were long. "Why don't you ask what happened the last time someone tried to fight me with a knife?"

Liam said, "Ah, yes, but the difference is: Captain Baskin isn't much of a dancer."

The dead man's empty hand shifted, and then it wasn't empty anymore, another knife held in its grip. He sank down in his knees a fraction, stretching the tendons, preparing.

Fulk had the awful sense that he was missing something. "Vlad..." he started.

But the prince was already in motion.

And so was the dead man. Both knives held in a backhanded grip, he moved quick, feet impossibly light on the carpet. He sidestepped, facing Vlad, forcing him to turn to keep up. *Captain Baskin isn't much of a dancer*, Liam had said, but this man clearly was. Had been.

Vlad seemed to gather himself, no longer ready to fling himself at an easily crushed opponent, but more reserved, calculating. He turned to keep pace with the dancer, mouth open as he scented the air.

"Vlad," Fulk said, as respectfully as possible, "let's just wait."

"You should listen to your wolf," Liam said, amused. "Sometimes he has the right idea about things."

"I'm *not his wolf*."

Liam ignored this. "You're looking well, your ladyship. It would appear the twenty-first century agrees with you."

Fulk snarled.

Anna said, "Shut up, Liam. Call off your damn zombie."

Vlad lunged, and the dancer leapt back, an efficient movement that sent him spinning away, knives flashing. Vlad made a low sound that could have been a growl or a laugh. He turned back to Liam, sneering. "So you made yourself a poppet. My uncle can do that, too. He wants to destroy half of humanity with them."

Liam's smile never slipped. "You're mistaken, your grace. Your uncle's – affliction, I guess you could say – eats a person's soul out of their body, leaving only disease and mindless violence. You call it the Absence, yes? Well, he's only a vampire, after all, playing at being a mage. I can assure you that when I raise someone from the dead, I bring their soul back as well."

Vlad looked again at the dead man, still poised for a fight.

Liam said, "Show them your face, Kolya."

The man stilled. He sheathed his knives at the small of his back, an efficient movement, and then reached up to push his hood back.

Fulk had seen the videos of the Absence-afflicted creatures in the desert. Mindless destruction; worse than animals – as an animal himself, he could attest that a creature's species had no bearing on its intelligence. Those things were, as Vlad had stated, poppets.

But this man, the skin of his face laced with scars, was very much present, if quiet and expressionless. Dark eyes; intelligent eyes...but lost. His hair hung shaggy and unkempt past his chin. He stood at attention, unmoving, like a soldier, like a –

Oh. Oh no.

"This," Liam said, "is Kolya Dyomin of Moscow. A Chekist under the command of Captain Nikita Baskin."

If either name meant a thing to him, Kolya didn't react, gaze fixed somewhere in the middle distance.

Fulk turned to Liam with another growl. "*What did you do?*" he repeated.

Liam sighed. "I brought you a soldier for your war. Now kindly shut up and point me toward the good whiskey."

<u>50</u>

CANDY-FRAGILE

"How's Brando?"

Everything about this, about having her here, was a marvel. Staring down at the top of her head, breathing in the scents of her shampoo and skin, was a revelation. The heat of her body pressed close to his side; the embrace of her arms around his waist; weight of her temple at his shoulder. He was fascinated by the glimpse of her bare ankles between the line of her pants and the tops of her black, borrowed sneakers. He couldn't stop shaking. Wasn't sure if he could ever stop.

Her hair rustled as she tipped her head back, propped her chin on his collarbone and smiled up at him. "I finally get here and you want to know about Brando?" she teased.

He couldn't respond in kind, his voice as shaky as his hands. "I want to know everything there is to know about you."

Her expression softened, smile going warm and a little self-conscious. "There's not much to know."

"I disagree."

She sighed, fond. "Donna texted me a little while ago to say that Brando misses me – which I doubt – and that the other girls are spoiling him. She also wanted to know if she needed to call the real police for me. Or maybe even the National Guard." She breathed a quiet laugh, but it was humorless. "I still can't believe this is happening."

She rested her head against him, lashes dropping low, and he could read the anguish in her. It was soft, but it was real, layered and confused. She didn't deserve it, he thought.

"Mia." He raised one unsteady hand and cupped it around the back of her head. Her skull felt candy-fragile, even given his own current weakness. "Your father isn't exactly the villain here."

She pulled back far enough to tip an angry, disbelieving look up to his face. "He's holding you prisoner–"

"Just as hundreds of others have done before him. He didn't put me in the cage, darling. He's merely keeping me here.

There are nearly six-hundred years' worth of files and rumors and security tapes on me, and none of them tell a story that would convince a rational person that I was some – innocent pawn in all this."

Her frown deepened, undeterred. "So? So you killed some people while you were in here, right? You said you did. That's – well, that's not ideal. But they were keeping you locked up. They were abusing you."

"Are you trying to convince yourself?"

"No." She braced her hand against his chest and pushed herself upright, so their faces were nearly level. "I asked you once before if you were trying to scare me off, and you're doing it again."

"I don't want you to forsake your family just because–"

"Val." She laid her hand on his face, and he couldn't help but lean into it. Her gaze sparked, as ferocious as any wolf. "Family is made of the people who love you. Who you love back. The people who help you, and hold you up, and accept you. I get to choose that. I get to choose you – to be on your side. Stop trying to convince me I shouldn't."

She vibrated with energy and emotion. Her look dared him to challenge her.

But then she realized what she'd said – how forceful it had sounded – and she shrank a little, hand sliding down to his chest, her touch light – not enough. "I'm sorry, I–"

He caught her hand in his. *"Mia."* He sounded ragged, and he didn't care. This was…she was…

She was *everything*.

The door opened at the top of the stairs.

"Mia, listen to me." He grabbed her shoulders tight. Shoved his face into hers. "I need you to think about what you want. What you *really want*. Not in fantasies and hypotheticals, alright? Decide. And trust my brother. He's an asshole, I know, but he's on our side."

Her gaze flicked back and forth across his face. Uncertain now. "I…"

The barred door creaked open and footfalls moved toward them.

Val shut his eyes and touched his forehead briefly to hers. "Decide," he said again, and then there was Vlad, come to collect her.

He looked especially stone-faced.

"What's going on up there?" Val asked.

"The mage is here," Vlad ground out. "And he has a revenant with him."

Val's stomach lurched, and he bundled Mia in closer. "Fascinating."

"More than you know: it's one of Baskin's Russians."

~*~

Talbot looked exhausted, and Fulk took a small amount of satisfaction in that. "Mr. Price," he said with a deep sigh. "I just...don't understand."

The revenant, Kolya Dyomin, stood against the far wall of the office, hands clasped loosely in front of him, gaze fixed unseeing in the middle distance. Fulk found him to be a collection of unsettling contradictions. He was very much alive, but he smelled like – not like a corpse. Not like rot. But like deep, dark earth that shouldn't have been disturbed. Things lived, and things fed, and things bled, and things died. Vampires slept, and healed, and overcame the most grievous of wounds. Wolves never aged. But things didn't die and come back – that wasn't natural.

Kolya was alert, and he moved quickly, as elegantly as the former ballet dancer Liam had claimed him to be. He could speak, and he breathed; his heart beat at a normal resting rate.

But to follow Liam here, to defend him, to remain stone-faced at the mention of his friends. He was not...himself. Fulk could tell that without ever having met him as he'd once been.

"It's really quite simple, Doctor," Liam said. "I meant what I said before about needing soldiers in your war. *Our* war," he amended, with a look toward Fulk that had Fulk shifting in his seat. "Whether mortal or immortal, I think it's safe to say that all the creatures living on this earth want to continue living. Therefore, the war must be a joint effort by all those capable of fighting. Kolya is a valuable soldier. And." He held up a finger, quietly triumphant. "He offers us leverage. Nikita Baskin's pet wolf – Sasha – was the original progeny of your little institute. Since you seem unable to keep him here by force, I thought we'd try a different tactic."

Fulk snorted. "By bribing him? 'Look, we have your dead friend, join us.'"

Liam looked over, serene. "Yes."

"Sasha Kashnikov is one wolf," Fulk said. "And not a very ferocious one at that. Have you seen him? He only gets riled up when his vamp is threatened."

Liam smiled. "So I've heard."

"What do you need them for? They're just two. Leave them alone."

The smile stretched. "Ah. So you haven't brushed up on your Roman history."

Fulk growled. "What are you talking about?" God, he hated him.

The fucker laughed. "How many Romes are there, Fulk?"

Oh…shit.

"It's three," Liam answered, gleeful. "Rome, then Constantinople, then Moscow. Remember, brother?"

"We are not brothers."

He waved, dismissive. "You're avoiding my point. Which is: Baskin brought a very special Russian with him to this manor house." He paused.

Fulk stared him down.

"Christ," Liam muttered, "Alexei Romanov. He brought the tsarevich with him." He held both hands up, triumphant.

"What is your point?"

Liam blinked at him a moment, then heaved a dramatic sigh. "The point, my dear brute, is this. Romulus has faced more than one would-be killer in his time, but none have ever been able to defeat him. One almost wonders if he really is half god, hm? Vlad stood the greatest chance – he was the strongest, of the original line of Rome, Romulus's own flesh and blood. But he only managed to put him to sleep. So this begets the question: can he be stopped?"

Talbot looked faintly ill.

650

"I have a theory about this. I think we've—"

"We?"

"—been going about it the wrong way all this time. The vampire, the mage, and the wolf." He ticked them off on three fingers. "What if a single hero can't defeat Romulus? What if it takes three Roman emperors to do so?" His grin was sly, his eyes bright, and...

Oh.

Something turned over in Fulk's stomach, and he couldn't decide if it was dread or hope.

Liam sat back, looking smug. "The Greeks in Istanbul have a legend. They believe – well, some of them do – that Constantine Dragases wasn't killed when the Conqueror sacked the city. That he went into hiding, inside a secret vault. And that in Rome's greatest hour of need, he shall rise again, immortal, the last Roman emperor come to slay the dragon."

"You stole that from the old Arthurian legend, didn't you?" Fulk said.

Liam chuckled. "Uncanny, isn't it? But I swear that it's true. History has a funny way of overlapping like that."

"So, what, Constantine was a vampire?"

"Oh, no. Quite human, and very dead. But the legend points to my larger theory: that the secret lies beyond the original city of Rome. It's more a representative thing. Three immortals in a working relationship: the triumvirate. The triumvirate of Rome. The three Romes."

"So you're saying..." Talbot started, leaning forward.

"I'm saying, doctor, that we need three very strong vampires, and their Familiars to take this bastard out. And I haven't met the boy, but Alexei Romanov is related, by blood, to the last emperor of Constantinople. I think that means something."

"And so you think..." Every gaze shifted toward Kolya Dyomin, who stood unflinching, still, against the wall. "That we can get to him through Nikita Baskin," Talbot said.

"I think," Liam said, "that if Baskin finds out we have one of his dearly departed brethren in the flesh, he'll become much more cooperative."

Fulk…couldn't disagree with his logic.

"Now," Liam went on, "someone please explain how you managed to lose my daughter."

~*~

"You look well, sister."

They'd been alone in the study for nearly ten minutes, and they were the first words Lily had spoken.

Annabel set her book aside; she'd only been pretending to read it anyway.

Her sister stood in front of the fire, firelight dancing up her smooth white arms. She dressed like an eccentric; Beneath the cloak she'd draped over the arm of a chair, her dress was simple, but finely made. It brushed the floor at its flared hem, and was cinched tight at the waist. A walking dress for a lady born well before their own original time.

She looked at Annabel with a small, fond smile, her gaze melancholy.

She smelled like a toasted marshmallow, and Anna fought not to scrunch up her nose. "No, I don't." She dropped her feet off the arm of the chair, chunky soles of her boots thumping onto the rug.

Lily's smile widened a fraction, patronizing in an innocent sort of way. "The house looks–"

"Do you really wanna make small talk?"

"We don't have to, if you don't want to."

Anna stifled a growl. Her hands wanted to – to do something, so she gripped the arms of the chair. Hard. Felt the leather give beneath fingertips that seemed more like claws. "Don't do that."

"Do what?"

"Act all innocent! Like – like we–" She forced herself to stop, and took a deep breath. "Lily," she said with more control, "we haven't spoken to each other in decades. How can you act like nothing ever happened?"

Lily sighed. As with all her gestures, it was delicate, feminine. Appropriate. "Isn't it better to be civil than to wallow in the past?"

Annabel got to her feet without meaning to. Her wolf strained inside her, wanting out, wanting to trade this fragile human skin for something that looked as ferocious as she felt. "Protecting myself isn't wallowing. And our past? That wasn't a couple of schoolgirl arguments. Don't you dare act like I'm supposed to get over that."

"Anna, we're sisters."

"So? When did that ever matter to you?"

"Always."

She did growl this time. "Then why did you choose that creep over your own family?"

Lily stood serene, hands folded in front of her, expression infuriatingly placid. "I could say the same of you."

"Do *not* compare Fulk to that bastard of yours. They're *nothing* alike."

"Hmm."

Disgusted, frustrated by her own short temper, Anna spun away with a snarl. She stalked all the way across the room and was nearly to the door when Lily spoke up behind her.

In an uncharacteristic, wavering voice, she said, "Did you meet her?"

Annabel started to turn around – but caught herself, one hand clenched tight on the crystal doorknob. "Who?" she asked, just to be contrary. She knew exactly, and that was why she couldn't turn and look at her sister's face, couldn't see whatever emotion colored it.

"My...my daughter."

I hope she never meets you, Anna thought, viciously. *I hope she never knows how heartless her parents are. You don't deserve her. She's the only good thing that ever came of Liam Price.*

But Anna said, "Her name is Ruby. Her boyfriend calls her Red." Then she left the room.

~*~

Vlad didn't so much walk as *stalk*, his gait that of a lion or tiger. Val, or at least his astral projection, had moved around Mia's apartment with a natural grace, but Vlad was more overtly threatening – even when she didn't actively feel threatened, like now.

She followed behind him as he made his way through the lab and back to the elevator, noting the way every staff member averted their eyes and hurried to get out of the way. Vlad didn't acknowledge any of them, but they all ducked and bowed and fled, as if from royalty. From frightening royalty.

He didn't speak to her in the first elevator, nor during the long walk to the second, and she sank down into her own thoughts.

Decide, Val had said. Decide *what*?

She still couldn't believe that she'd touched him. Leaned against him and felt his body heat. Felt the press of bones too close to the skin, and smelled the soap on him. She touched her neck, absently, and recalled the warmth of his tears there.

Val was real.

She didn't realize she'd closed her eyes until she bumped into Vlad's back. It was an embarrassing collision; she ran her face into his shoulder blade, and tromped all over the heels of his boots.

"Sorry, sorry," she said, stumbling back.

He sent her a flat look over one shoulder, but said nothing.

They'd arrived at the second elevator, and its doors slid open with a quiet chime. Mia hurried inside before she could do anything else as stupid as *run into* Vlad the Impaler.

He followed at a normal pace and pressed the button for the third floor. Once the doors were shut, he finally spoke, and she flinched before she could catch herself.

He chuckled.

The sound surprised her so much that she turned to look at him, to make sure, and, yep, he was laughing. It was low, and dark, and sounded half a growl, but he was *smiling*, dark eyes creased at the corners.

"What?" she asked, and felt her own disbelieving smile threaten.

654

He faced his own reflection in the elevator wall, smile still in place. "You're a brave one, aren't you?"

"Uh...I try to be." But her heart pounded, and she didn't want to turn her back to him.

"Hm. Trying is better than not, in most things."

"O...kay."

"My brother said that you are a talented horsewoman."

The change of subject surprised her – but, maybe it shouldn't have. Nothing about Vlad spoke of meandering segues and deft handoffs. "Well, that was nice of him."

"Are you?"

"Oh, um..." She had to sound decisive with this crowd. "Yeah, you could say that. I've worked hard at it."

He murmured a noise she read as approving. "We will go riding tomorrow."

Another surprise, more lurching than the motion of the elevator. "We will?"

"There's a stable, and I asked for horses to be stalled there." A note of imperiousness. A prince, after all. "I wish to take Val riding, and you shall come with us."

"Oh." Her heart bumped, part excitement, part worry. "Will they let you take him outside?"

"Do you always worry about what you're allowed to do?"

She sighed.

He smiled again – more of a smirk. "I can do what I want. Will you come with us?"

"Of course."

"Good." The elevator arrived and the doors slid open. "Wear something appropriate."

It wasn't until she was back in her room that it hit her: Vlad the Impaler telling her to wear something appropriate. Then she laughed so hard she almost choked.

~*~

She expected her dad to show up at some point, but it didn't mean she was glad when a knock sounded at her door just after eleven. Exhaustion dragged at her, and she was beginning to feel sick to her stomach, but she'd stayed up on purpose, leaning back against the headboard of the massive four-poster and trading texts with Donna. Donna was dead serious about calling in the National Guard. Mia hated that she was only just now realizing that her boss actually cared about her beyond her ability to warm up a horse.

She fired off another text to her mom, too, a quick check-in. She'd texted her before she boarded the plane in Colorado, her first chance to reach out, and told Kate she was *on the way 2 see Dad.* By the time they'd landed, she'd had twelve missed calls. Guilt gnawed at her, but she had no idea what to say to her mother; Kate couldn't help her now, and Mia wanted to be as clear-headed as possible right now.

When she heard the knock, she set her phone aside on the nightstand and called what she hoped was a grudging "come in."

Edwin cracked the door first, and peeped slowly around its edge before he finally shoved his whole head inside. He looked ridiculous. "Hello, dear. I wondered if I might have a word."

"Fine."

He came in smiling, though careful, walking gingerly across the carpet and settling in a claw-foot chair that looked two centuries old. He sat like an old man, legs spread so he could settled his linked hands between them, shoulders rounded beneath the white lab coat he still wore. Mia had a sudden, disturbing vision of herself like this, flabby and stoop-shouldered, hair thinning. Maybe it was because his brain was so industrious; his body had withered under the strain of all that thought. Or maybe it was just genetic. Had Mom's genes been enough to stave off his? Or would this be Mia, frail, and old before her time?

No, she realized with a sick inner laugh. She'd be dead long before she went gray and thin.

God.

"I hope you find your room to be comfortable," Dad began.

"It's very nice," she said without emotion.

"It's west-facing." He twisted his fingers together until they went white. He still wore his wedding ring, she saw. "I thought you might enjoy seeing the sunset."

She didn't respond.

He studied her a moment, expression strained. Then he slumped a little more. If possible, the lines on his face deepened. "Mia," he said, weary, "I know you're furious. I know you probably hate me. But can't we – can't we just talk? Not as doctor and patient, but as father and daughter?"

She had to take a few breaths. Then, as calmly as she could: "You have to understand that there's nothing you can say at this point. You know that, right? This isn't just about us, Dad. It's not father-daughter problems. What you're doing here – I can't get over that."

He looked terribly sad. "Is this really an issue of a wider morality for you? Or is it just about the prince?"

"I–" She hesitated, and that killed her entire argument.

"Mia," he sighed. "I know that you–" he winced "–have come to care for Prince Valerian in some way. But darling, he's nearly six-hundred-years-old. He's killed people, maimed them, *drank their blood.* He can manipulate minds. He was a sultan's concubine. How could you ever possibly believe anything he says?"

Concubine? She thought of that day in the stable, when he'd showed her his childhood. There were unpleasant, awful, shameful things he'd meant to show her, he said. But then he'd been snatched away, and her dad's goons had come to take her. What hadn't he shown her?

Whatever she felt – she was too numb to label it properly – it must have shown on her face, because Dad leaned forward in his chair, eager now. "I know you don't like me, and that you don't want to believe me. But I'm your father, Mia. You're my little baby. I would never lead you astray in this. Please trust me, for the sake of family."

"Family," she repeated. A word that left her cringing. Family had never mattered to him; his blood relation to her, his parental obligation, had never mattered as much as his work. And on some level, she couldn't even blame him for that. How could science march forward if it was weighted down by dirty diapers and bottle feedings?

She understood that, but she was still a daughter, one who resented her father.

And now…now, he was lying to her about an innocent man who'd been mistreated for an ungodly amount of time.

Decide, Val had said. She thought she knew what he meant, now.

"Yes, family."

"So…blood is the most important thing," she said, slowly.

"Mia, it is. Blood is *everything*."

"I'm beginning to see that."

He smiled. "Perhaps we can come to an understanding. Wouldn't that be nice?"

"Yes." And he didn't seem to notice that the word rang hollow.

<u>51</u>

EVERYTHING AND NOTHING

Vlad didn't sleep much. He'd slept for over five centuries, and felt no need to wallow in his bed now.

He forced at least three hours, for basic maintenance. It wouldn't do to let exhaustion set its hooks in him, not now that so much was at stake. But he usually awakened around four most mornings, and then went looking for something to do. Most nights, he went down to the training room in the main basement, and practiced his sword or knife skills, or pinned up paper targets so he could work on his archery, or worked with modern firearms. He didn't like the uncertainty of them, but he'd never met a weapon he didn't want to master. There was a pool in the east wing, and sometimes he swam laps until the muscles in his chest and arms burned. The woods called to him on some nights, dark and alive with the rustle of mammals, wind-tossed, filled with the call of owls.

But then other nights he sought the main house's rooftop, and the distant glimmering lights along the horizon, a peek at civilization that lay on the other side of the forest. He went to the roof now, drawn there by the scent of something old made new again. A revenant smelled like a human forged of ash and congealed blood, and he fought the instinctual urge to growl as he approached the parapet where a silhouette in a long black coat stood staring off across the compound.

Kolya shifted a fraction, glancing back over his shoulder, his eyes too bright in the dark. When he saw that it was Vlad, he faced forward again, and his shoulders relaxed.

Vlad drew up beside him. "Can you scent me, like a wolf?"

"No." His voice left his lips as a quiet rasp. The scars on his face, Vlad knew, meant that his flesh hadn't quite realigned as it had been in life. He imagined scars deep down in his throat, criss-crossing his insides. A patchwork man. "I heard you, though." Even softer: "I think – I think maybe I could always hear well. It's hard to remember."

"Do you remember your friends?"

"Bits and pieces. I – I remember a wolf. It was white. And – blood. War. But. There was a girl. We danced." A deep groove formed between his tucked brows, and he reached to rub it with absent fingertips. "I don't know."

Vlad followed his gaze out across the grounds. The stable lay behind the manor, so from here they had a view of the massive front stair, and circular drive, and the splashing fountain at its center. All of it was lit with torches that looked like the old pitch ones of his time, but which Talbot had told him were powered by underground gas lines.

Everything about the world had changed since he went to sleep.

And *nothing* had changed.

Vlad reached back into the waistband of his pants and withdrew the two sheathed knives he'd come up here to deliver. Kolya didn't start, exactly, but his head snapped around, and his gaze landed on them as Vlad held them out on a flat palm. "I believe these are yours."

The revenant studied them a long moment, and then slowly, hesitantly reached for them. He wore fingerless gloves, and even in the dark Vlad could see the faint pink scars around his nail beds. He didn't touch them, though; his hand hovered. "Are they? How did you get them?"

"Your captain had them when he fought me."

He lifted his head, and whatever he felt about Vlad, whatever Liam Price had told him, was swept aside in favor of his desperate search for information. "Fought him? That was – his name is Nikita, right? I…" He trailed off, gaze clouding. "He was here?" he asked in a small voice.

"He came to break his wolf loose."

His brows twitched, and drew even tighter together.

"I am told they are the only survivors of your original team. The vampire and his wolf–"

"*Vampire?*"

"You died before he was turned, then. Yes, he's of my kind. Bitten – not bred. He and the wolf, Sasha, live amongst mortals, I am told. The captain was a passionate fighter, if an inept one."

660

Kolya winced, as if his head hurt. He brought his free hand up to massage at his temple, and the other shook over the knives. "You – you didn't kill him, did you?" He looked afraid to know the answer.

"No. I have no conflict with him, so long as he stays out of my way. I had hoped to bind his wolf, but…" The revenant's eyes were wide, and half-wild, struggling to remember, Vlad thought. "Bound or not, your captain and his wolf are too closely bonded for another vampire to make any use of him."

"Oh. Alright." His gaze dropped back to the knives, and he hesitated another long moment before he finally took both hilts together in one grip. "Thank you."

Vlad let his hand fall to his side. "My brother knows where they are if you want to find them."

"I work for Mr. Price," he said, half-heartedly. "I…"

Vlad backed away. "Then stay with him, if that's what you want." He turned and walked to the hidden door that led into the stairwell, paused there and glanced over his shoulder one last time.

Kolya held the knives in one hand, down low along his thigh. The breeze stirred the tails of his coat, and his too-long hair. A portrait of the truth that the dead should be left to peaceful graves.

~*~

Val was awake long before the guard brought his breakfast. It was only fruit, bagels and lox, and his stomach fizzed with anticipation, but he forced down every bite, drained the accompanying milk and pig's blood, too.

Mia was here.

He was jiggling both knees by the time he scented his brother at the outer door, and was on his feet to greet him.

Vlad carried a canvas tote bag, an image so incongruous it startled a laugh out of Val.

"What have you got there?" He looked like a mother at Disneyland with that bag. A murderous mother with bulging biceps.

Vlad passed it over with an unimpressed look. "Suitable clothes."

Val set the bag on the cot and drew out a plain black t-shirt…and a pair of modern riding breeches, the kind with suede patches sewn inside the knees. At the bottom of the bag he found a folded leather jacket and…yes, a doubled-over pair of worn knee boots.

His pulse jumping, he looked up at his brother again. "Clothes suitable for what, Vlad?"

"Do you want to go riding or not?"

"*Yes.*"

"Here." Vlad snapped an elastic off his wrist, and pulled a hairbrush from his back pocket. "Do you want your hair braided?" He sounded grudging, but his own hair was braided down his back, and Val knew his warrior's fingers had always knitted the tidiest plaits.

Val sat down sideways on the cot in wordless answer, presenting his waterfall of unmanageable golden hair. He could have done it himself, though his arms would be shaking by the end, but the offer was…unimaginably important to him.

He dragged the boots into his lap and petted their butter soft uppers, eyes closed tight against the sting of sudden tears, as Vlad carefully brushed all the tangles from his hair and then separated it into bunches.

He'd always found it soothing to have his hair played with, the steady tug, the drag of warm fingertips across his scalp. He remembered Mama's slender fingers winding through his little-boy curls, her hummed bits of song that belonged to colder shores, and a culture she'd left behind long before giving herself over to the Roman traditions of his own youth.

"I invited your mortal along," Vlad said.

Val gasped. He opened his eyes and tried to twist around, only to have Vlad put a hand on his temple and shove him back. Oh, right, braiding.

"What did she say?"

A snort. "What do you think she said? Yes, she's coming. She was readying when I came down."

"God," he breathed. Then: "Wait, how do you have horses?"

His half-finished braid lifted, and he imagined Vlad shrugging. "There's a stable. I asked for horses, and now there are horses."

"*Asked?* You mean you demanded, and some poor intern went scrambling off with a trailer to get you some."

"It isn't my fault they're all afraid of their own shadows."

"Beg pardon, brother, but it's exactly your fault."

"You're one to talk. You're the one they think is a magical liar and traitor."

"Ah. Yes." Val sighed, and some of his excitement dimmed. "I suppose their fear of you is the only thing stronger than their fear of me, after all."

Vlad was quiet a moment, and when he spoke, there was almost something of an apology in his voice. "They are soft, these humans. They've never known a real traitor in their lives."

"Hopefully they won't ever have to."

Vlad made a noncommittal sound, and finished off the braid with a snap of the elastic. When he dropped it, the braid landed like a rope against Val's back, heavy and secure. An anchoring sort of feeling. "Get dressed." He then stepped to the corner of the cell and looked down at his boots. It was a silly bit of privacy, given he'd lowered Val into and out of a bath yesterday, but throughout his captivity, Val hadn't even been afforded this small gesture, so he took it to heart.

Drinking Vlad's blood yesterday had gone a long way toward strengthening him, but he still wobbled a little when he stood to tug the breeches up over his hips. They were meant to fit snug – he thought of Mia in hers, the thick fabric hugging every line and curve – but his legs were still too thin, and there were wrinkles where there should have only been taut material stretched over tauter thighs. Oh well. Perhaps Mia wouldn't find him too hideous.

The boots were a dream, already broken in by someone else. He tucked the shirt in behind his belt buckle and then, while Vlad's gaze was still diverted, slipped his hand mirror from beneath his pillow and checked his reflection. A little gaunt, too pale, but clean and presentable. More like himself than he'd looked in centuries, with his hair braided neatly and color blooming along his high cheekbones. It would do.

"Finished?" Vlad asked, and Val tossed the mirror down onto his cot, face heating.

He cleared his throat. "Yes." He tried to say it with dignity, but Vlad rolled his eyes and muttered "stupid" under his breath.

Just like old times.

When they reached the main basement, where the lab bustled away like a beehive that couldn't tell night from day, Vlad wrapped a strong hand around Val's bicep. A gesture that probably looked restraining, but which felt comforting to Val.

"Do not make a fool of me," Vlad said in warning, low enough that the humans couldn't hear.

"Of course not," Val said, and in this moment, he meant it. He may not have been the sweet, adoring little brother he'd been as a boy, but in this instance, free of cuffs and walking on his own two feet, being bratty was the absolute last thing on his mind.

Techs and doctors gave them a wide berth; some masked their horror, but a few gawked openly. No doubt they all were thinking of Val charging through this lab with his sword in his hands; throwing Major Treadwell across a room; slaying guards with his bare hands.

Vlad had always believed in the Machiavellian ideal: better to be feared than respected. Respect had never been in the cards for Val, not in any lifetime; a little fear, he thought now, wasn't such a bad thing after all.

He caught a whiff of Mia in the elevator, and his spine straightened unconsciously.

Vlad noticed. "This mortal—"

"She has a name, Vlad."

"Your *Mia*. Do you trust her?"

A snap answer formed and died on Val's tongue. It wasn't the simple question that it seemed – nothing ever was with Vlad. "Yes," he finally said, careful. "I do." He would list the reasons if he had to, but mostly it was a gut sense. He hadn't felt that way about anyone in a very, very long time.

Vlad nodded. "Will you turn her?"

His stomach lurched. "That's up to her to decide."

"It's the only way to keep her alive."

"I *know that*," he said through his teeth.

Vlad thankfully didn't say more, and the elevator deposited them into the library.

His pulse picked up with every step, a rapid hammer-beat that echoed through his ears and fingertips. Excitement. A rabid kind that elongated his fangs in his mouth and made him salivate, though there was nothing in him that wanted her blood. It was just – visceral, his anticipation of seeing her. Something as primal as all the vampire parts of him.

Vlad gave one low warning growl that meant *calm down* as they passed through the library and out to the vast atrium. But Val couldn't calm down. He–

There she was.

She was dressed as she normally was back in Colorado: buff breeches, and a casual t-shirt, and lovingly worn schooling boots. Someone had given her a black baseball cap with a little checkmark logo on it – Nike, he'd learned in his dream-walking; modern men and women were obsessed with the makers of things – and her honey-colored ponytail had been pulled through the hole in the back. She held herself a little uncertainly, arms folded across her chest, and she had dark smudges of exhaustion and creeping sickness under her eyes.

She was the loveliest thing he'd ever seen.

His breath left his lungs in a shaky rush. "Mia." It was the only thing he could think to say, struck dumb all over again that *she was here.*

"Good morning." She smiled, and her gaze trailed down his legs and back up. He wanted to preen a little under the attention; he might be a little sallow and thin, still, but he was pretty, and she noticed. When her eyes met his again, she was blushing, faintly. "I can't believe Vlad was able to find you riding clothes."

"He's very resourceful, my brother." His voice sounded breathless, smitten. He didn't care. Grinning, he said, "What do you think? How do I look?" And gave her a spin.

Her blush deepened.

"You can say 'fetching,' darling."

"Don't be arrogant," she chastised, but smiled.

He wanted to step in close to her, pull her into his arms, press his face into her hair and tattoo its fragrance into his brain. But he felt suddenly self-conscious with Vlad watching. And with–

Ah, yes. They had an escort. Sergeant Ramirez waited a few paces away, arms folded, expression one of tense, studied disinterest. She was dressed to ride as well, her ensemble entirely black, a gun strapped to her hip.

"What's she doing here?" Val asked.

Mia huffed an annoyed breath and said, "Babysitter."

"Sergeant Ramirez will be escorting us," Vlad said, and Val wondered if Ramirez knew how dangerous that tone was. "Apparently, she's the only military person here who can sit a horse and manage to stay on."

"I rode jumpers in high school," the woman said icily. "I can sit a horse just fine."

Vlad smiled – but it wasn't a smile at all, just a brief flash of fangs. "We shall see. Come." And all of them followed him like the prince he still was.

~*~

The stable was made of the same pale stone as the manor. The interior had been designed in the European style, with big box stalls paneled in tongue-and-groove and iron grillwork, U-shaped openings through which the horses could hang their heads and see who was walking up the brickwork aisle.

And the heads that hung over the doors weren't the tame cattle or plow horses she'd been expecting, but sleek warmbloods with trimmed manes and shiny coats. And someone had consulted with the staff about proper care of them; Mia spotted brand new plastic water buckets, slowly-spinning upscale fans overhead, and even saw a few bales of alfalfa peeking out of a cracked-open feed room door.

"Like I said," Ramirez said, and Mia sent her a sharp look. "I rode jumpers in high school."

"You don't have to be so defensive about it, though."

666

The other woman strode on down the aisle without reaction.

"How unpleasant," Val said, lightly, and Mia tightened her arm where it was looped through his. He hadn't wanted to admit it, but he'd been shaky on the walk down from the manor. She was glad to have him in out of the sun; now it was time to find him a horse that wouldn't try to buck him off. He could have been the best horseman in the world, but he hadn't ridden in centuries, and there was no way his watery muscles could hold him on in the event of a bucking bronco incident.

"When Vlad says 'jump,' they really say 'how high,' don't they?" she said, towing Val along the stall fronts, determined to push all thoughts of her father and his experiments and staff out of her mind. This morning was, so far, a kind of perfect she hadn't dreamed of when Val first appeared in her living room, and she wasn't going to waste it fretting.

He chuckled, and brought his hand up to cover the back of hers. His skin was soft save a distinct callus in the center of his palm; from holding the bars, she thought. Maybe even calling through them for food, or help, or mercy. She shuddered, and he gave her hand a squeeze in acknowledgement, tone determinedly cheerful when he said, "Everyone always has, ever since he was a boy. All save his tutors – whether it was people Father hired, or the mullahs, those men weren't all that impressed."

Mia snuck a glance at the prince and found him pushing back the door to a stall that held a tall, rangy black horse with a fat blaze down its face. The horse greeted Vlad with a few whuffed breaths and a gentle touch of his nose. Vlad cupped its jaw and murmured something low, haltering it with the ease of someone who, though royalty, was well familiar with saddling his own animals. It was a small checkmark in his favor.

She turned her attention back to Val. "See someone you like?"

"Maybe. Just up there."

The next stall held a lovely dappled gray mare with big, square knees and a thick neck. A sturdy hunter, from the looks of her, with massive hooves…and gentle, liquid brown eyes. She watched them approach with calm attentiveness.

Val lifted his free hand and offered his palm for her to sniff. "Hello, lovely."

She stepped up closer, thrusting her head fully over the stall door, so she could sniff Val's shoulder and face.

Val's resultant smile was beatific.

Mia thought of Brando seeing him, of her horse's quiet, curious regard of him. A lump rose in her throat and she swallowed it down. "You're a natural, aren't you?" she murmured.

"There's only a few things I'm good at," Val murmured, gaze far away. "This is by far the best of them."

~*~

Behind the stable lay a patch of flat ground, freshly-mown, glittering with dew drops. They started there, just to let Val get reacquainted with his "horse legs," as Mia put it with a smile.

He couldn't bring himself to believe this was anything besides a dream until he was seated in the saddle, reins drawn between careful fingers. He closed his eyes a moment, breathed in the scents of saddle soap and clean horses. Felt the mare's steady breaths, her ribs expanding against his calves. Her skin rippled beneath the touch of a fly, and he opened his eyes and squeezed her gently forward.

As a boy, he'd favored fleet-footed Arabs, but as a man and a warrior, he'd ridden the heavy destriers better suited to carrying an armored soldier. That's what this girl reminded him of, with her solid, swaying gait, sure of herself and unhurried. They'd found a stall chart in the tack room, and apparently her name was Gin Fizz – a Trakehner, which Mia had informed him was a very kind and eager-to-please German breed.

So far so good. She lengthened her walking stride with the softest pressure from his heels, stretching her neck politely down and forward, testing his grip on the reins. She steered into a circle with a thought, following his shifting weight as he turned his head. He was shaking, and he couldn't decide if he was already weakening, or if it was simple joy. He was riding again. *Riding.*

He urged Gin into a trot, and she obliged immediately, her gait huge and swinging. Sitting was hopeless, given the current state of his core muscles, and he bounced in the saddle. But he laughed, bright peals that echoed off the surrounding tree trunks. This was perfect.

He trotted a few laps around the mown grass oval, and tried a bit of canter. Gin had a deep, rocking gait that covered an immense amount of ground, though she wasn't hurrying. When he finally pulled up beside the others, Mia was watching him with wide eyes.

"I'm more than a little rusty," he said, face heating. He patted Gin's neck and her ears swiveled back; yes, they would get along splendidly, and hopefully he could keep from going jelly-legged and sliding right off of her. "A bit embarrassing." Or a lot.

But Mia shook her head. "You look good."

"Such flattery."

Ramirez cleared her throat.

Vlad said, "Will you stay on?" Flat and disinterested.

Val swallowed another laugh. He couldn't decide who looked less pleased with this outing: his brother, or the quietly furious Army sergeant. "Yes, I do believe so." He gave Gin's neck another pat and she craned around to nudge the toe of his boot affectionately.

"There's a trail," Vlad said, and turned his horse and started down it.

Val looked to Mia, who shrugged. "He's very imperious, you know."

"I've noticed."

There was indeed a trail, a narrow one that plunged into the trees, a grown-over game trail just big enough for them to proceed single file. Vlad led the way, and Ramirez held back to fall in last. Val didn't like her eyes on the back of his head, but was glad Mia was ahead of him so that he could serve as a buffer between the two women. Ramirez had her orders – but the second one of those orders put Mia in harm's way, Val would cheerfully kill her.

The track led them into a dense forest populated with a mix of hardwoods and pines. The underbrush grew dense and wild here, in a way that it hadn't in Romania. Birds trilled overhead. Sunlight pierced the canopy in thin fingers, the world a kaleidoscope of gold and green dapples. The leaves on the hardwoods had just started to turn, brittle in patches, brown at the edges. Val tilted his head back and stared up, fascinated.

"Don't get yourself knocked off by a low branch," Mia advised with a laugh, and he righted himself to see that she'd twisted around in her saddle to look at him.

He returned her smile; his face was starting to ache from smiling. "Same goes to you."

Vlad led them deeper, and the path began a slow rise, the way strewn with rocks, shaded by low limbs. After a time, Val picked up the gentle chuckle of running water, and soon after, its scent. Clear mountain spring water, coming down from the Virginia hills. Gin lifted her head and walked a little faster; it smelled nice to her as well.

The trail widened, and Mia dropped back to ride beside him. She was still smiling, but he could read the concern in the little groove between her brows. "You doing alright?"

"Fine," he said immediately, but he could already feel that he'd be sore later. The long muscles in his thighs had begun to twitch every few strides, and his shoulders ached. He hated the weakness, but gave her his brightest smile. "I could keep going for hours."

Her look said she knew that was a lie, but she let it slide. "How's it feel to be back in the saddle?"

"Like being able to breathe again."

Her smile turned soft and sweet. "I meant what I said about you looking good."

"I know, darling." He winked. "I look good riding other things, too."

Her mouth dropped open, and for a moment, Val wanted to kick himself. It was such a line, so crass and – and the sort of thing he said to men, just to fuck with them. (Usually right before they tried to actually fuck him.) He swallowed against a sudden surge of nausea.

But Mia blushed and glanced away. "Al*right*," she said with an embarrassed little laugh. "I didn't doubt that, but whatever."

"Didn't doubt it?" His own voice sounded hollow. "What do you mean?"

She breathed a disbelieving sound. "Are you serious?"

"Quite." She'd figured out that he was a whore, then. Doubtless her father had told her, or one of the officers who'd gone to collect her. It was common knowledge, wasn't it? Of the two brothers, one was a terrifying warrior, and the other was a pretty mistress. He swallowed again. "Mia—"

"You're gorgeous," she said, blush deepening as she stared fixedly ahead. "I know you know that. Unfairly so. I mean…" She made a vague gesture toward him. "And then you say stuff like that? You don't have to."

His heart pounded. "Why not? Do you dislike it?"

"I…didn't say that."

"Do you want me to stop?"

She didn't answer, instead bit down on her lip until he thought it might bleed, blush darker than ever.

Oh. Oh, she *liked* it.

"You don't have to," she repeated, softly.

Slowly, his panic eased, like a clenched fist opening. He smiled and leaned out of his saddle, getting in closer. "Sweetheart, that wasn't the question."

She turned her head to look at him, and beneath the brim of her helmet, her eyes were very blue. Why hadn't he kissed her yesterday? What kind of idiot was he?

But then they reached the stream, and he smelled the bear, and everything went to hell.

52

VLAD THE FUCKING IMPALER

Adela hadn't lied – she really had ridden jumpers in high school. And before that, too, all the way back to the jodhpur-straps and short boot phase of her equestrian career. Her Uncle Miguel had been a horse trainer in Cali, breaking rodeo mounts and pleasure horses out of a massive Quarter Horse barn owned by three rich white men who were nice enough, but didn't expect to break a sweat when they stopped in, lit cigars in-hand, to inspect their animals. Miguel had been part of a huge crew, from grooms, to stall-muckers, to other trainers like him. He'd taught her to ride in a big western saddle as broad as an armchair, and she'd taken to it with an almost violent passion. But then she'd seen one of the owner's girls riding English – jumping a big-boned chestnut horse over rails – and she'd known that was what she wanted to do. She'd scraped and saved every summer, and her own jumper, bought with her uncle's help when she was twelve, had been gray and rangy, with a bad tendency to bolt. She'd gone to Regionals at sixteen.

A natural, so many had said of her.

But then her father had died, and her mother had needed her help, and she couldn't afford to keep her horse.

And then the economy had tanked, and Mama had gotten sick, and even three fast food jobs hadn't been enough to keep them afloat.

And then she'd joined the Army. And she'd been good at it.

And then she'd lost her foot…

She hadn't lied, but she'd left a good many things out. Things like that fact that she'd been the one to pick the horses at Blackmere, and track down all the necessary tack; had guessed right about the size saddle Vlad the fucking Impaler would need.

A babysitter, the girl – Mia – had called her. And she was. She was also: scared out of her skin to be in the company of these two immortal monsters; and enjoying herself in spite of it, because a chance to ride was a chance to ride, no matter the company.

When the trail widened, Mia reined up so she could ride alongside Valerian, which meant Adela had to watch them flirt awkwardly with one another. Which...ugh. Yes, he had golden hair, and yes he was pretty in a *Lord of the Rings* kind of way, but what could the girl possibly see in him? He was a criminal, for God's sakes. And, according to what Talbot had told them, a one-time kept sex pet of his brother's worst enemy. That did not make him a catch in Adela's opinion.

They reached the stream – one that she'd scouted out the week before on her own, and found it to be wide, but not deep, its water clean and clear. That day, she'd dismounted and taken her boots off, rolled up her breeches, and waded in, towing her horse – a sweet-natured Bay named Ranger – in after her. It had been the best afternoon she'd had in years.

Now, she steered Ranger up past the lovebirds and to the water's edge. The gelding lowered his head and whuffed, eager for a drink. She loosened her reins, letting them slide through her fingers, spine relaxing...

"Wait," both brothers said at once.

Ranger flung up his head. He inhaled once, deeply, and let out a huge snort, like a frightened buck.

She tightened her reins in a single movement, winding her fingertips in a chunk of mane for good measure. "What?" But then she saw it. On the opposite bank: a bear.

She'd done a cursory review of Virginia's native wildlife one night in the manor, bored out of her mind and not wanting any surprises on a trail ride. Black bears were listed as indigenous, but the website had described them as "small and shy." This bear was *big*. Not grizzly-sized, no, but still broad and healthy, its coat shining in the dappled light, its shoulders and flanks well-padded with the fat that it was already gathering for winter. A bear didn't have to be *that* large to kill you, she thought, stupidly, in the tense moment that she and her horse both stared at it.

And then she saw the cubs. Two bright-eyed, fluffy things peeking around from behind their mother's back legs.

Oh shit.

Ranger snorted again, and attempted to duck and whirl away. She tucked her elbow into her side and held the rein fast. "It's alright, it's alright," she tried to soothe him, but she spoke through gritted teeth.

He backed up instead, hasty, unsteady steps over the loose rock of the bank, and bumped into one of the other horses.

"Control him," Vlad commanded, voice oddly quiet.

Adela put a leg into him, and murmured comforting nonsense, and grappled for control of the bit. The other horses were nervous and edgy, but only Ranger was losing his mind. He spun, a full one-eighty, kicking up a loud spray of water, and she caught brief flashes of the others' faces. Fear, surprise, grim resolution – that last was Vlad.

Ranger slipped and nearly went to his knees. "Shit." Adela braced her hands on his neck, trying not to throw him further off balance.

When he stopped, suddenly, she nearly fell off, still spinning, her weight thrown awkwardly half-out of the saddle. Vlad stood at Ranger's head, holding his bridle. He murmured something to him in another language. Ranger quivered, from nose to tail, but he froze, and his ears swiveled wildly between her, and the bear, and Vlad. Adela could see the white of one eye as he tried to shift his head. Vlad held him tight.

Vlad looked up at her, and their gazes locked. His eyes were almost gray in this strange forest light, and very calm. "Dismount," he instructed.

What an excellent fucking idea.

She nodded, and then began to ease her weight out of her right stirrup. Slow and steady, no sudden movements.

That was when the bear let out a furious sound and charged across the stream toward them.

Adela knew right then that she would fall, and that it would be bad, but it seemed to happen in slow motion, and she noticed everything in a hazy swirl, certain details leaping out with strange vividness. She noticed:

Vlad letting go of Ranger, turning to move *toward* the bear.

Ranger screaming, gathering himself to rear.

Val and Mia out of their saddles, Val reaching for Adela's reins.

But it was too late. Ranger reared, and his rear hooves slipped on the wet rocks.

Adela scrambled at his neck, throwing her weight forward, trying to force him back down onto all four legs. But with only one foot in the stirrup, she was off balance, and she slipped to the left.

No, no, no.

It happened in the span of a heartbeat. The horse toppled backward. She tried to throw herself free, but it was too late.

The last thing she saw, before they landed, was Vlad standing nose-to-nose with the bear, bent forward at the waist, shoulders jacked up around his ears. He was snarling like an animal.

And then her helmet cracked open on the rocks.

~*~

Mia hadn't seen someone take a spill like this in a long time; it wasn't something that ever got easier to watch. She didn't really like Sergeant Ramirez, but that didn't mean she'd wanted anything like this to happen.

The bay gelding scrambled up immediately, shaking off water, snorting, blowing, still panicking about the bear – the bear that was slowly slinking backward, head lowered, cowering in the face of Vlad's panther roar. Ramirez didn't get up, though. In fact, she didn't move. She lay limp as a doll in the first shallow inches of the stream, eyes shut, limbs sprawled out to the side.

"Here." Val shoved Gin's reins into her hand, and went for the bay.

Gin, and Mia's horse Astrid, were both nervous, blowing and dancing, but so far hadn't set so much as a hoof out of place. A few paces away, Vlad's big black stood stoic, reins dangling. Mia wondered if the vampires had put some sort of enchantment on them, and if so, decided she was glad for it.

The mother bear finally turned tail and ran, her cubs at her heels. Thank God.

675

Val snagged the bay's dangling reins and reeled him in, murmuring soothingly, pulling his flashing hooves away from Ramirez.

Who still hadn't moved.

Mia, horses in tow, walked over to the edge of the streambed to join Val, who'd managed to quiet the bay with some gentle words and pats to his neck. The black gelding joined them, nosing at his nervous friends, and that left Vlad with his hands free to see to Ramirez.

When the bear was gone for good, he turned and viewed the situation, made his way over to the fallen agent.

Closer now, Mia could see that her helmet hadn't survived the fall, cracked down the middle; a thin trickle of blood had slid out of her hairline and trailed across her cheek. And her right leg–

Mia glimpsed the slick white of bone protruding and looked away, swallowing hard. "Compound fracture," she said, and felt shock pulse hot and then cold under her skin.

There was a quiet splash, and she dared a look back to see that Vlad was on his knees in the water, lifting Ramirez's upper body into his lap. "Oh, you shouldn't move her," Mia said, startled into forward motion. Val's free hand landed on her shoulder. "She could have a spinal injury. She–"

"I know how to handle the injured, girl," he said, gaze trained on the sergeant's slack face. With a quick, but careful, movement, he unsnapped her ruined helmet and drew it off. There was a gash at her hairline, oozing bright red blood. It wasn't bad – but the head trauma beneath probably was.

Vlad cupped a hand around the back of her head, and leaned over her; for one sick moment, Mia thought he meant to put his mouth to her wound. But instead he thumbed open her eyelids with his fee hand and examined them closely.

"A concussion," he announced, sitting back on his heels. "At the very least." Then his gaze swept down to her leg, and he frowned. "She won't be able to keep the leg."

Mia said, "*What?*"

Vlad sent her an unreadable look.

"That – that kind of break is bad, I know. She'll need surgery. But usually doctors can save the leg."

He shook his head. "That leg isn't hers. It's a dead woman's. The vampire blood concoction your father gives her is all that's allowed her to keep it thus far."

A woman lost a foot, Dad had said. "Holy shit."

"We have to get her back to the manor," Val said, voice strained. He stared fixedly at the place where her leg was bent the wrong way, the bone jutting through.

Mia looked down, and saw thin little trails of crimson go swirling along with the stream's current.

"I'll carry her," Vlad said, lifting her into her arms without effort. "The two of you ride ahead. Tell them to make preparations."

<u>53</u>

CATS AND DOGS

Jake was...really tired of all this magic bullshit. Despite what Dr. Talbot had insisted during his initial debriefing – when he'd made the transition from patient to operative; before that disastrous trip out west to retrieve Ruby Russell – magic appeared to be completely uncontrollable for mere mortals. It was bad enough with the werewolves, and the girl, and the angry Marine, and those bow-and-arrow guys who'd stormed the place. Not to mention the resident vampires. But now here sat this red-haired shithead, and Jake was...pretty much done.

They sat in the upstairs study, the one in the main part of the house that Dr. Talbot used to entertain visitors he didn't want to drag through the chaotic, ugly lab area in the basement; the people he needed to schmooze. Jake didn't understand why he was here, and was doing his best to melt back into the flocked wallpaper.

Today, Liam Price was dressed in olive-colored slacks with a knife crease, a cream sweater, and had a black topcoat draped over his shoulders. He sat with his elbows braced on the arms of his chair, hands linked together in front of him. It was such a calculated, designed-to-impress pose, and Jake hated him for it.

"I'm assuming you still want me to perform the locating spell?" he said.

"Er, yes, please. If it's not too much trouble. I've already spoken with Lord Dracula about his use of electrical corrective measures in the future," Talbot said.

Price leaned forward a fraction, gaze going to the door. "Shall we do it now? No time like the present. Then we can begin searching for my daughter in earnest."

Talbot winced – Jake suspected mostly because the idea of launching another search for Russell, this time with her fire-wielding parents in tow, sounded truly awful. "Actually. Well. Prince Valerian isn't here at the moment."

That caught Price's attention. He turned back slowly, red brows lifted. "Beg pardon? I thought you had him chained up for everyone's safety."

"We did. We *do*. It's only – his brother's taken him riding this morning."

"His – *brother?*"

Talbot looked ashamed. "Yes."

"I was under the impression they hated one another."

"I'm not sure they don't."

Jake could still see Prince Valerian laid out on the library rug when he blinked. Arms and legs twitching, blood pouring out of his mouth and down his chin, matting his hair. A wound like a canyon, opening him at his neck, and shoulder, and chest. Jake had seen ribs. Jake had been to war, and that was part of the reason, he was sure, he'd staggered away and vomited into an ornate vase in the hallway.

It had seemed like the sort of wound delivered by a hateful hand. It was one thing to kill on orders, to drop an enemy in combat; it was another to savage an opponent like that.

But Price stroked his chin with one long finger and looked pensive. "Vampires often have strange relationships with one another. They love deeply, but they aren't pack animals. It makes for unusual personal dynamics."

Jake snorted despite his determination to keep quiet. "So werewolves are dogs and vampires are cats?"

"More or less," Price said, serious. "Is this the first time he's been out of his cell?" he asked Talbot.

"N-no. It's…the third."

Price lifted his brows, inviting an explanation.

Talbot sighed, looking caught between shame and dread. Like a scolded child, Jake thought. "Yesterday, before you arrived, Vlad unhooked his brother's restraints and took him up to his own room, to be bathed and cleaned and redressed. Before that…there was an escape."

"An escape? Dr. Talbot, did Prince Valerian contribute to the 'chaos' into which you lost my daughter?"

"Yes."

He thought that over for a moment. "I want to examine his cell."

"Of – of course."

They all trooped down to the dungeon. It sparked a knee-jerk, momentary panic in Jake to see the door of the last cell standing open. He hung back, and wasn't even ashamed of the fact, content to let Price walk into the cell and take a look around. This was his errand, after all.

The mage turned in slow circles, eyes tracking over everything. He leaned forward and picked something up off the cot. He smirked and then showed it to them: a small mirror, like a woman would carry in her purse. "Someone brought him a little gift for his vanity."

Talbot sighed. "That would be the baroness, I imagine. They're friends of a sort."

"Hmm."

Price found a comb under the pillow, and a small plastic container full of residue of what looked and smelled like salad dressing. A few empty glass Starbucks bottles under the cot, tucked into the shadows.

"I can't help but notice," he finally said, "that there are no restraints of any kind."

"Vlad had them removed."

"And you allowed it."

"He's taken personal responsibility of his brother's captivity."

Price smiled, thin and hard. "And you allowed him to?"

"He…"

"Vlad gets what he wants," Jake supplied. "That's just how things are."

Price's head snapped around, his gaze pinning Jake to the wall. The smile widened, sharp at the edges. "Is that so." It wasn't a question. He glanced away. "Tell me how he managed to escape this cell. He was chained?"

"Yes." In halting tones, Talbot explained what they'd been able to piece together from context clues, and Valerian's pained confessions.

"The mortal helped him? *Ruby's* mortal?" Jake didn't like the feral gleam that sparked in his eyes. "The soldier."

"Marine, actually," Jake said, and he wasn't sure why he'd felt the need to make the correction.

Deep down, he knew why, but he wasn't ready to examine that reason too closely just yet.

"Marine, yes." Price's voice raised all the hairs on his arms. "Tell me about him."

Something seemed to pass through the cell. A chill, but one with a presence. Jake felt it ripple through the stone beneath his boots, like a shock wave.

"He's no one important," Talbot said. "Just a mortal. A badly wounded veteran. He obviously feels some sense of responsibility for the girl–"

"Love."

"What?"

"Responsibility doesn't propel a man, unarmed, into a place like this, Doctor. Love does that. He loves her." His teeth set, a muscle in his jaw leaping.

How dare he, Jake thought, get angry and fatherly about the man who was probably sleeping with his daughter when he'd had her raised in a lab and never even met her face-to-face.

"Does that bother you?" he asked. "That someone loves her?" He thought of Rooster Palmer staring him down on a stretch of Wyoming highway, gun in one motionless hand, Ruby Russell's big green eyes peering over his broad shoulder. Yeah, Palmer loved her. A terrifying amount.

Price stared at him, inscrutable. "Why should it, Major?"

"You tell me."

Another grin; dangerous as a knife. "Word games. How charming."

"I assure you, Mr. Price," Talbot said, "we will find your daughter."

The mage laughed. "Oh, Doctor. You'd better."

~*~

So much of the house had been if not lovingly, then at least meticulously restored to its former grandeur and cleanliness. The new items purchased to replace those aged beyond repair were careful replicas of the original antiques; Annabel felt certain that someone had consulted a historian as to authenticity.

But the one area of the house so far untouched was the conservatory. With its patterned tile floors, and soaring glass walls and ceilings, it had once been an oasis of delights. Native plants, and English plants brought from the duke's manor in Cambridge, and exotic tropical flowers carefully tended by a team of gardeners. There had been a massive koi pond in the center, studded with lily pads and water hyacinths, fish longer than her forearm begging for food with gaping mouths.

The pond was nothing but a few inches of black sludge now. The plants had withered and crumpled and been left as tattered gray streamers spilling out of the planters. The fruit trees had been dead for decades, their bare limbs reaching for the ceiling like claws.

A dead, haunted place.

Small steps had been taken. The glass had been cleaned, so now it sparkled, and the gas torches, designed like old English lampposts, had been repaired, so the pathways were lighted. The old dead vegetation had been cleared out, wheelbarrow after wheelbarrow of it trucked out to a dumpster. It had been stripped down to the bones, to a starting place for someone with a green thumb to work magic.

Annabel had brought a basil plant out here a few weeks ago, picked a spot with plenty of daytime sun and carefully patted it into place. Had watered it. But she didn't have a knack for green things, not like her sister; that was how she knew she'd find Lily in the conservatory, and she wasn't wrong.

Lily sat on the stone lip of a planting box, heels of her brown boots peeking from beneath the hem of her emerald skirt. She leaned forward, hair falling around her face, her expression one of intense concentration. She held both hands above Anna's sad basil plant…and her fingertips seemed to glow. Slowly, slowly, visible to the naked eye, the plant's leaves broadened and darkened; its stems lengthened. The basil *grew*. When she finally sat back with a deep exhale, the sallow plant was thick and healthy. Thriving.

She lifted her head and sent a small, uneven smile toward Anna. "Hello, sister."

Annabel folded her arms and braced her shoulder against one of the (rather creepy) angel statues that had been cleaned up. "Trust you to find the one growing thing here."

Lily turned her smile on the plant and dusted invisible dirt from her palms. "It was doing fine. It just needed a little help."

"Help I didn't ask for."

A sigh. She lifted her gaze again. "Anna—"

"Why are you here?"

"Why did you seek me out if you just want to argue?" Lily countered, but calmly.

Anna's hackles went up — and she forcibly smoothed them back down. Lily had adopted her husband's infuriating habit of riling up those around him. Lily had always been able to do it, but now it was effortless. The worst part, always, was her guileless tranquility.

"I don't want to fight," Anna said, her own calm coming with difficulty. "I'm trying to figure out — okay, Fulk and I are here because these assholes threatened us. Did they threaten you? Because I'm getting the really bad feeling that you and Liam let them grow your kids like lab monkeys willingly."

Another sigh. Lily pulled her hands into her lap and looked up, her tone that of an adult explaining something complicated to a child. "I lost four children, Anna. The first time I didn't know. But after that, I tried — but there was always some reason I needed to use my powers. I can't carry my own babies, so I gave up on motherhood. There are other ways to find meaning in life, and I found them.

"Liam was in contact with the Institute early, in its first incarnation, before they went to Russia. He of course knew that you and Fulk were out there somewhere, hiding, but he told Dr. Ingraham that he didn't know of any living wolves. To spare you."

"Gee, thanks."

"It was a kindness," Lily insisted. "He let them go to Russia, let them make a new wolf. Nothing came of it. The Institute failed, reduced to a few boxes of singed files. We thought that was it, and for a little while, it was."

"Fine. That still doesn't explain the test tube babies."

Lily smiled, wistful. "Liam always loved the idea of having a family – one of our own. Mages with whom we could share our gifts. A family that we wouldn't...wouldn't outlive." She frowned; her gaze drew inward. "It was only a fantasy, but then – we met another mage." Her tone shifted, and it set Annabel's skin prickling. "He called himself the Roman. He nearly killed Liam."

Shame he didn't, Anna thought, but it was a hollow assertion. What could kill Liam? What could get close enough even for *almost?*

Lily swallowed; her face was very pale, freckles stark across her nose. "When Dr. Talbot approached us about his program, we felt like it was important to participate. Not just for our sakes," she rushed to say when Anna opened her mouth with a protest. "I know you think poorly of Liam, but he isn't one of those world-destroyer types. We want what you and Fulk want: to live in peace, for the world to keep spinning."

"Peace? Liam doesn't believe in peace."

"He does," Lily said, stubborn now. She had her jaw set at that angle their mother used to get when she was about to whack someone with her fan. "There are rumblings, Anna, things you haven't heard. There are some immortals who aren't content to just live and let live. They think that the mortals have had control of things for long enough, and that immortals should take power. That the people with the most physical power should be front and center, respected. Feared. The mage who calls himself the Roman thinks that, obviously. The time for immortals minding their own business is over. We all have to choose a side, and we all have to fight.

"So Liam and I donated our DNA, yes. We helped them grow soldiers. We're going to need those soldiers. And believe it or not, I do care about them. They're my children."

Anna's heart pounded hard against her ribs. All this talk of stirring, of a war, of choosing sides. It sent her spinning back home, to smoke in the sky, and the boom of cannon fire. Back to the taste of ash, and the constant panic turning her legs to water.

The burned-out ruin of Atlanta. She'd seen war, and she didn't want to see it ever again.

But she managed to keep her voice steady when she said, "If you care about them, how come none of them have ever met you?"

Lily's gaze dropped, russet lashes fanning down across pale cheeks. "I wish they had."

"One of them's dead, you know," Anna said, just to be a little shit, because she was so sick of Lily's calm, her self-assuredness, her unwavering faith in the man who she should have loathed.

Lily's head lifted, eyes wide.

"Nikita Baskin choked one of the boys to death in New York." And clearly, no one had told Lily that.

Slowly, her expression settled into a hard mask. "He'll wish he hadn't done that," she said, and Anna shivered.

~*~

Jake's radio crackled to life on his belt and he reached for it lazily, expecting another mundane update about shift changes or some such. But before he could get the thing unclipped, one of the upstairs guards shouted through it: *"Major Treadwell, it's Sergeant Ramirez! She's badly injured!"*

Jake turned away from Talbot and Price, their startled and curious expressions, and headed for the stairs, heart rate spiking. He thumbed the transmit button as he started up at a jog. "Where is she? What's her status? What happened?" Was he panicking? Yes, a little bit. She'd gone riding as escort with the princes and Talbot's daughter, and if Jake was honest, he didn't like the way Vlad looked at Adela. Like she was a meal.

Static. Hesitation. Then: *"The prince brought her in. They're going to wheel her into an operating theater. She, um..."*

Jake sprinted through the shadowed, musty subbasement that served as storage. "I'm on my way," he snapped into the radio, and slapped the elevator button.

The lab, when he finally reached it, was in a state of chaos. Techs and nurses in scrubs rushed around, gathering supplies. A young doctor with glasses and a harried expression guided a group of orderlies pushing a gurney toward the center of the room...

Where Vlad Tepes stood with a bloody, unconscious Adela held bridal-style in his arms. Blood on his shirt, blood all over her.

Jake's first thought was that Vlad had attacked her. All too easily he could envision those long fangs breaking her skin.

He charged forward. "What the fuck?" he demanded, reaching them, blowing like a racehorse. To Vlad: "What did you do?"

Everyone around them froze. Doctors, nurses, techs, everyone.

Vlad's mouth was clean, he noticed stupidly. The blood was on his shirt. One of the sleeves of his compression shirt had been torn off and was currently tied around Adela's shin. He met Jake's glare with a level stare of his own. "I carried her," he said, his voice low and unnerving, touched with a Romanian accent. "Her horse fell on her, and I carried her back."

Jake breathed harshly through his mouth.

"Excuse me," the doctor said, intervening between them. "If I can just – oh, my. Your grace, if you could please place her on the stretcher..."

Jake got pushed back in the shuffle of nurses as they laid Adela out on a stretcher and surrounded her. Her skin was too pale, her face slack. And she was wet.

Jake's panic rapped beneath his skin like a second pulse, skittery as a rat. "What happened?" he asked again. Beneath the tourniquet, he saw the white of bone protruding from her leg.

Vlad's eyes remained trained on her. He shook his head. "There was a bear. It frightened her mount. I frightened the bear away, but it was too late, and the horse fell on her. She needs blood."

"Sir, we have blood," a tech said, lifting a cold blood bag.

"No," Vlad said. He lifted his own hand, his own wrist, his own blood. "That's not what I mean."

The bespectacled doctor turned to a tech. "Fetch me–"

"Your serum?" Vlad said, mocking. "Don't bother. It isn't strong enough." And he motioned imperiously toward the OR. "Lead the way, Doctor. I will provide whatever blood you need."

Jake moved to protest – and was promptly swept aside in the tide of professionals.

~*~

It felt like someone was sitting on her chest. But it was a dull pressure. Nothing hurt; in fact, she felt mostly numb, but she couldn't breathe, and that was going to be a problem in the long run.

Around her: movement, frantic, but professional voices, beeping.

She cracked her eyes, and everything was a blur. Drugs, she realized. She'd been pumped full of something. Why was she awake? She…

She wet her lips, some sort of instinct, and her tongue passed over something wet and warm that sent a jolt through her entire numb body.

"Your grace!" someone shouted. "I told you we can't…" The voice flickered in and out. "…untested…vials of the serum!"

"Shut up. See to her leg." That voice she knew: the low, accented voice of Vlad Tepes.

Which meant that the hand that gripped her face was his. And that the warm, electrifying thing on her tongue? That was his blood. He pushed his slit wrist against her mouth, and she was too dopey and ruined to resist this time.

The blood went down her throat like good whiskey. Like fire. And then she fainted.

~*~

In the mayhem of getting Ramirez to the house, Mia and Val had been overlooked. She wished their stolen moment of alone time had come under better circumstances. But she would take what she could get.

She pulled the saddle down off the steaming back of Vlad's gelding, wincing when she saw the lather under the saddle pad. Vlad had ridden hard to catch up to them, effortlessly balancing

Ramirez's unconscious body in his arms. It had struck Mia as a distinctly medieval image.

"So let me get this straight," she said as she set the saddle aside and reached for the bucket and water and sponge that waited against the wall. The big black shivered when she swiped the wet sponge down his neck for the first time. "Dad's fancy drug keeps her body from rejecting a donated leg" – she couldn't wrap her head around that one just yet – "but she has to keep taking the drug all the time, and it won't be strong enough to fix this kind of injury."

Ramirez's bay was exhausted in the aftermath of his explosion, head hanging in his cross-ties as Val rubbed him down. Poor thing. Val worked a sponge in long strokes and frowned to himself. "We won't know what will happen until the doctors are done operating. She might lose the foot, yes. Your father's drug is – unpredictable."

"You mentioned side-effects before," she prompted.

He sighed. "Humans and vampires aren't so different. They can interbreed, after all. Sometimes, anyway. My brother Mircea was a half-breed. But…" He hesitated, expression pained.

"Val," she said, softly. "I want to know."

He sighed. "According to my father, my uncle tried countless times to mate, with both human and vampire women. He was never able to beget a child. I've heard other such stories. Breeding isn't always possible. Just like…" He paused, and turned to her, eyes bright in the afternoon sunlight that fell through the skylights. "Not everyone can digest vampire blood. You can turn anyone, but you can't always medicate them. No matter how badly your father wants it to be so, our blood is, ultimately, blood, and not medicine."

She wet her lips. She felt choked, like a fist was pressed to her windpipe. "What if – what if I could take the serum? Without side-effects? Then what?"

Val looked very sad. "Then you would have to take it the rest of your life. It's a temporary solution, Mia, not a cure."

Chills chased across her skin, and it had nothing to do with the cool water trickling down her arm. "But there is a cure. A very permanent one. That's what you meant when you told me to decide. Decide if I want you to–"

He silenced her with one quick wave. "I would not speak it aloud. I don't want to influence you."

"In – *influence* me? Val." She breathed a nervy laugh. "You're asking if I want to become a vampire. What other reason would I decide that if not for you?"

He recoiled physically, as if she'd struck him, expression wounded. "Mia…for *yourself*. Don't you want to live?"

"You're asking me to live forever," she said, as gently as she could manage, though her heart was pounding. "There's a big difference."

"I…" Slowly, he shut his mouth, and turned away, facing the horse. The sponge dripped, forgotten, in his right hand. He let out a little breath. "Yes." Voice distant now. "Forever is a long time. I've been held captive for most of it."

Her heart cracked. "Val–"

"We should get the horses put away."

So that's what they did. Got them all sponged off, cleaned up, and tucked into their stalls with generous flakes of hay. The sort of busy quiet that forced a person into her own head – forced her to think about the things she'd been pushing onto the back burner.

She had to face it: Val was offering her…immortality. A cure, yes, but also *forever*. The thing about it was, she was a human, and forever carried *weight*. It wasn't something you tossed out on a whim. Not something you shrugged and said "whatever" to. Forever was a big damn deal.

She didn't want to die. But did she want to live to be two-hundred? Three-hundred?

Val had been born in 1435…

She turned away from the laundry sink in the tack room and he was blocking the doorway, slim-hipped, and long-haired, and gorgeous. He had his arms folded, but it wasn't the overtly masculine pose that so many men made it; it was something almost sultry, and completely unselfconscious.

A wave of dizziness moved through her, and she steadied herself with a hand on the edge of the sink.

His brow furrowed. Concerned. "What's wrong?"

She smiled at him, and it felt like a stripped-bare expression. Too vulnerable, like her heart must show, pathetic and pounding, through her eyes. "You're beautiful."

He studied her a moment, and then, slowly, his expression melted into something warm and a touch self-satisfied. And then further, into surprise. Awe. "So are you."

They moved at the same time; he pushed off the door, and she started forward, and they met in the center of the floor, reaching. She pressed her hands to his chest. He was underweight, and still shaky, but her impression was of the warmth of his skin bleeding through the thin material of his shirt, his pectorals lightly muscled against her palms. *Vampire*, she thought, half-dazed. Healthier and more resilient than any human could have been in his circumstances.

He curled one hand loosely around the side of her throat, cupped her cheek with the other. Gentle, like she was made of glass.

His thumb moved feather-light beneath her eye, his gaze flicking back and forth across her face. Drinking her in – there was no other way to interpret it. But he hesitated. She read the tension in his face; felt the tremor in his fingertips. Holding back.

"Val," she whispered. "It's okay."

He exhaled in a rush, breath warm across her face, ducked down and kissed her.

Her eyes fluttered shut at the last moment, and it narrowed her world down to sensation. The racing of his heart under her hand. The softness of his lips against hers, slightly damp from his tongue. The flicker of his long lashes on her cheeks, press of his nose.

It felt like a very first kiss. Like something out of a storybook.

But unlike her first kiss, she wasn't a sweaty-palmed kid, and she knew what to do. What she *wanted* from this. From him.

She leaned into him with her whole body, and opened her mouth under his.

He hesitated just a moment longer, trying to be so gentle, the pads of his fingers warm and soft on her face. And then he groaned and slipped his tongue into her mouth.

She'd read somewhere before that the quality of a kiss didn't have anything to do with lips and teeth and tongues; it was *who* you were kissing that made it electrifying. And oh, did she ever understand that now. Because this? This was exquisite.

In a graceful stumble, they ended up on the closed lid of a tack trunk, Val sitting down and Mia straddling his lap.

He clutched at her hair, at the sleeves of her shirt. Pressed a line of wet, decadent kisses along her jaw to the soft patch of skin beneath her ear. Breathing raggedly, chest heaving under her hands. "Mia. God. I…" He opened his mouth against her throat and breathed. She felt the faintest scrape of teeth.

Fear. That's what she should have felt. He was a vampire, and he drank blood to live, and she felt the barest edge of a fang gliding along her pulse point.

Call it love, call it madness, but she wasn't afraid. She slid her hands up his neck and cupped the back of his head, held him to her.

"I want you," he murmured, and his voice was a big cat purr. "I want…God, I want *everything*."

Her neck felt weak, like she might swoon. Her sports bra was too tight, suddenly, all of her clothes itchy and stifling. Everything. Yes, she wanted that too.

He shifted upward again, bit gently at the hinge of her jaw and then recaptured her mouth. A kiss that devoured.

She rocked against him, slight, rhythmic little movements of her hips. She wanted to slide down to the concrete floor and pull him on top of her. Wanted to—

Footfalls echoed off the stall fronts, several sets.

Mia pulled back and saw that Val looked halfway to debauched: cheeks flushed, mouth red and damp, gaze heavy-lidded. She'd pulled hair loose at his nape, thick strands that had come free from his braid.

He sighed, and smiled faintly, and squeezed her waist. "We're lucky we had that long, darling."

She wanted to punch whoever was about to walk in on them.

He chuckled at her expression. "I know. Me too."

They disentangled and stood, and straightened their clothes. There was nothing to do about their heated faces and racing pulses. Maybe whoever this was wouldn't notice.

A moment later, two guards in black appeared in the threshold, shoulder-to-shoulder, not managing to pull off the intimidating looks they were going for. They glanced between Mia and Val. One, the younger of the two, lifted his brows a degree beneath the brim of his hat, and Mia knew they'd been busted.

The older guard cleared his throat. "Miss Talbot, we've been asked to escort you back to the manor."

She reached over and caught Val's hand in hers. "What about Val?"

The man's eyes darted to their linked fingers and then skittered away, as if frightened by the sight. He swallowed. "The prisoner is to return to his cell."

She opened her mouth –

And Val squeezed her hand. "Lead the way, gentlemen," he said, all politeness. "I'll go quietly."

<u>54</u>

FIXES AND MIRACLES

One thing Vlad would grant this century was its medical capabilities. The killing, crippling wounds of his time were no match for modern doctors.

Adela – Treadwell had called her that, hovering back with a stricken look before he was elbowed aside by a nurse – lay unmoving on the table, IV lines snaking from her arms. Someone had put a contraption over her nose and mouth – anesthesia. The doctors had stopped the bleeding; she was "stable," they said. They were worried about infection, which they shouldn't have been – the blood Vlad had given her, living blood, would kill anything. The real worry, Vlad knew, was the damage to the tissues of her leg. It smelled faint to him – like it was dying.

"We set the break," one of the doctors said, sighing behind his paper mask. He held his arms up, gloves slick with blood. "But the leg…" He doubted, just like Vlad.

Then the doctor looked right *at* Vlad, eyes wide behind his glasses. "The blood. Will it–"

"It might."

The man cursed under his breath and looked back at the offending limb. "We'll just have to medicate and see–"

"No," someone said, and Vlad looked up to find that it was Treadwell, red-faced and blowing like a horse that had just run a race. "I'm – I'm blind!"

He shook his head, clearly frustrated. "No, I mean…shit." He squeezed his eyes shut. Anguish of a kind Vlad didn't understand; he and Adela didn't smell of one another beyond the most cursory of ways. Co-workers, friends. They weren't mates.

Warrior obligation, perhaps. Women could go to war in this age.

When Treadwell opened his eyes again, he looked surer, more in control. "I'm blind. I am. I came home from Iraq, and I couldn't see a damn thing. And now I'm working again. I can *see.*

This whole facility is dedicated to miracle cures," he said. "So why can't you guarantee that you can fix her?"

"There are fixes, and then there are miracles, Major," the doctor said. "She can survive without her leg. And if she's able, once she's healed, we can try the procedure again. I'm sure by that point that Dr. Talbot's work with the serum will have been further refined, and—"

"I could save the leg," Vlad said, and all eyes swept toward him. "I could turn her."

The doctor resumed his work, dismissive.

But Treadwell stared at him, slack-jawed. "You – you mean – make her like you?"

"Yes."

His jaw firmed, mouth finally closing. "Why would you do that?"

"Does it matter?"

The doctor had stopped again, head turning back and forth as he looked between them. "Are you serious? Damn, you're serious. Look, that isn't approved. Doctor Talbot will never go for—"

Vlad spoke over him. "Major Treadwell, you know her best. Will she be able to stand living without this leg? Or will the disability slowly kill her?"

"I…" He faltered, looking down at her still face. "I don't know her that well."

"It makes no difference to me," Vlad said.

But it did. His plan would take place regardless of the surrounding circumstances, but it would be more likely to succeed if he had others on his side. Price's revenant had been a gift dropped into his lap. And here now, this woman, was another. At least, she had the potential to be.

The doctor straightened with a disapproving sigh. "This is ridiculous. A missing limb is not a death sentence. Amputees lead fulfilling lives every day."

"No one said otherwise, Doctor," Vlad said, scrutinizing Treadwell. "Decide, Major."

Treadwell bit his lip, and shook his head…but Vlad could already smell it in the man's stress sweat. He'd won.

~*~

Fulk found his wife in the conservatory. Alone, sitting on a low stone wall beside a thriving green plant. Her sister had been here, he could smell – the plant was her work. Annabel hummed quietly to herself when he sat down beside her, but didn't move, still staring into the middle distance.

Fulk whined quietly in the back of his throat, inquiring.

She didn't answer; instead climbed into his lap and looped her arms around his neck, tucked her face into his throat.

Fulk put his arms around her. "What is it, darling?" Words this time, and gentle fingers through her long hair.

"Just me being selfish."

Not for the first time, he wished he'd been able to convince her to leave with Baskin and his allies. But he pushed aside her hair and cupped the vulnerable curve of her throat with one hand because if she was selfish, he was doubly so, and he was glad she was here with him. "No you're not."

She sighed. "Please stop trying to see the best in me. Lily told me about the war – about what's coming. And I know what they want you to do here, and I'm just…being selfish. Because I want you all to myself. And I want us to go home, and pretend none of this is happening." When she blinked, he felt dampness on her lashes, tickling over his pulse. "And I just needed five minutes to get my head on straight so I could be strong for you."

Oh, Anna. He tightened his grip, bundling her in closer. He put his face against her neck in turn, scenting her, wanting that pack comfort. "You're always strong. You don't have to hide anything from me."

She chuckled hollowly. "What did I just say about seeing the best in me?" She pulled back, hands braced on his shoulders, so she could see his face. Fulk knew his smile was half-assed, but didn't have the energy to make it any better.

"Baby." She framed his face with her small, cool hands. "I want you to know, in case you go getting any other stupid ideas about me leaving, that I'm with you all the way. Even once—" Her voice hitched. "Even once Vlad binds you to him, and we go to war. I will *never* abandon you."

A low, sad sound rumbled in his chest, and he rested his forehead against hers, until her face became a blur. "I know, love. I know." He swallowed down a sudden flickering surge of hope, not wanting to give it any credence, not yet. "But I don't know if I'm meant for Vlad. I think…I think he's planning something."

~*~

Mia was tired. Part of it was the good kind of tired: riding, exerting herself…making out feverishly in a tack room. But also the bad kind: panic, fear, dread…and illness.

The massive house was eerily still – everyone down in the basement working on Ramirez, she supposed. She shuddered every time she thought of the gleaming white bone protruding from skin gone pale with shock.

The guards had taken Val back down, and left her alone. Without an escort, with no one watching, she rode up in the elevator and trudged down to her room, fatigue dragging a little more insistently with every step. Someone, hopefully Annabel and not a random staff member, had left a small pile of neatly folded clothes on the dresser in her room, all of it stiff and new; she picked a pair of jeans, a fresh t-shirt, and went to shower.

After, clean, but even sleepier, she flopped down across the bed to stretch out her back – and to think.

Decide. Did she want to become immortal? A vampire? A creature that needed to drink blood to live? Did she deserve to be turned? Was she more deserving than anyone else with a terminal disease? How could she think that she was so special that…

No. It wasn't about deserving. It was a gift, freely offered. Because Val cared for her. Wanted her.

She closed her eyes and the bed seemed to tilt beneath her; another dizzy spell. Why save *her*? He'd been alive almost six-hundred years. Was she just a convenience? Was…

She drifted off on a tide of worry and self-doubt.

When she woke, it was to the sound of a knock at her door, and to the churning of her empty stomach. Evening light slanted, hazy and heavy, across the rug, and the room spun around her. She was going to be sick.

She flailed upright and just barely made it into the bathroom in time to curl over the toilet and bring up a few mouthfuls of watery bile. Her stomach cramped and clenched on nothing, and she dry-heaved, tears stinging her eyes.

"Mia?" her father called from the bedroom, and she wished she'd been able to shut and lock the door.

She flushed, rinsed her mouth, and shuffled back out to find her dad standing awkwardly at the foot of the bed, wringing his hands. Seeing him there compounded her exhaustion. She wanted to sink back down onto the bed and sleep for a full twenty-four hours.

"Your condition is deteriorating," he said gravely.

"Yeah."

"Let me show you my lab. Let me walk you through the process. Please, Mia."

She steadied herself with a hand against the bedpost. "What happened to Sergeant Ramirez?"

He let out a long breath, shoulders slumping. "She'll make a full recovery." His voice came out heavy, unhappy.

"She'll keep her leg?"

"Yes."

Another wave of nausea struck, and she closed her eyes, waited it out. *Decide.* When she opened them again, she said, "Alright. Show me."

~*~

After a quick stop-off in the kitchen so she could choke down a handful of saltines and sip a little ginger ale, they headed for the basement and its assorted horrors. The massive lab wasn't the kicked-anthill of activity it must have been earlier, when Vlad brought Ramirez in. Mia was glad she hadn't witnessed that.

They walked past the tables and tables of quietly-working techs toward one of several medieval-looking wooden doors set in the far wall. Dad said, "We have a full OR here, with trauma center level equipment," he said, proudly. "As well as exam and patient rooms. We've managed to fit all the function of a hospital into one basement." He cast a proud eye over the work stations.

A dungeon, too, she thought.

The door, which Dad almost wasn't strong enough to open by himself, revealed a stone hallway lit by flickering wall sconces. It struck her as very *Frankenstein* and surreal, the juxtaposition of the modern equipment with the antique background. This place might have all the trappings of a hospital, but there was no mistaking it for one.

This hallway was lined with more studded wooden doors, and Mia had the sense that this basement wormed its way far deeper into the earth than she'd first imagined. It was a vast house, but the basement, she thought with an uneasy prickling at the back of her neck, was monstrous.

At one door, a completely out of place brass plaque with Edwin's name on it awaited them. He pushed it open with a flourish, beaming. "My personal lab."

It was dark in there, darker than the hallway at least, and Mia hesitated on the threshold. *I don't want to.* But she swallowed the now-perpetual lump in her throat and followed him in.

The door shutting had an air of finality to it – and well it should. *Decide.* She had to.

A long, low white table occupied the center of the room, lights on apertures angled over its surface at intervals. She spotted several microscopes, two laptops, a scattering of notebooks, and pens and petri dishes. Tidy chaos. Computer screens dominated the back wall, their blue glow the major light source for the room.

Windowless, stuffy, unnatural, and no doubt her father's favorite place on earth.

Decide.

"Here, sit, sit." He wheeled over a stool and ushered her into it. Offered her a bottle of water from a mini fridge tucked into the corner. "My assistants like to make sure I remember to eat," he said, fondly. "Now, allow me to show you..."

He showed her still photos, and video clips taken under microscopes. He explained vampire blood on a cellular level that she was too tired and woozy to fully grasp, walked her through his thought processes on a dozen different experiments.

He was so excited throughout it all. This meant so much to him. Meant *everything*.

Finally, when he was out of breath, and had stopped to sip water for his dry throat, when Mia was getting dizzy again and thinking she needed more crackers before the next bout of nausea hit her, Dad snagged another stool and sat down right in front of her. Close enough to set one tentative fingertip on her knee.

"Mia," he said, voice going heavy, and if she hadn't known he was capable of performing experiments on prisoners, she would have thought he looked like a kindly man – he did, despite all that she knew. That had always been one of the trickiest parts of his abandonment: he wasn't a snarling asshole. He was *nice*. It had always made it so much harder to maintain her insistence that he was the one in the wrong.

"I know," he continued, hesitant, delicate, "that you have very strong feelings about our past together. About my split with your mother, and about the work I'm doing here. I know that you–" here he winced – "might have some feelings about Prince Valerian as well."

"Dad–"

He held up a hand. "I don't want to dissuade you, or argue with you. This is just about you, now. Your health. I want to be a good father to you. I know it's too late for that. I know you can't love me." Sad smile. "But I do love you. Let me help you."

"Dad, I..." *Decide.* She took a deep breath. *Decide.* "You are...doing important work. I couldn't tell when I was a kid, but I think you always have been. There are terrible diseases out there in this world. Awful injuries. If you can help people with your research and your medicines, then I can't hold onto any kind of resentment. I missed you growing up, and I've been angry with you for a long time, yes, but this is more important.

"Your methods, though..." His gaze dropped; ashamed of what he'd done? Or ashamed to have been called out on it. "Dad, I won't even buy makeup that's been tested on animals. And this is...oh my God, this is..." She shut her mouth, clenched her teeth. She couldn't get sidetracked; it wouldn't change anything.

"I know, I know," he murmured.

"But that was your choice. "You made it, and there's no going back. In life, we all have to make our own decisions, and then we have to live with them."

His eyes widened. "Does that mean—"

"Yes. I'll let you help me."

55

I CALLED HIM NIK

On their way back through the main basement, they encountered a tableau that had all the techs and scientists staring: Vlad stood in the center of the room, arms folded, expression stony, while a well-dressed, whipcord thin redheaded man attempted to have a polite argument with him.

It at least sounded polite, comments laid down in a fastidious British accent, but each word had barbed tips. "I'm *saying*, you've seen what I can do. Why in the world would you take action this rash and irreversible when I was quite literally upstairs twiddling my thumbs?"

Vlad appeared unimpressed. As ever. "This didn't concern you, witch."

His laugh sounded more like a cough. "My dear man, everything in this whole bloody house concerns me."

"Gentlemen," Dad said, and both of them turned to him. "If this is about Sergeant Ramirez, then there's no sense arguing after the fact."

"What about Sergeant Ramirez?" Mia asked. She wasn't sure she really wanted to know.

"Nothing," Dad said, hurriedly. "She's fine."

Vlad looked...beneath his granite façade...pleased. Or maybe that was just her imagination.

The redhaired man frowned at her a moment, and then his expression cleared. In a blink, he was convivial, smile seemingly genuine. "Ah. Dr. Talbot, this must be your daughter. It's Mia, correct?" He extended one pale, manicured hand.

A pale, manicured hand she had to force herself to shake. She'd figured out who he was. "And you're the Necromancer."

He winced. "That old moniker again? Please. Liam Price, my lady."

She pulled her hand back.

"Dr. Talbot," Liam said, gaze hardening as it shifted to her father, "there are some things about this — latest development — that we need to discuss."

Dad sagged a little. "Yes, of course."

"I'll escort Mia," Vlad said — a command rather than an offer.

But at the moment, his was the company Mia wanted, needed, the most. "Yes, thank you." She slipped her arm through the one he offered her and let him lead her toward the elevator. She was alone with him, the cab moving upward, when she realized the enormity of what she'd done: grabbing onto Vlad the Impaler and letting him lead her away from her own father.

She tried and failed to squelch a laugh in her hand.

"What?" he asked.

She shook her head. "This is just crazy, is all. And I think it's time I stopped referring you to 'Vlad the Impaler' in my head."

When she snuck a glance, a faint smile was touching the corners of his mouth. "Vlad will suffice," he said, magnanimous. Then turned to face her fully. "Have you decided yet?"

Her stomach turned over, but this time it was nerves and not sickness. "I have. I want to take Val up on his offer."

His brows lifted in obvious, if quiet surprise.

"You thought I'd say no."

"I thought you'd say yes immediately," he countered. "Humans don't tend to take anything into consideration when the offer of unlimited health is dangled in front of them."

"Thanks for the vote of confidence."

He gave her a narrow, appraising look and faced the doors again. "I misjudged your eagerness." It almost sounded like an apology.

"Yeah, well. It wasn't a snap decision. I put a lot of thought into it." She didn't feel like she owed anyone an explanation beyond herself and Val. But Val had said to trust Vlad. And he *was* Val's brother. So she said, "I'm doing this because I love your brother. Because I want to help him get out of here. And — and be with him." That sounded corny, but it was the best she could do right now. She wasn't about to explain the revelation of kissing Val.

Vlad said, "My brother has never..." Uncharacteristic hesitance. "Been allowed to – to choose for himself. *Love.*" He said it like a curse. "He was a hostage. A slave. And it wasn't *love* that was forced on him...but I wonder sometimes if he believed it was. Unwilling romance is the only sort he's ever known." He turned to her again, and his eyes were fathomless. "He's chosen you. Now. Don't ever make him regret that choice." *Or else* hung unspoken between them.

"I'm not a monster."

He didn't blink. "Neither is he. I mean what I'm saying."

"I know."

She didn't draw a breath until he turned away from her again. Like a declaration: "I won't suffer any more tyrants when it comes to my brother. No one will hurt him again while I draw breath. I will burn this house to the ground, and I will kill everyone in it who ever touched him."

Mia bit back a gasp.

"Tonight. Get some rest, prepare yourself. I will bring him to you. I will see to it that the wolves take care of the rest."

Her pulse beat high and fast in her ears. She rested a hand against the slick wall of the elevator. "Okay."

"Whatever happens, don't look back."

Trust him, Val had said. And somehow, she did.

~*~

The grand dining room across from the library was not only ostentatious, but for Fulk, it held some memories he didn't like to relive unless absolutely necessary. He never spent any time there unless ordered to – how quickly he'd fallen back into the habit of taking orders. Of being in someone's service. He hated himself for that.

But, luckily, there was a small family dining room just off the kitchen. It had plum-colored flocked wallpaper, golden candlesticks gathered in clusters on the marble top of the buffet table. But it was overall modest when compared to the rest of the house. It was where he and Anna took dinner tonight, blissfully alone, candlelight flickering off silverware, a view of the glowing

703

conservatory through the window rendering the chandelier unnecessary.

Anna picked at her food, pushing the roasted potatoes around with her fork. It was nerves, he knew, because his own were making his stomach tight and restless. Like a dog sensing an oncoming electrical storm, he could sense the energy rippling through the old house. The knife-edge moment of *what's next*.

Fulk smelled the revenant long before he appeared in the doorway. Kolya Dyomin slid into the shadows of the threshold like a wraith. His hood was down, but he wore his long dark coat, and boots, the scars on his face gleaming faintly silver in the low light.

He stood, gaze somewhere on the table, not self-conscious enough to understand the awkwardness of the moment.

Fulk didn't take pity on him, but Anna did. "Do you need something?" she asked, just enough steel in her voice to tell him that they weren't really looking to help him. Fulk had nothing against the man – he'd once been a friend of Sasha Kashnikov, after all, and alpha wolf or no, that boy was impossible to dislike – but he'd dealt with Liam's playthings before. He didn't want to deal with this one.

Kolya blinked a few times, as if surprised by the question. His brain wasn't running on all its cylinders yet; that would come with time. So too would the memories, and then heaven help the poor wretch, he'd be distraught.

Maybe. He was Russian. Soviet at that. Maybe *distraught* wasn't possible.

"Lady Price said there was food." His voice was low and rusty; the voice produced by a throat that hadn't been recreated quite right. "She said I should eat."

Anna snorted and set down her spoon. "First off, she's not nobility, so you don't gotta call her 'lady.' Liam's not a lord either."

"Oh," he said, without inflection.

Anna cocked her head. "Sit down. I'll have someone bring you a plate."

As she got up to do so, Kolya pulled out a chair and slowly settled into it. He could move fast – Fulk had seen it firsthand –

but he tended to creep through the house, almost cautious. Like maybe he didn't quite remember what his body was capable of.

He folded his hands together on the edge of the table and cast a blank look around the room. Blank, but – candlelight caught in his eyes, a quick flash, and Fulk thought this blankness was born of intent. The gaze of a government agent trained to appear disinterested.

Fulk set his own fork and knife down, appetite gone. "Are your memories returning?" he asked, aiming for conversational.

Kolya turned his head a fraction, so their gazes met. The man was neither vampire, nor wolf, and definitely not a mage, but his stare wasn't human. Fulk was struck with a terrible sense that he was looking into the void; behind his dark eyes lay a place from which no creature was meant to come back.

He wet his lips, and took a long moment before answering. "Some. It's patchy."

"That's how it works, I'm afraid."

Slowly, with movements that seemed deliberate, he reached down inside his coat and came out with two long, wicked knives. Fulk tensed – but then recognized them. The ones Vlad had been playing with in the training room. The ones he'd knocked out of Nikita Baskin's hands.

Kolya laid them on the table with something like reverence. "These are mine. Vlad said. Or – they used to be."

Oh.

Fulk recalled the files Talbot had laid in front of him, the ones he'd tried to shove aside…but caught glimpses of anyway. Kolya Dyomin had favored knives and close combat. He'd been a ballet dancer…

"He kept your knives," Fulk said quietly, and Kolya's head snapped up. "Baskin. Your commander."

The man's bewildered gaze dropped to the blades again. "Nikita…*Nik*." He sucked in a quick, sharp breath. "I called him Nik." Slow at first, and then gaining speed as the memories tumbled in to fill the blank places in his mind. "We grew up together. Us and Dima…" A sideways, humorless smile tugged at his mouth. "Nik always liked him best, he was…and then he died…" He lifted a hand and wiped it down his face, pushed his long dark hair back. "Jesus. That asshole. He was totally in love with that kid, and he–" He caught himself, bit his lip. He looked up through his lashes. Voice thin and wavering: "They're still alive? They...?"

Fulk took a deep breath. He didn't want to feel sympathy, but it was unavoidable. This reincarnated *thing* – this *man* – was too pitiful to feel otherwise. "In 1942, you died in a field, along with most of your comrades. Rasputin and a mage named Philippe killed you all."

The air left his lungs in a rush, mouth open and gaping afterward.

Fulk pressed on. "One among your company, Sasha, was a wolf, like me. He killed the mage and Rasputin. And he used Rasputin's blood and heart to save your captain. The two of them still live, yes. They are immortals, as am I, and your Lord Price, and Vlad."

"They're..." His gaze darted, flicking over Fulk's face, around the room. "Nik and Sasha, they're okay?"

"Yes."

He nodded, slow, and wet his lips again. "Good. That's – that's good. Do they know...?"

"About you? I would assume not."

"But they're *alive*."

"Very much so."

His fingers, still long and slender – Fulk could envision them splayed artfully against a backdrop of stage lights, arms held aloft in some impossible ballet pose – but now crossed with faint, pale scars, moved over the blades. Familiarizing himself with them again. "I don't...Liam, he's the one who brought me back–"

"Kolya," Fulk said, as gently as he could manage. Scent aside, the poor Russian made a heartbreaking picture, clutching knives like lifelines, memory and confusion warring for supremacy in an outwardly visible way. "Liam didn't bring you back as a favor. You didn't ask for it. You don't owe him anything."

He swallowed, throat moving. "My friends..." Too somber for hope, more like grief. But longing all the same.

"Would like to see you, I'd imagine." They would be horrified, yes. And confused. But a man who walked willingly into this house with nothing but idiot children for backup was of the sort who'd like to know that a childhood friend was back from the dead.

Kolya pressed his hands flat over the hilts of the knives, and the faint tremors in his arms stilled. Soft, just a whisper: "I used to work for some really bad people."

"Yes, you did."

When he lifted his head this time, he seemed more deeply rooted in himself. More of the real him filling out the shell of his body. "I don't want to do that anymore."

Fulk opened his mouth to respond—

And Vlad stalked into the room. He never walked anywhere idly, but there was an extra level of intent to his stride now.

Kolya whipped around to face him, hands closing on the knives, white-knuckled.

Vlad shot him an unimpressed look before he turned to Fulk – and heeled the door shut behind him. "We need to talk."

Anna returned and set a plate heaped with roast beef, vegetables, and gravy in front of Kolya. "Talk about what?" she asked, sliding back into her seat.

Vlad cut a speaking glance toward Kolya.

"Don't worry," Fulk said. "I think he's about to jump ship."

"Is he now?" The glance became a stare. To his credit, Kolya didn't flinch away. "Do you want to see your friends again, Chekist? Do you want to leave his place?"

A muscle in Kolya's jaw twitched, but he nodded.

To Fulk, Vlad said, "I asked you before to think about your feelings toward my brother. I'll ask you again, but this time, you need to know."

It was quiet a beat, and then Anna breathed out, "Oh."

"Dr. Talbot got it wrong," Vlad continued, smug. "I never meant for you to be my wolf, le Strange. But my brother needs one. Two, even, if he's going to manage an escape."

56

DARLING

They'd taken his cat away. Val thought of Poppy often, wondering if someone had killed her, or if she, hopefully, wandered the manor's hallways, eating bits of table scraps from friendly hands. She was only a kitten. Could her association with him have earned her a death sentence? Stranger things had happened.

But he thought of Mia, too. Constantly. Thought of the firsthand sight of sunlight gliding down the slope of her nose. Thought of the heat of her pressed all down his front. Thought of her mouth, warm and sweet under his. He hadn't put a hand around himself for pleasure's sake in a very long time, but he was tempted now, just thinking of what they'd done, just the weight of her on his lap, and the soft sounds of kissing her.

He'd been aroused in his life, more times than he could count, but the rush of blood and heat had always been accompanied by shame. Fear. Revulsion. Pain – always pain. He'd hated himself for finding pleasure in torture, but it had been his body's way of coping. There had been moments when it had been good – welcome, even. But nothing had ever felt like the gentle, mutual wanting that spilled out of Mia in soft looks and quiet, delighted breaths.

His own want, by contrast, was nothing but violent.

He tipped his head back against the wall and stared at the damp stone of the ceiling. He'd never felt like this before; never wanted to consume someone. And it wasn't about the blood; he wanted inside her, a want so bad that it ached.

Vlad had said he would return, and the squeal of door hinges announced that he'd kept his word. He wasn't alone, though; Val smelled wolf.

Vlad appeared in front of the cell alone, though, keys jangling as he unlocked the door.

Val chuckled. "Did they give you those? Or did you take them?"

"What do you think?" He carried the tote bag from this morning, and tossed it to Val.

He had an easier time catching it this time. Stronger. Every meal, every drop of blood, every minute he was stronger than he'd been before. He felt almost like his old self – the version of himself that had killed Mehmet. That had fought sorties outside the walls of Constantinople.

God, Constantine…

No. Now wasn't the time.

"What's this?" he asked, peering into the bag.

"Clothes."

Val reached in and drew out a pair of very soft, thin black sleep pants and a robe of similar material. He shot his brother a raised-brow look.

"Those are for before. The others are for after."

Under the – well, they were pajamas, is what they were – he found a pair of jeans, t-shirt, leather jacket, and black sneakers. "Brother." He felt a slow grin overtake his face. "Do you want me to look cool?"

"I want you to take this seriously."

Val sighed. "I take everything seriously, I just don't look as miserable as you while doing it."

Vlad stared at him.

Val lifted his hands, palms-up. "I swear!"

Vlad studied him a long, tense moment. Then seemed to come to some sort of decision and nodded. "Before you go to your mortal, there's something else we have to do."

The baron and baroness edged into view, walking with small steps, pressed close together. Fulk, especially, looked pale and severe.

Val's pulse hiccupped. "What?"

"You've gone walking," Vlad said, "and you've seen much of the modern world, but you haven't lived in it. Mia will be newly turned, and likely overwhelmed. You'll need help – both to escape, and to continue to evade Talbot's minions. You need wolves, Val. Strange and his wife have agreed to become bound to you."

Val sat blinking, dumbfounded, hands clenched in the soft material of the robe in his lap. "But…" He turned to Annabel. "He doesn't ever want to be bound again. You told me that."

Fulk fidgeted, gaze caught between dark and frightened.

Annabel hugged his arm. "I don't think you'd try to act like our master, would you, Val?"

"No." His voice was faint. He couldn't believe this. He swallowed. "I wouldn't – but, Anna, dear girl…you don't have to do this."

She looked at him steadily, with nothing short of ferocity. "We do, actually. If we stay here, they'll just keep using my safety as leverage to make Fulk do whatever they want. We have to leave. And…if we're bound to you, then no other vampire can ever force us to work for them."

"That…makes sense." And it did. But. "Baron Strange. What are your thoughts?"

Fulk ground his narrow jaw, hands clenched into fists at his sides. Nostrils flared. "I think I want to get the hell out of here." Val waited, but he said nothing else.

"You see?" Vlad said. "They are willing." He waved and the couple shuffled forward, into the cell, until they stood side-by-side in front of him.

Slowly, struck hard by how surreal this seemed, Val set the clothes aside and smoothed his suddenly-damp palms down his thighs. His parents' wolves had considered him pack, had protected him, listened to him, and he'd loved them in return. But he'd never performed a binding; never bound a wolf to himself, personally. He'd wondered, felt a tickling urge at the back of his throat several weeks back when he finally came face-to-face with Sasha…but that would have been wrong. Sasha was meant for another.

He hadn't expected this.

"I would be honored," he said, quietly, voice shaking. His breath trembled in his lungs and he wet his lips.

"Do it," Vlad said.

Annabel shifted her weight–

And her husband caught her around the waist, held her still. "I'll go first," he said, and then slowly sank down so that he knelt on the cold stone floor between Val's parted legs.

He breathed quick and harsh through his mouth, gaze darting, restless. Val could hear the rabbit-fast beating of his heart. He was *terrified*.

Val felt his own shaking ease. He cupped the baron's chin in a gentle hand and tipped his face up. His pupils were pinpricks, sweat beading at his temples. The poor dear. He'd left off his usual red leather jacket, his neck long, and bare, and pale.

"It's alright, sweetheart," Val murmured. Fingers cupped carefully, but firmly under the wolf's sharp jaw, and he touched the pad of his thumb to Fulk's upper lip, lifted it up and sought the point of a canine. Pressed. Felt it elongate. Watched the blue eyes flare to life, a faint glow.

Val leaned in closer, and pushed every ounce of his crippling sincerity into his voice. "It really will be an honor to be a part of your pack. Will you accept me?"

Permission wasn't necessary – a wolf could be held down and forced to choke on blood, and be bound against his will.

But something eased in Fulk at the question. He settled deeper into his knees, and swayed forward, eyelids drooping. He let out a quiet, lupine chuff. His voice was nothing human. "Yes, your grace."

"That's a good darling." Val tucked his face down low, into Fulk's neck, guided the wolf's mouth to his own throat. They were pressed together, ear-to-ear, and their pulses pushed against one another there.

Val opened his mouth and bit with slow precision, fangs piercing skin. And Fulk did the same to him.

The first sip was an electric shove between his shoulder blades. But it quickly became a soothing warmth. He *felt* the baron, saw his wolf in his mind – great, shaggy black, blues eyes, a wary alpha. He held out a hand to it, smiled. *Hello, beautiful boy. I won't hurt you.*

The wolf approached in fits and starts, raising and then lowering his head. He growled, once. But then he was close enough to press his cold wet nose to Val's fingers and snuffle at them, breathe in his scent…and his intent.

Finally, the beast ducked his head and pressed the side of his face into Val's palm. Acceptance.

Val blinked back to the present, and sat back, swallowing a last rich mouthful of blood. The wound on his own neck tingled pleasantly, and when Fulk drew back, he looked drunk, lips red and wet, eyes closed.

He sighed and went boneless, and laid his head down on Val's thigh.

Val cupped a protective hand over his silky dark hair. And that was that.

~*~

Mia hated all this sleepiness, but she had to admit that this was a very nice way to wake up. She rose up out of a shapeless, unsettling dream to the sensation of someone petting a gentle hand over the crown of her head, again and again. She lay on her side, and the lamp was on, its light spilling over Val, who sat perched on the side of her bed, smiling down at her with so much warmth it made her throat ache.

She licked dry lips, and the first words out of her mouth were, "You look good."

And he did. His hair was loose, falling over his shoulder in a golden curtain, his face flushed with health, eyes bright, the awful bags beneath them gone. He wore a loose black robe, its sleeves pushed up past his elbows, the front open, his chest smooth and bare beneath.

His cheeks pinked in response to her words. Oh, he was *blushing*. It was precious. "So do you," he said, and smoothed her hair back from her face again.

Except there was no way she could. She'd seen herself when she first woke up. And here she was, face smushed into a pillow, possibly drooling on herself. Ugh.

She braced a hand in the sheets and eased up to a sitting position. Dizziness swamped her, and she closed her eyes against the sensation.

He put both hands on her bare shoulders – she wore nothing but a tank top and shorts – and steadied her. "It's getting worse."

No sense lying when that's why he was here. She cracked her eyes open, wincing and smiling – trying to. "Yeah."

His expression had grown serious. Grave. One hand slid up to her neck, holding her there. "Mia." Voice heavy. "I want you to know that I'm doing this for you. That I want you to be healthy. If you don't want anything from me beyond that, I'll understand."

Never been able to choose, Vlad had said. And he was choosing now. And he was going to do this monumental thing for her, save her life – even if she didn't want him in return.

She leaned in and knocked their foreheads together, lightly. "Val. Sweetie. I wouldn't be doing this if I didn't want to be with you."

He pulled back, eyes wide. "Oh *no*. You can't – it can't just be for *me*. You have to–"

"I *meant*." She laid her hands on his face, and he quieted. "That I trust you."

He studied her a long moment, gaze shifting over every part of her face, his own expression held in careful check. A muscle flexed in his jaw; she saw it, felt it leap against her palm. "Do you love me?"

"Yes."

"Do you mean it?"

"Yes."

He smiled, slow and sharp, fangs too long, but it didn't quite touch his eyes – which glimmered bright with tears for one fast beat before he blinked them away.

"Kiss me," she urged, and he did.

~*~

In his cell, with two freshly-bound, blood-drunk wolves propped against one another at his feet, Vlad had seen fit to share some brotherly wisdom.

"Turning a human is a powerful thing. It's intimate."

He knew that. But rather than talk of Arslan, a little blood-drunk himself, relaxed and cocky, Val had said, *"What sort of intimate are we talking here, brother?"* And thrown an eyebrow waggle in for good measure.

Vlad had doubled down on his scowl. *"You know what I'm talking about."*

"Does that mean you fucked that little soldier girl when you turned her earlier?"

Vlad scoffed. *"Intimate for others. Not me. You, since you care for the—"*

"Love."

"Since you love the girl, it will be powerful for you. And her, likely, if she's sincere in her affections."

"Brother dearest," Val had said, *"how is it that I'm the one who was used as a plaything most of my life, and yet it's you who doubts true love?"*

"I doubt most things," Vlad had deadpanned. Then had come the truly terrible part: *"Have you ever bedded a woman?"*

Val had straightened up from his relaxed sprawl, trying to gather his dignity, thin though as it was. *"Yes."* There had been a woman or two, during his long captivity. He'd been chained up, and they'd done most of the work, but he understood the mechanics of it. (And he knew the intoxicating heat and softness and wetness of the experience; desire coiled tight in his belly when he thought of having Mia like that, above him, hair loose on her shoulders…)

Stone-faced, Vlad had said, *"You understand that you're supposed to—"*

"Yes!"

He didn't want that conversation in his head now, one hand braced on the mattress, the other smoothing slowly up Mia's bare stomach, but it had stubbornly taken root, fed by his sudden self-consciousness. Because here he was, and he knew he was beautiful to look at, but she was stretched out beneath him, unclothed, willing, looking up at him with soft invitation, and she was *perfect*. What if he couldn't make her feel good?

Her hand slid up his naked shoulder – he shivered, leaned into the touch – and found his nape, fingers threading through the hair there. "Come here," she said, so gently, and he leaned down, grateful, to kiss her again.

He loved kissing her. It was lush and unhurried. She lifted into him when he ran his tongue behind her teeth. Pressed her breasts to his chest, skin to skin, and – oh, that was…

He opened his mouth against hers, panting. Her pulse raced against his hands, under thin skin and rib bones delicate as a bird's. He still wore his pants, but he lay between her parted legs, and he could feel the heat of her. Could smell that she was ready…ready for him to push through his doubt and touch her.

How many nights had he appeared to her as nothing but a conjuring? Wishing he could touch. And now he hesitated.

She pushed both hands through his hair and pulled him down to her, even closer. Took his lower lip delicately between her teeth, and *bit*.

He groaned. "God. Darling…" His response was immediate, and automatic; his spine moved like a whip-crack, a slow undulation that rubbed them together in all the right places.

The last bit of hesitance evaporated, and his hand slipped up the fretwork of her ribs to cup her breast.

She breathed a small, almost-startled sound into his mouth, and he drank it in; cupped her, squeezed, and drew out a whimper. He thumbed the hard bud of her nipple and she whimpered; her legs tightened on his hips.

She was reacting to him. She *wanted* him.

He trailed kisses down her throat, across her chest, moving over her like a panther. Bolder, hungrier. Salt taste of her skin blooming on his tongue, scent filling his nose; still sick, but not for long, no. He would heal her. He would make her *his*.

His hand slipped down between her legs and found her slick for him. He wanted to put his mouth there, so he did, shouldering her thighs wider apart, his hair falling around his face so all he could see, and smell, and taste was her.

He could have stayed there an hour, listening to the pleading sounds she made, feeling the rough scrape of her nails on his scalp. Giving her pleasure like this, hearing her ask for *more, Val, oh God* left him so hard he was panting against her sex, grinding his own hips mindlessly against the mattress.

When he lifted his head to take a breath, she tugged at his hair. "Val. Val, come here."

His fangs ached, and he couldn't take a deep breath, and he needed to come, and rational thought was out the window, and...That sounded like a brilliant idea.

He prowled back up her sweat-sheened body and cupped her face; kissed her. Too hard, too deep, too much – but she gave it right back, rising against him like the tide, nails dragging down his back. He could feel the scratches she was leaving; already wanted to turn and admire them in the mirror. That was his mate, his woman; she'd been the one so turned on she marked his flesh.

But later. Later.

Mia followed the lean dip of his back with both hands, until they slipped into the waistband of his pants and she could palm his ass. He gasped and his hips jerked, grinding down into her. She was so wet that her slick bled through the thin fabric. God, *God.*

He closed his eyes and panted against her mouth. "Please." Tremors skated across his skin. He felt fevered. He felt *everything.* "Mia, *please.*"

"Shh, I know, I know." Her voice was wrecked. She pushed his pants down his hips and wrapped a sure hand around his cock. Guided him, and then...

He growled when he entered her. She sighed, and she gave, and the hot, slick grip of her around him punched the air out of his lungs.

He hovered over her, unmoving, breath caught in his throat, for a seemingly endless moment, trying not to come right away.

She seemed to know it, murmuring low and soothing, words he was too overwhelmed to comprehend; petting his sides, and hips, and shoulders. Tucking his hair behind his ears.

Slowly, slowly, teeth clenched, he eased back from the edge. "...Val. Val, I'm right here."

He cracked his eyes open, and even through a blur of tears, he could make out her face, her half-lidded eyes, and her bruised mouth, and the long line of her throat, bared to him.

She was. She was right there.

With a low, deep purr, he settled over her and began to move. It was a rhythm engraved in his bones, even if he hadn't often been the one to set it. His hips knew the way to hitch, and roll, and her thighs were strong around them, her heels digging into the backs of his thighs. He tucked his face into her throat, pressed open-mouthed kisses against her pulse, where the scent of her blood was the strongest.

He'd been fucked more times than he could count, but nothing had ever been like this.

When he came, the astral plane tried to take him, its flickering stars and vast black reaches. But he fought it off; he wanted to stay in his body, to feel the wracking pleasure that shifted through him in tides.

Mia made a low, throaty noise, just after him, her walls clenching tight around him. He wanted to drown. And for a little while, he let himself, just drifting.

When his wits returned, he found that he'd slumped over onto his side, and that he'd hauled her up against him. His cock had softened, and he'd slipped out of her; they were wet and tacky, skin glued together. His face was buried against the side of her face; he had a mouthful of her hair. He snuffled and purred like a housecat, and couldn't find it in himself to feel embarrassed about that.

Mia's hand skimmed aimlessly up and down his arm. Her breath came in soft little puffs just beneath his ear. "That was…" she started.

"Mmm." He pulled back so he could look at her: her flushed cheeks, and bright eyes, and kiss-pink lips. "I've wanted to do that for a very long time," he admitted.

She smiled, lazy and sated, a little embarrassed. "Not as long as me, I can promise."

He traced her smile with a fingertip. "I didn't hurt you?"

"God, no."

But what he did next would. A little. At least at first.

It should have been a sobering thought, but was instead electrifying; his eagerness, the rush of blood to his face and his cock frightened him in its intensity.

He peeled away from her, reluctant, and pushed himself upright. "Stay here."

She didn't argue, closing her eyes and settling down in the sheets with a little hum of agreement.

Val felt wobbly as a new colt when he got to his feet, his knees threatening to give out. He braced a hand against the bedpost, and memory threatened to intrude – a night centuries ago, legs shaking, lungs shaking, stomach aching; Mehmet rolling away from him, candle shadows leaping up the tent walls. But no, that wasn't this. This was new and precious, and he wouldn't let the past scar it.

In the bathroom, he wet a cloth with warm water. His reflection was an unfamiliar one: color high, face soft, and tired, the light in his eyes warm. It took him a long moment, warm water rushing over his hands, to realize that he looked *happy*.

He shut off the taps, turned back to the door, and paused in the threshold.

Mia had turned onto her side and pulled the sheet up over her hip. Her hair fell loose over her shoulders, and the lamplight did artful things to the curve of her waist and breasts, her skin pearlescent with drying sweat. She looked like a painting, right down to the enigmatic smile she was sending his way.

She laid one arm across the mattress, toward him, palm-up in invitation. "Come back."

He did. It felt like she'd hooked him by the collar he no longer wore and towed him in, and he went unresisting. Willingly. Not an order, not an ultimatum, but a choice, and he grinned like a fool as he climbed onto the bed and knelt at her side. Slowly, reverently pulled the sheet down.

"Here, darling, let me clean you off."

She turned over, but blushed, slow to open her legs for him. "You don't have to do that."

"Oh, but you've awakened my inner gentleman, and I absolutely have to, I'm afraid."

She chuckled. "You're always a gentleman."

"Hmm. That's what you think."

"Pretentious, anyway."

"You wound me, darling."

He wiped her breasts, and belly, and between her legs with the cloth, tender and intimate, but without any kind of heat. He wanted her, yes, but he loved her too. Wanted to care for her. To take that awful taint of sickness from her blood, and to do every little thing she would let him, down to braiding her hair and bathing her skin. He would clean her with his tongue if it wasn't completely ridiculous.

The night table was topped with green marble, so he set the cloth there when he was finished, vowing to wring it out properly over the sink later – not that they would *be here* later, but it was the thought that counted, so often. When he turned back, he expected to find her blushing – and she was – but she was staring at him, her gaze trained between his legs.

Her brows scaled her forehead, but he thought her sideways smile was impressed. "Really? Already?"

He resisted the urge to squirm. "Vampire biology is…a little different. We can…um…yes. Also…" No, he couldn't tell her that.

"What?"

He bit his lip and realized his fangs were still fully descended. Blood welled up from the pinprick mark he'd left, and he swept it away with his tongue. Even though it was his own, the taste of blood only left him more eager, if that was possible. "Sexual lust and bloodlust can often be…linked. In a vampire's subconscious."

"Oh." She sat up, and subtly tugged the edge of the sheet into her lap, covering herself. It didn't look like a conscious move, but Val eased back, not wanting to frighten her. "And you're…?"

"It's only anticipation, love. But if you–"

She shook her head. Took a deep breath and let it out slow. Smiled at him. "I'm not afraid of you. I promise."

"I know. But it's overwhelming. I understand." The glow was beginning to fade, and he didn't want that to happen. He shifted around her so he could stretch out on top of the sheets, head resting on the pillow. "Will you lie down with me?"

She snuggled up to his side with a grateful-sounding exhale, head on his shoulder, hand on his chest, over the steady thump of his heart. The skin-to-skin contact soothed worries he hadn't known he'd had. It had been so long since he'd been touched with kindness or affection that even the simple act of his brother braiding his hair elicited breathless emotion. This, having her pressed to him in a long, warm line all down his side…that nearly brought tears to his eyes.

He blinked away the burn and tried to focus on the sensations: the softness of her skin, the weight of her breasts against his ribs. Her lashes tickling his throat as she blinked.

"Have you ever turned anyone before?" she asked, voice hushed.

He traced the back of her hand with his fingertips, little circles around her knuckles. "Yes. Once."

"Then it's just the first time for me, then." She pressed in closer, and in a very small voice said, "I'm ready. Just…whenever."

Val hooked an arm around her waist and pulled her onto his chest, hauled her up until her face hovered above his. He didn't expect her to look startled.

"You're really strong," she blurted out, and he grinned.

"You will be too, soon." Then sobered. "Physically. You're already strong in every other way."

She rolled her eyes.

Val cupped the back of her head and pulled her down into a kiss.

It started slow and easy, afterglow kisses. But then Mia slid her leg over so she was straddling him, planted her knees on the mattress and rolled her hips. Easy little movements, slow flexes, but the friction had Val curling his hand into her hair, chasing her mouth, lifting up to meet her.

Val caught her lip with his fang, and the taste of her blood bloomed across his tongue for the first time.

It did things to him. His insides were a riot; competing, visceral urges: bite, keep, claim, feed, mate. His growl started low in his chest, a deep rumble, and worked up his throat; she caught it in her mouth with a little gasp.

When she pulled back a fraction, her pupils were blown. A bead of blood welled up on her lip, and Val didn't think: he leaned up and licked it off with a slow swipe of his tongue.

The sound she made in response was incredible.

He was purring now, and the sound threaded through his voice. "Ready?"

"Y-yes." It was desire that made her stutter; he couldn't catch a trace of fear anywhere on her.

"Alright, darling." He turned them onto their sides. Swept her hair back over her shoulder to expose her throat. He could see the leap of her pulse beneath the skin, as beckoning as a sly look and a crooked finger. "We'll go slow." His voice was rough and awful, more animal than man, but she leaned into it, pressing her head into the pillow, offering her throat. "It won't hurt, darling. Just a little, at the start, but then it won't." Please God, let that be true. "I'll do it right. I promise."

The last he breathed across her skin, leaning down closer and closer as he spoke. He watched goosebumps form, smelled the rush of blood, and sweat, and skin, and sickness. He was going to pull that out of her – draw it into his own body and let his impossible immortality duel it to the death. He felt like an awful predator, poised above her, tip of his tongue tracing up her jugular, but she wasn't his prey. This wasn't a feast.

This was a beginning. The start of the rest of his life as a free man. As someone with a mate. As someone *loved* again, for the first time in so, so long.

Mia put her hand on his shoulder, and pulled him in that last half-inch.

Val closed his eyes and bit her.

<u>57</u>

ADMIRABLE

Dr. Edwin Talbot's upstairs office – the showpiece, some of the others called it – was above reproach in all manners. But in his downstairs office, the same office across which Major Treadwell had been thrown a few weeks before, he tended to let his packrat tendencies overtake his sense of decorum. Files sat stacked and precarious; at least two dirty dinner dishes had been set aside on the tops of file cabinets. A few cobwebs swayed in the high corners. He hadn't let the cleaning staff in here in two weeks, afraid they'd accidently trash something critical.

He knew where everything was, though, including the half-full bottle of Crown Royal in the bottom left cabinet. Liam regarded him with an intense amount of judgement when he pulled it and two mostly clean glasses out and thumped them onto his blotter.

"You aren't a teetotaler, are you, Mr. Price?"

"Obviously not." He sat like every elegant, martini-drinking British villain that had ever graced a movie screen. "But...Crown Royal? Really?"

"You are most welcome to go upstairs and find something more to your liking." Earlier, even this morning, Edwin might have offered to go get it for him. He'd overhead two of his technicians saying that he was a suck-up, and he couldn't really argue that he wasn't. But right now, he was tired in every sense of the word.

Liam sighed, but accepted the glass that was slid toward him. "Fine. But if you offer me a cola to mix it with..." He shuddered and took a delicate sip – and then shuddered again.

Edwin downed his all in one go and refilled it.

A good thing, too, because Liam said, "Alright, Doctor."

He threw down the second for good measure.

"Things are, apparently, a mad house around here, and you've managed to avoid me on this so far. We need to discuss my daughter."

Edwin really, really didn't want to do that. "The story hasn't changed since I told it to you last," he said wearily. "Though we'd put precautions in place, we were unprepared for the outside interference of—"

Liam sliced a hand through the air, cutting him off. "How could you have been anything *but* prepared? Doctor, when you called to tell me that she'd been taken into custody, you assured me that Major Treadwell and his team had neutralized her – her *bodyguard*." The word obviously left a sour taste in his mouth. Edwin imagined it was much like the taste in his own when he was forced to acknowledge that Mia and Prince Valerian were *friends*. "And yet the man was alive, and somehow managed to befriend Robin of Locksley."

"An unanticipated development, I assure you."

"It was unanticipated that your little toy soldier wouldn't follow orders?"

He poured a third round, resolving not to drink it – yet. At this moment, he longed for Vlad Dracula's blunt approach to conversation. The prince might have a reputation for brutality, but when it came to dueling with words, Liam Price was by far the more dangerous party.

"Major Treadwell is a decorated soldier. He jumped at the chance to resume an active duty position. He's the sort of man who comes to the military for a career, Liam. I had no way of knowing his emotions would compromise the mission. How could I?"

"Hmm." Liam settled deeper into his chair, elbows propped on its arms, hands steepled together. It should have been a cliché pose, but he lent it a particular gravitas. "She manipulated him? Magically, I mean."

"Not that I'm aware. But by the time she was here, she'd been contained by the cuffs, and we hadn't had a chance to fully test her capabilities. Is that something you can do yourself?"

Liam gave one of his enigmatic, infuriating little close-lipped smiles. "A mage can do all sorts of things."

Edwin wanted to bury his face in his hands. He said, "Not to sound callous, but there *are* other children. One of the boys – part of the same batch as the Russell girl – is showing great promise. The New York team thinks he's ready to send here for training."

"Excellent," Liam said, toneless. For a second, the lamplight caught his eyes so they seemed to glow. These damn immortals. "Though I'm troubled by the fact that you seem to think I care only for them as weapons. They are my children, after all."

"Yes. I know."

Liam cocked his head. "Do you doubt that I love them?"

"I…" Yes, he did. But how could he admit that considering the father he'd been himself? Deep down, he liked to think that, though he'd been absentee, he at least hadn't grown a whole hoard of children in a lab and entrusted them to the care of others. He'd made use of those lab-grown children, yes, but…that was only science.

If only Mia could *see that*…

Liam chuckled. "Doctor Talbot, you might be wise, but I've been alive for a *very long time*. I'm immortal, and so are my children. If I miss their first few years, that doesn't mean much in the grand scheme of things."

"Of course." But Kate had shoved more than one parenting book under his nose during Mia's early days, wanting him to be *present*. Mia hadn't needed his attention then, he'd said, when she'd been drooling and learning basic words. Resentment, though, was something he'd since learned could last well into adulthood.

"I suspect you don't believe me. I would say that you will understand one day, but I suspect you won't live that long."

Hand shaking, Edwin reached for his glass. "Suspect?"

He grinned with teeth. "Mortals can always be turned. But I doubt that will happen to you."

"Yes. As do I."

Liam lifted one elegant hand in a speaking gesture. "Your daughter on the other hand…"

"My daughter," Edwin said, firmly, "has agreed to undergo treatment. And frankly, she doesn't concern you."

"Yes, yes, of course not." A toothy smile. "Let us hope not, to be sure. In any event, we should be talking about *my* daughter."

Edwin sighed. "We're searching for her, I assure you."

724

"If she's joined up with Locksley and his crew, you won't find her."

Curiosity got the best of him. "About that. I always assumed Robin of Locksley was a myth. I never suspected that he was not only real, but an immortal and a werewolf as well."

Liam's smile was cutting. He flicked his wrist and conjured a palmful of fire. "Really? You find out there's actual magic in the world? You raise Vlad Tepes from his slumber, but you doubted Robin Hood?"

"Well…"

He laughed. "Rest assured, Doctor, I don't think anyone suspected he was still alive. We did know he existed, though. He might not be the most powerful, and certainly not the most ambitious, but Locksley is the wiliest creature to ever walk this earth." He grew pensive. "I wonder where he's been hiding all this time. And if he's still got Richard stashed somewhere."

Edwin stared at him; his face was beginning to feel heavy with exhaustion, the bones of his jaw hard to move as he spoke. This conversation had gone completely off the rails. And yet, his curiosity was still piqued. "I'm sorry, Richard who?"

Liam dropped his hands into his lap, expression alive with disbelief. "Richard the First? Tell me you've heard of the Lionheart. The Crusader King of England."

"Yes. Of course." He made a mental note to Google that later.

Liam's gaze drew inward, faraway in the past. "Truth told, I think the Western historians gazed upon him too favorably, having never met him. But he *was* resplendent. It was a personal sort of majesty, not merely the vampirism. A king in all ways. And," he added, conspiratorial, "I heard it said he was insatiable in bed. Man, woman, he didn't care so long as you were beautiful and you could keep up with his appetites. Not that I ever cared to test that theory firsthand, mind you." He chuckled.

Edwin took a deep breath and willed himself to speak calmly. "Liam. When we first sat down twenty years ago, I asked you for a list of the immortals you knew who might be able to help us in this fight." He opened the upper righthand drawer of his desk and pulled that list out now, laid it on the desk. He'd laminated it, so it was perfectly preserved. "There's not a king of England anywhere on it."

"And indeed there shouldn't be. I have no idea whether Richard is still alive. Up until your phone call a few weeks ago, I had no idea Locksley was still alive. I thought you wanted concrete information, Doctor, and not speculation."

"You know that I do—"

"Doctor." Liam sat forward, a sudden burst of movement that left Edwin shrinking back. The mage braced his hands on the edge of the desk and leaned in, his smile more a baring of teeth, his carefully smoothed hair shaking loose into untidy curls that framed his narrow face and turned its edges razor-sharp. His words came slow and precise, dripping with threat. "I admire the work you've done here. You've made great strides, for a mortal, and you have, perhaps for your own selfish reasons, given me children, when I never thought I'd be able to have any. But you are in so, so far over your head, and the water continues to rise.

"You want to save this world – humanity – and that is admirable. But you understand nothing of its history. Of the monsters that have shaped it down through the centuries. How can you hope to control a threat that you can neither understand, nor recognize? Do you think you can go around waking vampires and be thanked for it? That you can control them? Do you think for a second that *Vlad* answers to *you?*"

His voice had grown higher and louder, and he seemed to realize that now. He paused. Sat back, raked his copper hair off his face with both hands. "Forgive me, I – I have so very little patience with mortals these days."

Edwin lifted his glass and drained it. "What are you saying?"

"I'm saying that you've made a good start, all things considered. But that I won't allow you to fritter that away now, because you fail to grasp the enormity of your undertaking. I'm saying I'm taking charge of this Institute, Dr. Talbot, whether you like it or not."

<u>58</u>

VAL, MATE, MINE

During her fight with her first tumor, after her operation, Mia had taken the kind of opiate painkillers that sent her kaleidoscopic waking dreams, all awash in color and nameless pleasant sensations. That's what this reminded her of – only now that pleasure was acute and definable, and through the acid-trip glow of delight, she could see each detail with aching clarity.

Val pressed his wrist to her mouth again, and this time she could smell the blood in a way she'd never been able to before. The salt of it, yes, but she could read what it said on a cellular level, too: *vampire, male, Valerian, mine.* The knowledge bloomed in her head; she couldn't have explained it if she tried, but she *knew* these things.

His wound was red and ragged from her mouth, and from his – he kept reopening it with his fangs so the blood would flow fresh; she knew it must hurt when she opened her lips over it and sucked. It had just tasted like blood at first, salty like when she accidently bit the inside of her own mouth. But slowly, as they fed, passing blood back and forth, she could feel the beginnings of a change. It tasted now like something to crave: like wine or chocolate. Her head spun pleasantly, and she closed her eyes; held his arm with both hands, holding him to her, though he had no intention of pulling away.

"That's it, darling, take as much as you can." His voice was ragged; she could hear the desire in it; feel his want like a pulse in the humid air between them.

He knelt between her spread thighs, his free hand anchored on her hip. She had his blood in her mouth, but he wasn't close enough. *Intense,* he'd said of this process, and that had been an understatement. She needed more of him; needed everything.

She passed her tongue over the pulpy wound on his wrist and rested a moment, panting against his skin. "Val." A shameless plea. She was past the point of dignity – as was he.

727

"I know, I know." Breathless, his pupils tall, narrow, catlike slits as he stared down at her, free hand moving restless down her stomach and between her thighs, where she was tender, almost-bruised, but slick with need and aching for him again. "Drink," he said, and pulled her up into his lap, her legs falling over his hips, sharp bones pressing into the bruises he'd already left there. He slid into her with a low, rippling moan that turned into a growl at the end, head tipping back, eyes shut.

She took his wrist again, drawing his blood into her mouth. *Val, mate, mine, mine, mine.*

~*~

She didn't smell sick anymore. She smelled like blood, and sex, and him, his claiming of her, like a woman mated. But the sour tang of the tumor was gone. And in its place the scent of vampire, blooming slow like spring's first flowers beneath her skin.

Not just any vampire, but one born of his blood. His turning. His...everything.

"Mia...Mia..."

He was sitting up against the headboard, and had her in his lap. Thighs split over his hips, her wet heat gripping him so tight. She rested her hands on his shoulders, thighs flexing as she lifted in little increments and then seated herself again, working him over until it was all he could do to form words. He was getting close, but he didn't want to come yet; he was sore, and exhausted, and blood-drunk, but he wanted this to last.

And every bit of urgency that bled through his fingers where he touched her she gave back twofold. The turning was upon her, and it had left her ravenous.

She leaned in to kiss him, her hair tangling with his, so it was a curtain against the outside world. The change in angle did delightful things to the sex, and they both breathed punched-out sounds in response. He growled – and so did she, now; he could hear the feline harmonics undercutting her voice now.

It was a sloppy kiss, mostly just breathing against one another. "Do you," she started, "do you – again…?" And she tried to tip her head to the side.

His own voice was a brittle shell of its normal sound. "Once more. I think." The marks he'd opened into her throat thus far had half-healed, but the skin there was pink and tender. Carefully, gently, he tucked his face in and bit her again. She came when his fangs pierced her, walls squeezing tight around him. He found his own finish as he drank, a few last swallows to complete the circuit.

Stars burst behind his eyes, and Mia slumped down, her head on his shoulder.

When he finally gathered the strength to reach with one shaking hand and push her hair back, he saw that she'd swooned; dead asleep.

Her pulse thumped strong, though, regular and healthy. The scent of the cancer was completely gone.

Now, she only smelled like *his*.

Val bundled her close, tipped his head back, and let sleep claim him as well.

~*~

Fulk's weapons cache and several outfits a piece were all the belongings they'd brought with them to Virginia. Once both of them were back on their feet and no longer floating on the opiate-like tide of post-binding torpor, they began preparations for leaving. In what Anna hoped was a subtle way.

Fulk locked up his weapons chest and took it down a back servants' staircase. He was gone a long time, long enough that she had long since packed all their personal effects in one big duffel and was pacing back and forth across the rug by the time he returned.

She jumped when she slipped back into the room. "How did it go? Was anyone suspicious? Did they stop you? What did the guards say?"

He'd looked concentrated and battle-ready when he entered the room, but a smile slipped through now, as he gathered her into a hug and kissed the top of her head. "Yes, there were some guards, and I do think they were suspicious. But. I played it off well. I think. I hope." Doubt touched his voice. "In any event, the car is packed."

She nodded. Having it ready and running was his job, while she would see to their charges.

Not charges. Masters.

"Jeez." She let out a shaky breath. "You think they'll be ready in time?"

Val wasn't in her head per se – wasn't controlling her. But she knew that he could, if he wanted to. She felt his presence as the slightest weight in the back of her mind; it felt unnervingly like a collar. They were far enough from the room he currently occupied with Mia that she couldn't hear everything, but she caught vibrations through the floorboards, and the scents of sex, and blood, and aroused vampires were strong. She would have noticed these things anyway, but now, bound to him, she felt something almost like…obligation. Maybe gladness that he was enjoying himself.

And she *was* glad. She liked Val, and God knew he deserved a bit of fun after all his centuries locked away…

Fulk rubbed her back in long up-and-down sweeps. "You're thinking very loudly."

"It feels weird," she confessed against the stretch of collarbone his old faded t-shirt couldn't hope to cover.

He murmured a soothing noise. "I know. You'll get used to it."

She tipped her head back so she could look at him, chin resting in the hollow of his throat. His face was calm. "I thought you'd be…angstier about this," she admitted, and he cocked a single brow. "You didn't want this," she said, softly, guilt welling up in her chest. "You – you've worked really hard to keep us unattached for a long time." Her eyes burned. "Shit, baby, I'm sorry–"

He laid a finger against her lips. She hated to think it, knowing his thoughts on the matter, but he'd been almost serene since the binding. He was the sort of man who tried to carry the world, and struggled beneath the weight every moment of the day. Having that weight removed – passing it onto the shoulders of someone else – had smoothed the divot of stress from between his brows. "Darling," he said, achingly sweet. "All I've ever wanted, from the moment I met you, was to call you mine and keep you safe."

"The *very* moment? 'Cause I spit on you that day. More than once."

He chuckled. "And tried to stab me with my own knife, if I remember correctly."

They smiled at one another a moment, remembering. So much about those early days had been awful. The war, the duke, Liam…hell, dying. Or almost. She knew he still berated himself for turning her. But she didn't regret that, not ever. Sometimes a person had to go through hell to find the one thing she wanted to hold onto most. He was that for her. Everything else could be dealt with.

"We should try to sleep," he said. "It'll be a few hours more."

"Sleep. Right. That would be smart." She smoothed her hands up his chest. "Or we could–" The rest of her suggestion cut off into a startled laugh as he picked her up by the thighs and hoisted her onto the bed.

<u>59</u>

WHAT I THINK OF MAGIC

Vlad had always found exercise soothing. Grounding. It was so easy for the knowledge of what he needed to do to become a din of competing voices in his head. His mind was sharp – he knew this without boasting. It was simple fact. But that didn't mean he never wanted to run from conscious thought. He was a prince, and princes couldn't run; but he could work his body until exhaustion lulled him into a peaceful trance. Exercise had a way of whittling away all the noise until his decisions became clean, precise things shining through the cacophony; undeniable, unbendable.

He especially enjoyed sparring with an opponent.

Undead or not, so far, Kolya Dyomin made for a better partner than Fulk le Strange.

He was unaccustomed to fighting with swords, so they dueled with knives, up close and in each other's orbits.

Vlad ducked a wicked slice, intending to reach inside the man's defenses – only to have his hand batted away. He jumped back and felt the passing breeze of a knife swiping past his ribs, a hairsbreadth shy of making contact.

Vlad felt a smile break across his face. "You're fast." He struck again.

Kolya grunted, and bent backward at the waist, catching himself on the knuckles of one hand; Vlad's swipe went over him. And before Vlad could reroute, Kolya had executed a tidy tuck and roll, and sprang back to his feet three yards away, knives at the ready again.

"Again?" Vlad asked.

Kolya twirled one knife, idly, walking it down his knuckles. His fingers were the only parts of his body that moved. "Do we have time?"

"No." Vlad straightened with reluctance and slipped his own knives into the sheaths strapped to his thighs. Kolya's went to the small of his back. "We should make ready."

The revenant nodded.

The thing was, though, they were *already* ready. And if he wasn't sparring, or walking through sword exercises, he became unnervingly aware that there was a new, female vampire a few rooms away. One that he'd turned.

His nose was still full of the smell of her.

That man – Treadwell – was probably still sitting with her, waiting for her to wake.

Arousal had never been a distracting state of being for Vlad. In his own time, if it became pressing, he found someone to lie with, and had done with it. He hadn't felt the need since waking; there was a war coming, and none of his "allies" were prepared for it.

But now.

He took a deep breath in through his nostrils and let it out slow, going to the table where the rest of his weapons lay, freshly whetted and ready. He hefted his sword and turned it, light flaring down the blade in a bright wink.

"You're distracted," Kolya said, coming up beside him, a guileless observation.

Vlad sent him a sharp look – but found nothing there but blank question. An emotion almost like curiosity – but not quite.

"No," he said, firm. "I'm ready. Do you remember what you're supposed to do?"

"Escort your brother, his mate, and the wolves," Kolya said back, rote. "Protect them. Go with them." He blinked, and the first sign of life glimmered in his eyes. "Find my friends."

"You're to go with them. They'll decide if you can find your friends."

"Right."

"Though I suspect they will." Vlad looked back to his sword, turning its pommel in his hands. "Val has nothing."

But that wasn't true now. He had his new mate, and his new wolves, and a Russian werewolf in New York that he called his friend.

And he had Vlad, too, if hateful brothers were anything worth having.

~*~

Mia came awake with a start. Waking was a slow, labored affair these days, always accompanied by a terrible headache. It took a good face scrubbing and at least half a cup of coffee before she felt human. But not so this time. Her eyes snapped open, clear and focused, and she jackknifed upright, breath catching in sudden fright.

She registered the bed, its rumpled sheets, illuminated by the soft glow of the lamp on the table. Her sudden fright gave way to a sense of warmth, and safety, a sense of having something important very close by.

And then the *smells* assaulted her. All of them, stronger than she'd ever imagined, all of them tagged with dozens of individual markers, layered over one another in an impossible array. She could taste them; swore she could hear them.

She couldn't help it; she choked on nothing. Clapped both hands over her mouth.

The sheets rustled beside her, and then two warm arms wrapped around her; one across her shoulders, the other around her waist. She was naked, she realized, and so was he, skin-on-skin.

His breath stirred her hair; his scent – *Val, mate, mine* – overwhelmed all the others, and the urge to retch subsided.

"It's a lot to take in, I know," he murmured; the movement of his lips against her scalp was soothing. Everything about being pressed against him was. He huffed a laugh. "Well. I assume it's a lot. It's always been like this for me. But I've heard the turning is fairly magnificent."

"Fairly magnificent," she echoed with a shaky chuckle. "That's one way of putting it."

He rubbed her arm and her ribs, gentle, undemanding touches. "How do you feel?"

She let her hands fall to her lap – ended up curling them around his forearm, holding him to her midsection – and forced herself to take a deep, measured breath. She felt...pain-free. Energized. Only now that it was gone did she realize how debilitating her low-level headache and nausea had been. She'd been living with a fuzzy sort of disconnect, her eyesight blurry, her temples always throbbing.

"I feel...*fantastic.*"

She turned her head, faster than anticipated, and found his face right up against hers, his eyes blue, and deep, and glued to her like she was something special. "Val." She touched his cheek and he leaned into it. "I don't feel sick."

He beamed at her. "That's because you're not."

She leaned in to steal a kiss, and it was the sweetest thing she'd ever tasted.

~*~

"I'll go check with Vlad one last time," Fulk said, half-out the door already. "And make sure Kolya's ready."

"'Kay," Anna said, distracted, as she tugged on her boots. "I'll get the newlyweds."

"Anna."

She paused, and lifted her head.

"Be careful."

She sent him a quick grin. "You, too."

He slipped out.

It was late, the wee hours, really, and the house was quiet...but it never really slept. Someone was always moving around: rustling up a midnight snack; going to or from the bedrooms; flinging off the covers to run down for one last test. Scientists kept strange hours.

Fulk walked on silent feet down the long hallway, booted footfalls muted by the rug. He heard the house murmuring around him, its low, constant rhythm, but he didn't detect anyone until he was halfway down the grand staircase. And by that point, when the stink of a campfire filled his senses, it was too late. He paused a moment, hand on the bannister, cursing internally.

Liam called, "I already saw you. You might as well come on down."

"Fuck," he muttered. This was exactly why they'd split up, but he'd thought he might get farther than the foyer.

Fulk clomped down the remainder of the stairs, just to be petulant, however childish that was, and came to stand in front of his old nemesis on the black-and-white tile.

The shadows beneath his eyes marked Liam's fatigue, but he was otherwise as put-together as ever, today's long coat green velvet, his khakis tight enough to be breeches, and tucked into riding boots no less.

Fulk said, "You look ridiculous."

His brows lifted. "And you look like you're about to go on tour with Guns N' Roses, so I'd say we're even, old chap."

Fulk hated his guts.

Liam tilted his head, the motion as bird-like as ever. He'd always reminded Fulk a bit of a stork in that respect. "I would have thought you'd be all curled up with your little girl in a puppy pile by now. I'm surprised to see you up."

Fulk's fingers twitched, wanting to curl into fists, and he forced them to relax. Being around Liam left him feeling his least human: a moment from shifting, fangs long and prominent in his mouth. He swore he felt his ears growing pointed, that he had an actual ruff down the back of his neck that bristled. "She's my wife. And a baroness." *And your sister-in-law* he didn't say.

"I suppose you expect me to show a little respect."

Fulk said nothing.

"Tell me, Baron Strange, why *are* you out of bed?"

"Why are you?"

A smile cut across Liam's face, sudden and cold. "You're going to make him a terrible Familiar."

Oh. So that's what this was about. Well, Fulk could stall. "Who?"

"Don't play dumb. Even if you are. You and I both know why we're here."

"This is my house," Fulk said. "That's why I'm here."

Liam really was tired, because a flicker of temper showed through his façade, his jaw tightening. "Come now, brother. You woke Vlad. You know what your purpose is here."

Brother was a hard word to swallow, but Fulk managed. "Do I?"

A humorless laugh. "Oh. Poor fool. It will be easier if you stop resisting. We're going to work together again, you and I. Familiars for the same master." He grinned with all his teeth. "Like old times."

The idea was anathema. It was certainly what Talbot and his ilk had fancied: two strong Familiars, used to the task, with a history of obedience (or something like it), ready to serve as the guiding arms of a vampire with a tyrant's reputation.

But no one, not even the smug Liam Price, had counted on Vlad. No one had known him, and no one had anticipated that he was not only vicious, but sharp, and self-sacrificing.

Fulk felt a smile threaten, and let it break slow.

Liam looked confused. "What?"

"You are...*wildly* underestimating Vlad Tepes if you think he'll fall in line with that plan."

Liam repeated, "What?" Snappish this time.

"If you'd bothered to speak with the prince." Fulk couldn't help his chiding tone; it felt magical to be the one in the know. "Then you would understand that he would never lower himself to bind me. He thinks I'm weak, and indecisive. Weak because I worry about my wife. You have a wife, too, as it turns out. What makes you think he'll want you?"

Liam's smile was brittle, ready to crack. He held onto it steadfastly, though. "Vlad is a traditionalist. He'll want to do things the old way."

"Why? Just because he was asleep for so long? Just because he'll want to bring back the old days? Liam, did Vlad ever have a mage in those old days?"

"He—" Liam faltered.

Fulk wanted a plaque made to commemorate the moment. He said, "You see, back then, Vlad had a contingent of wolves. The same wolves that had served his father, and his mother. Family wolves. Their own pack. But a mage never darkened the door of the palace at Tîrgovişte. In fact, he's said he doesn't *like* mages."

Liam swallowed, the movement of his throat visible in the low light of the wall sconces. "He's no longer fighting a border skirmish against humans. He'll see the reason in having a true triumvirate this time."

"Or so you hope, lest you'll be out of a job. What happens if he doesn't want you, Liam? Do you get sent back to your bolt hole, tail between your legs?"

Liam's laugh sounded more like a cough. "Which of the two of us has a tail, hm? Vlad will want me."

"Yes, because he'll see reason, was it? And if the history books tell us one thing, it's how *reasonable* Vlad the Impaler was."

Liam opened his mouth to respond–

And an alarm sounded.

~*~

Mia pulled the zipper up on her second boot, free hand resting on Val's shoulder for balance, and an alarm went off. It wasn't on their floor, was obviously coming from somewhere much deeper in the house. But her reaction was immediate and instinctual: she slammed her foot down and clapped both hands over her ears. She felt a vibration in her chest, and it took her a moment to realize she was *growling*.

When she opened her eyes, she saw that Val and Anna were wincing, but hadn't resorted to covering their ears like big babies. Slowly, she lowered her hands, teeth gritted against the onslaught of the alarm. Having heightened senses was going to take some getting used to, and at the moment, she wasn't sure it was a good thing.

"You good?" Anna asked. She carried a long knife, unsheathed. When she'd come in the room ten minutes ago, she'd brought Val his sword, which he wore buckled over his shoulder; the blade was so long it had to hang down his back, rather than along his hip.

Mia took a deep breath. Yes, her ears hurt from the sound, but she was strong, and not sick, and she felt a humming energy under her skin like nothing she'd ever known before.

She nodded. "I'm good. Lead the way."

~*~

Blood. She could smell it, taste it; it was in her eyes, and thick in her throat, choking her. She heard the thump of rotors – medivac. Medivac for *her*. Everything hurt. She didn't know where the pain ended and her body began. Did she have a body? She had at least part of one, because hands gripped her arms, and shoulders, and supported her head.

Voices:

"Do you see her foot?"

"Just...pieces."

A warm hand touched her face – spanned it, really, thumb on her jaw, fingers along her temple – and pushed her head to the side. Not rough, but not gentle. Not tender. A military touch. The thump of the rotors grew louder. *Whump-whump-whump*. Hot air on her neck. Breath. And then pain there, stabbing, like needles, like...

Fangs.

She opened her eyes. Ceiling above: the stone of the basement, crawling with modern wires and tubes; harsh lights droning. Too bright. She squinted, and tried to bring her hand up to shield her eyes. Something tugged: an IV. Turned her head: a hospital bed, laid flat, machines humming and beeping.

She remembered the ride. The stream. The bear. The sense of not being in control, and hating the way it made her afraid. The fall...

She jackknifed to an upright position.

"Adela! Whoa!"

She'd awakened from more than her fair share of surgeries – they'd operated, right? Her right leg was encased in white bandages – and it had always been a slow, groggy, sick affair. Having to press the buttons on the bed to sit up, swallowing with difficulty, face numb. But right now, she was alert. Her heart throbbed in her chest and temples, and her vision was crystal clear, and adrenaline coursed through her veins; she wanted to leap off the bed, go running out into the hall. Wanted to...wanted to...

Something was *wrong*.

"Adela," Jake said. He'd stood up from his chair, and stood frozen in the middle of the room, open palms held toward her in a universal *calm down* gesture. He was too loud. She could *smell* him. "It's okay. Don't panic."

"I don't panic," she snapped. And then she *growled*. The sound started in her chest, a deep vibration, and rolled up her throat; slipped out through her teeth. She gasped afterward. "What – what the fuck – what did I–"

"It's alright," he said. "Take a deep breath, please, and I'll explain everything."

A deep breath, right. Her lungs worked like machines, perfect and strong. She wanted to claw her own skin off, the itchy, awful energy buzzing under it trying to get out.

"*What did they do to me?*" Her voice was an inhuman snarl.

One of the monitors, it must have been her heartrate, started to whine.

Jake inched closer, hands still held up – the posture looked more and more protective the closer he got; like he was shielding his face. "Easy now."

"'Easy now'? I'm not a fucking horse, Treadwell. What the fuck is going on?"

Another inch. She'd seen his face like this before: carefully blank save his traitorous eyebrows, which knitted together. "Do you remember coming back here? You were unconscious at first, and you'd lost a lot of blood."

She remembered...flashes. Hands gathering her. Rocking motion of the horse. Arms around her. A low, emotionless voice.

"Vlad."

Jake grimaced. "Yeah. Yeah, he carried you back on his horse. Like something out of a goddamn book," he muttered. "Listen, Adela." Serious again. Concerned. And his scent – man, and sweat, and metal, and something acrid she couldn't place and shouldn't have been able to place – projected a sense of fear. She'd seen him scared before, like he'd been when they faced Ruby Russell in Wyoming. But she'd never *smelled* fear before. She could now, and the knowledge cranked her panic up another notch. "Your leg was really fucked up. They couldn't save it."

She looked down, wildly, at her bandaged leg. She saw her toes – her donor toes – sticking out the end. She wiggled them, and the movement didn't hurt. In fact, *nothing* hurt.

The heartrate monitor went off like a tiny alarm, and it hurt her ears. She ducked away from it, wincing. "What's *happening?*"

"They couldn't save your leg," Jake said, in a rush, "but Vlad said he could, so he bit you. He turned you, Adela. You're a vampire now."

She sucked in a breath. "What—"

The door flew open, and in poured guards in their featureless black garb. God, she was starting to hate those fucking uniforms. The one in the front held a clear riot shield, and they all wore helmets, gleaming black like beetle shells beneath the lights.

Jake gestured toward them viciously. "Get out! What the hell? You'll spook her!"

Like she wasn't there. Like she was an animal.

Well, wasn't she?

The Institute clearly thought so, if they were sending guys with batons in to handle her when her heart monitor went off. No nurses with crash carts here, just a nice ass-beating.

No one had ever accused her of being indecisive.

She ripped out her IV. Blood beaded up on the back of her hand, and before she could question the instinct, she passed her tongue across it. The blood tasted – well, she couldn't think about that, even if it set off a sequence of snaps and pops in the back of her mind. When she lowered her hand, the pinprick wound seemed like it was already closing. She reached for the bandages on her leg next.

"Hey." Jake moved around the end of the bed, placing himself between her and the guards. He made an abortive reach for her hands, pausing when she growled at him. "Hey," urgent now, "you have to calm down."

"Why, or they'll knock me out? Lock me up like the fucking basement prince?" She was...so many things. Furious was just one element of it; she chose not to name the other emotions. They glittered, their edges jagged, and trying to lay claim to them would cut her like broken glass. "Where's Vlad? I want to talk to him." And something low in her belly tugged. She *needed* to see him.

"We'll find him later," Jake soothed. "Just sit tight. Let's figure this out."

She lifted her head, and saw that there were more guards, logjammed in the door, spilling out into the hall. Jake was starting to sweat, a sheen building along his temples.

"What do you all think I'm going to do?" she asked.

He swallowed. "We…we don't know."

~*~

The alarm didn't sound anything like war drums, but the sound of it had the same effect on Vlad's body. A tightening in his stomach, a quickening in his lungs…and then an intense flood of calm. He'd been terrified when, at seventeen, he'd laid siege to his own home city, wresting it back from Vladislav. But he'd been thrilled, too; he'd been born a boy with violence inside him, and having a chance to let it loose was always a blessing. An indulgence, like sex or good wine.

He'd been sitting too long, planning, scheming – things better left to his brother. Now it was time for battle, and he was past ready.

He was seated on the floor of the training room, cross-legged, alone, his sword resting across his thighs.

When the alarm went off, he got smoothly to his feet, and strode down the hall to the main part of the lab, hand steady around the pommel of his sword.

It was chaos.

Techs running away, guards running to, and in the middle of it, hospital gown sliding off one shoulder, freshly-healed leg trailing bandages across the floor, was Sergeant Ramirez.

Adela. That was her name. He'd turned the woman; might as well think of her more intimately.

She had her arms outstretched, feet braced: a defensive stance. There was blood on her hands, and Vlad knew it wasn't hers. The guards circled, wary, and there was Treadwell, trying to talk down a situation that had been doomed from the first.

There was shouting, and the alarm blaring overhead, red lights strobing along the ceiling as if the noise itself wasn't enough of a call to arms. But Vlad saw the moment she caught his scent.

She froze, and her head swung toward him, black hair fanning across her shoulders. Her nostrils flared and she showed her teeth, and her eyes went wide.

Slowly, the tension bled out of her face, and she stared at him, open-mouthed. She could feel his blood in her veins, same as he could feel hers. Whether it ever meant anything to either of them – and he guessed it probably wouldn't, knowing himself, knowing what he did of her – a link existed between them. The unbreakable kind.

Her moment of distraction gave one of the guards the chance to catch her in the side with one of the electrically-charged stun batons Vlad had used to threaten his brother. She gasped and staggered, reaching for her ribs.

The growl that rippled up his throat was mostly for his brother, for the memory of the pain he'd caused him, but some of it was for this girl, the fledgling vampire of his own making. In that way, she was his, and he didn't take kindly to having his things mishandled.

The guard reached in with the stun baton again.

The growl became a roar. It echoed off the walls, the floor, the ceiling, the stone sending it back harsher, deeper, more threatening.

Everyone froze.

Vlad crossed the distance in two long strides, lifted his sword in a long, smooth motion, and separated the baton-wielding guard's head from his shoulders. It landed with a wet, heavy sound against the stone, and then the body followed. The baton clattered to the stones, useless.

In the stunned silence that followed, Vlad could hear Adela breathing, harsh and fast through her mouth. He could smell her pain, and fear, and confusion.

And her yearning, too. Whatever happened now, he had her.

~*~

Annabel was slammed with a wave of déjà vu when they hit the top of the servants' staircase. Her feet knew these steps; her hands knew this black, velvet-flocked wallpaper. A half-dozen mortal lifetimes ago, Fulk had herded her down these stairs, energy frantic, but hands gentle as he steadied her. She'd been an eighteen-year-old human girl then, just before her turning. The sconces had held candles rather than electric bulbs, but it was otherwise the same: scents of beeswax and savory cooking odors from downstairs.

Her heart was pounding now, same as it had then, only now she had a wolf bristling beneath her skin, ready to leap out fang-first if her human shape couldn't handle whatever trouble they encountered. And it wasn't her mate behind her, but her master, and his mate.

Val's binding sat comfortably in the back of her mind; it felt like he smoothed a hand down the back of her neck, soothing. She was glad of its comfort as they hit the floor below, and found two black-clad guards awaiting them.

Shit.

She'd thought the alarm would draw everyone within jogging distance to the basement. That was the plan anyway. She had no great affection for Ramirez, but she felt a little bad that the freshly-turned vampire had been sacrificed as a distraction.

Vlad was down there; he would handle it.

Though she wished Vlad were here now, to handle this. It had been a while since she'd gone hand-to-hand with anyone.

"Hey!" a guard said, shouting to be heard over the wail of the alarm. His gaze was trained over her shoulder, on Val. "What are you—"

His sentence choked off into a wet gurgle, and the sharp point of a knife burst through his throat, just below his Adam's apple.

Val put a hand on her shoulder, and tried to push past her, but she held her ground, growled at him. He could have shoved her aside, but he didn't. He waited, letting her take point. Letting her watch the knife withdraw. The guard fell face-first on the carpet, breath dying with wet rasps in his ruined throat, and before his partner could even turn all the way around, the bloody knife was going into the side of his neck. Arterial spray up the wallpaper, shiny-black; heavy gun clattering to the floor.

Kolya withdrew his knife and wiped it carefully on the sleeve of his jacket. He looked up at her with his blank expression, face dead, eyes riotous.

When she could, Anna let out a deep breath. "You were supposed to disarm them, Fulk said. Knock them out. Not kill them."

"Oh."

"Wait." She heard Val inhale behind her, and this time when he urged her over, she complied. He took the last step down and came to stand in front of Kolya, who drew himself upright and went very still: poised to strike. Val opened his mouth, scenting the air. He smiled. "My God. Kolya Dyomin."

Oh shit, no one had thought to tell him. "Yeah, boss," Anna said in a rush. They had to keep moving. "That's him. Liam brought him back, but he's with us now."

Val lifted his hand, as if he meant to touch, and Kolya flinched. Val retreated. "It's true, then. He really is a necromancer."

"Yep, really true, come on, we gotta go."

Val laughed. "Oh, this is *perfect.*" He turned to Anna, grin wide and sharp. "When we show up in New York, we'll have quite the gift for our hosts."

She sighed...but felt herself smiling. His simple delight was infectious. "That's if we get out of here first. Come on. Kolya, try not to kill anyone else."

As Anna headed for the next set of stairs, she cast a glance back over her shoulder and saw that Mia held a hand over her mouth, face pale with shock. Poor thing, but she'd adjust soon enough. Shock was a luxury for those who'd lived dull lives. And after tonight, Mia Talbot's life would be anything but dull.

~*~

So. That was a head. On the floor. Fulk had seen many decapitated corpses in his many years on this earth, but he hadn't quite expected to see one here in the midst of this modern laboratory.

Vlad stood over a slumped Ramirez, sword bloody, shoulders thrown back in the sort of pose that rallied bone-weary troops on the battlefield. His clothes might have been contemporary, but there was nothing modern about this man. This prince. This son of old Rome.

"Jesus," Liam murmured beside him.

Fulk said, "I thought you didn't believe in him." He caught the arm of a tech who was attempting to belly-crawl his way toward the elevator. "Turn off that alarm." He let the man go, and a moment later, the alarm cut off abruptly.

The silence hummed. Several people were crying quietly; Fulk could hear their choked-off sobs.

Ramirez breathed in rough shudders, her ribs shaking under the thin gown she wore. She leaned sideways, and pressed her shoulder into Vlad's thigh. She'd chosen to align herself with him, then.

Good, Fulk thought. That would make this easier.

Sound of a throat clearing, obscene in the quiet. It was Talbot, stepping boldly forward, exposing himself to the slow, animal stare of Vlad...and to the reach of the bloodied sword.

Talbot took a quick, unsteady breath. "Vlad. Your grace. Please. I promise that no one meant Sergeant Ramirez any harm. I know this looks—"

"It looks like your people were going to beat her into unconsciousness," Vlad said, toneless. "This morning she was one of your trusted guards, and now you want to lock her up. Is it just because of what she is now? Or is it because I'm the one who turned her?"

Fulk smelled the sharp tang of fear sweat.

"I assure you," Talbot said, "that this is only a temporary measure. We don't want Sergeant Ramirez to hurt herself or anyone else. She's in shock. She's confused, and she's panicked. All perfectly reasonable reactions! But we have to contain her until she calms down. I'm sure you understand."

"*Contain.*" Vlad pronounced the word as if it offended him. "That's how you see vampires, isn't it, Doctor? Things to be contained. First my brother, and now her. Are you containing me as well?"

"N-n-no!"

"My Lord Dracula," Liam said, smoothly, stepping forward. Fulk knew, with that voice, that he was trying to compel the prince. "Be at ease." He walked straight toward him, without hesitation, confident in his power...

But he shouldn't have been. Vlad's eyes were hard and bright, and his gaze was completely his own.

For a moment, Fulk almost felt sorry for his mortal enemy.

The stupid mage kept talking, and kept walking. "Everyone here is–" He choked off, the very tip of Vlad's sword coming to rest in the center of his throat.

Vlad said, "Did I give you leave to speak to me, witch?"

Liam swallowed, and the skin of his throat moved against the sword-tip. A drop of fresh blood welled. "I mean no disrespect, your grace."

"Then hold your tongue."

Liam did...for a moment. His mouth formed the semblance of a smile. He said, "They're true, then: the tales of your viciousness."

Fulk had never been more grateful to be bound to a vampire than in that moment, because Liam's magic compulsion pushed through the room like a wave. The humans all went slack-jawed. Ramirez sat on the floor, drooping against Vlad's leg, her loose-curled arm around his calf all that held her upright.

But Vlad's gaze sharpened. His voice came out calm, conversational. "Did you ever hear the story of the mage Mehmet sent to treat with me? The one who tried to force my surrender?"

For the first time in a long time, panic flitted across Liam's face.

"I impaled him on a pike of ash," Vlad said, "and I planted him in the forest, so that brother-raper could get a good look at what I think of magic."

This was it, Fulk realized. This was the moment Liam finally met his end. He'd always thought, should he be fortunate enough to witness the occasion, it would bring him joy. But he felt only dread now, boiling like sickness in his belly.

Vlad drew his sword back.

Liam set himself aflame.

Vlad reached *through* the fire with his free hand, and gripped Liam by the face.

Liam screamed, and the fire went out, and Vlad dragged him in close as a lover, chest-to-chest. He ducked his head and bit the mage's throat. His arm was badly burned, Fulk saw, but the prince paid it no heed.

The humans snapped out of their stupor. Some shouted, others cowered.

Fulk didn't wait around to watch the rest of the binding. It was nothing like his own, kneeling quietly on the floor while Val petted his hair and called him *sweetheart*. Val was the gentle brother, in his own way – as gentle as a vampire could be – and Vlad had given Fulk and Anna to him. Vlad might be vicious, but he could be kind, too.

Fulk turned and fled, sprinting for the garage, and his Anna, and freedom.

~*~

"Hello, boys. Mind letting me through?"

Someone had shut off the alarm – a bad sign – and two more guards awaited them at the entrance to the tunnel. They'd scented them from around the corner, and Anna had said, "I'll get them." Her knife was stashed away in her boot, and to all appearances, she was just an unarmed, petite girl with a baby face. She wondered how much these two goons knew about werewolves.

Enough to be nervous, apparently. They made a good show of drawing themselves up, rifles held across their chests – *rifles*. No longer just handguns, but full assault gear. Their faces set at stern angles, looking down at her over the bulk of weapons and tactical vests, she could nevertheless scent fear on them.

A scared human was a more aggressive human, usually. But also a human who made mistakes.

"What for?" one of them asked.

"No one's allowed through the tunnel after hours," the other said. "You know that."

"Well, I *do*..." she drawled. She aimed for cute, hip cocked, big smile plastered on. She'd never been good at charming anyone, though; she firmly believed the only reason Fulk had ever taken a shine to her was because he thought her hissing-cat routine had been endearing somehow. "But. I figure that's just so none of the scientist guys can go running outta here with a buncha vampire blood and research notes, right?"

They went goggled-eyed. If the guards had been told about the existence of immortals, none of them seemed quite ready to believe it yet.

After a moment, the first one cleared his throat. "I'm afraid our orders stand. We can't let you through."

She sighed. "That's a real shame, boys." And she launched herself at them.

They reached for their guns, but she was already within their defenses. She grabbed one by the wrists, gripping tight, tighter than any mortal girl could have, and kicked off from the floor, twisting, catching his friend in the jaw with the heel of her boot. He fell back against the wall with a grunt. She swung around behind the other, and karate-chopped him in the back of the neck. He flinched, dropped down to his knees, and that gave her the chance to whip the knife from her boot and bring the hilt of it slamming against his temple. Hard. He fell, unconscious. And as his friend scrambled, she took him out the same way.

She straightened, and saw the others crowded together in the hallway. Mia looked numb. Kolya looked...the way that he always did. And Val had a hand on the pommel of his sword.

"We could have helped," he lamented.

"That's not your job. Come on."

He hesitated, looking down at the fallen guards. "Couldn't we just..."

"No." Anna turned and started down the tunnel at a jog; thankfully, she heard the others following.

The tunnel itself had existed in the duke's time, though then it had been a narrow, dark passage hewn into the earth and lined with stone, big enough for two to pass through it with shoulders overlapping and heads ducked beneath the low ceiling. Once the Institute moved in, modern equipment had been used to expand it. Now three could walk abreast, with room on both sides, and the ceiling was a standard eight feet, laced with wires and cables that ran electricity to the caged lights set at intervals. It ran under the conservatory and sloped slowly down, and eventually emptied out into an underground parking garage where a bevy of unmarked SUVs, sedans, and Humvees crouched on cold concrete.

"You don't actually think they'll let us drive out of here, do you?" Val asked from behind her.

"That's the plan," she tossed back over her shoulder. "Have faith."

"Yes, well…you'll forgive me if I have my doubts."

Anna huffed to herself and lengthened her stride. It felt good to run, even if now it was for the wrong reason. Her wolf, already straining to be let loose, wanted desperately to drop to all fours and *really* run. To streak through trees, and leap creeks, and meet the wind with open mouth and joyful, lolling tongue. If they got out of here – *when* they got out of here – she and Fulk were long overdue for a shift. Maybe even a hunt…

All such fantasies jolted to a halt when they entered the cavernous garage and were met by a lone figure. A red-haired woman in a green dress, arms down at her sides, still as stone. The smell of ash rushed to greet Anna; she'd always wondered if her sister had smelled like that from birth, and if it was only her turning that had allowed her to scent it. Humans claimed they couldn't sense it.

All her bubbling energy drained away. Her fledgling hope. "L-lily?" She'd expected more guards, a few more heads to bash. Maybe, if Fulk hadn't shown up yet, she'd even let Val have a drink from one of them. But for some naïve reason, she hadn't thought the final obstacle would be her own sister.

She should have. But she was stupid, and always would be when it came to her own flesh and blood.

Lily stared, calm and cool, her face like porcelain. "I'm sorry," she said, without even a hint of emotion. "I can't let you leave."

Anna took a deep breath, and then another, even though the smoke-smell was enough to choke her. Lily wasn't burning fire...yet...but her power surged within her, just below the surface. She could burn them all to a crisp at any moment – and the scary thing was, Anna thought she might, without hesitation.

"I–" This time, when Val put a hand on her shoulder, he pushed on their bond. *Stand aside.* Forceful this time, but not unkind. And Anna obeyed.

Val, to his credit, didn't place himself in front of her, but beside her. He was still thin, still weaker than he ought to have been. But in the moment he stood tall, relaxed, pleasant half-smile gracing his angular face. Even in jeans and a motorcycle jacket, he looked very much like a prince, golden hair cascading over his shoulders, and it had nothing to do with the sword across his back; it was just him, his bearing. His noble lineage.

He had a prince's grace with language, too. "Lily, is it?" He sketched a quick but correct half-bow. "Please take it as a compliment when I say that your daughter favors you greatly."

Mention of Red sent a flicker of emotion across Lily's face, there and gone again.

"I've had the pleasure of meeting her," Val said. "She even, in the short time she was here, tried to help me escape." His regretful frown was one born of long practice; a calculated expression that nevertheless looked genuine. "Obviously, we weren't successful."

A tremor moved through Lily, a tiny earthquake. She clenched her hands into fists. "You have to stay here." But her voice was threaded with cracks this time, unsure.

"I know that's what you've been told," Val soothed. "But the plan has changed."

"Whose plan?"

"My brother's."

If it was possible, she paled further.

"I know," Val continued, "that Dr. Talbot, and maybe even your husband, had grand ideas about arming Vlad with a wolf and a mage, and using him as a weapon. I confess I don't know what they want with me – perhaps just to keep me locked up for the safety of the world. But Vlad is in charge now. He's the one who will find Romulus and kill him. It's his wish that we be allowed to leave." He gestured to the rest of them with a slow sweep of his arm.

She stood her ground.

"Lily," Anna tried again. "You can do whatever you want. But, please...you don't need us. Fulk and I are bound to Val now."

Lily's eyes widened.

"Let us go." Inwardly, she wanted to scream. *Is this the way you want us to reconnect as sisters? With me as your prisoner?*

The sound of running feet echoed from down the tunnel behind them, and a moment later Fulk burst into the garage. Unharmed, thank God. Without missing a step, he said, "Lily, Vlad's just bound your husband, and probably drained half his blood. He'll need you." And he grabbed Anna's arm and towed her along with him.

Anna went with him. She didn't turn around to see what Lily did, but none of them were set on fire, so she figured they were being allowed to escape.

~*~

Vlad left him alive. Mostly. He was immortal; he would heal. When the mage swooned from blood loss, Vlad nipped his own wrist and pressed it to the man's slack lips. The blood filled his mouth and overflowed, running down his chin, pouring over his fancy clothes. But, finally, he swallowed a few times. Vlad pushed with his will, and the binding was done, whether Price wanted it or not.

He released the mage, and he crumpled to the floor, eyes shut and face pale beneath a faint mottling of newly-forming bruises. He felt sure he'd broken a bone or two, perhaps even his jaw. But yes, he would heal.

Vlad wiped his mouth with the back of his burned hand. The blood stung the wounds, badly; he would heal also. It was of no consequence. Pain was something he'd learned to tolerate long ago.

He lifted his head, and surveyed the humans standing around him – those that hadn't cowered beneath tables and covered their heads. Dr. Talbot, always so nervous, had finally been shocked into complete blankness of face. His expression gave away nothing, eyes glazed behind the lenses of his glasses.

It was to him that Vlad spoke, while Adela clutched at his leg, and Liam Price lay unconscious on the floor at his feet. "This moment marks a turning point, Dr. Talbot. Every one of your plans has crumbled, because you are a scientist, and not a leader. You woke me so I would fight, and I will…but I will do so on my terms.

"As of this moment, this house, and your entire Institute, are under my command. Your troops will obey orders. *You* will obey my orders. Is that understood?"

Talbot looked at him with something like hopelessness. His voice was a small, broken thing. "Yes, your grace."

"We are at war," Vlad said, "and if you think I'm cruel, then you should meet my uncle. Stopping him is the thing I care about; anyone who chooses to stand in my way rather than at my side can expect a similar fate." He reached to nudge the decapitated guard's body with the point of his sword.

"I – I understand, your grace."

Another alarm sounded, this one softer, a gentle chiming. All the computer and TV monitors in the vast lab switched to the same view: black and white footage of vehicle taillights.

"The perimeter alarm," one of the guards said, voice wavering. "Someone's leaving the garage, sir."

Vlad recognized the car: he'd seen it in the vast underground parking structure when he'd been given his initial tour of the compound; long, and black, and chrome, and described as "an old thing" by Fulk le Strange. His car, one he'd had since "it rolled off the line in Detroit." Whatever that meant.

"That would be my brother," Vlad said. There was a sudden scramble, a reflexive reach for guns, for radios. "You will not interfere," Vlad said, deep voice echoing off the walls. Everyone froze again. "My brother has been held as a prisoner his entire life, and that ends today. He's not the warrior – I am. You don't need him. Surely if there was anything useful to be discovered about his magic, you would have already done so. So yes, he's leaving, and you're to allow it."

753

He turned to Talbot again. "Valerian has saved your daughter's life." His mouth fell open. "And she's chosen to leave with him. As have the wolves: the baron and baroness are bound to Val now, a bond that persists until death."

"He – he–" The doctor gulped. "What did he…?"

"He turned her. As I said: he saved her life."

Talbot groaned and clutched at his belly, as if in pain. He sank backward into a chair, head hanging low. "God…oh my God…"

"Major Treadwell," Vlad said, and turned to find the man standing upright, though shaking. He stiffened when Vlad's gaze fell on him, but he didn't shrink away.

"Yes, sir?"

"See that Sergeant Ramirez gets safely to her room. You will do this alone, without any of the guards."

"Yes, sir."

"And then you will report back to me so that we may discuss strategy. If I'm going to plan a war, I will need the assistance of a modern military man, and not these doctors."

"Yes…sir."

On the screen, the car left the garage.

Vlad wiped his sword clean on the dead man's sleeve and thought, *finally*.

He would finally have his revenge for the evils his uncle had inflicted upon the world.

And, God willing, Val would never have to see any of them ever again.

~*~

Mia couldn't catch her breath.

The Cadillac went around the fountain with a spray of gravel, fish-tailing, and then roared up the drive, through the massive iron gates. No one tried to stop them. No one shot at them. Trees enfolded them, and the round yellow headlights, so delightfully old fashioned, carved a path through an alley of close-set tree trunks.

In the back seat, she leaned forward and put her head between her knees, struggling to get her lungs to work right.

Val cupped his hand around the back of her neck. "Darling." Laced with worry.

"I'm okay," she panted. "I'm okay, I just…" It was hitting her all at once. "I can't believe we just…*did that.*"

His squeezed once, gently, comforting. But he didn't give her any false platitudes or try to tell her how to think about it.

It would be…a while, she knew…before she could wrap her mind all the way around the entire chain of events.

She'd drunk blood tonight.

Become a vampire tonight.

Watched two men get killed tonight.

She cut a glance across Val's lap – he was sitting in the center of the wide backseat – to the silent man with the long dark hair on the far side. She'd watched him drive a knife through two throats, and here he sat, totally unbothered, staring at the back of Annabel's head.

She was still figuring out this whole incredible sense of smell thing, but he smelled…different. Like an attic trunk full of old books; a picnic tablecloth left out in the rain.

Val caught her gaze, the dark of the car more like twilight to her new eyes, and lifted his brows in silent question.

"I've never watched anyone…get killed before," she admitted.

His expression smoothed, warm with sympathy. He slipped his arm across her shoulders. "I see. It's an unpleasant thing, but sometimes necessary, I'm afraid."

She tried to smile. "Please don't tell me that I'll get used to it."

His smile went strained. "Alright. I won't tell you."

He pulled her in close, so they were pressed together, hip-to-hip, thigh-to-thigh, her head resting on his shoulder. "Take all the time you need, love," he murmured against her hair. "I know this is an incredible amount of change to take in."

It was. It was more change than most people ever saw in an entire lifetime, a thought that settled like dread in the pit of her stomach as Fulk drove them away from the unreal English manor house in the woods, and toward a more familiar civilization.

The drive snaked for several miles through the trees: ruts, and dips, and dark hollows like bowls brimming with moonlight…and shadows studded with blue-reflective animal eyes. Did Fulk and Anna's eyes look like that in the glow of headlights? Did her own?

The driveway terminated, unremarkably, at its juncture with a snaky, two-lane street that needed its lines repainted. There was no grand gate, no mailbox; just two of those circular reflective disks on long handles sunk in the ground. Passersby would have never suspected what lay at the other end of the rutted gravel turn-off.

When the front tires hit pavement, Fulk stomped the gas, and the big Caddy slung gravel, fish-tailing out onto the road. The engine roared, old but strong, well-loved. That was the only sound that filled the interior of the car for several long moments, automatic gears shifting as Fulk steered them through the turns, laying hard on the gas at every straightaway. That, and the breathing patterns and heartbeats she could hear.

Val kept his arm around her, but he twisted his head to look out the back window. Searching for pursuers. But none appeared.

Finally, Anna leaned over and switched on the radio. The station was staticky, but Mia could make out Led Zeppelin. "Black Dog."

Val's hand rubbed up and down her shoulder. "It will be alright. You'll see, darling." But his heart was beating fastest of all.

60

SAFE

Val had seen things in his years of captivity. His out-of-body wandering. In so many ways, he was well-versed in the modern world. So it was no great wonder to him when, after an hour of driving, at an Interstate exit on the other side of Richmond, Fulk pulled into the parking lot of a hotel. A La Quinta. Val had seen that name on tall, glowing signs before. He'd seen buildings like these: a five-story concrete box with lots of windows, a huge parking lot, glass-walled lobby and fenced-in swimming pool. A place for weary travelers, not too different from the inns of old.

But he'd never stood at the edge of a pool just before sunrise, staring down into the glowing blue waters, lit from below, bare toes wiggling against the cold, gritty concrete. He felt the breeze on his face; cool, scented with the season's first turning leaves. He hadn't smelled the seasons in *so long*. He was aware of the dim rumblings of activity in the hotel behind him: the kitchen staff preparing breakfast; businessmen up early for their day's meetings; families loading suitcases and kids and coolers into their overstuffed vans.

He smelled things he'd only ever been able to imagine: frying food, car exhaust, the chemicals they put in the pool to keep it sanitized.

He smelled his Mia; heard her walk up to him; felt the air stir as she looped her arm through his and leaned against his shoulder, joining him in his staring contest with the water.

"It's a swimming pool," she said.

"I know. It's lovely."

He felt her smile, the sweet shape of it pressing through his shirt and into his skin. "Do you want to go for a swim?"

"I'm an excellent swimmer, actually. Father had the wolves throw us into the moat as soon as we could walk. The water was freezing; it proved an excellent motivator."

She hummed a sad little sound. "That's not what I asked, though."

757

"I was under the impression that humans have to wear some sort of special bathing costume."

She chuckled. "Bathing suits, yeah. The concierge said there was a Target just up the road. We could get some. Water's probably cold, though." She shivered. "Fall's here, finally."

"You sound excited about that."

"I love fall. No more sweating through my clothes when I ride. And it's a lot easier on the horses…" She trailed off, and when he glanced down, she had her lower lip caught between her teeth, face touched with sadness. "But I guess I won't be doing that anymore, huh?" Her voice grew fainter with every word, only a breath at the end.

"Mia." Her hand tightened around the meat of his arm. "Mia, look at me."

When she did, her eyes were wet. She blinked furiously, and no tears fell, but she looked ashamed.

He reached to cradle her face, ran his thumb over the delicate skin below her eye. "I'm sorry."

"For what? You saved my life."

"But what about your Brando? Your life training?"

She turned away from him, and his hand slid down to cup her throat, the rapid pulse beating there. "I'll call Donna," she said in a strained voice. "I'm sure she'll…" She broke off, jaw clenched. After a moment: "I need to call my mom, too. She's been really worried. Maybe I won't tell her about the whole vampire thing…" She gave a weak, watery chuckle, and the tears finally slipped free, crystal droplets down her cheek, bright in the glow of the pool lights.

"Oh, sweetheart." He put both arms around her and pulled her into his chest. She trembled, and she stared down at the water, but she melted into him, head tucked in under his chin. Maybe he'd ruined her life, but he had her trust. A dark thought, one he dashed. No, he wouldn't think those things. This woman – his mate – was the one who'd seen him, believed in him, fought for him in all the quiet, determined ways that no one else ever had.

His mother would have loved her.

"I'm going to make you a promise," he said, and she started to protest. "And I'm going to keep it. I swear to you." He kissed the top of her head, and she went still. "Though I am immortal, I was born in a violent age. More violent than this age, if you can believe it," he tried to joke. "Living forever wasn't something we took for granted. It was easy to think that tomorrow might not come; to not want to put off the things we most wanted to do. It's equally easy, sometimes, to stare into the yawning maw of endless time and feel defeated by the inevitable boredom.

"So I promise you this: We will go home to your farm, and your Brando, and your training. Now that you're strong, and healthy. We'll ride horses together with the mountains in the background. Perhaps Donna won't be so frightened of me if her hand doesn't pass right through me."

Another weak laugh from her, but this one truer. "Perhaps." She heaved a deep sigh, ribs expanding beneath his arms. But when she spoke next, her voice was steadier. "I appreciate you saying that. It's what I want. But I know we can't do that right now."

"Oh?"

She tipped her head back, twisted, propped her chin on his collarbone. "I don't know if you noticed this, but we're fugitives."

"Not in the technical sense."

She gave him a small smile. "True. The cops aren't after us. Just some people *a lot* scarier."

"Vlad will see to that." And he was surprised to find that he felt confident about it. He and Vlad had seemed like enemies once…but that was in the past. And, after walking into his brother's memories, he knew it hadn't been true. "The second we left, he took that place in hand. They'll be following his agenda now, and he'll be turning his eyes to the east. Toward Romulus."

"Still. I don't want to take our baggage to Donna's doorstep just yet. I don't want to take…" She flushed and her gaze dropped; she pressed her face into his chest.

"Me?" he guessed.

"*Me.* I'm…different."

He ran his fingers through her hair. "How are you different, love?"

She made a disbelieving sound. "I'm a *vampire*, for one."

"So?"

She lifted her brows.

"You have different nutritional needs. And you're faster, and stronger. And you won't age. But you're still *you*, Mia. Nothing can change that."

She glanced at him again, a sharp, measuring gaze.

"We are animals, just like everyone else. We aren't the depraved creatures of novels and movies. Well." He rolled his eyes. "Some are. But so are some humans."

She stared at him.

"Darling, I would never have turned you if I thought I was dooming you to an eternity as a bloodthirsty monster."

She swallowed. "I know," she said, with quiet wonder.

His throat ached, suddenly. "I want you to have the life you deserve."

"I want the same for you."

His eyes started to burn, too. His sinuses swelled up. Nearly six-hundred years without crying, and he wanted to do it all the time now, from his brother's embrace to his mate's. He didn't know what to do with so much love at once; it was incomprehensible.

They both started laughing together, sniffling and dabbing at their eyes.

He hugged her close again. "We have time," he told her. "We can figure everything out."

"Yeah," she said, and he could *sense* her contentment. That was the thing about being a vampire, the thing she would come to learn: it was hard to keep secrets from one another. "But I think we should lay low for a little bit, before we try to head back to Colorado."

"Alright." He wanted to go to her home, to sit on her couch in person, sleep in her bed...do other things. Stroke Brando's handsome nose with his flesh-and-blood hand. But he was relieved in a way. Because even if Vlad had sent him off to live his own life, to escape this war...he didn't think he could just ignore its coming. And he wanted, badly, to have a visit with his two favorite Russians, and get a feel for the current state of affairs in the immortal world.

"I can *feel* you thinking," Mia said.

"You've caught me out. I was just thinking I know where we ought to go for now."

"Where?"

"How do you feel about New York City?"

~*~

They had two rooms at the La Quinta, one for each couple. They weren't even an eighth as grand as their quarters at the manor. But there was something to be said for stiff sheets and hotel soap when they came with total and complete privacy.

Fulk hadn't slept much. They'd arrived late, and had stripped down to undershirts and underwear, all but falling onto the bed. Anna had turned to him immediately, urging him onto his side so they lay front-to-front, her small head tucked into his chest, one of his arms draped around her waist. The skin-to-skin contact was important – essential, really, for wolves. Humans and vampires and mages enjoyed their pair bonds, the emotional support and stability provided. But wolves could go into deep depressions without a pack or mates. A pack would help, in place of a mate...but it was the mate that made them whole. Pack or not, with a mate, a wolf could gladly take on the world.

After high-adrenaline events, Fulk always felt himself drop into an almost dopey state: exhausted but restless, needy, clingy. Anna said it was the same for her, but she handled it more gracefully – as she did with most things.

He clung to her now, as the first gray light of dawn slipped through the gap in the hotel drapes, a sinuous glide across the bed. Pressed his nose and mouth into her hair and breathed in the scent of her, of them, their pack of two. They each had their own scent, colored by one another, and then there was a third scent, unique to their union. He drank that in now like water, slow sips through his open mouth.

He sensed when she woke, but she didn't say anything for long minutes, just breathing against his collarbone, warm, still-sleepy puffs. His hand moved of its own volition, unhurried strokes down her back, fingertips playing in the dip of her spine.

Finally, she stirred, the cold sole of one foot sliding down his shin. She shifted back far enough to tip her head and meet his gaze; he'd been watching her peaceful face for hours now, and he was sad to see her wake for the sake of her tiredness, but glad for the warm, forest green of her eyes.

"Hello, love."

"Mm. Hey, baby." She yawned, unselfconscious. Pressed her face into the hollow of his throat and sighed. "What time is it?"

The numbers on the bedside table clock glowed green. "Six-fifty."

She hummed; he felt the vibration in his teeth.

"Go back to sleep if you want."

"Nah." She slipped a hand up his ribs. Played idly with his nipple, hard and tight in the chill of the AC. "We should probably get moving."

They probably should. The more miles they put between themselves and the Institute, the better. Doubtless their new master would have some idea of where he wanted to go – Fulk envisioned a furious, pale-eyed vampire in a black coat, and a tow-headed, gentle-sweet wolf.

But exhaustion dragged at him. How easy it would be to bury his nose in her hair, close his eyes, and pretend nothing pressing awaited them.

"He'll want to go to New York," Anna said, voice wide-awake now. Low and warm against his skin.

"Yeah?"

"You know he will."

"Yeah."

They'd been there before, of course, because they'd been everywhere. The glaring, manmade light drowning out the stars; too many scents and sounds to catalogue, a kind of insulation of white noise around them. Cold iron bars of fire escapes and a too-fast pulse; a shared mug of whiskey passed back and forth in the wee hours, and rainy afternoons tucked into the corners of delightfully messy bookshops.

It was easy to get lost in New York. Easy for someone abnormal to fade into the tapestry. Who could dwell on the yawning maw of forever when the city too busy to sleep pulsed around you like a second heartbeat?

He pulled her in closer to him. "I'm okay with New York."

~*~

A crew of employees pushed carts through the hotel's dining room, unloading baskets of muffins, and bagels, and pastries; igniting the warmers under the chafing dishes and toting out eggs, and bacon, and sausage. Kolya sat alone at a table by the window, both hands wrapped around a steaming cup of black coffee. The heat and the smell were soothing; he hadn't added cream or sugar because he had no idea if that's how he took his coffee – Liam and Lily had never offered him any, and he couldn't remember from *before*.

Remembering was…difficult.

Some things were clear. The time *after*. His first awareness was of pain, and of light. The sense of being layered together from ash and electricity. He'd opened his eyes to a gray sky; his lungs had opened, and he'd known how to breathe. Instinct. A scraped-raw throat, and eerie, bloodless hands he'd used to reach up, up, out of the dark pit in which he'd lain.

The first faces he'd seen belonged to the Prices. Liam, with his copper hair, and laughing eyes, and narrow face. And Lily, worried but lovely, her hair a mane of fire down her back. *Kolya*, Liam had said. That was his name. And it had felt right.

But it was the only thing that had.

He'd been a grown man with no memory of childhood. He couldn't recall his mother's face, or his childhood friends. Couldn't remember his job, or his death. The kind of man he'd been.

What was a person without memories? Was it even a person at all?

They'd taken him into a city that frightened him. He had no memories, but this felt wrong. The cars, the buildings, all the lights.

"How long was I dead?" he'd asked in his ruined voice.

Liam had taken a careful sip of his tea and set his cup down slow, face warm with apology. "Seventy-five years."

"Oh."

"Your memories will begin to return in time. That's at least been my experience with this sort of thing. Some will return naturally – gradually. And others will be jolted to the surface by some stimulus. In time, you will remember exactly who you are. But until then, I think it's best if you stayed close with us. We'll be going to America soon, and you'll need to learn to speak English."

"What are we speaking now?"

"Russian. You are Russian, Kolya. We are in Volgograd." A pause. "You would have known it in your time as Stalingrad."

Stalingrad. Drone of Luftwaffe. Thunder of bombs. Screams. Rubble. Blood. A lab; a steel table. A boy, howling. Fingers digging into muscle, pushing back. *Let go of me, let go! They're killing him! Sasha!*

He blinked and he was on the floor, crouched low like an animal, his head in his hands.

Liam crouched down in front of him. "What did you remember?"

"Who's Sasha?" he croaked.

"One of your friends from before. One of the ones who is still alive. You'll get to meet him soon."

He hadn't met Sasha yet, but he remembered him now. Him and Nikita. Liam said they were the only survivors, that they lived together in New York.

Are they…? Kolya wondered, because the more distinct they became in his mind – Sasha's platinum hair brushing his shoulders, blue eyes scrunched up as he laughed; Nik's icy façade thawing just a little, too pale, and too shaky, and never enough to eat, but always a ghost of a smile for that boy – the more obvious it became that they'd loved one another. Did they still? Liam had said this age was different, that people could–

The chair across from him pulled back, drawn by an elegant hand, and the blond vampire prince slipped into it.

Kolya tensed, hands slipping beneath his jacket, seeking knives. He knew enough about before, now, to know that this was an instinct honed through years of violence. He knew he'd done terrible things, once, just because someone told him to; and that he was capable of doing them still.

The prince seemed unbothered by this. He held his own cup of steaming coffee in his free hand, and waved with the other. *Sit down, sit down*, the gesture said. His hair was braided, a thick golden rope draped over one shoulder of his motorcycle jacket.

Based on what he'd learned of this age, people didn't just look like the prince. He was more like something out of a storybook, and if the way the female employees gawked at him was anything to go by, it was a much-appreciated look at that.

"Good morning," the prince – Val, his name was Val – said, smiling wide enough to flash his too-sharp canines.

Kolya had a flash of memory: a bearded face, rancid breath, dramatic weeping and the smell of spilt wine. He suppressed a shudder.

Val, seemingly unbothered by the lack of response, turned sideways in his chair and crossed one long leg over the other. His gaze wandered out across the mostly empty dining room, following the progress of the staff as they moved to the kitchen and back, toting condiments and silverware.

"I haven't discussed this in any detail with our wolf friends, yet," he said, "but I should very much like to head north from here."

Kolya's heart thumped. Sometimes, stuck in the vacuum of his own missing memories, he thought he might not have come back...right. That there were larger pieces missing: emotions, and responses, and empathy. But here he was, *feeling*. Hoping.

"New York?" he guessed.

The prince lifted his brows and turned a surprised little smile on him. "Why, yes, how did you know?"

"You said I could see them again. Nik and Sasha."

"And so you shall." His smile slipped, and he turned his upper body around so he could brace his elbows on the table. Set his coffee cup down with a sigh. "Actually, that's why I'm here. I felt the need to...warn you."

More feeling. Ice in his belly, pins and needles in his lungs. "About what?" His voice had gained strength in the months since his rebirth, no longer a sound like barbed wire tangling over itself; but it creaked now; his throat ached.

"It's alright," Val soothed. "It's only – well, I think that your friends might be doubtful. At first. That you really are you."

"Oh." The breath left his lungs in a rush; he deflated.

"Nikita is, if you can remember, doubtful by nature. And he is wildly protective of his little family. He'll come around, I'm sure. But I wanted you to be prepared."

"Yes. Thank you."

Val tipped his head, smile searching now. "Are you alright?"

"What do you mean?"

Soft, sad. Kolya knew what those things looked like, even if he couldn't put his hands on them and claim them as his own. "Nevermind." Gentle. "You'll figure that out along the way. You're with us, now." He laid his hand on the table, near to Kolya's, but not touching. "You're safe."

Safe. A word that held no meaning – not now…and not even in his piecemeal memories.

61

SIRE

Jake was a practical man. Born of a practical family, a boy who'd played baseball, and gone to the homecoming dance every year with a pretty date on his arm. A stand-up, designated driver, mom friend kind of guy. Decent grades in all subjects, but excellent ones in history and politics. A guy who'd known right away that he wanted to enter the military, spurred by the same swell of indomitable post-9/11 patriotism that had propelled so many young people to their local recruitment offices. West Point to Iraq, to a German hospital bed. He wasn't one for fanciful thoughts. He'd never enjoyed books about made up shit, no *Lord of the Rings* or *Walking Dead* or *Star Wars*.

He hadn't been prepared for redheaded girls who threw fire out of their hands. Nor for vampires. A nerd could have found the proper mental drawers in which to file these impossibilities, but he'd had no such resources.

To keep from going crazy, he'd decided to think of vampires like this: as dangerous zoo animals. Like the lions and tigers that are never touched with bare hands; instead lured with meat, and clickers, transported in huge metal crates and forklifts, feral golden eyes watching through the round holes cut in the sides.

He suspected that was why Vlad chose not to make Talbot's study his headquarters. It smelled of another animal, of a male, and Vlad wanted to press his scent into a room as of yet untouched, his own area, and no one else's, one in in which he graciously allowed others to visit, but never to stay.

Jake felt very much like he was walking into a tiger's lair as he crossed the threshold of Vlad's designated study. It was a room at the front of the house, with a wall of mullioned windows. A former sitting room, the kind with dainty furniture and pale blue wallpaper, designed for ladies in frothy dresses with delicate teacups.

Vlad had found a desk somewhere, a heavy, dark, masculine one at war with the rest of the room's décor. He sat behind it, hair loose down his shoulders, poring over a map that took up nearly all the surface space, anchored at two ends with matching green lamps.

He afforded Jake only the barest of glances when he entered, a flat thing shot from beneath his brows, without lifting his head.

A small orange cat, the one the baroness had given to Prince Val, sat beside one of the lamps. It twitched its tail once, then stood, leapt down soundlessly, and disappeared somewhere near Vlad's feet.

Jake approached the desk with a kind of hesitance he hadn't even known in war. Cleared his throat. "You wanted to see me?"

Vlad hummed a sound of agreement and motioned to the chair across from his desk – powder blue with curved white legs. "I'm going over your modern maps."

Jake sat down slow, like the chair might bite him. It creaked. "I'm guessing they look a lot different from the maps you had in your day," he said, carefully. Because if Vlad was a tiger, then he was one who'd swatted at his keepers, and broken his latch.

Last night, Jake had dreamed of Vlad's sword cutting through that guard's neck. The wet *thock* sound of it, like a woodsman's axe notching a tree. The twin thumps of the body and the head hitting the floor separately. Blood everywhere. The awful stink of the dead man's bowels voiding.

Jake had seen lots of death in war, before the war eventually took his sight. But for reasons he couldn't understand, that death shook him to the core. The cage had come open; the tiger was loose.

The tiger was staring at him over a map of eastern Europe.

Jake swallowed with difficulty. "Do you need help with any of the new names for things?"

Vlad gave him an unreadable look, then dropped his gaze back to the map. He pressed his index finger to a city. "This is where I was born." He slid it over. "And this is where the palace was. Where Val and I grew up." His voice was still commanding and implacable, but softer, gruffer. "Here, Bucharest. I built this city from scratch."

Jake swallowed again and scooted to the edge of his chair, forearms resting on the desk so he could peer down at the map, some of the buzzing anxiety in his belly calming. "It's a major metropolis now. Modern. But some of the old buildings are still there."

Vlad looked up, sharply. "You've been there?"

"I looked at pictures when Talbot told me about you. I've never seen it in person."

A nod, and his gaze swept downward again. "There are some immortals who know that I buried my uncle. I had my wolves spread false rumors about the location, however. It is true that I rode to Damascus. I was seen riding east from there...and also west. The deserts of Egypt? The deserts of Arabia?" He tapped his fingertip. "That was a ruse. He's in Bucharest."

"He...he *is*?"

"If he hasn't been found, then yes, he is."

"But..." Images from the video Talbot had shown him flashed behind his eyes, shaky, visceral, repulsive. Undeniable. "The footage. The mountain village. Christ, that was in Pakistan! How...?"

"There's no way to know how many humans Romulus managed to turn before I put him in the ground. It could be dozens, or hundreds. Everyone he turns is eventually corrupted by whatever dark disease lies in his blood – and anyone *they* turn doubly so. They're little more than raving monsters."

"Zombies," Jake said, flatly, overwhelmed. "They're like – fuck, they're like zombies."

"Zombies?"

Jake made a vague gesture. "The undead. They eat people. There are movies about them."

"Movies." Vlad tasted the word.

"For entertainment. You had the theater back then, right?"

That earned him an unimpressed look.

"There's movies about zombies. And...about vampires."

His brows lifted. "I was under the impression that mortals at large are still ignorant as to our existence."

"They are. The movies are just pretend."

Vlad cocked his head, thinking it over, then finally shrugged and looked back at the map. "In any event, the first order of business is retrieving Romulus and killing him. If we can."

"There's a chance we can't?"

"I made only a weak attempt before," Vlad said, grim. "He's the son of a god, you know. He doesn't die as easily as the rest of us."

Faintly: "Right." He thought he might pass out. "What if – what if Romulus isn't there?"

"He will be. And then we will find and eradicate any of his spawn."

"Yes, your grace." The title came to him easily, to his surprise. He was used to calling someone "sir" or "ma'am." Vlad was unlike any CO he'd ever had in his military career, but he found himself responding to the presence of him as such all the same. He'd reached the limits of belief and just wanted, selfishly, to fall in line at this point.

Vlad eased back in his chair; a lazy, panther-like movement undercut with an energy just shy of a threat. Eyelids at half-mast, he should have looked relaxed, sleepy – but he didn't. He was terrifying. "There's no royalty here in your country. Does it pain you to call be by a royal honorific?"

"No. Sir."

"Hmm. You are a soldier, used to bending to authority."

"Yes, sir."

Vlad picked up a letter opener shaped like – oh, no, that really was a knife. Long, slender, double-edged, meant for stabbing rather than slicing. He walked the hilt down his knuckles in a quietly dazzling, deft movement, twirling the blade at the end in a fast arc and beginning again. Hypnotic. It felt intentional. "But you are repulsed by me." It wasn't a question.

"I–" Jake faltered.

"I can see it in your face. I can smell it on you. No need to lie."

It took a degree of effort not to squirm in his chair. As evenly as he could, he said, "You're not human."

Vlad waited.

"You drink blood. You cut off a man's head without a second thought – and maybe he was expendable, to you, and maybe he was a jackass, but he didn't deserve to *die*. And with Adela–" He bit off the rest; he'd already said too much.

"Ah." Vlad caught the knife's handle and it stilled, angled so the blade became a bar of reflected sunlight, its threat obscured. "This is about Adela, then."

Jake grit his teeth.

"You care for her."

"She's a fellow soldier and a member of my team. She's my subordinate. And you turned her without her consent."

This, of course, neither bothered nor shamed the prince. He said, "I asked you, Major. I asked what she would want."

"I *know*."

"The question then becomes," Vlad drawled, "which of us do you hate the most? Me for turning her, or yourself for allowing it?"

"It isn't that simple."

"Of course it is." Maddeningly calm. Jake gripped the flimsy arms of his chair until the tendons stood out in the backs of his hands; until the wood creaked. "Everything is simple."

Shaking, vibrating out of his skin with a fury so potent he couldn't hope to understand it, Jake said, "You really are insane."

Vlad said, "For most of my childhood, I was held hostage by my father's enemy. A man whose son would go on to defile my little brother and keep him as a concubine. My father's own people turned on him, killed him. My little brother nearly cleaved me in two six-hundred years ago, and then I returned the favor.

"These are things that happened. Because of selfishness – and because of protectiveness, also. Brutal things are always simple, Major Treadwell, even if your *emotions* are not. I saved Adela's leg; I made her immortal and ungodly strong. Now: are you glad of that, or do you wish she'd lost her limb?"

Jake bit the inside of his cheek and tasted blood.

"Are the two of you lovers?"

Shut up! he wanted to scream. He couldn't answer, afraid of what he might say if he opened his mouth – and what Vlad might do in retaliation.

But the prince was calm. He set the knife down on the desk and linked his hands together over his flat stomach. He had large, long-fingered hands, rough with prominent calluses in places not caused by modern weapons. His lips tipped up the slightest fraction in the corners, and he looked almost amused.

"No need to answer, Major, I can tell that you aren't. I would have smelled it if you were. I might think you wanted to be her lover, but that's not quite the truth, is it? You just don't want *me* to be."

"If you're mind-controlling her—"

"I can't do that."

The chair arms *groaned*.

"I possess no psychic abilities whatsoever," Vlad explained. "Though it appears I'm stubborn enough to resist the compelling efforts of mages even as strong as our stupid Mr. Price. I have no way to compel Adela, though."

Jake forced his fingers to uncurl from the wood; they were bloodless and aching from the pressure.

"I have done innumerable violent things in my life, and I'm not sorry for them. But I've never forced a woman against her will, and I have no plans to do so now. There are more important things at stake than sex," he said, dismissive, and turned back to his map. "I have need of a second in command, and I thought that might be you, if you are capable and willing enough." One last, lazy glance, only half-curious, but assessing.

Jake took a series of deep breaths, his heart pounding against his ribs so forcefully that it hurt. It hit him then, with an unreal sense that the floor was tipping out from beneath him, that he'd made a terrible error in judgement.

Tigers could kill, and tigers could escape. Tigers could creep up silent in the half-light of dusk and gut you open. But the thing he'd forgotten? Tigers were *smart*.

So was Vlad.

This was no rabid beast foaming at the mouth for violence. Not something depraved who feasted on chaos. Vlad was colder and more calculating than any military man Jake had ever met. Vlad weighed the odds and acted on logic.

772

And sometimes, logic was the most monstrous motivation of all.

~*~

Adela checked her watch and was surprised to find that it had only been five minutes since she'd checked last. She'd covered nearly two miles in that time. Earbuds pumping music, she lifted her head and pressed on. Nikes digging into the loose pebbles and hard-packed dirt of the trail, arms swinging, lungs working with a strength and regularity that was almost mechanical. She jumped a branch, skipped over a set of hoofprints, and started up the next hill with a fresh burst of speed.

She'd always been athletic, but this was...this was something else entirely.

Dr. Talbot hadn't wanted her to leave the mansion. Agent West had said "under no circumstance," his face pinched and pale.

But Vlad had stepped in. "She goes where she wants." And his word was law, now.

Agent West had been on the phone, hiding in corners, having hushed, furious conversations. She'd eavesdropped without any effort: calls to Washington, to the secretary of state, on hold with the president, requests to speak with the joint chiefs. There was a real possibility he might try to call in an airstrike on the manor just to get rid of Vlad.

But Adela knew this whole thing was bigger than ego or the lives of a few underlings. The US government had spent seventy-five years and uncountable millions trying to find Vlad Tepes; if he wanted to control a manor house, he could control a manor house.

She had no idea how the rest of it would shake out, only that she was now a part of it in a way she'd never expected, and there was no going back.

She flew the last distance, taking the wide stone steps two at a time. She was out of breath and tired when she reached the double front doors, but in a pleasant way. The familiar ache of lactic acid, the rush of too much oxygen in her lungs, the dizziness of dehydration, yes – but she wasn't going to cramp, or faint, or need a nap. She could feel energy in a reserve now, dormant in her blood, ready to be tapped into with a sit-down and a snack and a bottle of water. Vlad had told her she was strong now, and she was.

She paused in the vestibule to take out her earbuds and slip them in the pocket of her shorts. She looked down at her feet.

The surgeon who'd performed the transplant of the donor leg had done a magnificent job. The donor had been the same shoe size, and of a very similar build. She'd been Latina, and shared Adela's slender calves and ankles. Still, it hadn't been a *perfect* match; no such thing existed. The skin tone hadn't been an exact match; then there had been the scar...

When she'd stood in her shower, and looked down at her feet on the stark white tile, the difference had always seemed glaring. The success of the surgery, the fact that her body had accepted the new limb, had been miraculous. She'd been grateful.

But now...now her legs looked the same. The scar was still there, but the leg was *her own* in a way she'd never thought possible.

She went through the inner doors into the soaring atrium as Jake walked across it toward the grand staircase, head down, brows pinched with unhappiness. Discontent rolled off of him, a detectible aura that was part smell, part vibration along her nerve endings.

He paused when he saw her, hand suspended above the bannister, and offered a bare smile. "Good run?"

"Yeah."

"Good." He turned away, but not before his smile turned brittle and fell away. A part of her wanted to reach out, ask him why he looked and smelled and felt this way. But they'd never been close; just coworkers and team members; their only bond was military service and their place in the drug trial.

He started up the stairs, calling over his shoulder: "Vlad wants to see you. He's in his study."

Her stomach flipped. "'Kay. Thanks."

She looked down at herself again, her dusty sneakers and her orange tank top glued to her skin with sweat. She should shower first. But she knew that delaying the meeting would just make her jittery stomach worse. So she headed for his study.

Which she realized was a horrible, horrible idea the moment she rapped on the open doorframe and crossed the threshold.

His head lifted immediately, his nostrils flared, his gaze snapping up, a predatorial gleam in his dark eyes.

She hadn't showered, and her skin was slick with sweat, and her scent had to be *potent.*

She could smell him, his particular rich scent, like dark woods with deep shadows, cool streams on a mountainside a half a world away.

The moment stretched, long and tense, and she thought, at first, that she had intruded. Vampires – herself, even, she was realizing – were prickly about territory. Like big, solitary cats. Only mates and family and those they needed for some reason were welcome in their personal environs.

But then his head tipped, and his pupils expanded, and…oh. This wasn't about territory.

"Come in," he said, and dropped his head over his desk again, seemingly disinterested. He buzzed with energy, though, tightly-checked.

She'd never been a coward, and now didn't seem like a good time to become one – even if she was in over her head. So she walked up to the desk, head held up, strides sure. She would never cower, not for anyone or anything. If Vlad could tell that her insides quavered, so be it.

She didn't take the chair there, because she didn't think antique fabric and sweat were a good combo, instead stood at parade rest. "Did you need me for something, sir?" He held a fine-tipped green Sharpie and was tracing routes on the map with it. "I'm really better with weapons and battle tactics than I am with logistics."

He made a sound, and it took her a moment to realize he was chuckling. When he lifted his head again, he was almost smiling. His eyes were bright, if nothing else, the lines at their edges touched with humor. It was such a subtle thing, but it lit him up; he even smelled amused, if there was any such thing.

She bared her teeth in knee-jerk defense.

His chuckle tapered off into a purr, and it soothed her. A helpless, automatic reaction.

"What?" It came out softer than she'd intended.

"You are very different from the major," he observed, easing back in his chair, hands braced lightly on the desk's edge. "He wants to be rid of me, but you want to impress me."

"No, I don't," she scoffed, but her breath quickened. Betraying her. "We're both soldiers. We're both just following orders."

"Yes, but even the best of soldiers has his own ideas about the war he's fighting in. About his commander."

"Do you read minds, sir?" she snapped. "Is that what you're telling me?"

Unbothered, he said, "No, I can do no such thing. I'm merely well-studied in the art of observation."

"And you think I want to impress you."

"I think you want to impress everyone."

She'd already been preparing a rebuttal, but it just sort of…froze up in her throat. She swallowed it down. "What?"

His smile held no warmth, and she realized, in a moment of alarming clarity, that it reminded her of her own smile, on the rare, bitter occasions she flashed herself one in the mirror. "For reasons I don't yet understand, I think you're afraid no one will think that you are the fearsome warrior you've styled yourself. You are a harsh woman."

Stand down, a logical voice in the back of her head warned. There was never anything gained by goading a superior – much less a legendary one with a reputation for viciousness.

But. He wasn't wrong about her.

And she wasn't technically in the Army anymore. It wasn't like he could demote her.

(Kill her, sure. But. She wasn't going to think about that.)

"I thought you just impaled people. What's with all the riddles?"

He chuckled again. "Not riddles. Simple observations."

"Is that your trick?" She folded her arms. "You talked yourself in circles until your enemies got so frustrated they just impaled themselves?"

"You don't know anything about me, do you?" Hint of a purr in his voice, and Adela knew she was being baited. This was a game for him, and she sure as hell wasn't going to play it.

In what was maybe the riskiest, dumbest move she'd ever made, she turned her back to him and started for the door. "I know you're bullshitting me," she said over her shoulder. "Call me back when you actually want to talk strategy."

The thing about her new strength and speed? It had come from somewhere; it had come from *him*.

She heard him move, but she didn't react quickly enough. One moment her way was clear, and the next he was heeling the door shut and leaning back against it, blocking the way with his broad shoulders and implacable stare.

She pulled up short. Still…in for a penny, in for a pound.

She propped her hands on her hips. "Am I not allowed to leave?" She knew he could smell her fear and anxiety, probably sense the way it crawled across her skin, leaving goosebumps behind.

He didn't smile at her. She knew him well enough to know those were rare things; just because he'd flashed a semblance of one a moment ago didn't mean he'd show her one now. But his gaze *burned*. He didn't come into her mind; she knew herself well enough to know that she wasn't being manipulated. The way he looked at her, though – it tugged at her. Something visceral and blood-deep she didn't understand.

She gritted her teeth. "Stop."

He didn't.

"*Please.*"

He edged forward, into her space. Leaned down, so their faces were level. When he opened his mouth, his teeth were very white, his fangs very long; they seemed to extend as she watched, too big and prominent.

He said, "*Why?*"

A fine tremor stole through her; no doubt he could see it, feel it. "I don't like it."

A grin, slow and *awful*. His breath warm against her face. "Yes, you do."

Oh, God. What would his mouth taste like? What would it feel like to slide her tongue between his fangs?

He inhaled, scenting her, and she swayed forward–

Vlad straightened and stepped back. Stepped around her and headed back for his desk.

The bottom dropped out of her stomach. She turned, following him with her eyes, hungry, and aching, and hating herself. She watched him settle in his chair again, calm as ever, and it took her a moment to realize he'd spoken.

"What?"

"It's instinct," he said, bored, looking down at his maps. "I'm your sire, and you feel an instinctual urge to be close to me. Even if I repulse you, the instinct is there."

She braced a hand against the high back of a chair and just breathed for a moment, open-mouthed, feeling her fangs press into her lip. "You're joking."

He didn't look up. "I most definitely am not."

Shame came first, a hot wave of it flooding through her. She'd been – God, she'd been aroused. Still was. Had wanted to push her fingers through his hair and slide into his lap and… She cut the fantasy off with a forceful mental shove. This man – this monster – had slaughtered thousands. His own people. She'd watched him cut a man's head off just days ago. How could she want him? What kind of monster did that make her?

But then came the relief. It was only instinct. She couldn't help it. And clearly, he didn't feel the way she did, had only been toying with her…

She took a deep breath and drew herself upright. "Sir, what's our plan of attack? What's our objective?"

He lifted his head then, and she thought he looked approving. "I'm going to lead an expedition into Romania to retrieve my uncle. I could use someone with modern warfare experiences to help me work out the particulars."

Another deep breath. Just instinct. She was a soldier; things were different – she was different – but there was a war on, one in which she was needed. She could do this.

"Will you feel well enough to be a part of my team?" he asked.

She snapped a salute. "Yes, sir."

~*~

EPILOGUE

It was raining. A soft patter of autumn drops that drummed against the roofs of cabs and the umbrellas of pedestrians.

A man selling newspapers shouted and waved a polka-dot umbrella at them. "Great deal! Super cheap!" But Val waved him off with a laugh. He wanted to feel the rain in his hair, sliding down his skin, soaking through his clothes. Cold and real.

Beside him, Mia tugged her hood forward over her face.

"Darling, if you want—"

She squeezed his hand and smiled up at him. "I don't mind getting wet." She smelled like him, and like her, and like rain, and like heaven.

He kissed the top of her head and tugged her along down the sidewalk. They were almost there. Up ahead: the glowing gold neon of the sign: The Lion's Den.

Another laugh bubbled up in his throat; he couldn't *stop* laughing. Richard the Lionheart's wolf had broken into the manor, and here was the rampant lion over the door of a bar that Nikita and Sasha frequented.

Val had the sense they were being drawn together: a last bastion of immortals. Legends, and liars, and heathens. Perhaps the beginnings of an unholy family.

He would start with these, though, now.

He tugged open the door of the vestibule and ushered Mia inside with a hand at her lower back. She pushed her hood down and blinked raindrops off her lashes, sighing with relief. Here, in the air lock, the windows were fogged; umbrellas and dripping coats hung from pegs on the wall.

Val knew a moment of nervousness. He paused to let his lungs work, breathing in and out through his mouth. Scents of pub food, and liquor, and lots of bodies, smoke, damp.

Mia rubbed his arm. "It'll be okay."

His laugh came out like a cough. "I hope so."

"Come on." She looped her arm through his and they went through the inner door.

It was a delightful bar: dim, and crowded, and full of inviting nooks and crannies. His nose drew him around a bend and into a smoky main room, backlit bar gleaming gold along one wall. At a big round table in the corner, backs to the wall: there they were.

Sasha had a pack again, one built of misfits: Trina, Nikita's great-granddaughter, and her vampire partner, Lanny. The young, innocent bystander they'd taken in: Jamie. And of course the tsarevich, Alexei Romanov.

Sasha and Nikita sat side-by-side, shoulders touching, overlapping. Beneath the table, Val saw that Nikita's hand rested on Sasha's thigh, undemanding, but possessive. Their scents, even across the distance and tangle of other senses, were intertwined, undercut by the musk of sex.

Val smiled. *It's about time.*

Suddenly, Sasha's head snapped up, eyes wide and searching as he scanned the room, nostrils flared. He'd caught the scent of vampires.

And then his gaze landed on Val. He stared a moment; Nikita's gaze followed, hand tightening on the wolf's thigh.

And then…Sasha smiled. And then he laughed. "Val!" he shouted.

And Val was home.

THE END

~*~

This concludes *this* chapter in the
Sons of Rome saga. Be on the lookout for
Book Four, *Golden Eagle,*
Coming Soon

Afterword

Prince Radu Dracula, brother to Vlad Tepes, was raped at age nine by the Ottoman Sultan Mehmet. He was taken to the sultan's bedchamber, and, when the sultan's intentions became clear, young Radu was able to take up the sultan's own sword, and stab him with it. A non-lethal wound, but one that afforded Radu the chance to flee out into the garden. He spent the night hiding in a tree outside the seraglio, until Mehmet finally found him, and took him inside, and ravished him.

This is one of the true stories that inspired this book. Little is documented of Prince Radu's time with the Ottomans. We know that he was kept as a hostage until he was eventually placed on the Wallachian throne after his brother's arrest, and we know that he was an especial favorite of the sultan's, kept on as a lover during his captivity. We know, also, that the sultan took other hostages – the sons of nobles, even the cabin boys of merchant vessels – into sexual servitude. Sultan Mehmet was an intelligent man, one with a clever approach to warfare, creative and unbendable.

But when I read what he did to these boys…Dear Reader, I cried.

In fact, I cried an embarrassing amount while writing this book. It was the most difficult, the most emotionally draining project of my career to date. But I'm so proud of it, and I have learned so much about Vlad Tepes, about his family, that is never spoken about in popular culture.

I might have always wanted to write a book about Vlad the Impaler, but this particular book required two years of intensive research – and I'm sure there are details over which a historian of the period would find fault with me. Some bit of dress, or food, or social custom. But though I would like to be, I am not a historian. My goal was to portray this period, and these two conflicting kingdoms, with as much accuracy as possible, while maintaining the urgency and relevancy of the story.

In regards to names, I chose to write the sultans Murat and Mehmet with the T as opposed to the D which often appears in Western-based sources. My Eastern sources used T, and so that was the way I chose to spell their names. Likewise, the place name "Edirne" was used in place of "Adrianople" when it was being referred to by Ottoman leaders/captives, and as "Adrianople" in the mouths of purely Western characters.

I've used the term "crusader" to describe Vlad and his fellow Eastern European lords, because that was how they styled themselves. And while the battling back and forth was between Christian Europeans and Muslim Turks, I made a decision early on not to use religious rhetoric when describing the animosity between Vlad and Mehmet; in truth, I don't believe their conflict was ever *about* religion. Mehmet himself was quite secular in real life, even going so far as to attend Catholic worship services after he'd taken Constantinople. And while Vlad was born Eastern Orthodox, and converted to Catholicism so that he could join the Order of the Dragon, his hatred for Mehmet, and the Ottomans, was, I believe, wholly personal in nature. Therefore, this novel is not a commentary on the Christian/Muslim dynamic, nor on the Crusades in general, because the clash of the 15th Century had little in common with the first four Crusades that took place in the Holy Land. This book is instead a character drama; a battle between two kings, if you will, and God plays no part in it.

In regards to research, it was difficult to find sources that were not biased in some sense, be it Western or Eastern, and even then I found the wording to be, for lack of a better term, strange at moments. Oftentimes, it became quite clear that both Sultan Mehmet and Prince Vlad were capable of extreme butchery. Given that Vlad is a central protagonist of this book series, Mehmet must needs be the antagonist, and he is written as such.

In regards to dates, all battles, capitulations, and conquests are true to life. I also included as many real names and happenings as I felt was possible while maintaining the story's integrity. For instance:

Emperor Constantine was truly beheaded; the blockade-running captain Antonio Rizzo was truly impaled, and his scribe was truly taken into Mehmet's collection of sex slaves; Vlad's ally Mihály Szilágy was truly cut in half after having been tortured. The timeline of Vlad's multiple ascensions to the Wallachian throne begs to accuracy, as do events such as the killing of Albu the Great, and the forced labor of the boyars that Vlad then killed, and replaced with boyars of his own making, commoners raised up to these titles.

The Forest of the Impaled is a true story. As is Mehmet's retreat in the face of it. Think what you will of Vlad, and doubtless this act of mass impalement was monstrous; but turning back the Conqueror of Constantinople was no slight accomplishment for a Romanian prince. It is for this, among other things, that Vlad is not a villain in his native homeland.

I hope you'll think me fair, and I hope you'll overlook any anachronistic details. I also hope that you enjoyed this installment of the series, and that you'll press forward from here. In the next installment, we return to New York, and to Nikita Baskin's group of allies.

And I hope that you'll be curious, as I have been, about the story of the plucky Eastern European nations who stood against a monolithic empire. Who held their own. I hope you'll go forth and look up stories of Vlad, and Skanderbeg, and John Hunyadi. Prior to researching this book, I knew little of the history of Romania, because theirs is a history never told in American classrooms. I entered this project without one inch of skin in the game – this isn't my history; these aren't my ancestors. But what I found, when I started digging, was absolutely remarkable. In a world full of pro-expansionist dictators, the lords of Eastern Europe in the 15th Century stand out as rebels (though Hunyadi was a bit of an expansionist himself, I'm afraid). Those who would defy; those who would seek sovereignty, caught between the gears of political machines they had no hope of shaking off – but which they rattled all the same.

I hope that you will look up the Ottoman Empire, and its contributions to art, and science, and medicine. To culture, and architecture. And I invite every reader to draw his or her own conclusion about the real events that unfolded in this century.

But this is, after all, dear reader, a story about characters. About the men and women who populate this saga that I'm writing. And my loyalty must lie with them, as their muse and recorder, as the one chosen to tell their tales. Biased? I'm sure that I am. But so are all artists. Valerian is a creature of my own making, and to him I will always be loyal. And in regards to the true prince upon which my Valerian is based...I looked at all the facts, and I wanted to be his champion, too.

Thank you for reading. I'll see you when we get to *Golden Eagle*.

About the Author:

Lauren Gilley is the author of over twenty novels.
She writes contemporary and historical stories with a focus on found family, and overcoming tough odds. She blogs, sometimes, at hoofprintpress.blogspot.com, and accepts emails at authorlaurengilley@gmail.com. She lives in the South; when she's not writing, she's mucking horse stalls, or walking her giant dog.

You can also find her on these other social media sites:

Instagram: @hppress

Twitter: @lauren_gilley

Facebook: "Lauren Gilley – Author"

Other Novels From Lauren Gilley:

Sons of Rome Series:
White Wolf
Red Rooster
Dragon Slayer

Dartmoor Series/Lean Dogs Legacy Series:
Fearless
Price of Angels
Half My Blood
The Skeleton King
Secondhand Smoke
Snow In Texas
Tastes Like Candy
Loverboy
American Hellhound
Shaman
Prodigal Son

Walker Series:
Keep You
Dream of You
Better Than You
Fix You
Rosewood

Standalones:
Whatever Remains
Walking Wounded
"Love Is…"

Russell Series:
Made for Breaking
God Love Her
Keeping Bad Company